Dear Reader,

Thank you for choosing to celebrate more than a decade of award-winning romance with Arabesque. In recognition of its ten year anniversary, Arabesque launched a special collector's series in 2004 honoring the authors who pioneered African-American romance. With its unique 3-in-1 book format, each anthology features the most beloved works of the Arabesque imprint.

Intriguing, intense and sensuous, this special collector's series was launched with *First Touch,* which included three of Arabesque's first published novels written by Sandra Kitt, Francis Ray and Eboni Snoe. It was followed by *Hideaway Saga,* three novels from award-winning author Rochelle Alers; the third in the series, *Falcon Saga,* by Francis Ray; and concluded with Brenda Jackson's *Madaris Saga.*

In 2005 we continued the series with Donna Hill's *Courageous Hearts,* Felicia Mason's *Seductive Hearts,* Bette Ford's *Passionate Hearts* and in November, Shirley Hailstock's *Magnetic Hearts.*

This year we are continuing the series with collections from Arabesque authors Angela Benson, Lynn Emery, Monica Jackson and Gwynne Forster. The book you are holding—*Sweet Passion*— includes three classic romances from Angela Benson: *Bands of Gold, For All Time* and *Between the Lines.*

We hope you enjoy these romances and please give us your feedback at our Web site at www.kimanipress.com.

Sincerely,

Evette Porter
Arabesque Editor
Kimani Press

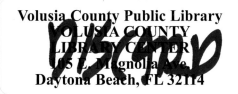

Other Arabesque books by Angela Benson

The Nicest Guy in America
The Way Home

ANGELA BENSON

SWEET PASSION

ARABESQUE®

SWEET PASSION

An Arabesque novel

ISBN 1-58314-738-1

© 2006 by Harlequin S.A.

The publisher acknowledges the copyright holder as follows:

BANDS OF GOLD
Copyright © 1994 by Angela Benson

FOR ALL TIME
Copyright © 1995 by Angela Benson

BETWEEN THE LINES
Copyright © 1996 by Angela Benson

CONTENTS

BANDS OF GOLD

Chapter 1

"They're pressuring me to change my mind." Christina sat in her office on the forty-first floor of Boston's John Hancock Towers, twirling the cord of the telephone handset as she spoke.

"Don't let them decide for you. It's your life."

"I know, Mom, but they have some good points. Maybe I should reconsider." Christina wrapped the telephone cord around her lower arm.

"Look, Christina," Louise began. "This is your mama talking."

Christina smiled. She knew what was coming.

"I've known you a lot longer than those people you work with and I'm telling you to do what you think is right. Go with your instincts. You know what I want, but it's not my decision. You do what's best for you. I'm with you either way. Got that?"

"I've got it," Christina answered. "Have I told you lately that you're a great mom?"

"You have, but I never get tired of hearing it," Louise replied.

"You're the greatest, Mom. Really." As Christina unwrapped the phone cord from her arm, she looked at her watch. Standing up, she said, "I have to hang up now. Walter's waiting. Wish me luck."

"You don't need it, but good luck. Let me know how things turn out."

"Okay, Mom," Christina agreed. She hung up the phone and walked out of her office.

Since her promotion to senior engineer in charge of new accounts, Christina had made the walk to Walter's office many times. Walter loved to talk; at least, he loved talking to her. He had become her self-appointed mentor, and he always wanted to know what she was doing. He had been a lot of help when she was first promoted and she appreciated that, but sometimes she felt that Walter went overboard in his concern.

"I don't want you to go," Walter began, as soon as she entered his office.

"I know, Walter, and I'm glad that you like having me around, but I have to go," Christina responded. She sat in the visitor's chair closest to his massive oak desk.

"No, you don't have to leave. You can stay here." Walter got up from his desk and took a seat next to her.

"We've been through this before. I'm going."

Trying another tactic, he asked, "What will it take to make you stay?"

"It's not about the money. You know that," she answered, shaking her head.

"I'm not talking about money. I'm talking about OPTIMA."

Christina leaned forward slightly in her chair. She had heard about OPTIMA. The high-visibility project could skyrocket the career of some lucky manager. "What about OPTIMA?"

Walter moved back in his chair and steepled his fingers across the bridge of his nose. "The board has agreed that OPTIMA is yours if you stay."

"You can't be serious. That would mean a two-step promotion for me. That's unheard of at Communications Limited."

"There's a first time for everything." Walter took her hand in his. "We want to keep you here, Christina."

Christina withdrew her hand. "You make it sound as though I'm defecting to an enemy camp. I'm only transferring to the Atlanta office."

Walter sat back in his chair. "Going to Atlanta is almost as bad as defection."

"It is not. How can you say that?" Christina stood up and walked towards the wall of windows that faced Copley Square. She saw specks of milling bodies that looked more like ants than people.

Walter spoke to her back. "You know you've done good

work—no, outstanding work—in the seven years you've been here. Some people, me included, are looking for you to occupy a VP seat some day. The quickest way to that seat is to stay in Boston. Atlanta may as well be another company."

Christina turned to face him. "I know what you're saying is true." She knew she was on the fast track at CL. She knew she was a good engineer. She had showcased her abilities on three high-profile projects. Things were going according to plan…maybe even better than planned. "OPTIMA could get me the VP seat a few years early, but Atlanta is something that I have to do."

"You're allowed to change your mind, you know." Walter stood up and shoved his hands into his pants pockets. "One phone call and OPTIMA is yours."

"Walter…"

He interrupted, "Which do you want, Christina, a direct path to a vice presidency, or a detour to Atlanta?"

Fifty-four-year-old Walter Thomas sat facing the windows, looking out but not seeing anything. He had been at Communications Limited, affectionately called CL by its employees, for some twenty-five years. When he had started, CL was a small, start-up operation. Today, it was a multibillion-dollar business with offices in twenty major cities across the country. Boston was its headquarters, and headquarters was where things happened. Why couldn't he get Christina to see that? He knew that he hadn't changed her mind. She still planned to go to Atlanta.

Young people, he thought. You couldn't reason with them when they got their minds set. What was Christina thinking about? Didn't she see the opportunity before her? Most engineers in her position would trade their right arm for a shot at OPTIMA.

Walter knew his reaction to Christina's planned move was as much personal as it was professional. He had watched her mature into a fine engineer. She reminded him of himself at her age. Because he considered her his protégée, he couldn't let her make the move to Atlanta, a move that could effectively stall her career.

"If I can't convince her to stay, I know someone who can," he said aloud. He turned around in his chair and dialed Rosalind's number.

Christina arrived at Mr. Chen's restaurant a few minutes late. She knew that Rosalind Jones would already be there. She gave the maître d' her name and followed him to Rosalind's table. Though she had been in the restaurant more times than she could count, she still felt awkward during the walk to the table. The back lacquered walls, the flower arrangements, the tuxedoed waiters and the spotlight-studded ceiling made a perfect picture. Too perfect. She always got the feeling that her slip was showing and that everyone noticed. Never had her slip showed, yet each time she came to this restaurant she felt the same way. It was just one of her little insecurities.

Rosalind looked up and saw her. Christina smiled. Rosalind Jones and Walter Thomas were old friends. They began their careers at CL around the same time and had achieved comparable levels of success. Both were vice presidents. Her rise to that post occurred before the Women's Movement, before the age of women "having it all." Rosalind had a job, a career, but she didn't have a husband or children.

As soon as the maître d' seated her, Christina began, "Why do I get the feeling this isn't a casual lunch?"

Rosalind laughed. "You're right, it's not. Walter has assigned me to the 'Christina project.' My job is to make you see the error of your ways and stay here in Boston."

Christina frowned. "I knew Walter had a hand in this." She was getting tired of explaining herself. "I'm hungry, so let's order before you get started."

"Fair enough," Rosalind consented.

After the women quickly placed their orders, Rosalind asked, "Why are you so hell-bent on going to Atlanta?"

Christina picked up her napkin and placed it in her lap. "As I told Walter, it's time. I've always wanted to move south. I grew up in Alabama and I went to college in Atlanta. I'm ready to go back."

"That's a strictly personal reason, Christina. Don't you see that it would be better for your career if you stayed here with OPTIMA?"

Christina rearranged her napkin in her lap. She was determined not to get upset. "I agree that OPTIMA is a great project, but ORION has its good points as well." ORION was the primary software project assigned to the Atlanta staff.

"How can you say that? ORION is in chaos. The Board just ousted Paul Bechtel. The guy practically ruined that project. Why do you want to step into the middle of that? OPTIMA is fresh, new. It would be yours from day one."

"I don't share your view of ORION, Rosalind. I consider it a challenge. I've been putting together a plan to turn the project around. It can still be successful for CL. I can make it successful."

"I don't doubt your ability at all, but I wonder at your judgment. Why do you want to go with ORION, whose chances of success are slim, when you can have OPTIMA, whose chances of success are great? The real question, Christina, is which you want more—a move to Atlanta, or a shot at the vice presidency?"

Christina sat back in her chair and clasped her hands in her lap. "I didn't know they were mutually exclusive. Are they?"

"All the data indicate your best bet is to stay here in Boston. You know the saying, 'Out of sight, out of mind.' Atlanta is definitely out of sight."

The arrival of their food interrupted the conversation.

As soon as the waiter left, Christina leaned forward and placed her hands palms down on the table. "Listen, Rosalind, I appreciate what you and Walter are trying to do, but I know what I want."

Rosalind shook her head. "I hope you do, Christina, because I'd hate to see you throw away your career."

Christina pondered Rosalind's and Walter's comments as she did the dinner dishes later that night. When she finished, she turned off the lights in the kitchen and went to her bedroom. She sat down on the side of the bed and removed a small black leather notebook from her nightstand. Turning to the page entitled "Personal Goals," she began to read. A few minutes later, she picked up the phone and dialed her mother's number. No answer. She hung up and dialed another number.

"Marshall's Nursery," her mother answered.

"Mom, it's me." Christina still held the black leather notebook.

"Christina, how are you, honey?"

"Great, Mom," Christian answered. She placed the notebook back in the nightstand. "I know what I'm going to do."

One year later

Christina and Louise arrived at Boston's Four Seasons Hotel for the Communications Limited Annual Awards Ceremony at seven o'clock. Since Christina was the guest of honor, she and Louise sat at the head of the table.

As soon as dessert was served, Walter moved to the podium. The tinkling of fork against glass got everyone's attention and he began.

"This evening we're honoring one of our own, Christina Marshall. She's being honored for her work on ORION. This time last year few of us were optimistic about the success of ORION. Gross mismanagement had the project behind schedule and out of focus. Christina changed all of that.

"Her success is no surprise. Stellar performance has marked each of her eight years here at CL, from her first assignment as associate engineer, to her job as project engineer, then senior engineer, and now managing engineer for ORION."

Walter turned to Christina. "Ladies and gentlemen, Christina Marshall."

Christina made the short walk to the podium amid a swell of applause. She wondered again at her wisdom in wearing the form-fitting blue sequined gown. Her first thought had been that it hugged her full breasts a bit too snugly, but Louise had convinced her that that wasn't the case. Now, making the trip to the podium, she was unsure again. Maybe the dress was too tight. Maybe she shouldn't have worn her hair up, exposing her long neck and smooth shoulders. Maybe…

Christina shook off the negative thoughts. She held her head high and stood tall, naked shoulder and neck be damned. Tonight was her night and she was going to enjoy it.

She viewed the award as confirmation of her instincts. She had been right to go to Atlanta. It had been a tough year, but all the hard work had paid off. The success of ORION had put her back on the fast track. "Thank you, Walter. Thanks to the board for this recognition. I share it with my staff in Atlanta. They worked tirelessly for the past year and the success of ORION is the result. We in Atlanta accept this award as a symbol of the faith that CL has in our operation. We will continue to serve CL with the professionalism and excellence that inspired this award. Thank you."

Another round of applause followed as Christina returned to her seat.

Rosalind took the podium next. "It's no secret that some of us were convinced that Christina shouldn't take the ORION position. We thought OPTIMA was the better project for her. Though she proved us wrong on the first point, we still think that she's the best person for OPTIMA. So, effective the first of next month, Christina Marshall is the new district manager for OPTIMA."

Louise smiled at Christina and squeezed her hand with joy. "I knew you'd make the right decision. Now you have OPTIMA *and* Atlanta. You have everything you wanted."

Christina returned pressure to her mother's hand. "Yes, Mom, everything I wanted." Even as she spoke the words, Christina knew they weren't true. She didn't have everything she wanted. Not yet.

Chapter 2

Christina looked at the clock on the microwave above the oven. Good timing. It was almost seven. Liza should be arriving any minute now, she thought, as she put her special green bean casserole in the oven.

It has been several years since she'd seen her old friend. She sighed over the fact that it had taken OPTIMA to bring them back together. She had her fingers crossed that Liza would take the job as one of her project managers. It would be good to have a girlfriend again. As if on cue, the doorbell rang.

"It's so good to see you again, Liza. Has it really been three years?" Christina asked, after they had shared hugs.

"Three long years," Liza said. "The last time we saw each other was the night we celebrated our promotions to senior engineer."

"Yes," Christina said. "A combination celebration and going-away party."

"You were lucky. You got to stay in Boston, but I had to move to Forth Worth."

"At the time, I didn't see myself as the lucky one. I would have given anything for a move back south."

"Yeah," Liza said. "And look what happened when you did move south. Congrats again on your promotion to district manager and your success with ORION. I'm sorry I couldn't make the banquet."

Christina waved her hands to dismiss Liza's apology. "Don't even think about it. You sent a card. I understand. Now tell me what you've been up to."

Christina led Liza to the family room, where they seated themselves on identical facing blue leather couches. They began to catch up on all that had happened while they'd been apart.

"You're getting married!" Christina practically shrieked at her friend's news. "I didn't even know you were seeing anyone. When did this happen?"

"You knew I was seeing someone, Christina. I told you. Remember? His name's Robert. I met him at a Professional Accountants meeting."

"Oh, yes, I do recall something about your going to some meeting to meet men."

Liza placed one hand on her hip and shook her finger at Christina. "I didn't go to meet men. I have a real interest in accounting."

Christina laughed. "Sure you do, Liza. Anyway, I'm not knocking it. Maybe I should try it. It worked well for you."

Christina got up from the couch. "I want to hear all about this guy of yours. How about something to drink first? This is an occasion for wine. Which do you prefer, white or red?"

"White."

"Two white wines coming up."

When Christina went to prepare the drinks, Liza got up and walked around the room. She was seated in front of the fireplace when Christina returned.

Taking a sip, Liza began her story. "You remember how much I hated Fort Worth when I first got there? After the first month, I was sure that going there was the biggest mistake of my life. Then I met Robert." Liza faced Christina. "He changed my life. It's hard to explain."

That single statement touched Christina in a secret place. For the first time, she was envious of Liza. To cover her feelings, she remarked in jest, "So, he was your knight in shining armor. He rescued you from the boredom of Forth Worth."

"No," Liza corrected, her voice soft, almost serene. "It wasn't like that. It may have started like that, but Robert and I had to work hard for our love."

"What do you mean?" Christina asked, now serious.

"From the beginning I liked him a lot. He was such fun to be with. We had common interests—I loved a good party, we found the same things funny. The laughter attracted me first. Then his cooking."

Christina was surprised. "He cooks?"

Liza nodded. "The man is a master chef. He started cooking for me after our second date. He said that I didn't eat right and he made it his business to see that I did. I liked that. It showed that he cared, and it felt good to have someone care." Liza's voice wavered as she said the last. She got up, swirling her drink around in her glass. Her eyes focused intently on Varnette P. Honeywood's *Jackie's Song,* hanging on the wall above the television, but it seemed her thoughts were miles away.

"What is it, Liza?" Christina asked.

Liza looked at Christina then. She smiled a smile that didn't quite reach her eyes. "He had problems with my weight at first."

"Oh," was the only comment Christina could make. She knew how the weight comments could kill a budding relationship. Obviously, though, Liza and Robert had gotten past them.

"He had this picture of the woman he would marry. She was a size 5 or 7 or 9. You know that I'm none of those."

Christina looked at her friend's two-hundred pound frame and understood how she must have felt. Though Liza was an attractive, well-proportioned woman with soft features, Christina knew that sometimes men only saw the weight. Christina had first-hand experience with that herself. She had been Liza's weight before and knew it was hell getting a relationship started and even tougher keeping it going. One could work through it, though. Liza and Robert were proof of that. "How did you two deal with it?"

"I fought for him. In the past, I would have backed out of the relationship to keep from getting hurt. This time I couldn't do that. Robert had become too important to me. It was too close to call for a while, but once Robert admitted to himself that he loved me, we knew we had it made." Liza smiled and lifted her glass in a toast. "Here's to women who fight for what they want."

"I'm for all that," Christina agreed, lifting her glass. "So, what about sex?" The question rushed out. If she had taken time to think about it, she would never have asked it.

"What about it?"

It was too late for Christina to take it back now. "That's what I'm asking you."

"Of course, we've made love. We're good together. What more can I say?"

Christina placed her glass on the table and rose from her seat. Though she wanted to have this conversation, she was beginning to feel uncomfortable. Vulnerable. "I don't quite know how to ask this, but I need to know."

"Just ask. It's obviously important to you. If I don't want to answer it, I won't."

The next words rushed out of Christina's mouth. "Was it hard to take your clothes off the first time?"

Liza didn't answer immediately. She took a deep breath and nodded in a way that made Christina think that the question brought unhappy memories. "It was a little difficult the first time. I knew that Robert cared for me, but I didn't know how he'd respond to the whole me, naked. His response…well, let's call it enthusiastic. After the first time, it was no longer an issue." Liza's expression brightened and she looked directly at Christina. "Why do you ask?"

Christina turned away. "It scares me, Liza. That's the reason, or at least that's one of the reasons, I haven't allowed anybody to get close to me. I'm afraid of the rejection. I've lost a lot of weight, but I still don't have a model's body and I don't know if I could handle rejection if it came at an intimate moment like that."

Surprised, Liza sat on the couch and placed her glass on the cocktail table. "Are you telling me you're still a virgin?" When Christina didn't answer, Liza continued, "What about you and Bruce?"

Christina took a seat on the couch facing Liza. "Nothing happened. We came close a few times. I just couldn't go through with it. I had mixed feelings. I liked being close, but I feared his reaction to my naked body and I was scared to death of becoming pregnant. There was no way I was going to get pregnant and have to quit school. My worst nightmare is being an unwed mother. I saw the problems my mom faced, and I don't want to face them. Neither do I want to put my children through them."

"There's such a thing as birth control," Liza reasoned.

Christina picked up her glass and ran her finger around its rim. "Yes, but nothing is a hundred percent effective. Anyway, with Bruce, fear of pregnancy wasn't the only hindrance. I wasn't sure I loved him. So, I couldn't make love with him."

"My, my," Liza clasped her hands together. "A thirty-year-old virgin. I'll bet there aren't many of you around."

"You'd lose your money. The June issue of *Cosmopolitan* had a survey that showed there are a large group of us."

Liza began shaking her head. "I don't see how you made it through college."

"In the words of my mother, I kept my dress down and my legs closed."

Laughing, Liza admonished, "Christina, you're awful."

"It's true, though now it's like a bad habit that I can't break."

"I've never heard virginity called a bad habit before."

"You know what I mean," Christina said. She drank the last of her wine and leaned back on the couch. "Once you get used to keeping men at arm's length, you find yourself doing it automatically, even when you don't want to. Now that I've waited so long, I find more reasons I shouldn't—my body, my age, AIDS. You name it."

"All people have insecurities, Christina, but they don't let those insecurities stop them from pursuing relationships. You shouldn't let yours stop you, either."

Intellectually, she knew Liza was right, but emotionally, she wasn't sure she was ready for that kind of advice. "It's so easy to fill my life with other things—the house, work—so that I don't have to think about how much I'm missing or how much I want a real relationship, marriage, and children."

"You can have all of that, if you're willing to work for it. You've got to get outside yourself and take a risk. Being vulnerable is the foundation of any relationship."

Christina knew there was truth in Liza's words, but it was too much for her to think about right now. To lighten the conversation, she asked, "Are you sure I can't have a relationship that's guaranteed not to hurt? I'm so used to formulas and equations that I should be able to create the perfect relationship."

Liza shook her head. "Sorry, my friend, it doesn't work that way. Everybody gets hurt. Some more than others. As they say, 'No pain, No gain.'"

"You must be getting tired, Liza. Isn't that an exercise slogan?"

Liza laughed. "What do you expect this late at night? You have to catch me in the morning for something original."

"I'll remember that." Christina stood up. "My famous green bean casserole should be ready about now. Are you hungry?"

Liza stood, too. "I thought you'd never ask. Lead the way."

The women ate a relaxed dinner as Liza talked more about her wedding plans. After dinner, Christina gave Liza the grand tour of her home. They ended up in the guest bedroom where Liza would sleep. The blue-patterned curtains and comforter were warm and suited the night and the night's conversation.

"You have a very comfortable and inviting home, Christina. I hope Robert and I can find something as good. We really want to buy a house. How long have you been here?"

"Seven months now. It seems longer, though," Christina answered.

"How so?"

"There's a lot of work to do when you live in a house. Yard work and housework. And there's not that much time left when you're working twelve- and fifteen-hour days. It might be easier for you and Robert, since there will be two of you."

Liza didn't agree. "That won't help. We're both going to be very busy when we first move here. Maybe we should wait a while before we buy?"

"That's what I did. When I first moved back, I lived in an

apartment in midtown, so I'd be close to work. I was working close to twenty-four-hour days then."

Liza sat on the edge of the bed and pulled off her shoes. "Why such long hours? I know there was a lot of work, but that much time is a bit extreme, even for you."

"I was determined to make a success of this move," Christina said, leaning against the chest nearest the door. "Walter and Rosalind were dead set against it. They didn't think it was a wise career move. I wanted to prove them wrong."

"Well, you definitely did that," Liza stated.

"So I did," Christina said. She *had* proved Rosalind and Walter wrong, but she still hadn't achieved her primary goal. Talking with Liza tonight made her realize that all the more.

"It seems like you're settling in for the duration."

"In a way, I am," Christina said. "I never considered Boston home. It was a stopover on my way back to Atlanta. Now that I'm here, I want to establish roots, settle down, build a future." Christina knew she sounded like she was on a soapbox. "Sound crazy?"

"Not at all. That's the way I feel. I want Robert and me to establish roots, settle down, build a future."

"You're lucky," Christina said. "You've already found that special person to share the future with you."

Christina and Liza rushed to the office the next morning. It was about a thirty-minute drive, in rush-hour traffic, from Christina's house to the midtown office of Communications Limited. Christina took Liza on a tour of the facility, introduced her to the staff, and then took her to lunch with the people who would be reporting to her. After lunch they went back to Christina's office.

"It's going to be at least four months before I can make the move," Liza said. "With my current project, the wedding and the honeymoon, four months is probably optimistic."

"We'll work that out. I'm just glad you want the job. Your delayed start won't present much of a problem if Jackson Duncan

can start immediately. The first six to nine months will be planning anyway, and Jackson will handle that. You'll handle the implementation."

"Has he accepted the job?" Liza asked.

Christina shook her head. She was interviewing Jackson Duncan for the other project manager position on her staff. "He'll be in tomorrow."

"I've heard only good things about his work. And though he has the reputation of being a ladies' man, I hope he takes the job."

"His reputation doesn't bother me," Christina said. "I'm only interested in what he'll do in the office. And I have a feeling that he's going to accept the job. Walter hinted that he'd recommended Jackson take it. And you know how Walter recommends."

Liza laughed. "I see what you mean." She looked at her watch. "The limo should be here to take me to the airport. I'd better go down now."

Christina rode the elevator to the lobby with her. "It's been good seeing you again, Liza. Thanks for the talk last night."

"Remember what I told you—don't let your insecurities stop you from going after what you want. You don't let it happen in your professional life, so don't let it happen in your personal life. Go after what you want."

After giving Christina a short hug, Liza got into the limo. Christina watched as the car pulled away. "Go after what you want," Christina spoke softly to herself. "Maybe I should do that."

"Excuse me, Miss Marshall." A security guard interrupted her thoughts. "Do you need any help?"

"No," Christina said. "I'm fine."

Christina returned to her office. She tried to review the paperwork on Jackson Duncan, but her mind still focused on her conversation with Liza last night. Since she wasn't accomplishing anything, she placed the Jackson Duncan file in her briefcase and left for the day.

* * *

Once home, Christina went directly to her bedroom and removed the small black leather notebook from her nightstand. She sat on the floor beside the bed, turned to the page entitled "Personal Goals," and began to read. The list read:

1. Move to Atlanta
2. Get established in job
3. Buy house
4. Get established in community
5. Make friends
6. Fall in love
7. Get married
8. Have 3 children

Of the eight entries, Christina had already accomplished the first three. The Outstanding Manager Award for her work on ORION indicated her success. Now she was a district manager and OPTIMA was her project. Not bad for one year.

She was working on numbers 4 and 5. Numbers 6, 7, and 8 were dearest to her heart. What Christina really wanted, and she was embarrassed to think it even to herself, was to be in love. She wanted to share her life with a special man. Not exactly modern or progressive thinking, but her thinking nonetheless.

As she sat on the floor beside her bed, she began to make a list of things she could do and places she could go to meet eligible men. Liza would be proud of her for making a move. Yes, making the list was the first step; acting on it would follow. Though she was afraid, she knew she had to start somewhere.

After finishing her list, Christina ate a light dinner and started on the Jackson Duncan file. He was twenty-eight and had been at CL for six years, and a managing engineer for two. Both years were spent on special projects for the president of CL. Quite impressive, Christina thought with a smile. According to his last manager, his arrogance was outweighed only by his effectiveness. Jackson Duncan was the stereotypical CL executive. His career path led directly to senior management.

He may be just what we need to get OPTIMA off the drawing board, she thought. The interview tomorrow should prove interesting.

It was nine-thirty in the evening. Jackson Duncan sat at the bar in the Georgian Hotel on Peachtree Street in Atlanta and thought about Christina Marshall. He had read her file on the flight in from Los Angeles. The file only confirmed what his friend, Walter Thomas, had already told him. Christina Marshall was a no-nonsense, get-the-job-done type. Her accomplishments impressed him, especially her work on ORION. The chance to work on OPTIMA with her convinced him that Atlanta wouldn't be a bad move.

OPTIMA was a career-making project, and Christina Marshall had Boston's attention. They would be watching her every move, which was fine with Jackson. He welcomed the attention. He knew that success with OPTIMA was key to a promotion and a district manager slot back in Boston. It was already agreed. He just had to bide his time with OPTIMA until a suitable position in Boston came open.

His thoughts came back to Christina Marshall. In some ways, his career followed hers. The lady must really be something, he thought. The interview tomorrow should prove interesting.

As Jackson finished his drink, he noticed an attractive black-haired woman with long legs sitting alone across from him. Before he could turn away, she looked up and smiled at him. Jackson recognized that smile. Why the hell not, he thought. He ordered another drink and walked over to meet the smiling lady.

Chapter 3

Jackson checked his appearance in the mirrored lobby walls. Not bad, he thought, for a guy who'd gotten only three hours of sleep. Mona, the black-haired woman from the bar, had kept him busy for over half the night. Not that he was complaining. No, work like that didn't cause a man to complain. Mona had been just the right kind of woman. She'd wanted only a good time for one night, no strings. And she'd been prepared. Jackson wondered if her name was really Mona.

The long, shapely legs and bouncing breasts of a woman crossing the street to the building interrupted his thoughts. He watched intently as the woman walked up the steps and through the lobby doors. He decided, as she entered the lobby door, that if she made eye contact with him, he would introduce himself. The woman didn't look his way. Obviously, she was in a hurry. Probably late for some meeting.

Jackson looked at his watch. Nine-fifteen. His interview with Christina Marshall was scheduled for nine o'clock. He checked with the lobby desk again. He didn't like waiting. And it was worse waiting today. He was hyped up about this assignment. Finally, a middle-aged woman, most like a secretary, walked up to him.

"Mr. Duncan, I'm sorry you had to wait. Miss Marshall can see you now."

Jackson followed the woman back to Christina Marshall's office.

When Jackson entered the office, he was surprised to see the woman he had watched crossing the street. She sat at the desk with the phone to her ear.

"Look, George," she was saying, "something is wrong with the car. Cars don't stop on the interstate for no reason at all."

The woman looked up and motioned Jackson to a chair in front of her desk. She went back to her conversation as he took a seat.

Jackson used the opportunity to get a good look at Christina Marshall. For some reason, he had never imagined how she looked. Until now, he had thought of her in sexless terms as an executive much like himself. This Christina Marshall was a lot different from him—in all the right places. She was a knockout in a nontraditional way. She was tall, about five foot ten. She wasn't overweight, but neither could she be called slim. He liked her fullness, the roundness of her shape, especially her breasts. The breasts he had noticed as she'd crossed the street were no longer bouncing, but they looked as soft as pillows. He wondered how it would feel to rest his head on them. His gaze moved from her breasts to her strong, inviting neck and on to her face. Her face was hard to describe, but Jackson liked it. It was delicate, yet it had strength. The full lips were colored with coral lipstick that accentuated her honey-brown complexion. He imagined kissing away every speck of the color. As he was thinking of the words to describe her silken black hair, Jackson realized he was having a physical reaction to Miss Marshall that could prove embarrassing to them both.

To stop staring at her and to stop the rush of blood to his groin, he got up and pretended interest in the art hanging on her office walls. It was no use. He could no more stop his mind from thinking about her than he could stop his body from responding. Giving her a glance and pointing toward the door, Jackson left her office for an emergency run to the bathroom.

He couldn't believe what was happening to him. He hadn't had such an immediate physical reaction to a woman since he was fourteen years old. *You are here to work with her on OP-TIMA while you wait for your promotion,* he reminded himself. *Starting something with Miss Marshall would be a mistake.*

Finished in the bathroom, Jackson made his way back to Christina's office. If Mona is any indication, there are plenty of women here in Atlanta, he reminded himself. So stay away from the boss.

"I can't talk about this any longer, George," Christina said. "Call me after you repair the car."

Christina placed the receiver on the hook. She was glad she had been on the phone when Jackson arrived. She couldn't believe he was the man she had noticed briefly in the lobby. She had thought him appealing and she had known that he had been watching her. That knowledge boosted her self-confidence. Remembering her conversation with Liza about going after what she wanted, she had considered making eye contact with the man and giving him a smile. Yet, she had checked herself with the reminder that she was late for an appointment. Besides, she knew nothing about the man. Anyway, she didn't want to start considering every man she met a possible prospect. She wasn't that desperate. Yet.

She admitted she'd been shaken when the man had walked into her office. She had intentionally kept the conversation with George going longer than necessary. She needed the time to compose herself. For a moment she had wondered if her mind was playing tricks on her, but no, that was Jackson Duncan. Her secretary guarded her door with a warriorlike force. Jackson Duncan would be the only man to walk through it.

None of her research prepared her for meeting Jackson Duncan in the flesh. He was a very attractive man, from the close-cropped wavy black hair to... His reentry into the room stopped her thoughts. As he strode purposefully toward her, she came around her desk and extended her hand.

"Please forgive the delay. My car broke down this morning. That was my mechanic on the phone. Can we start over, Mr. Duncan?"

He took her hand and squeezed it briefly before letting it go. "No need for that, Miss Marshall. And, the name is Jackson."

"Jackson it is, then. I'm Christina. Would you like to sit over there?" She pointed to a sitting area with two wing chairs and a small table.

"That's fine with me," Jackson answered.

After they were seated, she asked, "So, what do you think of Atlanta so far?"

"I could get to love it here. It's a beautiful city. Beautiful, and inviting."

Christina felt Jackson was talking about more than the city, but she didn't dare inquire. Using her most professional tone, she asked him about the work he had done as managing engineer. He gave her details of his two most recent projects. Although she already knew about them from her research, she wanted his description of his contribution.

He spoke with animation. Christina knew from the cadence of his voice and the twinkle in his eyes that he enjoyed his work very much. He wasn't selfish in his praise. He noted the contribution of others without downplaying his own.

"Did they brief you on OPTIMA and your role should you decide to accept the position?"

"I talked with Walter Thomas about it and Rosalind flew out to LA to convince me to take the job. I'd like to get your view, though. Walter and Rosalind tend to give only enough information to get you to do what they want you to do."

Christina found his observation amusing and accurate, but she didn't comment on it. "OPTIMA is aimed at manufacturing facilities. We plan to write the software for each customization to meet the specific needs of individual customers without massive rewriting. Because of your previous assignments, I'd want you to lead the planning effort. This project has been on the drawing board for two years now. It's time it became a reality. Your job would be to get it off the drawing board, to get the specifications into the hands of Liza Randall. Liza will be on board in about six months, and she'll be in charge of implementation."

"How would my role change during that phase?" Jackson asked.

Christina was impressed with the question. Jackson Duncan looked ahead. "I envision more planning. By the time Liza comes on board, we should have our first customers identified. You would interface with those customers to assure that our implementation met all their needs. It might be more accurate to describe your job as planning and deployment and Liza's as development and implementation."

He seemed to be deep in thought.

"Do you have any other questions?" she asked.

Jackson didn't hesitate. "How do you describe your management style?"

Christina smiled. "You mean, of course, am I going to give you the space to do your job, or will I overmanage you."

She thought she saw respect flash in his eyes. "Yes, that's what I meant," Jackson answered.

Christina described her management style and gave her expectations for how the two of them would work together. They agreed to meet weekly to assess project status.

"When do I start?" Jackson asked.

Christina stood. "Two weeks from Monday, if possible."

Jackson got up. "Sounds good to me."

"Now that the hard part is over, why don't I show you around the place? I'd like you to meet and talk with a few members of the staff before you leave today."

Christina took Jackson to lunch at Montclair's on Peachtree, the place of choice for midtown executives for lunch. While they ate, Jackson gave his first impressions of the project and the people.

Christina smiled. "I'm glad we meet with your approval."

Jackson put his fork down and looked at Christina. "Don't get me wrong, that wasn't a negative comment. I'm genuinely pleased with all the people I've met. I didn't mean that I didn't expect to find good people. I'm only giving my impression of the staff."

"You'll learn, Jackson, that I have very thick skin. You'll have to try hard to insult me."

Jackson smiled then. I'll remember that."

How did the man get such a wonderful smile? Christina wondered. His smile made you want to smile back. She hoped she wasn't grinning at him like an idiot.

After lunch Christina left Jackson with one of the senior engineers and went back to her office. The lunch rattled her. There was something about the way Jackson looked at her. She had stopped herself from covering her breasts a couple of times. Yet it was nothing he did. It was how he made her feel.

When he laughed, something tingled down her spine. When he accidentally bumped against her arm, she felt every hair stand on end. It was electric. And his smile. When he smiled, she felt at home. There were times during the lunch when she felt as if she had a huge grin on her face. She had to pinch herself under the table to get control of her emotions.

"God, Christina. Listen to yourself think. You sound like some moonstruck teenager. Jackson Duncan is only a man—nothing more, nothing less." If you say that enough, maybe you'll believe it, she thought.

Christina forced herself to stop thinking about him as she read the latest OPTIMA report. At the end of every paragraph, she saw his smile.

Jackson was just as deeply affected by lunch with Christina. His only memory was the sway of her hips as she'd walked away, leaving him to talk with the senior engineer.

A man could get hooked on a woman like Christina, he thought. But it wouldn't be him. He had seen first-hand what that could do to a man. His father had been hooked—too much—on his mother. Jackson wondered if his father had felt for his mother what he himself was now feeing for Christina. He never understood the hold his mother had had over his father. He swore that no woman would ever control him the way his mother had controlled his father. Ironically, that was part of his appeal to women. They viewed his aloofness as a challenge. Each woman felt that she would be the woman to change him. Jackson had proved them all wrong. That was why he didn't understand his reaction to Christina.

Jackson stopped Christina as she entered her office his second week on the job. "I need to talk to you for a few minutes."

"Sure, Jackson, come on in. Have a seat." Christina settled into a chair. "What's on your mind?"

At that moment Christina's breasts were on Jackson's mind. He could see the tops of them as she leaned forward to speak to him. Did she realize how she looked in that red silk blouse? "I may have to go to Boston. The OPTIMA transition team is dragging its feet. I have people here who are ready to work, and I can't get Boston to turn over all the plans."

Christina dropped her pencil on the desk. "I was afraid this would happen. Do what you have to do and keep me posted. If you don't get some cooperation by the end of the week, let me know."

Jackson flashed a smile. "Thanks, boss. I'm going to give it one more day before I make the trip."

His smile was contagious. "It's good having you on board, Jackson. Have you found a place to live yet?"

"Thanks and no. I'm living in a furnished apartment now."

"Feel free to take some time off to get settled if you need it," Christina offered.

"I'll remember that," Jackson replied and left the office.

Jackson Duncan had arrived at CL-Atlanta and every woman on the staff knew it. Christina noticed that the women always had something to say to Jackson. And Jackson always had time to listen. There was always a smile or a laugh involved and Christina noticed a touch or two. There was a visible electric charge between Jackson and any woman with whom he spoke. Christina began to wonder if the man had enough work to do. She certainly didn't have time to flirt with every man in the office. How, then, did Jackson find time to flirt with every woman?

With shock, Christina realized she was jealous. Jackson wasn't flirting with every woman in the office. He was flirting with every woman except her. In the short time he was on staff, he didn't even engage in light banter with her. For him, everything was strictly business.

Jackson stopped by Christina's office Friday morning. "It wasn't necessary for me to make the trip to Boston. The transition team released the plans Wednesday. Our guys are working with them now. We should have some results in the next two weeks."

"That's good news. Do you have an estimate for the staff you're going to need?"

"I've worked up some numbers for you, but they won't be ready until late this afternoon. Can we postpone our regular status meeting until then?"

Christina checked her calendar. "Four-thirty okay?"

"Four-thirty it is."

Christina didn't get out of her meeting until six. Jackson was waiting in her office when she got there.

"I'm sorry I'm so late, Jackson," she said with a smile. Her heart took a leap to see him looking so incredibly handsome in a blue Armani suit. "I didn't expect you to wait, but I'm glad you did."

"I wanted to go over these numbers with you while they were fresh in my mind." His real reason for waiting was that he wanted to get one final look at her to last him the weekend.

"Give me a second to recover from that meeting. We were there for five hours. It was a killer." Christina closed her eyes and leaned back in her chair. She began to turn her head from left to right as if to remove tension.

She looked so sexy sitting there with her eyes closed and her lips slightly parted. Jackson had often resisted unbidden thoughts of her like this. But for some reason he couldn't stop them. Something about Christina Marshall made her image fill his every thought. With that in mind, Jackson moved behind her chair and began to slightly massage her neck and shoulders.

It startled Christina at first, and she knew she should stop him, but she said nothing since it felt so good and she needed it so badly.

Jackson stopped and Christina opened her eyes. He had moved and now stood in front of her. His face reflected naked hunger.

Something inside Christina responded to that hunger and she wanted to reach out and touch him. As she moved to do just that, her phone rang. She looked at Jackson and she looked at the phone. She answered the phone.

When she had finished her call, Jackson showed her the numbers. He had projections through the next year. She gave him the go-ahead for the additional staff.

As Jackson gathered his papers, he casually asked, "It's late. How about getting a bite to eat?"

Christina didn't answer immediately. The question took her by surprise. She knew that Jackson and other members of the staff ate dinner together when they worked late. She had gone with them once or twice, but Jackson made her uncomfortable, so she had stopped going. "Tonight's not a good night. Maybe another night." That was a good answer, she thought.

Jackson wasn't fooled. She wanted to pretend that nothing had happened between them, and he wasn't going to allow it. Not tonight. "We can't deny what almost happened, Christina."

She lowered her eyelids to hide her surprise. "I don't know what you're talking about."

Jackson faced her. "You do know what I'm talking about. I'm talking about what almost happened before your phone rang a while ago."

Christina turned away. "Mr. Duncan…" she started.

Jackson spoke to her back. "I'm attracted to you, Christina, and you're attracted to me. If your phone had not rung, you would have kissed me."

Christina didn't deny it, but she didn't admit it, either. She turned around to face him. "You seem pretty confident of that."

"God, Christina, the tension between us is so strong that you can practically see it."

"I'm not saying you're right, Jackson. But even if you are, there can never be anything between us."

"Why? Because we work together? I had the same reservations, but—"

Christina interrupted him. "We don't just work together, Jackson, I'm your boss. You report to me. A less trusting person might suspect the motivation behind your interest."

Jackson rubbed his hand across his head. "Christina, I am very attracted to you. I am attracted to your smile, your eyes, the way you move, the way you handle business. And I think you feel the same way. I am not using you to further my career. Do you think I need to do that at this stage in my career?"

No, she didn't really think that, but she couldn't think of anything else to say. "Don't act so surprised. It wouldn't be the first time that it's happened."

"You mean something like that happened to you before?" he asked.

He was getting it all wrong. "Not to me, Jackson. I'm talking about in general."

"Generalities don't interest me. I'm interested in you and me."

"It's not that simple. I'm your boss. That's a complication."

"It doesn't have to be. Your position doesn't threaten me and I don't need to use you to get ahead. We both know that I'm already established here." He grinned. "And, as for you being the boss, there are benefits to a woman taking charge."

She rolled her eyes. "Be serious, Jackson."

"I don't want to be serious. I don't want *you* to be serious. I only want to see if what we feel is real." He took her hand and pulled her to him. Looking into her eyes, he asked, "Aren't you even the tiniest bit curious about it yourself? Don't you want to know?"

God help her, she did want to know. Jackson captivated her. He was so handsome, and he showed such sincerity. Being close to him felt good. She relaxed in his arms, then spoke so softly he had to lean closer to hear. "You know what they say about curiosity, don't you?"

"Tell me, Christina," he whispered. He was so close she could feel his breath on her face.

Christina abruptly stepped out of his arms and looked him square in the face. "Curiosity killed the cat."

Jackson stared at her. Then he laughed. Without saying anything else, he gathered his papers and walked toward the door. He turned back to face her. "You know what I think about that, Christina?"

When she didn't respond, he told her anyway. "A cat has nine lives, so a little curiosity won't really matter. Will it?" Without waiting for a response, he opened the door and was gone.

Chapter 4

Christina sat at her desk and rested her face in her hands. Curiosity killed the cat. Real good, Christina. That was a sparkling retort. Admit that Jackson has you rattled. He was right on every count. You're attracted to him and it's taking all of your energy to fight that attraction. And, yes, you would have kissed him if the phone had not rung.

She lifted her head from her hands. What am I going to do? she wondered. She knew that she shouldn't even consider a personal relationship with Jackson since he worked for her, but she was doing just that.

Maybe I met Jackson at a vulnerable time, she reasoned. Only a few nights ago I was pouring out my heart to Liza about marriage and a family, then along comes Jackson Duncan, everything a woman could want in a man. Well, almost everything, she argued with herself; your ideal man doesn't usually work for you. Except for that minor—no, major— point, Jackson Duncan would be a godsend. He was attractive, yes, but that was only part of his appeal. There was something about him, his self-confidence, maybe, that made her think he could handle anything. It instilled a sense of trust. It made her think Jackson would take care of her love if she ever gave it to him.

"I'm not too sure how easily Mr. Duncan would give his love, though," she said aloud. "Sometimes I think he carries as much baggage as I do in that area."

Christina got up from her desk and walked over to the window. She knew she should go home, but she didn't want to face an empty house this weekend. She needed to talk to someone.

I know what I'll do, she mused, I'll take a trip this weekend. And I know just the place.

She packed her briefcase and left the office feeling better than she had felt since Jackson Duncan had come to Atlanta.

Jackson began unpacking boxes in his new apartment that night. The confrontation with Christina had energized him. Now he knew how she felt. She felt the attraction, but she resisted it. He understood her apprehension, given their professional relationship. He had apprehensions, too, but he detected in Christina a fear that had nothing to do with their working relationship. All that talk about the job was a smokescreen. He was sure of it. What was she afraid of?

Maybe something happened in the past. Some guy she worked with probably mistreated her. Now I have to pay, he thought. I hate that women do that. One man does wrong, and the next man who's interested pays the price. Sometimes it makes a guy contemplate celibacy. Why even bother?

We bother because we need women. "Can't live with 'em, can't live without 'em" applies to women, too. It's hard to find a good woman. When a man finds one, he'll take all the bull that she dishes out because he knows she's worth it. Too many women are looking for someone to take care of them, financially and emotionally. That burden is too big for any man. A strong woman with her own goals and her own identity is a treasure more than worth the wait and the hassle.

"Hold on there, Jackson," he chided himself. "You're thinking like a man ready to settle down. That's not you. You're going to be in Atlanta at most two years, and then it's back to Boston with a promotion. Now concentrate on unpacking those boxes before you get yourself in trouble."

It was a five-hour drive to Mobile in her recently serviced car. Christina's first choice had been to visit her mother in Selma, but Louise was going to the Nursery Owners' Convention in Memphis. Mobile was her second choice. Christina had promised herself that she would "see the South" this year. She planned to do it in a series of weekend trips. Among other cities, she had already visited Asheville, Savannah, and Birmingham. Mobile seemed a reasonable next place.

The drive down was uneventful. She arrived at the Malaga Inn in downtown Mobile a littler after one in the morning.

After a good night's sleep, Christina faced Saturday morning, late Saturday morning, with excited anticipation. She decided to take an escorted tour to get an overview of the historic downtown area and then to visit the battleship. The tour bus was one of those open air buses patterned after the nineteenth-century horse-drawn trolleys. She took an empty seat about midway the bus. There were quite a few people on board, three older couples, four couples about her age, and about two groups of two together. She was the only person alone. Though she regularly traveled alone, sometimes she envied the couples and friends traveling together. She had tried vacationing with girlfriends before, but it had never worked out. You needed to be pretty good friends with somebody for it to work.

Christina's attention was drawn to the front of the bus as a tall, dark man got on. She watched him as he moved down the aisle to take a seat. As he passed her, she averted her eyes so as not to make eye contact. When she realized what she had done, she cursed herself. Damn, she thought, I could have smiled at him. He's alone; I'm alone. We could have shared this tour together. At least I would have had someone to talk with.

The tour went down Dauphin Street, circling the park at Bienville Square before stopping at Horst House on Conti Street. After getting off the bus, Christina consulted her tourbook. A deep voice interrupted her.

"An amazing restoration job, wouldn't you agree?" It was the man from the bus.

"I was thinking the same thing. I can't imagine anyone ever living here, though," she said with a nervous laugh. "It's too formal."

"I prefer a place that's a bit more casual myself," he said, "but it is impressive."

"Like fine art. You enjoy looking at it in a museum, but you would never be comfortable with it in your home."

"Yes, that's it exactly."

Christina walked over to get a closer look at an odd-looking object that may have been a vase, but it contained no flowers. The man followed her.

"Do you have any idea what it is?" he asked.

God, the thing is ugly. She frowned. "No, I don't. It's kind of…interesting looking."

He smiled. "It *is* ugly, isn't it?"

She returned his smile. At least he was honest enough to speak his mind.

"I'm Reggie Stevens," he said, extending his hand to her.

She shook it. "Christina Marshall."

"Nice to meet you, Christina. How about me following you around for the rest of this tour? Maybe you can teach me something about history and art appreciation."

She saw the kidding in his eyes, so she laughed. "I don't know about my teaching you anything. It may be a case of the blind leading the blind, but you're welcome to follow me around."

He bent at the waist in an exaggerated bow. "Thank you, madam. After you."

Christina and Reggie spent the rest of the tour together. He was funny, and she enjoyed his company. From Oklahoma City, he was in town for an interview with International Paper. Having never been to Mobile before, he had come in early to see the city.

When the tour ended, Reggie asked, "What are your plans for the rest of the day?"

She pulled her tourbook from her purse. "I'm going to Battleship Park. What about you?"

"I was planning to visit there myself. Mind if I tag along?"

Christina hesitated. She was sure she wanted his company, but she wasn't sure if that was wise. A woman alone could never be too careful.

Reggie jumped in before she could answer. "We can take separate cars. That way, you can dump me if I begin to bore you," he said with a smile.

She considered his request. He's a pleasant man and we won't be traveling together, she reasoned. Oh, what the hell? "Sure, it ought to be fun."

They drove to Battleship Park in separate cars, with Christina leading the way. She wanted to take the harbor tour of Mobile Bay.

"I'm sorry, the last tour was at one-thirty," the reservationist said.

"I thought the last tour was at three-thirty," Christina responded, her disappointment obvious. "I'm sure I read that somewhere."

"You probably got our schedules mixed up. We only have the three-thirty tour in June, July, and August."

"I hate that I missed it." She looked at Reggie, who hadn't said a word. "I really wanted to go out on the water."

"Maybe we could do it tomorrow."

Christina noticed with a grin that he had said, "we." So he was planning to spend time with her tomorrow. She liked that.

Reggie turned to the reservationist. "What's tomorrow's schedule?"

"We have tours at eleven and one-thirty. We also have a dinner cruise tonight at seven. You'd probably enjoy that more. You don't get the narrated tour, but it's pretty out there at night. Couples enjoy it. There's plenty of food and good music. You can even dance if you like."

"Sounds like it might be fun." Turning to Christina, he asked, "What do you say?"

Christina still wondered at the reservationist's assumption that she and Reggie were a couple. She liked the thought of being part of a couple. Jackson's smile registered in her brain. She pushed the thought aside. "Okay, let's do it." She turned to the reservationist. "How much is it?"

The reservationist told them the price and they paid. Reggie offered to pay for Christina, but she declined with a polite smile.

Reggie checked his watch. "We don't have to be back until six-thirty. That gives us three hours. Let's get started."

The tour of the battleship took ninety minutes. Reggie had spent two years in Navy ROTC, so he had first-hand information about ships that made the tour more enjoyable.

"You weren't lying when you said you were planning to come here, were you?" Christina asked.

His eyes widened in surprise. "No, I had planned to come. Did you think I was lying?"

"I didn't exactly think of it as lying," she said, not wanting to hurt his feelings. "I thought of it more as a pick-up line."

He laughed. "I might have used one if you'd said you were going somewhere else, but fate was on my side and I didn't have to."

She lifted a questioning brow. "You think it was fate, do you?"

"Of course. How else can I explain an attractive woman like you on a tour bus *alone,* in Mobile, of all places, at the same time that I am in Mobile on that same tour bus? The gods must be watching out for me."

"I take that to mean you've enjoyed my company."

He took her hand and led her toward the submarine. "That's the understatement of the year."

"I'm starving," Christina said, after the tour of the submarine. "What time is it?"

Reggie turned his wrist so he could see his watch. "It's about six. We still have some time before the cruise. Can you hold out, or would you like to get something to drink?"

"I'd better get something to drink." She looked around. "Where can we go?"

"I remember a snack bar near the entrance." He took her hand and led her to it.

They took a seat after getting their drinks. Reggie told her about his upbringing. She had a warm feeling as she listened to the stories of his happy clan.

"Do you have a close family?" he asked.

"It's only my mom and me. We're very close. Over the years we've become friends as well as mother and daughter. She's one special lady."

"That's the way I feel about my mom. My dad's also a good guy. They've been married for forty-two years. That's good in anybody's book."

Christina envied Reggie his parents. Not that her mom wasn't fantastic, but she missed having a father. The more she thought about having a family of her own, the more she thought about her father. How she wished she could have known him. "I can't even imagine a marriage lasting that long. I'm only…" She stopped before revealing her age.

Reggie laughed. "You can tell me your age. I promise not to hold it against you." He raised his right hand. "Scout's honor. To make it easy for you, I'm thirty-seven."

"I'm thirty."

"I would have guessed that you were younger."

"Flattery will get you everywhere. Now, back to your parents. I can't imagine being with someone that long. Their marriage is older than I am. What's their secret?"

"I wonder at that myself sometimes. I think the key is openness. They don't keep secrets from each other. They talk about everything."

"Ummm…" Christina wondered what sharing your life with someone for forty-two years would be like. She hoped she'd get to experience it. Maybe with someone like Jackson. Christina felt her face flush. Now where did that come from?

Reggie pushed aside his drink cup. "We'd better start making our way back to the boat now." He stood up and helped her with her chair.

Christina welcomed the short walk. She needed the time to clear her mind of thoughts of Jackson.

They heard the music before they saw the boat. There was already a crowd. Reggie found a table near the crowded dance floor.

Before they took a seat, he asked, "Is this okay?"

She nodded and took the chair he was holding for her. She searched for the buffet table; she was starved.

"Would you rather eat or dance first?"

Christina moved her gaze to him. "Food first."

They made their way to the food and helped themselves to generous servings. They didn't talk much as they ate. Christina took the opportunity to observe Reggie more closely. She liked him. He was easy to talk to, and he liked to laugh. Strong and confident like Jackson, but much more open. Christina shook her head at the comparison. Why was she thinking about Jackson?

"Something wrong?" Reggie asked.

His voice brought her attention back to him. "I was thinking about the fun we've had today. It's been a real pleasure, an unexpected, but welcome pleasure."

"You talk like the night is over. Not yet, Cinderella. How about a dance?"

"I'd like that."

It had been a while since Christina had been out dancing, and she was enjoying herself. The music was good, and Reggie was a smooth dancer.

They danced for a long while, then took a walk on the top deck away from the dancers. They held hands but didn't speak as they watched the Mobile city lights shine in the distance. Christina liked the sense of togetherness she was feeling. It's been too long, she thought. She had almost forgotten what it felt like to be with a man like this. It was definitely something she could get used to.

The night passed quickly, and soon the cruise was over. They walked hand-in-hand to Christina's car. Reggie hadn't kissed her all night, though he'd had many opportunities. Well, if he doesn't kiss me, I'll kiss him, she decided.

She didn't need to worry. When they got to her car, Reggie leaned over and kissed her. A short, sweet kiss on the lips. He pulled back and looked into her eyes. "I think something special is happening."

Christina started to speak, but Reggie put a finger to her lips. "You don't have to say anything. I'm not rushing you. I'm only telling you what I'm feeling. Will I see you tomorrow?"

Christina wasn't sure what was happening, but she liked it. "I'm leaving early in the afternoon."

"Why don't I meet you for breakfast?"

She nodded as he ushered her into her car. She rolled down the window to say a final goodnight. He leaned in and gave her another kiss. "Sweet dreams," he said, and walked to his car.

He followed her to her hotel and waited in his car until she was safely in the lobby. Without any attempt at further conversation, he drove away.

Christina had sweet dreams that night. She dreamed of her and Reggie. At some point in the dream, Reggie began to look a lot like Jackson.

Jackson considered it a stroke of luck that the Atlanta chapter of his fraternity was having a picnic this Saturday afternoon. He had finished unpacking this morning and had called a fraternity brother who was a friend of a friend. He hoped to meet some interesting people, maybe some women to take his mind off Christina. After rethinking the situation last night, he decided it would be best for him and Christina if he didn't pursue her. If she'd been a little more receptive, he might have gone through with it. If he had been looking for a long-term relationship, he might have gone through with it. Since neither was the case, he was going to leave it alone.

"Hey, man, you must be Jackson." A smiling light-skinned man in an Omega T-shirt with the name "Maddog" written across the front was speaking to him. "I'm Ellis."

Jackson gave the fraternity handshake. "How did you know who I was, man? I didn't describe myself when we talked this morning."

"Maybe I'm psychic," Ellis joked. "Really, man, I called Tom in LA last night and he told me your line name." Ellis pointed to the name "MackDaddy" printed on Jackson's T-shirt.

Jackson laughed. "What else did Tom tell you about me? I haven't talked to him since I've been here."

Ellis turned away when someone called his name. He turned back to Jackson. "They're here. Let's get this meeting over so we can party. The women will be here in a couple of hours and we need to have the business finished then."

Jackson followed Ellis over to the other guys. They had a large chapter. Over two hundred on the roll, and nearly seventy-five at this meeting. Once again his fraternity affiliation was helping him settle into a new area.

As Ellis had said, the women started to arrive a couple of hours later. There were wives, girlfriends, and female friends. There were mostly couples, but that didn't bother Jackson; he liked going out alone. Usually a wife or girlfriend knew someone they would love to fix him up with. He took it all in stride. Today was no different.

"I know you'll like her," Betty was saying. Betty was Ellis's wife and she was talking about Angela, one of her sorority sisters.

"What makes you think an Omega man would be interested in an AKA woman?" he teased. "Omega men want Delta women."

"Please! Delta women are out. Ellis and I are the perfect example of what a good match you'd make with Angela. Are you free tomorrow night? We can have a few people over. A smaller group in a more intimate setting."

"Tomorrow's great. I appreciate your hospitality."

"Hey, it's my pleasure. Besides, I want to make sure that you meet Angela before one of these other women introduces you to one of their single girlfriends. AKA women watch out for each other." She laughed and was starting to say more when someone called her name. "Ellis will call you with directions. See you tomorrow. Again, welcome to Atlanta."

Jackson watched Betty as she rushed away. Ellis has done well for himself, he thought.

Jackson enjoyed the picnic. He ended up with three dinner invites, not counting tomorrow with Ellis and Betty, and at least fifteen "we must get together"s. With a little effort, he'd keep so busy that he wouldn't have time to think about Christina.

"I want to keep in touch with you, Christina," Reggie said over breakfast at the Malaga the next morning. "Maybe come to Atlanta. I've been through the airport a few times, but never a real visit."

"I'd like that, Reggie. You'd love the city, and I'd enjoy being your guide."

He reached his hand across the table and rested it atop hers. "Seeing the city wouldn't be my reason for coming. I'd be coming to see you."

Christina liked his directness. The feel of his hand against hers wasn't so bad, either. "I know, and it pleases me."

He removed his hand and continued eating. "Now that that's settled, what do you want to do for the rest of the morning?"

Christina checked out of her hotel and packed her car, and they drove down Spring Hill Avenue to the University of South Alabama. They strolled the campus.

"It's about time I get on the road for home," she said sometime later.

"I've been dreading those words, but I know you have to go. Let's head back for the cars."

As they made their way to the cars, Christina thought about the kisses they'd shared last night and felt her cheeks burn at the memory.

Today's kiss was more intense than last night's, holding a promise of future kisses and caresses. She liked the feel and the smell of him. And she liked his taste. Too soon she was in her car and Reggie was waving after her. His "I'll call you" seemed much more than a polite gesture.

Christina stopped to gas up a few miles outside Montgomery. While at the station, she called to see if her mother was home.

"I got back early," her mother said. "Why don't you stop over on your way back? You can drive to Atlanta Monday morning."

"Sounds like a good idea, Mom. I'll do that. Look for me in about an hour."

Exactly sixty-six minutes later Christina pulled into the driveway of her mother's house. She hadn't grown up in this house, so she'd never thought of the place as home. It was simply her mother's house, but she felt safe and comfortable here. The absence of the Ford Bronco in the driveway told Christina that her mother was out. She shook her head as she thought of her mother in the Bronco. Louise had bought a small Chevy truck when she'd first opened the nursery. Last year she'd gotten rid of her truck and gotten the Bronco. She'd said a lot about needing the Bronco for deliveries, but Christina could tell by the way Louise drove and by the way she cared for the car that it was her toy. It was unlike Louise to splurge on herself, and Christina was glad that she had.

Christina got out of her car and walked to the back of the house. She reached under the azalea pot on the back porch for the key. It was there. Small towns, she thought, as she opened the back door.

As soon as she walked into the kitchen, she heard Louise pull up out front. She went to open the door for her mother, and saw Louise taking packages from the back seat of the Bronco. My mom is a beautiful woman, she thought. She could easily pass for forty.

For as long as Christina could remember, people had asked if she and Louise were sisters. It had bothered her during her teen years, especially since she was taller than her mom even then, but as she'd grown older and more confident, it hadn't mattered as much. She'd never thought of Louise as anything but mom. As she looked at her today, she was reminded that Louise was so much more than just her mother. She was an attractive and desirable woman. There had been a couple men in Louise's life over the years. Christina wondered why there had never been anyone special.

Louise was also a successful businesswoman. She had worked as a nurse for almost thirty years before taking early retirement two years ago to open the nursery. That risk had proved profitable. The nursery had been operating in the black for the last year. Business was so good that she now had three full-time workers and was thinking about expanding. Yes, Louise was much more than just her mother.

Coming out of her reverie, Christina asked from the doorway, "Need any help?"

Louise looked up. "Hello, sweetheart. I thought I'd get back before you got here. I went to the post office and stopped off to get us a bite to eat. I hope you're hungry."

"I'm always hungry for the Colonel, Mom. You know that." Christina took the barrel of Kentucky Fried Chicken. "Let me help you. You take the mail and I'll take the food."

"How was your drive?" Louise asked, as they walked back into the house.

"Uneventful about sums it up."

"I don't like the idea of your traveling up and down the road by yourself. It's too dangerous."

"Mom…"

Louise held up her hand. "I know what you're going to say. You're a grown woman. You can take care of yourself."

"That's right. I *am* a grown woman and I *can* take care of myself. Besides, I'm careful. I don't take risks. I always make sure I have a tank of gas. I keep my car serviced and I have the single woman's substitute for a husband, Triple-A."

"Yes, but do you have to do so much traveling alone? Why don't you go with friends? That would be safer."

Christina placed the bucket of chicken on the table. "I know that, but I can't always wait until someone else is free. I don't want to wait. It makes me feel that I can't live my life. Do you understand what I mean?"

Louise looked at Christina. "Sometimes I forget how independent you are."

Christina smiled. "I'm like my mother."

Louise gave a small laugh. "Sometimes I forget that, too. So, how was Mobile?"

"I'm going to tell you about Mobile and the latest happenings in Atlanta, but first let's eat and talk about Memphis."

Louise took potato salad from the refrigerator and plates from the cabinet. She talked about the conference while they ate. She planned to take a Thanksgiving cruise with some people she had met at the conference.

"How can you plan a cruise with people you've known less than two days? Mom, you're the one who needs to be careful."

"It's safe enough. The Nursery Owners of Greater New Orleans are planning the trip. They plan something every year."

Christina retreated. "That's more like it."

"I met a couple there that had recently opened their second nursery. It made me rethink my position. Maybe I should expand. What do you think?"

"You want to expand. I know you can make a go of a second shop. Give your attorney a call next week and see what he says."

"I was thinking of doing exactly that. It'd be fun to have another shop. A lot of work, but a lot of fun."

Christina envied her mom's sense of purpose, her excitement with her work and her life. "I hope I find as much fulfillment in my life as you've found in yours. How do you do it, Mom? Tell your daughter your secret."

"There's no secret, sweetheart. Life is what you make it. Aren't you fulfilled?"

Christina sighed. "I thought I was. As long as I was planning for what I wanted, I felt that I was on track. I knew what I wanted and I was going after it. I felt good, but now that I have what I planned for, I feel there ought to be more. I feel like I've won a prize that I worked hard for only to question whether it was really worth it."

"Are we talking about something more than work, darling?" Louise asked gently.

Christina got up from the table and rinsed off her plate. When she was done, she leaned back against the sink. "God, Mom, sometimes I feel that work is all I have. It used to be enough, but it's not anymore."

"What's happened to change everything?"

Christina thought about Liza's upcoming wedding. "The work hasn't changed, so I must have changed. I don't know, Mom. I only know that I'm very discontented right now."

"You do know, Christina," her mother said.

Christina heard the challenge in her mother's voice. She moved away from the sink and crossed her arms. "What's that supposed to mean, Mother?"

"Don't 'Mother' me. You know why you're discontented. You just won't voice it."

"I don't know what you are talking about."

Louise shrugged. "If you say so. How about some dessert? I have chocolate cake in the fridge."

Christina wouldn't let it go. "I don't want cake, Mother. I want to know what you're talking about."

"All right, Christina, if you won't say it, I will. You're lonely, sweetheart. Now don't get insulted. It's not like I've said you have bad breath. A lot of people are lonely. It's a curable malady."

Christina uncrossed her arms and dropped them to her sides. She knew her mother was right. "I'm not lonely, Mother. I'm alone, but I'm not lonely. There's a difference."

"I know, Christina. You've been alone a long time, but now you're lonely. To be alone is to be happy to be by yourself; being lonely is being unhappy to be by yourself."

Christina didn't speak immediately. Finally, she asked, "Has it been that obvious, Mom?"

Chapter 5

"It's obvious to me because I'm your mother and I know when something isn't right with you."

Christina returned to her seat at the table. "How long have you known that something was wrong?"

"I've seen it coming for a while, Christina. It had to happen.

"You had to realize that the job wasn't enough." Louise took her daughter's hand. "Christina, sweetheart, you need to build a life for yourself apart from that job. You need to make friends."

Christina jerked her hand away and stood up. "You mean male friends, Mother?"

"You said it, I didn't."

"For your information, Mother—" she practically sneered the word "mother" "—I met someone, a male, this weekend."

"I hope he was a nice man, dear, but that's not really the issue, is it? We're talking about you and how you feel about your life."

Christina looked at her mother and her heart filled with all the love she had always felt. Leave it to Mom to stick to the subject. Christina had learned early how to avoid painful discussions. Her mother caught on and stopped it at home. In the outside world, Christina could control her interactions with people, but at home, Louise always made her face her fears. It was a pain in the butt sometimes, but Christina loved her mother for it because she knew that her mother did it out of love.

Christina gave in. "You win, Mom. You always do." She ran both hands through her hair and threw her head back. "God, where do I start?"

Christina started with her response to the news of Liza's wedding and ended with a description of her weekend with Reggie.

"I'm glad that you're opening your eyes to your surroundings and finding people that interest you, but I think you could have been a bit more cautious. What do you really know about this man?"

"Not again. I was careful, Mom. I've never been much of a risk taker, but I have to learn to follow my instincts more." She pulled out a chair and sat directly in front of her. Taking her mom's hand in hers, she said, "I'm going to need your support."

Louise squeezed her daughter's hand. "You know I'm here for you. What do you want me to do?"

"That's just it. I don't know." Christina stood up again. "I'm having so many new emotions. I feel like a teenager who needs guidance in dating. I'm a thirty year-old professionally competent woman who handles multimillion-dollar projects, but I can't seem to get a handle on this man-woman thing."

"It's only natural, Christina. You learn how to deal with men by dealing with men. You've never really dated, so you don't have much experience."

Christina thought about that awhile. How she wished her father was here. "It feels strange to want a husband and a family. A part of me feels I should be content with what I have, but another part of me would seriously consider chucking it all to be a housewife and mother. I feel like a heretic and a traitor for thinking that way."

"There's nothing wrong with your feelings," Louise said. "Women have choices. You can choose to have a career, or you can choose to have a family, or you can choose to have both. The only responsibility you have is to yourself. You've got to decide what you want and go after that. You can't let other people's expectations dictate your life."

"I know you're right, but these thoughts make me feel like a weakling. It's disgusting."

"Growing pains are natural. Don't think for a minute that needing people makes you weak. Your strength is shown in your doing what makes you happy."

Christina sat down again. "How did you do it, Mom? You're happy and fulfilled, but you don't have a man. You never really did in all the time that I was growing up."

Louise looked away from her daughter. "There's not a special man in my life and there hasn't been for a long time." She turned back to face Christina. "I had you, Christina, and you made the difference. You filled spaces, provided love, and provided a way for me to show my love. Though there was no special man, there was an outlet for my love and that outlet was you."

Christina knew a daughter's love and a lover's love were two totally different experiences. "Was it enough?"

"I made it enough. As you got older, I developed other interests. Now that you're gone, I have the nursery."

"You love the nursery, Mom, but the nursery can't love back."

Louise nodded. "I know. I've been doing some thinking of my own lately. I wonder if I didn't do us both a disservice by not having an intimate relationship. At the time it seemed the right decision to make, but as I look at you and me now, I wonder if it was."

Christina paused before she spoke. "Do you ever think about him?"

"Who?"

"You know who, Mother. My father. Do you ever think about him?"

Louise was silent for a minute. "At times. It still hurts. All this time and it still hurts. I loved him and I still miss him." Louise took a napkin from the table and wiped away the tears that had quickened in her eyes.

"I don't want to make you sad, but I need to talk about him. Is that okay?"

Louise nodded.

Christina got up again and walked around the room. She got anxious when she thought about her father. "I've been thinking about him lately. Tell me about how you met and what happened."

Louise paused for a moment before speaking. "I met him the

summer after my freshman year at Alabama A&M. I was working as a nurse's aide at the hospital in Bottoms. I went to a voter registration rally with one of my girlfriends. Thomas Evans was the speaker. His electrifying speech inspired me to become a volunteer voter registrar. I met your father at the orientation for registrars. I remember my girlfriend nudging me when she first saw him looking at me. He was gorgeous. A tall, bulky man. So handsome. All the women thought him attractive and smart. I had no interest in him because I thought he was conceited. My lack of interest attracted him to me. I think. He asked me out for over a month before I agreed to go out with him.

"I fell in love with him the night of our first date," Louise said, as if in her memories. "He was so much more than what I thought. He had character, substance. I remember the fervor and strength of his thoughts, his plans. I knew that night that I wanted to spend the rest of my life with him. It was love at first sight, but not the kind of sight that had to do with your eyes. I saw inside to the man that he really was, and I loved that man. I've never felt that way again."

Christina had heard the story many times before, but it warmed her heart to hear it again. If only she had known her father. "When did you know he felt the same way about you?"

Louise gave a teary smile "He told me that first night. When we said goodnight, he told me that he loved me and that he wanted to marry me. I couldn't say anything, but I knew he meant it. Does this make sense to you Christina?"

"It makes a lot of sense. Go on."

"After that first night, we were practically inseparable. Your grandparents thought he was going to move in. They fell in love with him as fast as I did."

"How did you make it after he died?"

"It almost killed me. He never knew about my pregnancy. It was such a fluke. At a time when young men were dying in riots, Christian died of pneumonia. He had come to visit during Thanksgiving vacation. We made love the first time during that visit. He wanted to wait, but I didn't." Louise paused. "I got my way and I got you."

Christina wiped at the tears in her eyes. She nodded to signal her mother to continue.

"I don't know how I made it. I didn't realize I was pregnant until February. Fear was my first emotion. But your grandmother really came through for me. It took all of my courage to tell her. She held me while I cried, and told me that she loved me. She even told your grandfather for me. If he was angry, I never knew it. He supported me just like your grandmother did. How I wish you had known them longer!"

Christina went to her mother and held her. Through her tears, she said, "Me, too. I was so young when they died. I wish I had known my father. I miss him so much sometimes."

"He would have loved you so much. I named you Christina so you would always have him with you." Louise pulled away so she could see her daughter's face. "I love you, Christina, and I've never regretted having you. You made the suffering bearable. Knowing that I would always have a part of Christian with me kept me going. Even through the deaths of your grandparents."

"I love you, too, Mom, and I know that you love me and that Big Mama and Big Daddy loved me. What about my other grandparents?"

"Big Mama and Big Daddy decided it best that we not tell them. Christian was dead. Your grandparents and I were your family, and after they died, you and I were a family."

Christina wanted to ask more questions. But she saw something that looked like fear in her mother's eyes. She didn't know the reason for the fear, but she felt that the time for questions had passed. She reached for her mother again and they held each other as they cried.

Jackson called his father early Sunday morning as he always did on the first Sunday of the month.

"Morning, Dad," Jackson said, right before he heard the phone drop.

"That you, Jackson?"

"Yeah, Dad, it's me. What's that noise?" Jackson heard something, maybe music in the background.

"I got some of your mother's old records on the record player. Your mamma sure could dance. She loved to dance, too."

"I know, Dad, I know."

Jackson stopped listening as his father went into his age-old storytelling. When he drank, he thought about his wife. Maybe when he thought about his wife he drank. Either way, when he thought about her, he had to talk about her. Jackson's emotions for his father went to extremes. Sometimes he was overwhelmed with love for the man that had been his father for the first fifteen years of his life. At other times, he was overcome with anger and hatred at the man who had been his father for the last thirteen years. Mostly, he felt pity for the man who had loved a woman who after twenty years of marriage decided she no longer loved him.

His feelings for Sarah (he rarely thought of her as his mother) were more definite. He hated her. He hated what she had done to his family. He hated what she had done to his father. Most of all, he hated what she had done to him. What had she really done? She had left her husband and son, showing them clearly she didn't love them. He could understand a woman leaving a man, but he couldn't understand a woman leaving her child. For that he hated her.

His dad was saying something. "Yes, I know what you mean, Dad. I have to go now. I'll talk to you soon."

His Dad mumbled "G'bye," and they hung up.

Jackson hated making the monthly phone calls. He never knew if his father would be drunk and sad or sober and depressed. Either way, his father was a lost cause. He refused to get over Sarah. Jackson had long given up trying to help him. His father didn't want help. He wanted to wallow in pity, and nothing was going to stop him.

Jackson picked up the Sunday *Journal-Constitution* in an effort to clear his head. It worked, and soon his thoughts centered on the adventures of Doonesbury and Curtis.

* * *

Jackson arrived at Ellis and Betty's around two. Betty answered the door. "Welcome. We're all out back. You're in luck, Angela's already here."

Jackson laughed. "You don't give up, do you?"

"Haven't you figured it out yet, Jackson?"

"Figured what out?"

Betty wagged her finger at him. "And you the man about town. Shame on you. Haven't you heard that matchmaking is the married woman's way of staying single forever? You get to date, albeit vicariously, without guilt. And sometimes you even get your husband's help." She winked at him and led him out to the patio.

"Hey, everybody, the guest of honor is here. Jackson Duncan, meet Michael and Jewel Taylor and Angela Ware. Mike's an Omega. Jewel and Angela are AKAs. I'll leave it to you to take the subtle hint."

Betty started to say more, but Ellis covered her mouth with his hand and the others laughed.

Angela walked over to Jackson, her eyes twinkling. "Welcome to Atlanta. I won't hold it against her," she said, referring to Betty, "if you won't. Deal?" She extended her hand.

He took her hand. "Deal." He dropped her hand and gestured toward Betty. "Is she always like this?"

"No. Betty is in rare form today. You really impressed her at the picnic. She thought you were a good guy. Your response to that introduction proved it."

Jackson assessed Angela. She was an attractive woman, tall, brown-skinned, slim, with a sexy voice and legs that were pretty but not as full as Christina's. Wrong thought. "When did Betty become your matchmaker? I would think you'd have men lined up around the block."

Angela gave him a half-smile. "There was probably a compliment in there somewhere, but I tell you, it's pretty hard to find."

"I apologize. I only meant that you're a very attractive woman and I wouldn't think you'd need the services of a matchmaker."

"That's better," Angela responded. "Betty and I were college roommates. We've always watched out for each other. I introduced her to Ellis. She's trying to return the favor."

Jackson was about to comment again on Betty and her matchmaking, but Angela spoke first. "Excuse me, I see Jewel and Betty heading into the house. If I don't help, I'm dead meat." She winked and was gone.

Jackson watched her walk away, thinking he'd have to thank Betty for introducing him to Angela.

"Get over here, Jackson," Ellis called. "I have a feeling you're going to need the counsel of married men to make it through this afternoon."

Mike and Jackson watched as Ellis plopped the steaks on the grill. "You have a nice spread here, Ellis," Jackson commented. "How long have you lived here?"

Ellis looked up from the grill. "Thanks, man. Betty found this place about four years ago when there was still a family living here. She decided then that we would own it. When it came on the market two years ago, we got it."

"Betty is something else," Michael commented. "Jewel is getting to be a lot like her. We're looking for a house now and yours is the standard. God, I hope we find something before the year 2007."

Jackson listened as Mike and Ellis exchanged funny stories about their wives. It was obvious that both men were deeply in love. Jackson felt left out and a little envious.

"When will the monsters be back?" Mike was asking.

Again Ellis laughed. "You call mine monsters, but I bet your tune will change in about six months. E.J. and Anne will be back tonight. Betty's parents took them for the weekend. For Betty and me, it's been a honeymoon around here. We spend as much time in bed as possible. Unfortunately, for most of that time, we're asleep."

"Sure, man," Jackson said with sarcasm.

Ellis threw another steak on the grill. "I wish. Wait until you have a working wife and two toddlers. Any break from the kids is a time to catch up on sleep. Not that we didn't have some fun. A man takes what he can get."

"The times at my house have only gotten better," Mike said. "Jewel has this new surge of passion since she found out about the baby. It's great."

"You'd better enjoy it while you can," Ellis advised. "And prepare yourself for that dry period that's going to start sometime in her ninth month and last until the baby is about six weeks old."

"You guys are something else," Jackson said. "Do your wives have any idea what you're talking about out here?"

Mike and Ellis chuckled. Mike answered, "Jewel gives guidelines on what I can and can't say."

Ellis pointed his spatula toward the house. "What do you think they're doing in there? You can bet a month's pay they aren't discussing the best way to make potato salad."

Mike pointed to Jackson. "I'd bet my pay that they're discussing you, big boy. By now, they're probably deciding how many children you and Angela should have."

"He *is* cute," Angela agreed. He was more than cute, but she'd never tell that to Betty and Jewel. They moved into overdrive when they learned she was attracted to someone.

"Cute? Honey, that is one fine man. If only I weren't married," Betty chimed in.

Jewel spoke next. "You'd better jump on that one quick, Ange. The women are going to be out for that man."

"Ellis says he has some executive engineering position at Communications Limited downtown," Betty offered.

"I haven't heard of Communications Limited," Jewel said.

"Ellis says their offices are in the Peterson Building. Anyway, Ellis says it's a good company and Jackson has a good position."

Jewel and Betty looked at Angela.

"Why are you two looking at me like that?" Angela asked.

Jewel and Betty looked at each other. They shrugged their shoulders, then each grabbed a casserole dish and headed for the patio. Betty spoke, "If you don't know, girlfriend, we can't help you."

* * *

Mike and Jewel were standing. "We hate to eat and run, but we promised Jewel's parents we'd stop by tonight."

Ellis stood. "It's okay, man. Now is not the time to irritate the grandparents-to-be. They make the best babysitters."

Betty punched him in the leg. "Ellis, you're so bad."

Mike extended his hand to Jackson. "It was nice meeting you, man. You'll have to go out on the course with Ellis and me sometime. I could use the competition."

"Thanks, man. I'd like that. Give me a tee-off time and I'm there."

Jackson noticed Jewel whisper something to Angela before saying goodbye to everyone else. While Ellis walked Mike and Jewel out, Betty began clearing away the food. She declined Angela and Jackson's offer to help.

Angela smiled and Jackson noticed she had a very pretty smile. "If Ellis is not back in ten minutes," she said, "we can safely assume that he and Betty are giving us some time to get to know each other better."

"It really doesn't bother you, does it?"

"This matchmaking stuff?"

Jackson nodded.

"Not really. They're my friends. They're trying to be helpful. Like I said before, if you can handle it, so can I. How does it make you feel?"

"At first it was funny, but I'm beginning to think they're serious."

Angela laughed. "They are, but don't get too scared. We haven't set a wedding date yet. Let's talk about something else. How do you like Atlanta so far?"

Jackson gave Angela his first impressions of the city and found that they shared common interests and viewpoints. Angela was easy to talk to, and before long they were talking like old friends.

"You'll have to visit Auburn Avenue and the AU Center. They're pretty close to your apartment building."

"Soon, too." Jackson decided to flirt. "Will I need a guide?"

Angela went along with him. "I think you might."

Ellis and Betty walked out of the house and joined them. "What are you two talking about?"

"Angela was telling me of some sites I need to see. I think she volunteered to be my guide."

Betty nodded approval then asked, "Is she taking you to Stone Mountain?"

"I hadn't thought about Stone Mountain," Angela said.

"Everybody has to see the Laser Light Show," Ellis added.

"Laser Light Show?" Jackson asked.

"A fireworks display only with lasers," Betty explained. "You'll like it."

"Sounds like fun," Jackson said. He looked at Angela. "What do you think, tour guide?"

"That could be our first outing. Since we're right here at Stone Mountain, we could even do that tonight. That is," she looked at the three of them, "if you guys are up for it?"

"I'm game," Jackson said. Looking at Betty and Ellis, he asked, "How about you two?"

Ellis opened his mouth to answer, but Betty beat him to it. "We can't tonight. My folks are bringing the kids back any minute now. Why don't you two go on, though?"

"Sounds like a plan to me." Jackson winked at Betty, then turned to Angela. "Ready to go guide?"

The ride to Stone Mountain Park took about fifteen minutes. After they entered the main gate to the park, Jackson said, "You give good directions. How long have you been a guide?"

Angela smiled and directed him to the parking lot nearest Memorial Lawn. "We got here at the right time. The show started at nine-thirty, but as you can see, people are already getting in place. I'm glad Betty thought of this."

Jackson studied her for a long moment. "I'm glad, too." She *is* attractive, he thought, even if her build is not like Christina's.

"Shall I get the blanket so we can get seated?" he asked, needing to remove Christina from his thoughts.

"Yes, we'd better stake out a spot. Thanks to Betty, we can have cider and cheese while we wait."

Jackson grabbed the blanket and Angela took the picnic basket. She picked a spot and they spread the picnic blanket. Jackson opened the basket and poured them both a glass of cider.

Neither spoke for a while. They looked at the people around them as they nursed their drinks. Jackson saw a man and woman in their early thirties with a child. He assumed they were a family. The child, a red-haired boy, carried a blue balloon on a string and had what appeared to be chocolate ice cream smeared around his mouth. Attractive family, he thought. His gaze went to a couple seated not far from them. They were young, early twenties. They shared an intense embrace, kissing as if they couldn't get enough of each other. Young love, Jackson thought. He turned to see Angela looking at the same couple.

"Ain't love grand?" he commented, finishing off his cider.

"Nothing like it. At that age or ours."

"Have you ever been in love, Angela?"

She laughed. "Many times. How about you?"

Jackson answered seriously. "Never."

"Not even as a teenager?"

He shook his head.

"That's sad, Jackson, and a little hard to believe."

An image of Christina flashed in his mind. "It's true."

"I bet you've broken a lot of hearts, though."

He raised his right hand. "I plead the fifth." Lowering his hand, he said, "Tell me more about Angela."

"What do you want to know about her?"

Jackson rubbed his chin, pretending to think hard. "Well, I already know she's beautiful, she's smart, she has a good sense of humor, she gives great directions, she has close friends, and she has a sexy voice." He snapped his fingers. That's it, he thought. "I knew your voice sounded familiar. You're on the radio, aren't you?"

Angela unfolded her legs and stretched them out on the blanket. "Don't pretend Betty didn't tell you. She tells everybody. She used to introduce me as her friend Angela who's on the radio station WAOK."

Jackson leaned back on his elbows and laughed. "That sounds like Betty, but I swear she didn't tell me."

"Good. It really bothers me when she does that. We've had more than a few heated discussions about it. Maybe she finally understands. I'm glad she didn't tell you."

"You're such a good sport about the matchmaking. Why is this a problem?"

Angela brushed a nonexistent spec from her slacks. "I like to keep my personal and professional lives separate. Once people find out that I'm in radio, they turn into groupies and want the inside scoop on some artist. That can get old real fast."

"I understand the need to keep your work life separate, but I find it impossible to do in reality." He was thinking about Christina.

"It works, but you need a strict set of guidelines and you have to follow them religiously."

He could use all the help he could get. "For example?"

"I don't date anyone that I work with. Nothing but problems."

"Is that conclusion based on experience?"

"No. I've come close a couple of times, but it was never worth the risk. If the personal relationship doesn't work, what happens to the professional relationship? If the personal relationship does work, what happens to professional competition? My career is very important to me and I don't want to jeopardize it."

Let's go fishing, Jackson thought. "What if your attraction to the person was strong and you thought it might be the real thing?"

"That's never been the case. In each situation, for me at least, the chance of something lasting was never really high, so why risk it? There are plenty of other men out there."

And there's plenty of women. The problem is that all women are *not* created equal. "You've thought a lot about it."

Angela crossed her ankles, then inclined her head toward

him. "I have. I don't know how it is for men, but I've found that professional women have to be above reproach, and sex with co-workers falls in the reproachful category. It's the old 'she slept her way to the top' story."

"That's archaic thinking."

"Haven't you noticed that this country still holds a somewhat archaic view of women? And it's worse for black women." She looked around. "The show's about to start. Get ready to enjoy it."

"I'm ready," Jackson said. His thoughts went back to Christina. If she would risk it, he would pursue a relationship with her, but she had made her intentions clear. He looked at Angela as she watched the show. She was good people. He liked her and thought that she liked him. Maybe Angela was the person he needed to keep his mind off Christina.

When the show ended, Jackson drove Angela to her home in Decatur.

He walked her to the door. "When's our next outing?"

"Are you serious about my being your guide?"

"Very serious. How about it?"

"Let me think about it. I'll call you early in the week and we can make plans."

"Are you really going to call, or are you letting me down easy?" he teased.

"Somehow, Jackson Duncan, I don't think you've ever been turned down." She reached up and gave him a quick kiss. "Goodnight." She entered the house before he could say or do anything more.

When Jackson got home, he pulled out his briefcase and began to prepare for work. It only brought back thoughts of Christina. He wondered how he was going to approach her, given what had happened Friday. What did she expect him to do? What did she want him to do?

His thoughts turned to Angela. She was going to help him forget Christina. Well, maybe "forget" was too strong a word. The most he hoped for was that Angela would keep him distracted so he wouldn't think about Christina as much.

Angela was almost right when she had said that he had never been turned down before. His record had been perfect until Friday with Christina. God, he loved a challenge. Could he do the right thing and leave Christina alone, or would he follow his emotions? Only time would tell.

Chapter 6

The offices at CL were dark when Christina arrived Monday morning. She switched on the lights in her secretary's office and proceeded to her own office. She was more tired than usual. Leaving her mom's house at three o'clock in the morning had seemed like a good idea since she couldn't sleep, but now her body was rebelling.

She looked at her watch. Seven o'clock. That was actually late for her; she was usually in by six. She used the time to catch up on reading, go over her schedule for the day, and prepare for any meetings. Today she had to plan for the afternoon staff meeting. She liked getting together with her people on Mondays to make sure the week started right and to identify any issues that need her intervention. The meetings worked well. She had tried Monday morning meetings, but they didn't give the staff any time to wrap up the loose ends that invariably cropped up late Friday. She and Jackson met on Fridays, she remembered. A heated flush graced her cheeks as she recalled their last meeting.

Christina headed straight for the couch. Once she would have considered an office like hers extravagant. Now, she realized it was only functional. Since she spent so much time there, she needed the space and comfort.

Christina sat down, slipped off her black pumps, opened her briefcase, and began to read. She yawned and wished she had some tea. In forty-five minutes Penny, her secretary, would bring her morning tea. She yawned again and closed her eyes. She didn't know when she slipped into sleep.

She woke up when the door opened. She didn't bother to open her eyes or make a comment. It must be seven forty-five, she thought. Penny would place the tea on the desk and quietly leave the room. If she didn't hear Christina moving around by eight o'clock, she'd come back to check on her. Christina waited to hear Penny do her task and leave. When it seemed to be taking a long time, she called to her. "Penny, what are you doing?"

A masculine voice answered, "Penny's not here yet. It's only seven-thirty."

Christina opened her eyes and quickly sat upright. A tall, gray-haired man stood near her desk. If she had met him under other circumstances, she would have thought him distinguished looking. In the present circumstances, she thought he looked a bit misplaced, even weird. There was a haunting look in his eyes, too.

Christina stood up as he walked from the desk where he was standing toward the couch. "Excuse me. Are you looking for someone?" she asked.

The man hesitated a second, then extended his hand. "Paul Bechtel."

The name sounded familiar to Christina, but she couldn't place it. The man must have concluded as much from the look on her face. He said, "This used to be my office." He looked around the room. "Though it's changed a lot since I was last here."

Now she remembered. Paul Bechtel was district manager for ORION before her. She never knew the details, but he had been fired before her arrival. She assumed it had had to do with the state of the product then.

"Mr. Bechtel." She shook his hand. "I'm Christina Marshall." She slipped on her shoes and went to stand behind her desk. "What can I do to help you this morning?"

Bechtel said nothing and merely looked at Christina. She was beginning to get nervous. What was he doing here? How did he get in? Before she could say anything else, Penny walked in with the tea.

Penny saw Christina first. "Good morning, Christina. How was your weekend?" Then she saw Bechtel. She stopped in her tracks. "Mr. Bechtel…what brings you here?"

Christina saw Bechtel smile for the first time. "You haven't changed at all, have you, Penny?" He walked toward her. "I've been feeling homesick for the place and thought I'd drop by." He looked at Christina. "Sorry if I frightened you, Ms. Marshall. I only wanted to see the old place." With that, he walked past Penny out the door.

Christina realized she'd been holding her breath. She let it go. Looking at Penny, she said, "That was spooky."

"What?" Penny placed the tea on the table. "Oh. Mr. Bechtel being here?"

Christina wrapped her arms around herself. "Yes, it was spooky waking up and finding him standing here. The way he looked at me was eerie. How did he get in here, anyway?"

"I really don't know," Penny said. "He doesn't have a badge, but one of the security guards may have remembered him and let him in."

"Well, they shouldn't do that. Check with security. I need to know who let him in. We can't have unauthorized people roaming around our office. There's a lot of proprietary work going on in here."

"I'll call them," Penny said. "Is there anything else you need?"

Christina was still thinking about Bechtel. Remembering his comment about Penny not being in until seven forty-five, she asked, "Did you bring Bechtel tea every morning, too, or was it coffee?"

Penny shook her head. "I didn't work for Bechtel. Doris was his secretary." Doris now worked for Jackson.

Christina opened her mouth to ask another question when the phone rang. "I'll take it," she said to Penny. Penny nodded and left the office.

Christina sat and talked with Walter in Boston. She brought him up to date with the schedules. Before hanging up, she thought about Paul Bechtel. She told Walter about the incident this morning.

"Bechtel is an idiot. Don't worry about him. Be sure you tell security not to let him in the building again. Damn it. That man never should have been allowed in. What kind of security do you have down there, anyway?"

Christina wanted to find out more about Bechtel, but sensing Walter's irritation, she decided not to pursue that at this time. "I'm checking with them now. I'll have some answers before the end of the day. Don't worry."

With that they hung up. Christina sat for a while thinking about the morning. Jackson interrupted her thoughts when he burst into the office.

"Look what just arrived for you." He was carrying a bouquet of pink roses. "You must have an admirer." He placed the flowers on her desk.

"Where did you get these?" Christina asked. She wondered if they were a gift from Jackson himself. Maybe a peace offering.

"They came when Penny was in your office earlier. She would have brought them in, but you were on your call with Walter."

"You seem to know a lot about what I'm doing," she commented.

He touched one of the rose petals. "So, who are they from?"

Christina lifted a brow. "You didn't read the card?"

Jackson clutched at his heart. "You wound me. I only deliver; I don't read."

Christina didn't open the card. She waited for Jackson to speak.

Finally he said, "I think we should clear the air concerning Friday."

Christina didn't comment.

Jackson continued, "I was out of line. Will you accept my apology?"

Christina felt a little hurt. What was he really saying here? "No apology needed. I haven't even thought about it."

Was that a twitch she detected? No, it must not have been, because now Jackson was smiling. "Good," he said. "Now I can get back to work." He walked to the door. Looking over his shoulder as he walked out, he said, "Don't forget to read the card."

Jackson walked from Christina's office to his own, greeting everyone he met with a smile. Inside he was seething. He walked into his office and slammed his fist on his desk. On Friday she had wanted to pretend nothing was happening, and this morning when he'd played it that way, she'd actually looked hurt. What in the hell was going on here? Jackson sat at his desk.

She recovered quickly enough, he thought. I haven't even thought about it, she says. I know she's lying and she knows she's lying, but we're both going to pretend that the whole incident was nothing. Well, it was something to me.

Reggie was also something to him. So he'd lied about reading the card. Who the hell was Reggie, anyway? Was this somebody she'd been dating for a while? Or was it somebody new? He wondered if it was serious. It probably was. Somehow, he couldn't imagine Christina in a casual affair. She was much too rigid for that.

Jackson wondered what had happened to his control. Christina Marshall was doing a number on him and he doubted she even knew it. This weekend he had figured it all out. The conversation with Angela removed any doubts he'd had. Christina Marshall was off limits. He could deal with that. She wasn't really his type anyway. He liked his women a lot less stuffy than Miss Christina Marshall. Someone more like Angela. Yes, Angela. Thinking of her, Jackson dialed her number.

"I know you said you'd call, but I couldn't wait. When's our next outing?" he asked.

Angela laughed softly. "You're impossible. I haven't had time to make plans yet."

"If you don't think of something, I will. That's a threat."

She went along with his teasing. "And what will you think of?"

"How about lunch, for starters?"

"If it's tomorrow, you have a date."

"I'm flexible. Tomorrow it is."

Jackson hung up the phone feeling better. He liked Angela a lot and he looked forward to spending more time with her. If anybody could keep his mind off Christina, Angela could.

I was out of line, he'd said. Christina drummed her fingers on her desk. So, was that what it was? I'm glad I didn't give in to the moment. Then where would I be? Would he have come in here and said that making love to me had been out of line? Men, ha!

Christina remembered the flowers. She opened the attached card and read it. "I miss you already," it read. It was signed, "Reggie." Christina smiled as she thought about her weekend. She'd had fun with Reggie. She checked the time and decided it wasn't too early to call Oklahoma City. Reggie answered on the second ring.

"I love the roses," she said.

"It's good to hear your voice, Ms. Marshall. It means that you remember me."

The smile she heard in his voice made her feel giddy. "How could I forget you, Mr. Stevens? It's not everyday a girl gets picked up on a tour bus in Mobile."

Reggie laughed at that. "I didn't pick you up."

She teased. "What do you call it, then?"

"I call it two people meeting each other, liking each other, and spending time with each other. How about that?"

"A rose by any other name…"

He took that opening to change the subject. "You like the roses?"

"They're beautiful." She rubbed a petal between her thumb and forefinger.

"Like you."

Christina beamed. She wondered if he could hear it in her voice. "Thank you, Mr. Stevens."

She heard him smile again. "When can I come visit?" he asked.

She hesitated before answering. "Reggie, I don't want to rush into anything."

"I'm not rushing you, but I want to see you again." He paused. "Soon."

"Let's take it slow for the time being."

"You can call the shots," he conceded. "For now."

They talked a while longer and Reggie promised to call again before the end of the week. Christina hung up with her confidence restored. At least Reggie didn't say he had been out of line the past weekend.

The staff meeting started promptly at two. Jackson watched Christina. She was good at what she did. She ran her team like an army general, but the troops treated her like a benevolent dictator. They did what she told them to do because they felt she had their best interest at heart. Even though Jackson didn't know a lot about Christina, he felt she was good people. He didn't know her favorite color, although he guessed it was blue, since she wore the color often. He didn't know her political inclination. He didn't know how she felt about the death penalty, but he would bet his life that she was honest, trustworthy, and dependable. He wanted to get to know her. To see more of her soft side. To share her goals and dreams, even her fears. He looked at this woman and he knew somewhere deep inside himself that they connected. He couldn't explain it, but he knew it as sure as he knew his name. He felt that she knew it, too.

"Jackson," Christina was speaking to him now. "I need to talk to you after the meeting."

Jackson nodded. When everyone else had left, Christina said, "We have to go to Boston in two weeks."

That got his full attention. "What's going on?"

"Walter has called a summit."

"How long will we be there?" he asked.

"Two days, Thursday and Friday. Penny has the dates. She's getting the information to Doris. You, Liza and I will meet Thursday morning. Later that afternoon we'll meet with Walter and

Rosalind. They expect the meetings to last through Friday. Will that be a problem for you?"

"No, I can arrange it. There's plenty of time to adjust my schedule."

"Good. That's all I had. Is there anything you need to tell me?"

"If you have a few minutes."

"Sure, take a seat." She pointed to the two wing chairs where they'd had their initial interview. "Is there a problem?"

They each took a chair. "No, there's no problem. I just wanted to tell you how much I'm enjoying working on OPTIMA with you. I remember our interview, and I have to say that you've been true to your word. You've given me the freedom to do my job and you've supported me all the way."

"It's been good working with you, too, Jackson. I can tell that you're in your element here. You know that Walter and Rosalind are working hard to get you back to Boston. It'll be a great career move for you, but I'm really glad you're here and I'm going to hate to see you go."

Jackson looked at her for a few minutes, thinking of the things they hadn't said. They were doing a good job of pretending Friday had never happened. He stood up. "That was all I wanted."

Jackson left and Christina remained seated. She hated and loved being alone with Jackson. She loved it because she felt so at home with him. She felt as though she could take off her shoes, get comfortable, and be herself. She hated it because she had to fight the urge to give in to that feeling. She had to keep it strictly professional with Jackson or she'd be lost. She had mixed emotions about the trip to Boston. She knew she, Jackson, and Liza needed to meet, but she also knew the trip held the potential for her and Jackson to get to know each other in a semisocial setting. She was a little afraid of that.

I'll worry about it later, she thought. For now, I'm going to concentrate on the work that has to be done.

While the staff meeting was going on in Christina's office, Penny and Doris had a meeting of their own at Penny's desk.

"I would have sworn that something was going to happen between the two of them," Doris was saying. "The electricity between them was practically scorching everything in its path."

"When I left Friday, he was in her office," Penny added.

"I would love to have been a fly on the wall for that," Doris said.

"Well, he did look a little put out at the roses she got."

Doris was encouraged. She leaned closer to Penny. "Tell me more."

"She got flowers—pink roses—this morning."

Doris was all into it now. "Who were they from? Did you see the card?"

"Of course I saw the card, and you know I didn't read it." Penny looked insulted.

Doris didn't back down. "I know you, and that's why I asked."

Penny looked around. She whispered, "The signature on the card said 'Reggie.'"

Doris whispered, "Who's Reggie?"

"I don't know. I've never heard the name before. It's the first time she's gotten roses. At work, at least. There must be something to it."

Doris leaned in still closer. "I overheard him talking to someone named Angela this morning."

"Maybe we misread the signs and there's nothing between them," Penny wondered aloud.

Doris didn't buy it. "It ain't over till it's over. I still say those two have something going."

Penny nodded.

Angela came for lunch Tuesday. Doris led her to Jackson's office to wait for him.

A moment later, Jackson rushed into the office. "Sorry, I'm late. I got tied up in something. How long have you been waiting?"

Angela stood up. "Don't worry about it. I haven't been here long. If today is bad for you, we can reschedule. I know how the days can get out of control."

Jackson gave her a kiss on the cheek, then smiled at her. "No,

I don't want to reschedule. I do appreciate your understanding, though." Jackson looked at his watch, then back to Angela. "How much time do you have?"

"Actually, I have the rest of the day. I have a promo to record tonight, so I'm free until about seven."

"That's great. If you'll give me about thirty minutes, I promise I'll make it up to you."

"I think I can manage that. Can a girl get a cold drink around here?"

Jackson had Doris bring in sodas for them both. Angela worked on her promo while Jackson finished his report. He was almost done when Christina entered his office.

Christina was about to speak when she saw Angela. "Excuse me. I didn't know you were busy."

Jackson stood up. Was that irritation he saw in Christina's eyes? He knew it couldn't be jealousy. Or could it? "Christina Marshall, my friend, Angela Ware." He gestured to Angela. "Angela Ware, my boss, Christina Marshall."

Angela stood and the women greeted each other.

"You're on the radio, aren't you?" Christina asked.

Angela glanced at Jackson, who shook his head. "That's me," she answered.

"You have a great voice," Christina said. They exchanged niceties, then Christina asked Jackson a few quick questions about the proposal he had prepared.

After Christina left, Angela looked askance at Jackson. "So that's your boss?"

Jackson nodded.

"She's a very attractive woman."

Jackson didn't like the way this was going. He began shuffling papers on his desk. "Yes. If that's your type."

Angela kept on. "And what type is she?"

Jackson hedged. "You know. All work, no play."

"How do you know?"

Can't we change the subject? He silently pleaded. "I never see her with anybody. She's kind of uptight."

Angela continued. "That's not the impression I got."

Jackson stopped shuffling the papers. "What did you think?"

"She came across as a very together woman, but there was also a certain warmth about her. Not exactly charismatic, but close."

"Someone you think you'd like to be friends with?"

Angela thought about it. "Yes. I think Christina and I would hit it off if we were thrown into a social situation," she answered with a smile.

Jackson winced. "I'm done here. Let's go before you decide you'd rather have lunch with Christina."

Angela took Jackson to the King Center for lunch. Since it was his first visit, they toured the memorial and the house where Martin Luther King, Jr. had grown up. Afterward, they walked up and down Auburn Avenue.

"Sometimes I wish I'd been born earlier so I'd have stronger memories of the events of the early sixties," Jackson said.

"I know what you mean," Angela responded. "It's our heritage and it should be as fresh now as it was then."

"Fresh is a good word. We have to keep it fresh so it'll always be real to us."

Angela finished his thought, "Then it'll keep its value throughout all the coming generations."

Jackson thought about his problems with his father and his nonrelationship with Christina. "If we kept it fresh, we wouldn't get sidetracked on trivial issues."

"It would keep us looking at our sameness and not at our differences."

"I wonder what Martin and Coretta's relationship was like," Jackson wondered aloud. "I wonder how he courted her. What he was looking for in a woman; what she was looking for in a man. I bet the words 'love' and 'forever' had different meanings then." Jackson was thinking about his mother and father. His mother should have known what "love" and "forever" meant.

"You sound like a man who's been hurt."

Jackson didn't want to open up yet. He played it light. "All men have been hurt at some point. It started with Adam and Eve."

Angela was direct with him. "If the conversations get too personal, Jackson, let me know and I'll back off."

"I'm sorry. I didn't want to get into it."

"Next time just say that."

Jackson stopped and tilted her face up to his. "You're a special woman, Angela."

"I know, but it's good you know it, too."

Chapter 7

Jackson arrived at Hartsfield International Airport an hour before his scheduled six-thirty flight Wednesday night. He had had enough bad experiences with checked luggage that checking his garment bag was not even a consideration. With his briefcase in one hand and his garment bag thrown over his shoulder, Jackson walked from the main concourse to the gate.

When he arrived, he looked around for Christina. He didn't see her, so he got his boarding pass and took a seat. He opened his briefcase and pulled out the newspaper, going straight to the comics. *Curtis* and *Doonesbury* were his favorite strips. He never missed them. He smiled as he read the day's installments.

"Must be good news."

He looked over the top of his paper. Christina smiled down at him. She wore casual blue slacks and a pink sweater. She looked like the calm after a long rain. "When did you get here?"

"I just walked up and got my boarding pass." She looked at the seats on either side of him. One held his garment bag, the other his newspaper. "Mind if I sit here?"

He removed the newspaper from the seat on his right.

Christina placed her garment bag in the seat with his and sat down.

"You don't believe in checking luggage either, I see?" He glanced toward her garment bag.

She shook her head. "Not on your life. I could tell you horror stories."

He laughed. "We could have a competition. Something like, 'Can you top this?'"

She laughed with him. "Maybe we could get the airline to give bonus frequent flyer miles to the one with the best story."

Jackson felt good sharing a joke with her. "I'm sure they'd go for that. Are you looking forward to getting back to Boston?"

"Not particularly. I never felt like I belonged there. I always knew I was only passing through."

"Passing through to where?"

"Atlanta, of course." She crossed her legs and began swinging her foot back and forth. "I'd been looking for an opportunity to get back here for the last three years. Actually, I wanted to stay in Atlanta after I graduated."

"You went to school here?"

She nodded. "Spelman and Georgia Tech."

"I can't picture you as a Spelman woman."

She stopped swinging her foot and eyed him. "I don't quite know how to take that. You'd better explain yourself."

Jackson smiled at her pretend pique. "It's nothing bad. Somewhere along the way I picked up that Spelman women were a bit—how shall I put this—bourgeois?"

"Bourgeois?" Christina laughed, uncrossing her legs. "Is that your way of saying stuck-up?"

He smiled. "I was trying to be diplomatic."

"No need to mince words. There are many different views on the Spelman woman. Like us or not, you have to admit that for the most part, we have a strong sense of self and an assertiveness that is matched only by the arrogance of the Morehouse man."

Jackson thought back to his college days. "There are times when I wish I'd gone to a black college. I thought about Morehouse, but at the time an all-male school was not my idea of a good experience."

"Spelman was a good experience for me. There's something about an environment with all women—all black women. People on the outside looking in only think of the similarities of the student population—all women, all black; but within the gates, we celebrate our differences. I was amazed at the diversity among us." She paused. "Do you understand what I'm saying?"

"I think so. At Oberlin, I could look around and see the differences, but then I also saw how much alike we all were."

They were silent for a while, then Jackson spoke. "So you fell in love with Atlanta when you were a student, and always wanted to come back?"

"That's part of it. I grew up in Selma. I really wanted to be close to home, and Atlanta was close without being too close."

"Sounds like somebody is still concerned about the apron strings. Is it Mom or Dad that's holding on too tight?"

She raised her brow. "Mom. Though I'm not sure if it's her or me who's holding on too tight."

Jackson understood that. Once again, he wished he could have been closer to his father after his mother had left. "Has the move met all your expectations?"

Christina thought before answering. Atlanta had been all she'd expected, but *she* hadn't been all she'd expected. Maybe this relationship with Reggie would work out and she could move forward with her goals. "In some cases, yes. In others, no."

"Your success at work has to be one of the yes ways. What are the no's?"

"I haven't gotten as involved in the community as I'd like. I've pretty much focused on work."

"It's only natural, given the new job and all."

"I know, but I always envisioned myself being real active in the community, in the local alumnae chapter. That hasn't been the case."

Jackson sensed that she didn't want to talk about this anymore. Maybe it was getting too personal. He looked toward the gate. Noticing a change in the flight time, he said, "We're going to be late getting out of here. They've pushed our departure time to eight-thirty."

Christina looked toward the gate. "A two-hour delay. I can't believe it." She stood up. "I'll check with the attendant."

Jackson watched her walk to the gate. He was glad she was in control again. Miss Marshall didn't like to get too personal.

Christina needed to get up. She knew something like this would happen with Jackson. She felt too comfortable with him. Now, with this flight delay, she'd have even more time to spend with him. She couldn't keep her guard up all night. After inquiring about the delay, she walked back to her seat.

"There's a thunderstorm in Boston. They don't know when we can leave. Right now, a two-hour delay is their best guess."

"It'll be midnight before we get to our hotel."

"At least," Christina agreed.

"Are you hungry?"

Such a simple question. Christina remembered the last time Jackson had asked her to go eat with him. She hadn't gone then and she wouldn't go now. "Not really, but you go ahead."

"I hate to eat alone. Come watch me?" he pleaded.

"Who'll watch our bags?"

Jackson smiled. "It's amazing how accommodating an airline becomes in situations like this. They'll let us leave them behind the counter."

"That I don't believe."

"Let's bet, then. If they let us leave the bags, you go eat with me; if they don't, you stay here with the bags." He held out his hand. "Deal?"

She shook her head, but took his hand. "Deal."

She watched him walk over to the gate counter. He said something that she couldn't hear and the gate attendant shook his head. I knew it, she thought. Jackson flashed a smile and said something else. The next thing she knew, Jackson was placing the bags behind the counter.

Jackson looked over and beckoned her to come over to him. She got up and walked over. "What did you say to guy?" she asked.

"In my own kind and gentle way, I reminded him of a long-standing principle of customer satisfaction. Now, let's find a place to eat."

Christina wondered exactly what Jackson had said, but before she could inquire further, Jackson was leading her into an eatery.

"Any preference where we sit?" he asked.

She shook her head and he led them to a table in a corner.

They sat facing each other. She watched him while he studied the menu. He had nut-brown skin and a clear complexion. He didn't have any hair on his face. She liked that. Sometimes she felt that bearded men were hiding behind their hair. Mustaches were okay, but a clean-shaven man was best. His shoulders were wide, giving him an aura of strength. She knew from memory that his waist was tapered and his buns tight. She smiled to herself.

"Must be a good thought?" Jackson inquired.

She was so intent on studying him that she forgot that he could study her as well. How long had he been looking at her? She felt exposed. Did he know what she was thinking? Had he seen her staring? Was she that obvious? "I was thinking about the last time I was here."

"What happened?"

She hedged. "It's one of those stories that loses something in the telling. What are you going to have?"

He looked at the menu again. "Nachos and a beer."

She laughed lightly. "You don't look like the beer type. Unless, of course, it's some expensive imported beer."

He laughed, too. "Not even close. I like good domestic beer. Are you going to get something?"

"Maybe a Coke."

"Not a Diet Coke? A woman of the nineties. You can share my nachos."

When the food arrived, Jackson coaxed Christina into sharing the nachos with him. "They're better with beer," he said.

She raised her Coke in mock salute. "Things go better with Coke."

They continued in gentle banter while they ate. She enjoyed his company. She could tell. She had slipped off her shoes, a telltale sign. She looked at her watch. "We've been here almost two hours. I didn't think it had been that long. We'd better get back to the gate."

They got back to the gate to find the passengers boarding. The weather had cleared up in Boston. Jackson got their bags and they boarded the plane.

They got to the hotel around midnight, as Jackson had predicted. Christina checked in first. The hotel had run out of king-sized rooms, so she ended up with a suite. She waited while Jackson checked in. They needed to make plans for breakfast.

"What do you mean I don't have a room?" Jackson was asking.

"I'm sorry, sir, but your reservation wasn't guaranteed."

"There must be some mistake. Of course my reservation was guaranteed." Jackson was adamant.

"I'm sorry, sir. Under ordinary circumstances we'd be able to accommodate you, but we have a convention booked. I can try to find you a room at another hotel. It'll be difficult, though."

"By all means, make the calls. I have to have a room."

Christina walked closer. She knew what was going on. She also knew that she had a suite, but she didn't think it wise to mention that to Jackson. "Is there anything I can do to help?"

"Not unless you want to give up your room or share it with me," he joked.

Christina didn't smile.

The clerk interrupted, "I've tried two hotels with no luck. I may be able to get you at a comparable hotel a bit farther away. What do you think?"

"Do I really have a choice? Just find me a room."

Christina checked her watch. It was close to one o'clock. "Look, Jackson. It's late. I have a suite. You can take the sofa in the living area. Otherwise, you're not going to get much sleep."

Jackson looked as surprised at her offer as she felt making it. "Are you sure you don't mind? I'd owe you one."

"Sure. We'll have to flip for the shower."

The desk clerk interrupted again, "Ms. Marshall, yours is actually a two-bedroom suite with two baths. You shouldn't have any problem with privacy."

Shows what you know, Christina thought. This clerk must not have seen *It Happened One Night.* "Thank you," she said.

If Jackson hadn't been so tired, he would have worried about the sleeping arrangements. But it had been a long day and a long night. All he wanted was sleep. He looked over at Christina. She had to be tired, but she looked fresh and relaxed. He admitted her offer surprised him. He guessed the sleeping arrangements bothered her, too. He noticed she had visibly relaxed when the clerk said hers was a two-bedroom suite. He yawned. "Thanks again, Christina. I probably would have been up all night had you not made your offer."

"Don't think about it. We have a busy day tomorrow and we both need a good night's sleep."

The elevator reached their floor and they got off. Christina unlocked the door to their suite. "Not bad," Jackson said, giving the place the once-over. He inspected both bedrooms and pointing to the one on the right, he said, "You take that one. It has the bigger bathroom." Jackson began to feel refreshed. He wanted to talk some before going to bed.

It was not to be. Christina picked up her bag and headed for her bedroom. "Goodnight, Jackson. See you in the morning."

Jackson stared dumbfounded at the bedroom door as Christina closed it. He stood there a few minutes before flopping down on the sofa. He yawned again. I really should to go bed, he thought. He heard Christina's shower come on. With vivid thoughts of Christina in the shower, he took himself off to bed.

Christina stepped into the shower. The water felt good against her skin. Her aching muscles and worn nerves welcomed the warm water. She thought about Jackson in the next room and wondered if he was asleep yet. He looked tired, real tired. And women were supposed to be the weaker sex. You'd think the man had been working in the fields somewhere. She smiled. Tough and aggressive in the boardroom, a baby in the bedroom. She shook her head. Jackson might be a baby in the bedroom, but she knew he wouldn't be a baby in bed.

When Christina stepped out of the shower, she looked at herself in the mirror, something she didn't often do. Her breasts were not as firm as she would have liked, and her belly could have been tighter. But overall, not bad for a thirty-year-old woman who had at one time weighed more than 220 pounds. She wondered what Jackson would think of her body. Tired of looking at herself, Christina put on her nightgown. She liked the way the silk felt against her skin. There was something sensual about it. When she rubbed the fabric against her skin, she felt a tingle throughout her entire body.

Shutting off the light in the bathroom, Christina headed for bed. She settled herself under the covers and closed her eyes. She jerked her eyes open and stared at the ceiling. God, she was fantasizing about Jackson. She'd done it before, but never with him this close. He was so close she felt he knew what she was thinking. She turned over on her stomach, afraid to close her eyes again.

You are a successful, intelligent woman, not some starry-eyed schoolgirl, she told herself. Get a grip on yourself. Jackson is only a man. You've known men before.

She stopped there. That was the problem. She hadn't known, in the biblical sense, a man before. Horny at thirty. She could see the headlines now. FEMALE EXEC ATTACKS MALE EMPLOYEE. That made her smile. She didn't think she'd have to attack Jackson. He'd be more than willing to help her out. She guessed he'd be a thorough lover. God knows, he was thorough in his work. No, it wasn't the night of love that concerned her; it was the day after. She didn't want to think too closely about that.

Christina and Jackson arrived at CL headquarters at eight-thirty. The day had gotten off to a good start. Breakfast had been surprisingly easy for Christina. She and Jackson had dressed in their respective rooms with no embarrassing moments. He had been seated on the couch in the living room when she'd walked out of her bedroom. They ate breakfast in the hotel while going over the day's agenda. The awkwardness of the previous night had passed. They were back on safe ground.

They took the elevator to the fortieth-floor conference room. Liza was already there.

She stood up when Jackson and Christina walked in. "Good to see you both this morning. How was your flight?"

Christina looked at Jackson. He held up both hands. "I'm not the person to ask." He extended his hand to Liza. "It's about time we met."

Liza shook his hand. "Good to meet you, Jackson. I'm eager to get to Atlanta to work with you and Christina."

"We're ready for you to start, too," Christina said. "We have our work cut out for us." Christina looked from Liza to Jackson. "I know you two want to get to know each other a little bit, but for the sake of time, can we get started now with business and plan to have a relaxing dinner together tonight?"

"It sounds good to me," Jackson answered. "How about you, Liza?"

"Great. Robert, my fiancé, came to Boston with me. He's taking this time to get to know my parents. We had planned to take you two to dinner tonight, anyway."

They seated themselves at the conference table and started to work. As the morning progressed, Christina marveled at the way they clicked. Not that they always agreed. That was not expected with minds like theirs, but they were able to reason together to reach consensus pretty quickly. That boded well for the project.

The morning passed quickly. When it was time for lunch, Liza said, "I can't go to lunch with you. Something came up late yesterday that I have to address. I'll be back for the afternoon meeting, though."

Jackson and Christina walked to Walter's office. Christina was nostalgic as she walked the corridors. She paused to look in her old office. Someone new had moved in and the office now bore no resemblance to the place where she'd worked for over four years. Nothing stays the same, she thought.

They met Rosalind at the door to Walter's office.

"Perfect timing," Rosalind said. "Walter's waiting." She led them in.

Walter turned around in his chair. He beckoned them to seats while he finished a telephone call. After he hung up, he said, "We're having lunch in the private dining room." He looked at his watch. "We'd better get going."

Christina walked alongside Jackson and they followed Walter and Rosalind to the dining room. Though Christina had eaten there many times before, the room still overwhelmed her. It was too much, too rich. She felt out of place. She took a seat quickly. She actually hated eating here. She worried that she'd spill something on the thousand-dollar tablecloth or break one of the hundred-dollar crystal glasses.

Walter's voice brought her out of her thoughts. "So, Jackson, is Atlanta all that we told you about?"

Christina watched Jackson. "It's a good city," he answered. "The people are open and friendly." He nodded in Christina's direction. "The work is great."

Christina commented, "I'm glad Jackson joined us. He's been a great asset to OPTIMA."

Walter nodded. "I knew you two would make a good team. Things will only get better when Liza gets there."

They spent the rest of lunch talking about OPTIMA. Christina listened as Jackson shared their accomplishments, his concerns, and his ideas for bringing the product to market. She loved listening to him. He was really excited about his work. Though his gestures were toned down a bit, his voice exuded excitement. There was something charismatic about Jackson. You believed him; you trusted him; you knew he could do it. And, most important, you wanted him to do well. Christina smiled at him.

Walter listened to Jackson. He and Rosalind had talked a lot about the best team to support Christina in Atlanta. He knew their recommendation of Jackson and Liza was a winning combination. He looked at Christina. She had done a hell of a job in

Atlanta. The woman had a career at CL, if she wanted it. Sometimes he wondered what Christina Marshall really wanted. She was excellent at her job, but Walter had the feeling there was something more she wanted. That something was behind her decision to move to Atlanta; he was sure of it.

At that moment, Walter noticed a soft smile cross Christina's face. It took him by surprise. The smile carried a vulnerability that he'd never before associated with her. Walter followed her gaze and saw that the smile was directed towards Jackson, who was wrapped up in a discussion with Rosalind. Walter shook his head slightly. Who would have ever thought of it? He glanced in Rosalind's direction. He wondered if she had picked up on anything. He couldn't believe it. Christina and Jackson. Of course, he didn't know anything for sure, but he'd bet something was going on. His next thought was of the effect their relationship would have on OPTIMA. He knew Christina and Jackson were consummate professionals, but intimate relationships in the workplace… Yes, he'd have to talk to Rosalind about this.

Chapter 8

Christina and Jackson got back to the hotel around seven o'-clock. Jackson stopped at the desk to inquire about a room. Luckily, they had one for him.

Jackson took the key from the clerk and turned to Christina. He held the key up to her. "Looks like you've lost your roommate." He could have sworn she looked disappointed.

"I'm glad you have a room," she said. "Where is it?"

"I'm on the eleventh floor," Jackson answered. "Let's go. I can move my clothes, get settled, and be ready to meet Liza and Robert for dinner, if we hurry."

They were silent for the elevator ride up. When they got to her room, Jackson packed his bag while she waited in the living room.

"That's about it," Jackson said, walking out of the bedroom. "Thanks again for letting me stay."

"No problem. I'll see you downstairs for dinner." She checked her watch. "In exactly fifteen minutes."

"Yes. I'd better get hopping."

Christina stared at the door after Jackson left. So much for *It Happened One Night*. She wondered again if ignoring her feelings for Jackson was the right approach to take. She stopped looking at the door and dropped down on the couch. She closed her eyes and cleared her mind. Then she got up and changed for dinner.

When Christina walked into the bar, Liza and Jackson were seated with a man Christina assumed was Robert. Liza glanced around as Christina walked up.

"There you are, Christina." Liza waved her forward. "Come here, we've been waiting for you. I want you to meet Robert."

A tall, dark, bearded man held out his hand to her. "Glad to meet you. Liza has told me a lot about you." He pulled Liza to him, placed his arms around her shoulder, and squeezed.

Christina was happy for Liza—a little envious, but happy. "It's about time, Robert." Christina took his hand, "Liza sure can keep a secret."

Liza smiled and leaned into Robert. "I wasn't keeping him a secret, Christina. We just lost touch for a while."

Christina tapped Liza on the shoulder. "I'm only kidding. I'm happy for you two." She turned to Robert, "So, what do you think about moving to Atlanta?"

Robert told Christina of his plans to open a public relations office as the group moved to their table.

"Liza's lucky to have you," Christina said. "Not many men would have been agreeable to relocating with their wives."

Christina was surprised when Liza chimed in. "You're right. I *am* lucky." Liza was seated on the other side of Robert. Her hand covered his on the table.

Robert looked at Liza, smiled, then turned back to Christina. "I'm the lucky one. I'd follow this woman anywhere."

"Are there any more like him stashed away anywhere?" Christina asked Liza. "I'd like to get in line for one."

Jackson answered for Liza. "That's easy, Christina. There are plenty more like Robert. He's an Omega, and there are thousands of us around."

Liza laughed. "Can you believe the first thing they learned about each other was that they were in the same fraternity?"

"Surely they couldn't tell by looking at each other," Christina said. "Did they bark?"

Liza laughed harder. Robert answered with mock sternness. "Omegas don't bark. It was the pin. We're both wearing frat pins."

Christina looked and sure enough they both wore frat pins. "Do you always wear yours, Jackson? I don't remember seeing it before."

"I rarely wear it to work, but I usually wear it to social functions."

"I guess that means you two don't see each other much outside of work?" Robert asked. "I thought you two ran in the same social circles."

"No," Jackson answered. "This is the first time Christina and I have been out for a social evening."

"This evening is not really social," Christina clarified. "It's business."

"If this is a business dinner, I'm leaving," Robert said. "I want to relax tonight and I want my baby to relax, too." He looked from Jackson to Christina. "How about it?"

Jackson answered first. "Sounds good to me, man. How about it, Christina?"

Christina hesitated. "What does it matter what we call the evening, business or social?"

Robert held up four tickets. "If it's social, I have tickets to the late show at a comedy club in Cambridge. If it's business, we have to leave early because I have an early meeting."

Liza punched him softly. "When did you get the tickets? I thought the show was sold out."

"That's me. I'm your miracle man. I pulled a few strings and got us tickets." He looked again from Christina to Jackson. "What'll it be, guys?"

Jackson looked at Christina with a silent question. They all waited for her answer. She knew she was making a bad move, but she wanted to enjoy the evening. She liked being with Robert and Liza; she liked looking at their love. It was something tangible. She could feel it and she could see it. It made her wonder what she was missing. She looked at Jackson and saw that he was still looking at her. "Which comedy club is it?"

"Jackson's a great guy," Liza said. She and Christina had taken a run to the powder room during intermission. "What's he like at work?"

"As arrogant as he is here."

Liza gave her a puzzled look.

Christina knew that look meant Liza would probe until she had the answer to her question. "There's something about that man. Don't get me wrong, we work well together, but he's so, so…"

Liza finished for her, "So attractive? So manly? So fine?"

Christina rolled her eyes. "That's not exactly what I was going to say, Liza."

Liza snapped the cap on her lipstick and placed it back in her purse. "You mean you don't think that's a fine brother out there?"

Christina hedged, "Sure, he's attractive."

"I hear a but in there somewhere. What's wrong with the man? He's attractive. He's fun to be with, easygoing. He has a good job. Damn, if the man were any more perfect, he'd be Robert."

Christina laughed. "You and Robert have something really special, don't you?"

Liza stood behind Christina and watched as she freshened up her makeup. "I can't explain it. We're one in every sense of the word. When relationships are good, they're real good, and right now we're real good. It gets better everyday."

"The man looks at you like he could eat you up. If I wasn't so jealous, I'd be nauseated."

Liza laughed. "Robert isn't the only man looking hungry tonight."

Christina stopped putting on her lipstick and studied Liza's reflection in the mirror. "What do you mean by that?"

"Come on, Christina. I see the way Jackson looks at you."

Christina resumed putting on her lipstick. "I don't know what you're talking about."

Liza inclined her head. "Sure you don't. So, what's up between you?"

"There's nothing but business between us."

"Right," Liza said with obvious sarcasm. "That man was not giving you business looks out there."

"What kinds of looks was he giving me?"

"That territorial thing. 'Me, Tarzan; you, Jane. I want to jump your bones.'"

Satisfied that her face was together, Christina placed her lipstick back in her purse. "That's terrible, Liza. He's giving me no such looks," Christina lied. She knew Liza was right. Jackson had given her a few looks tonight that had almost scorched her. She just didn't think anyone else had noticed.

"If you say so." Liza let it drop. "Let's get back out there before the men think we've flushed ourselves."

Christina followed Liza out of the restroom. They made their way through the crowd back to their table. Jackson and Robert were in intense conversation when they walked up.

"Hey, what are you guys talking about?" Liza asked.

Robert looked up at her. "I was telling Jackson how great being engaged is."

Liza looked at Christina. "They're not going to tell us. Compliments like that are a sure sign."

"Now, wait a minute, Liza," Jackson said. "Robert *was* telling me how good being engaged is. He practically had me wishing *I* was engaged." He leaned closer to Liza. "Of course, there probably aren't many women like you around."

Liza slid her gaze to Christina. "I don't know about that. There are still some women out there who haven't been taken."

Jackson followed Liza's gaze to Christina.

"No telling how long they're going to remain available, though," Liza continued. "Good things are usually snapped up pretty quickly."

Still looking at Christina, Jackson said, "I hear you."

"Now who's keeping secrets?" Christina asked. "What are you and Jackson whispering about?"

Liza answered, "I was giving Jackson pointers on making art acquisitions." She leveled another look at Jackson. "Good pieces last only when they're hidden. As soon as people know where they are, they snap them up. You'd better get that piece before someone else does."

Christina sensed they were discussing more than art. "What have you found, Jackson?"

"A unique piece by a new artist. I've seen the work for a while now and it's growing on me. I made an offer to buy it once, but the artist wasn't selling."

"You should try again," Christina said. "He may have changed his mind."

Jackson studied Christina for a long second and then let his gaze go back to Liza. "Maybe I'll do just that."

Robert stretched out on the bed and watched Liza read. "How much longer are you going to be baby? I want to get some sleep."

Liza looked up from her notes. "You're nothing but a big baby yourself. You can go to sleep without me."

Robert crossed his ankles and put his arms behind his head. "I know I can sleep without you, but I don't like it. I sleep better when you're near."

Liza closed her notebook and placed it on the table next to her chair. "Are you sure you want to sleep?"

Robert didn't change his position. "Of course I want to sleep. What else could I want?"

Liza sashayed over to the bed. "Oh, I can think of a few things." She began to undress. "What did you think of Jackson and Christina?"

"I liked them. It's a real coincidence that Jackson and I are in the same fraternity. He says they have a strong chapter in Atlanta. He'll introduce us to some people."

Liza stood in her bra and panties. "What did you think of Jackson and Christina as a couple?"

Liza watched Robert as she unhooked her bra.

"I didn't think of them as a couple. I only think of us as a couple." Robert raised up and put his fingers to her nipple.

Liza moaned softly. "Couldn't you tell there was something between them?"

Robert took her nipple in his mouth. "There's too much between us. Take off those panties."

Liza pressed closer to him. "Robert, I'm serious. Don't you think they're attracted to each other?"

Robert eased his hand into her underwear. "I think I'm attracted to you."

"I know that. What about them?" Liza took his head in her hand and brought his face to hers. "What do you think?"

"I think Jackson wants to be in her panties as much as I want to be in yours." He rubbed his fingers against her wetness to make his point. "What do you think?"

"I think her panties are probably as wet as mine."

Robert looked into her eyes. His gaze never left her face as she leaned down to remove her underwear.

Naked, Liza lay down next to him, not touching. "Goodnight," she said.

Robert rolled over until he was poised over her. He began kissing her. "It's going to be a good night, all right," he said. Then he began making those words come true.

Jackson and Christina got back to their hotel a little before eleven. "The bar's open. How about a nightcap?" Jackson asked.

"Good idea," Christina answered, to Jackson's surprise. He hadn't expected her to take him up on his offer.

He led her to a booth and ordered drinks for them. "Did you have a good time tonight?"

"I did. It was good seeing Liza again. I didn't realize how much I'd missed her."

"I like them. Liza and Robert are good people." He paused. "You were different tonight."

"Different how?" she asked.

"I can't really describe it. Most of the time you're so in control, so staid. Tonight you relaxed. You were a bit like that in the airport last night, but tonight you reached another level."

"I did, did I?" Christina said. She slipped her shoes off and leaned back against the booth. "I needed to get away from the office. Even if this is business, I feel more relaxed."

"It wasn't all business," Jackson reminded her gently.

Christina closed her eyes. "No, it wasn't, was it?"

Jackson watched her sitting there. She looked good enough to eat. "How long have you known Liza?"

"We started at CL together. That makes it about eight years," Christina answered. Her eyes were still closed.

"This was your first time meeting Robert?" It was a question. Jackson didn't really care about the answer. He just wanted to keep her talking, keep her here with him. The feelings she'd awakened in him refused to be put back to sleep. He was going to have to deal with them...and so was she.

"Yes. I found out Liza was getting married when she came to Atlanta to interview. We lost touch the past couple of years. She was in Fort Worth. I was in Boston. We were both busy."

"Two career women. Work came first."

Christina opened one eye. "I think Liza found time for a little more than work." She closed her eye again.

"She and Robert appear to be happy together."

She opened both eyes. "They love each other. I can see it. I can feel it."

Jackson wondered at her tone. "Have you ever been in love?"

"Sad to say, but no."

But he'd bet plenty of men had fallen in love with her. He wondered how many men she'd cast her spell over. "And why is that?"

Christina shrugged her shoulders. She wasn't going to answer that. Finally, he said, "I could offer a guess or two."

"I'm probably going to regret asking this, but what's your guess?"

"It's no deep insight," he said. "You've probably always focused on your career and never taken the time to invest in a relationship. Too much time and too much energy."

"Sounds like experience talking. Have you ever been in love?"

Jackson shook his head. Never been that unfortunate, he thought. "Never been that unfortunate," he answered.

"Your work a problem?"

"That's part of it." The smaller part.

"And what's the other part?"

"I've never met a woman I knew I could trust."

"Ah, trust."

Jackson didn't say anything. He watched Christina close her eyes again. She was a beautiful woman. A part of him believed he could trust her. He wondered what she would do if he kissed her. He knew she'd taste sweet. At that moment, she opened her eyes as if she'd heard his thoughts. She didn't move. He leaned across the table and kissed her. He was right. She was sweet.

He pulled back to look into her eyes. She leaned toward him. He took her lips again. This kiss was longer and sweeter. He moved closer and wrapped her in his arms. This time when he pulled back, she followed.

"We're acting like teenagers," he said. "Let's go upstairs."

Christina nodded. Jackson left money for the drinks and led her upstairs.

Christina couldn't think. She knew she was in the elevator with Jackson. Correction—she was in the elevator wrapped in Jackson's arms. She knew she had kissed him. She knew she liked it. She knew this was probably the wrong move to make, but she couldn't stop herself. She wanted to be with him. She loved being in his arms.

The elevator stopped. She looked up and saw that it was her floor. He gave her a short kiss and led her down the hallway. He kissed her again at her door. Somehow, she found her keys and opened the door. He walked in with her, closed the door behind them, and kissed her again. God, she loved it. He was good at this. He must have kissed more than a few women in his time.

"God, Christina, you taste so good," he said between kisses. "I knew it would be like this."

Her answer was to return his kiss.

"Ohh…" he moaned. "I want you, Christina, like I've never wanted any woman."

"Yes…" she answered. She was still kissing him. She couldn't get enough.

He raised his head and looked down at her. "I want to make love with you."

She heard him, but she didn't want to answer. She wanted him to kiss her again. She put her hand behind his head and pulled him closer until his mouth touched hers.

He gave her what she wanted. The kiss was electrifying. She felt it in her heart, her head, all over her body.

He pulled back again. "Let's go to bed."

Christina looked deeply into his eyes. She could love this man. "I'm sorry," she said. "I'm not ready for this."

Jackson smiled. "Yes, you are. Do you want me to show you how ready?" He kissed her again.

She responded with everything she had.

He lifted his head. "You're ready." He leaned down and kissed her again.

God, I could do this forever, Christina thought. Jackson began to unbutton her blouse. Next, he took off her bra. His large hands caressed her full breasts. Her nipples hardened as he flicked his forefinger back and forth across them. The pleasure was unbearable. He kissed her again. He started with her lips, moved down her chin, her neck, her shoulders, her breasts. When his tongue touched the tip of her nipple, her knees went weak. She'd never felt anything like this before.

Suddenly, he picked her up. He kissed her mouth again as he carried her to the bedroom. He laid her on the bed and looked down at her. He looked obsessed. His eyes were full of passion, his breathing ragged, his need obvious.

She lifted her arms to him and he came to her. He laid his full weight on her. She loved the feel of him. His hands rubbed her breasts, moving down her stomach to her panties. He passed his hand against her femininity.

He moaned. "I can't wait any longer." He stood up and began to undress.

The ringing telephone stopped him. He looked at Christina and then he looked at the phone. She sat up and answered it. He didn't move. He watched her full breasts heaving.

"Hello," she said, her eyes never leaving his face. "No, Walter, this isn't a bad time. What do you need?" She paused. "Hold on a minute, Walter, I have to get my notebook." She laid the phone down and looked at Jackson. "I have to take this," she whispered.

"I can stay," he offered.

Her head was clear now and she couldn't let what was happening between them continue. "I don't think that's such a good idea."

"Is that the way it is?" he asked, a frown settling around his mouth.

"That's the way it is," she answered.

Jackson just stared at her. He opened his mouth as if to speak, but closed it without saying a word. He buttoned his shirt and righted his clothes. "You'd better watch yourself, Miss Marshall. You're beginning to look a lot like a tease."

As he walked out of the bedroom, Christina went back to the phone. "Okay, Walter, I'm ready."

Chapter 9

"Your admirer again, Christina. This time red roses. He must not have wanted you to get tired of pink ones," Penny said, as she arranged the bouquet on Christina's desk.

Christina looked up from her work. The roses were a welcome surprise. Roses from Reggie had been at her house when she'd gotten back from Boston. They'd been a well-needed lift after the fiasco with Jackson. She had called to thank him and ended up talking for over three hours. By the time the conversation had ended they'd planned his visit to Atlanta.

She smiled as she reached for the card. Reggie was going overboard, she thought. She loved getting them, but she'd have to tell him to stop. Maybe. "Ugh…" Christina moaned, as she slumped into her chair.

"What is it? Are you ill?" Penny asked. She walked behind the desk to get closer to Christina. "What's wrong?"

Christina said nothing. She handed Penny the card. Penny read to herself. "I can't believe this. Who would send this?"

Christina tried to regain her composure. "I have no idea. Who delivered the flowers?"

"They were on your desk when I arrived this morning. I didn't see the delivery boy."

A knock at Christina's door interrupted them. "Come in," Christina said. Jackson walked through the door. It was the first time she'd seen him since the flight in from Boston.

He was talking as he walked in. "I need to talk to you before the staff meeting this afternoon. Do you have some time?"

Christina didn't answer immediately. Staff meeting. This afternoon. Oh, yes. "What do you want to talk about?"

Jackson sensed something was wrong. He looked from Penny to Christina. "Did I interrupt something?"

"No."

"Yes!"

Both women answered at the same time. The no belonged to Christina; Penny gave the yes.

Again, Jackson looked from one woman to the other. "What's the problem?"

Penny looked at Christina who said nothing. "It's the roses," Penny said.

Jackson noted the red roses on Christina's desk. "I don't get it. What's wrong with them?"

Penny handed him the card. "This came with them."

Jackson opened the card. The word "Bitch" was printed in big red letters. Jackson looked directly at Christina. "When did you get this?"

"They were here when Penny came in this morning."

"They were here in your office or out on Penny's desk?" Jackson asked.

"They were here," Christina answered.

"Did you see anybody?" Jackson asked Penny.

Penny shook her head. "I was the first one in the office this morning. I even beat Christina, which is unusual."

Christina thought about her late-night conversation with Reggie. "I did get in later than usual this morning."

"That's true," Penny said. She looked at Christina. "I saw the roses when I came in with your tea. I was surprised you weren't here."

"How long had you been here before I walked in?" Christina asked.

"I came in with the tea at seven-forty-five, as usual. I had just walked in when you arrived."

"You didn't see anything suspicious?" Jackson asked.

Again Penny shook her head. "I saw the roses, but I didn't

think much about them." She looked at Christina. "You've been getting roses regularly. I assumed these were from the same person."

Jackson focused his gaze on Christina. "Who sent the other roses?" Jackson remembered the name "Reggie," but that was all he knew.

"A friend," was Christina's only answer. "I'm sure it wasn't him." Christina spoke to Penny. "Check with security to see who was in the building this morning. Don't look so worried. No harm was done."

"If you say so, Christina," Penny said. "I'll call security."

Penny left the room. Christina spoke to Jackson, "So what did you want to talk to me about?"

"You really have no idea who could have sent the roses?"

Christina shook her head. "No idea at all. I thought they were from Reggie. I don't understand it."

That was the first time she'd spoken Reggie's name to him. "I don't understand it, either, and I don't like it."

"There's nothing we can do about it now, so let's get down to business." She asked again, "What did you want to talk about?"

Jackson wanted to inquire more about the roses, but seeing Christina seated at her desk, he realized it was time to get back to work. "The status meeting. I wanted to talk with you about it. We need to split the groups now, before Liza gets here. The people can get a head start on their new work. What do you think?"

"I've been thinking the same thing. Liza would probably prefer picking her own people, but we don't have time for that. Let me talk to her and see what she thinks."

"Sounds good to me." He started for the door. Looking at the roses, he asked, "Are you sure you're okay?"

"I'm fine." She nodded toward the roses. "I should have Penny throw those out."

"Let security get rid of them. They might lead them to the culprit."

"You're right. On your way out, ask Penny to come back in here. At least she can take them out of my sight."

Jackson left the office wondering who wanted to scare Christina. He was sure those roses were meant to scare, not to harm. He still hadn't ruled out this Reggie character. He stopped at Penny's desk. "Christina wants you to remove those roses from her office." As Penny got up to go into Christina's office, Jackson stopped her. "How often has she been getting roses?"

"She's been getting a dozen every week for about a month now. The others were pink. This is the first dozen that's been red."

"Do you think they're from the same person?"

"When I first saw them, I thought they were from the same person, but now I don't know. If he cares for Christina, why would he do this? If he didn't care for her, why would he have sent the others?"

"Maybe they're having a fight or something?" Jackson offered.

"I don't think that's it," Penny responded. "Christina was happy when she saw the roses. Like she expected they were from the same person. I don't think that's it."

Since Penny was being so open, Jackson continued, "Have you ever talked to this Reggie before?"

"I've taken calls from him a couple of times. He's a nice man."

"Okay," Jackson said. Nice man. What could you really tell from a voice over the telephone? "I'm just concerned about Christina's well-being. Don't forget to make that call to security."

"I won't," Penny said. "I'd better go remove those roses now."

Christina sat alone in her office. Penny had removed the flowers, but Christina still had the card. Who would do such a thing? She couldn't believe it. She'd heard of things like this happening in the movies, but not in real life. Somebody wanted to get to her. Why? Though she thought hard, she could come up with no answers. There was a positive side to the incident, though. Her meeting with Jackson had a focus other than their weekend fiasco. She had dreaded seeing him, unsure what affect the Boston trip would have on their relationship this morning. She was touched by his concern. She twirled the card in her fingers. Yes, she thought, there was a positive side to this nasty incident.

Christina sat in the restaurant at Hartsfield Airport. She thought of the last time she was here, the day she and Jackson had flown to Boston. They had eaten lunch in this very restaurant. She smiled thinking about it. Today she was meeting Reggie's flight. She had waited at the gate until she'd learned his flight was delayed. Now she sat in the restaurant to pass the time.

She thought about Jackson and she thought about Reggie. She wondered what would have happened if she'd slept with Jackson. She replayed the scene over and over in her mind. What if, what if, what if? She was glad she hadn't. The relationship would have been too complicated. Her best bet was to see what happens with Reggie.

She and Reggie had talked regularly since Mobile. She felt she could come to love him, but she knew she wasn't there yet. Reggie knew his feelings were more serious and told her so. She had to make him take it slowly.

She checked her watch and headed back for the gate. The flight had just touched down. Reggie would be coming out any minute now. She took a quick stop by the restroom to freshen up. She wanted to look her best.

"You look gorgeous," Reggie said, before he kissed her softly on the lips. "I've missed you."

"You have, have you? We'll have to see how much," Christina teased.

"I hope that's a challenge, because I'm going to prove to you this weekend how much I've missed you. Now, where are we going for dinner? I'm starving."

She laughed. "I thought you'd want to check into your hotel first."

"Let's eat first. Who knows? Maybe I won't have to stay in a hotel, after all."

Christina played dumb. "Oh, you have friends in the city?"

"I've got one friend that I think can be persuaded to let me bunk with her."

"It's a her, is it? Just who is this friend?"

"A very special woman. If you're good, I might introduce you. I think you'd like her. You're a lot alike."

"That's what scares me."

Reggie laughed. "Enough, woman. Let's eat."

Knowing Reggie loved southern cooking, Christina took him to the Beautiful Restaurant on Cascade. He had barbecued ribs, potato salad, collard greens, cornbread, and, for dessert, apple pie.

"God, you should be as big as a house. I would be, if I ate that much."

"I'm a growing boy," Reggie said, taking the last bite of potato salad. "I have to eat."

"Do your brothers eat like you?"

"Now that you mention it, we all have healthy appetites. So does my dad."

"You men probably kept your poor mom in the kitchen all the time."

He laughed. "Mom has a pretty good appetite herself. She loves to cook, loves to eat, and she loves feeding her family."

Christina stirred her tea idly. She wondered what Reggie's family was really like. "I'd like to met your family, especially your mother."

"You're invited to come to visit anytime you want. I know my mom would love you."

"You probably say that to all the women."

Reggie wiped his mouth with his napkin, then spoke earnestly. "That's not so. I can count on one hand the number of women I've taken home to meet Mom. That's too special."

Christina was caught off guard by his sincerity. "So, why do you think she'd like me? Are we alike in some way?"

Reggie thought for a moment. "On the exterior, you're nothing alike. My mom has never worked outside the home. She's the ultimate homemaker and caretaker. She's content that way. Now that her children are grown, she takes care of my dad and the grandkids. She's fulfilled. There is something almost serene about her. There's something about you that gives off that same sense of serenity."

"That sounds good, but I don't really understand it."

"Let me say it this way: my mom's her own woman. She chose her life and she lives it because she wants to, not because she has to. You're your own woman, too. You've just chosen a different track from my mom."

Christina wondered if Reggie had her confused with someone else. She must be putting up a good front if that was what he saw. "So, you think I'm my own woman?"

"Sure you are. Look what you've accomplished. You had to have a great deal of self-assurance and skill to accomplish what you have."

"Who do you think made the better choice, me with my career, or your mom with her family?"

Reggie stopped eating. "There's not a better-or-worse. It's what's right for the individual. You're you, and my mom's my mom. You're both doing what's right for you."

Reggie's words sounded right, but Christina wasn't sure she agreed with him. Maybe at one time work had been enough for her. But not now. She wanted more.

"You could have your own family—husband, children, career, everything," Reggie was saying. "It all depends on what you want."

Christina hoped Reggie was right, but this conversation was making her uncomfortable. Reggie was getting too close to the truth. She decided to play it light. "So, you think I can be Superwoman?"

"Not Superwoman, but a very happy woman."

Christina didn't answer, but she thought about what he'd said for a long time.

"What are we doing tomorrow?" Reggie asked. He sat on the couch in Christina's family room.

She put the popcorn in the microwave and set the timer.

"There are a couple of ways we could go. Which do you prefer, cultural or entertainment?"

"How about entertainment on Saturday and cultural on Sunday?"

"Okay. Tomorrow, we can either do the great Six Flags, Stone Mountain, White Water, or the zoo. Pick one."

"That's an easy one. Six Flags. It's been ages since I've been to an amusement park. I loved it as a kid. How about you?"

"I never went much. My mom and I went once, and I went one time with a group from school."

Reggie walked over to her and took her face in his hands. "Tomorrow will be your day as much as mine. We'll both be kids." He kissed her, then he raised his head to look at her. He rubbed his hands down both her cheeks and smiled. "I like you, Christina Marshall. I like you a lot. Now, let's get that popcorn and get ready for this movie before I get myself in trouble."

Christina reached up and kissed Reggie again. "I like you, too, Reggie Stevens." She stepped out of his embrace and got the popcorn.

They cozied up on the couch to watch an early Robert Townsend video. The movie was Reggie's idea. Christina knew it was a ploy to get into her house, but by that time she had decided to invite him anyway.

Christina enjoyed watching the movie with Reggie more than she had imagined. Afterward, they talked for a while.

"We'd better get some sleep if we're going to tackle Six Flags tomorrow." She looked askance at Reggie. "Or, we could sleep in and go later?"

"No, way," Reggie said. "We're going to do this like real kids. What time does this place open?"

"Eight or eight-thirty," Christina answered.

"We ought to be there when the gates open, but I'll live with getting there at nine."

"You're serious about this, aren't you?"

"You'll find that I'm always serious about my fun. We'd better get ready for bed."

Christina knew Reggie hadn't forgotten he was staying in the guest room. "What do you mean by that?"

"This." He leaned over and covered her mouth with his. It was the most passionate kiss they had shared. He continued kissing her for a few minutes. "We're going to have to stop or I'm going to need a cold shower before I go to bed."

Christina punched Reggie in the chest playfully. "Oh, you…"

"Don't stop," Christina moaned. "It feels so good."

"Those words do things to me," Reggie responded. He was massaging Christina's feet and legs.

She closed her eyes and gave herself over to his touch. "Reggie, I ache all over. How do kids do it?"

He laughed. "You're not used to all that walking. Are you feeling any better?"

"As long as you keep doing what you're doing, I'll recover. Stop and my muscles may all lock up."

Reggie continued to massage. "It was fun, though, wasn't it?"

She opened her eyes and blessed him with a smile. "I wouldn't have missed it for anything. I had a great time. Amusement parks weren't this much fun when I was a kid. Those rides! God, how do kids do it?"

"You didn't do too badly. I thought my eardrums would burst on that Ninja roller coaster. Other than that, you were a real trooper."

"Uhhmm," she said. "Guess what?"

"What?"

Touching her fingers to her lips, she said, "I want to kiss you, but I'm too tired. What do you think of that?"

"I think we'd better get you to bed and get some rest. Tomorrow promises to be a good day."

Jackson saw her as soon as he walked in the restaurant. She was with a man, but he saw only the back of the man's head. He thought for a moment, then decided to go over and say hello. To Angela, he said, "I see Christina over there. Let's say hi before we get a table."

Angela nodded and followed Jackson to the table. When Jackson reached the table, he saw the man's face. "Reggie? Reggie Stevens, is that you?"

Reggie looked up. "Jackson? What are you doing here?" Reggie stood and the men clapped each other on the back.

"I live in Atlanta now. What are you doing here? It's been ages since I've seen you. How's your family?"

Reggie held up his hand. "Hold a minute. Let's take it one question at a time. I'm in town visiting a friend."

"How do you two know each other?" Jackson asked Christina.

Reggie's face registered his confusion. "You know Christina?" he asked Jackson.

Christina finally spoke up. "Jackson and I work together." She included Angela in the conversation. "Angela, it's good to see you again. This is Reggie Stevens."

"Hello, Reggie," Angela said.

"I'm sorry about the way Jackson and I went on," Reggie said. "I'm glad to meet you, Angela." He looked at Jackson. "Why don't you two join us?" Including Christina in his glance, he asked, "You don't mind, do you?"

Christina shook her head. "Not at all. You and Jackson have a lot to catch up on, and I can get to know Angela better." She made the invitation again. "You two should join us."

Jackson looked at Angela. She agreed, and so did he. He realized neither Reggie nor Christina had answered his question. It didn't matter, really. It was obvious Reggie was in town to visit Christina. Reggie. Reggie was "Pink Roses" Reggie. He shot Christina a quick glance.

Reggie motioned for the waiter to bring more chairs, and soon they were all seated. "How long has it been?" Reggie asked.

"It seems like forever, man," Jackson said, getting his mind back on the conversation. "I haven't talked with your brother since his wedding."

"My mom asks him about you now and then. She adopted you back then, you know."

"Your mom was good to me." Jackson explained to Angela and Christina, "Reggie's youngest brother, William, and I went to Oberlin together. I spent many holidays at their house in Oklahoma City." He asked Reggie, "Your mom still cooking those great meals?"

"Does the sun still shine? Mom's still cooking and still loving it. She always said she liked cooking for you because you ate like one of her boys."

"Those were some special times that I spent at your house, man. You and your family will never know how much it meant to me."

Christina watched the interchange between Jackson and Reggie. Neither she nor Reggie had answered his question, but she knew by the scathing glance Jackson had sent her that he realized who Reggie was to her. She couldn't help but be satisfied with his response.

"How long have you been working with this guy?" Reggie's question brought her out of her thoughts.

"About six months now," Christina said.

"Don't be modest, Christina," Jackson said. "Reggie, I actually work for Christina. She's the boss."

Reggie looked at Christina, but his question was for Jackson. "Is she a hard taskmaster?"

"She carries a whip, but she rarely uses it."

Reggie laughed and gave Christina a quick wink. "I'll bet." He then asked Angela, "So how did you get mixed up with this character?"

Christina had wondered that herself. She silently thanked Reggie for asking the question.

Angela smiled then. "The wife of one of his fraternity brothers introduced us."

"Actually, the wife fixed us up," Jackson added. "She thinks Angela's wife material."

Angela joined in. "My friend has us married with two kids." She smiled at Jackson. "We became friends in spite of her."

Christina sneaked a glance in Jackson's direction and saw him return Angela's smile. They couldn't be considering marriage, could they?

"How did you manage to surround yourself with such beautiful women?" Reggie asked Jackson.

Jackson grinned a purely masculine grin and said, "What can I say, man? I'm lucky."

Reggie smirked. "That's an understatement. What are you two doing today?"

"Angela has been showing me the sights." He turned to Angela. "What are we doing today, guide?"

"Today's the Atlanta University Center. They're having a campus production of *Dreamgirls*. I thought we'd tour the campus and see the play." She looked from Christina to Reggie. "Why don't you come with us?"

Christina didn't want to spend Sunday with Jackson and Angela, but she knew from Reggie's expression that he wanted to do exactly that. "I was going to take Reggie to southwest Atlanta today, anyway," Christina said. "It sounds like a good idea." She turned to Reggie. "What do you think?"

Reggie looked at Jackson. "Do you think it's a bad sign that our women don't want to be alone with us?"

Chapter 10

"I can't believe you're actually checking your garment bag," Christina said.

Reggie tipped the skycap before responding to her. "I have better things to do than carry luggage."

"Like what?" she asked.

He walked over to her, put an arm around her shoulder, and began walking. "Like this."

Christina looked up at him, but kept in step. "This only takes one arm. You could have carried your bag with the other."

Reggie squeezed her to him. "Are you being difficult?"

"No," Christina answered. "I'd just hate to see your luggage get misplaced."

Reggie stopped walking. Using both arms this time, he pulled Christina to him and gave her a long kiss. When he lifted his head, he said, "That's why I need two arms free."

Christina didn't miss a beat. "Well, I think people are overly cautious about their luggage anyway. There's only a small chance that the airline will lose it."

Reggie threw back his head and laughed. He gave her another kiss on the nose and started walking again.

Christina was glad Reggie had suggested they walk to the gate instead of taking the train. She liked being close to him like this. There was a homey feeling about Reggie. She was comfortable with him. Comfortable, but not attracted sexually. She liked kissing him, but there were no sparks for her.

She looked up at him as they walked. He was an attractive

man, fun to be with, but something was missing. He must have sensed her looking at him, because he smiled down at her.

"What are you thinking about?"

She decided to be honest. "Us."

"What a coincidence. I was thinking about us, too. What do *you* think about us?"

How do I tell this man that I don't feel anything sexual for him? "I like you, Reggie," she began. "I like you a lot."

Reggie dropped his arm from around her shoulder. "Somehow, I know a 'but' is coming."

Christina took his hand in hers. "I like you, but I think you're going faster in this relationship than I am."

"I'm not rushing you. I admit that I haven't tried to deny or hide the way I feel about you. That's the kind of guy I am."

She brushed his knuckles with her hand. "I know that and I don't want you to change. I just want you to know where I am. I don't want either of us to get hurt."

"It's a little too late for that," he said. "If this doesn't work out between us, I'll be hurt."

"You don't sound bitter or disappointed at that."

"Why should I be? That's the way relationships are. If you're involved, you've got to be vulnerable. If you're vulnerable, you might get hurt. If the relationship works, the risk is well worth it."

With his hand still in hers, they resumed their walk to the gate. After they had gone about five feet, Reggie placed his arms around her shoulders again. Christina smiled.

Jackson arrived early for the Monday afternoon staff meeting. Christina was in her office.

"I asked, but you didn't answer," he began. "How did you meet Reggie?"

The question surprised and annoyed Christina. They were bringing personal matters into the office. She lifted her gaze to him. "We met in Mobile."

Jackson nodded. "Reggie is a good guy. I was relieved to know that he sent the pink roses. That means he didn't send the red ones."

"You thought Reggie sent those?"

Jackson shrugged. "You have to admit it was a reasonable conclusion."

She leaned back in her desk chair. "Maybe. It never crossed my mind that it was Reggie." Though I did think for a moment that it might be you, she said silently. The roses did come right after our fiasco in Boston.

"You and Reggie," Jackson mused aloud. "He's a good guy, but it's hard for me to picture you and him together."

"What's that supposed to mean?"

"Well," Jackson continued. "It's hard for me to envision you with him the way you were with me in Boston."

Christina gasped. She couldn't believe he'd brought up Boston.

"Have you been with him that way?" he asked.

"That's none of your business."

Jackson kept coming. "Reggie's a decent, patient man, but I doubt even he'd put up with a stunt like the one you pulled in Boston."

"I knew this would happen," Christina commented.

"Knew what would happen?" Jackson asked.

"I knew it would create problems if we started something personal. Now here you are, bringing up personal matters in the office."

"I have to bring it up in the office. I don't see you anyplace else."

"You saw me this weekend."

"Are you saying you wanted me to bring this up in front of Reggie?"

"I mean that I wanted this office to remain a place of business and nothing else."

"You owe me an explanation, Christina. Either we meet after work to discuss this or we discuss it here. The choice is yours."

"There's nothing for us to discuss."

"You don't lie very well. Did you sleep with him?"

Christina ignored that question. "As I said before, there's

nothing for us to discuss. You've started something with Angela, why are you still pestering me?"

"Jealous?"

"God, no!"

"Then why bring up Angela?"

His grin told her he still believed she was jealous. She took a deep breath. "Look, Jackson. I'm going to say this once. There's nothing between us. There has been nothing between us." Jackson started to interrupt, but she didn't let him. "Boston was a mistake. It should never have happened. It's the best proof I have that we should stay strictly professional in our dealings with each other. Nothing is going to happen between us."

"I hear your words, Christina, but I also remember how you felt in my arms in Boston. I don't want to complicate your life, but we have to deal with what's between us." He paused to let his words settle around them. "For now, I'm going to play it your way. I'm going to keep it professional. I want you to remember that this is the way you wanted it. And don't ever tease me again. A man can only take so much."

She would not be intimidated. "I guess we understand each other, then?" At Jackson's nod, she said, "Let's get to work. We need to go over the agenda for the meeting."

"Have a rough day, man?" Ellis asked.

"That's an understatement," Jackson answered.

"What's up? Work, or women?"

Jackson laughed. He was glad he'd met Ellis for drinks after work today. He needed to talk to somebody. "How did you know?"

Ellis took a swallow of his drink. "That's easy, man. What else causes us trouble? Work because we have to eat, and women because we have to sleep. What gives?"

"I think I've screwed up."

"I thought you and Angela were getting along well. If there were any problems, I'm sure Betty would know. That leaves work."

Jackson shook his head. "It's not Angela. It's Christina."

"Christina, as in your boss Christina?"

"Yeah, man, one and the same."

"I feel for you, buddy. You've managed to wrap up women and work in a single problem. How'd you get involved with your boss, anyway?"

"I'm not exactly involved with her. It's complicated."

"I bet it is. There's no way sleeping with the boss couldn't be complicated."

"I'm not sleeping with her," Jackson clarified. "I just want to really badly."

"I advise you not to go that way. There are plenty of available women without you going after your boss."

"You sound like Christina. You make the word 'boss' sound like 'monster.' God, it's a job, a title. You'd think we were living in the Dark Ages."

"Regardless of how it sounds, you'd better be careful. You're screwing with your career. What if this relationship doesn't work? She's in a position to affect your career. And if it does work and everybody finds out, what will it do to office morale? No matter how you cut it, you can't win."

Jackson had heard all the arguments before. They didn't help. He took another swig of beer. "What if Christina is the one?"

"You've got it bad, haven't you?"

"There's something that draws me to her. I've told myself to leave her alone. She's told me to leave her alone, but I can't. I dream about this woman, man. It's like I'm obsessed."

"Damn."

"It's not that bad. She has no idea how she affects me. She knows I want her, and she knows that I know she wants me, but she's determined to keep it professional. She's doing a damn good job, too. She let her guard down when we went to Boston, but she threw it back up so fast that I thought I had dreamed the whole thing."

"What happened in Boston?" Ellis asked.

"Nothing. We came close, but she backed down." Jackson remembered how it felt to hold Christina in his arms. Hell, he'd done nothing but think about it since it happened. The woman haunted his nights and his days. It seemed the more he tried to get over her, the more she ruled his thoughts. He was going to have to do something—soon.

"Consider yourself lucky, friend," Ellis said, interrupting Jackson's thoughts. "Leave it alone. Aren't you and Angela getting close?"

"I like Angela. If Christina weren't in the picture, more might be happening with her. But I can't get Christina out of my mind."

"Angela's a good woman, Jackson. Don't lead her on if nothing can come of it."

"We're friends," Jackson explained, but he wondered how Angela would react to his description of their relationship. "I think Angela feels the same way. I don't think she's ready to get serious."

"Make sure you're right. Angela is a friend and I'd hate to see her head get messed up in this."

"I hear you, man. I'll make sure things are on the up and up with Angela. Now, let's cut this talk. What chance do you think the Braves have this year?"

"We need to talk," Jackson said. He and Angela had just finished dinner at her place and they were settling in to watch television.

"Sounds serious," was Angela's response. "What do we need to talk about?"

He pointed his finger from her to him. "Us. This relationship."

"Oh. One of those conversations."

He touched a hand to the back of her neck. "Help me out here, Angela. Be serious."

"Okay." She closed the *TV Guide* she was reading and gave him her full attention. "I'm serious."

"I like you a lot, Angela," he said, taking her hand in his. "We have a lot of fun together, but I'm not ready for anything more than that."

She blinked twice. "And you think I am?"

Jackson wasn't really sure. He knew she liked him, but he didn't know how much. "No, but we've never really talked about it and I wanted—no, needed—to get it all out. I'd like for us to be friends a long time. I don't want to screw it up by getting our signals messed up."

Angela was silent.

"So, say something," Jackson prompted. He hoped he hadn't hurt her feelings.

"Is there somebody else?" Angela asked.

"Not really," Jackson responded. His thoughts went immediately to Christina.

"Does 'not really' translate to 'not yet'?"

Jackson smiled. "How come you're so smart?"

Angela removed her hand from his. "I got the impression early on that there might be somebody else."

Jackson wondered at the signals he was sending. Angela couldn't know about his feelings for Christina, could she? "And what impression was that?"

"I thought you had a thing for Christina."

"Christina? What makes you think that?"

"Something I picked up the day you introduced us. I was more convinced after that Sunday evening we spent with her and your friend Reggie."

Jackson remembered that he'd been especially careful that day. What could Angela have seen? "I didn't show any special interest in her either time. And I know she didn't show any in me."

"Maybe that was it. You were both trying too hard not to pay attention to one another."

So much for his being careful. It was Jackson's turn to be silent.

"Am I right?" she asked. "Is there something going on between the two of you?"

"Would it matter if there were?"

"Look, Jackson, it's okay with me if we're just friends. There doesn't have to be anything romantic between us. But you've got to make up your mind which it will be. Sometimes I think you want romance, and at others I think you want a buddy. If we're going to be friends, you've got to be straight with me."

She was right. He had been trying to play it both ways, but he would stop that today. "I'm sorry, Angela. Can you forgive me? I really value your friendship."

She pursed her lips in a pout. "I don't know if you deserve forgiveness."

Jackson sighed in relief, knowing her pout was done in jest. "We can be friends, then?"

She picked up the *TV Guide* again. "Only if you let me choose what we watch tonight."

Christina received an unexpected call from Angela the next week. She was making notes from a lunch meeting she'd just attended.

"I've been thinking a lot about what you said the last time I saw you," Angela said.

Christina closed her folder. "I'm sorry, Angela, but I don't know which thing you're talking about."

"How we can be more supportive of our colleges."

Christina remembered now. After learning Angela was a graduate of Clark College, she'd wondered aloud about what more they could do to support their schools. "What have you come up with?"

"I have a great idea for a fundraiser."

"The schools always need money. What's the idea?"

"I'd rather not get into it over the phone. Are you free tomorrow night? Maybe we could meet for dinner and I can tell you about it."

"That's a good idea." Christina flipped the pages of her appointment book. "Tomorrow night looks good. Can't you tell me more about your idea now?"

"Wait until tomorrow, when I'll have time to lay the whole idea out for you. We can meet at the Pelican Club on Peachtree. Let's say six."

"I hope my curiosity doesn't get the better of me between now and then."

Angela laughed. "It won't. I'll see you tomorrow."

"See you then," Christina said, and hung up the phone. She was curious about Angela's fundraising idea. The ringing phone got her attention.

"Christina, it's Liza. I called to get your flight schedule for the weekend. We're lining up rides."

She flipped open her appointment book again. "Right, Liza. I arrive at four o'clock. I can always take a limo, if that would be better for you."

"No, four is great. My dad would have a fit if he thought I was making people take limos. He'll be there to get you."

"Okay. I'll look for him when I get there. How are you holding up?"

"I can hardly believe I'm still functioning. Panic won't set in until the rehearsal Friday night."

"I'm so excited about it, too. I've told you before, but I'm honored that you asked me to be a bridesmaid. God, I hope I don't fall and ruin your whole wedding."

Liza laughed. "You won't, but even if you did, it wouldn't ruin this wedding. Robert is determined to get married this Saturday."

"How's he holding up?"

"If he says one more time that we should have gone to the courthouse, I'm going to bash him over the head."

Christina laughed at that. "Men! You'd think they'd understand why the ceremony is so important."

"Actually, Robert is more excited about this than he's letting on. We haven't had sex in three weeks. You'd think the man was going without food!"

"Liza!" Christina admonished. "I guess the abstinence was your idea."

"It was my suggestion. We wanted to go on a fast, I guess you could say, before the wedding. Don't be surprised if we leave immediately after the ceremony and don't come back."

Christina burst out in giggles. "Liza!"

"Robert has threatened to do that. Let's hope he's joking."

"God, I'm so envious of what you and Robert have. You're so good together. I know you'll be happy."

"Thanks, Christina. I believe we'll be happy, too. It feels so right. It's making me believe in destiny. But enough of that, I'm going to hang up now. See you Friday."

"See you Friday."

Christina left work the next day at five-thirty to make her dinner date with Angela. Angela was waiting for her when she arrived.

"Let's get a table," Angela said. "I'm starved." A hostess seated them in a booth. "I don't even have to see a menu. I'll take the salad bar."

"I'm with you. Let's go for it."

Both women got up. When they had filled their plates and were seated again, Christina said, "Now tell me about this fundraising idea."

Angela took a bite of macaroni salad. "We can have a radio-thon."

"A radio-thon?" Christina repeated.

"Yes, a radio-thon. We'll do it in conjunction with a phone-a-thon. We'll plan a variety talk show format for the radio and couple it with a phone-a-thon."

"I'm familiar with phone-a-thons. Spelman has one every year, but this radio-thon idea is new. Is WAOK giving us the airtime?"

"I wish," Angela said. "We can use the Clark Atlanta University station."

"How'd you manage that?"

"One of my old professors is still in the communications department. Well," Angela continued, "I talked with him. He thought it was a good idea and has agreed to give us a twelve-hour block of airtime."

Angela gave Christina the details of her plan as they ate. Once they had agreed on the major points, Christina asked Angela about her job at the radio station.

"I started as a gofer," Angela said. "My mom thought I had lost my mind. All through college she kept telling me to get a teaching certificate, get a teaching certificate. I thought she'd die when I took the job at the radio station."

"I bet she's proud of you now, though," Christina said.

"You'd think it was her idea."

"That's mothers for you," Christina agreed. Louise had encouraged her to be a teacher or a nurse. But once she'd settled on being an engineer, Louise had supported her.

"Your mom's like that, too?"

Christina nodded. "That teaching certificate was the key to success for their generation. They just wanted us to have that security."

"In my business there is no security, but I love the work. How about you?"

A few years back, Christina would have answered a resounding yes and meant it. Things were different now. "Yes," she answered, "I like my work a lot." Which was true. Amazing that a person could tell the truth and still not be honest.

Chapter 11

"Thanks, Jackson," Christina said. "I'm glad you could meet with me this morning."

"It worked out well for me, too," he responded. "I'm planning a long weekend for myself."

"Good. Let's move forward with the marketing projections." She wondered what his plans were but didn't dare ask. It had been her suggestion to keep their relationship professional and she was determined to stick by it.

Jackson sat next to Christina and placed the graphs in front of her. He leaned in to talk through the findings. His eyes met hers and he shifted in his chair.

"Maybe you should use the viewgraph machine," Christina offered. "That might be more comfortable for both of us."

Although Jackson didn't ask what made her uncomfortable, he was sure he knew. He took her suggestion and used the viewgraph machine to show the charts that he had drawn up.

"All the numbers indicate that we should start first in semiconductor manufacturing. It's the growth industry for the next decade. The market now has two giants, as you can see, and hundreds of small-time players. That means the competition is fierce. They'll be open to OPTIMA."

Christina studied the charts in front of her. "The numbers look good, and as usual, your research is thorough. Let me think on this and we'll talk about it again at next Friday's meeting."

"Okay," Jackson responded. "But I don't see what there is to think about. The numbers are clear."

"To you, maybe," Christina said, without looking up from the charts. "But I need to study them for a while." She had to get firm with Jackson sometimes. He seemed to think she should fall in line with every recommendation he made without evaluating it for herself. "Now, is there anything else?"

Offhandedly, he asked, "Why did you need to move up the meeting?"

Christina looked up at him then. It was none of his business. "I'm leaving for Boston today."

"More meetings?"

"Not this time. Liza's wedding is Saturday. Why all the questions?"

"No reason. Just wondering. I knew it had to be something important." He stood up and prepared to leave. "Have a good trip." He stopped when he reached the door. Looking at Christina's wastebasket, he asked, "What's this?"

Christina wasn't looking at him. She turned around. "What's what?"

"Those." He pointed to the red roses that had been thrown in the wastebasket.

"What do they look like?" Christina had hoped the incident would pass unnoticed. She'd already called security.

"What are they doing here? Since they're in the garbage, I guess they're not from Reggie."

"You guess right. They aren't from Reggie." She could see the wheels of his mind turning.

"What did the card say this time?"

"That's none of your concern."

He asked directly, "It was like the other card, wasn't it?"

"If you really must know, yes, it was."

"Have you called security?"

"Of course. By now they expect a call."

"What do you mean by that?"

She mentally kicked herself for even opening up this conversation with Jackson. "I've been getting the roses every week since the first delivery."

"What!" Jackson exclaimed. He strode toward her. "You've been getting these roses every week?"

"Yes," Christina said. She moved from the conference table to her desk. "Don't overreact. It's probably someone I let go when I first came here."

"I'm not overreacting. How did you come up with that answer?"

Christina shrugged. "It wasn't difficult after I settled down. I just thought of people who had a reason to get back at me."

"How many people did you let go, Sherlock?" Jackson asked.

"About twenty were let go and fifty more were reassigned. Security is checking into all of them. It's only a matter of time before we uncover the culprit."

Jackson checked out the roses in the wastebasket, then turned back to Christina. "I don't like it, but I guess you're right. Have you had any other problems?"

Christina shook her head. "Only the roses."

"You still need to be careful. It bothers me that they're still coming."

"You're overreacting," she said again. "Security has it under control."

Jackson raised his brow. "You sound pretty confident of that."

She was concerned, but only a little. And there was no reason for her to tell Jackson. He was not her protector; he was her employee. "I am. Security is running a thorough investigation. I'm looking for a breakthrough any day. Now, are there any more questions?"

His eyes met hers again. "I care about you, Christina. I don't like this at all."

She felt weak at his words. She was glad he cared, but she couldn't let it go beyond that. "I appreciate your concern, but there's no need. It's under control."

"I won't stop being concerned until we find out who's sending the roses. Will you keep me posted?"

Christina nodded with impatience. "Anything else?"

Jackson looked at the wastebasket one last time. "I guess not."

* * *

Jackson yawned. He was one of the first to arrive at the church. Last night had been a late night. The bachelor party for Robert had been unreal. What a night! Jackson didn't get back to his hotel until six this morning. Sleep had been quick coming but too quick over, given that he wanted to get to the church early. Before Christina. Robert had told him that she was a bridesmaid. Jackson hadn't wanted her to know he was here until later. He had plans for Miss Christina Marshall. He looked at his watch. Eleven o'clock. One hour until the fireworks. He could hardly wait.

"It's time, ladies and gentlemen," Mrs. Tremont said, clapping her hands together. "Let's get in place. We've had the rehearsal. This is the real thing. Everybody, take your places."

Christina took her position behind Liza's younger sister, Karen. Karen turned around. "Is my hair all right, Christina?"

Christina looked at the beautiful girl. She thought Karen must be more nervous than Liza. "Your hair looks great. Don't worry."

Karen wrung her hands. "I'm so nervous. What if I trip or something? Liza will never forgive me." The girl looked terrified.

"You'll do fine. Everything's going to be perfect." Mrs. Tremont walked by and handed bouquets to them. Christina said to Karen, "You'd better turn around. We're going to be marching in any minute now."

Christina watched as Karen turned around. The girl immediately began rocking from side to side. Christina smiled. Karen was refreshing. A bit spastic, but appealing.

Now that Christina no longer had to reassure Karen, she was getting nervous herself. Last night and today had been bittersweet. She was happy for Liza and Robert, but she felt as though life was passing her by. She thought about Reggie. She had wanted him to come with her, but his work wouldn't allow it. His presence would have helped keep Jackson out of her thoughts. Jackson was there, always looming in her thoughts. She wondered where he was today, what he was doing.

Christina looked back and saw Liza. It was the first time she had seen her in her wedding dress. She was a beautiful bride. The gown was extraordinary, with a beaded lace brocade, but it was the radiance of Liza herself that was beautiful. Liza practically beamed. She saw Christina looking at her and gave her a private wink. Christina winked back, then turned around. The music started and they began to march into the church.

The church was full. As Christina walked down the aisle, she couldn't help but imagine that it was her own wedding. She imagined her mom decorating the church with arrangements from her nursery. Christina wouldn't need a church this large, though, maybe a small chapel.

When she reached her position in the front of the church, she stopped. She didn't know if she sensed him or saw him first. She wasn't even sure it was him, but it was. Jackson was here. Her heartbeat raced and she quickly faced forward to focus on Liza and Robert. She didn't know why she was so surprised—or so excited. Robert and Jackson were fraternity brothers. Maybe they had kept in touch since their trip to Boston. Maybe Liza had invited him out of professional courtesy. Either way, Liza had known he was coming and had never mentioned it to her. Why was that?

"If there is anyone here who knows a reason why this couple should not be…" the minister was saying. Christina turned her head slightly and looked directly into Jackson's eyes. Again she quickly turned back. She felt his eyes piercing her back. He was challenging her!

Jackson saw her as she entered the church. She was captivating in the dusty rose gown. The neckline was cut low in the front, giving an almost teasing view of the tops of her breasts. The sway of her hips as she walked by took his breath away. This was his woman. He would not be denied.

He concentrated on her as she stood with the others at the front of the church. He was determined to make her feel his presence. It worked. He saw the ever-so-slight turn of her head. He knew the moment she saw him. In the next moment he was inside her eyes, inside her head. In that split second, he knew he had communicated with her. His feelings were verified when she jerked her gaze away from him and back to the altar.

Jackson heard nothing the minister said. All his energy went into communicating his message to Christina. Today was the day to force her hand. He hoped she wouldn't deny him or herself on this day. Yes! he thought, as he saw her head turn again. For the short moment that she met his gaze again, he thought he saw acceptance in her eyes. He knew he saw fear, but he thought he saw acceptance, too. She turned too quickly for him to be sure. Mentally, he reassured her. In his mind, he held her in his arms and addressed all her fears. He had done all he could do. It was now in her hands.

As Robert kissed the bride, Christina watched with tears in her eyes. Tears of happiness for Robert and Liza. Tears of fear for herself. She sensed that this was the last time Jackson would pursue her. After today, it would be all professional, as she had wanted.

She still felt Jackson's eyes on her as they proceeded out of the sanctuary. She kept her eyes averted so she wouldn't see him. She needed this time to think. She knew the decision she made today could change the course of her life.

Jackson arrived first at the reception. He had purposely left the church quickly. He didn't want to be around while the wedding party took pictures. He was giving Christina time. The decision was hers: either she chose to be with him, or he'd let her go.

He saw Rosalind and Walter when they walked into the ballroom. He walked over to greet them. Extending his hand to Walter, he asked them both, "Enjoying yourself today?"

Walter answered, "Sure are. How about you?"

"Other than being a bit tired, I'm having a great time. It was a beautiful wedding. Robert looks as if he relishes the shackles of marriage."

Walter laughed at that. "I have to agree. He does look like a happy man."

"And Liza was a beautiful bride," Rosalind added.

One of the ushers walked up. "Jackson, can you give us a hand for a few minutes?" he asked.

Looking to Rosalind and Walter, Jackson said, "Excuse me. Hope you two enjoy the rest of the day."

Christina didn't know what to make of Walter and Rosalind. She had never seen them embrace before. She could see the tears falling from Rosalind's eyes. She walked over. "Is something wrong?" she asked Walter.

Walter looked up but did not take his arms from around Rosalind. He smiled, "Things have never been better."

Confused, Christina asked, "Why is Rosalind crying?"

Rosalind seemed to cry harder. Walter said, "Rosalind needs to make a trip to the powder room. Why don't you go with her?"

Walter gently pushed Rosalind away from him. He looked down into her face and said, "I'm sorry it took me so long to realize what was important."

Christina was amazed when Rosalind leaned up and kissed Walter smack on the lips. The kiss went on forever. She couldn't stop staring at them. Finally, Rosalind pulled away. No longer crying, she beamed at Christina, "We're getting married."

Christina couldn't find any words. "Married?"

Rosalind nodded vigorously, "Married."

Christina's mouth was open, but no words came out.

"Get ahold of yourself, Christina," Walter commanded. "Rosalind and I are getting married."

"I didn't even know you were seeing each other. When did this happen?"

Rosalind took a handkerchief from Walter's pocket and wiped her eyes. "It's a long story. We'll tell you some other time. Now," Rosalind looked at Walter, "Walter and I are going home to celebrate." Looking back at Christina she said, "Give Robert and

Liza my love. Tell them we'll have them over when they get back from the honeymoon."

Christina said nothing. She stared after them as they left the ballroom. She couldn't believe it—Walter and Rosalind. She wondered how long this had been going on. How could she have missed the signs? Surely there had been signs. They were gone now, but Christina continued to stare at the door, shaking her head. The next person to enter was Jackson. She turned away quickly. She wasn't ready for their confrontation. She needed time to think.

"You see, the ceremony was perfect," Christina said, as she picked up a cup of punch.

"I'm glad it's over," Karen said. "I'm still nervous."

"Want to know a secret?" Christina asked. At Karen's nod, she said, "I felt my knees knocking while we were standing at the altar."

"You may have felt yours, but I heard mine," Karen said, and they laughed.

"Excuse me," Jackson said. Christina had not heard or felt him walk up. He extended his hand to her, "Dance?"

Christina looked at his hand and then moved her gaze to meet his. She placed her cup on the table, took his hand, and followed him to the dance floor. Jackson pulled her into his arms and began to move. Neither spoke. Christina knew that after tonight they would move forward in a more intimate relationship or they would put to rest forever this sexual foreplay in which they had been indulging.

As if he could read her thoughts, Jackson exerted pressure to her lower back in agreement. She looked up to see him looking down at her. It was all in his eyes: they contained a controlled passion. They also held a question. He wanted her, but it was her decision. Christina couldn't take her eyes from his. She was caught up in his feelings, his thoughts. She wanted to be inside him. She wanted to let him inside her. Suddenly she stopped moving. A different question was now in his eyes. In answer, she took his hand and led him to the door. She asked only one question: "Do you have a car?" When he nodded, she told him the name of her hotel. Jackson squeezed her hand and led her outside.

Neither spoke as he drove the short distance. They made the walk to the elevator without speaking. Christina pressed the button for her floor. Still they said nothing. At her floor, she led him to her door. Once there, she took the key from her purse and handed it to him. He took the key and opened the door, then led her in and closed the door behind him. They stood looking at each other. Jackson's eyes still held a question. Christina knew what he wanted. She moved to stand in the circle of his arms. His hands rested lightly on either side of her waist. The questions were gone from his eyes and all she saw now was passion. She lifted her arms to place them around his neck and leaned forward so her breasts lay against his chest. At his soft moan, she pressed harder against him. She pulled his head down to her and kissed him.

For the first few moments she wondered if he was going to make her do all the work. Then she felt him respond. His hands were now tight around her waist and her body was flush with his from breasts to thighs. His hands moved down to cup her buttocks and pull them tighter against him. She heard his moan as she felt his hardness. She pulled back from the kiss to look into his eyes. He growled. The look in his eyes now was uncontrolled passion and something that she thought was relief. He pulled her back to him and picked up where they left off. When his hands moved from her buttocks to her breasts, it was her turn to moan. She heard something that wasn't a moan from him or her. What was it? She heard it again. The phone was ringing. Jackson pulled back and looked at her. His eyes were glazed with passion, but she saw the question in them.

He finally spoke. "What's it going to be, Christina?"

Chapter 12

Christina looked at the phone, then back at Jackson. In answer to his question, she pulled his head back down and continued the kiss. Jackson moaned, and held her even tighter. When the phone stopped ringing, Christina pulled back. She stepped out of the circle of Jackson's arms and walked to the phone. She picked it up and dialed the front desk. "Hold all calls for this room."

She stood then to face Jackson. He opened his arms to her and she walked into them. Pressing her cheek to his chest, she held him as he held her. They stood that way for a while. When he squeezed her, she pulled back to look up at him. His mouth swooped down to possess hers. She became one with him in that kiss. It was as if everything, every nerve ending, every emotion, every thought that she had was wrapped in that kiss. Only she and Jackson and whatever this was between them existed. Nothing else mattered.

She knew the inevitable end of this evening was near. She had gone over it before in her mind. She had thought she would be apprehensive, but she wasn't. She knew it would happen and she wanted it to happen. Only the how was unknown. Would he pick her up and carry her off to bed? As if he'd heard her thought, he pulled back and gazed intently at her. No, he wasn't going to pick her up and carry her off. She was going to have to make the next move. There would be no way she could say this was his idea.

She stepped out of the circle of his arms and moved to his side. She placed her arm around his waist and leaned into him. He placed his arm around her waist then and they walked together to the bedroom. When they got to the bed, Christina moved away from Jackson and turned so her back faced him. He began to place little kisses on her neck. Christina shivered at the touch of his mouth. He made a trail of kisses down her back to the zipper that started midway her back. All the while his hands fondled her breasts through the fabric of the dress.

"God, you're so soft," she heard him say. A trail of kisses followed the zipper as he took it down her back. When the dress fell from her breasts, he squeezed her nipples. She moaned, not in pain, but in desire. The trail of kisses stopped when the zipper was fully undone at the base of her back. As the dress fell to the floor, Jackson fell to his knees behind her and pressed his face full against the base of her spine. His hands moved down her front from her breasts to her belly, caressing all the way. He then wrapped his arms around her belly and pulled her tighter against him.

Christina felt her knees buckle as his hands moved farther down her front to caress her femininity. She needed to touch him. She would die if she didn't touch him. She reached back to touch his head, but it wasn't enough. She turned to face him. When she turned around, his face was in her womanness.

Jackson was enraptured. He held the woman of his dreams in his arms. She felt so good, so soft. God, he could caress her breasts all day. All day. He would never tire of them. He longed to linger over them, to taste them, to savor them, but he could linger. He had to touch her all over. Her body was to him as a room full of toys to a kid. So much to play with, so little time to do it.

He groaned aloud when she turned and the center of her womanhood pressed against his face. He felt her wetness against his face. He had to have her now. He was already straining against his pants. He needed her. Slowly he rubbed his tongue across her nether lips. In response, she moaned and pulled his head even closer to her. He darted his tongue into her. When she trembled, he held her tighter so she wouldn't fall. She was so wet. His tongue took bolder strokes and she trembled more. He had to stop or the night would be over before it started.

He pulled his head back and looked up at her. Her head was thrown back and her breasts were thrust out. She was an Amazon. A strong woman. A beautiful woman. More than anything, he wanted to push her back onto the bed and enter her wetness. He was so taut he knew he would come immediately. Deliberately, he rose from his knees, caressing his way up her body. His hands reached her cheeks at the same time his mouth reached her lips. Passion filled her eyes. He had her full surrender. It was a powerful feeling. When he could bring himself to stop the kiss, he pushed her to the bed so that she lay on her back. There was a question in her eyes when he pulled back to stand looking at her.

"It's all right, sweetheart," he said. He began to unbutton his shirt. His jacket was already discarded. "God, you're beautiful. I could look at you all day."

Christina watched as he undressed. She felt alone and exposed, now that they weren't touching. She wanted him to touch her. She wanted to touch him. All over.

His shirt fell to the floor first. God, she wanted to bury herself in his chest. She wanted those strong arms wrapped around her. Next came his belt, then his pants. His erection was obvious in the bikini briefs. When he slid them off, he stood tall and erect. She felt her heartbeat increase. He was so big. The first inklings of fear began to surface. What if it hurt? What if she didn't please him? What if he didn't please her?

The fear he saw in her eyes surprised him. He eased himself down on the bed next to her. "What's the matter, sweetheart?" he asked.

Christina couldn't tell him she was afraid so she shook her head.

He knew there was something wrong and he set out to ease her fears. He started with light kisses all across her face while his hands caressed her body. He felt the tenseness in her. Something had changed and he had no idea what. He pulled back and asked again, "What's the matter, sweetheart? You can tell me."

Christina said the words in her mind, but no sound came out of her mouth.

"I want you, Christina," he said, "and I want you to want me. This is what you want, isn't it?"

Christina nodded.

"What's the matter, then?"

"Nothing," she said. To stop the questions, she reached up and kissed him.

Jackson didn't like the desperation he felt in her kiss. He pulled away and sat up. "We can't start this way, Christina. We shouldn't be here if you can't talk to me. I want more than one night with you."

"Oh, Jackson," Christina said. He wanted her to trust him. The decision to make love with him was much easier than that request. "I'm a virgin."

Jackson wasn't sure he heard her right. "What?"

"I'm a virgin," she repeated.

God, Jackson thought. How could this beautiful woman be untouched? He couldn't think of anything to say.

"Is that a problem?" she asked. She knew some men preferred experienced women. She hoped he wasn't one of them.

Jackson shook his head. "It's not a problem, but it is surprising. How did you manage it?"

Christina picked up a pillow in an attempt to cover her nakedness. "I don't know how to answer that."

Jackson took the pillow away. "No answer needed. It was a rhetorical question. I never expected you were a virgin, that's all."

"How does it make you feel?" she asked.

Jackson knew he had to be honest with her. "It makes me scared, actually. I wanted to please you before. Now that I know it's your first time, I feel that I have to please you." He smiled then added, "If I don't, you may decide never to have sex again, and that would be a real tragedy."

Christina relaxed at his words. She reached up and ran a finger down the side of his face. "Oh, I don't know about that. I may just decide that I don't want to have sex with you again."

Jackson could see she was teasing, and he was relieved. She was back with him. "That would be an even greater tragedy."

She lay back on the bed. "So, do you want to make it with a virgin or not?"

Jackson stared at her naked body, beautiful in its openness and precious in its purity. "I want to make love with you more than I've ever wanted to make love to a woman. Are you sure you want your first time to be with me?"

She pulled him down to her. "More than you know, Jackson. More than you know."

Christina awoke first. Jackson woke her with his snoring. He snored loudly. She couldn't move because one of his arms was thrown across her breasts. She contented herself by studying him in his sleep. Never again would she look at him and not think of this night. Never again would she look into his eyes and not remember the passion they had held for her. Never again would she look at his lips and not remember the ways and the places they had kissed her. Never again would she look at his hands and not feel the sensations they made her body feel. As her gaze moved lower on his anatomy, she knew she'd never think of Jackson without thinking of this, her first experience of love. He made it very special.

Thoughts of the past night were having an effect on Christina. She wished Jackson would wake up, but she wasn't bold enough to wake him. Instead, she moved so her breasts were massaged by the hand that rested on her chest. Soon her nipples were erect. She looked over at Jackson. His eyes were still closed and he was still snoring. Frustrated, she focused her eyes on the ceiling and began counting sheep. Maybe she could get back to sleep. One, two, three…

Jackson awoke with a start. He thought he heard someone counting. He looked over and saw that Christina was the culprit. She was staring at the ceiling. He turned his head to look at the ceiling.

"What are you counting?" he asked.

She stopped and looked at him. "Jackson? I didn't know you were awake."

"What are you counting?" he asked again.

"Sheep. I've been trying to get back to sleep."

"You must not be sleepy if you're counting sheep."

"I'm not, but I couldn't get up without waking you, so I tried to get back to sleep."

Jackson looked at the arm spread across her breasts. He tweaked an already erect nipple. "I see what you mean."

She was suddenly shy. "Now that you're awake, I don't have to worry about that." She removed his arm and got up from the bed.

Jackson raised up on an elbow. "Where are you going? Come back here, it's not time to get up yet."

Christina looked back at him. "Some things can't wait." She closed the bathroom door.

Jackson kept his eyes on the door. He thought Christina had forgotten that she was naked. He hadn't. He wanted to see her walk back to the bed. She walked out of the bathroom wrapped in a towel. "No fair," he said. "I was waiting for the view."

She sat on the bed next to him. "You've seen enough already."

"I could never see enough of you," he said, as he unknotted the towel. When she was naked, he kissed her and began again the melody they had started earlier.

Christina was lying across Jackson's chest when he woke up. He could tell by the steady rhythm of her heartbeat that she was asleep. She was exhausted and he was satisfied. She had lost control more than once during the night. He was certain that her first experience at lovemaking had been good for her. It had been for him, too. Her inexperience showed, but she had a natural passion that overcame all her inexperience.

A wave of apprehension passed over Jackson as he thought about the Monday afternoon staff meeting. How would Christina act once they were back in Atlanta? Would she regret this weekend? He didn't have the answers and he didn't want the questions to ruin what was left of the weekend, so he pushed the thoughts aside.

He slapped Christina playfully on her soft bottom. "Wake up, sleepyhead. You're going to sleep the day away."

Christina grunted but didn't open her eyes. Jackson decided to let her sleep a little longer. He gently moved her from his chest to the bed. He looked at her for a few moments, then he got up.

She was still asleep when he came back in the room forty-five minutes later. He carried a tray to the bed and placed it next to her. He gave her a soft kiss on the lips. "Wake up, sleepyhead," he said again. "I have a surprise for you."

She rolled over to face him, but she still didn't open her eyes. He tickled her nose with a rose. She shook her head to get rid of the irritant. He tickled her again. She shook her head again. He tickled. She shook. She looked so funny that he laughed. She opened her eyes then.

"What are you doing?" she asked.

He pointed to the tray, then handed her the rose. "I'm serving you breakfast in bed," he said.

She gave a smile that didn't reach her eyes. "A red rose."

Jackson remembered then. How stupid could he be? He took the rose back. "I'm sorry, Christina. I wasn't thinking."

She smiled a real smile and took the flower back. "Maybe it's a good thing. Now when I see red roses, I'll think of you."

"Are you sure you want to keep it?" He mentally kicked himself for being so inconsiderate.

"I'm sure," she answered. "It was a sweet idea." She gave him a short kiss. "Thank you."

He gave her a kiss in return. "You're welcome. Now, let's feast on this breakfast that I've prepared with my own hands."

Christina raised a brow. "Your own hands?"

He held his hands up to her. "These hands picked up the room service menu. These hands dialed the room service number. These hands opened the door for the bellhop. These hands tipped the bellhop. If that's not preparation, I don't know what is."

Christina laughed before taking a bite of the French toast. "That's one way of looking at it."

After they finished eating, Jackson slid over to Christina and pulled her into his arm. "It's never been like this for me before. You were the virgin, but you made me feel like one." He took her face in his hands. "Being with you was like making love for the first time."

At her look, he felt the need to clarify. "Making love, not having sex."

"Are you saying you're in love with me?" she asked.

"I don't know much about love," he answered truthfully. "I know I've never felt this way before. I've never been with a woman the way we were together last night."

"So, you're saying you're not in love with me but you feel you made love to me. That doesn't sound right."

He pulled her closer. "I know it doesn't sound right, but I have a problem with love."

"You want to talk about it?"

He shrugged. "What's the use? It won't change anything."

"It'll help me understand you better."

He squeezed her shoulders. "It sounds stupid when I say it."

"Say it anyway."

Jackson lay back on the bed and pulled her with him so she lay across his chest. He rubbed his hand back and forth in her hair. "It goes back to my parents."

"What about your parents?" Christina asked.

He was silent a while, trying to decide what to say.

"Jackson..." Christina softly whispered.

He spoke slowly. "I have a lot of good memories of the three of us—my mom, my dad, and me. When I was fifteen, my mom left. She just left. One day she was there, the next she was gone. To this day I don't understand it. She said she loved my dad, she loved me, but she left us. What does that say for love?"

Christina heard his pain. "It says that your mother made a mistake, Jackson. That's all it says."

Jackson continued as if she hadn't spoken. "My dad never got over it. He's never been the same. He stopped smiling the day she left. He stopped laughing. When she left, she took all the love with her."

Christina hugged him to her. "Your dad made a mistake, too."

"You're telling me. He should have gotten on with his life. He should have showed her that he didn't need her. Instead, he flushed his life down the toilet."

"That's not the mistake I'm talking about. His mistake was not seeing that his wife hadn't taken everything. She left you. His mistake was in not seeing that you were there to receive his love and to give him love in return."

"Well, I didn't need him." Jackson spat out the words. "I went on with my life."

Christina knew Jackson wasn't ready to face how much his dad, not his mother, had hurt him, so she let it go for now. "It was only my mom and me. I never knew my father," she said.

"You didn't miss much."

There was a chill in his voice and she knew he was still thinking about his dad.

"I think I did. I don't even have those early memories that you have. I used to dream about having a dad like everybody else."

"What did your mom think about that?"

"She never really knew how much I missed him. She only talked about him when I asked questions."

"Did he die when you were young or something?"

"He died before I was born. Before he and my mom could be married. My mom was a single mother before it was fashionable." Christina gave a hollow laugh.

"Was that hard for you?" he asked.

"Teasing from kids, that's all," she answered in a quiet voice.

He hugged her closer. "That can be a lot for a little kid to handle."

"I weathered it all right."

"No scars?"

Scars, yes. And a lingering emptiness that had followed her all her life. "I wouldn't go that far."

They held each other for a while. "What do you want to do today?" she asked finally.

Jackson leered at her. "I'll give you three guesses."

"You have a one-track mind, Jackson Duncan."

He nuzzled her behind her ears. "But what a track it is."

"Stop, I'm serious. We can't stay in bed all day."

"Why can't we?" he asked, his tongue in her ear.

Christina felt her resistance slip a notch. "Because it's so, so…decadent."

He laughed.

"Don't laugh."

He continued laughing. "Is that a virginal flush I see on your face?" He nuzzled her again. "I thought we'd gotten rid of that last night."

Christina inclined her head to give him better access. "Don't you have to check out of your hotel or something?"

He stopped nuzzling. "Damn. I had forgotten about that. I'd better get dressed and get over there." He kissed her on the nose. "Want to come with me?"

Christina shook her head. She needed time alone to get her feelings together. "You go ahead."

"Come with me," he urged. "What else do you have to do?"

She saw something akin to fear in his eyes. "I'll be here when you get back," she said. "You are coming back, aren't you?"

He grinned. "I'll be back before you know I'm gone." He got up then and began to dress. "What time are you checking out of here?"

She sat on the bed and watched him dress. "Around three. I asked for late checkout because I have a late flight, eight tonight."

"Why so late?"

"I'm having dinner with Walter and Rosalind. Business."

"Oh." Jackson momentarily stopped buttoning his shirt. "And I'm not invited?"

She didn't miss the flash of annoyance that crossed his face. She'd have to talk to him about this attitude, but not today. "Not OPTIMA business, Jackson. New project planning."

"Oh." Jackson was dressed now. He looked at his watch. "I should be back by noon."

"I'll be here when you get back," she assured him.

Christina watched Jackson leave the hotel room. As soon as he closed the door, she flopped back on the bed and thought, Oh, God, what have I done?

Jackson felt as though he could run the distance to his hotel, he had that much energy. There was something right about him and Christina. He knew she still had reservations, but he also knew that she was more involved than she wanted to admit. She was not a woman to sleep with a man when she had no feelings for him. Plus, she had been a virgin. Jackson grinned when he remembered his concern about pleasing her. She had been pleased, all right. Once she'd gotten the hang of it, which didn't take long, she had more than enjoyed it. A man likes to know that he pleases his woman, and he was sure that he had pleased Christina.

There was no doubt that she pleased him. She had been so giving and so responsive. He hated being away from her now. He found acceptance in her arms. He needed that as much as he needed air to breathe. His euphoria began to fade as he realized how quickly he had connected with her. He shook off the dark thoughts and set himself to enjoy the relationship while it lasted.

Christina met him in the lobby. When he saw her standing there in blue, all he wanted was to be back in bed with her.

"I decided to wait for you here," she said. "Let's go to one of the Harbor Islands and have a picnic."

"That's a good idea. Did you check out?"

Christina shook her head. "I'm staying another night."

All right, Jackson thought. She doesn't want this to end yet, either. Maybe. "Does your staying have anything to do with us?"

She shook her head again. "Walter and Rosalind postponed the meeting until tomorrow. Rosalind called after you left."

Jackson hoped his face didn't show his disappointment. "Must be something big, for Rosalind and Walter to cancel a meeting. What's up?"

"You'll never guess."

Jackson wasn't in the guessing mood. He was uncomfortable with Christina having meetings with Rosalind and Walter that didn't include him. "I believe you, so tell me."

"Walter and Rosalind are getting married."

Jackson turned to give her an amazed look. "I didn't know they were anything more than friends. When did this happen?"

"I have no idea when it started. They told me yesterday at the reception that they were getting married."

"You knew yesterday?"

Christina nodded.

"Why didn't you mention it before now?"

Christina shrugged. If Jackson only knew how large a role that news had played in her decision to invite him back to her hotel... "It slipped my mind."

"I find that hard to believe. This isn't the kind of news that slips your mind."

She lifted a brow at him. "There were other things occupying my thoughts."

Jackson smiled then. "I can see how you could have been distracted." He shook his head. He couldn't believe it. "I had no idea. Walter and Rosalind. Who'd have thought it?"

"I never would have."

"They did a pretty good job of keeping their professional and personal lives separate. They're an example for us."

Christina looked at him. "What do you mean?"

"If Walter and Rosalind can pull off a romantic relationship and a professional relationship without any negative consequences, there's no reason why we can't do it, too."

Chapter 13

Christina didn't say anything. She had been thinking the same thing since she'd found out about Rosalind and Walter. It scared her. All her reasons for not having a relationship with Jackson were crashing down around her. All her excuses were gone. She watched Jackson as he led her to the car. She liked everything about him. His looks. His height. His professionalism. His easygoing nature.

"Why so quiet?" Jackson asked, as he opened the door for her.

She slid in. She was glad that he had to walk around to his side of the car. It gave her time to think. "Things are happening so fast," she said, when he was seated next to her.

"By things, I guess you mean us?"

"Yes, I mean us. It's happening too fast."

"Getting scared?"

It was uncanny how easily he had read her emotions. "Fear is just one of the emotions I'm feeling."

"Can you tell me about it?"

She bit her lower lip. *Again, he wants me to open up.* "I don't know if I can. I can't even explain the feelings to myself."

"Do you like what you feel when you're with me?"

She could only stare at him. "What do you think?"

"I want to know what you feel."

Jackson reminded her of her mother in his ability to keep her focused. "Yes, I like the way I feel when I'm with you."

He smiled and she thought she saw relief in his eyes. "It feels good to hear you say that," he said. "How are you feeling now?"

She wanted to tell him. "Honestly?"

He nodded.

"Like I could lose myself in you." Then, to lighten the conversation, she said, "Maybe first sex at my age damages the brain cells."

He didn't laugh. "Do you regret it?"

She knew the answer, but she paused before telling him. How could he think she regretted it? He was a most gentle and tender lover. She felt warm all over when she thought of the night they had shared. She covered his hand that rode on the shift column with her own. "No, I don't regret it. It was beautiful. Thank you." She reached over and gave him a kiss on the cheek.

He didn't say anything. He just turned his hand over to enclose hers. They rode in silence.

"I want to stay with you tonight," Jackson whispered. They sat under a tree on Harbor Island. She was positioned between his legs, her head resting on his chest, his arms around her waist.

"Do you think that's wise?" she asked.

He kissed the top of her head. "Does it matter if it's wise or not?"

She lowered her head. Jackson was determined to be a part of her life. She wanted it, but she was afraid. What would happen if it didn't work? What would happen if it did?

"Do you want me to stay?" he asked.

"I do, but I don't know if I should."

"I want to and you want me to, so I will."

She raised her head and looked back at him. "It's that easy, huh?"

"That easy."

She turned back around and rested her head against his chest. "What are we doing, Jackson." She wanted to know what he wanted out of this relationship.

"We're going with the magic," he said.

"Magic?"

"That's what it is—magic. I felt it long before this weekend, and I think you did, too. I felt it the first day we met. It was almost as if we were destined to be together."

He was right. She felt it. She hadn't named it, but she had felt it.

"Am I staying tonight, or do I fly out of here?" he asked again.

"Why do you do that?" she asked.

"Do what?"

"Force me to make my intentions clear. You either wait for me to make the first move, or you make me say what I want. Why is that?"

"We have to be open and honest with each other, Christina. There are already too many things that could play against us. We don't need to add anything more to the list."

She knew he was talking about their work. "What's going to happen when we get back?"

"What do you want to happen?"

"There you go again."

He laughed then. "All right, I'll answer that one first. When we get back, we'll continue with what we've found here. We'll see where it takes us."

"I'm scared."

"I know. I'm scared, too." He paused, then asked again, "Do you want me to stay with you tonight?"

Jackson awakened her the first time with an intense bout of lovemaking. She reveled in it, so much so that she wondered if there were something to the sex addiction concept that was being talked about. Maybe she was a sex addict.

Before Jackson left for the airport, they made plans for dinner in Atlanta. It was important that they be together their first night back. Tonight would set the pace for their relationship.

The ringing phone woke Christina the second time. Wake-up call. She dressed, had a room-service breakfast and took a taxi to the Hancock Towers.

Walter's door was open, so she walked in. He was seated at his desk. "Good morning," she said. When he looked up, she added, "And congratulations."

Walter stood up. "Good morning, and thank you, Christina. I bet we surprised you, didn't we?"

"That's an understatement. I had no idea, no idea at all. How long has this been going on?"

"You wouldn't believe me if I told you."

"Wouldn't believe what?" Rosalind asked, as she walked into the room.

Walter walked from behind his solid oak desk to greet Rosalind with a kiss on the cheek. He placed his arm around her. "Christina wants to know how long our relationship has been going on."

Rosalind stepped out of Walter's embrace. "He's right. You wouldn't believe it if we told you." She looked at her watch. "We'd better get started if we're going to finish by noon."

Christina nodded. She wanted to hear more about this relationship, but she could see that Rosalind wasn't going to discuss it now. Ah, well, Christina thought, maybe some other time. She turned her attention to the work.

"Let's go out for lunch," Rosalind said to Christina, when the meeting ended. Walter had another meeting, so he couldn't go with them.

Rosalind and Christina took the elevator to the lobby. "Walter and I have done a good job keeping our relationship out of the office," Rosalind explained. "I want to keep it that way."

"Do you think you're going to be able to keep it that way after you're married?" Christina asked.

Rosalind gave a small laugh. "You saw Walter this morning. I don't think so."

"Walter surprised me when he held you like that. I had no idea he was so affectionate."

"He's really surprising me these days, too. I like it, but it makes me wonder how different our lives would have been if he had always been this way."

"Sounds like you two have a long history," Christina said.

"We do. I hope you and Jackson handle yourselves better than we did."

Christina pretended ignorance. "Jackson and me?"

"No need to deny it. Walter suspected something after your first trip here. And he saw something at the wedding that convinced him."

Christina didn't say anything until they were off the elevator. "We're that obvious?"

"Maybe to us because we're in the same situation."

Rosalind led her out of the building to Toffee, an intimate café nearby.

"So just how long have you and Walter been seeing each other?" Christina asked, after lunch had been served.

"Since his wife died ten years ago," Rosalind answered.

"How did it happen?" Christina asked. When Rosalind didn't answer immediately, she added, "It's really none of my business. You don't have to answer that. I'm sorry."

"I don't mind. Maybe it'll help you and Jackson not to make the same mistakes."

"What mistakes?" Christina asked.

"Choosing a career over a relationship," Rosalind answered. After a sigh, she began, "When I started at CL, women didn't have the options they have today. You were a wife and mother, or you had a career. Maybe you could teach and still be considered a good wife, but that was about it. I always thought I would get married. I went to college thinking it would happen, then on to graduate school, but it never did. I intimidated most of my male classmates. Dating was difficult. I wouldn't suppress the real me to be the fluff they seemed to want."

As Rosalind spoke, Christina realized it could have been her life that Rosalind talked about. She, too, thought she would end up married with children. The only difference was that Christina thought she would have the family, the children, and the career.

"You came to CL right out of college?" Christina asked.

Rosalind nodded. "I was so excited to get the job. I was one of the first women engineers hired. I worked hard to show them they had made the right decision in hiring me."

"That's when you met Walter?"

"Yes. He started about six months before I did. He thought

he'd show me the ropes. Actually, he wanted to boss me around."
She smiled then as if she was reliving those days. "We had a few
rows early on. I determined that he wasn't going to roll over me."

"Were you attracted to him even then?"

Again Rosalind smiled. "Was I ever! Walter's still an attractive man. Then, he was what you'd call 'fine.'"

"Was he attracted to you?"

Rosalind's smile faded. "Yes."

Christina sensed her sadness, and to cheer her up, she said,
"You're fortunate. Now you have each other."

The comment must have helped, because Rosalind smiled
again. "We did, but it wasn't an easy road. Walter didn't want a
wife who worked, especially a wife who worked where he
worked. CL didn't hire married people at the time. If we were
to be together, one of us had to quit."

"You put your career first?"

"Walter never gave me that option. He married somebody
else." Rosalind shrugged as if past pain was pain forgotten, but
the hurt in her voice spoke the truth. "I honestly don't know if
I could have done it if he had asked me. In those days I was so
determined."

"How could Walter have done that to you? He should have
talked to you about it first. He owed you that much."

"You're right, he did. And for years I hated him. After he married her, I considered leaving CL. I didn't know if I could handle being around him. But I didn't leave. I threw myself into the
job instead. It worked."

Christina saw herself in the picture painted by Rosalind's
words. "How did you two get back together?"

"I hated him, but I never stopped loving him. After his wife
died, we came back together. He never stopped loving me, either."

Christina couldn't imagine pining for a man for all those
years. "Why have you kept it a secret for so long?"

"When Walter and I started at CL, dating between employees wasn't allowed. Though the rules had changed when we got
back together, Walter and I were still the same. At first it was

too personal, too new, too private, to bring into the open. Later, it was just too complicated. We wondered what everybody would think. What effect it would have on the people working with us. We focused on all the negative consequences of our relationship. Maybe we should have looked for the positive."

"I know what you mean." Christina was thinking about herself and Jackson now.

"I have you and Jackson to thank for my upcoming marriage."

"How's that?"

"Walter wanted me to talk to you about the problems of office affairs."

Christina's face burned with embarrassment. It was as if she and Jackson had worn neon signs. Everybody knew about them. "You and Walter have talked about us?"

"Walter talked about you. I talked about Walter and me. His response to your relationship made me angry about ours."

"Why hadn't you told him before?"

"I didn't realize how much I resented the secrecy until then. Don't get me wrong—I never doubted Walter's love for me. When he began to talk about you and Jackson, I realized how much I was missing because of the restrictions on our relationship."

Christina gave a sad smile. "I'm glad we could help."

"How are things between you and Jackson?"

"There was nothing between us until this weekend," Christina answered honestly. She wanted to share this with Rosalind.

"How do you feel about him?"

Christina placed her napkin on the table. "I don't know. Right now my emotions are everywhere."

"Are you two going to see each other when you get back to Atlanta?"

Christina nodded. "We're going to see where this relationship takes us. I admit I'm a little scared about seeing him tonight and going into the office in the morning."

"What about that scares you?"

Everything. "I don't know."

"Are you in love with him?"

Christina pondered that question. Was she in love with Jackson? She wanted to be with him. She missed him even now. She believed she could trust him. But did she love him? "I don't even know what love is." She repeated Jackson's own words.

"Do you want some advice from someone who's been there?"

"Yes," Christina answered.

"Hiding your feelings won't make them go away. If you love him, say it and get used to saying it. You aren't going to hurt any less by not saying it, and you'll find more joy in your love if you do say it."

That made sense to Christina.

"Has he told you how he feels?" Rosalind asked.

"He says it's magic and he wants to see where the magic takes us. I think he's afraid, too."

"I'm glad that you see that. Jackson's a good man. I've known him a long time. Be good to him."

She's telling me to be good to Jackson? Christina thought to herself. This I don't believe. "If anybody's in over their head in this, Rosalind, believe me, it's not Jackson."

"Just be careful, Christina, and be good to each other."

Christina sat by the window on the flight back to Atlanta. She looked out and thought about Jackson. She had called him from the airport and he was meeting her flight. She couldn't wait to see him. He said he had a surprise for her.

She saw him as soon as she entered the gate area. He greeted her with a kiss. "Welcome back, stranger," he said. "I've missed you."

She kissed him back. "You saw me this morning, Jackson. How could you have missed me that quickly?"

"I missed you all right. Did you miss me?"

"I just saw you this morning," she said.

He pulled her into his arms and looked into her eyes. "Did you miss me?"

Her first instinct was to tease him, but she saw he was serious. "I missed you. A lot."

He grinned then. "Good. Now we can get going."

"Where are we going?"

"It's a surprise," he said.

When he opened the car door for her, she said, "I'm impressed. A red Porsche. Somehow, I should have known."

Jackson grinned again. "Even grown-ups have toys. If you're good, I may let you play with it. Now, buckle up."

Jackson got on I-85 and drove downtown. When he got off at Fourteenth Street exit, Christina asked, "You're taking me to the office, aren't you?"

Jackson shook his head. "Work is the farthest thing from my mind right now."

"Then where are we going?"

"You'll see," was all he said.

He pulled into the private garage at the Midtown Terrace Apartments. "Do you live here?" She remembered that he lived near work. This apartment complex was compatible with his Porsche.

"We're almost there," he said, getting out of the car. He opened her door and said, "You sure do ask a lot of questions."

She stepped out of the car. "You do live here, don't you?"

He used his key to open the elevator and they stepped on. "Yes, I live here," he answered finally.

"Looks pretty expensive," she said.

"Maybe you could tell my boss that I need a raise," he said, with a teasing smile.

"Close your eyes," he said, when they reached his door.

"Close my eyes? Why?"

"Will you just cooperate?"

She did. He led her through the door and across the room. She felt a light breeze and Jackson said, "You can open them now."

She couldn't believe what she saw. A table had been placed on the balcony. There were candles, red roses, and what seemed to be chilled wine or champagne. Plates and flatware were on the table as well. "Did you do this?"

He lit the candles and pulled out a chair for her. "A special night for a special woman." When she sat, he bent to kiss her on the lips.

He sat across from her and poured for them both, then lifted his glass to her. "A toast." When she lifted hers, he said, "To beginnings."

Christina couldn't believe this was happening. She took a swallow of the drink. It was champagne. She had to say something, and looking out into the Atlanta skyline, she said, "You have a beautiful view from here."

"It *is* a beautiful view," he said thickly.

She looked at him. He was not looking at the skyline. He was looking at her. No, he was devouring her with his eyes. She looked away again.

"Don't turn away," he whispered. "I like looking at you. You're a beautiful woman, Christina."

Christina knew she wasn't beautiful. She was average looking. Maybe pretty, but not beautiful. There was something in the way he said it, though, that made her feel beautiful. She turned back to look at him.

"If you continue to look at me like that, we may not get around to dinner," he warned.

She continued to look at him. He cleared his throat and got up from his chair. "I'm going to check on dinner."

Jackson walked into the kitchen. The evening was turning on him. He had intended to seduce Christina to christen their first night back in Atlanta, but the looks she was giving him threatened his control. They had been together this morning, but he wanted her again. He wanted her badly.

He looked in the oven. Not ready yet. He stayed in the kitchen longer than necessary to calm down. He had to get control if this was going to be the special night he had planned. He turned on the stereo on his way back out to Christina.

The notes of a soft ballad floated onto the patio. Jackson held out his hand to Christina. "Dance?" he asked, repeating the question he had asked at the reception.

She got up and walked into his arms. As soon as he felt her against him, he knew he'd made a mistake. Now he had to get through this dance and then through dinner. He could do it, he told himself. He knew he could do it.

Christina leaned her head against his chest and tightened her hold on him. He groaned aloud. She looked up at him. "I think it's going to be a while before I'm ready for dinner. How about you?"

"I'm sorry about your dinner, Jackson."

He leaned over and kissed her. "I'm not complaining. We just had dessert before the main course." They sat on his bed, eating his home-cooked meal. He was in his undershorts; Christina wore one of his shirts.

"When are you going to take me home?" she asked.

"Do you have to go? You could stay. Waking up with you is something I could get used to."

"I like waking up with you, too, but I have to go home. There's work tomorrow," she said.

He slapped his hand against his forehead. "Oh, work. I forgot about that."

"Now, I know you're lying. You'd never forget work."

"You make me forget everything, woman. Why don't we take the day off and spend it right here? We could use a vacation."

"You can't be serious," she said.

"Why not? When's the last time you took a day off?"

She tilted her head and looked at him. "It's been a while, but we can't take a day off. They'll know we're together."

"Who'll know?" He reached over and pulled her into his arms. It was manipulative, but he felt he had a greater chance of getting her to agree if she were in his arms.

"Everybody in the office," she said. "Penny and Doris have probably already figured out that we spent the weekend together in Boston. There would be nothing but gossip if we both took the day off."

"They're going to find out about us sooner or later. Why not sooner?"

"I'm not ready for that yet, Jackson. Let's keep a low profile for now. Just us."

He squeezed her to him. "I want to spend a lot of time with you. Is that what you want?"

"Yes," she answered, a bit too hesitantly for his taste, "but I need to take it slowly. I can't handle us and the world right now. Let's stick to us for a while."

He didn't like it, but he sensed that was all he was going to get. "Just us. You've got to remember that."

"Are you going to take me home now?" she asked.

He pushed her back on the bed. "Not yet. We need a little more time together."

Chapter 14

Christina saw the pink roses first. Reggie, she thought. What am I going to do about Reggie? She walked over to her desk and picked up the card. "Sorry I missed the wedding," the card said. Christina sat at her desk. She wondered what would have happened if Reggie had gone to the wedding with her. She certainly wouldn't have spent the weekend with Jackson. Maybe Jackson was right. Maybe they *were* destined to be together.

"When are you going to tell him," Jackson asked. She hadn't heard him walk into her office. She looked up to see him standing next to her.

She considered playing dumb. "Soon." It was too early in their relationship to play games.

"What are you going to tell him?"

"I don't know yet. What should I tell him?"

"I can't help you there."

"Did you want anything special?"

"Yes. I wanted to say good morning. Maybe get a kiss. What do you think?"

After closing her office door, Christina walked to him. She reached up and kissed him softly on the mouth. "Good morning."

When she moved to pull away from him, he pulled her back. He kissed her again then set her away from him. "Now it's a good morning. See you later," he said, and left the office, leaving the door open.

Christina looked after him. I want this to work, she thought. I really want this to work.

Penny stuck her head in the door then. "You have a call, Christina. Do you want to take it now or should I take a message?"

Christina hadn't heard the phone. "Who is it?"

"Reggie Stevens."

Not now. "I'll take it," she said, and picked up the receiver.

"Reggie, thanks for the roses. How are you?" she asked. She dreaded what she had to tell him.

"I'm great, now that I'm talking to you. How was the wedding?"

"Enlightening would be a good word." Invigorating would be another. Intoxicating would be another.

"What did you do in Boston?"

"I spent some time with friends." Well, more time with one friend than another, she elaborated in her mind. "Actually, I spent a lot of time with Jackson."

"I didn't know Jackson was going." She detected a slight change in his tone.

"I didn't, either. Robert must have invited him. They're fraternity brothers, you know."

"No, I didn't know. So, what did you two do?"

She didn't answer immediately.

"Is there something you need to tell me, Christina?" Reggie prodded.

She knew that he knew. "Jackson and I started seeing each other this weekend, Reggie."

"Started seeing each other? What does that mean?"

She gave a heavy sigh. "It means we're seeing each other exclusively."

Reggie didn't say anything.

"Reggie?"

"How long have you been seeing each other?"

Christina heard his pain and she regretted she had caused it. "I didn't want to tell you like this, Reggie. It wasn't planned. It just happened."

"I don't know why I'm surprised. I could see there was something between you when I was in Atlanta. Why couldn't you tell me then?"

She had no idea he had noticed. "It's not like that. There was nothing going on between us then. We weren't even friends. Not really."

"Well, you sure moved fast."

She tried not to take offense at Reggie's words. She knew she'd hurt him, but she also knew that she hadn't made any promises to him. "I'm sorry."

"It doesn't help, Christina."

"What else can I say? What can I do?"

"You could love me instead," he said.

She heard him take a deep breath and she knew he wished he could take those words back. "I care about you, Reggie, but I'm not in love with you. We've talked about this before."

"I know. And I thought I'd handle this better. Let's talk about this later, okay?"

"Okay." She held the phone in her hand after he had hung up. Was there a better way to handle this? What else could she have said? Why do things have to be so difficult?

Christina kept herself busy for the rest of the day. She didn't even eat lunch. It was after six when Jackson stopped by her office.

"Ready to go?" he asked.

"I think I'm going to stay a little later," she said, without looking up from the papers on her desk. "You don't have to wait for me."

He walked over to stand next to her. "How much later?"

"Maybe an hour or so. You don't have to wait." She still hadn't looked up.

"What time did you get in this morning?" he asked casually.

"I don't know. Probably around six."

"And you're going to work till…say, eight?"

"That's right."

"That's thirteen, fourteen hours. When do you sleep?"

"I'll have plenty of time for sleep. I don't need much anyway."

"What about time for me?"

She stopped working and looked up at him. "We'll have time together."

"When?"

She didn't know when. "Okay. We both have busy schedules. What do you suggest we do?"

"The way I see it we only have two choices—either we cut back to more reasonable-unreasonable hours or we move in together."

Live together? She was flabbergasted. It was impossible. "What's your idea of more reasonable-unreasonable hours?"

"Something less than fourteen hours a day, for sure."

"That going to be hard, Jackson. There's a lot of work to do around here."

"What about the other option?"

"It's too soon for us to move in together. We'd be rushing it. We need time."

"I agree that we need time, but where are we going to get it?"

"We'll find ways," she said.

"Be sensible. You don't want us to spend any personal time together during the day. You're working until late into the night and we live a half-hour apart. Where's the time?"

She considered the options. "What if we worked together?"

"I thought you didn't want people in the office to know."

"I don't. We can work together in your apartment. It's near here. We can leave work each day around five, have dinner out or at your place, finish up on any pressing work, and then I could drive myself home."

"I don't like the idea of your being out all hours of the night."

"You need to be sensible now, Jackson. If I was working late in the office, I'd be driving home alone. What's the difference?"

"Why don't we go to your house and I'll drive back each night?"

She smiled. She liked his consideration, but it wasn't necessary. "You're not a sexist, are you, Jackson? Why don't we split it—two days at your place, two days at my place, and one night apart? The weekends we play by ear."

"That's a good idea. I guess that's why you're the boss."

The words caught Christina off guard. His tone didn't sound malicious, but neither was the teasing spirit there. "Is there something wrong?" she asked.

"Not a thing," he answered. "Are you ready to go now?"

Maybe she had misheard him. "Give me a couple of minutes."

Christina began putting her papers in her briefcase. She would get some reading done tonight. When she finished packing the briefcase, she locked it. "I'm ready."

Jackson walked to the door and held it open for her. As she walked through it, he asked, "Your place or mine?"

Christina thought about her first night at Jackson's apartment. She wanted to plan something special for their first night at her house as well. "Yours."

Jackson rode with Christina. He never drove to work. He lived close enough to walk, and he enjoyed the exercise.

Jackson pulled Christina into his arms as soon as they were in his apartment. "You're like a drug. The more I have you, the more I need you."

Christina returned his embrace. She needed this, too. She hadn't realized how much.

She pulled back to look at him. "I think I'm falling in love with you." There, she said it. She hadn't planned to say it. She meant it, but she wondered if she had said it too soon. She had an uneasy feeling.

He spoke directly to her heart. "I know. I'm falling in love with you, too."

She laid her head against his chest. "Don't you think it's too soon for this?"

"Who sets the time schedules? When is the right time? It's not too soon. It's not too late. It's just how it is."

It's just how it is, she thought, as they stood holding each other. The ringing phone intruded on their time together.

She moved to pull back, but he kept her pressed close against him. "Stay here. The machine's on."

Christina heard Jackson's voice on the machine. She realized that she had never called his home, never heard his machine voice, never left a message. There was so much they didn't know about each other. She then heard a familiar voice.

"Jackson, this is your tour guide. How was your trip to Boston? I have some new plans for you. Call me." The machine clicked off.

"You haven't talked to her since you've been back." It wasn't a question.

"No, I haven't had time," he answered anyway.

"I talked to Reggie this morning."

"How did he take it?"

"Not well," she said. She stepped out of his arms and moved to sit on the couch. "Reggie's a good man. I didn't like hurting him."

Jackson stood looking at her. "I know you didn't, but he had to know. Maybe I should call him. His family was very good to me when I needed them."

"I suggest you give it a few days, Jackson. He needs to work through his feelings right now. What about Angela?"

"What about her?"

She inclined her head toward the answering machine. "You haven't told her about us."

Jackson sat down then. "Actually, she told me about us."

"What?"

"After the Sunday the four of us spent together, she guessed there were some unresolved feelings between us."

Christina was shaking her head. "Did everybody see something? Liza did. Rosalind and Walter did. Reggie did. Angela did. God, I wonder who else has?"

"What did Rosalind and Walter see?"

"They picked up something during our first visit to Boston and then later at Liza's wedding. I wonder if they're talking about us in the office."

"Probably, but it's mostly innocent speculation. I'd bet Penny and Doris are doing most of the talking."

Christina nodded. She knew that was true. She just wondered how long it had been going on. "I don't doubt it. It's kind of scary that people were seeing things that we weren't even acknowledging to ourselves. What's going to happen, now that we're lovers?"

"Lovers, Christina?" Jackson asked, a gleam in his eyes.

"Well, what do you call it?"

"I like the image that 'lovers' conjures up."

She held up her hand to stop him. "I'm not even going to ask what images. Now, what else did Angela say?"

He nuzzled her neck. "I don't want to talk about Angela."

She let him nuzzle. "I'm meeting with her next week."

Jackson stopped nuzzling to ask, "About what?"

His tone surprised her. "Oh, just girl talk."

Jackson sat up then. "This doesn't sound good. You and Angela. Girl talk. I hope I don't live to regret this."

Christina laughed. "What do you think we're going to do? Compare notes?"

Jackson grunted. "There are no notes to compare."

"You never slept with Angela?" His answer was important to her, she realized.

He shook his head.

Though she would have understood if he had, she was glad that he hadn't. "Why not?"

"My relationship with Angela isn't like that. We're friends."

Though Christina couldn't imagine that Jackson and Angela weren't physically attracted to each other, she decided not to pursue it. "What are you going to tell your friend Angela about us now?"

"Knowing Angela, I think she'll know by looking at me. If she doesn't I'll just tell her that I took her advice. Can we stop talking about Angela now?"

"Sure. What do you want to talk about?"

"Who said I wanted to talk?" Jackson leaned over and started a conversation that Christina found all consuming.

He liked watching her sleep. She snores, he thought. Not a loud, obnoxious snore, but still a snore. He'd be sure to tell her about that when she woke up. He wondered what time it was and looked over at the clock. Nine-thirty. Nine-thirty and neither of them had done any work. He hated to do it, but she'd be upset if he didn't. "Wake up, sweetheart." He shook her lightly. "Christina."

She awoke slowly. She had a grin on her face. She reached up for him. "A girl can get used to this."

He wanted to oblige her, but she had to know the facts. "It's nine-thirty."

She blinked as if she didn't understand. "Nine-thirty? I just got here."

He stroked her breasts. "That's not quite true, sweetheart. You've been here quite a while, and you've been quite busy."

She stopped his hands. "I'm hungry." She lifted a brow at him. "We've got to start eating first."

"I do eat first," Jackson said. The gleam in his eye told her not to pursue that one.

She got out of the bed. "What do you have in the kitchen?"

Jackson consumed her naked body with his eyes. He was glad she didn't reach for something to cover herself. He would never tire of looking at this woman.

"Stop looking at me like that."

His eyes moved to her face. "How was I looking at you?" he asked innocently.

Like I'm the most beautiful woman you've ever see, she answered in her head. Like you could devour me. Like you love me. "You know how. Now, are you going to feed me, or what?"

They microwaved last night's leftovers. "I should get ready to go now, Jackson."

"You're right, but I don't like it."

Christina gathered her belongings. "I haven't even opened this briefcase. You're a bad influence on me."

He was right. She didn't mean it. There was nothing in that briefcase that couldn't wait until tomorrow. "You think you know me so well?"

He nodded. "Better than you think."

"I'd better watch that. A predictable woman quickly becomes boring."

He kissed her goodnight. "I never said you were predictable. And there's no way I'd call you boring. You're exciting enough for me. Any more excitement and I just might have a heart attack and die."

Angela called Wednesday of the following week. "Can we get together tonight to work on our fundraising idea?"

Christina wondered if Jackson had spoken with her yet. He hadn't mentioned it. "Tonight looks good for me. What time were you thinking?"

"How about six? We can do dinner, like we did before."

"Good idea," Christina said. "If you like, we can meet at my house. That way we can work and eat and probably get more done than if we were sitting in a restaurant."

Christina gave directions to her home. When she and Angela hung up, she called Jackson.

"Are you missing me, or is this a work call?" Jackson teased.

"Angela's coming over tonight," she said.

"Girl talk, I imagine. Do I still get to come over, or what?"

"Sure you can come over. What have you told Angela about us?"

"I told her that love wasn't turning out to be such a bad thing," Jackson answered.

"You told Angela you were in love with me?"

"Don't sound so surprised. It's not exactly a secret."

"Jackson, you've never told me that you love me."

"Yes, I have. I've told you lots of times. I told you the first night we were together. I knew it then."

Christina couldn't believe Jackson was saying this. "You did not say you loved me. You said making love with me was special. You said you were falling in love with me, but you never said you were in love with me. Believe me, if you'd said it, I'd remember."

"How can you not know how I feel, Christina?"

She did have an inkling about his feelings for her. "I made some assumptions, but it's good to hear."

"I love you, Christina Marshall," Jackson said.

"You do?" Christina was grinning now. "Well you'd better, because I love you, too."

"Music to my ears, sweetheart. Are you sure you have to meet with Angela tonight? I feel the need to celebrate."

She understood the celebration he had in mind. "She won't stay all night. We'll have plenty of time to celebrate. You know what they say about anticipation."

"You'd better be ready for a long night, Miss Marshall. I hope you got a lot of rest last night."

He knew she hadn't gotten a lot of rest last night because he'd kept her up half the night. "I haven't been getting a lot of rest lately, but if you have the stamina, I'm sure I do."

"We'll just have to see, won't we?" was Jackson's response.

The doorbell rang just as Christina finished tossing the salad. Exactly six o'clock. Angela was punctual.

The doorbell rang again when Christina and Angela were about halfway through dinner and their agenda. Christina knew who was at the door. She looked at Angela.

"Something wrong, Christina? Were you expecting company tonight?"

Christina got up to get the door. "I guess you could say that. It's Jackson." She paused, then added honestly, "This feels awkward."

"It shouldn't," Angela said. "Jackson and I were never more than friends. There might have been something there, but I always figured he had a thing for you." The doorbell rang again. Angela smiled. "You'd better get that before he kicks the door in."

The doorbell rang again and Christina laughed. "I think you're right. I'll be right back."

Jackson kissed her in greeting. "Are you about done?" he whispered. "I've been anticipating all day."

"Behave yourself," she said. "You're going to have to wait a little while longer. Come on back, we're in the family room."

Christina deliberately let Jackson walk ahead of her. She was still unsure of this platonic relationship he and Angela shared. "Hi, Angela," was Jackson's greeting. No hidden message in that, Christina thought.

"Hi, yourself," Angela said. "If I had known you two had plans tonight, Christina and I could have gotten together another time."

"It's not a problem. We just decided today." He looked at Christina. "Sometimes things come up."

That wasn't just a look he gave Christina. It was a promise, a threat, and a dare, all rolled into one gaze. Christina cleared her throat. "We're almost finished," she said to Jackson. "You want something to eat? We have some left."

"Don't let me rush you. I'll get a bite and watch some television. Never let it be said that I came between a woman and her work. Or in this case, two women and their work."

Christina looked at Angela to see if she had picked up on the double entendre. She didn't look as if she had. Christina looked back at Jackson, which was a mistake. He was slowly seductively licking mayonnaise off his knife. Christina felt a shiver go down her spine.

Chapter 15

Christina leaned against the armoire in her bedroom with her arms crossed. "You were bad tonight, Jackson," she scolded. Angela had just left.

"Actually, I was pretty tame. I could have been a lot worse," Jackson reasoned from his seat on her bed. The bed tray in front of him held a newspaper and his discarded dishes. "How did your meeting go?"

"Good." She dropped her arms and walked over to the bed. Jackson put the bed tray on the floor to make room for her. "We came up with a pretty detailed proposal for what we want to do. Angela has some other people she wants to involve. We did enough tonight to take the proposal to those people."

"It's a pretty big project, but a great way to raise money. You two will probably be a big hit."

"I don't know about all that. We're going to need a lot of support. Are you sure you don't want to help?"

"No way. That's yours," he said quickly.

"Just thought I'd check again," she said. She hadn't really expected him to help. They had talked about the project and agreed that Jackson wouldn't get involved. Their lives were too intertwined as it was with work and this romance. There had to be room for separate interests.

Jackson touched his hand to the back of her neck. "Has the celebration started yet?" Jackson asked.

"I was thinking that we'd go out tonight. Maybe dancing." Her eyes twinkled. "What do you think?"

"I think we have different ideas of what a celebration is. Mine don't include leaving this room."

"I think we're becoming limited in our activities, Jackson. All this time in one room isn't good."

"Speak for yourself. It's very good for me."

She rolled her eyes. "That's not what I'm talking about and you know it."

Jackson's nimble fingers began a gentle massage of her neck. "Do you really want to go out?"

"Well…" she teased. "Not really."

Jackson shook his head. "Then why are we having this conversation?"

"Because we need to look at how much time we spend in bed. Maybe we're having sex too often?"

Jackson laughed. "Sweetheart, there is no such thing as too much sex."

"Don't laugh. I'm serious, Jackson. What if all we have is sex? What if we don't have a real relationship?"

"That's not the case and you know it," he said in a serious tone. "What's brought this on?"

She moved so that his hand fell away from her. "I think about it all the time."

"Sex?" he asked.

"Making love with you," she clarified.

"What's so bad about that? I spend a great deal of my time thinking about making love with you. It's natural. We're in love."

Christina wasn't too sure about it being natural. "I wonder if Liza and Robert have sex this often."

"From what I saw in Boston and from what I remember from their wedding, I'd say they have sex at least as often as we do. Probably more."

Christina couldn't imagine more. "Why do you say more?"

"Their relationship is more established. They've found a rhythm for their lives together. I'm not just talking sex, I'm talking their lives. Look at Robert's ease with relocating to Atlanta."

"Are you saying we're going to have sex more often than we

do now? That I can't imagine." Christina made a mental note to talk to Liza about this.

"What about the celebration?" Jackson asked again. "When does it start?"

Christina stood up. "I do have a surprise for you. Don't move." She went into her walk-in closet and closed the door.

When she walked out she was wearing a purple teddy trimmed with black lace. The gleam in Jackson's eyes told her that he liked it.

He gulped. "Did you buy that especially for me?"

She walked around the bed. "I bought it for myself, but I knew you'd like it." She bent over from the waist to pick up something from the floor. She knew she gave Jackson a good view of her derriere and her thighs. She stood up when she heard him moan.

"Everything all right, Jackson?" she asked innocently.

"I want to touch you," he said quickly.

"Not so fast," she admonished. "Tonight I'm going to make love to you."

Liza began work the following Tuesday, two months after her wedding.

"When did you guys get into town?" Christina asked, over coffee in her office that morning. She and Liza were seated in adjacent chairs.

"Saturday night. We're still in a hotel. We looked at a couple of apartments yesterday. I think we're going to end up at the Midtown Terrace Apartments."

"That's where Jackson lives. You're going to love that building. It's close to work."

"Robert will like living close to Jackson. How is he, anyway?"

"He's great. The two of us want to take you and Robert out when you get settled."

Liza lifted a brow. "The two of you? Is anything going on here?"

Christina couldn't stop the grin that spread across her face. "As a matter of fact, there is."

"Details," Liza said, leaning closer. "I want details."

"Jackson and I are seeing each other."

"Seeing each other? What does that mean? Are you sleeping with him?"

Christina found Liza's eagerness amusing. "Yes, I'm sleeping with him."

"So, you finally did it. How was it? That was a stupid question. It must have been good, or you wouldn't still be seeing him. So, how was your first time? Was it as difficult as you imagined it would be?"

Christina felt as giddy as a schoolgirl. "That's the thing, Liza. I didn't have any reservations at all. I didn't think about my body or possible pregnancy or AIDS or anything. I just wanted to be with him." Christina paused, then added, "There were a couple of moments when I was apprehensive, but Jackson helped me through them. He's a considerate lover."

Liza reached over and hugged her. "Oh, Christina, I'm so glad it was good for you." Liza pulled back. "I have one question. Did you use protection?"

Christina nodded. "Jackson came prepared. Since then I've seen the gynecologist, so we're okay."

"Are you in love with him?"

"Yes, I love him. There are times, though, that I wonder if it's him I love or the sex. Liza, I never even considered how much I would like it. It scares me sometimes."

"Don't look for trouble where there is none," Liza advised. "Be thankful that you and Jackson are sexually compatible. There are thousands of women out there who'd love to be in your shoes, or maybe I should say, in your bed."

"So you think this is normal?"

"What's normal? As long as it makes you happy, it's normal and right for you."

"Are you and Robert very active?" Christina asked. It seemed that she was always asking Liza about her sex life.

"Very, and you don't hear me complaining. Making love binds you. It doesn't make the commitment, but it cements it. Making love also helps you keep your perspective. It's hard to fight when you're making love. And it's hard to remember what the fight was about in the afterglow."

Christina stored those comments in her memory bank. "I always thought that communication was the cement that held a relationship together, not sex."

"Making love is a form of communication. It's the most intimate conversation two people can have. It comforts, it relaxes, it reassures, it soothes, it excites, it stimulates. It can do all those things depending on the needs and wants of those involved. It can't be the only form of communication in the relationship, but it's a vital form."

"So you think I'm worrying needlessly?"

Liza nodded. "How does he feel about you?"

"He says that he loves me, too."

"Sounds like there's a but in there somewhere. What's the problem?"

"It all happened so fast. We've only been together since your reception."

"Who cares about time? There's no timetable for your emotions. You have to take love when it comes. Cherish it, don't question it away. Be happy. Isn't this what you wanted?"

"It is," Christina answered. "Sometimes I wonder why all these good things are happening to me."

Liza put her cup down and took Christina's hand. "Good things are happening to you because you deserve good things."

"I'm glad you're here, Liza. Jackson's a good listener, but I need to talk to another woman sometimes."

"I'm glad I'm here, too. I've missed your friendship. And I'm glad Jackson and Robert like each other. We can do some foursomes. That makes it all the better."

"Don't forget Jackson and I want to take you two out. Just give us a date. Let us know, too, if you need help with anything." Christina took a slip of paper from her desk and wrote her and Jackson's phone numbers. She handed the paper to Liza. "Call us anytime."

* * *

"Did you see Liza today?" Christina asked from her desk in Jackson's apartment. They were now spending weekdays at his place, since it was closest to work and weekends at her place. They had fallen into the comfortable routine of bringing work home and working until all hours of the night.

"In passing. We didn't get to talk, but she mentioned they were thinking about moving in here. That would be great, wouldn't it?"

Christina nodded. "We should plan something special to welcome them to Atlanta. I just have no idea what."

"We can have a party for them. Introduce them to some people. Not a lot of people, just a small dinner party."

"We'd host a party?" It made them seem like an official couple. Not that they weren't, but giving a party for his fraternity friends made a statement.

"Sure. Don't you like the idea?"

"It's not that. This'll be the first time we've hosted a party."

"I say it's about time. It would be a good time for you to meet Betty, Ellis's wife. I hate that you two haven't met each other yet. Let's pick a date that she and Ellis can definitely make it."

The plans began forming in Christina's mind. "Do you want to have it here, or at my place?"

"It doesn't matter. You decide."

Christina weighed the pros and cons. "We can have a larger group at my place. How many people were you thinking about?"

"No more than ten, including us. Ellis and Betty, Michael and Jewel, Robert and Liza, you and me, and one other couple. Who do you suggest?"

"Why don't we invite Angela? She's seeing somebody, isn't she?"

"I don't know, you spend more time with Angela than I do."

Christina detected his hesitation. "Does that bother you—my friendship with Angela?"

"Not at all. I just wonder if she'll feel awkward when we're with Ellis and Betty, Mike and Jewel. Jewel and Betty are the ones who wanted to pair me up with Angela originally. I don't want her to be hurt."

Christina remembered the first time she and Jackson had gone out with Mike and Jewel. She had sensed a need to win Jewel over. She had done it, and she now had a new friend. "She may be more hurt if we don't invite her. Jewel and Betty are her friends, too."

Jackson picked up his newspaper. "If you think that's best, let's do it. I'll talk with Ellis tomorrow and get some dates and we'll work it from there. Okay?"

"Okay," she said. She hoped Jackson hadn't acquiesced just to appease her. "Are you about ready for bed?"

"I have more reading to do. You go on ahead." He looked up from the paper. "Just don't go to sleep before I get there."

When Christina awoke Sunday morning, Jackson wasn't in bed with her. Maybe he's in the bathroom, she thought. Or the kitchen. She waited awhile, then, sensing something was wrong, got up to look for him. She found him in the family room. She stood in the doorway and watched him hang up the phone, then lean forward and place his head in his hands.

"Bad news?" she asked, as she walked toward him. He lifted his head from his hands and turned in her direction after she spoke.

"Just another call to my dad. Every call affects me this way."

She took a seat on the couch next to him and pulled him back so his head rested against her breasts. She began rubbing her hands across his chest. There was nothing sexual in her touch this morning, she only wanted to comfort him. "What did he say?" she asked.

"Why can't he get over her?" Jackson demanded to know. "She left fourteen years ago."

She heard the pain in his voice and she wished she had answers for him, but she didn't. "Neither of you have heard from her in all this time?" Christina found it hard to believe that his mother had just disappeared.

Jackson shook his head. "I haven't heard a word, and I don't think Dad has, either."

"How do you know nothing happened to her? Maybe she didn't leave willingly."

"She left a letter. I never read it. My dad sat me down and told me she was gone. He said she left a letter saying she needed her own space. Wanted to find herself," he said. "Can you believe that? The old man didn't even care enough to lie to me. How can you tell your fifteen-year-old kid that his mom just up and left. That she doesn't love him?"

Christina held him tighter. "It was cruel of your mother to leave, and your father handled it badly," she agreed. "Didn't you want to find out for yourself? Didn't you want to talk to her yourself?"

"Yes, and that talk led to the deterioration of my relationship with my dad. I called him a liar. I told him my mom did love me. I told him she left him, not me. I told him I was going to find her."

Christina wished she could absorb some of his pain. She hoped talking about it helped him. "What did you do?"

"I set my sights on getting out of that house and looking for my mom. I told myself that she didn't leave me. She was out there waiting for me somewhere. My dad was the bad guy."

"You never found her?"

"I didn't say that. During my second year in college, I hired a private detective. Can you believe that?" He didn't wait for an answer. "She was living in Los Angeles, married with two kids—twins."

Christina knew the ache he'd felt when he'd learned the truth was still there. Time had dulled it, but it was still there.

"She was pregnant when she left my dad," he continued. "She'd been having an affair. I didn't even want to know how long it had been going on. That day my mom died for me."

"Oh, Jackson, that's so sad."

"Not really. I learned how strong I was. I didn't need a mother."

Christina didn't believe Jackson didn't need his mother. The pain in his voice told the real story. "What happened between you and your dad?"

"Nothing. I wanted to forget her, all my dad wanted to do was remember her. That's the way it is now. He can't get over her."

"He must have loved her a great deal," Christina offered.

"If love did this to my dad, who needs love?"

The bitterness in his tone made Christina cringe. "What does it mean when you say you love me, Jackson? You don't have a real high opinion of love."

He sat up then and looked at her. His feelings for her were real. "I know that everything that's called love isn't love. I've seen the effects of false love in my mom and dad."

"Why did you pursue me, then? What were you looking for? A good time?" Christina wasn't sure she'd like the answers to those questions, but she wanted them.

Jackson must have sensed her uneasiness, because he turned and pulled her into his arms before he answered. "I was first attracted to you when I saw you walk in the building that morning before the interview. I liked the way you moved. Your legs and your breasts." He squeezed her left breast with his hand. "They bounced as you walked across the street."

Christina remembered that morning. She had known he was watching her.

"I was surprised to find that my mystery lady was also my boss. That information should have stopped me, but I couldn't help myself," he stated simply.

"Be for real, Jackson."

"I'm serious. You were on my mind constantly. When I started going out with Angela, I hoped she would help me not think about you so much. It didn't happen. The more I tried not to think about you, the more I thought about you. You got under my skin real quick, lady."

Christina liked hearing that. She turned and gave him a quick kiss.

"To answer your last question, I wouldn't have pursued you

if all I wanted was a good time. I pursued you because I sensed there was something special between us."

"Magic," she whispered. She remembered he had called it magic.

"At the time, I didn't want to put a label on it. Somewhere in the back of my mind, I thought that we had a chance to have something as solid as Reggie's parents have. I'd never felt that before."

Warmth spread over her at his words. "Do you ever think that we'll end up like your parents?"

He didn't answer immediately. She gave him time. "Sometimes, when I'm thinking about how well we fit, I begin to wonder if it's all in my mind and I get scared. It's possible we'll end up like them, but I don't think we will."

"What makes you so sure?"

"A lot of little things. We share the same work ethic. We talk about everything. We're sexually compatible. I love being with you. We don't have to talk. We don't have to do anything. I just like being with you, being in the same room with you. Being in the same house and knowing that you're in the house, even if you're not in the same room. I like going to bed with you and I like waking up with you. You're good for me, Christina."

Christina pressed closer to him. "I feel the same way. I can't imagine coming home without you. It's as though you're a part of me. It's scary, but it's good." She peeked up at him. "You make me feel beautiful."

"You *are* beautiful," he said.

"You make me believe that," she said.

"You know that we're sounding like an old married couple, don't you?"

"I can't imagine feeling more committed to you than I do now."

"I feel the same way," he said.

She listened to the regular thump of his heart and felt content to be in his arms, glad they had shared what was in their hearts. He surprised her when he spoke again.

"Do you want to get married?" he asked.

Chapter 16

"Married?" Christina's first thought was that this was a proposal.

"Yes, do you want to get married?"

"Now? Someday?"

"This wasn't meant to be a difficult question, Christina," Jackson said dryly. "Let's try 'someday.'"

"Sure, I want to get married," she said offhandedly. "There are a lot of benefits to having a man around."

"You don't have to be married to have a man around. You have me now and we aren't married. Do you want to get married?"

Christina thought again that Jackson was a lot like her mother. He always brought her back to the real issue. "Yes, Jackson, I want to get married. I've always wanted to get married."

He heard the wistfulness in her voice. "You didn't have any role models for marriages as a child, either, did you?"

"Not really. My mom was a great mom, but I missed having a dad. I've developed a lot of theories about the role a father plays in his daughter's life."

"That's only natural. You look at what you missed and you think he may have filled that. The reality is that even if he were there, he might not have filled those roles."

"You're probably right," Christina said. She often fantasized about life with a father. She wasn't ready yet to give up those dreams.

"Tell me your theories," Jackson said.

Christina pulled away from him to look into his eyes. "Are

you sure you want to hear this? I've had a lot of years to develop these theories. It may get a little long."

Jackson kissed her softly on the lips. "We've got all day and all night."

Christina rested her head back against his chest. "My first theory is that girls learn to relate to boys by watching their mothers relate and interact with their fathers. Growing up in a house with no males make boys more foreign and, in some ways, more frightening. They're really an unknown quantity."

"That makes sense. All kids learn about the interaction of the sexes from their parents' model. You and I are proof of that. What's your next theory?"

"Well, I think that a little girl's confidence in her sexual self is given to her in her father's eyes."

"That I don't understand," Jackson said.

"It's difficult for me to express. The father is the first man in a girl's life. She wants to please him in all ways. His acceptance or rejection of her is what she expects to find in other men. If Daddy thinks she's smart and pretty, there's no reason for her to expect other men will think any differently. If Daddy thinks she's dumb or ugly, there's no reason for her to expect that other men will be any different in their view, either."

"What if Daddy isn't there?"

Christina had first-hand knowledge of that case. "If Daddy isn't there, the girl's first experience with a male is one of rejection."

"Not all fathers are absent because they want to be," Jackson reminded her. "What about cases where the father dies?"

She shook her head. "Children don't understand the difference. It's still rejection. The result—the little girl's expectation—is that every man will reject her."

"Is that how you felt?"

Christina expected the question. "I think so. I've never had to depend on a man, so I never had the experience of him being there when I needed him. You know, I remember a girlfriend in college saying that I had a lot of male friends. When she said that, I thought about it. She was right. I was friends with a lot of guys—none of them romantic, though. I was a friend who listened, but I didn't trust them and I didn't respect them."

"No trust and no respect. That's pretty cold, Christina."

"I know, but you have to remember my theory," Christina explained. "My expectation is that men will either reject me in the beginning or they'll reject me in the end. That kind of thinking doesn't allow for much trust or respect."

"Well, I hope your opinions have changed now."

"Of course they have. I know there are good men out there. I have professional relationships with men that I trust and respect."

He squeezed her to him. "What about personal relationships? What about me?"

She turned to face him. "You're a whole new experience for me." She turned back around.

"How's that?"

She heard the smile in his voice and turned to face him again. "You make me feel things that I've never felt before. You make me think all my dreams will come true."

Jackson kissed her then. "I want to make them come true, Christina, if you'll let me."

Christina searched for the words to express to Jackson how much he had given her already. He had taken her dreams for love, marriage, and family and brought them so close that she could touch them. "I wish I could tell you how much I love you."

"I know, Christina. I love you, too."

She smiled. "And how are you so sure that I love you?"

He gave her a smug masculine smile. He touched her eyes. "I can see it here. They light up when you see me." He touched the corners of her mouth. "I can see it here. You have a smile that's reserved just for me." He ran his forefinger up and down her cheek. "You've taught me what love is."

She felt his intensity. At that moment, she was overwhelmed with love for him. She couldn't say anything so he put all her emotions, all her love, into a long, wet kiss. When it was over, she turned around and burrowed into his chest. "There's no place I'd rather be than in your arms."

He squeezed her. "Sometimes I want to take you away so I can have you all to myself. Someplace where I wouldn't have to share you. You'd be all mine. All the time."

How beautiful that sounded. Beautiful and unrealistic. "You'd get tired of me."

"Never."

The forcefulness of that one word shook her. She knew he meant it. She realized he wasn't going to allow her to minimize his feelings for her. "Your love for me is hard for me to get a handle on."

"What do you mean by that?" he asked.

"I know you love me, but sometimes it's hard for me to understand and to believe that you have as much invested in this relationship as I do. I always think of the woman as having the greater emotional investment."

"I don't know who has the greater investment, but I'm as committed to this relationship as you are. I can be hurt as easily as you."

Christina waited before saying, "Rosalind told me not to hurt you. I thought it odd for her to say that. I thought she should have been more concerned with your hurting me. She also said that we should be good to each other."

"We're doing that."

Christina nodded. She picked up one of Jackson's hands that rested on her stomach. As she began counting his fingers, she asked, "Do you want children?"

"A couple."

"Boys or girls?"

"I prefer boys, but as long as they're healthy I won't complain."

"What do you have against girls?" she asked.

"I'd rather spend the next twenty years telling my boys to stay away from other people's girls than spend them telling other people's boys to stay away from my girls."

She pinched him. "I want children, too. One boy and one girl." Christina thought for a while. She turned to look at Jackson. "Can you picture me pregnant?"

Jackson turned her so she faced him and her body was fully flush his. "I can't picture how you'd look pregnant, but I can definitely picture you getting pregnant."

"I checked with Betty, and next weekend is good for us," Ellis said.

"Good. It's about time she and Christina met."

"Betty's eager to meet her. Once she accepted that you and Angela weren't getting married, she was pretty receptive to hearing good things about Christina."

Jackson laughed, then signaled the waiter for a fresh drink. "Has Mrs. Matchmaker found another mate for Angela yet?"

"No, and between you and me, I think Angela's told her to butt out for a while."

"Good for Angela."

"Is she coming to this get-together?" Ellis asked.

"Yes. She and Christina are working together on a fundraiser. They like each other."

"You and Christina must be pretty serious if you're giving parties together," Ellis said, popping a pretzel in his mouth.

"We're pretty serious. I asked her to marry me the other night."

Ellis slapped Jackson on the back. "I don't believe it! What did she say?"

"She didn't understand the question, or maybe she chose not to understand the question. I'm still not sure which it was."

"What do you mean, she didn't understand the question?"

Jackson shrugged as if it didn't matter, but it did. "I asked her if she wanted to get married, and she said yes. Somehow, it was never clear that she wanted to marry me."

"I don't understand. Did you ask her to marry you or did you ask if she wanted to get married?"

"I asked if she wanted to get married. Who would I be talking about, if not myself?"

Ellis shook his head. "You have a lot to learn, man. Christina probably didn't understand your question. Imagine yourself in her position. What if she had said she would marry you and you had said, 'Well I wasn't talking about marrying me, I was talking about marriage in general?' When she answered in general terms, you should have told her the question was about the two of you. Why didn't you do that?"

He didn't do that because he'd been unsure what her answer would be, especially after their conversation about rejection. "I got scared, man. I hadn't planned to ask her."

"Join the club. I felt that way with Betty. I wanted her, but I never would've married her if I thought I could keep her without marrying her."

"That's the difference with me and Christina. I've never wanted to get married, but I want to spend the rest of my life with her."

Ellis slapped him on the back again. "Well, you'd better practice proposing if you want to get married, because what you did last time was a bust."

"Calm down, Christina," Jackson said. "Everything's going to be perfect."

"Maybe we should have had it at your apartment, after all. We spend most of our time there anyway."

Jackson walked over to her and took both of her arms. "Why are you so nervous? It's only a party. They're people we already know."

She pulled away from him and leaned against the kitchen sink. "You don't understand, Jackson. This is more than a party."

He looked at her. "I'm not usually dense, but you'll have to explain that one to me."

"This is the first event we've held as a couple. We're inviting people to the home that we share together. It's not just a party." She wiped at her tears.

"There's no need to cry," Jackson said, and then he laughed softly.

"Don't laugh at me," she said between her tears.

"I'm not laughing at you, sweetheart," he said. "I love you too much for that. I'm laughing because you're so unpredictable. Sometimes I think you're two different women."

Christina sniffled and asked, "What do you mean by that?"

He pulled her to him. God, he loved this woman. The love had come quickly, but it was in no way shallow. She was a part of him now and he was determined to keep her. "Don't take it wrong. You're different at work than you are here at home. At work, you're all strong and in control. At home, you're just as strong, but nowhere near as in control." He wiped her tears and smiled. "I'm laughing because I'm so glad that I have you."

"You really think this is going to go okay?" she asked.

The doorbell rang then. "I do. Now I'm going to greet the first guest. Take care of your eyes, we don't want the guests to think that I beat you."

Jackson went to the door. He opened it to see Liza and Robert. "Glad you guys got here first." He looked at Liza. "Christina's in the kitchen. She could probably use a friend right now."

"Okay, I'm off for the kitchen," Liza said. "Don't you two get into any trouble."

Jackson led Robert to the living room. Before they could sit, the doorbell rang again. This time it was Jewel, Michael, Ellis, and Betty. "We drove together," Ellis explained.

"Come on in, Robert and Liza are already here," Jackson said.

Christina and Liza came out of the kitchen and Jackson made the introductions. When they had all been introduced, the women went back to the kitchen.

"Jackson told us that you were a frat. We'll look to see you at the meeting next week," Ellis said to Robert.

"I'll be there," Robert said. "Where's it going to be?"

"Paschal's on MLK," Ellis answered. "Where do you live?"

"We were fortunate. We found a place in Jackson's building downtown."

"You and Jackson can come together, then."

Jackson spoke up. "I planned to do that, though we're usually out here on weekends."

Mike clapped Jackson on the back. "Yeah, he and Christina live in their downtown quarters during the week and they come to their country place on the weekend."

The men all laughed.

"You joke, but it's working well," Jackson explained. "Christina likes not having the long commute everyday, and I love being out here on the weekends."

"So, when's the big day?" Robert asked. He was looking at Jackson.

"Big day for what?" Jackson asked.

"The wedding, of course. You're acting married, you're talking married, you're living married. When are you going to get married?"

Jackson glanced at Ellis. He wasn't ready to talk to the other guys about his feelings. "We haven't talked about dates yet. We're enjoying being together."

The three married men all shook their heads. "He's a dead man and he doesn't even know it," Mike said.

"He thinks they're just enjoying being together, and I'll bet you Christina's already picked out the wedding dress," Robert added.

Jackson hoped they were right. "You guys don't know Christina. If she was ready to get married, I'd know. There wouldn't be any games."

Again the three married men all shook their heads. "Has she started naming the kids yet?" Mike asked.

Jackson shook his head. "No, we've only talked about how many we'd like to have."

"That's it, man, when you start talking about babies, it's all over but the ceremony," Robert explained. They all laughed. "We're kidding you, man. I, for one, wouldn't trade marriage for anything. You and Christina have a good thing going. We wish you all the best."

"Thanks, man," Jackson said. He knew he and Christina had something special. And more and more each day he wanted to make it permanent.

"I didn't think I'd like you, Christina, since you busted up what was probably my best matchmaking effort, but I like you a lot," Betty said.

Christina didn't know to respond to that, but found she didn't have to.

"You'll get used to Betty, Christina," Jewel explained. "She has a tendency to say what she thinks without thinking about what she says."

"She's right," Betty agreed. "I didn't mean anything bad. Angela told me that I'd like you, but I wasn't too sure."

"Well, I'm glad we all get along, since our men are such good friends," Christina said. "Have you heard from Angela today? I expected her to be here by now."

"She didn't call you?" Betty asked.

Christina shook her head.

"She must have gotten tied up," Betty explained. "She's meeting with the producers for her talk show tonight. It came up suddenly and she couldn't get out of it."

"That's great—the show, I mean," Christina said. "I hope this means it's really going to happen."

"I think that's what it means," Betty said.

"I'm happy for her," Jewel added, "but I wanted to meet her new guy."

"Yes," Betty said. "So did I. This is the first guy Angela's dated who works at her station."

"This guy works with Angela?" Christina asked. "I didn't know that."

"She probably decided to give it a shot since it's working so well for you and Jackson," Betty said. "What's it like working with him and living with him?"

"It's good. You know, we've only been doing it for four months, but it seems like we've been doing it forever. He understands my day, I understand his. We support each other. I had my apprehensions, but now I recommend it highly."

"Ellis says you're his boss," Betty continued. "What's that like?"

"We don't think of it that way," Christina responded. Betty did ask a lot of questions, she thought. "Because of the nature of our work, we don't really have to deal with the boss-employee roles." Christina knew she wasn't being completely honest, but it wasn't Betty's business.

"That's right," Liza interjected. "I work for Christina, too, but we're also friends. It can work if you want it to." Christina gave Liza a thank-you smile, then Liza added, "I'm a newlywed and I'm missing my man real bad right now. Can we go and see what they're up to?"

They all laughed. "Newlyweds," Betty repeated. "I'm surprised you two were willing to get out of bed to come here."

Liza winked at Christina. "It was tough, but we couldn't let Christina down."

"You were a hit tonight," Jackson said to Christina. She was in the bathroom, so he couldn't see her.

"It did go well, didn't it?" He heard the water come on.

"More than well," he replied. "What's taking you so long in there?"

She walked out of the bathroom then, turning off the light as she did.

"What are you so impatient about?" she asked. She sat on the side of the bed and began to lotion her legs.

"Let me do that," Jackson said. "Lie back."

Christina lay back on the bed and Jackson began applying the lotion to her legs. "You didn't warn me about Betty," she said.

"I didn't know I needed to. What did she do?"

"It's not so much what she did as what she said."

"I know she's a talker, but I thought she was basically harmless."

"She is. There's not a malicious bone in her body. She's just a bit more outspoken than I expected."

"Turn over," Jackson said. He began applying the lotion to her hips and the backs of her legs. "What did she say?"

"She said she liked me even though I did bust up her perfect couple, you and Angela."

Jackson laughed. "Betty said that? And what did you say?"

"I was at a loss for words. What could I say? I told her I was glad we got along since our men were such good friends."

"Did you like her?"

"I don't know if I'd use the word 'like.' She's a nice person. I don't know if I could be around her for an extended time, though."

"Well, I'll make sure you don't have to. We'll only see them at fraternity events and get-togethers like tonight's. How did she and Jewel get along with Liza?"

"They got along well. Liza enjoyed keeping Betty in line. And you know Jewel, she gets along with everybody."

Jackson slapped Christina softly on the buttocks. "Finished." She turned over. He smiled at her and added, "Too bad Angela couldn't make it. She would have helped Liza keep Betty in line."

"I wish she could have come, too. Jewel and Betty said Angela was dating a new guy, somebody she worked with. Did you know that?"

Jackson shook his head. "I hadn't heard. It doesn't sound like Angela, though. She had strong convictions about dating co-workers. If it's true, this guy must be something special."

Christina reached up and touched his face. "Betty said she was following our example."

Jackson covered her hand with his own. "We set a pretty good one, don't you think?"

She raised up and kissed him on the lips. "I sure do." When she moved to lie back down, Jackson followed her. He was about to kiss her again when she asked, "How did Robert get along with the guys?"

"I think they got along well. He's a frat, and that makes it easier." He kissed her above each eye. "They had something else in common, too."

Christina closed her eyes and let herself enjoy him. "And what was that?"

He continued with kisses all over her face. "They're all very much in love with their wives. It's obvious."

Christina tilted her head to give him better access. "Same with the women. Three solid marriages right before our eyes."

"They seem to think that we should be next," Jackson said casually. His kisses continued.

"What did they say?" she asked.

"They said we're obviously in love and we're acting married, so we may as well get married."

She opened her eyes then. "What do you think?"

Jackson stopped kissing her and looked into her eyes. "I think they're right."

She didn't say anything. All she could think was that it was too soon. They had known each other six months and they'd only been together for four months. Marriage now would be a disaster. It just wasn't done. They needed more time to get to know each other.

Jackson asked, "What do you think?"

"I love you, Jackson, but it's too soon to think about getting married." At his pained look, she added, "You haven't even met my mother. I haven't met your father."

"I don't want to marry your mother. I want to marry you."

Christina couldn't think of anything to say. She had dreamed of hearing those words from this man. But it was too soon, wasn't it? Didn't they need more time to be sure? What if he decided later that he'd made a mistake? It was better to be sure than to make a mistake and end up in divorce court. That she couldn't handle. "I couldn't marry you before you've met my mom or I've met your dad. It wouldn't be right."

Jackson sat up. His back was to her. He admitted his surprise, his disappointment, at Christina's hesitation. Was she looking for an excuse not to marry him? Maybe she didn't want to marry him. "I don't understand. We're living like we're married already. What would change?"

"I don't know," she said softly. "I do love you and I'm committed to you. I want to marry you and have your babies. I want to grow old with you, but I need time to get used to this." When he didn't respond, Christina added, "I don't want to lose you. Tell me I'm not going to lose you because of this."

Jackson turned to face her. He saw the fear in her eyes and knew that a part of her expected that she would lose him. That was the past. He was the present. He couldn't erase the past. All he could do was hope that she would believe in his love for her. "You're not going to lose me, Christina."

Christina sat in her office preparing for the Friday status meeting with Liza and Jackson. Today they had to select the first application site for OPTIMA. Christina studied the papers. She hoped they could agree.

"Let's start with site selection," Christina said, when Liza and Jackson were seated in her office. "Who wants to go first?"

"I will," Jackson said. He spread out four charts that he had pulled together. "We should start with E-Manufacturing. They're aggressive and they're prepared to do a full conversion within six months."

"That's what concerns me about E-Manufacturing," Liza said. "They're too aggressive for a new product like OPTIMA. We need to start on a smaller scale. Maybe Kenner Limited. They have one line that they want to bring up, then see what happens. We could use that time to work out the kinks."

"The kinks ought to be worked out before we deliver to the field," Jackson explained. "Kenner Limited won't be a showcase site for this product. E-Manufacturing will give us the cover page of every major manufacturing journal in the country."

"You're right, Jackson," Liza said, "but it's too risky. We shouldn't go that big until we're sure."

Jackson knew it was no use talking to Liza. She was much too conservative. He turned to Christina. "What do you think?"

"There's merit to Liza's concerns. We need the extra time that Kenner would give us. We go with Kenner."

"Surprise" didn't adequately capture Jackson's response. Had Christina gone conservative on him, too? He definitely did not like the way the scales had been tilting around here lately.

Jackson walked out on the balcony of his apartment to talk with Christina. "That's the second time this week that you've sided with Liza against me."

Christina turned from the railing to look at him. "What did you say?"

"At the status meeting today...you sided with Liza. It's the second time that you've done it."

"I didn't side with Liza. I made the best decision for CL. Nothing more, nothing less."

"So you think Liza's judgment is better than mine?" He vowed not to get angry, but he felt his temper rising.

"Not really. I think she's more cautious than you some of the time."

In his opinion, Liza was cautious to a fault. "You think I don't use caution."

"You're deliberately misunderstanding me, Jackson. That's not what I'm saying at all. You're good at your job. Liza's good at her job. Most of the time we're able to come to a consensus. When we can't, it's my job to decide. Sometimes it'll be in your favor, sometimes it'll be in Liza's favor. I'm not being disloyal to you, if that's what you're implying. This is business, plain and simple."

"Whatever you say, Christina," Jackson said smugly. "You're the boss." He turned and walked back into the apartment.

Chapter 17

"It's not the end of the world, Christina," Liza said. "All relationships have problems. You've got to find out what your problem is and fix it."

Christina looked across the conference table at her friend. "Easier said that done."

"How's the sex?"

"It's been better. We go through the motions, but I can tell something's wrong and I know he can, too."

"Have you talked about it?"

"We've talked around it. I think it's a lot of different things."

Liza nodded. "I thought something was up."

"You did?" Christina didn't know why she was surprised. From the beginning, outsiders knew what was going on with her and Jackson before they did.

"I've noticed lately that you two aren't as relaxed with each other as you were before. The staff has noticed, too. I overheard Penny and Doris talking about it."

"Penny and Doris? What were they saying? Do they know we're living together?"

"There's speculation, but no one really knows. They know there's tension between you that wasn't there before."

Christina stood up and walked to the windows. Looking out, she said, "I knew this would happen."

"Knew what would happen?"

"I knew we couldn't keep this relationship out of the office. That's part of the problem."

"What are you talking about, Christina?"

She turned around and looked at Liza. "I think Jackson resents my being his boss."

"That's a pretty serious charge. You need to talk to him about this."

"I know. That's why I can't bring it up."

"Keeping it bottled up inside isn't going to work. You've got to talk to him about it."

Christina began to pace. "Our relationship was going so well. It was almost too good to be true. Maybe it was."

"Don't blow this out of proportion now. Remember that you love this man and he loves you. Whatever's wrong can be fixed."

Christina stopped pacing and looked back at her friend, wanting very much to believe her words. "I wish I were as sure as you, Liza. I wish I were as sure as you."

"What do you want to do this weekend?" Jackson asked. He and Christina were in his apartment.

"I don't care. What do you want to do?" She wondered if she had imagined the friction between them.

"I was thinking about taking in a ball game with Ellis, Mike, and Robert this weekend. Mike has tickets for Saturday and Sunday."

Then again, maybe she wasn't imagining it. "Don't worry about me. I understand you want to spend some time with your friends."

"Are you sure you don't want to do something else?" he asked.

"I'm sure. You go and have fun. Maybe Liza and I'll do something."

He walked into the kitchen. "And since the games are downtown, I thought I'd spend the weekend in town."

"Oh," was all she said. Our first weekend apart, she thought. We've only been together five months and he wants a weekend alone. This is the beginning of the end.

"Don't say it like that."

"Like what?"

He walked back into the living room. "Like I've said I don't love you anymore."

She didn't say anything. *Is that what you're saying, Jackson?*

"What are you thinking?" he finally asked.

I'm thinking that maybe you don't love me anymore. "This will be the first weekend we've been apart since we've been together."

"I'm only going downtown, not across the country," he said. The irritation in his voice made her angry.

She got up. "That's not the point."

"Since you know so much, you tell me. What is the point?"

"You know as well as I do that things between us have been strained for the past couple of weeks. I wonder if this is your way of dealing with it."

Jackson took a deep breath. "I'm beginning to feel crowded. We could use some space, Christina."

First he wants to get married and now he's crowded. Bull... "Crowded?"

"Maybe 'crowded' isn't the right word. We're together all the time. We need some space."

Doesn't sound like a man serious about marriage. She was right not to consider his proposal. "We? So now you're speaking for me?"

"All right. I need some space." He turned her to face him. "I love you, Christina, but I need some space and some time to figure out where this relationship is going."

"A few weeks ago you were ready to get married. What's going on here, Jackson?" Christina feared asking the next question, but she had to. "Have you stopped loving me?"

"I love you, Christina, but I wonder if that's enough. Maybe you've been right all along. Maybe this is moving too fast."

Christina felt each of his words like a dagger in her heart. Jackson wasn't supposed to leave her. They were supposed to be together forever. "You've felt this way and you've never mentioned it to me?"

"I didn't know where to start. I couldn't talk about it."

"Can you talk about it now?"

"No more than what I've said. It's not you, it's me. I'm not feeling good about myself lately. I've got to work through it."

"You have to work through it alone? Without me?" Tears were in her eyes, but she was determined not to let them fall.

Jackson nodded.

"If that's the way it has to be, there's nothing I can do." Christina began putting her papers in her briefcase.

"What are you doing?" Jackson asked.

"What does it look like I'm doing? I'm going home."

"You don't have to leave."

"What good will my staying do? Maybe you're right. Maybe we both need some space. My staying here tonight wouldn't be right."

She wanted him to take it all back. She wanted him to say that it was all a joke. He didn't. He looked at her with a sad expression on his face.

She gathered her belongings and went to the door. She opened it and walked out without saying anything more.

When she closed the door behind her, her knees buckled. She held on to the wall for support. It was over! She and Jackson were finished. The tears she held back fell freely now.

When she got into her car, she rested her head on the steering wheel and cried. She cried for herself, for what she had, and for what she had lost. After about fifteen minutes, she started the car and began the drive home. As she drove, she played and replayed the past couple of weeks in her mind. What if she had done this differently? What if she had done that differently? What if? What if?

Her tears were all gone when she reached her house. All she had now was a heart that felt as if it weighed two tons. She walked into the house. She missed him already. She saw him in every room. She dreaded going into the bedroom, but she finally decided to get it over with. She walked in and flipped on the light. Jackson's jacket was lying at the foot of the bed. She smiled. He could never decide which jacket to wear. If they'd spent weekdays here, her bed would probably be full of jackets. She picked up the jacket and held it close. It smelled of him. Chastising herself, she took the jacket and hung it up in the closet, their closet. His clothes were now mingled in with hers. It was amazing how quickly and completely their two lives had become intertwined.

She lay down on the bed. It, too, smelled of him. She remembered the nights they'd slept together in this bed. She remembered the night she had worn the purple teddy for him. God, it had been so good then. She lay there thinking of him until the tears came again. She was asleep before they stopped.

Jackson lay alone in his bed and missed her. Though their relationship hadn't been too good the last few weeks, he preferred being with her to being without her. He replayed tonight's conversation. He could think of any other way he could have handled it.

He loved her. There was no doubt about it. He just couldn't handle the new emotions he was feeling. He didn't like the way he felt when Christina chose Liza's judgment over his. It felt like a slap in the face. They had disagreed before Liza had come on board. But it was one thing for your woman to disagree with you when it was just the two of you. It was a whole other thing for her to do it in front of a friend. Liza probably went home and told Robert about it, too.

Jackson turned over onto his stomach. He missed her softness pressed against him. He knew he had no one to blame but himself, but he couldn't talk to her about it. How could he tell her that it made him feel less a man when she overruled him on a matter? How could he tell her that he needed her to respect his opinion?

He had told her that he could handle her being the boss. He had even joked about it. It was no joking matter. How did a man resolve his need to protect and care for his woman with the reality that his woman didn't need or want his protection? He rolled over onto his back.

He had changed a lot since he'd met Christina. He thought he wanted an independent woman. Maybe he did, but he also wanted a woman who looked up to him, a woman who knew she could look to him for help. Christina didn't need him. She might not know it now, but she would come to that conclusion sooner or later, and then she would leave. Just as his mother had left, she would leave.

When Christina awoke she didn't know where she was. Then she remembered. She was home. Alone. She lay there looking at the ceiling for a while. She knew thoughts of Jackson would come. She couldn't stop them and she wouldn't try. She turned, opened the top drawer of her nightstand, and pulled out her small black notebook. She rubbed her hands up and down the cover, then opened it and turned to the page labeled, "Personal Goals." She read numbers 4, 5, and 6: fall in love, get married, and have three children. She had certainly fallen in love. She closed the notebook and put it back in the drawer.

She closed her eyes and let the tears come. She opened them when the phone rang. She considered not answering, but she did.

"Hello," she said.

"I called to see how you're doing." It was Jackson.

Maybe he's calling to say it's all a big mistake. "I'm doing fine. How about you?"

I've been better, he thought. "I'm fine. Are you sure you're okay?"

Strangers. They were talking like strangers. She was pissed at herself for getting her hopes up. "I'm a big girl, Jackson. You don't have to worry about me."

"That what I thought," he said sadly, and then hung up.

Christina held the phone in her hand. The nerve of that man. Was that sadness she heard in his voice? What did he have to be sad about? I'm the one who's been wronged here. Men.

Christina didn't feel like going to work today. She dreaded the staff meeting with Jackson and Liza, but she'd be damned if she'd let him think she was home crying over him. She got up and dressed for work.

She arrived in her office later than usual. Penny was not at her desk. When she walked into the office, she saw a bouquet of red roses on her desk. Her heartbeat sped up. Maybe he wants to make up. She rushed to the desk to read the card. She held it to her heart and wished. Then, she opened it and dropped down in her chair. "Not again," she said aloud. "Not again."

Christina couldn't bear to see Jackson today. She told Penny to tell him and Liza that the status meeting was canceled and left the office.

When she arrived at her house, she went straight to the kitchen. She needed something cold to drink. She placed her briefcase on the counter, took a glass from the cabinet, and went to the refrigerator. She stood with her back to the counter as she drank. From her position, she could see her front porch. And something on the porch caught her eye. She went to the front door. "Oh, my God," she said.

She was still seated at the kitchen counter when Jackson let himself into the house a few hours later. "I was worried when you canceled the meeting this afternoon," he said. "I called. When nobody answered I came to check on you. Is everything all right?"

She looked at him and wondered who this man was. "Thanks for the roses," she said dryly. "There was no need to send two bouquets."

"What are you talking about?" Jackson asked.

She pointed toward the dining room. "See for yourself."

Jackson saw the roses through the open dining room door. "When did you get these?"

"They were here to greet me when I got in from work."

"Where's the card?"

It was on the counter. She pushed it in his direction. He read it, then asked, "Have you called the police?"

She shook her head. "I got more roses today at work. I called security."

"What did they say?"

"They came to a dead end in the last investigation, but they did come up with one bit of information that you might find interesting."

"And what's that?" he asked.

"The last bouquet came from Wall's Flower Shop in the Midtown Terrace apartment building." That bit of news had sent her home early. Security should have given her this news as soon as they found out.

"My building? The roses came from my building?"

"You sound as surprised as I was to get that piece of information."

Jackson looked at her then. The look in her eyes was one he had never seen before. "Christina, you can't think…" he began.

"I don't know what to think. Maybe you can help me." Christina knew her voice was calm. She was falling apart inside, but her voice was calm.

"You can't think I sent them," he said.

There was something in his tone that made her want to go to him and wrap him in her arms. She didn't give in to the feeling. "Who do you think sent them?"

"I don't know. What would I gain by sending them?"

"I've been asking myself that same question."

"And what answer do you come up with?"

"I don't have an answer. I just have a lot of pieces that make a real ugly picture."

"What pieces? What are you talking about?"

"When I thought about it, I began to see a pattern. The roses started after our fiasco in Boston the first time. I stopped getting them after our weekend together at Liza's wedding. They started coming again after our first real fight. What do you conclude from that, Jackson?"

"There's no need for me to say anything. You've figured it all out yourself."

"You don't have anything to say?" she asked. She wanted him to deny it, to explain it.

"You're a smart woman. You've figured it all out. What more could I possibly add?"

She didn't answer.

"I didn't think so," he said, and turned to leave. He stopped when she spoke, but he didn't turn to face her.

"Leave my key on the table on your way out," she said.

He turned then to look at her. She saw the plea in his eyes, but she chose to ignore it. He turned, put the key on the table, and left the house.

Christina remained seated at the counter after he had gone. She waited for the tears to come, but they didn't. She waited for the overwhelming sense of hurt and pain to come, but it didn't. She finally realized that she was numb. She felt nothing. She didn't know if she would ever feel anything again.

Jackson made it to his car. He drove out of the driveway and down the street. He made it about one mile before he had to pull over in a Denny's parking lot.

He shook with anger. How could she think that I would do something like that? he asked himself. What kind of man does she think I am?

Jackson leaned his head back against the headrest. Memories of times he and Christina had shared passed in his thoughts. He saw her face the first time she'd had an orgasm. He heard her voice when he'd told her he loved her the first time. He remembered her anxiety the day of their first party. He felt the same emotions he had felt when the events had occurred. He patted his face because it felt funny. When he looked at his hands, they were wet.

Christina needed to talk to someone. She considered calling Liza, but Liza was too close to Jackson. She picked up the phone and dialed. "It's me," she said. "Are you going to be home this weekend?"

"Yes," her mother said.

"I should be there in four hours," Christina said.

"Is something wrong? Did you and Jackson have a fight?"

"I don't want to talk about it now, Mom," Christina said. "I'll tell you everything when I get there."

It was dark when Jackson opened his eyes. He looked at his watch. He'd been sitting there for more than three hours. He felt his face. It was dry. He looked in the rearview mirror and couldn't believe what he saw. Though his heart was crushed, he looked the same. Shaking his head, he started the car.

He considered stopping by Ellis's house, but decided against it. He and Betty were too close to him and Christina, and Robert was out of the question. Then Jackson had an idea. Instead of taking the Interstate downtown to his apartment, he made a detour.

Chapter 18

Jackson arrived at the Oklahoma City Airport at 2 A.M. He rented a car and took a room at a nearby hotel. He admitted that he may have been a bit rash in taking the flight out, but now that he was here, he was going to make the best of it. He had no clean clothes and no sleepwear. "What the hell." He pulled off his clothes and went to bed nude.

The light streaming through the hotel room window greeted him when he awoke. He sat up in bed and wondered again that he had decided to fly out to Oklahoma without any clothes and without telling anyone that he was coming. He looked at the clock. It wasn't too early, he decided. He walked over to where his pants hung on the chair and pulled his wallet out of the pocket. He sat back on the bed, shuffled through the wallet, and found the number. Jackson weighed the decision. What were the chances he'd be there? It didn't matter. He needed to talk and the Stevens were the closest thing to a real family that he had. He picked up the phone and dialed.

"Stevens' residence," a young male voice answered.

"Hello, this is Jackson Duncan. Is Mr. or Mrs. Stevens around?"

He heard the phone drop and the young voice yell, "Grandma, telephone."

"Hello," a familiar voice said.

Hearing her voice made him feel better. "Hello, Mrs. Stevens. This is Jackson."

"Jackson?" she asked.

"You've forgotten me that quickly? I'm crushed. It's Jackie Duncan."

"Jackie? Is that you, Jackie? How are you doing boy? Where are you calling from?"

She was the only person who called him Jackie. Hearing the enthusiasm in her voice, Jackson was transported back to his college days. "I see you still ask a lot of questions," he said. "I'm doing fine and I'm here in Oklahoma City."

"You're here in Oklahoma City," she repeated. "What are you doing here? Where are you staying? You're welcome to stay with us, you know."

Jackson was relieved she hadn't changed. Her home was still open to him. "I'm at a hotel now, but I'd like to come visit."

"What are you doing in a hotel? You should have stayed with us."

"My flight got in late last night. I didn't want to disturb you."

"You wouldn't have been a bother. George stays up all hours of the night, anyway."

"How is Mr. Stevens, by the way?"

"George is fine. He retired last year. He's been around here worrying me to death, but he's doing fine."

"I can't wait to see you both again. Do you still live in the same place?"

She laughed a rich, full laugh. "You know better than to ask that. Where would we go? All our kids grew up here, and now the grandkids. This is home for the rest of our days. Now, when are you going to get over here?"

"I should be there in the next couple of hours. I have a few errands to run first."

"Take your time. We're not going anywhere."

The shopping took longer than he'd expected, and he arrived at the Stevenses' an hour later than planned.

"We were beginning to wonder if you'd gotten lost," Mr. Stevens said, after he and Mrs. Stevens had given Jackson big hugs.

"I had no problem at all getting here. It was like being on automatic pilot. I got in the car and it brought me here."

"It sure is good to see you again, son," Mr. Stevens said. "Reggie told us that he saw you when he was in Atlanta. How long have you been there?"

"Almost eight months," Jackson answered. *But it felt like a lifetime.* "My job transferred me there."

"How do you like it?" Mrs. Stevens asked. "I've never been to Atlanta. Always wanted to go, but I never got around to it."

A month ago he would have given an enthusiastic, "I love it," but now… "It's a good city. It grows on you."

"Reggie liked it, too. He was dropping hints about moving there for a while," Mr. Stevens said.

Jackson knew the reason for that. "Is Reggie around this weekend?" he asked cautiously.

Mrs. Stevens shook her head. "He's out of town today, but he'll be back tomorrow. I hope you get to see him."

"Me, too," Jackson lied. Reggie was the last person he wanted to see. "How's William? Reggie told me married life was treating him well."

"He and the wife and kids are fine," Mrs. Stevens said. "They're out of town this weekend, though, and won't be back until Wednesday."

"I hate that I won't get to see them."

"Their oldest answered the phone when you called. He left about a half-hour ago to spend the weekend with one of his friends," Mrs. Stevens said.

"You missed out all the way 'round," Mr. Stevens added.

Jackson looked from Mr. Stevens to Mrs. Stevens. He was glad they were still the same happy family. "I didn't miss out at all. I have the two of you to myself this weekend."

Mr. and Mrs. Stevens laughed, and then Mrs. Stevens stood up. "Do you still have a good appetite, Jackie?"

Jackson smiled and patted his stomach.

"Good. Let me go see what I can rustle up for you."

* * *

Jackson stood in the garage of the Stevenses' home with Mr. Stevens. He watched from a seat on the workbench as Mr. Stevens tinkered with his lawn mower.

"What really brings you out here, Jackson?" Mr. Stevens asked casually.

Jackson stood up at that question and walked the length of the garage. He didn't know how to get started. "You don't buy that I'm just in the area?"

Mr. Stevens looked up and Jackson saw the concern in his eyes. "I have three boys of my own. I know when a man needs to talk."

Jackson sat back down and clasped his hands in front of him. "I don't even know where to start, Mr. Stevens."

Mr. Stevens stopped working on the lawnmower and sat next to Jackson. "It helps to start at the beginning."

When Jackson didn't say anything, Mr. Stevens added, "You can start with her name."

Jackson looked up at him. "How did you know it was a woman?"

Mr. Stevens's eyes gleamed. "I might be old, Jackson, but I'm not dead."

Jackson gave a half smile at that, then looked back at his hands. "Christina." From Mr. Stevens's response, or lack thereof, Jackson assumed that Reggie hadn't mentioned Christina before.

Giving him more help, Mr. Stevens asked, "Do you love her?"

"Very much." There was no doubt in Jackson's mind about his feelings for her.

"Does she love you?"

Jackson raised his head and looked straight ahead. He shrugged. "I really don't know. She did. Now, I'm not so sure."

"Did something happen?"

Jackson stood up again. "A lot happened."

"Just start at the beginning," Mr. Stevens coaxed.

"She's my boss," Jackson explained. "I work for her. We both knew it was risky to start something, but we were attracted to

each other. We fought it as long as we could." Jackson thought
about his early advances and Christina's rejections. He wondered
now if it would have been better for both of them if he'd left her
alone. He had thought that he couldn't live without her. Now he
wondered if he could live after losing her.

"That's understandable, Jackson. Emotions don't know positions."

Jackson was so lost in his thoughts, he'd almost forgotten Mr.
Stevens. "She's the first woman I've ever loved. I thought we
could get past any problems our professional relationship might
cause. We did, at first." I couldn't handle it though, he added
silently.

"What happened to change that?"

Jackson knew that question was coming. "Me. I changed. I
thought I could handle her being the boss. At first I could, I really could. If we disagreed and she overruled me, it wasn't a problem. We were colleagues working together. I could handle it."

"What happened?"

"Liza happened," Jackson said. He couldn't handle Christina
choosing Liza's opinion over his.

"Who's Liza?"

Jackson looked back at Mr. Stevens. The concern and love in
his eyes were comforting. "Liza works with us. She and I report
directly to Christina. Initially, Christina and I decided everything
together. Now, there are three of us who have to work together."
Jackson began to pace. "I thought I could handle it. I had no idea
I would feel this way."

"Hold on there, Jackson. I think you're leaving something out.
What couldn't you handle?"

Jackson stopped pacing. "I couldn't handle Christina choosing Liza's opinion over mine." Jackson shook his head. "If anyone had told me this would happen to me, I would have laughed.
I thought I was a bigger man than this."

"Doesn't have anything to do with how big a man you are,"
Mr. Stevens said. "It's about feelings. Did you talk to Christina
about it?"

Jackson shook his head again. "I couldn't. I knew that what I was feeling was irrational. How could I explain it to her?" Jackson didn't wait for a response. He knew the answer; he couldn't explain it to her. "Christina is a smart woman. She has her life together. She really doesn't need me. I knew that from the beginning, but I also knew she loved me and respected me. That was enough for us. When her decisions started falling with Liza's opinions instead of mine, I began to wonder if she still respected me. And if she didn't respect me, I began to wonder if she would soon stop loving me. The more she agreed with Liza, the greater my insecurities became."

"Is that why you don't think she loves you now?" Mr. Stevens asked.

"That's part of it, probably the smaller part," Jackson answered. "I mentioned my feelings to her once and she said, as I knew she would, that it wasn't personal. She was making what she thought were the best decisions for the company."

"And that made you feel worse," Mr. Stevens finished for him.

"That's right," Jackson said, glad somebody understood what he'd been feeling. "Finally, I told her I needed space. Our relationship was strained, but we were going on as if nothing was wrong. I had to do something."

"You decided to leave her before she could leave you," Mr. Stevens concluded wisely.

Jackson jerked his gaze to Mr. Stevens. "That wasn't my intention. At least, not my conscious intention. But that's exactly what Christina thought. I tried to tell her that I still loved her, but she didn't buy it."

"Can you blame her?"

Jackson lowered his eyelids. "What do you mean by that?"

"Think about it. She knows something's wrong. You won't talk about it and then you want to leave. What did you expect her to think? It probably didn't look like a man in love to her."

He looked up again. "I do love her. I even asked her to marry me."

Mr. Stevens held up both hands. "Hold on a minute here. You asked her to marry you?"

Jackson nodded.

"What did she say?"

Jackson gave a hollow laugh. "She said it was too soon. She said she loved me and wanted to marry me, but she needed more time."

"How did you feel about that?"

"I was disappointed, of course. And hurt." And he still hurt. "But I understood her reasons."

"Are you sure you understood her, or did you just let it go?"

Jackson didn't answer immediately. He had tried to understand Christina's reasons. He wanted to understand them. He told himself that he did. A part of him knew her childhood scars were the cause of her fears and cautiousness. Yet another part of him wanted her love for him to be stronger than all that. "Maybe I just left it alone."

"Why do you think you did that?"

Jackson knew why. "Because I was hurt. And I was afraid. What if she really didn't love me? That's why I'm here, Mr. Stevens. I have to figure out how to handle my feelings, my fears."

"That's where you're wrong, Jackson," Mr. Stevens said. "Your feelings aren't your problem, your refusal to share those feelings with Christina is the problem. I've been married for forty-two years, and I'll tell you this, talking about it might cause a problem, but not talking about it causes even greater problems."

Jackson didn't respond immediately. "It did lead to bigger problems."

"Always does, my boy, always does."

Jackson thought Mr. Stevens was getting carried away. "Now she thinks I've been sending her red roses with offending cards."

"Why would she think that?"

Jackson told Mr. Stevens the story of the roses and how Christina thought that he sent them.

"Whew, you do have yourself in a pickle," Mr. Steven said.

"That's what happens when you don't talk about things. One person starts wondering what the other is thinking and drawing conclusions from everything. Things that aren't even related."

Jackson nodded. "You're right about that. How could she even think I sent those roses? I'm in love with her."

"That's what you say, Jackson, but that's not what you've been showing her lately. All she's seen lately is your discontentment, your silence, and then your decision to leave. I'm not saying that she's making rational decisions, but she's using what you give her."

"I wish I knew who was sending those damn roses," Jackson said. He started to pace again.

"I wish you did, too," Mr. Stevens said.

Christina was exhausted when she reached her mother's house. She pulled into the driveway and sat there a few minutes trying to get herself together. She couldn't understand how or why Jackson had betrayed her as he had. When the front porch lights flicked on, Christina gathered her belongings and headed for the house.

"How long had you been sitting out there?" her mother asked, after Christina had put her bags down and sat on the bed in the guest bedroom.

"Only a few minutes, Mom," Christina answered. "I'm so tired."

"It's late. Do you want to go to bed now, or do you want to talk?"

Christina thought about that. "The truth, Mom? Right now, I could use a hug."

Louise sat next to her daughter and opened her arms. Christina leaned into them and her tears began again. She let them flow freely as she rested in the protectiveness of her mother's embrace.

When the tears finally stopped, Christina remained in her mother's arms. "It's over, Mom," she said slowly. "Jackson and I are finished."

Louise brushed her daughter's hair with her hands. "What makes you say that?"

"He said that he needed space."

"That doesn't mean it's over. It means he needs space."

Christina tightened her embrace on her mother. "That's not all, Mom. Do you remember the roses I was getting a while back?"

"Yes, I remember. I thought those had stopped."

"So did I." Christina paused to get her breath. She was choking up again. "Well, I got two dozen today. One at work with a card that said *'Bitch,'* and another at home with a card that read *'Whore.'*"

Louise's hold on Christina tightened. "Oh, no, darling. Have you reported this to the police?"

"I don't need to report it to the police. I know who sent them."

"Christina, you can't possibly think…"

"Jackson sent them, Mom," Christina interrupted. "That's the only explanation."

"Could you be jumping to conclusions? What makes you think it was him?"

She explained the incidents to her mother as she had explained them to Jackson.

"Those could be coincidences," Louise said. "There's no real evidence implicating Jackson."

"Looks like evidence to me," Christina corrected. "Anyway, he didn't deny it."

"You accused him of sending the roses?" Louise asked. Her tone expressed her surprise.

At that tone, Christina became wary. Maybe she had gone too far with Jackson. "I didn't exactly accuse him. I merely laid the information out to him and asked him to explain it."

"And what did he say?"

She'd never forget the scene or the look in his eyes. "He didn't say much. He actually had the nerve to look affronted, like I was in the wrong. That man is a good actor."

"Either that, or he's innocent."

Christina pulled back to look at her mother. "You can't seriously believe that he's innocent, Mother. Have you heard a word I've said?"

"I heard you, Christina. I heard you loud and clear."

"Then how can you say he could be innocent?"

"I'm not saying whether he's innocent or not. That's your call to make, but do you think you've given him enough room to explain himself?"

"Why should I do that? So he can tell me more lies? What do I owe him?"

"You don't owe him anything. This isn't about Jackson. This is about you and what you owe yourself. A few days ago you were in love with this man. You were thinking marriage. Now you're ready to believe him guilty of the vilest of acts without even really discussing it with him. You owe yourself more than that."

Christina was beginning to get uncomfortable with this conversation. Why was her mother saying that she had been hasty? "I did discuss it with him, Mother. I told you, he didn't deny it."

"It's your decision, Christina."

Christina was silent for a while. She pulled away to sit next to her mother. "I hate it when you do that."

"Do what?" Louise asked.

"Back down like that. You know you're not really backing down and I know you're not really backing down. Why don't you just say what you mean?"

"I have said what I meant. You don't like it and now you want me to change it. I can't. You haven't said anything here tonight that makes me believe Jackson sent you those roses."

Christina stood up then. "So you think I'm overreacting?"

"No, not overreacting. Maybe reacting to the wrong thing."

"And what do you mean by that?"

"I wonder how you'd be feeling now if Jackson hadn't said he needed space."

Christina didn't say anything immediately. "That wouldn't have changed the facts."

"No," Louise agreed, "it wouldn't have, but it might have changed your interpretation of those facts."

When Christina didn't respond, Louise said, "We've had enough talk for tonight. You need to get some rest. A good night's sleep will do you good. We can talk about this tomorrow, if you like." Louise kissed her daughter on the forehead and left the room.

Christina watched as Louise walked away. She didn't understand her mother's reaction. Why was she taking sides with Jackson? Well, it doesn't matter, Christina thought. I'm not going to give Jackson another chance to hurt me. He did send the roses. I'm sure of it.

Christina was up early the next morning. She hadn't slept well. Her mother's questions had caused her considerable unrest. Had she been too hasty in her decision? Did Jackson deserve a chance to explain? No, she thought, she had given him a chance. Jackson wanted space; well, he'd gotten space.

"Up early, aren't you, Christina," Louise asked, still dressed in her gown and housecoat.

"I didn't sleep very well," Christina said.

"Thinking a lot, huh? Did you come to any conclusions?"

Christina shook her head. "No conclusions, really. Even if Jackson didn't send the roses, it's still over. He doesn't want to be with me anymore. He said so."

"That's not what he said," Louise corrected.

"He needs space. I think that's a euphemism for 'I need to get out of this relationship.'"

"I think you're reading more into it than necessary. Why didn't you ask him what he meant?"

Christina got up and poured herself another cup of tea. "We had practically stopped talking, Mother. He wasn't sharing his thoughts."

"When did this start?"

Christina shrugged. Maybe it was there from the beginning. Maybe it was never as good between her and Jackson as she'd wanted to believe. "I don't know exactly when it started. It's been the last month or so. It all happened so suddenly. Our relationship was going great, then it hit bottom. I don't understand it."

"That sounds strange. You have no idea what happened?"

Christina shook her head. "He went from asking me to marry him to accusing me of siding with Liza at work. That was ridiculous. I told him I wasn't siding with anybody."

"What did he say to that?"

Christina searched her memory. "I don't remember him saying anything."

"Maybe that's where your problem is, Christina," Louise reasoned.

Christina was not ready for her mother to analyze her problems. "Jackson and I are articulate adults, Mom. He's had more than enough time and opportunity to speak with me if he had a problem. Why should I go looking for a needle in a haystack? If he can't talk to me, it wasn't much of a relationship in the first place."

Chapter 19

Jackson was sitting on the top step of the Stevenses' front porch when Reggie came up the walk.

Reggie stopped in front of him, his legs apart, his arms crossed. "I'm surprised to see you here."

"Not as surprised as I am to be here," Jackson said. His apprehensions about this meeting with Reggie were proving well founded.

"We may as well get this out of the way," Reggie began. "How's Christina?"

Jackson didn't want to talk to Reggie about Christina. It was obvious Reggie still had feelings for her. "Christina's fine."

"That's not a very enthusiastic answer. Is something wrong?"

Jackson raised a brow in his direction. "Nothing's wrong."

Reggie dropped his arms. "So how is she? Why didn't she come out here with you?"

"You're overly concerned with Christina, aren't you?"

"You know that I had a thing for her, Jackson. That's no secret."

Jackson leaned back on his elbows and stretched out his legs. "And you know that now she has a thing for me."

"That what you say, but you're here and she's still in Atlanta. Maybe things have changed."

"And if they have?"

"Well, if she's not seeing you anymore, maybe she'll see me again."

"So you'd move in on my woman like that?" Jackson asked.

He knew Reggie would do just that, given the chance. There were no rules when it came to women.

"I don't remember your holding back when I was in the picture," Reggie minded him. "As I see it, what goes around comes around."

Jackson knew Reggie was right. He pursued Christina even after he'd realized Reggie was in her life. From Jackson's viewpoint, though, Christina was his before she was Reggie's anyway. "I'm not going to argue about this, Reggie," he said. "Just know that I'm in love with Christina and she's in love with me."

"If you say so, man," Reggie replied, but Jackson saw the challenge in his eyes.

The ringing telephone greeted Christina when she entered her house Sunday night. "Reggie," she said. "I'm glad to hear from you." She sat and cradled the phone in her arm. She had been tempted to call him, but she didn't want to hurt him any more than she already had.

"I've been thinking about you a lot," he said. "I wanted to apologize for our last conversation. I didn't handle what you had to say very well."

"There's no need for apologies. I'm glad to hear from you again. I'd hate to think we couldn't be friends."

"Oh, no, the dreaded friends," he said. "I guess Jackson was right. You're still in love with him."

Christina sat up straighter in her chair. "Jackson? When did you talk to Jackson?"

"I saw him this weekend."

Christina didn't understand. "You were in Atlanta?"

"No," Reggie said. "Jackson was here in Oklahoma City."

Christina slumped back in the chair. "Jackson was in Oklahoma City? What was he doing out there?"

"Your guess is as good as mine. I walked into my parents' house this afternoon and there he was."

She wondered what Jackson was doing out there. "He thinks highly of your parents."

"Well, he had them all to himself for two whole days. My mom can't stop talking about him. Dad, either. They had a good time with him."

"I'm glad he got to see them," was all Christina could say.

"It's none of my business, Christina, but are things between you and Jackson okay?"

"Things aren't as good as I'd like them to be," Christina said, hedging. She didn't know what Jackson had told them.

"Do you want to talk about it?"

Christina considered that offer. "I don't think it would be such a good idea."

"Maybe you're right," Reggie admitted. "I wouldn't be an unbiased listener. I still care a lot about you."

Christina wished she loved Reggie, but she didn't. She was still in love with Jackson. There was no future for them, but she loved him. "I know you do, Reggie, and I don't want to hurt you again."

"I'm a big boy," Reggie reminded her.

Christina didn't want to argue, so she changed the subject. "What's going on with you?" When Reggie didn't answer immediately, she thought he might not make this easy for her. When he said, "Nothing much," she breathed a relieved sigh, glad they could have friendly conversation.

Christina arrived at the office at her regular time Monday. A part of her hoped to get roses. If she got them today, she could be sure that Jackson hadn't sent them. He wouldn't be stupid enough to send more. She didn't see any roses on Penny's desk. Maybe they're on my desk, she thought. She opened the door to her office cautiously and looked around the room. No roses anywhere. She walked to her desk and sat down. Who's sending those damn roses? she asked herself. If not Jackson, then who?

She looked up when there was a knock on the door. Jackson stood in the open doorway. "It's open," she said. "You didn't have to knock."

He walked in. "I didn't know if I was welcome."

"You know I have an open-door policy. Every CL employee is welcome."

"That the way it is, then?" he asked.

"This is a place of work, Jackson. We should confine our conversation to work-related topics. Don't you agree?"

"If not here, then where?"

"Where what?"

"Where and when are we going to talk?"

"I did all my talking Friday. You haven't talked in a while. Are you sure we have something more to say to each other?"

"We need to talk, Christina." He walked closer to the desk. "I have something—"

"Excuse me, Christina," Penny interrupted. "Walter's on line 1. He says it's urgent."

Christina stared at Penny. She hadn't heard her come in. "All right, Penny, I'll take it." To Jackson, she said, "We'll have to continue this later."

"You can bet on it," Jackson said. He walked out of the office, closing the door behind him.

Christina picked up the phone. "Walter," she said. "What's so urgent this morning?"

"There's good news and bad news," Walter said. "Which do you want to hear first?"

"Let's try the good news first."

"Rosalind and I are getting married three weeks from Saturday and you're invited to the wedding," Walter said gleefully.

"Congratulations," Christina said. "I'm so happy for you and Rosalind. Give her a big kiss for me." Christina deliberately did not say she'd attend the wedding. It was too soon after her and Jackson.

"I'll do that," Walter said. "This is going to be some wedding."

"I bet it will be," was her reply. That was noncommittal enough, she thought.

"Now the bad news. Jackson's promotion has come through and he has to be back in Boston by the end of the week."

"The end of the week? That's too soon," she said. Too soon for me to let him go.

"I'm sorry, but there's no other way. You knew this was coming. Have you looked over any of the résumés we've sent you? You're going to have to pick a replacement."

"I haven't even started looking at résumés. I thought Jackson would be around until the demo was done. You can't do this now."

"It's done, Christina," Walter said. "You'd better get started on that replacement because if Jackson wants this job, he has to be in Boston by Friday. Now, who's going to tell him, me or you?"

It was all happening too fast. "You tell him."

"Who knows, Christina, maybe he'll turn down the job and stay in Atlanta."

"Be serious. You know as well as I do that Jackson is going to take the assignment."

"Yes, I do think he's going to take it, but I'm sure he'll talk with you about it. Anything else we need to discuss while I have you on the phone?"

"No, I can't think of anything."

"Okay, I'll talk with you later in the week. And don't forget the replacement."

Christina hung up the phone. Everything was falling in place for them to be apart. He wanted space. Well, there was definitely a lot of space between Boston and Atlanta. One week. Less than a week and he would be gone.

She stood and looked out the window. She could see his apartment building from her office. She remembered the first time she'd been in his apartment. Everything. The dinner he'd prepared and the dessert they'd shared. It was only one of the memories that bombarded her thoughts this morning. She wanted to hold on to every one of those memories because she knew there would be no others for her and Jackson. And that made her sad, very sad.

Jackson stood in the door of Christina's office later that day. He was glad Penny wasn't at her desk. This gave him time to study the woman he loved. He never figured he'd fall in love so deeply and so quickly. He smiled as he remembered the first morning he'd seen her. That seemed ages ago, but it was only eight months, less than a year. She'd gotten to him when no other woman could. She found a place in his heart that he hadn't even known existed. As he looked at her now, he knew he'd always love her.

Then why, he asked himself, are you leaving her? Jackson had been surprised at his own reaction to Walter's news. He'd wanted this promotion for a long time. His joy at hearing the news was dampened by the knowledge that it would mean leaving Christina. If their relationship was going well, it would have been hard to leave her, but they could have worked at a long distance relationship. Since it wasn't going well, he knew this would be the end for them. He had asked for space and he'd gotten space. Be careful what you wish for, he reminded himself.

Christina looked up when he cleared his throat. Her face didn't hold the smile it usually held for him, and that made him sad. "I just talked to Walter."

She stood. "Congratulations. I know how much this means to you, and I wish you the best."

"Thanks," he said. "I'm sorry I have to leave so quickly. I know you'll be shorthanded." *I feel like I'll be leaving a part of myself.*

"I knew this day was coming. I just didn't think it would be this soon. We're really going to miss you around here."

"I'm going to miss you, too." He saw by the way her eyes widened that she understood he meant it personally.

"Do you think we should announce it at the staff meeting today?" she asked.

"We need to tell Liza before then. You and she are going to have your hands full until you get a replacement, but I'm sure you'll handle it."

"I know we'll do it, but we'll miss you. You added a lot to this project. Where we are with OPTIMA now is largely due to the work that you did when you first came on board. Even before Liza got here."

He knew that, but it was good to hear her say it. He wondered how often she'd have to say it before he believed she meant it. "Thanks. That means a lot to me."

"It's true, and I know Liza feels the same way. When do you think you'll be leaving?"

"Walter wants me to report Friday, so I need to leave Thursday night." He paused. They were talking about work, not daring to discuss the personal issues between them. What cowards they were. "You, Liza, and I will need to plan some type of transition."

"This is going to be near impossible. You know that, don't you?"

And not just the work. It was going to be impossible to leave her. "I'll do what I can to make it easy. I'll make myself available after I'm back in Boston. Do you have anybody in mind to replace me?"

"I haven't thought about that, Jackson. To be honest, I haven't wanted to think about it."

He was glad for that. "I'm going to clean out the apartment soon, too. What do you want me to do about your belongings?"

She didn't even blink. They could have been discussing the weather. "I can pick them up over the weekend while you're away, if that's okay. I'll leave your key on the counter."

He was disappointed they were discussing this so unemotionally. Didn't their love deserve more? "That's fine. When can I pick up my stuff from your place? I no longer have a key."

Christina took the hit. She remembered asking him to return the key. "I'll be in every night this week, so you can come over anytime."

"I'd like to take you to dinner before I leave," he said. He needed her to agree to dinner, at least.

"I don't know if that's such a good idea, Jackson."

He couldn't let it end like this. "Christina, we've shared too much, been too close for me to just leave. There's still a lot we need to talk about. I'm still in love with you."

"Don't say that, Jackson," Christina pleaded. She was determined to make it through this with her dignity intact. It was all she had. "You wanted space and you're getting it."

"I know, but I don't want us to be over. Not yet. Not like this."

She wanted to believe him, but too much had happened. "So, you don't need space?"

"Yes, but I need to know that you'll be there for me. I don't want this to be the end."

"That's not fair, Jackson. You want your space to think, but you want me to wait for you. What am I supposed to be doing while I'm waiting?"

He wanted her to continue doing what she was doing, but he didn't want her to see other people. This made no sense, even to him, but it was how he felt. And he couldn't tell her. She'd really think he'd lost his mind.

"I don't know, Christina. I just don't want to lose you."

"You didn't lose me, Jackson," she said, close to tears. "You threw me back."

Jackson came over Wednesday night. He had called, so Christina expected him. She had most of his stuff packed.

"Thanks," he said. "You didn't have to do that."

She knew it was easier than watching him do it. "It was nothing."

"I…" Jackson began.

"Let's not make this any harder than it has to be. We have some problems that we can't work out long distance. Let's just call it quits and leave it at that."

"Is it that easy for you, Christina?" Jackson asked.

"It's not easy, Jackson, but it's easier than you want it to be."

"We need to talk," he said.

She shook her head. "We needed to talk last week. So much has changed since then. Talking is not going to change anything."

"Don't you want to give it another chance?"

More than anything she wanted to try again, but she didn't have the courage to say it. "What's the use, Jackson? You're leaving, I'm staying."

"That's the way you want it?"

No. "That's the way I want it."

He looked at her for a long while. Then he moved as if to come closer, but changed his mind. "Goodbye, Christina," he said and left.

"Goodbye, Jackson," Christina said. When she heard the door close behind him, she added, "I still love you, too."

"We're glad to have you back, Jackson," Rosalind said, directing him to a chair in front of his desk.

"It's good to be back, I think," Jackson said. It was his second week in Boston.

She sat down after he was seated. "Are you having any problems getting settled?"

"No, the work is fine."

"What's the problem, then? I expected you to be happy in your new job."

"I am happy, but not as happy as I thought I'd be. This is all I've wanted for the last three years. I've got it and I'm on my way, but it feels hollow." He shrugged. "Maybe my expectations were too high."

"Or maybe you've found that work is not enough."

He studied her. "You know about me and Christina, don't you?"

She nodded. "Christina and I talked the weekend of Liza's wedding. Are you two not adjusting well to the separation?"

"Not exactly. We decided to end the relationship."

"Why would you do that? You wouldn't be the first couple in a long distance relationship."

"There were other reasons and she…we thought it was best to end it."

"What do you think now?"

"I miss her. I miss her a lot. I miss working with her. I miss being with her."

"Have you told her this?"

He couldn't count the number of times he'd picked up the phone to do just that. "No, I haven't told her, and I can't tell her. She wants something I can't give her right now."

"Well, Jackson, you've got some decisions to make. I'd advise you to make them quickly. Christina is not going to wait forever."

"What makes you think she's waiting now?"

Rosalind smiled like she had a secret. "Remind me one day to tell you the story of a woman who waited twenty-five years for a man."

Jackson saw Robert and Liza first. "Hey, you two, how's it going?"

"No complaints, man, no complaints," Robert answered.

Jackson let his gaze roam the ballroom. "This wedding was almost as nice as yours."

"Almost," Liza said, and smiled at Robert.

"It's one thing to watch and another thing to be in it. That was the most special day of my life," Robert said. He put an arm around Liza's waist and pulled her to him. "We're an old married couple now."

Liza pushed against him. "Hardly. We're still on our honeymoon."

Jackson watched them. They were as in love today as they'd been the first time he'd met them, as they were on their wedding day. He used to wonder if he and Christina would be as good a couple as they were. Thinking about her, he asked, "Did Christina come?"

Liza looked at Robert before answering. "No, she decided not to come."

Jackson voice registered his concern. "Is she sick or something?"

Liza placed her hand on his. "She's fine, Jackson. She just didn't feel up to a wedding right now. She sent her love to Rosalind and Walter, though."

Jackson understood. Christina didn't attend because she didn't want to see him. She was really trying to get him out of her system. "She's okay?" he asked again to be sure.

"She's fine," Liza reassured him.

Chapter 20

Christina sat on the examination table in Dr. Johnson's office. "I feel tired all the time and it's getting worse each day," she said. She'd dismissed her fatigue as depression at first, but when it had gotten progressively worse, she'd become concerned.

"Any other problems?" Doctor Johnson asked.

"None that I can think of. Maybe I need vitamins or iron tablets."

He flipped open her chart, and scanned it, then closed it. "Before I prescribe anything, I'm going to take some blood and do a physical. It's about time for one anyway. How does that sound?"

"Right, now Doctor, I'd go for anything that was going to make me feel better."

"Give us a little time, Christina, and we'll figure out what's wrong."

Three days later, Christina got a call from Dr. Johnson. "I may have found the reason for your fatigue, Christina. Are you sitting down?"

My God, Christina thought, I must be dying. "Is it serious, Doctor?"

"Not exactly. You're pregnant, Christina."

Christina thought she had misheard him. "What did you say?"

"You're pregnant. I don't know how far along you are, you'll need to see your gynecologist."

"Pregnant? You must be joking, Doctor. How can I be pregnant?"

Dr. Johnson laughed. "You don't really need me to answer that, do you?"

She was pregnant. It must be a joke, a cruel joke. She and Jackson had been so careful. "Oh, no. I know how other people get pregnant, but how could it happen to me?"

"The same way, I'd say."

"That's not what I mean, Dr. Johnson. I wasn't planning to have a baby. Not yet, anyway."

"I thought you'd be happy about this, Christina."

Christina wondered if he was crazy. "Doctor, I'm a single woman with no marriage prospects. What makes you think I'd be happy about this pregnancy?"

"Every day single women are making choices to have babies. You're financially and emotionally capable of raising a child. It's conceivable that you'd be happy about it. Surprised, maybe, but happy."

"A word of advice, Doctor. The next time you tell a single woman that she's pregnant, try to tone it down a little." She hung up. The doctor was right about one thing. She was definitely surprised.

Pregnant. Christina couldn't believe it. She was pregnant. She touched her hand to her abdomen. A baby is growing in there, she thought. Jackson's baby. She took her hand away. *What am I going to do?*

"How about a movie?" Liza asked. "Robert is out doing some male-bonding so I'm free to do some male-bashing. Are you game?"

Christina gave a wry laugh. Male-bashing. She could really get into that now. "I'm not up for it tonight, Liza."

"Tired?"

"More tired than I've ever been," Christina said morosely. She was seated on the bed with the phone propped between her shoulder and her ear.

"What's wrong, Christina?"

I need to talk about this. "I'm pregnant, Liza."

"What? You're kidding."

"I wish I were. I found out today. I'm pregnant."

"Do you want some company?"

Very much. "Thanks, Liza, I could use a friend right now."

Forty-five minutes later, Liza sat in Christina's kitchen.

"How do you feel about it?" Liza asked.

"I don't know. I certainly don't feel pregnant."

Liza didn't comment.

"I feel stupid. How could I let myself get pregnant? I'm a grown woman, Liza, an intelligent woman. I swore I'd never end up in this situation. How could I let this happen?"

"What did happen, Christina? Did you and Jackson get careless?"

Christina shook her head. "I was faithful with the birth control pills. Before that, Jackson faithfully used condoms."

"That may be it."

"What?"

"Did Jackson always use a condom even after you started taking birth control pills?"

Christina shook her head. "Most of the time, but not all of the time." She paused, then added, "But I faithfully took the birth control pills."

"Unfortunately, they aren't one hundred percent effective."

Christina lifted a brow. "I remember telling you that once before."

"I remember, too. Too bad we didn't know Betty then."

"What does Betty have to do with this?"

"She was taking birth control pills when she got pregnant with her youngest, Anne. Now she jokes that even though she's still on the pill, Ellis can't come near her without a condom."

Christina knew Liza and Betty got along, but she didn't know they were as close as this conversation indicated. "You and Betty have been talking about birth control?"

Liza nodded. "You know Betty. She has an opinion on everything. When I told her that Robert and I didn't plan to have children anytime soon, she shared the Anne story with me.

Needless to say, the condom is now Robert's constant companion."

Christina smirked. "One of you could have clued me in."

Liza lifted her shoulders and let them drop slowly. "It happens less than point-three-percent of the time. I just figured it would be my luck to be one of the point-three."

"Well, it seems I made it into that lucky group." Christina smiled. "I have an idea for one of Angela's shows. Women who got pregnant while taking the pill."

Liza laughed. "Probably put a scare into the whole female population."

Christina laughed, too. "I'm glad you came over, Liza. I was getting depressed about this. You're helping me feel better."

"Have you decided what you're going to do?" Liza asked.

"Not really. I'm only beginning to believe I'm really pregnant. I've been thinking that maybe the blood tests got mixed up, maybe it's a tumor." She laughed again. "Maybe this is *Dallas* and it's all a dream."

Liza didn't laugh. "I know the feeling."

Christina looked around, surprised. "You've been pregnant before?"

Liza turned away. "Once."

"I didn't know. What did you do, Liza?" There were only three options—adoption, abortion, or miscarriage.

"Abortion," Liza said quickly.

"I never knew," Christina said.

"No one knew. Not my parents. Not the guy. Nobody."

Christina could see the memory was painful for her friend. She was sorry to have caused her to think about it. "You went through it by yourself?"

"I had to. There was nobody to go through it with me."

"Why didn't you tell the guy?"

"He didn't love me and I didn't love him. It happened at a bad time in my life."

At the sadness in Liza's voice, Christina walked over and put her arms around her. "I'm sorry, Liza."

Liza's eyes filled with tears. "Don't be. I knew what I was doing. It was a painful time in my life."

Neither woman said anything for a few long minutes.

"Abortion actually crossed my mind," Christina said softly.

Liza looked at her then, "You can't be serious."

Christina nodded. "It seemed the easiest way. You know how I felt about becoming an unwed mother."

"But you decided against it?"

"Yes. It was only a passing thought. I really want children, Liza. I just wanted a husband to go with them."

"I want them, too," Liza said. "I just didn't want one then, and I don't want one now. That's why Robert and I use birth control. Now, about the husband. When are you going to tell Jackson?"

Christina looked away.

"You *are* going to tell him, aren't you, Christina?"

"I haven't decided yet."

"What do you mean, you haven't decided? You *have* to tell him. It's his baby."

Christina shrugged.

"It is his baby, isn't it, Christina?" Liza asked.

Christina let out a deep breath. "Of course it's his baby."

"Then you have to tell him."

Christina had been debating this with herself. Jackson deserved to know, but she didn't want him back just because of the baby. There had to be more than that. "Why should I. You didn't."

"That was different. You and Jackson are in love. He deserves to know, regardless of the problems you're having now."

Christina wrapped her arms around herself. She wasn't sure of Jackson's feelings for her. "I'm not sure Jackson would think this is good news. If he felt crowded when it was just me, how's he going to feel about a baby?"

"I can't answer that, Christina, but you have to tell him. What if he wants to be a father? Don't you want your baby to know its father?"

Christina flinched. That hit a nerve. More than anything she wanted her baby to have a mother and a father. She hadn't planned this pregnancy, but she was going to handle it the best way she could. "Liza, I want my baby to grow up in a happy home, but I can't use this baby to force Jackson back to me. He wouldn't be happy with that, and neither would I."

"So you're planning to raise this baby alone? Without a father?"

Unwed motherhood would not have been her choice, but this was the hand she was dealt and she was going to play it. "My mom didn't do too bad a job with me, did she?"

"You can answer that better than I can, Christina. Do you want your baby to have the kind of childhood you did? Can you keep your baby away from its father? Your mother didn't have an option, your father was dead. Jackson is very much alive."

Christina knew she couldn't risk Jackson rejecting her or the baby. It would hurt too badly. "What if he doesn't want this baby, Liza? What if he doesn't want me?"

"I believe he'll want you and the baby."

"I'm not so sure about that. I'm not sure I want him."

"Come on, Christina," Liza pleaded. "You're still in love with Jackson. Even if you aren't, you can't keep your pregnancy a secret. He's bound to find out."

A plan began to form in Christina's mind. "Don't be so sure about that, Liza."

"What are you thinking, Christina?"

"I can't tell you now, Liza, but you have to promise not to tell anybody about my pregnancy." She paused, "Not even Robert."

"That's not fair. I don't like keeping secrets from Robert. Especially something like this."

"It's really not his business, Liza. Besides, he might feel obliged to tell Jackson."

When Liza didn't respond, Christina added, "I need your help on this, Liza. Promise me you'll help."

Walter slammed his fist on her desk. He had come down to Atlanta. "It's out of the question."

Christina forced herself to remain calm. A calm head would get her what she wanted. "It can work, Walter. I know it can."

Walter began to pace the room. "You want to take a year's leave of absence and you say it can work." Walter stopped, looked at her and shook his head. "Have you lost your mind?"

She thought Walter was going too far, but she was not going to lose her temper. "It will work. Tom Haydn has fully assumed Jackson's duties and he's doing a great job. Liza can take over my responsibilities. She's due for a promotion, anyway. We both knew we'd have to replace her."

"Not this soon, Christina."

"Now's a good time. The major OPTIMA milestones have been met. The demo was a success and the first office application site selection is complete. Now's the perfect time for a change."

Walter sat in the chair across from her desk and began tapping his pencil on the desktop. Christina knew he was trying to think of more reasons for her not to leave. She also knew he was having a difficult time.

"What about your career?" he asked. "What will taking a leave of absence do to your career?"

She wasn't surprised. She knew Walter would end up here when nothing else worked. "You tell me, Walter. What will happen?"

He started slowly. "All you've done here will be forgotten. You'll have to build everything again. People will wonder if you're dedicated. They'll wonder how important CL's work is to you. It will be hard to get back to where you are now."

Christina knew Walter had spoken honestly. "Do you think I could do it, Walter? Do you think I could get back to where I am now?"

Walter looked away from her and she knew she had won. "It'll take time, but you could do it," he answered. He paused. "What do you want, Christina? Sometimes I get the feeling Rosalind and I want the vice presidency for you more than you want it for yourself."

"I've been asking myself that same question. I can't give you any answers now. I love my work, but beyond that I don't know.

Angela Benson   231

Maybe the time off will help me focus and decide what I want to do."

"There's nothing that I can do to get you to change your mind, is there?"

Christina shook her head. "No, Walter, I've decided." At his look, she added, "And neither can Rosalind."

"Does your leaving have anything to do with you and Jackson?" Rosalind asked. She and Christina were having lunch.

"Jackson and I are no longer together," Christina answered. She wasn't telling Rosalind any more than she's told Walter.

"I know you think Walter sent me here to convince you to stay, but that's not the reason I'm here."

Christina was skeptical. "Walter didn't send you here?"

"Walter told me about your conversation," Rosalind explained. "But it was my idea and my choice to come and see you." She reached over to touch Christina's hand. "I'm here as a friend today, not as a colleague."

Christina looked at the hand that covered hers. She wanted to believe Rosalind. "I'm listening," was the best she could do.

"Leaving CL is not going to help you get over him. I know; I've been there."

"I'm not running away from Jackson, Rosalind. Jackson's already gone."

"Can you honestly say that you don't feel anything for him?" Rosalind challenged.

Christina enfolded Rosalind's hand in her own. She knew her friend was trying to keep her from repeating her and Walter's mistakes. "Jackson will always have a place in my heart. He's the first man I've ever loved. A part of me will always love him." And I'll have his baby, she added to herself.

Rosalind was slow to speak, and Christina knew she had given in. "What are you going to do during this leave?"

Christina gave Rosalind's hand a quick squeeze, then pulled away. "I'm going home to spend time with my mother. She'll probably work me to death. She's opening another nursery."

Rosalind smiled. "So you're going from the boardroom to the greenhouse."

Christina laughed lightly. "I guess you could say that. It'll be good for me."

"Do you think you'll come back to CL?"

Christina didn't expect that question. "It's my plan to come back, but I don't know what will happen. Maybe I'll find that I prefer greenhouses to boardrooms."

"So what do you think, Liza?" Christina asked.

"I don't know what to say," Liza said. She stood and looked out of Christina's office window. "I'll have to talk it over with Robert."

"You say that like you think he might object. Do you?"

Liza turned around to face her. "Just the opposite. He'll go crazy with the idea. He's been pressuring me lately to cut back on work."

"The house won't exactly help with that, will it? You can still work long hours."

Liza nodded. "I could, but not living so close to work will help some."

"So what's the problem?"

"I just can't believe you're taking a leave of absence. What about your job?"

Christina lifted her hands. "What about it? It'll be here when I get back. Besides, look how my leave benefits you. You get my job. Haven't you wanted it?"

Liza smiled. "You know I've wanted it. Not your job, but I wanted a promotion. I'm glad about that."

"Then what's the problem?"

Liza shook her head. "I can't believe you're doing this. Not at this point in your career."

"Well, I am. There's more to life than a career. I hope you haven't forgotten that."

"Now you're beginning to sound like Robert. Of course, I haven't forgotten. It's just that I want it all—the career and the family. And right now the career needs most of my energy."

Christina didn't want Liza to sacrifice her relationship with Robert for her job, but she knew she was in no position to give advice. "So when do you want to move in?"

"I like being downtown. It's so convenient to work. I don't know."

"The commute from Christina's house wouldn't be that bad," Robert said. "You need to put some space between you and your work anyway. You overdo it sometimes."

Liza got up from her seat on the balcony and stood next to Robert at the railing. She ran her fingers through his hair. He needed a haircut. "I know I've been working long hours. I appreciate your being a good sport about it."

He caressed her face with his hand. "That doesn't mean I like it, Liza. Will this promotion mean more hours for you?"

Liza thought before answering. She was ambitious and she was willing to work hard for what she wanted. And she wanted Robert, her job, and someday, children. "It doesn't have to."

"What does that mean?"

"It means it's my choice. I can set the pace and the schedule that I want to work."

He dropped his hand from her face. "What are you going to do?"

She thought again. If she was going to have it all, she was going to have to do one hell of a balancing act. But she was determined. "I'm excited about this promotion, Robert, and I want to do a good job. I want to be a vice president at CL one day, the sooner the better. That's going to mean a certain amount of commitment from both of us."

Robert turned away from her. "What about us? Do we rate as highly as your work?"

She moved so he faced her. "How can you ask that, Robert? Our marriage is much more important to me than the work, but I don't want to have to choose between them. I want both."

"I don't have a problem with that. I just don't want to lose you to your work."

She hugged him to her. "You won't. I'm going to need you to

keep me honest, though. We need to have talks like this when you feel that I'm getting out of balance. I love you and I want us to be happy together for the rest of our lives."

She felt the tension ease out of him. "I love you, too, Liza."

They stood holding each other for a long while. Robert broke the silence. "What are we going to do about Christina's offer?"

"We should move out there. You're right. Some distance between me and work would be good."

She felt Robert's arms tighten around her and she relaxed. It was hell being Superwoman.

Chapter 21

"Hi, Mom," Christina said into the telephone. "How'd you like to have a houseguest for a few months?"

"Depends on who the guest is," Louise responded. "Are you thinking about taking a vacation?"

"A very long vacation."

"Well, that's hard to believe. I've never known you to take more than a couple of days at a time. What bring this on?"

"I've got some news for you."

"By the tone of your voice, I'd guess it's happy news."

"It is."

"Are you going to tell me now or are you going to make me wait?"

"I'll tell you now. Are you sitting down?"

"No, I'm not sitting down," Louise answered. "Are you sure this is good news?"

Christina laughed. After all her initial misgivings, she was finally feeling good. Good about the baby. Good about her decision to take a leave of absence. Good about life. "I'm positive it's good news, but you'd better take a seat."

Christina held on while her mother found a chair. "I'm seated now, Christina. Tell me your good news."

"I'm pregnant, Mom. Can you believe it? I'm going to have a baby."

Christina enjoyed being back in Selma. She spent most of her days in the new nursery with her mother. She liked not having to dress for work every day, not having to prepare for meetings, not having to direct employees. She worked in the nursery and she thought about her baby. It was the good life—with one exception: Louise was upset. She was happy about the baby, but she disagreed with Christina's decision not to tell Jackson. For once, Louise wouldn't leave it alone.

"How long are we going to continue like this, Mom?" Christina asked one night after dinner.

Louise didn't pretend not to understand. "Until you come to your sense and tell Jackson about this baby."

"This is *my* decision, Mom," Christina said gently. "I'm doing what I think is best. Can't you support me in this?"

Louise shook her head. "Not this time. I don't want you to make the same mistakes I did."

Thinking Louise was talking about her pregnancy, Christina explained, "I don't think of it as a mistake anymore, Mom. It's an unplanned but welcome surprise. I wanted a baby and I wanted a husband. At least I'm getting one of them."

"It'll be all my fault," Louise said.

"It's not anyone's fault. I loved Jackson and I got pregnant. Unfortunately, our love ended before we found out about the pregnancy."

"It's a cycle," Louise said. "I have to break this cycle."

Christina didn't know what her mother was talking about. Again, she assumed it was her pregnancy. "You were a great mother to me and I'll be a great mother to this baby. I hope I can be half the mother that you are."

Louise stood up. Christina had no idea what she was mumbling about. "I should have told you the truth. I never should have lied."

As Christina watched her mother, a nervous feeling settled in the pit of her stomach. "What are you talking about, Mother? What should you have told me? What did you lie about?"

"I'm so sorry, Christina," Louise said. She was crying softly now. "I thought I was doing the right thing."

Christina rubbed her hands across her head. "What are you talking about?"

"I hope you don't hate me, Christina. I thought it was the right thing to do."

Christina went to her mother. "Tell me what you're talking about." *Please don't let it be bad. God, please don't let it be bad news.*

"It's your father." Louise looked directly at her daughter. "Your father is alive, Christina."

Christina couldn't believe her ears. Surely she had heard wrong. "Alive?"

Louise didn't look away. "Yes, Christina."

Christina heard a ringing sound in her ears. "Alive? He can't be alive. All these years you told me he was dead."

"It was a lie. All these years I lied."

Christina couldn't stand any longer. She sat down and stared at her mother. "You lied?" she asked softly. "Why did you lie?"

"I had to."

"Alive," Christina repeated. "All these years and my father has been alive. All these years that I've needed him and you told me he was dead. Why did you do that to me, Mother? Why? Did he not want me? Is that the reason?"

Louise shook her head. "He never knew I was pregnant, Christina. I never told him."

"You never told him," Christina repeated, dazed.

"You can't make the same mistake I did, Christina. You must tell Jackson about this baby."

Christina just stared at her mother. "All these years you were lying. How could you do that to me, Mother? How could you do it? What about all the stories you told about the two of you? Were they lies, too?"

Louise had dreaded this anger, but she understood it and she had known she would see if it Christina ever learned the truth. "No, Christina, they weren't all lies. I loved Christian and he loved me."

"Then why didn't you tell him about me?" Christina demanded.

Louise hoped Christina would understand. "It was the best

thing that I could think to do. There was no way Christian and I could be together."

"Then what kept you apart?"

"My parents didn't approve of him. And his parents wouldn't have approved of me."

"Why didn't Big Momma and Big Daddy like him? What did he do?"

Louise saw the confusion on her daughter's face. "It's not what he did, Christina. It's what he was. They liked him, they just didn't approve of our relationship."

"What was he, Mother? An ex-convict?"

"No, he wasn't an ex-convict. He was a law student, like I told you."

"Why don't you just tell me, Mother?"

Louise took her daughter's hand. "Your grandparents didn't approve because Christian was white."

"White? White?"

"Yes, dear. He was, is, white."

"My father is a white man?" Christina's mind felt numb.

Louise nodded. Please God, don't let my daughter hate me, she prayed.

"I don't believe you, Mother. How can that be? I don't look white."

"That's an ignorant thing to say, Christina. There's no doubt about it, Christian is your father, and he's white."

Louise watched Christina absorb this news. She saw pain, disbelief, begrudging acceptance, and then anger cross her daughter's beautiful face. Anger was the emotion that remained.

"If you knew there was no hope for the relationship, Mother, why did you sleep with him?"

"I loved him, Christina. You don't choose the person you fall in love with. You should know that. It just happens."

When Christina didn't speak, Louise continued. "If he'd known I was pregnant, he'd have defied his parents and married me. That's the kind of man he was. I wanted so much for you to know him."

"You had a strange way of showing it," Christina said. "What makes you so sure he would have married you? Maybe he didn't love you. Maybe it was curiosity. You saw *Jungle Fever*."

That stung. That question had haunted Louise over the years. She knew Christian loved her and she believed that he wanted to marry her, but there was still a niggling doubt. "It wasn't like that; he asked me to marry him. He asked me. He asked, and he didn't know about you."

"If you loved him so much, you should have married him."

She's so young, Louise thought. "It wasn't as easy as that. We would have had to give up so much and face so much. It may have killed our love. I couldn't risk that."

"For the sake of love, you decided to have an illegitimate child?" Christina asked, her pain evident. "Did you lie to me all these years because you loved him? Did you think I'd want to see my daddy and that might cause him some discomfort? Is that what you thought, Mother?"

"I can see you're distraught, Christina. Maybe we should talk about this later."

Christina shook her head vigorously. "No, I want to talk about it now. Why did you lie to me?"

Louise knew she had to make Christina understand. "I didn't even tell him. What was I going to tell you? How could I tell you he was alive when he didn't even know about you? You would have wanted to see him."

"Of course, Mother. He's my father. I'm a part of him." Christina broke down then and tears streamed from her eyes. "All these years I've dreamed about my father, he's been alive. He's alive, and he doesn't even know that I exist."

Louise got back to the reason she had told Christina this news. "Don't make the same mistake I made, Christina. You have to tell Jackson about this baby."

My father is alive, Christina thought. He's out there some-where. My father. My father. She placed her hands on her abdomen. She knew she had to tell Jackson. Her mother was right, she couldn't deprive her baby of its father.

Christina was still angry with her mother. Louise should have told her before now. A knock on the door interrupted her thoughts.

"Come in, Mother," Christina said.

Louise poked her head through the door first. "Are you sure it's safe for me in here?"

Christina smiled, almost. "Come on in. I don't have any lethal weapons."

Louise walked all the way into the room, closing the door behind her. She sat on the bed, facing Christina. "What have you been doing up here? I've been worried."

Christina saw a pattern here. Jackson breaks my heart, and then he wonders how I'm doing. My mother breaks my heart, then she wonders how I'm doing. Why do I have to love crazy people? she wondered. "I'm not going to do anything stupid, Mother." She aimed for humor. "I told you there were no lethal weapons in here."

"That's not what I meant, Christina. How long are you going to be angry with me?"

"I really don't know. Let's see, you lied to me for thirty years. Don't I at least deserve to be angry for thirty days?"

"You do have a right to be angry, Christina, but I'm not used to this tension between us. It's been a week."

Christina picked up a pillow from the bed and pulled it to her. "Me either, Mom. You were always the person I could count on. It's hard for me to come to grips with your lying to me. I can understand your not telling me when I was a child, but I'm thirty years old. I deserved to know."

"You're right. I should have told you sooner, but I was afraid. What was I supposed to say, 'Christina, by the way, your father's not dead, pass the salt?' I didn't know how and I was afraid I would lose you." She paused, then added, "I love you, Christina. Whatever wrong I've done or whatever else I've lied about, I do love you."

Christina heard the sincerity in her mother's voice. And the pain. She just wasn't ready yet to give Louise the forgiveness that she wanted. "Will you tell me about him now? The truth, this time?"

Louise took her daughter's hand. "Everything I told you about Christian was true, except that we didn't meet in Selman, we met in Huntsville. We were attracted to each other from the start. We couldn't really date in the open, so we attended rallies together and worked on a lot of the same work teams. Our feelings grew as we came to know each other. Though it was difficult, we found ways to be together. He told me he loved me early on, and even proposed, but I couldn't even think about that. As the summer went on, I realized he was serious and so was I. We made love once, the night before he left to go back home. It was beautiful." She squeezed Christina's hand. "I have never regretted what we shared or the result of it."

"You mean you got pregnant that first time?"

Louise nodded. "I've always considered myself fortunate."

Christina couldn't ignore the similarities in their situations. Her mother and Christian. Her and Jackson. History was repeating itself. "You considered being an unwed mother fortunate?"

"No," Louise said. "I consider having the child of the man I loved fortunate. I knew society, his parents and mine, would never allow us to be together. Having you allowed me to have him. It was worth all I suffered."

Christina wanted to know more. She could understand her mother's feelings because they were much like the feelings she had about Jackson and their baby. "What was it like, Mom?"

Louise breathed deeply. "It was hard, Christina. For me and your grandparents. When they found out about Christian and me, they told me to end it. They said some awful things. That Christian was using me. That a white man only wanted one thing from a colored woman. It was awful."

"But you didn't end it?"

"I couldn't. I was young and in love. I was reckless."

"How did they find out?"

"Your grandparents?" Louise asked. At Christina's nod, she answered, "Gossip. I never knew who, but people were talking about us."

"So what happened after he left?"

"He promised to write, and he did. While he was away, I came to my sense. Or maybe your grandparents' influence just affected me more. When I found out I was pregnant, I was scared. Your grandmother knew before I did. She and your grandfather sat me down and told me they would disown me if I told Christian about the baby, but they would help me if I didn't tell him. They said there was no way those white folks would want a black baby in the family, even if it was part white. Soon, I was believing them."

"What did you do?"

"The hardest thing I've ever done. I wrote Christian and told him that I was mistaken, I didn't love him. That it was wrong. That it was a sin for us to be together. White folks and colored folks don't mix, I told him. I never heard from him after that."

That didn't make sense to Christina. If Christian had really loved her mother, he wouldn't have given up so easily. "Why didn't he write you back or try to get in touch with you?"

"Because of what I said. It was the thing about it being a sin for us to be together. The whole basis of our relationship was that somehow God had ordained the two of us to be together. To say it was sin denied the entire relationship. What could he say? I never expected an answer."

"What did you do then?"

"Your grandparents sent me away to have the baby. We never told anyone about the father. After you were born, I came back home. People talked for a while, but it soon died down. So much was going on then that people really didn't care."

"That's it?"

"That it. The rest, as they say, is history." Louise smiled, then asked, "Do you think you can ever forgive me?"

* * *

"He's not in the office today, Miss Marshall," Jackson's secretary said. "He took the day off."

Christina felt relieved. She had decided to tell Jackson about the baby, but she wasn't looking forward to doing it. This was a welcome reprieve. "Thanks," she said, and walked toward the elevator.

The elevator doors opened and she saw Rosalind standing there.

"What are you doing here, Christina?" Rosalind asked. "Tired of greenhouses already?"

Christina laughed. It was good to see Rosalind. "Not yet. I think I'm growing a green thumb."

"Good for you," Rosalind said. "I'm glad all is well. What brings you here?"

Christina considered her answer. "I'm here to see Jackson, but he's out today."

"You can find him at home. Do you have his new address?"

Christina didn't, so Rosalind gave it to her.

"I wish I had more time to talk," Rosalind said, "but I'm on my way to a meeting. Are you going to be in town long? Maybe you can have dinner with Walter and me."

"Maybe another time. I'm leaving tonight." I'm here just long enough to tell Jackson about the baby, she added silently.

"I'm sorry we can't get together this time. Let me know the next time you're going to be in town and we can plan to get together. Good luck with Jackson," Rosalind said, and walked away.

Christina looked at Jackson's phone number and address as she pressed the button for the elevator. She debated calling first. She decided to just show up. She didn't have enough nerve to call first. By the time she got on the elevator she had changed her mind, she was going to call first. When she reached the lobby, she had changed her mind again, she would just show up. She hailed a taxi.

Chapter 22

"Christina?" Jackson asked. He couldn't believe it. What was she doing here?

"Hi, Jackson." She met his gaze and he saw the flicker of uncertainty in her eyes.

He stood looking at her for a few long moments. She was as beautiful as ever. Looking at her reminded him how much he missed her.

"Are you going to invite me in?" she asked. She was smiling now and he felt like an idiot.

He stood back so she could walk in. "I'm sorry, yes, come on in." When she was in, he pointed towards the sofa. "Have a seat. Would you like something to drink?"

Christina sat on the sofa. "No, I'm fine right now."

Jackson couldn't get his fill of looking at her. It was so good to see her again. He thought he'd gotten over her, but now he knew that wasn't true. And, God knows, he had tried to get over her.

What brings you to my apartment? Jackson wondered. "What brings you to Boston?"

She didn't answer immediately. While he waited, a noise from behind got his attention. God, he'd forgotten that quickly.

"Jackson," the sexy voice called, "where do you keep the shampoo?"

Jackson didn't answer. He looked at Christina and let his gaze follow hers to the hallway. Angela walked into the doorway. She stopped when she saw Christina.

Angela pulled the towel tighter around her. "Hi, Christina."

Jackson looked at Angela. He couldn't look at Christina. He could guess what she was thinking. Angela wore a towel and nothing else.

"Hi, Angela," Christina said. She stood up. "Congratulations on your TV show. I've seen it a couple of times and I've liked it."

"Thanks. I'm sorry I had to cut back on my help with the fundraiser. I know you guys have been working hard."

Jackson looked from one woman to the other. He couldn't believe they were carrying on this conversation as if they had met in a restaurant or something.

"You got us off to a good start," Christina was saying. "I was supposed to contact you about doing a spot on the variety show."

"I hope I can. Call me next week and I'll let you know."

"I'll do that," Christina said. She turned to Jackson. "I guess I'll be going now. It was good seeing you." She included Angela in her goodbye. "You, too, Angela."

Jackson followed Christina as she walked toward the door. "Don't rush off."

Christina looked up into that face that she knew so well. "I think I'd better go. I didn't know you had company. I should have called."

Jackson was shaking his head. He knew she couldn't stay, shouldn't stay, but he didn't want her to leave yet. "Wasn't there something you wanted to talk to me about?"

Christina looked at him. There was no way she could tell him about the baby today. "It can wait."

Jackson saw something in her eyes that could have been pain. He wanted to comfort her, to tell her that what she saw was not what she saw. He couldn't, so he let go.

"It was good to see you, Christina. Take care of yourself." I still love you, he added silently.

Jackson stared at the door after she had gone. He turned quickly when a hand touched his shoulder. Angela was standing next to him. He'd forgotten she was in the room. His mind and his heart were with Christina.

"It was harder than you thought it would be, wasn't it?" she asked.

He nodded. "I thought I'd gotten over her."

Softly, Angela said, "So did I."

Jackson looked down at her then. "I'm sorry, Angela. I didn't…"

Angela raised her hands. "Don't apologize, Jackson. That'll only make it worse."

"I do care about you."

"I know you do." They were both silent for a while. "I should leave tonight," she added.

Jackson thought it might be best. He needed some time alone, but he didn't want to hurt her feelings. "You don't have to go."

He could tell from the look in her eyes that she knew what he was thinking. "We've always been honest with each other, Jackson. Let's not start lying now."

What could he say to her? Beautiful Angela. He could love her if he didn't love Christina. He wished he did love her. It would be easier. "You're a special woman, Angela, a very special woman," was all he could say. He knew it wasn't enough, but there were no words to express what he felt. Angela had been there when he'd needed her. She'd listened to his pain and she'd comforted him. And when she'd believed him ready, she'd made love with him. As he looked in her eyes now, he knew she regretted that. He regretted it, too.

It was a long drive home from the Montgomery Airport to Selma. Tears fell freely from Christina's eyes as she drove. She hadn't thought it would hurt this badly. Or this long. But it did. She wondered if the pain would ever stop. It had to. She knew she couldn't continue these emotional highs and lows. They weren't good for her and they weren't good for her baby.

Louise walked out the door as Christina pulled into the driveway. Great, Christina thought. I don't need this right now. "Hi, Mom," she said with mock cheerfulness when she walked up to the porch.

"How did it go?" Louise asked, the anxiety evident in her voice.

"It didn't," Christina answered.

"What? Didn't you see him? Didn't you tell him?"

Christina walked past her mother and into the house. "Yes, I saw him, and no, I didn't tell him."

Louise followed her into the house. "What do you mean, you didn't tell him? You went all the way to Boston and you didn't tell him? Why not?"

Christina sat down before answering. "It wasn't the right time or place, Mother."

"What's that supposed to mean?"

"It means he had guests. Rather, he had one guest."

"A woman?"

"How'd you ever guess?" Christina asked, with a tinge of sarcasm.

"I'm sorry, Christina."

"Don't be sorry. I should have known he'd be seeing someone else by now. It's been almost three months." *I just didn't know it would hurt so much.*

"Just because he was with a woman doesn't mean he's sleeping with her."

"Oh, but in this case I know he is. She walked out dressed only in a towel. She looked pretty comfortable, too."

"That still doesn't mean anything. Men have needs," Louise reasoned. "It doesn't mean he cares for this woman. He's only known her a short time, anyway."

Christina shook her head. "Good try, Mom, but wrong. Jackson has known this woman for a while. It was Angela, from Atlanta. Jackson wasn't just having his needs met, he's starting a relationship, a life, with someone else."

"Angela? Your friend from the radio?"

Christina nodded. "She was Jackson's friend first. It was her." Christina could still see Angela standing there in that towel. She had wanted to double over. She felt like someone had punched her in the stomach.

"That really doesn't change anything, Christina," Louise said calmly. "You still have to tell him."

She stood up. "I know that, Mother. I couldn't tell him then. I just couldn't."

"When *are* you going to tell him?"

Christina placed her hands across her face. "I don't know." How could she tell him now?

"It's not going to get any easier. The longer you put it off, the harder it'll be."

Christina lashed out. "You're a fine one to talk, Mother. You never told Christian."

"I did."

Christina stood then. "When will the lies stop, Mother? You told me the other day that you didn't tell him. Which is it?"

Louise was not affected by Christina's outburst. "I hadn't told him then, but I have told him now."

"What?"

"I told Christian about you."

"How? When?"

"I called him right after you left for Boston."

Christina sat down. Things were moving too fast for her. "You knew his phone number."

Louise nodded.

"How?"

Louise looked away. "A while back I had a private detective do some work for me."

Christina was incredulous. "You tracked him down? Why?"

"I was thinking about him a lot. I always think about him around your birthday. In the year you graduated from high school, more than ever."

Christina stared at her mother. She was learning so much about her these days. "Where was he?"

"Chicago. He runs a law firm there."

"Was he married?"

"No," Louise said sadly, "he wasn't."

"Did you call him? Let him know you were thinking about him?"

"Not then."

"Why not? He was single."

"Because so many years had passed. So many things had changed. What would I say?"

Christina thought about that for a while. "I guess you really couldn't just walk back into his life, could you?"

"No, but I wanted to."

"You loved him that much?" Christina was beginning to understand how long it took for love to fade.

"It surprises me, too. I haven't seen him in more than thirty years, but in my heart we've never been separated." She looked at Christina. "A lot of that has to do with you."

Christina walked over to her mom. "Do you still keep up with him?"

Louise nodded.

"Where is he? What's he doing?"

Louise didn't answer.

"Did something happen to him?"

"Nothing happened to him."

"Then where is he?" Christina asked again.

"He's at the St. James."

"The St. James Hotel?" Christina asked.

Louise nodded.

"Here in Selma? What's he doing here?"

"I called him and told him about you. He wanted to meet you, so he came here."

He's here. My father's here, she thought. "You what?" she asked.

"I called him."

"You should have talked to me about this first, Mother."

"No, this was my decision."

Christina spoke rapidly, her words matching the beat of her heart. "What's he doing here?"

"I told you he wants to meet you."

"Why?"

"You'll have to ask him that. He's coming for dinner tonight."

"Tonight?" It was too soon. She needed time to prepare. She

wasn't ready for this yet. "How did you know I'd be back tonight?"

"I didn't. It was just going to be the two of us. He wants to know more about you. Now, he can go directly to the source."

Christina couldn't speak. She was going to have dinner with her father tonight. She was going to see him for the first time. She looked at the clock on the wall. It was five o'clock. "What time is he coming?"

"He'll be here around six."

That's not long, she thought. Then she commented, "You aren't excited or nervous about this. Why is that?"

"The telephone call was the hardest part. Seeing him yesterday was easy compared to that. I look forward to seeing him tonight. I want you two to know each other."

I want that, too, Christina thought. "Don't get your hopes up too high, Mom. It's a little late for us to become a family." Having said that, she turned and left the room.

Christina found herself watching for him. She passed the front window more times than necessary and stopped to peek out each time. She couldn't keep still. I hope he likes me, she thought, then chided herself for the thought. She didn't like how important this night was turning out to be. A car pulled into the driveway then. Christina stepped back from the window. If it was him, she didn't want him to see her looking. A tall, sandy-haired man stepped out of a blue four-door Chevy sedan.

She watched him stride up the walkway to the door and ring the doorbell. I should answer it, she thought, then decided against it. He rang the bell once more before Louise opened the door. Christina heard Louise lead him into the living room, but she couldn't hear what they were saying. While she was debating whether to go in now or to wait, Louise came to get her.

"He's here, Christina," Louise said, "and he's eager to meet you."

Christina took one step toward her mother, then stopped. She couldn't do it.

"What's the matter?" Louise asked.

"I'm scared, Mom. When I was small I used to dream that he wasn't really dead. That he would come back for me. Now that he's here, I'm scared. What if we don't get along?"

Tears formed in Louise's eyes. "He already loves you, Christina. He loves you because you're his daughter. He just wants to get to know you."

"I've wanted a father for so long. What if he can't be what I want him to be?"

"You can't make up for the time you were apart, and I'll always blame myself for that, but you can start something new here today. Don't you want to try?"

Christina didn't say anything. Louise extended her hand and Christina took it. They walked into the living room together.

Christian stood as they walked in the room. He smiled. "Hello, Christina. I'm Christian."

Relief washed over her. One of her worries was what to call him. His introduction made it easy. "Hello, Christian."

Louise ushered Christina into the room so the two of them stood facing Christian. "I'll get tea." She looked at Christian. "You still drink tea, don't you?"

Christina could have sworn that her mother blushed when he nodded. She watched as Louise left the room.

"She's giving us some time alone," he stated.

Christina looked at him and knew where she got her height from. And the texture of her hair. "I know."

"Shall we sit then, and get to know each other a little bit?"

Christina sat, but she could think of nothing to say. Fortunately, Christian could. "Louise tells me that you're on a leave of absence from your job. Are you enjoying yourself?"

Christina wondered what else her mother had told him. "I needed the break. I'm something of a workaholic."

Christian smiled at that. "I can believe that. I'm known to be somewhat of a workaholic myself."

"Mom says you have a law practice in Chicago. What's that like?"

"I like it. I've been doing it for nearly thirty years now."

"What kind of law?"

"Family law."

"Divorce?" This was stupid. She really didn't care about his law practice.

"Some divorce. I also do estate planning, wills, adoptions. That kind of thing."

"Did you love my mother?" Christina surprised herself with the question.

"Very much," Christian answered. "I've never loved anyone else."

"What did you think when she called you?"

"Shocked. Angry. Scared. Expectant. All those emotions."

Christina relaxed then. "I felt the same when she told me about you. I used to dream about you when I was a little girl."

"I bet you never quite pictured me, though."

Christina smiled because he did. "You're right about that. I imagined you were tall, though. I always thought I got my height from my dad."

"I thought that when I first saw you myself. You've probably been taller than Louise for a long while."

Christina nodded and laughed softly. "I passed her around eighth grade."

"Have you forgiven her yet?"

"She told you?"

He nodded. "She loves you a lot. She made a mistake, but she had the best intensions. At the time, it was all she knew to do."

"I'm not the only one she lied to. Have you forgiven her?"

"In my case there was nothing to forgive. I was there. I understand the pressure she was under. I regret not spending my life with the two of you. I was angry and hurt that Louise didn't feel confident enough to tell me she was pregnant, but I understand. I blame myself, anyway."

"Why is that?" Christina asked. How could he blame himself if he didn't even know?

"In my day, a man showed his love for a woman by waiting

until marriage. We didn't do that. If we had, none of this would have happened."

"And maybe I never would have been born."

Christian smiled again. "I like to think that you would have been born, but you'd have been born to a family, a mother and a father, who cherished you. I envy Louise the time she had with you."

"She was a great mother to me," Christina said. Her anger subsiding now.

"That doesn't surprise me. She's a great woman."

Christina detected that Christian's feelings for Louise were still strong. "What was she like when you met her?"

"She hasn't changed. She's as beautiful now as she was then, and unless I'm mistaken, she's as strong-willed now as she was then."

Christian smiled and Christina felt they were sharing a secret. It was a good feeling.

"She is," Christina agreed. "She's always done things her own way, been her own person. And she's managed to be happy."

"She tells me you're a lot like that yourself. You've built quite a career for yourself."

"I've done well in my profession, but there's more to life than work."

He nodded. "There should be. I've found that work can fill up a lot of places when other parts of your life aren't working right."

"Right about what?" Louise asked, when she walked back into the room with the tea.

"Christina and I were just comparing notes on work," Christian answered.

Louise set the tray on the cocktail table. "Things must be changing, since you both have taken leaves from your work."

Christina looked at Christian. This was the first she had heard about a leave. "How long are you planning to be away?" she asked.

Christian looked from Louise to Christina. "As long as it takes for me to get to know you. I've got nothing but time."

Christina was at a loss for words. She didn't know what to think.

"I think I'm the real winner in this," Louise said with a lilt in her voice. "I get to have time with both of you."

Christina looked at Louise. Her mother wore a shy smile. She looked at Christian. He wore a contented smile. What's going on here? she wondered.

Chapter 23

"How is she?" Jackson had been on the phone with Robert for almost fifteen minutes. He couldn't wait any longer.

"She?"

"You know I'm talking about Christina." Jackson hated putting Robert in the middle like this, but he needed to know.

"She's fine. Why do you ask?"

"She was in Boston last week and she came by my apartment." Jackson couldn't shake the feeling that Christina had wanted to discuss something important with him. When she saw Angela, she had closed up.

"What happened?"

"Nothing happened. I'm trying to figure out why she came by. Do you know anything?"

"Not really," Robert said slowly.

Jackson didn't believe him. "Come on, man. I need to know."

"Why do you need to know? I thought you and Christina had broken up. Liza said you were seeing Angela again."

News travels fast, Jackson thought. "I was seeing Angela, but I'm not anymore. I'm still in love with Christina, Robert. I need to know if there's still a chance for us."

"Then shouldn't you be talking to her?"

"Yes, but she's not talking to me these days."

"What happened?"

If he asks one more question, I'm hanging up, Jackson thought. "Angela was here when she came to visit. I could tell she wanted to tell me something, but after she saw Angela in my apartment, she changed her mind."

"Oh, man, do you have bad timing!"

"Tell me something I *don't* know," Jackson said. "What's going on, Robert? Do you have any idea why she was here?"

"Did you know that she has taken a leave of absence from CL?"

Walter and Rosalind didn't talk to him about Christina anymore. They kept this news from him as well. "A month or so ago. Liza took her old job. She's pretty excited about it, too."

"Give her my congratulations," Jackson said absentmindedly.

"And we've moved into her house in Decatur," Robert added.

"You've moved into her house? Where is she? Why did she take a leave of absence?"

"You should be having this conversation with her, Jackson," Robert said.

"You do know something, don't you?"

"I may have heard something from Liza," Robert said. It was obvious he didn't want to give away any information.

"Come on, man," Jackson pleaded. "This is important."

"She's pregnant, Jackson."

Jackson jumped up from his chair. "Pregnant? Christina?"

"Yes."

"When? Who?" Jackson asked, but he already knew the answers.

"I'd think that you'd know that better than me."

"Are you sure? She's pregnant?"

"That's why she took the leave. She wanted to get away…"

Jackson sat down. *God, did I have bad timing. First I need space, and then those damn roses.* "She didn't want me to know, did she?"

"You really should be having this conversation with her, Jackson. I only know bits and pieces."

Christina came to tell me about the baby, Jackson concluded. In spite of all that had happened between us she wanted me to know about the baby. That meant there was still a chance for us. "That's all right, man. You've helped a lot."

"What are you going to do?"

I've got to move fast, Jackson thought. First, I've got to find out who sent those roses. "I don't know yet, but I'm not going to let her keep me away from my child. I'm going to be a father." Jackson thought back to Christina's visit. She hadn't been showing then. "Do you know how far along she is?"

"No, man. I've told you all I know."

"I appreciate it, Robert. Thanks a lot."

Jackson continued to hold the phone to his ear even after Robert hung up. I'm going to be a father, he thought. Christina and I have made a baby. The recording signaled him to hang up.

He wondered what kind of father he'd be. He'd be better than his father, that's for sure. His father. Today was the first Sunday of the month and Jackson had yet to call his dad. Now is as good a time as any, he thought. He picked up the phone again.

"Good morning, Dad."

"Good morning yourself, Jackson. How you doing?"

His dad was sober. "I'm doing great, Dad. I've got some news for you. I'm going to be a father."

"A father? I didn't even know you were married."

"I'm not yet, Dad, but I soon will be."

"Who is she?"

"Her name's Christina."

"I don't recall you mentioning her before. How long have you been seeing this woman?"

"For a while now. I just haven't talked much about her."

"Do you love her, son?"

"I do, Dad. I love her a lot." The words seemed inadequate to express the depth of the feelings he had for Christina.

"Be careful. I loved your mother, too."

That was the closest thing to criticism his father had said about his mother in a long while. Maybe he was getting over her, Jackson thought. He wasn't going to bet on it, though. "I know, Dad."

"A woman can hurt you real bad, Jackson. You be careful."

"You'll have to meet Christina. She's not like that. We're going to be together forever." Jackson prayed he was right.

"Just be careful, son."

"I will, Dad." Now that he was an expectant father, Jackson wanted a better relationship with his own dad. "What are you doing next weekend?"

"Nothing much."

"How about my coming for a visit?" Jackson hadn't seen his father in more than two years.

"I'd like that, son. I'd like that a lot."

Jackson heard the surprise in his dad's voice and he smiled.

"Your move," Jackson's father, Jim, said.

Jim and a friend had been playing checkers on the porch when Jackson drove up. After the friend had left, Jim coaxed Jackson into a game. Jackson wasn't playing very well. He was distracted because he still hadn't come up with a plan for finding out who had sent the roses. He moved one of the red men without much thought.

"How long are you gonna be staying?" Jim asked.

He had an appointment with a private investigator Monday morning. "I'll be leaving tomorrow afternoon."

"That's a short time to stay after such a long flight. You must have plenty of money." Jim jumped two of Jackson's men.

"I do all right, you know that." Jackson studied the board. He didn't have a free move left. He could only prolong the inevitable.

Jim nodded. "Always knew you'd do good for yourself."

Jackson was surprised at that comment. Jim didn't hand out praise often. "Did you, Dad?"

"Too stubborn not to do good." Jim jumped all of Jackson's men with a single man. The game was over. "But you didn't do too well in this game."

"I was not stubborn," Jackson argued.

Jim began setting the board up for the next game. "Yes, you were, too. When you got something on your mind you were like a dog with a bone. Wouldn't give up until you had it whipped."

Jackson was surprised at the pride on his father's face. He couldn't recall ever seeing it before.

"Remember when you first joined the track team?" Jim continued.

"Yeah, I remember. You told me I wasn't going to be any good."

Jim laughed at that. "Proved me wrong, though, didn't you? Came in first in every race."

"I didn't even know you kept up with the races." Jim had never come to any of his meets.

Jim smiled as if remembering. "I knew about 'em, all right."

Jackson could only stare at his dad. He wondered at his dad's tone. He sounded as if Jackson should have known that he kept up with his activities. "You never mentioned them to me."

Jim picked up a checker and twirled it in his hand. "We argued about everything back then."

Not everything, Jackson thought, *someone*. "You still love her, don't you?"

Jim didn't answer immediately. "Too much." He was quiet again. "And too long."

Jackson agreed. "Don't you think it's time you stopped?"

Jim pointed to his heart. "I loved your mama way down in here."

Jackson didn't think Jim had really tried to get over Sarah, but he didn't want to get Jim on his soapbox about her, so he changed the subject. "How about me taking you out to dinner? Catfish?"

"Your mama made the best catfish in town. Did I tell you that?"

Jackson groaned. It was going to a long visit.

"So she thinks you've been sending the roses?"

Jackson had been determined not to spend the entire dinner listening to Jim cry over Sarah, but he couldn't believe he'd told Jim the full story of him and Christina. "That's what she thinks all right."

"If you ask me, any woman who'd believe something like that about her man doesn't know what love is. I say, be glad to get rid of her."

That wasn't the response Jackson wanted. "I'm not exactly rid of her, Dad. She's pregnant, remember?"

"How do you know it's yours?"

There'd never be any doubt about that. "It's mine, all right."

"You'd best be careful, boy. Women, these days, you can't trust 'em. They'll do about anything to get a man."

Jackson put two hushpuppies in his mouth to give him time to prepare a suitable response to Jim's negative comments. "Christina doesn't need to trap a man, Dad. She doesn't need me." That's the problem, Jackson added to himself.

"Don't be too sure about that. She don't have no man, does she?"

Jackson knew this conversation was going nowhere. "How about apple pie for dessert? They used to have the best in town."

Jim nodded. "They have good apple pie, right enough, but your mama made the best apple pie, in town."

"How did you know where to find me?" Christina asked. She had just come in from a day at the nursery.

"I ran into Angela in the Atlanta Airport last weekend," Reggie answered.

She sat down in the chair next to the telephone table. "Angela told you were I was?" She wondered if Angela had also told Jackson.

"She mentioned it in passing. She was on her way to Boston."

That figures, Christina thought. Angela must have found out from the Radio-thon Committee. "You were in Atlanta?"

"No," Reggie answered. "I was on my way to D.C. I'm spending a lot of time in airports these days. As a matter of fact, I'm in one now."

"Where are you?"

"Montgomery."

"Montgomery? What are you doing in Montgomery?"

"I'll give you three guesses."

Christina didn't need three guesses. "Reggie…"

"If you invite me to dinner, I can be there in less than ninety minutes."

Two hours later they were seated in Rob's Steakhouse. "I thought you were going to cook for me."

Christina laughed at that. "I don't cook anymore."

"How are you going to be a good mom if you don't cook?"

Christina had been pleased with Reggie's response to her pregnancy. He had looked at her and smiled. Her emotions had gotten the best of her and she had begun to cry. He had pulled her into his arms and let her do just that and he hadn't asked any questions…yet. "I didn't say I can't cook, I said I don't cook. Anyway, I can handle milk and formula. How many babies do you know that come here eating solid food?"

"You have a point there," Reggie conceded. "But they tell me babies move from milk to solid food pretty fast."

"I don't think that's a problem. Mom can cook and she's going to spoil this baby rotten."

"Aren't you going back to Atlanta and your job after the baby is born?"

Christina leaned back against the booth. She had thought a lot about that. She didn't know if she could go back to the memories and she didn't know if she wanted to go back to CL. "I don't know. It surprises me, but I really don't miss work. I thought I would."

"What would you do?"

Christina pushed her plate away. "Oh, I don't know. There are a lot of things I could do. I could go into business with my mom. She's thinking about opening another nursery in Montgomery."

"You could go from being a top business executive to running a small nursery?"

"In a heartbeat. I've even thought about opening a preschool. That way I could be with my baby all day."

Reggie reached over and took her hand. "I knew it."

"Knew what?"

He squeezed her hand before letting go and settling back in his chair. "You're more like my mom than I thought."

She remembered him telling her something like that before. "Maybe a little."

"More than a little. Don't tell me you haven't thought about being a full-time mom."

"More like dreamed about it. That's not a choice for a single mom, though."

"You don't have to be single," Reggie said.

"I've decided. Jackson's not going to be a part of this baby's life." She had come to her decision and she didn't want to get into a discussion of Jackson and the baby. She'd had that conversation often enough with her mother.

"I'm not talking about Jackson."

Christina didn't know what to say. "Reggie, you can't be serious."

"Oh, but I am," he said.

She placed her hand on her extended belly. "Why would you want a wife who's pregnant with another man's child?"

"I don't want a woman who's pregnant with another man's child. I want you, and I'll love this baby like my own."

This was all happening too fast for Christina. "You only found out about the baby today. How can you make such an offer?"

"I've been in love with you for a while, Christina. You know that."

She did know it. "I know, but…"

"There are no buts. My hat's in the ring. I want to marry you. I want to have other babies with you. Now what do you want?"

She wanted marriage and she wanted a family. But she also wanted it with a man she loved, and she didn't love Reggie. "This isn't right, Reggie."

"It *is* right, Christina. You can turn me down, but you can't ignore my proposal. We can go shopping for a ring tomorrow."

"Reggie—" she began.

He interrupted her. "Don't turn me down out of hand. Think about it. We could have a good life together. I love you. You like me. You could grow to love me."

"It's too much," she said.

"All I ask is that you think about it. Will you do that?"

She saw the sincerity in his eyes and nodded. "I'll think about it."

* * *

"He's a nice man," Louise said later, after Reggie had brought Christina home. He had stayed awhile, talking with them.

"He asked me to marry him."

Louise put down the paper she was holding. "What?"

"He asked me to marry him."

"Doesn't he see that you're pregnant?"

Christina put her hand on her stomach. "The man isn't blind. He sees."

"The baby isn't his."

"He's not stupid, either. He knows the baby isn't his."

"You told him no, of course."

Christina put her feet up on the ottoman. They tended to swell by the end of the day. "I tried."

"What do you mean, you tried? Either you told him or you didn't. Which is it?"

"I didn't exactly tell him no," Christina explained. The more she thought about Reggie's proposal, the more she convinced herself that it wasn't such a bad idea. A lot of marriages started with less than the friendship she and Reggie shared. Maybe they could make it...maybe...

"What did you tell him?"

"I agreed to think about it."

"I don't believe this, Christina. You can't seriously be thinking of marrying this man when you're carrying Jackson's baby."

"I don't know, Mother. Maybe I am."

"This isn't right, Christina. You need to tell Jackson about this baby."

"I'm not getting into that with you again. As for Reggie's proposal, I'm thinking about it."

"I don't believe you."

"I'm not thinking seriously about it, but I am thinking about it. Is that so wrong, Mom? He loves me."

"Do you love him?"

No, I don't love him. "I could love him if I tried."

"Sometimes you're so young, Christina. Love doesn't happen that way."

Reggie spent the next day at the nursery, helping Christina do the books. "Has your mother ever thought about expanding out West? Oklahoma City could use more nurseries."

Christina looked up from the ledger she was working on. "Reggie…"

"Just trying to help you make a business decision. Maybe I should talk to Louise about this."

"Maybe you shouldn't."

He laughed. "Maybe you're right. Last night I thought she liked me, but this morning she treated me like I have the plague.

"Let me guess. She doesn't think it's a good idea?"

Christina smiled at him. "Let's just say she thinks it's bad timing."

"The baby?"

She nodded. "And the baby's father."

Reggie got up from the desk where he was working and walked over to the table where Christina sat clipping stems. "We haven't talked about that."

"I know, and I'm glad."

"Why haven't you told him?"

She remembered Angela in the towel. There was no way she could share her baby with Jackson and Angela or whoever he chose as his wife. No, that would be too painful for her. "Jackson has moved on with his life. I'm his past. The baby was an accident. Why should it haunt him now?"

"Is that what the baby is to you, an accident?"

"No." This baby was her life now. She loved it already. She'd transferred all the love she had for Jackson to their baby. It didn't end the pain and hurt she still felt, but it did lessen it.

"Then why do you think he would look at it like that?"

Christina didn't like the way the conversation was progressing. She didn't want to think about Jackson and Angela. It was all she could do to take care of her own feelings. "Do you really want me to tell him?"

Reggie moved closer. "No."

Christina turned to look at him. She hadn't expected his honestly. "Then why are we having this discussion?"

Reggie scratched his chin. "Want to get married?"

She threw a plant stem at him.

Five weeks passed and Jackson was no closer to finding out who'd sent the roses than when he'd started. He hadn't talked to Christina, and he was getting restless. He needed to see her, but he was afraid to go to her without having some concrete information about those roses. He'd have a hard enough time explaining what had gone on with Angela. He picked up the phone and dialed. He was glad to hear Robert's voice. He got right to the important stuff. "What's the latest on Christina?"

"You haven't talked to her?"

"No. There are some loose ends that I need to tie up before I see her."

"You'd better hurry up and tie them. Christina's engaged. She might even be married by now."

Jackson jumped out of his chair. "Engaged? What the hell are you talking about?"

"Don't yell at me, man. I'm just telling you what I heard. She's getting married."

Jackson pinched his nose with his fingers. Things have gone from bad to worse. "To who?"

"I don't know. Liza doesn't tell me anything. She doesn't want us in the middle."

"How would you two get in the middle?"

"You know, her taking Christina's side and me taking your side."

"You're not taking sides. You're doing the right thing. I was supposed to know about the baby. It's also my right to know about this engagement. She can't be engaged when she's pregnant with my baby."

"I'm just telling you what I heard."

Jackson sat down again. He needed to be calm if he was going to get the information he wanted. "Who is he? She couldn't have met somebody new this quickly, could she?"

"Maybe it's somebody she already knew. I don't know, man."

"I can't believe she'd actually plan to marry somebody else and keep my child from me. That doesn't sound like Christina."

"Maybe I got it all wrong. Maybe she's not engaged."

Jackson didn't believe that. Christina was engaged. She was going to have the baby without telling him. And she was going to marry some man and give that man his child. "Thanks for the info, buddy. I owe you one," he said.

Jackson hung up the phone slowly. "So Christina is planning to get married. Over my dead body."

Chapter 24

Christian walked up behind Louise and placed his hands on her shoulders. "You can't live her life for her, Louise."

Louise leaned back against him. "I want her to be happy, Christian. I don't want her to make the same mistakes that I did."

Christian gently turned Louise around. "It's her decision."

"I know, but can you believe she's really thinking about marrying this Reggie character?"

Christian spoke calmly. "He's a good enough fellow. You can see that he loves her."

"She doesn't love him, though. She's still in love with Jackson."

"How can you be so sure? She and Reggie get along very well. And he's excited about the baby. He's been there for her. That has to count for something."

"He's a good friend. You can't build a marriage on that. You need the passion."

"Are you talking about Christina or yourself?"

He was right…she was thinking about herself. She'd never married because she'd never felt the passion she felt with Christian with anyone else. "I'm talking about Christina."

Christian put his arms around her waist and pulled her to him. He placed his chin on her head. "You still feel it, too, don't you?"

Louise placed her hands on his. "It's almost like it was yesterday."

"I love you, Louise."

She knew it. She had known it from the first phone call. Theirs was a forever love. "I love you, too."

She knew he was going to kiss her. She leaned up on her toes as he leaned down to her. He tasted the same. She remembered it. She lifted her arms around his shoulders. He was bigger, wider, more muscular. He had been a boy then; he was a mature man now.

When he lifted his head, she saw tears in his eyes. She wiped them away with her fingers and smiled. "Now, what are we going to do about our daughter?"

Christina placed her hand on her abdomen. "Reggie, it's moving. My baby's moving."

Reggie moved his hand next to hers. "Let me feel."

She looked at Reggie's hand resting next to hers. "It's a miracle."

Reggie moved his hand across her belly. "I don't feel anything."

"He's stopped," Christina said. "You missed it."

Reggie pulled his hand away. "What did it feel like?"

Christina smoothed down her top. It felt like she had a bad case of gas. "It felt like...I can't describe it. It felt like something moving inside me."

"Next time, tell me as soon as it starts."

She put her hands on Reggie's face. "You're disappointed, aren't you?"

He placed a hand atop hers, but didn't say anything.

"What are you thinking about?" she asked.

He looked at her. "Are you going to marry me, Christina?"

"That's not the right answer for either of us, Reggie."

"It is. I already love this baby and he's not even born yet. And you know I love you. I'd be a great father and a great husband."

"But I don't love you," she whispered.

"I think you do," Reggie responded. "You can't tell me that you don't feel more for me now than you did a few months ago."

Christina knew her feeling for Reggie had intensified. He had been there when she'd needed him. That meant a lot. But. There was always a but. Jackson. He was never out of her thoughts.

How could she marry someone else when she was carrying Jackson's child? Their child. "You're right. I do feel more for you now, but how do you know that it's love?"

"It's a start." He leaned in closer to her. "I can help you forget him, if you let me."

She wondered if he knew how often she thought about Jackson. She pulled her hands away and looked at her stomach. "How could you do that? The baby is his. I can never forget him."

"Maybe you don't want to forget him."

The accusation in his voice surprised her. "What does that mean?"

"You have to start living your life, Christina. If you want Jackson, you should go to him. If you don't want him, you've got to stop pining for him. It's not helping you. And it's not helping the baby."

Christina had said as much to herself. "I'm not going to tell him."

"Then you've got to start thinking about this baby and what you want. The baby needs a father."

"That's where you're wrong. I can provide everything this baby needs."

"I know you're more than able to provide financially for you and the baby. You even have enough love to give, but that's not enough for you."

She had to hand it to him, he knew her well. "I don't know. That sounds like all the bases have been covered. What more could I want?"

"You want the little white house with the picket fence. You want a traditional family."

"You know a lot about what I want. What do you want?"

"I want what you want. I want what my mom and dad have."

Christina massaged her stomach. "Sometimes I think I'm trying to make up for my childhood. I want to give my baby what I didn't have, and that's a father."

"I can be that father."

She stood then. "You don't understand, Reggie. I want it all. I want passion. I want fireworks."

Reggie stood next to her. "What about commitment? What about being there? Don't they count?"

"Why do you want to marry a woman who keeps telling you she doesn't love you?"

"That's an easy one. As I said before, I think you do love me. We have different definitions of love. If you can stop fantasizing about Jackson long enough, you'll see that we have more than enough to build a life together. Can you do that? Can you stop the fantasies?"

The following week Christian came to visit Christina at the nursery.

"You've been away from your work a long time," Christina said to him. "If you're away any longer, you may lose all your clients."

Christian leaned against the counter and watched Christina sort the day's mail. "I doubt that. I haven't taken a real vacation in the last twenty-five years. This time has been good for me. It's been more than worth whatever it may cost me in clients."

Christina saw the sincerity in his eyes. "Do you still love her?"

"I've loved her forever," Christian said, the love evident in his eyes. "That's why I've never married. Louise was my first and only love."

"If you loved her, really loved her, you could have come back for her."

Christian had wondered the same thing over the years. Had he been a coward? "The world was a lot different then. Louise and I knew our chances were slim. The only way it would work was with one hundred and fifty percent from both of us. When I got her letter, I knew it was over. I couldn't fight her, my parents, her parents, and God. It was best to leave it alone."

"So what's going to happen now?" Christina asked.

"I'm going to spend as much time as possible getting to know my two girls."

"Your two girls?"

"Yes, you and your mother. I know it's too late for me to be a father to you, Christina. Louise has raised you well. You're a beautiful woman and you don't need me. Not as a father. I would like to be your friend, though. Do you think that's possible?"

Christina wasn't so sure she didn't need a father. She looked up at him with hope in her eyes. "I don't know how to go about being your daughter, either, Christian. I think friends may be a pretty good place to start."

Jackson saw them through the front window. His first thought was that this was the man Christina was going to marry. He couldn't hear them, but he recognized the look in the old man's eyes. It was love, pure and simple. Christina's eyes showed a deep caring. Jackson shook his head. An old white guy. Who would have thought it? What could she possibly see in this guy? he wondered. Well, he was going to put a stop to this right now.

The chimes sounded when he entered. They both turned to look at him. The man's eyes were clear. Christina's registered astonishment and something else he couldn't quite place. Probably guilt, he reasoned.

"Surprised to see me, Christina?" Jackson asked. "I really don't know why." He looked at Christian, then he allowed himself a long look at Christina's extended belly. It hit him that she was carrying his child. That belly carried the result of their love. He wanted to reach out and touch it. He looked back up into Christina's eyes. "You're carrying my baby." He looked again at Christian. "You did know it was mine, didn't you?' He extended his hand. "I'm Jackson Duncan. Who are you?"

Before Christian could answer, Christina asked, "What are you doing here, Jackson?"

"Where else would I be darling?" His words dripped with sugar. "You're here, the baby's here. It's only natural that I'd want to be with my family."

"Your family? What are you talking about?"

He looked directly into her eyes, daring her to challenge him. "The three of us. You, the baby, and me. We're a family. I figure we'd better have the wedding pretty soon, though." He nudged Christian. "The preacher ought to beat the stork, if you know what I mean."

Christina stood staring at him. "Have you gone crazy? How dare you come walking in here, talking about a family? How dare you make any claim to me or my baby? You can leave now."

Jackson controlled his anger. He was going to play this scene his way. "I know you're upset it's taken me so long to get here, sweetheart, but I'm here now and we'll never be apart again."

"Uggg…" was all Christina could say. She looked at Jackson, then at Christian, then stormed out to the office in back of the nursery.

Jackson watched her waddle away. He had definitely ruffled her feathers. He glanced at the other man, who also watched her. Jackson took this opportunity to study the man. He didn't appear too upset by the things Jackson had said and he still had that dumb love look on his face. "I'll ask again," Jackson said. "Who are you and what are you doing here with Christina?"

Christian smiled as he answered. "I'm Christian Van Dorne, Christina's father."

Jackson couldn't believe his ears. "Christina's *father?*"

"Who else would I be?"

Jackson spoke before thinking. "I thought you were the man she planned to marry."

Christian shrugged, but kept smiling. "And I thought you said she was going to marry you."

"I know what I said. If you're not the man she's planning to marry, who is?"

"You'll have to ask her that."

Jackson wondered what the guy was smiling about. "You're her father?"

Christian nodded. "That I am."

"I thought her father was dead."

"As you can see, I'm very much alive."

"How can you be her father?" Jackson asked. The man was white, after all.

"Young man, if you don't know the answer to that, you're in

much more trouble than I think you're in." Christian inclined his head toward the back room.

"She didn't look too happy to see me. Did she?" Jackson asked.

Christian shook his head slowly. "Happy is not the word I'd use."

"Maybe I should go back there and talk to her?"

Grabbing Jackson's arm as he turned to go after Christina, Christian asked, "Want some advice?"

"Given the way this has started, I need all the help I can get. What's your advice?"

"Don't go in there now. She was shocked to see you. Give her some time to get her feelings together. She, her mother, and I are having dinner tonight. Why don't you join us? I know Louise would love to meet you."

Jackson wondered at the man's helpfulness. "Tonight? I have to wait until tonight?"

"That's best. You could probably use the time to do some adjusting of your own. You won't be able to browbeat her into doing what you want. You need to come up with another strategy."

Jackson didn't like having his style critiqued. "Why are you being so helpful?"

"She's my daughter. I want her to be happy, and she has to reconcile her feelings for you if she's going to be happy."

Jackson nodded. Maybe this guy would turn out to be an ally, he thought. "Are you going to tell me about this guy who wants to marry her?"

Christian shook his head. "I can't do that, son. That's between you and her."

Jackson looked closely at Christian. "Are you sure you're her father?"

Christian laughed.

Christina heard the chimes again. She hoped Jackson was leaving. She tensed up when she heard the office door open.

"He's gone, Christina," Christian said. "You can come out now."

"You make it sound like I'm hiding. I'm working."

Christian walked all the way into the room. "What are you working on? That book in front of you is upside down."

Christina looked up at Christian. "Okay. I was hiding. What did he say before he left?"

Christian shrugged. "Nothing much."

"Oh…"

"I invited him to dinner with us tonight."

Christina tried to jump out of her seat, but her stomach was a hindrance. She eased herself up instead. "You *what?*"

"I invited him to dinner with us tonight."

"You had no right to do that!"

"I'm sure Louise wants to meet him."

"Then the three of you can go to dinner. I'll stay home."

"If that's what you want."

Christina had expected Christian to offer to withdraw Jackson's invitation. "You don't want me to come? I thought this was a family dinner."

"You can't keep running from the man, Christina."

"Why can't I?"

"Because it's his baby."

"It always comes back to that, doesn't it?"

Christian nodded. "As it should."

Christina wondered if Christian was talking from his experience with Louise. "It would have been so much easier if he'd stayed away."

"You really think so?"

Christina sighed. "Not really."

"Do you still love him?"

"I don't know how I feel. This morning I was seriously considering Reggie's proposal. Now Jackson's here. It complicates things."

"You were really thinking about marrying Reggie?"

Christina sat down again. "Not really. I don't love him that way."

"Does Reggie know how you feel?"

She nodded. "I've told him more than once."

"And he still wants to marry you? He must love you a lot."

"I've told him it's crazy, but he won't listen. He's turned into a great friend, but it'll never be more than that. I know that now for sure."

"Because of Jackson?"

Christina covered her face with her hands. "I still love him. I never stopped. I knew it from the moment he walked into the shop. I guess I always knew it."

"Then why are you fighting it so hard? Being in love should make you happy."

She dropped her hands from her face. "Only if the person you're in love with is in love with you."

"And you don't think Jackson is in love with you?"

How she wished it were true. "He took his own good time getting here, didn't he?"

"You can't very well hold that against him. You didn't tell him about the baby. How did he know you were here?"

Her first thought was Liza or Robert. Most likely Robert. Maybe Angela. But she didn't like to think of Angela and Jackson together. "I don't know. My guess would be that friends in Atlanta told him."

"From his display of ownership when he walked in here, my guess is he loves you, too."

Christina wished Christian was right, but she couldn't bet on it. "There's a lot you don't know about Jackson and me. It's a lot more complicated than that."

"Do you want to talk about it? I'm a good listener. That's what friends are for."

Christina really didn't want to talk now, but there was something Christian could do for her. "Could you hold me for a while? I could use a good cry about now."

Christian walked over and for the first time in his life, he pulled his daughter into his arms. It felt good. It felt right.

Christina's tears started immediately. She cried for herself and Jackson, for her and her father, and for her mother and her father. She cried for all the times as a child when she had needed her daddy to hold her. She cried until she could cry no more.

Chapter 25

Jackson broke the silence. "It was good of your parents to give us this time alone."

They could have been a little less obvious about it, Christina thought. Louise practically fawned all over Jackson throughout dinner. Then Christian's bright idea was for him and Louise to go for a walk. "Maybe they didn't do it for us. Maybe they wanted to be alone."

"Do you think they'll get back together after all these years?" Jackson asked, his gaze on her stomach.

"It looks that way." Christina wished Jackson would stop staring at her stomach. He was beginning to make her nervous.

"Theirs must be a really strong love. If circumstances had been different, your parents would have been married for more than thirty years now."

"Thirty years is a long time." Not as long as Reggie's parents, she thought, but a long time. "I heard that you had been to Oklahoma City."

"I was out there. How did you find out?"

"Reggie told me."

Jackson lifted his gaze to her face. Reggie. He wondered why it hadn't occurred to him earlier. "You've seen Reggie?"

She nodded. "He's visited."

"He's been here, to Selma?"

Her nod was so slight he almost didn't see it.

Jackson moved from the chair across from her to sit on the couch next to her. "What was he doing here?"

"That should be obvious. He was here to see me. We're friends."

"Friends? Nothing more?"

"Friends." No need to mention Reggie's proposal. He knew the answer, but he asked anyway. "Is Reggie the guy you were thinking about marrying?"

Christina picked up on his controlled anger and moved closer to the end of the couch, away from him. "He has asked me."

"And you're considering his proposal?"

"I don't have many options, Jackson."

"The hell you don't. You have me. I'm the baby's father."

"You have a short memory. I did come to you. You were otherwise occupied at the time." Christina could still see Angela wrapped in that towel. The pain she had felt that day was still with her. "How is Angela, by the way?"

"I wouldn't know. I haven't seen her since that day in Boston."

Christina didn't respond. Why should she believe him?

"It's true, Christina. I haven't seen her since then."

"You slept with her, though, didn't you?"

Jackson knew he'd have to answer that question. "I did, and I'm sorry it happened."

"Well, I hope you didn't tell Angela that. It's cruel, Jackson. That's not your style at all."

"You know Angela and me. I didn't have to tell her. She knew."

It still hurt that Jackson had taken Angela to his bed so soon after their breakup. "Why did you sleep with her, Jackson? Didn't what we had mean anything to you?"

He heard the pain in her voice and for the hundredth time regretted what he'd done. "I thought it was over with us. I was trying to go on with my life."

She couldn't hold that against him, since she was trying to do the same thing herself. "When did you decide it was a mistake?"

"The day you came to the apartment. I still love you, Christina. I faced it that day. There was no place for Angela in my heart. It all belongs to you."

She wanted to believe him. These were the words she had waited so long to hear. "You sound pretty fickle to me, Jackson. First, you tell me you need space. Then you sleep with Angela. Then you tell Angela it was a mistake. Now you come back telling me you want us to be a family. How do I know you won't change your mind tomorrow?"

That hurt. He deserved it, but it still hurt. "I'm not fickle, as you put it, Christina. It was easier for me to give you the 'space' story rather than discuss the real problem with you. If I had done that, maybe none of this would have happened. We'd still be together."

"What was this real problem?" Christina asked.

Jackson moved closer to her and took her hand in his. He was relieved she didn't withdraw it. "It took me a while to figure it out myself. A part of it had to do with the way our work relationship was changing."

"But I told you that I wasn't siding with Liza against you. I was just making the best decisions for the company."

"I know you said that. And it hurt me that you did."

Christina was confused now. "I didn't say it to hurt you. I was trying to reassure you."

"It wasn't reassuring to know the woman in my life thought my judgment was unsound."

"I didn't think that. In some cases, I agreed with Liza's position."

"I know. I was there. Remember?"

"I'm not understanding, Jackson."

"I felt threatened, Christina." He wouldn't let her interrupt. "I found out some things about myself that I didn't like. I felt threatened. I felt I was going to lose you."

"Now I'm really confused. You left me because you thought you were going to lose me?"

"Don't try to make sense out of it. It doesn't really make sense. I thought I was losing you and I couldn't bear to wait around for the end to come. So I bailed out first."

"I loved you, Jackson. Leaving you never crossed my mind."

"You're a pretty intimidating woman, Christina. You don't really need anybody. You could have your pick of men and I feared one day you'd think you had made the wrong choice."

Christina was beginning to understand. She knew many of Jackson's insecurities stemmed from his mother's desertion. "You could have talked about this before now. Why didn't you?"

"I tried to a couple of times."

She remembered the conversations. "You could have tried harder."

"Maybe you could have listened a little better, too?"

She thought about that. "Maybe."

"Are you going to marry Reggie?" he asked.

"No, Jackson. I'm not going to marry Reggie."

His relief was obvious. "Are you going to marry me?"

She looked at him and she thought about her parents. Did she want her and Jackson to end up like them—trying to recapture a love that they lost for no good reason? "I haven't received a proposal from you."

Jackson remembered the pain from the first time he had asked her. "Yes, you have. I asked you before and you turned me down. That's the other part of what was bothering me. After you turned me down, I became convinced that you didn't really love me."

"Oh, Jackson," Christina cried. "How could you have thought that I didn't love you? I didn't turn you down. I just said your timing was off."

Keeping her hand in his, he got down on his knees in front of her. "I love you, Christina. Will you marry me?"

"I like him. How about you?" Louise looked up at the starry sky as she and Christian walked along Main Street.

"Yes, I like him. I hope they can work out their differences."

"So do I. It's obvious he's in love with her and more than obvious that she's in love with him. One day they'll regret the time they wasted."

Christian took her hand and they continued to walk. "You're thinking about us, aren't you?"

"Their situation is like ours in many ways." She looked up at him. "There are differences as well."

"Do you think we have a chance, Louise?"

She'd been asking herself the same question. Thirty years was a long time. She was old and set in her ways, and so was he. "There are so many things to work out. Where would we live? Your business is in Chicago. Mine is here."

"People are relocating everyday. We could work that out if we wanted to. The real question is whether you want to take a chance on me again." He stopped walking and tilted her face up to look at him. "I want to spend the rest of my days with you, Louise. We can't make up for our lost past, but we can have a future together. I love you. Will you marry me?"

"I love you, too, Christian. After all these years I still love you. Though some things have changed, a lot of things remain the same."

"You're talking race now?"

"Yes. The social environment will be more tolerant, but not any more accepting than it was thirty years ago. Are you sure you want to go through that? What about your business? Would it be affected?"

"I'd like to think my clients judge me by the work that I do. Honestly, I can imagine some effects, though. I may lose a few clients, but it doesn't matter. I've managed to build a sizable business and I seriously doubt that our marriage will cause it to crumble."

If it did, you'd hate me, she thought. "What if it did? What if you lost your business?"

"That's not going to happen. If it did, it wouldn't matter. I love what I do, but I stopped doing it for the money years ago. We'll have more than enough to last us the rest of our days." He smiled then. "There'll probably be some left over for our grandchildren. Now, what's your next problem?"

Louise turned and started walking again. He kept up with her. "You aren't taking this seriously, Christian."

"Yes, I am," he corrected. "You're worrying about the wrong

thing. We made a mistake thirty years ago. Do you want to make the same one again?"

She had known that one day he'd blame her for the decision she'd made. "So, you think I was wrong not to tell you about the baby?"

"Not exactly. I think we didn't trust our love enough. I think it would have survived. It would have been difficult, but I believe we would have made it."

Tears filled Louise's eyes. "I'm so sorry, Christian," she said. "I did what I thought was best."

Christian stopped walking and pulled her into his arms. "I know you did, Louise. I'm not blaming you. You did what you had to do, and I accept that. I just don't want you to turn me away again. This is our last chance."

She knew he was right. It was a miracle they'd found each other again, a miracle their love still lasted. More than anything, she wanted to be with him. She squeezed him to her. "I love you so much, Christian, and I want to be your wife, but I need time to get adjusted to the thought of marriage." She looked up at him. "Will you give me some time?"

He smiled and she knew it was going to be all right.

Jackson scooped dirt from the barrel. Helping in the nursery was not as easy as he expected. "We haven't talked about the roses."

Christina dreaded talking about them. "I know."

"Do you still believe I sent them?"

She answered honestly. "A part of me thinks it's possible." He visibly flinched at that and she added, "Another part of me doesn't believe you would ever hurt me."

"Which part is stronger?" he asked.

She reached into her heart to find the answer. "The part that trusts you."

He visibly relaxed. "That's good to know. Now, what will it take to get rid of the doubts?"

Christina moved to sit next to him. She was amazed at how

quickly they had fallen back into their relationship. It was almost as though they'd never been apart. They were back to their preproblem days now. Only better. Now, they talked about things, especially things that hurt, instead of allowing them to fester. "Do you think we can find out who sent them?"

"I've been thinking a lot about it. Someone set me up. They wanted you to think I was sending the roses."

"Why would anyone want to do that?"

"I don't know. That's what I'm trying to figure out. Who would want to break us up?"

She spoke her first thoughts. "Reggie and Angela, but I won't believe either one of them did it."

"They crossed my mind, too, but I dismissed them immediately. Maybe the answer is professional, not personal?"

"I never considered that. So, you think someone thought that causing problems in our personal relationship would affect the work we were doing at CL?"

"Possibly. Frankly, I'd rather think that over the other. I've hired a private detective."

"When? What has he found out?"

"I hired him after I learned you were pregnant, but he hasn't come up with anything yet."

"How did you find out I was pregnant?"

"Robert."

She had guessed it was Robert. "I knew it. I knew Liza couldn't keep it from him."

"You shouldn't have kept it from me, Christina. Regardless of our problems, I deserved to know."

She knew he was right. She shuddered to think that she would have had this baby without telling him. "I know. I came to Boston to tell you, but when I found you and Angela together like that, I couldn't. If you could fall into bed with her so quickly, I began to wonder if you ever really cared for me. I couldn't risk finding out that you didn't."

"We've both made mistakes in this relationship. Let's make a pact now to keep doing what we've been doing since I've been here—talk, even when it hurts. That's the only way we're going to make it." He extended his hand to her. "Deal?"

"Deal," she said.

He pulled her into his arms and kissed her when she reached for his hand. "If you get any bigger, my arms won't go around you," he teased.

"Are you happy about the baby, Jackson? It wasn't something we planned."

He pulled back to look at her. "Very happy. I think I'm going to be a great father. I've been practicing."

She chuckled. "Practicing?"

"Yes. I even went to see my dad."

"Your dad? When?"

"Right after I found out about the baby. I don't want any estrangements in our family."

"How did it go?" she asked. She was glad that he was building bridges.

"Dad hasn't changed, but he's not so bad. I learned a lot about him that weekend. With a little training, he'll do okay as a granddad."

"It's all working out, isn't it, Jackson? You and your father, my mother and father, you and me. Everything is falling into place."

He hugged her to him. "Almost everything. We still don't know who's been sending the roses, and unless I'm mistaken, Reggie still thinks you might marry him."

She lowered her eyelids. "I don't like the idea of hurting him. He's been a good friend to me and the baby."

Jackson knew, on some level, that he should be grateful for the way Reggie had supported Christina, but he just wanted the guy out of their lives. "I don't like to think about that. I appreciate that he was there for you when you needed somebody, but I don't like that he's always hanging around you."

"Jealous?" she teased.

"Maybe. The man planned to be a father to my child. I don't like it. Did he tell you that we almost came to blows on my visit to Oklahoma City? Mr. Stevens told me to talk to you, tell you how I felt."

"You could have done that."

"Not then. My feelings about our work relationship got mixed up with my feeling about my own manhood. I needed to work that out. And the situation had been complicated by the roses. I didn't know what to do. Then the Boston job came through and I took it."

Christina put her hand to her mouth. "Your work? I had almost forgotten about that. When do you have to get back?"

"I left it open. We have to decide what we're going to do. Are you going to marry me?"

Her mind went to the roses. Her heart went to his eyes. She wanted a life with him. It all boiled down to whether she would trust him to share his life with her.

"Yes," she answered.

His eyes lit up. "When?"

"Soon."

He reached down and touched her belly. "I'd say the sooner the better."

She laughed. "I agree."

They stood holding each other for a while. "Jackson," she said. "I have to tell Reggie first."

Jackson began nibbling her on her neck. "I understand that. Tell him."

"Jackson?"

"Umm…" He was still nibbling.

"Reggie's coming to town this weekend."

Christina met Reggie at the airport. "We need to talk," she told him as soon as he greeted her. "Let's go to the lounge."

When they were seated in the lounge, Reggie said, "This has to be bad news."

Christina reached over and touched his hands. She felt the tears puddling in her eyes. "You're the best friend a girl could have, Reggie. I love you for all you've done for me and the baby, but I can't marry you."

"Has something happened?"

She nodded. "Jackson came to town a few days ago." She knew this would hurt, but she had to tell him. "I still love him, Reggie, and he loves me."

She was surprised to see a half smile form on Reggie's face. "I half expected this," he said. "I knew you loved him, I just hoped you'd get over it."

She smiled through her tears. "You don't get over love, Reggie. I hope you find someone and learn that for yourself someday. You deserve more than I could have given you."

"Is Jackson still here?"

She nodded. "He's waiting in the car. I wanted to talk with you alone."

"I'm not ready to congratulate him yet. Do you understand that?"

She did. "And so does Jackson. Neither of us wanted to hurt you."

"I know. Why don't you leave now? I could use the time alone before I take the next flight back to Oklahoma City."

"Are you sure that's what you want?"

"I'm sure," he said, and then he smiled. "You'd better get back to Jackson. He's probably thinking I've convinced you that I'm the better man. Any minute now he'll come storming through the door."

There was so much Christina wanted to say. She wanted to tell him how much he had helped her. She wanted to tell him that if it were not for Jackson she could have loved him. Instead, without saying anything, she stood up, squeezed his hand again, and left.

Tears began to fall when she thought of Reggie and Angela, two innocent people who had been hurt because they had cared for her and Jackson. She wished they could find a love like the one she and Jackson shared.

Jackson met her at the exit door. "What happened? You were gone so long I thought something happened. Why are you crying?"

"Everything's all right, Jackson," she said through her tears. "Let's go home."

Chapter 26

"Remind me never to marry a pregnant woman," Jackson teased. They were in his hotel room following their wedding.

Christina chuckled. "It's your fault. This would never have happened if we hadn't had the honeymoon before the wedding."

"I'm dying here, Mrs. Duncan, and you're making jokes."

Christina was undressing in the oversized closet. "It's funny, Jackson."

Jackson stood and began to undress. "I haven't made love to you in over seven months. That's not what I call funny."

"It is when you think about it. Just think, you only have about seven more months to go."

Jackson stopped unbuckling his pants to stare at her. "Seven more months! You must be kidding."

"Doctors don't recommend sex for six months after the baby is born," Christina stated with authority. "We've still got one month till the birth."

"When is your next check-up? Your doctor and I need to have a talk. I'm not waiting six months. Is this a woman doctor?"

Christina walked out of the closet and sat on the bed to remove her hose. She thanked God for knee-highs. "What difference does that make?"

"Big difference. Is the doctor a woman?"

"She's a woman, but…"

"But nothing. That explains it. I'll have a little talk with Madam Doctor. Six weeks maybe, but not six months."

She looked at him. "Poor Jackson. Having such a hard time dealing with marriage."

"You'd better show some more understanding, woman," he teased. "Since we haven't consummated this union, I could have this marriage annulled."

"I doubt that, once they see the pregnant wife. Maybe even a baby."

"I'm talking legal here, not moral. Treat me right, or you'll find yourself a single woman again. For starters, why don't you waddle over here and give me a kiss?"

The first time he'd said "waddle" she'd taken offense, but his continued sexual interest in her took away her concern. "I guess I can be generous with kisses, since that's all you're going to get."

When she was standing in his arms, he said, "Make it good, too."

She did. "You have to stop now, Christina. I can only take so much."

She smiled deceptively. "I have to make sure you don't lose interest in your wife who waddles, who's so big your arms won't go around her."

"I'm interested. All right. More than interested. Now, let's talk about something else before I have to take a shower."

Christina gave a quick glance and saw his problem. "Stop looking at me like that," Jackson commanded. "You're only making it worse. Now, think of something else to talk about."

Christina went to the bathroom to remove her makeup. "I'm glad your dad came to the wedding."

"Me, too." He laughed lightly. "He still thinks you tricked me into this marriage."

"Why does he think that?"

Jackson stood by the bathroom door and watched his wife. Love filled his heart. It pained him to think that they could have lost each other. "Remnants from his past, Christina. He'll come around."

"I hope so. He didn't bring up Sarah once."

Christina touched Jackson's arm. "Did you think a lot about her today?"

Jackson answered honestly. "I thought about her. A couple of times I wished she were here. Strange, huh?"

Christina shook her head. "Not strange at all." She was glad Jackson was allowing his loving feeling for Sarah to surface. Maybe one day she could be a part of their lives.

"How do you feel about your parents getting back together?" he asked.

"I'm happy for them, but I'm still getting used to my father being alive. To his being white. To his loving me. To his loving Mom. To Mom loving him."

"Don't think about it too much," Jackson said. "Consider yourself and your parents fortunate. Not many people get a second chance."

She knew he was right. She shuddered to think that they could have missed their chance. "We did."

"We were lucky, too. We came too close to losing each other."

"I like to think that we would have found our way back to each other somehow," she said.

"I'm glad we did, and I'm glad it didn't take us years. Thirty years! That's a long time to be separated from the one you love."

"I know."

Christina's thoughts went to Rosalind and Walter. She had been happy they'd made it to the wedding. Rosalind and Louise had cried buckets of tears. Christina knew Rosalind's tears were tears of sorrow as well as tears of happiness. Tears of sorrow because Rosalind knew she would never give Walter a child. Tears of happiness because Christina and Jackson had been blessed to find each other before too much time had passed. After her talk with Rosalind at the reception, Christina had sworn she would never again take her family or her family's love for granted.

Jackson came up behind her then and she shook off all thoughts that didn't include him. When she finished removing her makeup, they walked back to their bed. They lay together, she in his arms.

"I think the soccer player is acting up again," Jackson said.

"You can feel him, too?"

"How could I not? He kicks like a veteran."

"He *has* been pretty active lately. The doctor says it's normal."

"Does it bother you much?"

She shook her head. "It's reassuring to know he's moving around in there."

"We haven't thought of a name for him."

"I have. We could name him Junior."

Jackson frowned. "I don't like that. Let him have his own name."

"I'm glad you feel that way."

"You didn't want to name him Junior?"

"That wasn't my first choice. How about Marcus James?"

"For my dad?"

Christina nodded. "I know it would mean a lot to him."

He leaned down and kissed her. "Thank you. You don't think your dad will feel left out, do you?"

Christina shook her head and smiled impishly. "Christian's middle name is Marcus."

Christina went into labor exactly three weeks after her marriage. She was in labor twenty-four hours. Jackson knew she did most of the work, but he was pretty tired himself. He wouldn't have missed going through it with her for anything in the world. It was more than worth all the time he'd taken away from his work. He felt that he and Christina had brought their baby into the world together.

As Jackson looked at his wife, her parents, and their baby boy, his heart overflowed with love. His and Christina's love grew every day. He was confident their love had finally overcome all the childhood fears they had carried into adulthood.

He knew Christina's love for him was constant. She would always be there for him. He expected they would have problems, but he was confident they would meet each one head-on. He knew Christina's feelings had changed, too. She expected him to be there when she needed him, and she let him know it. That was a big move for a woman who practiced not expressing her needs for fear they wouldn't be met. Yes, he and Christina were on their way.

They still didn't know who sent the roses, but it didn't matter now. They had their new baby. All was right with the world.

Louise's baby talk ended his musing. "Isn't he the cutest baby?" she was asking.

"I've never seen a cuter one," Christian agreed.

Jackson looked at Christina. "If I didn't know they were exactly right, I'd say they were biased."

Christina laughed. "He's ours, and he *is* a cute baby. I'll agree with that."

"Have you called Jim yet, Jackson?" Christian asked. He and Louise stood on one side of Christina's bed. Jackson stood on the other.

Jackson touched his son's cheek. "Right after this little fellow was born. He got choked up when I told him the name. He's flying in tomorrow."

"I was a bit surprised at the name myself," Christian said. "You two will never know how much it means to me."

"It means a lot to us that you're here, Christian," Jackson said. "Marcus J. is going to need all his grandparents."

"We'd better get out of here and give you two some time alone," Louise said. She looked at Christian. "Buy me lunch, Grandpa?"

"I guess I can do that, Grandma." He turned to Jackson and Christina. "We'll be back later this afternoon."

Jackson watched them leave hand in hand. "We may have another wedding soon," he said to Christina. "How would you feel about that?"

"It'd be great. I think you're right. They're probably waiting for the right time to tell us."

Jackson looked at his son and then at his wife. "You've made me the happiest man in the world, Christina. I'll be good to you and the baby."

"I know you will, Jackson."

"Are you sure about moving to Boston?"

She nodded. "I'm not ready to go back to work yet. I want to spend some time with this little guy."

"You're not worried about your career?" he asked, to be sure.

She reached out and touched his chin. "Before you and," she looked down at Marcus J., "this little guy, work was all I had. That made it very important to me. It's not that important now."

"You're going to be content staying home with the baby?"

"I think so. I'll consider it my second career. If I find I'm not happy with it, I can always go back to work." At his look of uncertainty, she added, "Relax. I'm sure."

"I want you to be happy. Now that I'm sure of your love, I can handle your career. I don't want your concern for my feelings to keep you home."

His words endeared him to her even more. "That's not it," she said. "I want to stay home. I've waited all my life for what I have now. Let me enjoy it."

"If you're sure."

"I'm sure," she said. "Don't you see that everything is working out perfectly for us? We don't even have to worry about the house in Atlanta."

"Robert and Liza's offer was a great wedding gift. They love the place."

Christina nodded in agreement. "Oh, Jackson, I hope they can be happy as we are. But it looks like they're moving in different directions."

"I know. Robert wants to start a family and Liza doesn't. It's causing a strain in their relationship, because he thinks she's too wrapped up in her career."

Christina had feared that would happen. She didn't know how they were going to work it out. "I wish there was something we could do for them."

Jackson leaned down and kissed her. "There's nothing we can do. They have to work it out themselves."

Christina just nodded. More than anything, she wanted Liza and Robert to work it out. She wanted everyone to be as happy as she and Jackson were.

"What are you thinking about?" Jackson asked.

"Rosalind and Walter. Their generous donation to the radio-thon was a welcome surprise. Now, I'll be able to give a substantial donation even though I won't be able to participate."

"You're right, Mrs. Duncan, everything is working out for us."

"I'm glad you see it. Now I have a surprise for you."

"Now you're talking. I love surprises."

"I'd like to have more babies. At least two more."

Jackson leered at her. "We can start on that sooner than you thought. I talked with Dr. Gray the other day."

Christina laughed while her husband nibbled on her ear.

Jackson arrived at the hospital early the next morning. Christina and Louise had volunteered to pick up his dad at the airport so he, Christina, and the baby could have some time alone. He stopped by the nursery first. When the crib for Baby Duncan was empty, Jackson smiled and headed for Christina's room. He saw the roses when he first opened the door. He looked at the bed and saw that Christina was still asleep. The baby wasn't in the room. Fear bubbled in his stomach as he walked toward the roses.

Please, God, no. Not again.

He took the card and turned it over in his hand before opening it. *You lose, Bitch,* he read silently. He closed the card. Inside he screamed. He looked at Christina sleeping peacefully. He knew he had to wake her and tell her, but he couldn't. Not yet. Maybe he was wrong. He left the room and headed for the nurse's desk.

"The Duncan baby is not in the nursery or my wife's room. Is he taking tests or something?"

Jackson went to hell and back during the time the nurse checked. When she told him that one of the nurses had the baby, his knees buckled in relief and he had to hold on to the counter for support.

"Did you see a man take flowers to my wife's room?"

The nurse nodded. "After he delivered the flowers, he asked for directions to the nursery."

Jackson's heartbeat raced as he turned to run to the nursery. When he got there, a nurse holding a baby was arguing with an older, well-dressed man. The man's back was turned to him.

"What's going on here?" Jackson asked.

"He wants to hold your baby, Mr. Duncan," the nurse said. "I've told him it's against the rules."

The man turned then and the hate-filled look in his eyes told Jackson that this was the man who had sent the roses. "Did you leave the flowers in Mrs. Duncan's room?" Jackson asked.

"Sure I did," the man said. "There's no law against it."

Jackson drew back to hit the man, but he stopped himself. What was the point? They had the man now and the incidents would stop. He didn't want revenge. He just wanted his family safe. "Call the police," he told the nurse. "We have a criminal here."

They held a celebration in Christina's room that night. "How do you like your grandson, Jim?" Louise asked.

"Fine-looking boy," Jim said proudly.

"Good set of lungs, too," Jackson added.

"Wait until we get him home and he needs to be fed at three o'clock in the morning," Christina said. "I'll see what you think of his lungs then."

"I can hardly wait," Jackson said. He added for Christina's ears only, "I'll be able to watch my beloved wife feed our beloved son from her beloved breasts."

"If you're good, I may let you watch. Now stop being bad," Christina whispered back to him.

"They've started whispering to each other," Louise announced. "That's our cue to leave. They need their privacy."

"Don't go, Mom," Christina said, "the party's just starting. Jackson and I have the next fifty years to be together. We want you all to stay."

"If you're sure?" Louise questioned.

"We're sure," Christina said.

Jim was still holding Marcus J. "Tell us what happened with that guy and the police."

"You'd never believe it," Christina told them. Thinking about it made her shiver. "Paul Bechtel sent the roses and the notes."

"Who's Paul Bechtel?" Christian asked.

"Paul is the guy I replaced when I came to Atlanta. He couldn't find another job, and that caused him to have a nervous breakdown. In his mind, I was responsible for his problems."

"We're lucky," Louise said. "There are many stories of people losing their jobs and doing much worse."

"I had the same thought," Christina said. "I'm grateful nothing happened to us or to Marcus J. Can you believe he was actually here in the hospital? Just thinking about it gives me chills."

"How did he know when to send them?" Christian asked. "Wasn't he trying to make it look like you were sending them, Jackson?"

Jackson nodded. "He was working with Doris, my secretary. She had been his secretary when he worked at CL."

"Was she in on it, too?" Jim asked.

Jackson shook his head. "He used her to get information about Christina and me."

"Poor Doris," Christina said. "She's probably never going to gossip again. That just might kill her."

They all laughed at that. Jackson looked around the room and saw all the smiles. He was happy, happier than he'd ever thought he could be.

He saw Christian whisper something in Louise's ear.

"We have an announcement," Christian said.

Jackson looked at Christina. His eyes said, "I told you so."

"Louise and I are getting married next week."

"That's great! I'm happy for both of you," Christina said. "Come over here so I can give you a kiss."

They did just that and Christina kissed them. Jackson shook hands with Christian and gave Louis a kiss, and Jim did the same.

"Does this mean I can call you Dad now?" Christina asked Christian.

Jackson saw the tears that quickly formed in Christian's eyes.

"I think that's exactly what it means, daughter."

Chapter 27

Six months later, Christina sat on the floor of their townhouse in Boston. Marcus J. was asleep, and Jackson was at work. The house was quiet, a welcome sound to her ears. She looked at the stack of boxes before her. She opened the one closest to her and pulled out a small black notebook. She smiled when she saw it. She took it out of the box, opened it, and turned to the page entitled "Personal Goals." She read:

1. Move to Atlanta
2. Get established in job
3. Buy house
4. Get established in community
5. Make friends
6. Fall in love
7. Get married
8. Have 3 children

Christina looked at the list. She had accomplished all the items on the list but one, number eight. She didn't have three children. Yet. She was working on it, though. All her dreams were about to come true. She closed the notebook with a smile on her face. She got up and went over to her dresser. She opened the third drawer and pulled out the purple teddy with black lace. "Who knows?" She asked aloud. "Maybe tonight we'll get lucky."

FOR ALL TIME

Chapter 1

Fired. Joshua Martin couldn't believe it. After nine years of dedicated service to General Electronics, he was being fired. "When will you make the announcement?" he asked Marvin Callahan, his boss and friend. At least, he had thought Marvin was his friend.

Marvin looked away. "I'm meeting with the management Monday morning. We'll tell the staff Monday afternoon."

That's fast, Josh thought. Too fast. "When's our last day?"

"Two weeks, Josh. They're giving everybody two weeks."

Marvin continued talking, but Josh didn't hear him. I can't believe this is happening to me, he thought. Not to me. I've done everything right. I've worked hard for General Electronics, done more than was required of me. And what do I get? Two weeks' notice.

Josh shook his head. Nine years to build a career and *two weeks to watch it die.*

"The severance package isn't what it should be," Marvin was saying, "but I'm sure you won't have a problem finding another job. I'll give you an excellent recommendation."

Josh could think of nothing more to say. He straightened the tie that was now feeling tight around his neck. He needed to get out of Marvin's office. He was suffocating.

As if Marvin had heard Josh's thoughts, he stood and extended his hand. Josh took it.

"It was great working with you, son," Marvin said. "You deserve better than this."

Josh dropped Marvin's hand and headed for the door. After

he opened it, he turned and faced Marvin. "Your right, Marvin. I do deserve better than this."

Josh made the long walk back to his office, not quite believing what had happened. He had gone into Marvin's office expecting to discuss his upcoming promotion. Man, had he been wrong. He couldn't have been more wrong.

When he reached his office, Grace, his secretary and the one person who still had a job, was still at her desk. "That was a short meeting," she commented.

Josh gave her a grim smile. "Why don't you knock off for today? I'll see you Monday."

Not waiting for Grace's response, Josh walked into his office and closed the door behind him. He sat at his desk, threw back his head, and stared at the ceiling. You're no better than your father, he thought.

"Wait up a minute, Gloria."

Hearing her name, Gloria Martin turned to see her friend Portia rushing down the hallway in a swirl of flowers. Gloria shook her head. Portia and her clothes, she thought. The solid navy jacket lessened the effect, but the rainbow of colors in the drop-waist dress was eye-catching. "Hi, Portia. I haven't seen you all week. You must be very busy."

Portia tugged at the button on her jacket as if she were uncomfortable in it. "I am, girl, but no more than you. I've been trying to reach you all morning. Dexter and I are planning a dinner party two weeks from today and we want you and Josh to come."

Gloria smiled. "No can do. Josh and I will be on our second honeymoon in two weeks."

"Second honeymoon, huh? How long have you been planning this?"

When Portia reached Gloria's side, they strolled together down the hall toward their offices. "A year."

"A year?" Portia rolled her eyes. "You've only been married a year."

Gloria nodded her head. "That's right. Before Josh and I got married we decided we would celebrate every anniversary as another honeymoon."

Portia wrinkled her nose. "Whose idea was this? Yours or Josh's?"

"Josh's."

"I knew it," Portia said. "Josh is such a romantic. I've told Dexter he needs to spend more time with Josh. I'm hoping Josh will rub off on him. Dexter is about as romantic as a lamp post."

Gloria laughed at Portia's exaggeration. She knew Portia and Dexter had a good marriage and they were deeply in love with each other. "You'd better stop putting Dexter down. One of these days you're going to hurt his feelings."

A soft expression came across Portia's face. "The big lug knows I love him, but that doesn't mean he couldn't bone up a little in the romance department. All the romantic ideas are mine and that gets to be tiring."

"I can imagine."

"No, you can't," Portia said, "but thanks for saying it."

When they reached the point where they would have to part company to go to their respective offices, Gloria looked at her watch. "I have to call Josh about our dinner date tonight. Why don't you come by my office? We can catch up on the office gossip."

Gloria led the way to her office. She motioned Portia to a seat at the conference table next to her desk, then she picked up the phone.

"Hiya, handsome," she said when Josh answered.

"Hi, yourself."

Gloria noticed that Josh's voice didn't hold the contained excitement that usually marked their conversations. "Is everything all right?" she asked. "You sound funny."

"Odd you should ask that question," Josh said in a resigned voice so unlike himself. "Things could be better."

"What's wrong?" Gloria was concerned. It wasn't like Josh to be down.

"Nothing that can't wait until I see you. How about Mick's at six?"

His words didn't reassure her. "Mick's is fine, Josh. Are you sure everything is all right?"

He paused and she heard him release a deep sigh. "It's nothing that can't wait," he said. "Now get back to work. I'll see you at six."

Gloria held the phone after Josh hung up.

"Something wrong?" Portia asked.

Gloria looked upset. She had forgotten Portia was in the room. "Josh is upset about something."

Portia stood and moved toward the office door. "Call him back. We can do lunch next week and catch up on the news."

Gloria waved Portia back to the table. "There's no need for that. I'm not meeting him until six. He wouldn't tell me what's wrong over the phone anyway."

Portia remained standing. "Are you sure?"

Taking a seat at the conference table, Gloria smiled. "I'm sure. Josh will tell me over dinner. Whatever it is, we'll work it out."

Portia sat next to her. "In that case, I have some news for you."

"What did you hear?" Gloria leaned forward, eager to hear the latest gossip.

"I'm up for a promotion," Portia said, a satisfied grin on her face.

"A promotion? Portia, that's wonderful. Which department?"

Portia hesitated, then whispered, "That's where the news is. I'm not sure yet, but it'll be either Trusts or Commercial Lending."

Gloria sat back in her chair and straightened her back. "Commercial Lending? That's my department. How can you get promoted into my department? That would mean you'd get my job."

Portia's grin grew wider. "That's right. I'd get your job."

Gloria didn't say anything. She didn't know what to say.

Portia laughed then. "Don't look so confused, you goose. The word is that you or Bob in Trusts will be promoted to Commercial Investments Second Vice President."

Gloria breathed a relieved sigh. "Where did you hear this?"

"I have my sources."

Gloria studied her friend. Portia was well connected in the office grapevine, so she was usually right on the money with her news, but this news was too good to believe.

"Nothing's final," Portia cautioned her. "So don't decorate your new office yet."

Gloria laughed because Portia knew her so well. "If this news of yours is true, when will we know?"

"Two months, tops."

"Two months, huh? Well, I hope you're right. This really would be good news for us. Josh is up for a promotion, too. Wouldn't it be great if we both got promotions? We sure could use the money."

Portia rolled her eyes. "You and Josh have more money now than you can spend. What do you mean, you need the money?"

"Josh and I want to start a family soon," Gloria confided. "And when we do, I want to stay home with the kids for at least a few years. We need the money so I can do that without changing our lifestyle."

"You—a stay-at-home mom? That I can't picture."

"And why not?" Gloria knew Portia too well to be peeved by her comment, though it did rankle just a bit.

"You're too much of a career woman. I thought you'd have the baby Wednesday and be back to work Friday."

Gloria laughed at that. "At one time, maybe, but Josh and I have talked a lot about it. We both grew up in households with working mothers. Mothers who worked a lot. We don't want that for our children. Besides, I can always return to work if I change my mind or if I get bored. What about you? Have you and Dexter been talking about babies?"

Portia slid her chair closer to Gloria's. "We've been trying to get pregnant for the last six months."

"And you haven't told me?" Gloria asked with a smile. "I'm insulted."

"Don't be. We haven't told anybody. We don't want to talk about it until I'm pregnant."

Gloria saw uncertainty in Portia's face. "There aren't any problems are there?"

Portia shook her head. "I'm getting anxious, but the doctor says there's nothing to worry about yet. I've stopped taking the pill and my body has to adjust."

"You guys will get lucky soon," Gloria said, touching Portia's hand. "So, will you continue working or will you stay home?"

"That's another reason we aren't talking about it. I knew a promotion of some sort was in the works for me and I didn't want my manager to know how immediate our plans for a family were. It might make him think I'm not serious about my career."

Gloria nodded. It was the new millennium, but corporate America still functioned as though it was the Dark Ages when it came to women and pregnancies. "I know what you mean. You still haven't answered my question, though. What will you do after the baby is born?"

Portia's slight shoulders drooped and her usually bright eyes dimmed. "We haven't decided. Dexter wants me to stay home. I want to stay home for a while, but I'm not sure I could do it for more than a year. I'd miss work too much. We're considering the part-time option."

"Good for you," Gloria said. "You'll find a solution that works for both you and Dexter. All the books say the best environment for a baby is a happy home, whether that's with a working mom or a stay-at-home mom."

"I'm glad you said that. Sometimes I feel guilty about not wanting to stay home, as though I'm putting my baby second."

"Don't think that way, Portia," Gloria said. "If you stay home, stay because it makes you happy, not because you think it's expected. If you're happy, your baby will be happy."

Portia reached over and hugged Gloria. "You're a good friend. Even with all the work we have, we should make time to talk more often."

Gloria pulled back and smiled at her friend. "You're right. Let's do that."

"I'm leaving now," Portia said, getting up from her chair. "You'd better go too, if you want to make your date with your husband."

Gloria looked at her watch. "You're right. I have a couple of things to do first and then I'm out of here. I hope you and Dexter have a good weekend."

When Portia left the office, Gloria returned to her desk and began reviewing contracts. After about an hour, she stopped and pushed her chair back from the desk. "There's nothing here that can't wait until Monday," she said to herself. "I'm going to meet my husband."

When Gloria walked through Mick's bright orange doors, she scanned the after-work dinner crowd for her husband. Her eyes found him seated at a table near the windows. He was staring into his glass, apparently deep in thought.

As she walked toward him, her heart swelled with pride. Joshua Martin was everything a woman could want. He was a handsome man, her husband. And he was hers. All of him. His close-cut wavy, black hair. His smooth, clean-shaven, brown, almost black, skin. His beautiful brown eyes. He lifted those eyes to her when she reached him and she saw that they were troubled.

"Hiya, handsome," she said as she leaned down to give him a kiss on the jaw. "Have you been waiting long?"

"Not long," Josh said. He stood, pulled out a chair for her, and gave her a long, wet kiss before he took his seat again. "Do you want a drink?"

Still reeling from that kiss, she pointed to the glass in front of him. "Whatever you're having."

Josh beckoned the waiter and ordered Evian for Gloria. Since she knew what she wanted, they also placed their dinner orders. When the waiter left, Gloria asked, "Do you want to tell me what happened?"

When Josh looked at her, Gloria saw the debate in his expression. "Not yet. Why don't you tell me about your day first?"

Something is terribly wrong, she thought. It's unlike Josh to hedge my questions. Maybe good news will help. "I talked to Portia today."

That brought a smile to his face. "How is she? It's been awhile since we've seen her and Dexter."

Gloria smiled because Josh was smiling. "Portia's Portia. She and Dexter invited us to a dinner party, but I told her about our anniversary trip. Have you decided where we're going?"

Josh's smile widened into a grin as he pulled airline tickets from his pocket. He waved them toward her, but when she reached for them, he pulled them away and put them back in his pocket.

"So, we're flying?"

Josh put a finger to his lips. "I'm not saying any more."

Gloria pouted. "If you don't tell me where we're going, I won't know how to pack."

"It doesn't matter. You won't need clothes. We'll spend most of this vacation inside anyway."

Josh's grin was now a leer. Gloria began to relax. Maybe nothing was wrong after all, she thought. "Maybe so, but I have to know what to wear to the airport."

"I'll do your packing for you."

Gloria laughed and shook her head. "I don't think I'll risk that. If I leave it to you, I'll have nothing but lingerie and probably very little of that."

Josh clutched at his heart. "You wound me!"

"Wound me, nothing. I know you, Josh Martin."

Josh's look turned serious and he reached for Gloria's hand. "I love you, Gloria. More each day."

Gloria saw the troubled look in his eyes return. "What is it, Josh? You can tell me."

"I know, Gloria, but I don't know how to tell you."

"Start at the beginning," she said in what she hoped was a calm voice. Josh was making her nervous, afraid even. *Please, God, don't let it be something terrible.*

Josh applied pressure to her hand. "Marvin gave me some news today," Josh began, but before he could continue the waiter returned with their salads and Gloria's drink. Josh released her hand and picked up his fork.

"Marvin gave you some news today," Gloria prompted after the waiter was gone. "What's news?"

Josh took a bite of his salad before answering. "The company has decided on more cuts. This time my department."

Gloria didn't know how to respond to this news. The last time downsizing affected Josh's department, he was promoted. Obviously that wasn't the case this time. "What's going to happen?"

Josh placed his fork on the table and sat back in his chair. "Everybody has to go but one person."

Gloria lifted the glass of Evian to her lips. She didn't say anything. That one person had to be Josh. He was the best thing to happen to General Electronics in years.

"That person is Grace."

Gloria spilled her drink on the front of her dress. "You can't be serious." She placed her glass on the table and picked up a napkin to dab at the water spot expanding on the front of her dress.

Josh gave a wry grin. "Do I look like I'm joking?" He didn't wait for an answer. "Marvin told me this afternoon. He'll make a general announcement Monday. We have two weeks to clear out."

Gloria stopped dabbing at the water spot and lifted her eyes to Josh. "Two weeks! That's criminal, Josh. This doesn't happen to professionals."

"That's what I thought, too, but apparently we're wrong. There are no rules of etiquette when it comes to salvaging the corporate bottom line."

Gloria picked up her glass and took a long swallow, wishing she had ordered something stronger. "Marvin could have told you sooner. Surely, he knew something. You deserved to know when the talk first started."

Josh returned to his salad, as if they were discussing inclement weather. "Don't be angry with Marvin. He's doing his job. He's out too. Forced retirement."

"I don't believe it," Gloria said, picking at her salad with her fork. "Everybody but Grace. What saved her?"

Josh shrugged. When he finished chewing, he said, "They used some service formula and Grace met the criteria. Marvin and I were pushed out on opposite ends of the spectrum. He had too much service, I had too little."

"Is there any chance you can find work someplace else in the company?"

Josh shook his head. "That's not an option. They want us off the payroll."

Gloria wished they were home now instead of in a public

restaurant. She wanted to be comforted. And she wanted to comfort her husband. She knew him well enough to know that even though his demeanor said "calm," he was shaken up. "I love you, Josh. We'll make it through this. Together."

Josh returned pressure to his wife's hand. "I love you, too. This thing blind-sided me. I walked into Marvin's office expecting to talk about my upcoming promotion. This was the farthest thing from my mind."

Gloria's thoughts went to the promotion she and Portia had talked about. She decided now was not the time to mention that to Josh.

Chapter 2

The moonlight shone through the bedroom window, giving Gloria a clear view of her sleeping husband. His relaxed expression gave a sense of peace. He looked like a carefree little boy. But he wasn't a little boy. He was a man. Six-feet-three inches of gorgeous, black man. And he wasn't carefree, at least not this morning. This morning he had more than his share of worries. She wanted to reach out and caress his face to reassure herself that everything was going to work out, but she knew her touch would wake him.

She was still steamed about his treatment from General Electronics. It wasn't fair. Josh had done everything right—more than right. This shouldn't be happening to him, to us.

She studied his face. From the look he wore, she assumed his dreams were pleasant, peaceful. Maybe pictures of the two of them on some secluded island filled his mind. She lifted her hand to touch him and withdrew it a whisper from his cheek. She wasn't going to wake him.

Gloria turned to lie on her back, her eyes focused on the ceiling, her mind on her marriage. She and Josh were a good team. They were best friends as well as husband and wife. They brought out the best in each other. She knew Josh would need her to make it through this job ordeal just as he had needed her tonight. Their lovemaking had taken on an ethereal quality. Josh was doing more than making love to her. He was claiming her, making sure that she was real and that she was there.

"Two dollars." The smooth silkiness of Josh's voice interrupted her thoughts. She turned her head in his direction to see him leaning on his elbows looking at her.

She turned fully toward him. "My thoughts are worth more than two dollars this morning."

Josh gave her a quick kiss on her mouth. "How much more?"

She returned his kiss, giving him one that was longer and wetter than the one he had given her. "Money's not everything, Josh."

"I love you, Gloria Martin."

Gloria saw the sincerity in his eyes. She never doubted his love for her. When he said it like this, though, it brought out something primitive in her. She rolled toward him until her body was flush with his, her lips so close to his that she felt his breath on her face. "I love you, Joshua Martin."

Josh wrapped his arms around her and pulled her atop him as he rolled over onto his back. "You're a beautiful, sexy woman, wife."

"I feel like a beautiful, sexy woman in your arms."

Josh rubbed his hands up and down her buttocks and thighs. "You probably say that to all your husbands."

Gloria moved so her breasts feathered across his chest. "What did you say?"

Josh groaned. In retaliation, he pushed his hardness more firmly against her. "I can't remember."

Gloria moaned as she met his hardness with her softness. "Fortunately, you remember the important things."

Josh met Gloria's gaze and held it. "You know you're in trouble, don't you?"

Gloria pressed her breasts flat against his chest and kissed him fully on the mouth. "When are you going to stop talking?"

Josh pushed up off the bed and rolled over until Gloria was under him. He stared into her eyes and saw a reflection of the love and desire he felt. "I've stopped."

Gloria placed her arms around his broad shoulders and pulled him to her. Josh reveled in the kiss she gave him, a kiss that made him feel she wanted to devour him. God, that was a heady feeling. This was his woman. With all the uncertainty in his life right now, he could be sure of this woman who purred so sweetly beneath him. She was his and she would be his forever.

She was his. That was the last thought Josh had before he erupted inside her.

* * *

Later, Josh smiled at his sleeping wife sprawled across the bed. Her normally well-coiffured hair was a mass of disarray around her face. Her lips were curved in a sensuous smile. The small, black mole above the right side of her upper lip was so enticing that he leaned over and kissed it. She stirred, but she didn't awaken. He pulled away and let his gaze wander down her naked body. He only got as far as her maddeningly sexy, full, round breasts before he was fully aroused. That didn't surprise him since simply talking with Gloria could awaken his arousal. It had been that way since he had first seen her strolling along McCosh Walk at Princeton.

"Who's that?" Josh had asked his friend Walter.

Walter looked in the direction of Josh's stare. "I can't believe you're even interested, Mr. Iceman."

Josh continued to stare at the tall, slim beauty with curly black hair that waved around her face. She was talking to Gwen, a fellow student. Even from a distance, he could see her happy smile and feel its warmth. "Are you going to tell me who she is or will I have to have Gwen introduce me?"

"Someone has finally gotten to the Iceman. I don't believe it," Walter said, shaking his head and laughing. "She really has your number, doesn't she, Josh?"

Josh began to walk away from Walter and toward Gwen and the beauty. "Her name, Walter. All I want is her name."

Walter called after him, "Gloria. Her name is Gloria."

"Thanks for nothing buddy," Josh responded without looking back.

Gwen greeted him when he reached her and Gloria. "Hi, Josh. Have you met Gloria?"

Josh directed his smile to Gloria. "Not yet."

"Now you have," Gwen said. "Gloria Adams, Josh Martin."

Josh felt fortunate to have that brilliant smile and those bright eyes focused on him.

"Hi, Josh."

He knew he was staring, but he couldn't help himself. That

312   *Angela Benson*

black mole against her warm, brown skin mesmerized him. "Will you have dinner with me tonight?"

Gloria's eyes registered her surprise.

Gwen laughed, then said, "You don't waste much time, do you, Josh?"

Josh's gaze didn't leave Gloria's face and he didn't answer Gwen. "Tomorrow night?" he offered when Gloria didn't answer.

The twinkle in her big, brown eyes told him that she was laughing at him, but he didn't care. He wanted a date with her. He had to have a date with her. "Okay, you pick the night."

Gloria laughed, a happy, full, feminine laugh that made him want to laugh with her. "I think I like you, Josh Martin. Tomorrow night is fine."

Actually, they went out ten nights in a row. On the tenth night, Josh surprised himself. "Will you marry me, Gloria Adams?"

From her look and her answer, the question didn't surprise Gloria. "When?"

"June, seven years from now."

Gloria didn't hesitate. "Yes, Josh. I'll marry you."

Josh remembered the day as if it had been yesterday. He and Gloria had been so young, so arrogant and so full of dreams. Walter had laughed when Josh had told him of their engagement.

"Seven years? You expect that gorgeous woman to wait seven years? You're crazy. Some other guy will come along and snap her right up."

Josh was undaunted. "You're wrong, Walter. Gloria and I *will* marry in seven years. She'll date other men and maybe I'll date other women, but in seven years you'll be the best man at our wedding."

Walter shook his head. "I believe in planning as much as the next guy, but you take it too far, Josh. You can't fit everything into your Day Planner for life. Some things won't fit. I don't want to see you hurt, man."

"You don't understand. Gloria and I want it this way. She has things she wants to accomplish before we get married, and so do I."

"But seven years is such a long time," Walter countered.

Josh shook his head. "Not when you think about it. Gloria has two years of school and then five years of work to accomplish her goals before we get married."

"What about you? How are you going to handle seven years?"

"Working. I'm taking that job with General Electronics in San Francisco. I'm up to my eyeballs in debt. Seven years should give me more than enough time to get established financially. By that time, I should have arranged a transfer to Atlanta."

"Atlanta? I thought you wanted to live on the West Coast."

"Hey, buddy, I'm in love, remember? Gloria wants to move back to Atlanta. You know she went to Spelman."

"I don't know, man. Seven years is a long time."

"It'll work for us. I'm sure of it."

Josh still remembered Walter's skeptical look. He had reminded Walter of that look many times over the last two years. "Surprised" didn't adequately describe Walter's reaction when Josh had asked him to be best man at his and Gloria's wedding. Of course, Walter had agreed. And on June tenth, seven years after she had accepted his proposal, Gloria Adams became Gloria Martin.

Everything had gone according to plan for them. They'd had their time apart and they had begun their time together. Their goal for their first year of marriage had been to save for a substantial down payment on a house large enough for the family they wanted to start by their third year of marriage. They had accomplished that first-year goal with the recent purchase of a five-bedroom contemporary in Atlanta's South DeKalb area. Their second year's goal was to save enough money for Gloria to leave work to raise their children. The size of their portfolio suggested they were well on the way to accomplishing that goal.

Thinking about their goals brought Josh's job situation to the forefront of his mind. For a while last night and this morning Gloria had helped him forget. But Josh knew he couldn't spend the entire weekend making love to his wife to forget his troubles. No, Josh Martin needed to do what he did best. He needed to make a plan.

Angela Benson

* * *

Gloria reached for Josh, but he wasn't in bed with her. She opened her eyes and looked around the room. He sat at the desk in the alcove of their bedroom, writing intently. It was a familiar sight.

"Working, Josh?" she asked.

Josh looked up then. "No need for that now."

Gloria ran her hand through her hair and sat up fully in the bed. Had she really forgotten that Josh had lost his job? "What are you doing?"

Josh placed the pad on the desk and walked over and sat on the bed. He pulled Gloria into his arms and kissed her forehead. "Planning to find a new job."

"Have you come up with anything?"

"Not much," he answered. "I've been thinking more than anything else."

"You were writing up a storm a few minutes ago."

"Just getting my thoughts together. Writing helps."

"What were you thinking about?" she asked.

"How naive I've been. Given the churn at General over the last few years, I should've had a contingency plan."

Gloria responded immediately to the self-directed guilt she heard in his voice. "There was no way for you to know, or even suspect, you'd be terminated."

Josh winced. "Ouch. I guess I'd better get used to that terminate word."

Gloria was instantly contrite. "I'm sorry, Josh."

He squeezed her to him. "It's not your fault. You have nothing to be sorry for." Josh was silent for a while. Finally, he spoke. "I started a list of contacts to explore. It doesn't look too promising, though. Most of the companies I listed are downsizing, too."

"You know as well as I do, Josh, that companies hire with one hand while they're laying off with the other. We'll have to use our inside contacts to find out what's really going on."

Josh gave a hollow laugh. "I sure hope that our contacts, as you call them, know more about what's happening in their companies than I knew about what was happening at General."

"Stop talking like that," Gloria said, pinching him on the arm. "There was no way for you to anticipate this. God, Marvin had been talking to you about a promotion."

A promotion, Josh thought. It was almost laughable now. Almost. "I'll start making calls Monday. All I want this weekend is to be with you. Is that all right?"

"Let me see," Gloria teased, glad that Josh was coming out of the doldrums. "Do I want my husband's full attention this weekend? Surely, I can find something better to do with my time."

Josh patted her bottom. "You can, can you?"

She felt him relax. "Easily. But since you need me, I'll put those plans on hold. What do you want to do today?"

"We could spend the day in bed." He reached out his hand and tweaked her left nipple. It immediately puckered.

Gloria pushed away from him, although she was tempted to go along with his suggestion. Very tempted. "We could, but we're not. Let's do something wild. How about Six Flags? I love amusement parks. We haven't been in ages."

Gloria got up from the bed and paraded to the bathroom. Josh called after her, "There's probably a good reason for that. I hate amusement parks. Let's take the boat out instead."

Gloria stepped out of the bathroom, her toothbrush in her mouth. She didn't want to spend the day on the boat that General Electronics made available to its executives. "That's not true, Josh. You hate the idea of going to the Park, but once you get there you enjoy it as much as I do."

"But I want to be alone with you and Six Flags will be so crowded."

Gloria pulled the toothbrush out of her mouth, relieved Josh hadn't mentioned the boat again. "Sure, there are lots of people there, Josh. It's a park, for God's sake. Now get up and get dressed. We can spend the whole day there."

Josh got up from the bed and went to his closet. "I don't believe we're doing this. Where has the romance gone in this marriage when the wife prefers Six Flags to a quiet, private day on the lake with her husband?"

Gloria put her hands on her hips, knowing that since Josh was in his closet, the trip to Six Flags was a done deal. "We're going to Six Flags, Joshua Martin, and you're going to love it."

The relaxed feeling Josh had experienced over the weekend wore off as soon as he walked into the office Monday morning. He dreaded the morning meeting with Marvin to discuss the specifics of the "termination," but more than that he dreaded the afternoon meeting when he had to tell his staff they'd be out of work in two weeks. Everybody but Grace.

"What's wrong, Josh?" Grace asked after he was seated at his desk.

"What makes you think something is wrong?"

"Well, for the first time in the three years I've worked for you, I beat you into the office. Second, there was no new work on my desk this morning."

Josh smiled. He usually worked on weekends, leaving work on Grace's desk for Monday mornings. Things were changing already. "Close the door, Grace, and have a seat."

Josh gave Grace the news.

"I don't believe it, Josh. I'm the only one staying on. How can that be?"

"They're doing this strictly by service times. You're the only one who meets the criteria. Everybody else will be terminated or forced to retire."

"Not you too, Josh?"

"Yes, me too." The stricken look on Grace's face only made him feel worse. If Grace took it this way and she was keeping her job, he didn't want to think about how the others would take it.

Josh stood, a signal for Grace to do the same. "The managers are meeting with Marvin this morning to discuss the details. Call a staff meeting for one this afternoon. I'll tell everyone then. I want you to be prepared, Grace. This won't be easy. Our people have a lot invested in this company and they aren't going to take the news well. I'll need your help to deal with them."

Grace nodded. "Just tell me what to do."

"Don't mention our conversation to anyone. I don't want the rumor mill to get this before this afternoon's meeting. And don't make a big deal out of the meeting; just make sure everybody's there. I'll handle the rest."

Josh walked to the door and opened it. Grace followed him. Before she left the office, she said, "I should feel relieved for myself, Josh, because I do need this job, but it doesn't seem fair."

Josh agreed. But nobody had ever said business was fair. "Fair or not, Grace you have a right to be happy. It's my job to deal with the fairness of the issue, not yours."

Josh closed the door and returned to his desk. He knew Grace was still upset, but there was nothing more he could say. He was upset himself. Though he had only worked with these people for three years, he felt close to them. He knew they had families. Jack Johnson's wife had been hospitalized for the last six months. What would this news do to him? Lora Taylor was a single mother with two children in college. How was she going to cope?

Josh turned around in his chair and faced the windows. It was a clear day and he could see Stone Mountain. The thoughts he had kept at bay since hearing the news flooded his mind. How had his father felt when he had been laid off? Josh remembered very well the two years of his childhood that his father had been out of work. He tried not to think about that time since the memories brought pain. One memory was more painful than all the others.

The sounds of his parents arguing had wakened him. He had gone part of the way down the stairs and peeked through the rails to the living room. His father had been yelling and his mother was in tears. It had happened so fast. Josh had stood up to say something, to stop his father, but before he could open his mouth, his father had slapped his mother so hard that she had fallen to the couch.

Josh never told anyone what he had seen that night, but it had changed him. He had gone from a carefree child to a young man who had failed to take care of his mother. That night, he had promised himself he would never let her down again. He became his mother's protector. His father became a nonentity to him.

When Josh was away for his second year of college, his parents were killed in a car accident. Josh blamed his father and himself. Again, he had failed his mother. It's easier not to care, he had reasoned. That's when he'd gotten the nickname *Iceman*. He had never dated much, but he had stopped altogether after the death of his parents.

Things had changed when he met Gloria. Something about her caused the gates of his heart to open. Beyond a doubt, it had been love at first sight for him. He had promised himself that he would take better care of Gloria than he had taken of his mother, better than his father had taken of his mother.

I'm not going to be like him, Josh thought. I love Gloria. We're not going to end up like my parents.

Josh turned around to his desk. He pulled out a pad and began to make notes for the meeting with his staff. He knew that words wouldn't make it easy, but maybe they could keep things from being too painful—for him and for them.

Nothing could have prepared Josh for how painful it really was. The meeting started as any other staff meeting. Then he dropped the news. The immediate reaction was silence or maybe stunned disbelief. Then came the questions.

"Why?"

"Why didn't you tell us before now?"

Next, the accusations. "You knew before now and you didn't tell us."

Then, worst of all. "I have three kids—how am I supposed to make it?"

"My husband has already lost his job. How will we live?"

Josh had no answers for them because he had no answers for himself. He repeated the company line. "This is the last day…This is the severance package…These are the reasons I've been given…I'll write each of you a personal recommendation…"

When Gloria met Josh for dinner at Mick's later that evening, she immediately saw the change in his attitude since the morning. "Bad day?"

"That's an understatement."

"Want to talk about it?"

"Not now. Maybe later."

Though Gloria wanted him to talk about it, she followed his lead and didn't push. "Okay."

"Are you ready for our anniversary trip?"

Gloria had wondered if Josh still wanted to go. She had mixed feelings about it. Though it was a perfect opportunity for them to get away and clear their heads, she wondered if it was the right time for a trip, given the change in their finances. "I'd under-stand, Josh," she said, "if you didn't feel up to the trip."

"No. I still want to go. Don't you?"

If he wanted to go, she thought, they needed to go. The time away would be good for them. "I do."

Josh nodded. "My last day of work coincides with the begin-ning of our trip. Ironic, don't you think? A celebration of be-ginnings and endings."

Gloria winced at the dry laugh that Josh gave. "Celebrating our first year of married life should be a happy time, Josh. We're not turning it into a wake because you're losing your job. When we married, we promised to use these trips to celebrate the past year and to plan for the next year. Finding a new job for you will be a challenge that we'll face together, but it won't overshadow our relationship or this trip."

"You're right, Gloria, and I'm sorry. I promise not to let what's happened ruin our anniversary trip."

"We can work this out, Josh. I know we can." She reached for his hand. Even though she believed her words, she knew that Josh didn't. "Did you make any calls today?"

Josh shook his head. "I was in meetings all day. Tomorrow I'm having lunch with Dexter. He should know something. Have you told Portia yet?"

"No, I thought you'd want to tell Dexter first."

"Thanks for that," Josh said. "You know, I'm thinking about giving Walter a call. He may be able to help."

"I wouldn't think Walter had many contacts in Atlanta. He's been in San Francisco since you graduated."

"I know, but maybe there's something in San Francisco. How do you feel about relocating?"

Gloria thought about the promotion Portia had mentioned. "How do *you* feel about it, Josh? We've always planned to plant roots in Atlanta. We've bought a house. Atlanta is home for us."

"We need to keep all of our options open. What if I can't find a job here?"

"You'll find a job here," Gloria said with confidence. "Let's not talk about moving until we've exhausted all possibilities here. Call one of those executive search firms. They should know about openings at your level."

"I may do that later. Dexter and Marvin will be my first steps. Marvin has contacts in the city. He's making some inquiries."

"He owes you that much, Josh. I still believe he knew about this long before he told you. He could have given you more notice."

Josh shook his head again. "I disagree with you on that. These decisions are made at levels a lot higher than Marvin's or mine. They come down and everybody is affected. I don't blame Marvin."

Gloria still didn't buy it. Marvin was a department head; he had to have known. "Who is Marvin talking to?"

Josh told Gloria of his discussion with Marvin. Her thoughts wandered as he talked. Josh's job loss was already affecting their relationship. She wasn't being straight with him about her feelings. She hadn't told him about her possible promotion. And she was sure there were things he wasn't sharing with her. The idea of moving unsettled her. She didn't want to move. She loved Atlanta. She loved their life here in Atlanta. She loved her job. Everything was perfect. Correction. Everything had been perfect until Josh lost his job.

"You haven't heard a word I've said, have you, Gloria?"

His question brought her thoughts back to him. Thoughts she didn't want to share with him. She handled it the way she was handling a lot of her feelings these days. She lied.

Chapter 3

Grace closed the bottom drawer of the file cabinet in Josh's office and stood up. "I still don't believe this is happening. It's been two weeks since you told me and I still don't believe this is happening."

Seeing the strain on her face, Josh walked over to her. "Grace, you have to get over this. It's not that bad. We'll find other positions."

Her eyes registered disbelief. "I know you will, Josh, and so will some of the other engineers, but what about the others? It's a tough market out there now. The more education you have, the better off you'll be. Some of these people don't have the education you do. I don't know what will happen to them."

Josh hoped Grace was right about his finding a job with ease, but he doubted it. He knew she was right about one thing though—it was a tough market now. For everybody. "You can't worry about everybody, Grace. It's not your fault."

"But I feel so guilty. Why do I get to keep my job when nobody else does?"

Josh looked at the gray-haired woman who had been his secretary for the past three years. She worried about him. She worried about all the workers. He pulled her into his arms for a big hug. "One of the saddest things about leaving this job is that I won't see you every day." He pulled back from her to see her teary eyes. "You've been more than a good employee, you've been a good friend and I'll miss you."

Grace wiped at the tears in her eyes. "I'll miss you too, Josh."

Josh tapped her on her nose. "Gloria and I will make sure that we continue to see you."

Grace nodded as her tears fell more freely. "You're all packed up here. I'd better get to my desk and finish my packing."

Grace turned and walked out of the office. Josh closed the door behind her, then walked back to his desk. He remembered the day he had moved into this office. He and Gloria had come in over the weekend to decorate. She had wanted the office to say "Josh." He had laughed at her, but her excitement had been contagious.

"I'm so proud of you, Josh," she had said from her seat at his desk.

He sat on the edge of the desk, facing her. "I'm proud of you too," he had responded.

"Josh, I'm serious. You've accomplished a lot in a short time. The youngest Chief Engineer in General Electronics' history. One of only four African-Americans. That's something to be proud of. Aren't you excited?"

Josh smiled at her. "I'm excited, but I don't express my excitement the way you express yours."

"You can say that again. That's why you need me. You need someone in your life to express emotions. That way you can maintain your macho exterior."

Josh leaned toward her and kissed her. "I do need you."

Gloria pulled away. "You're so bad. That's not the kind of need I'm talking about and you know it."

Josh smiled at the memory. He had known what she was talking about. And he knew she was right. She *was* the emotion in his life. She saw joy and made him see it. She felt pain and made him feel it. She had a courage that left him in awe. She was proud of him. Josh gave a wry laugh. *No, Gloria, I'm proud of you.*

Gloria had been proud of him then, but he wondered how she felt now. He knew she loved him. That wasn't the question. He also knew this job thing had her worried. He had seen fear in her eyes the day he had mentioned moving, but he hadn't responded to it. How could he? He didn't have the answers. All he could do was find another job. Fast.

Marvin's entry into his office brought Josh out of his thoughts. "Do you have a few minutes?"

Josh gave a grim smile. "I've got nothing but time."

Marvin took the chair in front of Josh's desk. "Have you made any plans yet?"

"I've put out some feelers, Marvin, but no responses yet. It's short notice to find another job."

Marvin winced. "I guess I deserved that."

Josh stood up and stretched to relieve tension. "I'm not blaming you."

Marvin waved his hand. "No matter. I'm not here to talk about that. I have some news for you. I've made a few calls."

Josh sat on the corner of his desk and faced Marvin. "What did you find?"

Marvin handed him a slip of paper. "There are four names on that list. No promises have been made, but they're all willing to talk with you."

Josh looked at the list of names. He recognized all of the companies, but only one of the names. He put the list in his wallet. "Thanks, Marvin."

"No thanks needed. What are friends for? We are still friends, aren't we?"

Josh extended a hand to him. "We're friends, Marvin. I know you couldn't have prevented this. It just came as such a surprise that it threw me off balance."

"I know, Josh. I had planned to stay around another year or so before retiring, so I wasn't ready to leave either. We'll both have to make adjustments, though I won't be in the market for another job."

Josh nodded.

"How's Gloria handling all this?"

"As expected, she's being a trouper. She's positive we'll find something better. I hope she's right."

"I know she's right," Marvin said. "It may take awhile, but you'll land on your feet. You're like me in that respect. We rise to the challenge every time."

"Especially when there's no other choice."

Marvin laughed. "When are you leaving?"

"Around three. Gloria's picking me up. We're going straight to the airport."

"Oh, yes, your anniversary trip."

"We're off to Aruba. The trip couldn't have come at a better time. Since we found out about the termination, there's been a black cloud hanging over our heads. This trip will give us a chance to focus solely on each other."

Marvin stood. "I'm happy for you, Josh. And I wish you the best. If you need me for anything, just call. Martha and I will be there for you."

"I appreciate the offer, Marvin." Josh patted his coat pocket. "You've done more than enough by giving me this list."

Portia drank the last of her coffee. "I'm so envious."

"You have no reason to be. You and Dexter travel a lot," Gloria reminded her.

"Never to some romantic place Dexter has picked out. I can't believe you haven't found out where he's taking you."

Gloria pushed her plate away, placed her napkin on the table and looked away. "Well, I…"

"You found out, didn't you?"

Gloria laughed. She knew Portia wouldn't stop until she had an answer. "I found out. We're going to Aruba."

"How did you find out?"

"I…ah…sorta…went through his closet. He has a box where he 'hides' things. The tickets were in the box."

Portia laughed. "You've only been married a year and you already know Josh's secret hiding place? Shame on you."

Gloria shrugged her shoulders. "Shame on Josh. He ought to stop using the same place. He puts everything in that box."

Portia nodded her head knowingly. "That's the difference between men and women. A woman would never use the same place twice."

"I'm glad Josh does. Thinking about this trip has kept me sane these last two weeks."

Portia sobered then. "Do you want to talk about it?"

Gloria shrugged again. "What's there to say? Josh lost his job."

"There's more to it than that, isn't there?" Portia probed.

"I don't know how to talk about it, Portia. Josh is different, but he's not really different. He says the right things but I know there's a lot he's not saying."

"You can understand that, can't you?"

"Of course, I understand, but I feel shut out and helpless."

Portia reached across the table and touched Gloria's hand. "All you need to do is be there for Josh. He loves you, Gloria. He needs your reassurance that you love him."

Gloria squeezed Portia's fingers. She needed her friend's reassurance now. "I'm trying, Portia, but it's hard. It's only been two weeks and I already feel a breach between us."

"You're blowing this out of proportion," Portia said softly. "This is the first real trial you've had in your marriage. You'll deal with it."

Gloria removed her hand from Portia's and needlessly adjusted the napkin she had placed on the table. "Josh doesn't trust me as much as I thought he did."

"What makes you say that?"

Gloria placed her hands in her lap. "Sometimes he just sits and stares. When I ask what he's thinking, he shrugs and says nothing."

"You already know what he's thinking, Gloria. The man has lost his job. Give him a break, will you? You can't expect him to act as if nothing has happened."

Gloria picked up her napkin and placed it in her lap. She was feeling sorry for herself and she knew it, but she couldn't stop her feelings. "I know that, and I understand it, but it doesn't change the way I feel. Josh and I have always talked about everything."

"You need to wake up, Gloria. You can focus on how things *were* or you can adjust to how things *are*."

"Maybe that's it, Portia. My marriage, my life, is changing and I'm not adjusting very well."

"But you will."

Gloria nodded because she knew Portia was right. She had to adjust to this new situation. "I will because Josh loves me and I love him, but I don't like this feeling of helplessness. I didn't want my marriage or my life to change. Things were great the way they were."

"And things will be great in the future," Portia finished for her. "They'll just be different."

Gloria could feel the tears puddle in her eyes. "I feel so stupid and so selfish. I should be concerned about Josh and all I can think of is about me."

"There's nothing wrong with that, Gloria. One thing I've learned in five years of marriage to Dexter is that you have to know what your individual needs are as well as those of your marriage. Any time you need to sound off, I'm here for you."

Gloria smiled at her friend while managing to keep her tears at bay. "Thanks, Portia. I'm going to need a friend through this. You see, Josh isn't the only one holding back these days. I've been holding back my feelings as well."

"That's probably for the best. Honesty may be the best policy, but there's something to be said for timing. Josh may not need you to be honest now. Just be supportive. You can be honest with me."

Portia's words sounded right. Gloria hoped they were. "I've always told Josh everything. I feel dishonest not telling him everything."

"Growing pains, that's all. You're not telling Josh things that Josh can't handle right now."

"That's the problem. How do I know he can't handle them if I don't give him a chance?"

"I don't know," Portia answered. She put her hand across her heart. "You feel it somewhere deep inside. You know Josh better than anybody. Do you think he's ready to hear what you have to say right now?"

Gloria thought about it. How would Josh respond if she told him her fears? He would probably want to protect her, to ease her fears. Would that put additional pressure on him? Gloria nodded slowly. It would. And Josh didn't need any more pressure right now.

"What's the answer?"

"You're right. What I want to say to Josh now wouldn't help at all. I'm going to take your advice and ride it out. I'll be there for him. And you'll have to be there for me."

Portia smiled. "That's what friends are for. Now tell me more about Aruba."

Gloria welcomed the change to a more pleasant topic. She told Portia what she knew of the plans for the trip. "My major concern now is putting on a believable performance when we get to the airport. I'm supposed to be surprised."

Portia laughed. "You'll pull it off. And if you don't, Josh will have a good laugh at your, ah…inquisitive nature."

Gloria laughed too. "That's my incentive to put on a good performance. If Josh finds out what I've done, he'll never let me forget it."

Gloria arrived at Josh's office a little before three. He was standing before the window, his back to her. She watched him and wondered what his thoughts were. She hoped they were happy thoughts, thoughts of them and their life together. She quietly walked over to him and placed her arms around his waist.

"I didn't hear you come in," he said with a smile.

"Lost in your thoughts?" she asked.

Josh turned, keeping her arms around him. "Thinking about you."

Gloria smiled up at him, pleased to see the sparkle in his eyes. "Those are words a wife likes to hear."

"For the next fourteen days, Mrs. Martin, all you're going to get are sweet words and even sweeter actions."

"Promises, promises."

"What do I have to do to convince you?"

"How about a preview of coming attractions?"

Josh moved until his lips were almost touching hers. She felt his breath on her face. "Consider it done."

Before Gloria could give a retort, Josh captured her lips with his own for a kiss that left them both wishing they were somewhere other than his office.

When Josh pulled back, Gloria saw the passion in his eyes. "We've never…ah…christened…your office," she said.

Josh looked at his desk. Gloria knew the thoughts running

through his mind. When he turned back to look at her, he said, "If only we had more time."

"As I said, promises, promises."

Josh playfully swatted Gloria's bottom and pushed her away from him. "Get away from me, woman." He picked up the packed box on his desk and headed for the door. Gloria didn't move. "Are you coming?"

She debated asking how he felt about leaving his office for the last time. Remembering her conversation with Portia, she decided not to. If Josh wanted to talk, she'd be there for him, but she wasn't going to force it.

"Are you coming?" Josh asked again.

"Almost," Gloria answered as she sashayed past him and out the door.

His laughter covered the sound of the office door as he closed it.

The moonlight on the water made the white sand beach sparkle. This is as close to heaven as I'll get while I'm alive, Josh thought. What more could a man want? A beautiful night. A private beach. A beautiful and loving wife next to him.

After making love on their private beach, neither of them had the desire or the strength to go back to their cabana. He knew Gloria was awake but he didn't feel the need to speak to her. There were really no more words to say. The important things had been said. Though he had been afraid his joblessness would cast a pall on the trip, their two weeks in Aruba had been a healing balm for them, for their marriage. "All I need to do is find a job."

"You'll find one, Josh."

Josh didn't realize he'd spoken aloud. He turned on his side to face Gloria. "It may take some time, though."

"We have plenty of time. All of our lives."

Josh smiled. "I hope it doesn't take that long."

Gloria leaned on one arm and playfully slapped Josh across the chest. "You know what I mean."

"Yes, I do. I feel much better now that I have a plan. Monday, I'll call the contacts Marvin gave me and follow up with Dexter."

"Sounds like a good start to me. I'm glad Marvin made the effort."

Josh had been thinking about Marvin's list. It was unlikely any of those companies were looking for a Chief Engineer. "I may not get the position I want, so I may have to settle for something less."

"What do you want, Josh? A position like your last one?"

"I enjoyed being Chief Engineer, but I'd have to be very fortunate to find an equivalent position."

"If not management, would you go back to engineering?"

Josh shrugged. He preferred using his management skills, he was a natural planner and negotiator. That was his passion. "That's not my first choice. An engineering position would pay a lot less than a management position. How would you feel about that?"

Gloria squeezed his hand. "I want us to be happy. If you want to go back to engineering, that's fine with me. With both of us working, money shouldn't be the deciding factor."

"What about the baby?" he asked. Though he had been thinking about their plans for a family, this was the first time in weeks he'd had the courage to voice his thoughts.

"Baby?" She had been thinking about babies lately, but she wasn't ready to share those thoughts with him. She wasn't sure he was ready to hear them either.

"The baby we were planning for next year," he answered. "You were going to stop working after we had the baby."

"I don't have to stop work to have a baby, Josh. There are alternatives."

Josh stood up. "There may be alternatives, but our plan was for you to stay home."

Gloria looked up at his back. "Maybe we need to reevaluate that plan. Is it a wise idea for us to put all of our financial eggs in one basket? If I keep working, we'll have more options."

Josh walked to the water's edge. "You don't trust me to support us, do you Gloria?"

I'll have to watch what I say to him, Gloria thought as she went to him. "That's not it, Josh. I trust you. I don't trust the economy. I don't trust corporate America. We have to learn from this experience and what I've learned is that we can't depend on anything. There's no need for you to carry the financial burden alone. I won't be the first working mother and I certainly won't be the last."

Josh continued to stare out over the water. He needed the calm that smooth waves provided. "It's amazing how much can change in four short weeks. Four weeks ago, you never would have said what you just said. You didn't want to be a working mom like your mother. You wanted to be there for our children."

Gloria had thought about her mother a lot lately. Maybe she had been too hard on her. "My childhood wasn't all that bad," she said. "Things have changed, Josh, and we are affected. Maybe we'll change a little, too, but we'll change together. We won't let adversity separate us or distance us. Our love is stronger than that. You do believe that, don't you?"

Josh turned to face her. She was the most beautiful woman he had ever seen. Her eyes shone in the moonlight and his heart expanded at the love he saw in them. "I want to believe it, Gloria. I love you more than you'll ever know, but I worry that I'm not keeping the promises I made to you when we married."

Gloria's eyes flashed her annoyance. "Don't you dare say that, Joshua Martin. You've given me everything any woman could want and a hell of a lot more than most women have. Do you know that my friends are envious of me?"

"Because of me?"

Gloria gave an annoyed sigh, but when she spoke, her tone was soft. "Yes, because of you. Because of the ways you show your love for me. This trip is a perfect example. Portia is practically green with envy because Dexter never does anything like this. You go out of your way to make me feel special, to make me feel loved. You *are* keeping your promises. We both made promises. We promised to love forever. I'm still holding up my end of that promise and you'd better hold up your end."

Josh pulled her into his arms. "Is that enough?"

"It's more than enough," Gloria said as she snuggled in his

arms. "Sometimes I worry about us, Josh. We're both so practical and logical."

"What's wrong with being practical and logical?"

"There's nothing wrong with it, but it's not always right. I don't want us to allow our logic to make decisions that may not agree with our hearts. Our love may force us to go against logic sometimes and we have to be open to that."

Josh knew that logic and practicality had gotten him where he was today. "That might be hard for me, but I'll try."

Gloria hugged him tighter. "That's good enough for me."

When Josh didn't say anything more, Gloria asked, "Are you all right?"

"I'm better than I've been in the last few weeks. I'm beginning to see some light at the end of the tunnel. Maybe this will turn out to be a good thing after all."

Gloria pulled away from him and looked up into his eyes. "I've been thinking, hoping, the same thing. Our relationship will be stronger because we'll have faced a trial together and you may even end up with a better job."

Josh turned, put his arm around Gloria's waist, and led her back to the cabana, stopping only to pick up their blanket. "I've been having thoughts like that myself, but I've been a little afraid to voice them."

"I'm not. I feel it, Josh. This will all work out for us. Just wait and see."

Later that night when Josh and Gloria were in bed, Josh asked, "So, Portia's jealous?"

"Yes, she is. She says Dexter could take lessons from you in planning surprise romantic getaways."

Josh was silent for a while. Gloria heard the smile in his voice when he asked, "How long have you known about my secret box in the closet?"

Chapter 4

"You have an outstanding résumé, Mr. Martin," Thomas Williams, Vice President of Operations at Micro Systems Limited, said.

Josh merely nodded but had a sinking feeling.

Williams closed the résumé folder, pulled off his glasses, and placed them on his desk. "I'm sorry we don't have a position open for a man with your experience. Of course, we'll keep your résumé on file."

Josh was numb. Williams was the last name on the list of contacts Marvin had given him. As such, he was Josh's last hope. But Josh didn't have any hope these days. He'd had hope two months ago when he had started his job search with Marvin's contacts and his friend's support. He'd had hope on the first interview, then the second interview and then the third interview. Each time, the message was the same. "You're great, but we can't hire you." Josh had hoped, prayed to hear something different today.

"The openings we have would be an insult to someone with your expertise and the pay would be a drastic comedown from your previous salary."

Josh had heard that before, too. He had priced himself out of the market. It was a Catch-22. On one hand, his salary at General Electronics had been so substantial that few positions could match it. On the other hand, if he took a position at a salary less than that, his negotiating powers for a higher salary elsewhere would be severely hampered. What was he to do?

Josh stood. He no longer waited for the interviewer to stand first. Extending his hand, he said, "Thank you for your time, Mr. Williams."

Taking Josh's outstretched hand, Williams stood. "Good luck, Mr. Martin."

Josh walked out of the office to the elevator. He stood there a few minutes before realizing he hadn't pressed the button. He stepped into the empty car, selected the button for the first floor, and leaned against the back wall. He studied his reflection in the mirrored walls of the car. Anyone looking at him would think he was a busy executive on his way to a power lunch. He still had the look. The close-cut haircut, the strong, hairless face, the power suit, the expensive attaché case, still named him a man to be reckoned with. He had the look, but now he didn't have the power to go with it.

The elevator doors opened and Josh stepped off. He stopped in front of the bank of telephones, then moved on toward the revolving doors. He couldn't talk to Gloria right now. He needed her support and she was giving it, but he still felt pressured to be as successful in finding another job as he had been in everything else. Gloria believed in him and he needed that, but each time he gave her bad news, he saw the light dim in her eyes. Sure, she covered it up with words like, "Next time" and "Their loss," but he saw it.

He understood her feelings. The money he had received in his severance package was gone. They were no longer putting Gloria's salary in the bank. Instead they were living on it. Since her salary was less than his, soon they would have to dip into their savings. Josh didn't even want to think about that. Their savings represented their plans for a family. What if they had to use it all?

"I'm glad you dropped by, Josh," Dexter said as they settled themselves at a picnic table in the park a couple of blocks from his office. "I needed to get out of the office for a while. The fresh air feels good."

"It sure does." Josh had pulled off his suit coat so he could enjoy the cool breeze.

Dexter took a huge bite of the submarine sandwich he had purchased. "What are your plans now?"

Josh took a long swallow of beer. Being out of work meant he could have a drink in the middle of the day. "That's a good question. I have to do something so we don't end up spending all our savings."

Dexter nodded between bites. "Be glad that you having savings to fall back on. What's the money for, if not for when you need it?"

"The money isn't for this, I can tell you. The headhunter says I should be prepared to wait nine months to a year to find a job. That's a long time to skim off your savings."

"Whew," Dexter said. "Why does he think it will take that long?"

Josh mimicked the headhunter's coached voice as he repeated the reasons to Dexter. "It's a tight market, Mr. Martin, especially for middle managers like yourself. You're going to have to wait this one out if you want to find a comparable position here in Atlanta. If you would settle for less pay or if you were open to relocating, we could reduce the time."

"Are you?" Dexter asked.

"Am I what?"

"Willing to settle for less or to relocate?"

Josh wiped the sweat from his beer can with his napkin, then wadded up the napkin and tossed it in a garbage can about five feet from their table. "That's a good question. The truth is, I'm not ready to do either yet."

"Which one do you think you'll be ready to do first?"

"I'd rather relocate for a comparable position with comparable pay than take a pay cut."

"What does Gloria think?"

That was Josh's concern. Gloria didn't want to move. "Gloria thinks I'll find a job here."

Josh saw Dexter's eyebrow raise slightly. "And if you don't?"

"We don't discuss that. We keep hoping I find something." When Dexter didn't comment, Josh added, "We've got to get a better handle on our money. I don't want to use all of our savings."

"Have you talked with your financial planner?"

Josh shook his head. "Not since the news with the job. We probably need to."

* * *

Gloria placed the fluffy, white towel around her neck and stepped on the treadmill next to the one on which Portia stood. "It's been awhile since we've done this."

Portia was out of breath. "Too long. I think my heart is about to burst. How do you do it?"

"I'm consistent, Portia. It would help if you came more than once or twice a month."

Portia started walking again. "How do you find the time? On the days that I don't work through lunch, I usually have some errand to run."

Gloria upped the speed on her treadmill. "Exercise is important to me so I make time."

"Now that Dexter and I are working on a baby, I need to get started on something that I can continue after I'm pregnant. Walking seems like the answer."

Preparation for pregnancy had been one of Gloria's reasons for exercise too. She wanted to give her baby a good start and a healthy body was part of that. But as she was learning these days, her baby also needed a happy and stable home life. Once she would not have questioned her and Josh's ability to provide that. Now, she wasn't sure.

"Did you hear what I said, Gloria? You look as though you're a million miles away."

"What? Yes, I heard you."

"Come on. Let's have it. What's on your mind?"

Gloria slowed her pace. "Josh."

"What about Josh?"

"It's taking longer that I thought for him to find a job."

"And…"

"To talk to Josh, you'd think we were destitute or something. He wants to put our lives on hold until he finds a job. I'm working. We're getting by. And we're far from being destitute."

"Have you told him about the promotion yet?"

Gloria shook her head. "I'm not going to bring it up until it's a sure thing. I never thought I'd say this, but I don't know how Josh will react."

"Come on, Gloria. He'll be happy for you."

Gloria wished Portia were right. Keeping secrets from Josh was not fun. "I'm not sure. Josh is turning out to be a little chauvinistic in his attitude. He doesn't look at the money I bring in as our money. It's my money. When he was working and we were saving my salary, it was our money. Now that my salary is all that we have, it's my money. It doesn't make sense."

"Did you two talk about money before you got married?"

"Of course we did. But any time we talked about us being a one-paycheck family, it was always Josh's paycheck."

"Does it bother you that much?"

"Yes, it bothers me. What does Josh think I am? I have an education. I'm capable. I don't need him to take care of me. I thought we were taking care of each other. Now, Josh won't allow me to enjoy sharing this burden with him. I know it's hard for him, but he needs to think about me."

"What do you want him to do, Gloria?"

Gloria shrugged her shoulders and reduced the speed on the treadmill. "I just want him to acknowledge that our marriage is a partnership. We support each other. He's making it seem so one-sided."

When Portia didn't comment, Gloria looked at her. "You don't have anything to say?"

"I wonder if there's something else bothering you."

"Like what?"

"Maybe your talk with Eleanor this morning. Did she mention the promotion?"

If anyone but Portia had asked this question, Gloria would have thought they were being nosy. But how could Portia be anything other than nosy? Well, it wasn't really nosiness, it was friendly concern. "How did you know about Eleanor? God, you and office gossip. Does anything get by you?"

Portia laughed. "Not much. What did she say?"

"You don't know?"

"I couldn't put a glass to the door, now could I?"

Gloria laughed at that. "We talked about changes at the bank."

Portia straddled the belt of her treadmill. "You got the promotion?"

"No, I didn't get the promotion. Yet. Eleanor and I had an unofficial career planning session. She talked about possibilities."

"Did she give specifics?" Portia turned off her treadmill and leaned against one of the handrails.

"Not really. Nothing's final. But she did talk timeframes and numbers."

"Come on, Gloria. Don't keep stringing me along. What did she say?"

"Everything should be final in four weeks. If things work out, I'll get the promotion and a thirty-five percent raise."

"Thirty-five percent? That's great. You should be ecstatic. Why aren't you?"

Gloria had asked herself that same question. A year ago, she would have been planning a party. But not now. "I've learned that nothing is sure until it's done. I'm not celebrating until it's official."

"You're thinking about what happened to Josh, aren't you?"

"How can I not think about it? Josh was expecting a promotion and look what happened. Nothing is certain."

"You're becoming cynical, Gloria. It doesn't sound like you."

"Not cynical. Realistic."

"*Not me.* I'm making Dexter take me out tonight as sort of a pre-celebration," Portia said. "Good news for you is good news for me. Hell, I may even start planning to redecorate my new office."

Gloria shook her head. "You're one of a kind, Portia."

"That's what Dexter says. Are you going to give Josh the news?"

"Not now. I told you, I'm waiting to celebrate and I don't know how Josh will react to the news." And the way Gloria figured it, there was no need to stir the pot until something was definite.

"I think it's funny."

Gloria turned to Portia. "Enlighten me, then, because I could use a laugh. I don't see anything funny about the situation."

"Not funny ha-ha, but funny interesting. If Josh were content to sit on his butt while you worked, you'd be furious. You'd think he was using you. But when he wants to be the provider and feels badly because he can't be, you're furious. I'm beginning to wonder if Josh is in a no-win situation."

"It's not like that at all. Sure, I want Josh to find work. I'd be pissed if he didn't look for a new job and he expected me to support us indefinitely. But I need to know that we're a team. I want to be there for Josh in all ways—including financially. Why can't he just accept it? It won't be forever."

"If you feel this strongly about it, you need to talk to him."

"I know that and I've been putting it off. After Aruba, I thought we had crossed the biggest hurdles, but they don't seem to end. There's one thing after another."

Portia laughed and shook her head. "I have to keep reminding myself that you're a newlywed."

"What's that supposed to mean?"

"It means you haven't learned yet what marriage is all about. Somehow you think it's a straight road to a predetermined destination, but it's not. There are no guarantees where you'll end up, what roads you'll follow to get there or that you'll make it there together."

"And you call me a cynic?"

"I'm not saying marriage isn't great. I love being married, but I also know that it's a day-by-day commitment to stay together and follow the road wherever it leads."

Josh was in the kitchen when Gloria came home from work. "In here," he called when he heard the front door open.

Gloria walked into the kitchen and greeted him with a kiss. "How you doing, handsome? Let's go out to dinner tonight."

Josh smiled at her before turning to set the temperature on the oven. "Are you getting tired of my cooking?"

Gloria took a seat at the table. "I love your cooking, but it's been ages since we've gone out."

Josh nodded. They hadn't been out once in the last couple of months, but he didn't feel comfortable going out. All he thought about was how much things cost and how much they could save if they stayed home. "I've already prepared dinner. We can go out another night."

"But I want to go out tonight," Gloria cooed.

Josh took the salad fixings out of the refrigerator. "What's so special about tonight? We can go out another night."

"You've been saying that for a while, Josh, but we never go."

Josh pulled a huge salad bowl from the cupboard. "We need to watch our money. The headhunter said nine months to a year."

"But does that mean a year without going out?"

"No, but we can't go out as much as we did before."

Josh turned on the faucet to wash the lettuce. They were not going out for dinner.

"I know that, Josh, but we never go out anymore. We can afford this. I'm working. We have savings."

I'm working. I'm working. Those words echoed in Josh's mind. She had finally said it. He didn't know why he was surprised. He knew it would finally come to this. Leaving the water running, he turned to face her. "So it's your money and you should be able to spend it any way you want to? Is that what you're saying, Gloria?"

He heard her frustrated sigh before she said, "It's our money. We should be able to enjoy some of it."

Josh turned off the water and slammed the salad bowl on the table. "If you want to go out, then we'll go out." He walked out of the kitchen. "I guess you'll pick up the check?"

Gloria rushed after him. "Don't be like this, Josh."

Josh turned around unexpectedly and she bumped into him. He grabbed her by both arms. "Like what, Gloria? You don't want me to be concerned about money because you've got it covered. Okay, I won't be concerned about the money. You happy?"

Gloria jerked away from him. She rubbed her arms as if he had hurt her. "What's wrong with you, Josh? Why are you talking to me like this? I'm trying to continue our lives and you want to curl up and wither away. It's not going to work."

Josh knew he was wrong, but he couldn't stop himself. "Since you seem to know everything, then you tell me what will work."

"I can't talk to you when you're like this," Gloria said. She grabbed her purse from the couch. "I'm going out. You stay here and think about what's happened. You owe me an apology." With that, Gloria raced out of the door, leaving it open behind her.

Josh heard her car start as he slammed the front door. "Good riddance."

Josh stormed to the couch and flopped down. He grabbed a pillow and punched it repeatedly. He stood up, still holding the pillow, and paced back and forth in front of the couch. *I'm working* she had said. *Well, I know she's working. There's no need for her to rub it in. Damn! Who the hell does she think she is? I'm trying my damnedest to find work and she throws it up in my face that she has a job. To hell with her.*

Josh threw the pillow on the couch and pounded into the kitchen. He jerked open the refrigerator door and pulled out a beer. After popping the tab, he threw his head back and took a long swig. "Now, that was good." He closed the refrigerator door, leaned back against the sink and opened his mouth to down the rest of the can. As he lifted the can to his lips, he remembered another beer can in another hand. How could I have forgotten that? he wondered. His dad had held a beer can in his hand the night he had struck his mother.

Josh turned around and poured the contents of the can down the drain. He was not going to be like his father. He was not going to try to drink away his troubles and he was not going to take his frustrations out on his wife.

Is that what I did tonight? he asked himself. Was the fight all about me and my problems?

Josh walked slowly back in to the living room. Memories of the evening flashed through his mind. How had things gotten out of hand so quickly? One minute he was preparing a romantic meal for his wife and the next she was storming out of the house. He flopped down on the couch again. Why had he forced his wife to leave like that? Why had he done it? What if she hurts herself? Oh, God, where could she have gone? She shouldn't be driving in her condition.

He stood up again, went to the door, and looked out the side panels. What if she had an accident? He felt fear rise up in him.

No, I won't think like that. She's fine. She probably went to Portia's. I'll call and see. Josh stalked over to the phone, picked up the receiver, and dialed Portia's number. He hung up before the first ring. I'm blowing this way out of proportion, he reasoned. Gloria is a grown woman, more than capable of taking care of herself. He looked at the phone. He moved to pick it up again but changed his mind and went back to the couch and sat down. *Where the hell is she?*

"What the hell is Josh's problem?" Gloria asked aloud as she floored the Beamer down the street, no destination in mind. "I've bent over backwards to be supportive and he treats me like this. Just who the hell does he think he is?"

Gloria pulled into the parking lot of Viner's Diner, less than a mile from her home. She walked in, smiled briefly at the waitress, and took a table near the back.

Their first real fight. She and Josh were having their first real fight. They had argued before but never like this. Never with her storming out. Never with Josh yelling at her, grabbing her. Never with them being unable to talk.

Josh had scared her tonight. The things he had said and the way he had said them. Things had gotten out of control. She hadn't liked what she had seen. It was a glimpse of a side of Josh that she hadn't known existed. No, her Josh was controlled and direct. Their only major fight, until now, had been over the car.

"It's not practical, Gloria," Josh had said, leaning against the powder blue Corvette.

"You mean, I'm not practical, don't you, Josh?"

"That's not what I mean at all. It's not practical for both of us to buy sports cars. One of the vehicles has to be general purpose."

"But why does it have to be my vehicle? Why don't you get the general-purpose vehicle and let me get the sports car."

"Let's be reasonable about this. We'll be keeping this car for at least six years. During that time, we'll have two or three children. We need to buy a car now that will hold those children."

"We can trade in your car and get a 'reasonable' car. You don't need a Turbo Saab."

"Be reasonable, Gloria. Who'll stay home with the children? Who'll drive this car most?"

Gloria had eyed Josh then. She hated when he was right. "We could buy the sports car now and trade it in when I get pregnant."

"That wouldn't make sense and you know it. We'd lose money. If you get a new car now, it should be the Volvo wagon. There's nothing wrong with the Beamer that you have now. Why not keep it a few more years?"

"But the Corvette is...it's me."

Josh had laughed at that. "If you really want the car, of course, we can get it. But it'd be a waste of money."

"I knew I should have bought my convertible before we got married. My friends all said things would change. I didn't know how right they were."

Josh laughed again. "I'm not keeping you from getting the car, Gloria. Get the car. I want you to get the car."

"You know you've won, Josh. I'm not getting the car. How could I after all your practical arguments? I'd never be able to drive it and have any fun. I'll keep my 325."

Josh had hugged her to him and laughed again. "I knew you'd make the right decision."

She had pretended to be piqued. "I want you to know, Joshua Martin, that you won't win all our arguments so easily."

As Gloria thought about it now, she realized Josh had always controlled the money. We'd probably be fighting about money even if he hadn't lost his job, she reasoned. I should have gotten that Corvette.

Gloria requested a Diet Coke when the waitress took her order. She would drink the soda and then she would go back home. She and Josh needed to talk.

By the time the waitress returned with the Coke, Gloria's appetite had returned. She was hungry enough for two dinners. Hungry enough to stay in the restaurant for a good three hours. She smiled to herself. That should give Mr. Martin enough time to put together a decent apology.

Chapter 5

When Josh saw the headlights in the driveway, he stood and faced the door. After what seemed to be more than an hour, he heard the car door open and close. Next, the click of heels against the walkway. The clicking stopped right outside the door. There was a period of silence before he heard the key turn in the lock. He rushed to the door.

"Gloria…" he began when she walked through the door. She met his eyes, then brushed past him. He turned and watched her flop down on the couch, dropping her purse on the floor next to her. She leaned her head back and closed her eyes.

"Gloria," he began. "I'm sorry about what happened."

"What did happen, Josh?" She spoke without opening her eyes.

Josh sat on the cocktail table in front of her and placed his hand on her knee in supplication. She moved and his hand fell away. "I've said I'm sorry. What more do you want?"

She opened her eyes and sat up straight. Her eyes were red and he knew she'd been crying. "Why won't you say something?" he asked.

He stood up and walked away from her, frustrated by her unwillingness to talk to him, to forgive him. "To hell with it, Gloria. Why did you come back if you're not going to talk to me?"

"I asked you a question," she said softly.

He walked back to his seat on the cocktail table. He didn't know what had happened, so he stalled. "What did you ask?"

"Oh, Josh," she said, as if it were some major calamity that he didn't hear or didn't remember the question.

"Ask me again," he said, placing his hand on her knee once

more. He was relieved and encouraged when she allowed it to remain there.

"What happened here, Josh? Why were we fighting? It's more than my wanting to go out to dinner."

Josh moved to sit next to her on the couch. He placed his arm around her shoulder and attempted to pull her into his embrace. She pulled away. "This isn't helping," she said. "We need to talk."

"Can't I hold you while I talk?" Josh needed the physical contact of her body against his to assure him that everything would be all right.

She got up from the couch and stood in front of the fireplace, her back to him. "You don't need to hold me in order to talk."

Josh heard the pain in her voice. She was hurting but she was wrong. He did need to hold her. And, he decided, she needed him to hold her. He followed her steps to stand behind her. He reached his arms around her waist and pulled her back against him, resting his head on top of hers. "I love you, Gloria," he said softly. "I'm sorry for the things I said earlier."

She turned in his embrace so that she could face him, but she didn't pull away. "Why did you say them?"

He wiped away a tear that was about to fall from her eye. "I don't know, but I'd never deliberately hurt you. You have to know that." Josh felt his heart contract with pain at the disbelieving look in her eyes. What's happening to us? he wondered. What more can I say?

Before he could say anything, she moved as if to leave his arms. He relaxed his hold on her and she stepped out of his embrace. She continued to stand in front of him, but they were no longer touching. "You don't have to protect me, Josh. I'm a big girl. You have to talk to me. We can't go on like this."

Fear welled up in Josh. "Go on like what?"

Gloria shook her head in dismay. "Not talking. Pretending everything is okay."

Josh wasn't ready for this discussion. He didn't want to talk about the problem until he could provide the answer. But actually, he argued with himself, he knew the answer. The answer was for him to get a job and return their lives back to the way they were. Unfortunately, he couldn't do that just yet. What was the point in talking about it until he could? He looked away from her. "I know things are different since I've been out of work, but they'll get back on track once I find a job."

"That could be months. Do you think we can go on like this for much longer?" When Josh didn't answer, Gloria replied for him. "I can't."

What does that mean? Josh wondered. "What do you want from me, Gloria? I'm doing the best I can."

Gloria smiled sadly. That was the problem. Josh was doing his best, but it wasn't enough. She looked at this man she had loved since she had first met him over eight years ago. She had thought he could handle anything, do anything. Now, she wondered if she was wrong. Was Josh one of those men who functioned well as long as things were going well, but who fell apart at the first sign of adversity? No, that wasn't it. Josh was strong; Josh was sure. Josh's problem was that he kept his emotions bottled up inside. She had known that from the beginning. If she wanted him to open up, she had to open up first.

She took a step toward him, put her arms around his waist and laid her head on his chest. She opened the floodgates and let the tears she had been holding in flow freely. She felt his arms pull her even closer, as if he wanted to pull her into his body. She heard his words of comfort, but her tears wouldn't stop. She hadn't realized how much she needed this. How much she needed to cry in Josh's arms. She stood there, in his arms, her tears falling, for what seemed to be hours, but was probably only minutes.

"It's going to be all right, Gloria. I promise you. Our lives will be back to normal soon."

If only that were true, Gloria thought, then we could keep up this charade. But it's not true and we have to face reality. "It's been almost four months, Josh, and the headhunter says it could be up to a year."

She felt him stiffen at her words, but she knew she couldn't back down now. She pulled back to look at him. "We have to accept that for the next few months we'll be living off my pay-check." At Josh's chagrined look, she added. "That's not a bad thing. I'm happy to help out. We've been living off your salary since we married. We ought to be glad we have a second salary to fall back on."

Josh tried to pull away from her, but she refused to release him. "It's not that easy for me," he finally said. "I'm the man, I should be supporting you."

She touched her hand to his face. "Support is more than money, Josh. I need your emotional support as well."

Josh gave that dry laugh that was becoming his trademark. "I never thought of myself as chauvinistic, but I'm showing tendencies, aren't I?"

Gloria nodded. "It's endearing in some ways. I'm glad you want to protect me, to provide for me, but it's not necessary."

Josh pulled away and this time Gloria let him do so. He took her hand and led her to the couch, where he seated himself before pulling her onto his lap. "I know it's not."

"If that's true, why can't you accept my being the breadwinner for a while?"

Josh gave a long sigh. "What do you want me to do?"

"I want you to have some fun. We have enough money to do most of the things that we want to do, Josh. It won't break us to go out once in a while."

"But what if we have to use all our savings?"

"That's why people have savings. If we have to use it, we will."

"If we use the money, we'll have to delay our plans for a baby. How would you feel about that?"

Gloria had other ideas on the subject of babies, but now was not the time to discuss them with Josh.

"Maybe we will, Josh. Then again, maybe we won't. We won't be extravagant with our money, but we won't be tightwads either."

When Josh didn't respond, Gloria asked, "What area you thinking about?"

"Money. We need to see Jerry Thomas. If we have to dip into our savings, I want professional advice before we do it."

"If that's what you want, we can do it."

"That's what I want."

They were both silent for a while, then Josh said, "I don't want what happened tonight to ever happen again. It scared me, Gloria."

She heard the fear in his voice. "It scared me too."

He hugged her to him. "I shouldn't have touched you like that. Did I hurt you? I swear it'll never happen again."

Gloria shivered, remembering his action. "You didn't hurt me physically. Your words hurt me."

"I'm sorry sweetheart. This job thing has me in knots."

Gloria was glad Josh was opening up. She decided to remain silent and let him talk. She wasn't going to push.

"I've tried to be big about the whole thing," he continued, "but I'm so angry. And the irony is I have no one to be angry with. I can't be angry with Marvin, it wasn't his fault. I can't be angry with General Electronics, a company. That's senseless. I can't be angry with the companies that won't hire me. So then I'm left being angry with myself for not seeing what was coming."

"You have valid reasons to be angry, Josh. Just don't turn that anger inward or toward me. Use it to find another opportunity."

"I've been trying to do that. Not very well, I guess. The more I look, the more it seems that there's no opportunity. At least, not here in Atlanta."

They were back to that again. "Well, I'm not ready to give up on Atlanta yet. I know you'll find something."

"You want me to do what?" Josh slammed his fist on Jerry Thomas's desk.

"You have to sign up for unemployment benefits, Josh. It's a reasonable move to make."

"We came here for financial planning advice, not advice on how to 'milk' the system."

"Jerry is offering a suggestion, Josh. We should consider it," Gloria said.

Josh turned on her. "You can't be serious, Gloria. You want me to apply for unemployment benefits...social security...welfare? Never."

"It's not welfare," Gloria clarified.

"To hell it's not."

"Josh," Jerry Thomas interrupted, "Gloria is right. Unemployment benefits are not welfare benefits. Every working American pays into the Social Security system through FICA taxes. Unemployment benefits are provided through those taxes."

Josh looked at Jerry as if he were a two-headed monster. "I know how unemployment benefits are funded and I don't care. I won't go that route."

"That's your decision, Josh. You came to me for advice on making the best use of your savings while you're unemployed. One way to do that is to bring in more income. A source of such income is unemployment benefits. If you choose to ignore that source, then you'll reduce your savings that much faster. You won't get rich on unemployment benefits but every penny that you get in those benefits will be money that you won't have to take from your savings. The choice is yours."

"Why did we go if you're not going to take the man's advice?" Gloria asked later that evening. They had eaten dinner at home and were seated on the couch.

"I thought he'd give us some fresh insights on managing withdrawals from our savings and investments. All he did was tell me to get unemployment."

"It's not a bad idea, Josh," Gloria said. "It is your money."

Josh gave her a skeptical look. "You really want me to do this? You don't find the whole idea degrading?"

"No, I don't, and I don't know why you do. What is it?"

Josh gave a pained expression. "My dad was out of work often when I was a child. We went on relief a couple of times. I swore I would never do that. You don't know how it felt to stand in those lines and have people talk to you like you're the scum of the earth."

Gloria was amazed. This was news to her. She knew Josh came from a modest background, that his parents had been simple, working-class people, but she never guessed that they had slipped into poverty. "Why didn't you mention this before now?"

"I've tried to forget, Gloria. I've worked hard to build a life far above the life I lived as a child. I can't go back to that. I won't."

Gloria knew Josh was adamant. "It's not the same thing. It's not a handout."

"My mind knows you're right, but my heart can't see the difference. To me, it's all the same."

"Well, you can let your benefits sit there while we go through our savings or you can overcome your fears. Like Jerry said, it's your decision."

Josh drove around the unemployment office four times before pulling his Saab 9000 Turbo into the lot. I should have borrowed a car, he thought as he watched the other cars pull up. His gaze followed the people who entered the office. He made a game of giving backgrounds to everyone who entered the building. The woman with the three children had been deserted by her husband. The well-groomed man with the attaché case was the program director. Josh looked down at himself; glad he had dressed casually in slacks and a sports jacket. He opened the car door to get out, but closed it when he saw another man walking toward the entrance door. The man was also dressed in slacks and a sports jacket. Josh wondered whether he was an employee or a claimant.

Josh opened the door and stepped out of the car, closing the door behind him. He walked to the entrance of the building, took a deep breath, and opened the door. He walked through the door, but he didn't enter the room. He was not one of these people. He was different. Wasn't he?

He wanted to turn around and leave, but he couldn't. He had driven by the office for the last three days and today was the first day he had mustered enough courage to come in. It wasn't really all courage; Gloria's urging had a lot to do with it. He couldn't let her down in this. He had to do his part.

"May I help you?" a uniformed guard asked, interrupting his thoughts.

"Uh…yes. I'm here to file a claim for unemployment benefits."

The guard pointed to his left, to a line of about twenty people. "Over there."

"Thank you," Josh said. He moved slowly toward the line. Perspiration beaded on his brow, though he knew the room was cool.

"Hello." It was the guy in the slacks and sports jacket Josh had seen when he was outside. "This must be your first visit."

Josh was surprised that he was able to smile. "Is it that obvious?"

The guy grinned. "You do have the look of a first timer." He extended his hand. "I'm Elliot Wells."

Josh took his hand. "Josh Martin."

"I'm a veteran here now," Elliot said. "I've been out of work for almost a year. How about you?"

"Almost four months, but it seems longer."

"I know the feeling. I never guessed it would take so long to find work. What business were you in?"

"Electronics manufacturing. You?"

"Automotive manufacturing. Fifteen years. Worked there since high school. Worked my way through college. Never even thought about being laid off."

Josh gave a relaxed grin. "We have a lot in common."

"I know it seems impossible now, but you can make it through this. I'm living proof."

Josh nodded. "What do I do now? How do I sign up for these benefits that are going to make me a rich man?"

Elliot laughed outright at that, which was Josh's goal. The conversation had turned too serious too quickly. "Here." Elliot handed Josh a form. "Fill this out and then get in line."

"What are you going to do?"

"I'm going through the jobs digest. I'll wait around until you're done. We can go for coffee and share war stories."

"Sounds good to me," Josh said. "Now, I'd better get to filling out this form."

"I can see you made it through the interview," Elliot said when Josh walked out of the door.

"Talk about war zone," he said. "You would think the woman was paying the money out of her own pocket."

Elliot shook his head in what Josh guessed was disgust. "I know. It takes all the courage we can muster to even walk in there. Then they try to make us feel that we're the dregs of society. Just remember we've paid into the fund. The money is ours."

"Somebody needs to tell Mrs. Hitler that," Josh said with a suppressed laugh. "I finally had to tell her that I paid her salary so she should treat me with more respect."

Elliot's eyes shone with respect. "You didn't? What did the old bitty say then?"

"She gave a 'humph.' Only after I suggested that I talk with her superior did she get her act together."

Elliot clapped Josh on the back. "You did good for a first-timer. It took me three visits to get enough courage to demand some respect. Now, how about that coffee?"

The two men walked to a nearby café. Seeing Elliot's wedding ring, Josh asked, "How's your wife handling all this?"

"It was tough there for a while, but I think we're on track now. Marilyn has been very supportive. I don't know how she does it and I know I don't deserve her."

Josh thought about Gloria. Did he deserve her? "Gloria, that's my wife, has been supportive too. Almost too supportive. Do you know what I mean?"

Elliot nodded vigorously. "Do I ever? There were times when I wished she would scream at me, curse me, leave me. That I could handle. The constant support and positive thinking almost drove me crazy."

Josh was glad to find someone who finally understood. "How did you get past it?"

Elliot shrugged. "I allowed Marilyn to help me through it."

"Sounds simple enough, but I know it wasn't. Gloria and I are at that stage now. I didn't know I was a male chauvinist until this came up."

"I know what you mean. A lot of your stated opinions on marriage and women's roles are put to the test. I came up short, too."

"Has Marilyn been supporting you two the entire time?"

Elliot nodded. "She's trained me not to say it like that. I'm supposed to say we're a single-paycheck household. She says she'll get her turn when my business takes off."

"You've started your own business? What is it?"

"I've been tinkering around with a formula to improve fuel efficiency in automobiles. I have a small lab set up in my garage. We've done some testing, but not enough. It takes money, more money than I have, to do the kind of testing that's required. So, now I'm looking for seed money. I've talked to some investors, but nothing yet."

"I'm impressed. I wish you luck finding an investor."

"Thanks. There's no need to be impressed, though. It's amazing what a man can do when there's nothing else to do. After I was unemployed for six months, Marilyn encouraged me to pursue this. She says it makes her supporting us seem more like an investment in our future."

"So, you've always had an entrepreneurial spirit?"

"I guess I have. Being wrapped up in Corporate America doesn't leave much time nurturing that spirit though. Marilyn said being out of work took away all my excuses. I had to take my shot."

"I want to meet Marilyn. She sounds a lot like Gloria. Why don't you two come over for dinner one night?"

Elliot pulled out a business card with his number on it and handed it to Josh. "Give us a call and we'll be there."

Chapter 6

Gloria watched Portia dance into the bathroom ahead of her, checking each stall. "Looking for somebody, Portia?" she asked.

"No, girl," Portia answered, walking away from the last stall. "I just wanted to make sure no one else was here. I'm so excited, I could scream."

"Why don't you? Nobody's here but us. I'll even guard the door to make sure no one comes in."

"Oh, God, this is the best news I've had in years. I called Dexter's office, but he's out. I'm about to burst. Hey, why aren't you excited?"

Gloria leaned back against the vanity. "I'm excited, Portia. This is good news."

"What did Josh say?"

Gloria looked away. "I didn't call him yet."

"You didn't call him? Why didn't you?"

"I don't know what to say. I don't know how he'll react."

Portia froze in her tracks. "I thought you and Josh had worked through the money issue. What's wrong?"

"We've made strides, but we still have a ways to go. Josh accepts that I provide enough for us, at least for the time being. But I know it's painful for him. I just don't know how he'll react when I tell him about the promotion."

"What are you afraid of?"

"I'm scared Josh will fake excitement. I'm afraid this will send him back to the doldrums. I'm afraid of everything." Gloria covered her face with her hands. "Oh, Portia, what am I going to do?"

Portia pulled Gloria to the settee and they sat down. "What makes you think it will be so bad?"

"When I get home, Josh will tell me about his first day at the unemployment office. How can I tell him about my promotion?"

"You make it sound as though you and Josh are in some kind of competition."

"I don't know what we're doing, but I do know that my promotion reinforces just how much our lives have changed. Josh was supposed to be getting promoted."

"I don't think you're giving Josh enough credit. He'll support you in this. He may feel a tinge of envy, maybe even some hurt, but he'll support you in this and be happy for you."

"I hope you're right," Gloria sighed.

"I know I'm right. Now, when are you going to tell him?"

Gloria hedged. "I'll tell him."

"Tonight?"

Gloria smiled through her tears. "You don't give up, do you?"

"Not when it comes to my favorite couple. Now, why don't the four of us get together tonight for a celebration?"

"I'm not sure tonight is a good night. Not with Josh's visit to the unemployment office today."

"Why don't you give Josh a call and see what he thinks? Maybe a night out is what you both need." When Gloria would have restated her refusal, Portia added, "You don't have to decide right now. Call me at home before seven and let me know. We'll probably do dinner and dancing. Wouldn't that be fun?"

Before Gloria could answer, the door opened and a woman walked into the bathroom. Gloria took that opportunity to walk over and check her face in the mirror. She expected to look like a raccoon, but her makeup was still intact. "We'd better get out of here, don't you think?"

Portia grinned. "Why not? I've done all my screaming."

Portia got up from the settee and they left the bathroom. Before they parted for their respective offices, Portia said, "Don't forget to call me. You and Josh will have a great time. Trust me."

"I'll call you, Portia. Promise."

When Gloria got back to her office, she sat at her desk. This should be one of the happiest days of my life, she thought. Under normal circumstances, it would have been. But circumstances aren't normal. They haven't been normal for a while. God, when will things settle down? When will I stop walking on egg shells around my husband?

A knock on her office door brought her out of her thoughts. "I hear congratulations are in order," Foster Dixon said.

Gloria smiled. She had known Foster for over five years. He was both a competitor and a friend. Once he had wanted more than friendship, but she was already in love with Josh. "Thanks, Foster. You didn't have to drop by, you could have called. How did you hear?"

Foster walked fully into the office and took a seat. "I've known for a couple of weeks now. Thought I'd wait until you knew before I told you."

"And you were able to keep a secret that long?"

"That's me. Tight-lipped Dixon. I'm known far and wide for my ability to keep a confidence."

Gloria chuckled. "You're known far and wide for a lot of things, but I don't think being tight-lipped is one of them. What's the real reason you didn't tell me?"

"Eleanor threatened me."

"My boss told you before she told me?"

Foster nodded, smiling all the while. "How does it feel, Madam Vice President?"

Gloria gave a slight smile. "Quite honestly, I don't feel anything right now, Foster."

"That doesn't sound like the Gloria I know. My guess was that you and Portia would be bouncing off the walls by now. I bet Portia is."

Gloria laughed again, feeling more relaxed than she had felt in a long time. "You're right. Portia is bouncing off the walls."

Foster laughed then, a rich, full, male laugh, something Gloria had not heard around her house in a long time. "What's keeping your feet firmly planted on the ground?" he asked.

"I'm excited, even if I'm a tad more reserved than my usual self."

"I know about Josh."

The statement surprised her. "It's not a secret."

"I was sorry to hear about it. He got a bad break."

Gloria moved an inch away from him. She didn't buy Foster's sympathy. He and Josh were not friends. "Since when have you been concerned about Josh?"

"I'm not. I'm concerned about you and I know that you love Josh. I know that really well."

If anyone knew of the depth of her love for Josh, it was Foster. He had tried everything thinkable to win her away from Josh, but nothing had worked. "There's no need for you to be concerned about us. We're both fine."

"Your lips say that, but your eyes tell another story."

Gloria debated discussing this with Foster. Maybe getting a man's perspective would help. It took only a second for her to dismiss that idea. Another man's perspective, maybe, but not Foster's. She didn't want to confuse things with them. As if sensing her thoughts, Foster said, "I want to be your friend, Gloria. Nothing more. You chose Josh and I've accepted that."

"Josh and I are fine, Foster." Seeing the skeptical look in his eyes, she added, "Really."

"I don't believe you, but I care enough about you not to push it. Let me take you to lunch to celebrate your promotion."

"No thank you. That wouldn't be wise."

"Are you afraid to have lunch with me?" Before she could answer, he added, "If you need a chaperon, Portia can come with us. I know she won't turn me down. How about it? Give a guy a break, will you?"

Gloria couldn't resist his puppy dog expression. "You win. If Portia is free, we'll go to lunch."

Foster grinned then. "Who said Christmas comes but once a year? Having lunch with two gorgeous women makes any day Christmas for me."

Gloria looked at her watch. Six-thirty. Josh was late. Today was the first day she had beaten him home since he lost his job. How much things had changed! A few short months ago, six-

thirty would have been early for Josh to get home. No use thinking about that now, she thought. I just hope everything is all right.

She had already called Portia and told her that she and Josh
wouldn't make the celebration. She wanted to be alone with Josh
when she told him anyway. If things went well, they could have
a private celebration.

"Gloria," she heard Josh call when he opened the door.
"Where are you?"

She hadn't heard his car. "I'm in the kitchen."

She pulled off her apron and walked out of the kitchen to meet
him. She was taken aback when she saw him. He practically
beamed at her.

"Sorry, I'm late," he said, gathering her in his arms. "I had a
good day today."

"I can tell. What happened? You look like you won the lottery?"

He kissed her on the lips. "I said I had a good day. If I had
won the lottery, I think the word would be great."

He brushed her lips with his again.

"Whatever happened today sure has you in a good mood," she
said. "You didn't go to the unemployment office?"

Josh palmed her bottom and pulled her tighter against him.
"Of course I went. I told you I was going, didn't I?"

Gloria licked Josh's lips. "But you weren't too happy about
it. It must not have been as bad as you expected."

Josh wrapped his arms around her waist and walked her to the
couch where they sat down. "It was worse. God, you'd think I
was the scum of the earth."

"You say that, but you don't sound upset about it. What
gives?"

"I met a guy in the unemployment office. We really hit it off.
His name's Elliot and he's been out of work for almost a year."

"What's so special about this Elliot guy?" It was unlike Josh
to be so excited over meeting someone.

Josh shrugged. "It just felt good talking to someone in the
same situation as me. Someone who understands how I feel."

I've tried to understand, Gloria thought. "I'm glad for you."

"Elliot was a middle manager at Welco Automotive. He lost his job when they shut down his division. That was eleven months ago."

"And he hasn't found a job yet? He can't be too happy about that."

"Of course he's not happy about it, but he's making the most of it. He and his wife, both. I told him that we'd have them over for dinner soon. His wife's name is Marilyn. From the way he talked about her, I'm sure the two of you will hit it off."

"You think so?" Gloria was skeptical. Josh had just met this Elliot guy and he was already inviting him over.

"I *know* so. You have something in common—out of work husbands." Josh hugged her to him, adding, "I know this hasn't been easy for you, Gloria. You probably need someone to talk with as much as I do."

"You make it sound as if I've been suffering, Josh. It hasn't been that bad." At Josh's skeptical look, she added, "Maybe a little."

"It's been more than a little, Gloria. You've said it before. Our lives are changing and we've had no power over it. Talking with Elliot today, I realized the feelings I'm having are normal."

"Of course they're normal. I've told you that."

Josh caressed her shoulders. "I know you have, Gloria. You've been very supportive, but today with Elliot was different. We talked about fears, fears that only another man in the same situation could understand."

"You can share your fears with me, Josh. I want you to," Gloria said, her voice rising.

"I know you do and sometimes I've wanted to share them with you, but I was afraid. Afraid that you would think I was weak. Hell, I was afraid that I was weak. That's why talking with Elliot helped so much. As I listened to his story, I accepted that he wasn't weak, that he wasn't a failure. Accepting him gave me room to accept myself. Can you understand that?"

Gloria nodded in understanding. Josh had found someone to share his deepest thoughts with and that someone was not her. She was happy for him, but she was also a little hurt that he hadn't felt secure enough to share those things with her. "Of course I understand. I'm glad you and Elliot hit it off. When do you want to invite them over?"

"How about next week? I really want you to meet his wife. Did I tell you Elliot is starting a business?"

Gloria shook her head. "What business is he in?"

Josh proceeded to tell her about Elliot's business. She heard his words, but she focused more on him than the words he was speaking. It had been a long time since she had seem him this excited, this animated.

"Marilyn knew about his dream, and when he couldn't find work after looking for a while, she encouraged him to follow the dream."

"She sounds like a remarkable woman. What kind of work does she do?"

Josh laughed. "You know, Elliot didn't say and I didn't ask. We'll find out when they come over. Why don't I call him now?"

"Sure. Call them. It won't take much to prepare a small dinner party."

Josh kissed her on the lips and got up from the couch. "Don't worry about the preparation. I'm doing the cooking. All you have to do is show up. You can do that, can't you, sweetheart?"

Gloria smiled at Josh's lightheartedness and her jealousy toward his new friend vanished. She knew she was going to like Marilyn and Elliot. She already liked them. She'd never be able to repay Elliot for what he had done for Josh.

While Josh was on the phone, Gloria remembered that she hadn't told Josh about her promotion. He was so happy tonight. Why bring that up now, she reasoned? "I'll tell him later. When we're in bed. After we've made love."

It was six o'clock before Gloria arrived home Thursday night. "I'm sorry I'm late, Josh."

"No problem, sweetheart. Everything is under control. They won't be here for another hour. Why don't you change and relax?"

Gloria dropped down in one of the kitchen chairs. "God, I'm

tired. Do you know what I'd like? A nice, hot, relaxing bubble bath."

"Why don't you do it? You have plenty of time. Relax. I want you to have a good time tonight."

The promotion, Gloria reminded herself, tell him about the promotion. "There's something I want to talk to you about first. It's important."

"Not so important that it won't wait until you're out of the bath. Now get to it."

"But, Josh…"

Josh took Gloria by both arms and pulled her from her chair. "No buts allowed. Tonight is for fun and relaxation."

Gloria didn't resist because she didn't want to. She should have told Josh about her promotion last night, but the right moment had never come. It had probably been the right moment all night, but she hadn't wanted to chance spoiling their interlude. She had given herself the same excuse since she'd learned of her promotion a week ago. Josh had been his old self again and she had reveled in it. He was still like his old self now. "Okay, Josh, I'm going to my bath now, but we'll talk when I'm out."

"Fine. We'll talk when you're out. Now get out of here."

Josh walked into the bedroom and found Gloria standing in the doorway of her closet, dressed in her bathrobe. "Sweetheart, they're here. Why aren't you dressed?"

Gloria pulled dress after dress out of the closet. "I know they're here. I heard the bell. Why didn't you wake me?"

"How was I supposed to know you were asleep? I thought you were taking a leisurely bath."

"That's the problem. It was too leisurely. I fell asleep in the tub. Now I'm not ready and I don't have a thing to wear."

Josh looked from the pile of dresses on the bed to the full closet and shook his head. "Well, I'm sure you'll find something, but hurry it up, okay?"

Gloria dropped another dress on the bed. "Go back down and entertain them, Josh. I'll find something to wear."

He walked to the door. "Don't be too long. They're waiting to meet you."

Josh walked down the stairs to the living room and his guests. "You'll never guess what happened? She fell asleep and now she's scrambling to get dressed?"

"You're probably going to get in trouble for telling us that, Josh," Marilyn said from her seat on the couch.

"That's only if she finds out," Josh responded.

"You know women, Josh, they stick together. Marilyn will tell her."

"I will not, Elliot. You're so bad."

Josh watched the couple's playful interchange. Once again, he told himself that meeting Elliot had been a good thing for him. For them. He could see the two couples' lives intertwined for a while. He smiled at the thought.

"What are you thinking about, Josh?" Marilyn asked. She looked up as though she knew.

"He's probably wondering where his tardy wife is," Gloria answered from the doorway. "I'm sorry I'm late, everybody. It's all Josh's fault."

Elliot laughed first, then Josh joined in. "How is it my fault?"

Gloria gave Marilyn a "you know men" look, then extended her hand. "I'm Gloria and I'm glad to finally meet you. Josh has done nothing but talk about you and Elliot since they met."

Josh walked up behind Gloria, placing his arm around her waist. "And that guy over there is her worse half. Elliot, meet my better half, Gloria."

Elliot shook Gloria's hand. "Josh talks a lot about you, too," he said. "I see he didn't exaggerate your beauty."

At Gloria's blush, Josh added, "We're fortunate men. How did a couple of ugly mugs like us get such beautiful women?"

Marilyn spoke to Gloria. "Only men secure in their looks talk like that. Sometimes it's burdensome being married to such an attractive man."

Gloria agreed. Marilyn and Elliot were an attractive couple. The petite Marilyn was much shorter than Elliot. She fit under his arm perfectly. Elliot was an inch or two taller than Josh but in Gloria's opinion, he was nowhere near as attractive. Though he was good-looking in his own right. "I know what you mean, but let's not tell them we've noticed that they aren't exactly a pair of dogs," Gloria whispered loud enough for the men to hear. "We don't want their heads to swell."

Josh released Gloria and motioned to Elliot. "Since our women are talking about us like we're not here, why don't you follow me to the kitchen. I prepared the dinner; you can help me serve it."

Gloria and Marilyn watched their husbands leave the room. "They're good guys, aren't they?" Marilyn said.

Gloria smiled. "I think I'll keep mine. You know why they left us alone, don't you?"

"Yes, I know. Elliot had done nothing but talk about Josh since they met. It's very important to them that we like each other."

"I know. Josh has never taken to anyone the way he's taken to Elliot."

"It's the same with Elliot. You'd think he and Josh had known each other for years."

Both women were silent for a minute. "It's the job loss, isn't it?" Gloria asked softly.

Marilyn nodded. "In all the time that Elliot has been out of a job, I never considered his need for a support group. I thought I was enough support for him. I thought he was doing fine, but I've seen the difference in him since he's met Josh."

"The same with Josh. I never thought it could make such a difference."

"I admit to feeling a twinge of jealousy when Elliot first began talking about Josh, but now I'm beginning to understand."

"I was jealous too." Gloria smiled at Marilyn, then added, "He said you and I would get along and I think he's right."

"Has it been hard for you?"

Gloria didn't have to ask what Marilyn was talking about. "The hardest thing I've ever faced. If there were something I could do, we could do, to change the situation, it wouldn't be so bad. It's the helplessness that kills me."

"Don't I know it. When Elliot was first out of work, I kept trying to fix things, to make them better. I finally realized there was nothing I could fix. Life didn't stop. I had to go on."

Gloria thought about her promotion. "That's so easy to say. How do you do it? How do you share your professional accomplishments with him without making him feel bad about his situation?"

"I learned the hard way, I can't make Elliot feel bad. That's something only he can do. I finally stopped caring for his feelings and started caring for my own. And guess what? It didn't kill him."

"Then why does it feel like it will?"

"It's us. We have to take care of everybody's feelings at the expense of our own. That doesn't help the marriage. I found myself resenting Elliot and hating the sacrifices I was making."

Gloria nodded. She understood very well the tings Marilyn was saying. "I got a promotion last week and I didn't tell Josh." The words surprised Gloria. She hadn't planned to tell Marilyn.

"Why didn't you tell me?" Josh asked. He and Elliot stood in the doorway.

Chapter 7

Josh closed the door behind Elliot and Marilyn. He didn't know how he had made it through the evening. He couldn't believe it. Gloria hadn't told him about her promotion. What was happening to them? God, things were getting out of hand.

"We need to talk," Gloria said, interrupting his thoughts. She walked hesitantly toward the couch. "Shall we do it down there?"

Now she wants to talk. "What's there to talk about? Everything has already been said." He knew he was being a bastard, but he couldn't stop himself. "Congratulations again on your promotion. You deserved it."

Gloria sat on the couch, looking at her hands. "I wanted to tell you." She looked up at him. "I tried to tell you."

Josh didn't want to hear her excuses now. He wanted to get out of this room, out of her presence. Instead, he walked over and sat next to her on the couch. "Why didn't you tell me?"

He saw the tears forming in her eyes when she looked up at him. "I didn't know how you'd take it," she said.

He looked away, not wanting to see her tears, wanting to hold on to his anger. "What's that supposed to mean? You didn't think I'd be happy for you?"

"I had my doubts," Gloria whispered.

He jumped up from the couch and began pacing in front of her, careful not to look directly at her. "Doubts? You had doubts? Why didn't you tell me how you were feeling? You're a good actress. I thought things were good between us."

"They are."

He stopped pacing for a moment and stared at her. "The hell they are." He shook his head and resumed pacing. "My wife gets a promotion and how do I find out about it? An overheard conversation with people we barely know. Things are definitely not good between us. What the hell is going on here, Gloria?"

"Nothing is going on. I only found out about the promotion last week. I didn't want to give you the news on the same day that you went to the unemployment office, so I put it off. And I kept putting it off. No time seemed like the right time. Portia kept after me to tell you and—"

"Hold on a minute," Josh interrupted. "Portia had to convince you to tell me? I don't believe what I'm hearing."

"Listen to me, Josh," Gloria pleaded. "I had planned to tell you the day I found out, but you were so happy about meeting Elliot. We were having such a good time. I didn't want to risk bringing you down. My actions may have been wrong, but my intentions were sincere."

Josh never thought Gloria would ever deliberately do anything to hurt him, but she had hurt him tonight. It wasn't only that she had kept the news of her promotion secret. It was the way he had found out. He had felt like a fool. Elliot probably thought him a fool.

"Aren't you going to say something?" Gloria asked when he didn't respond.

"I've said congratulations. What more do you want?"

"I want to know how you feel. Talk to me."

Josh shook his head. "There's nothing to talk about. I'm okay." Josh stopped pacing and walked toward the kitchen, effectively ending the discussion. "I'd better do the dishes."

Gloria got up from the couch. "I'll help."

Josh lifted a hand in her direction to stay her. He didn't want her company right now. "There's no need. I can do it. Why don't you go to bed?"

Gloria looked at the clock. Two o'clock and Josh still hadn't come to bed. She had known he was angry, but she hadn't known how angry. A part of her wanted to go down and talk to

him, but another part, a larger part, saw no reason to beg for
Josh's forgiveness. She had apologized. He'd have to get over
it. She was getting tired of Josh and his feelings. She had feelings too.

She looked at the clock again. Two-oh-two. When was he
coming up to bed? What was he doing? She was tempted to tip-
toe downstairs and see. Maybe he was sleeping on the couch or
in a guest room. She turned over on her stomach.

Josh drank his second beer. He wasn't going to get drunk, but
he needed to relax. These incidents, fights, were happening on
a regular basis. When will the arguing stop? he wondered. Will
things ever get back to normal?

Josh took the last swig of beer, crushing the can before throwing it into the garbage. He walked out of the kitchen and up the
stairs. As he got closer to the bedroom door, he softened his
steps. The door was opened and he saw Gloria lying on her
stomach. If she got any closer to the edge of the bed, she'd fall
out, he thought. Even in her sleep, she pulls away from me. The
hell with it. He took one last look at her and walked past the open
door to one of the guest rooms.

Gloria heard the water running in the shower. Not their
shower, but the shower down the hall. At least he had spent the
night at home. Not much, but these days she was thankful for
anything she could get. Well, Josh might put if off, but he'd have
to face her before he went to work. All his clothes were in their
bedroom closet. Gloria shook her head at the direction her
thoughts were taking. Would she ever get used to it? Josh wasn't
going to work today. She had no idea what he planned to do. She
hoped he'd look for work. She hoped he'd find another job. A
good job. They needed some good news.

She heard the water go off in the shower. A little while later,
she heard the sound of Josh's footsteps coming down the hall.
When he walked through the bedroom door, she was amazed at
her reaction to him. God, her husband was an attractive man. The
towel he wore this morning showed off his narrow waist and

broad shoulders. His legs, strong like a swimmer's legs, weren't bad either. No, Josh Martin was an excellent physical specimen.

Josh lifted a brow in her direction and she knew he knew where her thoughts were. Their physical attraction to each other was never something they denied. Far from it. They celebrated it. Often. The physical side of their marriage was strong. Or it had been. Even though she hadn't wanted to acknowledge it, even that had changed. They still aroused each other, but their lovemaking had taken on a desperate tone as if it were the only thing that held them together. Yet it wasn't working. Instead of bringing them closer, it amplified their distance. She wondered if Josh felt it too. Now was not the time to ask, though. She wondered how to play the morning—should she bring up last night or wait for him to make a move?

"I'm going to visit Walter," he said. Turning to look at her, he added, "We can use some time apart."

Maybe he was right. "So you're running away. We need to talk. Your leaving won't help."

"It'll help me. I'm going because I need to go. Seeing Walter will do me good." He pulled a suitcase from the closet. "He may even be able to help me with a job."

She couldn't believe it. "In California? A job in California? I thought we decided you'd limit your search to the Atlanta area."

He began pulling clothes from the closet. "Not we. You. I knew I had to keep my options open. I've looked. There's nothing for me here in Atlanta. I'm reduced to unemployment. Do you have any idea how that makes me feel?"

Before she could answer, he continued. "I need to feel like a man again, Gloria. I'm losing my edge. I've got to get it back before it's too late. For us. For me."

"California isn't the answer. Don't give up yet."

With the suitcase packed, Josh dropped the towel he was wearing and began to get dressed. "My flight leaves at ten."

She recognized that tone. There was nothing she could say to change his mind. "Does Walter even know you're coming?"

"I called him last night."

She should have known Walter would welcome Josh on a moment's notice. He would love for Josh to move back out there. "How long will you be gone?"

"At least a week."

She was surprised at the length of the trip, though she shouldn't have been, given the amount of clothing he had packed. "Does Walter already have an interview lined up for you?"

Josh looked at her from the mirror as he straightened his tie. "A couple."

"You've already decided, haven't you, Josh? If they make you an offer, you're going to take the job."

"I don't see that I have any choice. Unless you know something that I don't."

"What about me, Josh? I just got promoted."

"They have banks in San Francisco. You could find something."

Something. Sure she could find something. But she didn't want something. She wanted what she had. "That's your answer—I'll find something?"

He turned to look at her for the first time since he had heard about the promotion. "I don't want to fight about this. I'm going to California to see Walter and to check out some job possibilities. Let's just leave it at that."

"You're coming, aren't you?"

Gloria opened her eyes. The sauna was so relaxing that she had almost fallen asleep. "I'm sorry, Portia, I was a million miles away. What were you saying?"

"The party next weekend. You and Josh are coming, right?"

Gloria didn't feel like a party right now and she had no idea what Josh would think. "I'll have to see what Josh says."

"Well, I'm not taking no for an answer. We deserve a celebration for our promotions and we're going to have it."

"I don't even know if Josh will be back by next week," Gloria said. "He may decide to stay longer in California."

Portia would not be put off. "You'll just have to call him and tell him to get his butt back here. I'm not kidding, Gloria. You have to be there. This party is for you, too."

Gloria looked at her friend in the multicolored, striped towel and smiled. Portia had done it again. She'd made Gloria feel good about herself. "We'll be there."

"That's more like it. This party might light a fire under Josh. Remind him what a treasure you are."

Gloria laughed outright then. "And just how are you going to do that?"

"I won't have to do anything. Foster will do it all by himself." Portia nodded. "That should knock some sense into Josh."

Gloria knew Foster would attend the party. And she knew that he would flirt with her. "There was never anything between Foster and me and Josh knows that."

"Yeah, he may know it, but when he sees Foster mooning after you like some star-struck teenager, he'll wise up. Nothing like a little territorial struggle to get a man back in line."

Gloria wasn't too sure she agreed with Portia's thinking, but she didn't feel up to debating. Portia was giving a party, and if her other parties were any indication, it would be great. "Do you need me to do something for the party?"

"Do?" Portia laughed as if that was an outrageous idea. "I've already called the caterers and everything is taken care of. The only thing you have to do is find a dress that'll knock both Foster and Josh off their feet." With a twinkle in her eye, she added, "I have a new outfit myself and I can't wait to see what you think of it."

Josh's flight didn't get in until two hours before the party. He rushed home from the airport and dressed quickly. Gloria took his breath away when he saw her in the black *thing*. He wasn't sure he should call it a dress. There didn't seem to be that much to it. It was cut square across the top of her breasts, just high enough to make you wonder if you would get a glimpse of heaven if you looked down at her. It hugged her body from her breasts to just above her knees, showing off every perfect curve. Then there was the back, or where the back was supposed to be. The spaghetti straps led to a balloon-looking drape that fell in swirls at her waist. No way was she wearing a bra with that dress.

Not that she needed one. No, Gloria had firm, round breasts. They jiggled when she walked and her nipples jutted out when she was aroused. God, Josh was jutting out himself just watching her put the finishing touches on her make-up.

She turned around to face him. "Are you ready? We're running…ah…late."

He knew she saw his erection and he saw her reaction. Those perfect nipples immediately puckered against that perfect dress. "We could be later," he said, with a casualness he didn't feel.

Gloria couldn't seem to pull her eyes away from him. Her tongue slipped out to moisten her lips, damaging the lipstick line that she had so patiently constructed.

He walked over to her and bent his head to kiss her. "Since you started it, I'll finish it." At her puzzled look, he added, "Your lipstick. You started removing it. I'll take the rest of it off and then you can reapply it."

Josh kissed her then and he felt some of the tension between them fall away. He hadn't told her about his trip to California and he knew she was worried, though he couldn't tell it by her kiss. She had given him what he wanted in that kiss.

Her eyes were glazed when he pulled away from her. In them, he saw desire and love. That made him happy. "Let's talk when we get back tonight. We have a lot to talk about."

Gloria didn't know what had happened in California, but the trip had done Josh a world of good. She liked him like this, but she didn't want to think what a job in California would mean. Somehow they'd work it out, but not now. Now she just wanted to enjoy. She looked around for Portia, who was conspicuous by her absence. It wasn't like her to be out of the action. She was a world-class hostess and saw to each of her guests, but Gloria hadn't seen her tonight. She had asked Dexter about her, but he had only said she was "around somewhere."

Gloria turned and finally saw the face she had been looking for. Portia was coming through the patio doors. She looked different somehow. What was it? she wondered. Her dress. That's it. Why was Portia wearing that shapeless dress? It wasn't her style at all. Typically, Portia's dress made Gloria's look like schoolmarm attire. Gloria remembered Josh's reaction to her dress and smiled. He certainly hadn't been thinking "schoolmarm."

Portia walked up to Gloria and took her arm, but before Gloria could say anything to her, Dexter swished Portia away and moved to the center of the crowd. He tapped fork to glass to get everyone's attention. "Tonight we're celebrating Gloria's and Portia's promotions. So let's drink to the ladies of the night."

Gloria saw Foster Dixon lift a glass in her direction and wink, all the while wearing the biggest grin.

"That guy needs to get his own woman. He's been making eyes at you all night."

Gloria hadn't known Josh was nearby until he spoke. His words sent a shiver down her spine. "Jealous?"

Josh placed a possessive arm around her waist and lifted his glass to her. They drank together, never losing eye contact, thinking of the way this night would end.

They were brought back to the present when Dexter spoke again. "We have a second item to celebrate tonight." He hugged Portia to him. "We're pregnant."

Everyone in the room seemed to flock to Dexter and Portia. Everyone but Gloria and Josh. Gloria felt Josh's arm drop from her waist and she knew he was thinking what she was thinking— if things had worked according to their plan, she'd be pregnant now, too.

Realizing she hadn't congratulated her best friend, Gloria walked away from Josh and moved through the crowd to get to Portia.

She had tears in her eyes but she was genuinely happy for her friend. "Why didn't you tell me?"

Portia had tears now. "Dexter made me promise that I wouldn't. He wanted to make the announcement. We only found out two weeks ago. I'm three months along." Portia pulled back from Gloria and turned around slowly, holding out the flared skirt of her dress. "How do you like it?"

Gloria laughed. "Oh, Portia. That's it. You're wearing a maternity dress. It's beautiful."

Portia lifted a questioning brow. "Not exactly my style, though, is it?"

"It's not that bad."

"I don't know, girl. I may have to start my own line. But I couldn't resist wearing it tonight. I'm not showing or anything but I had to wear this dress."

Gloria knew exactly what Portia meant. Wearing that dress made it real and announced it to the world. Portia was having a baby.

"How was the trip?" Gloria asked, after a quiet ride home. It seemed Portia and Dexter's announcement had taken the shine off her and Josh's evening.

"I didn't turn up anything concrete, but I did get some leads."

"That's good," Gloria answered.

Josh wondered if she'd even heard what he'd said. From the lazy way she was undressing, he knew her thoughts were far away. He had a good idea where her thoughts were. She was thinking about the baby. Not Dexter's and Portia's baby. No, Gloria was thinking about their baby. The baby they didn't have. More than anything, that showed how much his job loss had changed the course of their lives. He might as well bring it up. "That's good news for Portia and Dexter, isn't it?"

"Yes, it's good news. She told me a couple of months ago that they were trying. They deserve this."

He heard the unspoken "And we don't."

"We'll have children."

"Don't, Josh, not now. Let's not talk about it now." As if to soften the words she had spoken, she added, "Let's talk about your trip. What were you saying?"

Josh hesitated, then decided to follow her lead. "I talked with Walter's AVP. They didn't have any openings out there, but the AVP gave me the name of a manager in Raleigh. It seems they're looking for someone with my qualifications and experience."

"I don't see why you don't concentrate your efforts here, Josh. What good will a job in North Carolina do us?"

"You can't be serious. All our problems are because of my job situation. Once we get that back in line, everything will be all right." Josh prayed that he spoke the truth. "Once I get a job, we can start our family. Continue with our lives."

"How was Walter?"

Josh recognized the change in subject for what it was. She didn't agree with him, but she didn't want to argue. Things had just gone from bad to worse.

Gloria lay on her side facing away from Josh. She could feel his eyes on her back, willing her to turn to him for comfort. But she couldn't. Not yet. Not until she reconciled her feelings. God, what was she feeling? There was the initial envy. Next came the great relief. She was glad she wasn't pregnant. Glad. How could she tell Josh that? She couldn't. He'd want to know why and she just couldn't bring herself to tell him.

She felt more than heard him turn away from her, giving up on comfort tonight. She knew she had hurt him. Tonight had shown all the signs of being a fresh start for them, but it was not to be. It seemed that every time they were about to turn a corner, something else came up. Would they ever again be able to just enjoy each other?

Gloria admitted to herself that she feared for her marriage. She and Josh were not handling this problem well. Instead of pulling together to get through it, they were pulling apart. A lot of the fault rested at Josh's feet, but she shared a part of the blame as well. She laughed softly to herself, in most situations identifying the problem meant you had crossed the biggest hurdle. Unfortunately, that didn't seem to be working for her and Josh. They both knew what the problem was. They even agreed on the solution. It was just the path of getting from the problem to the solution that was causing all the havoc.

Josh couldn't sleep and he knew Gloria was asleep. He could feel her turmoil. She wanted a baby. If he had a job, they could have a baby. But he couldn't find a job. At least, not here in Atlanta. And every time he even hinted that he was considering a move, Gloria pushed him in another direction. He wasn't going to find a job here and Gloria had to realize that. They were going to have to relocate.

Chapter 8

Just as Josh was leaving the unemployment office, he saw Elliot walking in his direction. Elliot had called a few times and Josh, embarrassed over the dinner party fiasco, had begged off each of his invitations.

"Just wanted to thank you again for having us over the other week," Elliot said when he reached Josh. "Marilyn and I want to return the favor."

Josh felt duly chastised. "I'm sorry, Elliot, but Gloria and I have been pretty busy lately."

"Don't sweat it, Josh. What happened the other night didn't bother me or Marilyn. You have to remember that we've been through a lot of the things that you guys are going through."

Josh knew Elliot was trying to make him more comfortable, but it wasn't working. "Let's say the evening opened my eyes to some things."

"Sounds like you're having an ego problem, my friend. How about a cup of coffee while we do some male bonding?"

Josh looked at his watch but his decision was already made. "Let's take separate cars. I have an appointment in about ninety minutes."

Once they were seated at the coffee shop, Elliot asked, "What happened when you talked about it?"

"We didn't exactly talk about it."

"Not good man."

You're telling me. "It doesn't matter now. Things are starting to look up."

"You've found a job?"

Josh shook his head. "Not quite, but I have a lead."

Elliot slapped Josh on the shoulder. "Congratulations. What's the deal?"

"An old college friend hooked me up. I have an interview in two weeks. Comparable in position and pay to my old job." Josh didn't see a need to mention that the new job was in North Carolina.

"Good for you. Seems the bad stretch is over. And I was just thinking of asking you to consider a partnership with me."

"Doing what?"

"Management, general business. Right now I'm working out of my garage, but after the papers are filed with the Commission, things will start rolling. I thought we'd make a good team. We hit it off so well."

"Well, you're right about our hitting it off, but I don't think I have the stomach for entrepreneurship. At least, not while this job possibility is in front of me."

"From where I'm sitting, I think you need just as strong a stomach to work in Corporate America."

"You have a point there. Nothing is stable these days. Anyway, tell me more about what's happening with your business. Maybe I can help out even if I'm not ready to be a partner."

"What are you so afraid of, Gloria? I don't see how my interviewing for this job will make anything worse."

Gloria took the basket of laundry from Josh and began stuffing clothes in the washer. "I can't believe how selfish you are."

"Selfish?" he responded, his voice rising. "You call me selfish. What's selfish about a man wanting to take care of his family? What's selfish about a man wanting to get his life back on track? Tell me how that's selfish."

Gloria dropped the basket on the floor and turned to look at him. "What about me, Josh? What about my job? Have you thought about that? I don't want to move. I've just been promoted. I want to stay here."

"I hear what you're saying and you have a point, but we can't go on like we are. This is tearing us apart. Something has to change. Do you have any better ideas?"

"You can continue to look for work here."

Josh lifted his hands in the air. "What kind of answer is that? Where have you been for the last six months? I've looked. There's nothing here for me. When are you going to face that?"

Gloria knew he was right, but she was afraid. Her life wasn't supposed to be like this. Josh wasn't supposed to be like this. They weren't supposed to be like this. "So, you expect me to quit my job and move to North Carolina if you get this job?"

"I expect you to do what's best for our marriage, for us. I know about your promotion. I even remember the night I found out about it. We both have to compromise in this situation. You've got to decide what's more important—keeping this marriage together or keeping your job. I can't make that decision for you."

"Are you saying that our marriage is not as important to me as it is to you?"

"I'm not saying that at all, Gloria. It's just that right now something has to give. You'll admit that my being out of work is not working for us?" After Gloria's slow nod, Josh continued, "Well, I have to do something about that. Right now my best opportunity is in North Carolina. If I get the job, we'll have to figure out how to handle it. But I can't not try. I have to go. Can you understand that?"

She knew he was right, but she was right too. Why did it all have to be so complicated? "It makes sense, Josh, but it's so scary. I just wish things were back like they were."

"That wish is *not* going to come true. You have a lot of thinking to do while I'm gone. I'm open to discuss any ideas that you may come up with, but we've got to do something."

"He's right," Portia said from her seat on the floor next to the treadmill Gloria walked on.

Gloria looked down at her. "You've supposed to be my friend."

"I am your friend, but the truth is the truth. You and Josh have got to make some changes if you're going to work this out. Girl, you're changing in ways that I never would have imagined."

Gloria straddled the belt, turned off the treadmill, and sat on the floor next to Portia. "You told me that we would change because of this. I'm proof that you were right."

"Don't put that on me. I don't know what's going on with you these days. I could tell my pregnancy threw you, but you haven't even wanted to talk about it."

Gloria looked away, embarrassed. "I didn't know I was being so obvious."

"I'm your friend. Your best friend. You can't hide something like that from me. I know you. Do you want to talk about it now?"

Gloria looked around the gym. There weren't many people out tonight. A couple of guys lifting weights, she and Portia. One of the guys caught her eye and smiled. She looked away. "Hearing about your pregnancy made me realize how much my life had gotten off track. If things had gone according to plan, Josh and I would be pregnant by now. But now I don't even know if I want to have a baby."

"Sure you want to have a baby. What are you talking about?"

"You're right, I do, but I don't know when. I just know now is not the time. Josh has it in his mind that when he gets a job we can pick up with our original plans. I don't know if those plans still apply for me."

"Have you told Josh this?"

Gloria shook her head. "All we've been talking about lately is this trip of his to North Carolina."

"Not good."

"That's an understatement. Josh is sleeping in the guest room."

"You didn't tell me that. How long has this been going on?"

"He moved out the night of our dinner with Elliot and Marilyn. He came back to our bed the night of your party but that only lasted a couple of nights. We haven't made love since before that dinner."

When Portia didn't say anything, Gloria said, "What? You're speechless. This I don't believe."

"I didn't realize how serious things were between you. Are you two going to be able to work this out?"

Gloria couldn't count the number of times she'd asked herself that same question. "I don't know. I just know I don't want to move to North Carolina."

"Do you love Josh? Do you want your marriage to work?"

If it was only that easy, Gloria thought. "I love him, but it's more complicated than that. There's no guarantee I'll find a job in North Carolina. What am I supposed to do then?"

"If you feel that strongly about it, you won't go. You and Josh will find another option."

Gloria laughed. "Like what? Josh will live in North Carolina and I'll live here? What kind of marriage would that be?"

"You're laughing, but it's not so uncommon these days. With both spouses needing to work, sometimes they end up in commuter marriages."

Gloria shook her head. "That doesn't seem right to me. How can the relationship survive the distance? Marriage is about togetherness."

"Of course it couldn't go on indefinitely, but until you find something there or until something else up turns up for Josh here, you could give it a try."

"I don't know, Portia," Gloria said, but she didn't dismiss the idea.

"You don't have to decide now, but it's an option for you to consider. Don't count it out yet." Portia got up then. "Time for a shower. Come on."

"I'll be along in a minute," Gloria said, but she didn't move. A commuter marriage, she thought. She and Josh in a commuter marriage. Would it work?

"We're preparing for our descent into the Atlanta area," the pilot's voice announced on the intercom. "We should arrive at the gate in twenty minutes."

Josh relaxed in his first-class seat. The interview had gone well. He was pretty confident he would get an offer soon. He felt better than he had felt in months. This was his shot and he had to make good on it. He liked everything about the job. He already liked his prospective boss, Carla Stevens. It would be the first time he'd worked for a woman but he didn't think that would be any problem at all. He and Carla had hit it off. She was only a couple of years older than him and she was already Plant Manager. Josh could see himself as her Chief Engineer. He knew that she could see it too.

Carla was an attractive woman. Not as attractive as Gloria, but attractive. And single. Not that it mattered to him. He was happily married. Happily married. Ha! These days he knew he couldn't describe his marriage as happy. He and Gloria fought too much.

Originally, he had thought finding a new job would put an end to the fighting, but it seemed that it had only introduced a new topic to fight about. He didn't know how Gloria would react when the job offer came. He had talked to Carla about helping Gloria find work. Unfortunately, the company had a policy of not hiring couples, so a job for Gloria with Carolina Microelectronics was out. But they did have a relocation counselor who helped spouses find work. Josh's talk with the guy had been promising, but tentative. He hoped this was enough to pacify Gloria. If it wasn't, he didn't know what else he could do.

There was no way he could pass on this job. He just couldn't. He couldn't give up his marriage either. But he knew his marriage couldn't take much more of his being out of work. He wondered if the marriage could handle his taking an out of town job.

It seemed that everything was stacked against him and Gloria. She was his love, his life. And he wanted to make his marriage work. It seemed it had been ages since they'd made love. He ached for her sometimes, but she pushed him away. Never with words though. She was just never there. When he wanted to reach out to her, he could feel her pull away. That scared him.

Josh looked out of the window as the plane pulled up to the gate. He knew Gloria would be waiting for him and he wondered what kind of greeting he would get.

He saw her as soon as he walked through the gate door. She looked happy to see him, though the question in her eyes was obvious. She walked toward him and he opened his arms, almost afraid she wouldn't walk into them, but she did. They held each other for a long time like that. Gloria broke the embrace, pulled away and looked at him. There was a smile on her face and the question in her eyes was dimmed by tears.

Josh lifted a finger to wipe the tears. "Happy tears I hope."

Gloria nodded. He wasn't sure whether she was answering his question or acknowledging it. Being in a positive mood, he chose to believe the former. He smiled at her, put an arm around her waist, and began the walk down the concourse.

"How did the interview go?" she asked.

"I impressed the hell out of them." He felt her stiffen at his words, but he continued. "We'll probably get an offer in the next few days."

"Josh…"

"I know you have reservations about it and we'll talk about them when we get home, but let's celebrate tonight. We need to celebrate."

"Okay," she said hesitantly.

"I missed you while I was away. Did you miss me?"

He felt her smile. "I missed you, Josh."

He squeezed her to him. "Where do you want to go for dinner?"

"It doesn't matter. As long as we're together."

He believed her and he felt relief. They just might make it through this.

"It was fun tonight, wasn't it?" Josh asked.

"Uh-hum." Gloria snuggled closer to him on the couch in front of the fireplace. It had been a glorious night. After dinner, Josh had taken her to BE's in Underground to listen to some jazz.

"Ready for bed?" Josh asked.

"Uh-hum, bed would be nice."

"Tired?"

"No." Gloria wasn't tired, but she was ready for bed.

Josh stood and lifted her in his arms. "I can take a hint."

"I kinda figured that, loverboy."

When Gloria was seated on the bed watching Josh disrobe, she began to feel nervous. It had been so long since they'd made love. She wanted him, but she was scared.

"What are you thinking about?" Josh was standing beside the bed now.

"You. Us."

"Good thoughts, I hope."

"It's been a long time, Josh. I was just thinking how long it's been since we've made love."

He put his hands to her face and looked into her eyes. "But I've wanted you every day, every minute." At the surprise in her eyes, he added, "I love you, Gloria. I've never stopped. I've been scared a lot lately about what I've seen happening to us. I don't want to lose you."

"I don't want to lose you either. We're going to make it through this. We'll compromise and we'll go on. Is that good enough for you?"

Josh shook his head. "I need more than that."

He saw the light in her eyes fade. "I don't know that I can commit to more than that."

"Do you love me?"

The light returned. "Of course I love you."

"Well, I haven't heard you say it in a long time. I need to hear it."

Her relief was obvious. "I love you, Joshua Martin. I think I've loved you forever."

He kissed her then. A kiss that said he loved her too. A kiss that said he cherished her. A kiss that said she was important to him. A kiss that said this was a beginning for them. A kiss that was only the beginning of their night of love.

"I love you in white," he said, tracing a finger around the lace at the neck of the white bodysuit she wore. "When did you buy this?"

"Yesterday, in anticipation of your return."

Josh fingered the lace from the collar to the waist of the suit. "Too bad you spent all the money for nothing."

"If you like it, it was worth the money."

"I like it, all right. You're just not going to get much wear out of it."

"Why not? If you like it, I'll wear it a lot."

Angela Benson

Josh pushed the straps down her shoulders. "Somehow I don't think so. Even though white is great, I prefer you in brown—as in skin." He felt her shiver when her breasts were exposed. He touched them both with the tips of his fingers and their nipples puckered. He rubbed his fingers back and forth across their firm tips. Soon his mouth replaced his fingers. He felt electricity when his mouth touched those peaks. He was home.

When she was fully naked before his eyes, he studied her every curve. It had been too long since they'd been together. Too long. He vowed never to let anything keep them apart again. This, being with her, making love to her, was too important. It was life sustaining for him.

He captured her gaze with his own and maintained it as he entered her. His look spoke words that were too voluminous to be spoken now. It spoke of his love, his need, his desire to protect her and keep her safe. She was his haven and he wanted her to know that he was hers.

She responded beautifully as she always did, arching against him, meeting him thrust for thrust, her concern and care for his pleasure obvious. When she lowered her eyelids, he kissed her. A kiss that sealed their bodies and hearts together in all the places that mattered. It seemed right that at that moment they shattered together.

Chapter 9

Josh smiled. His wife was working her magic in the early morning hours. It had been awhile since she had welcomed the morning this way. He kept his eyes closed while his hands moved to her waist to help with her movements and they fell into a rhythm of their own. When he knew he couldn't take it anymore, he opened his eyes and pleaded with her to come with him. She looked as if she was going to deny him, but in the end, they went together to that place of warmth and peace. He pulled her to him, kissed her sweaty brow, and fell back asleep.

When he awoke the second time, she was propped on an elbow looking at him. "Good morning, sweetheart," he said.

She stroked a finger down his chest to his waist. "Just good? Surely it was better than that."

Josh stopped her finger before it moved into dangerous territory, and he placed it to his lips for a kiss. "Maybe that was an understatement. How about earthshaking?"

She placed a finger between his lips, pulled it out, and pushed it back in again. "Better."

Josh sucked on her finger, moving his tongue up and down its length. "Maybe you need to refresh my mind."

Leaving her finger in his mouth, she moved to straddle him once again. "Remember anything now?"

Josh groaned as she pushed her pelvis against his. "My memory seems to be coming back."

She laughed a carefree laugh that he hadn't heard in a while. "Seems to me more is coming back than your memory."

Josh raised his hands to touch her nipples while he returned her thrusts. "It's getting warm in here, isn't it?"

Gloria covered his hands with her own, encouraging him in his ministration. "I don't feel warm."

Josh took that statement for the dare that it was. He rose up and pulled her down so he could take her breasts in his mouth. At her first moan, he asked, "Not warm?"

She groaned again, all the while undulating against him. "Maybe a little warm."

Josh moved from one breast to the other, his hands all the while massaging down her back to her hips and thighs. "Getting warmer?"

Gloria groaned again, a sexy sound from the back of her throat.

Josh rolled so that he was poised over her while she lay on her back. "I thought so."

"Now, Josh. Now."

He rolled off her, onto his side and drew circles around each breast with his fingers. Her skin was hot to his touch. "What's the hurry? We've got all day."

"Josh…I can't wait."

Josh moved his hands from her breasts to her flat stomach and drew more circles around her button navel. When he moved to kiss her there, she moaned and lifted her hips.

"Just a little while longer," he said. His kisses moved lower until he touched the wet covering of her mound.

"Josh…"

Josh moved until he was full between her legs, his mouth never leaving that wet place. He was able to maintain his control, at least partially, until she heaved against his mouth. Then he lost it. He pushed her thighs apart and sank into her warmth.

Gloria met him thrust for thrust. They were one. Together. Soon they were soaring.

It was heaven to wake with Josh's head on her breasts, their bodies entangled, the smell of sex all around them. She wished they could stay like this forever, but she knew they couldn't.

They hadn't talked about his trip to North Carolina and she knew they had to. Thoughts of the talk didn't scare her as they once had. She knew they'd work through it. Together.

"What are you thinking about?"

Josh's question surprised her. She thought he was still asleep. She smiled and answered. "You."

He gave her a quick kiss. "Good try, but what were you really thinking about?"

"Us."

His look told her knew there was more. "How about us and North Carolina? Do you want to talk about my trip now?"

She nodded. As if sensing her need, Josh pulled her into his arms before he began talking. "They're going to make me an offer."

That part she had figured out. "Are you going to take it?"

"I want to. What do you want?"

She pulled out of his arms and looked at him. "I want all our mornings to be like this morning, with our only concern being how to pleasure each other."

"But what do you want me to do about the job?"

"I want you to be happy. I want us to be happy."

This was harder than Josh had expected. "It's a great opportunity for me. The position is better than the one I had at General Electronics. They haven't given any specific salary numbers, but I know it'll be a significant increase over my old salary."

"I don't want to leave my job." There. She'd said it.

"They have a relocation counselor who helps with placing spouses. The company has a policy against hiring couples, but they've promised to help find something for you in the Raleigh area."

"But I was just promoted. How will I ever find a job as good as the one I have?"

"Believe me, Gloria, I understand," Josh said, his hand caressing her shoulders. "This isn't something that I ask lightly. I just don't see that we have many options. Either we stay here or we go to North Carolina. I've pretty much exhausted all my resources here. I just don't think I'm going to find a job in Atlanta."

"And you think I'll find something in North Carolina?"

Josh nodded. "I think you will. There are some big banks there. With your track record, you'll find something."

"I don't doubt I'll find something, but I don't want something." Gloria knew she was whining, but she couldn't stop herself. "I want what I've established here."

"I don't know what else to say."

Gloria silently thanked God for Portia. "I have another option for us."

"Well, don't hold back. Tell me what it is."

Gloria spoke slowly and softly. "You could go to North Carolina and I could stay here."

Josh felt his muscles tighten. Were his worse fears actually coming into being? "You mean separate? You want a separation?"

She pulled back and looked up at him with widened eyes. "No, Josh, that's not what I want at all. I'm talking about a commuter marriage."

"A commuter marriage?"

"Yes. You go to Raleigh and I stay here. I'll look for work in Raleigh and you'll continue to look here. The first one that finds something will move."

"A commuter marriage? Isn't that a contradiction in terms? Marriage means together."

She lay her head back on his chest and tightened her arms around him. "We'll be together in spirit and we'll see each other often. We just won't go to the same home each night."

"Or to the same bed. Is this what you really want? You want a commuter marriage?"

"No, it's not what I want, but what other choice do we have? It would be a mistake for me to move without having a job lined up as much as it would be a mistake for you not to take this job. This is only a temporary solution."

That was the first mention of the word *temporary*, Josh thought. Maybe they could make it work temporarily. "How temporary? How long will we have this commuter marriage?"

"We could set a time limit. Six months, nine months, a year.

If, after that time, neither one of us has found work in the spouse city, we'll decide who'll give up their job."

"Seems like we're just postponing a hard decision."

"That's a defeatist attitude, Josh," she said, hugging him tighter. "You just said you thought I'd find work in Raleigh. If you really believe that, you shouldn't be so upset."

She had him there. She was right. Though he didn't put too much stock in his finding work in Atlanta, he felt pretty confident she would find something in Raleigh. "I want to go on the record as saying I don't think this is a good idea, but I don't see any other option. We'll try it, but only for a specified amount of time. How about three months?"

"Come on, honey, that's not reasonable. We'll need more time. How about nine months?"

"Let's compromise. Six months?"

"Okay, six months."

Josh felt as if he had made a pact with the devil. How would they make this work? Married people were meant to be together. He understood Gloria's position, but a part of him was disappointed that she wouldn't even consider leaving her job to follow him.

"They made the offer. I start the new job in two weeks."

Elliot looked up from the workbench in his garage. "You aren't wasting any time at all, are you?"

"I've been out of work for almost eight months. I think that's enough waiting."

"Point taken. Have you figured out how you're going to manage the separation?"

He and Gloria had talked the issue to death. Josh knew she was as afraid of doing this as he was. Neither one of them had voiced the one concern that hung between them. What if their marriage, their love, couldn't handle the separation? "Yeah. We have a plan. We'll be together each weekend, and of course, holidays and vacations. One weekend, she'll go to North Carolina. The next weekend, I'll come here. It'll work out."

Josh saw the skepticism in Elliot's glance. "Are you trying to convince me or yourself?" Elliot asked. "Are you having doubts about this?"

Josh knew Elliot thought he and Gloria were crazy to even consider a commuter marriage. "It'll only be for six months."

"And what if neither of you finds anything? How will you decide who should quit their job and relocate?"

Josh shook his head. He and Gloria had come close to discussing this more than a few times, but they never had. Instead, they focused their energy on positive thoughts about one of them finding suitable work. "We'll work it out."

"If you say so, man."

Josh knew Elliot wanted to talk more about it, but since Josh didn't, he changed the subject. "Have you found a partner yet?"

"Not looking for one," Elliot said. "After you turned me down, Marilyn and I decided to go it alone. Now, if you were to change your mind, I might reconsider. What do you say?"

Josh shook his head. "Not this time. See me in six months. You might be the answer to all my problems."

Elliot laughed. "If you ever want in, just let me know. Did you get to look over that proposal I gave you?"

"It's in the car. I made a few changes and reworked the numbers. It looks good. Really good. Gloria looked it over, too. You should call her at the bank. She might be able to help you out."

Elliot's eyes lit up. "She really thinks I have a shot at getting the money?"

"From her response to your proposal, I'd say your odds were better than that."

Elliot grinned then. "What do you know? Maybe I should ask Gloria to be my partner?"

"I'm glad you two came over tonight," Marilyn said, pouring coffee for herself and Gloria.

Gloria felt guilty about the times since that first fateful dinner that she and Josh had turned down their invitations. "I'm glad, too. I'm embarrassed it's taken us so long to get over here."

Marilyn handed Gloria a cup. "Elliot knew Josh was out of sorts because of what happened that night. We didn't want you two to be embarrassed. We've been where you are and we know what you're going through."

"I guess that's why it was so easy for me to talk with you. I've wanted to call a couple of times since that night, but I never did."

"Well, you're here now and that's what's important. Let's not worry about the past. When are you and Josh leaving for North Carolina?"

"I'm not going this weekend." Josh had suggested she go up with him, but her work schedule wouldn't allow it. "I'm in the middle of a closing and I can't take time off right now. Josh is driving up Sunday and he'll be back Friday night. I won't be able to go up until the following weekend."

"Has he found a place to live yet?"

Gloria shook her head. "He's staying in a hotel. He'll look at some places but we'll make the final selection the weekend I go up. That way it'll seem more like our place."

"Well, it seems like you're getting off on the right foot."

Gloria put down her coffee cup. "I hope so, Marilyn."

"Having second thoughts?"

"Not second thoughts. It just doesn't feel right. Josh shouldn't be leaving like this."

"He's not leaving. He's going to work and he'll be home in a week."

"That's what I keep telling myself. Sometimes I'm convinced this will all work out, but sometimes I wonder if we're putting our marriage at risk."

"Are you and Josh having problems?"

Gloria shrugged and stood up. "No new problems. I just don't know if we've worked through the old ones."

"I'll listen if you want to talk about it," Marilyn encouraged. "Just remember our husbands are in the garage."

Gloria laughed softly, thinking of the last time she'd shared a secret with Marilyn. "I won't say anything that I don't want Josh to hear."

Marilyn smiled with her. "Just wanted to remind you. Now what's going on?"

"We're relying so much on this new job. Almost like it's going to get us back on track, but I know that Josh has as many reservations as I do. If things were good between us, it wouldn't matter. But things aren't."

"You aren't getting along?"

"Recently we've started to put the pieces back together, but now we're going to be separated. Is this separation going to bring us closer or pull us farther apart?"

"You want to know what I think?"

"Of course."

"I think this will be a good time for the two of you. A break will do you good. Josh needs this, Gloria. Elliot has his fuel. Josh needs this to feel like a man again. You have to let him go and you have to be happy about it."

At the sound of the men coming in from the garage, Gloria sat back down on the couch. "Thanks for saying that. I needed to hear it."

Chapter 10

"Two bottles of your best champagne, please," Josh said into the telephone.

"Josh, you're being too extravagant," Gloria said. "We don't need champagne."

Josh sauntered over to her; happy this trip was turning out so well. When he and Gloria had boarded the plane five days ago, he had told her they were going to Raleigh. He had failed to mention the stopover in Bermuda. Her response and their time together made the entire trip worth it. "I'm hosting this party and I think we need champagne." He pulled her from her seat on the bed and into his arms. "Nothing is too extravagant where you're concerned. I love you and I don't want you to forget it because I'm not going to be around much."

Gloria looked up at him, the love in her eyes plain for him to see. "I'm going to miss you so much."

"I'll miss you too. We have to make the best of this situation until one of us finds another job. I'll try my best to make your weekends in Raleigh special."

She smiled then. "You're so good at making me feel special, Josh. Thanks for this weekend."

"There's nothing to thank me for. We've gone over a rough patch and we made it. A little worse for the wear but we made it."

"It was rough going for a while there, wasn't it?"

He squeezed her to him. "That's all behind us now."

"I hope you're right, Josh. I'm nervous about my interview next week."

He pulled back to look at her. "I don't see why. You're going to knock them dead, sweetheart."

"I don't think that's an objective evaluation," Gloria said.

"It may not be objective, but it's true. You know as well as I do that there's not much in a bank that you can't do."

"That's another thing that has me so nervous. I have no idea what position I'm interviewing for."

"I can hardly believe that myself, but it must be something similar to what you do now. Why else would they want to interview you?"

"I hope you're right, Josh," she said.

"I know I'm right. But even if I'm wrong, it won't matter. We have time for you to find the job that you want. Not just anything that's available. We're going to make this commuter marriage seem like the best thing since our honeymoon."

She pulled back then and looked up at him, her eyes full of skepticism. "Huh?"

"I'm planning some special weekends for you in Raleigh. This trip is just the beginning of what I have in store for you, Mrs. Martin."

"Is that a challenge, Mr. Martin?"

He shook his head. "A challenge means you have a reasonable chance of outdoing me. I can tell you now that's not possible."

"I think that's a challenge and I'm taking you up on it. The weekends I plan for us in Atlanta will rival anything that you plan."

"I doubt it, but if you want to try, by all means, do so."

"You think you're hot stuff, don't you?"

He nibbled at her ear. "Hmm…"

So this is Carla Stevens, Gloria thought. Under ordinary conditions she was the kind of woman Gloria would naturally gravitate to. Self-assured, aggressive, no-nonsense. A woman who knows where she is and where she's going. A woman on her way to the top.

But there was something about Carla that caused unrest in Gloria. Carla Stevens was also the kind of woman that caused envy to well up in other women. The woman was drop-dead gorgeous. She couldn't be more than five-four and probably didn't weight one hundred and fifteen pounds soaking wet. The pounds were, Gloria noticed, well distributed. No, Ms. Stevens wasn't lacking in any endowments. Gloria was grateful for one thing though. Carla didn't play up her good looks. On the contrary, she played them down. The severe cut of her suit, the hair pulled back in a bun, with only a hint of makeup. Clearly, Carla was all about business.

"It was good meeting you," Carla said in a voice that sounded caring and friendly. Gloria could imagine this woman as a caregiver—a doctor or a nurse. "We're happy that you and Josh decided to join the Carolina Microelectronics family. If there's anything we can do to help you get settled, just let us know."

"Thank you," Gloria said. She knew she should have gone on more about how they were so happy to be here, but she couldn't.

"We're looking for temporary housing this afternoon," Josh added, "so we'd better get moving." With that, he and Gloria said their goodbyes and headed for the elevators.

"Good going, Gloria," Josh said when they were out of Carla's earshot. "What's the matter with you? You could have shown a little more enthusiasm."

Gloria knew Josh was right. She was being a bitch and she had been since the interview yesterday. It had turned out to be a total waste of time. To say she was overqualified for the position was an understatement. And then to come here and see this woman that her husband was going to be spending more time with than he spent with her, well that made her angry. "What did you want me to do? Kiss her feet?"

Josh punched the button for the elevator and put his hands in his pockets. "You know how important first impressions are. What were you thinking about?"

The opening of the elevator doors saved Gloria from having to answer that question. The ride down the four floors was quiet since there were others on the elevator. Gloria was glad for the reprieve.

The elevator doors opened again and they got off. Josh raced through the revolving exit doors ahead of her. She had to hurry her steps to catch him as he crossed the street to the car. Once they were in the car and buckled up, he asked, "Are you sure you want to look at the townhouse? Maybe it would be better if you went back to the hotel."

She knew he was upset. "Of course I want to see the townhouse. That's why I came up here, isn't it?"

"I'm beginning to wonder about that myself. So your first interview wasn't what you expected. Hell, I've been having disappointments like that for almost a year."

"And you've handled them so well," she replied, the sarcasm heavy in her voice. The nerve of Josh to complain about her attitude, given the way he had acted.

"What's it going to be? The hotel or the townhouse?"

She didn't want to visit this place that her husband would be living in without her, but she knew she had to go. "The townhouse, for God's sake. I'll be living there too. Rather, I'll be living there every other weekend."

They drove the remainder of the trip in silence. Josh decided to focus on his new job. He couldn't believe Gloria's attitude. Especially since their week had gone so well until now. Hell, it had gone better than well—it had been great, until she'd gone on that interview. He knew she was upset, but it wasn't the end of the world. It really wasn't. He was confident she'd find something. Soon.

Well, he wasn't going to let her ruin this opportunity for him and he wasn't going to let her ruin his good mood.

He was excited about this townhouse. It reminded him of the one he and Walter had shared when they started work in San Francisco. The one Gloria had helped pick out. He had been excited about showing her this place, wondering if she'd remember. Now he just wondered if they'd make it through the rest of the day without a fight.

When he turned onto Sycamore Street, he saw the owner's car parked on the street in front of the townhouse. He had intended to pull up behind the owner, but when the garage door began to go up, he pulled into the driveway and into the garage.

The owner greeted them when they got out of the car. Josh introduced Gloria and the owner led them through the garage door into the kitchen.

Though the tour was for her, Josh didn't think Gloria was interested at all. After they were done with the walk-through and were once again in the kitchen, the owner produced a contract, which Josh promptly signed. All the formalities completed, the owner left Josh and Gloria to enjoy their new home.

"It could be the same place," Gloria whispered.

"Did you say something?" Josh asked. He wondered what she wanted to bitch about now.

"I said this could be the same place. It's almost identical to the place you and Walter had in San Francisco. The exterior is different, but that's to be expected, East Coast, West Coast stuff, but the interior—it could be the same place."

She *had* remembered. Some of Josh's anger began to fade. "I noticed it right away."

"Is that why you decided to take it?"

Josh nodded, hoping that some of her anger was beginning to fade as well. "I knew immediately. It seemed like an omen of sorts. Maybe this will be a new start for us. Our love survived my six years in San Francisco with visits and telephone calls. Surely, it can take this commuter marriage for six months."

Gloria turned away from him to walk to the bay windows in the breakfast room. "That was actually a good time for us. Even though we were apart, I didn't feel separated. We had such a strong bond."

"Had? What about now?"

She turned around to face him. "I'd almost forgotten that we've spent most of our relationship apart. I always felt that you were there with me."

"What about now?" Josh asked again. He wanted her to stop talking in the past tense.

"I don't know. For the past few months, I've felt apart from you a lot of the time even though we were sharing the same house and the same bed; that is, until you moved out of our bedroom."

She was right. He, too, had felt more distant from her in the last months than he ever had during the separation before the marriage. Maybe the difference was being married versus only being engaged. Maybe their expectations were different now. "I felt closer to you when we were in Bermuda than I have in a long while. I thought you felt it too."

She smiled and the tension between them lessened. "I did, Josh. And it made me so happy. It's just that the interview yesterday was a real letdown for me. I don't want to be separated from you."

He went to her and pulled her into his arms, soothing them both with his touch. "I don't want to be separated from you either. But our love has survived a separation before and it will again. Finding this townhouse was a sign. Do you like it?"

She pulled away from him and walked around the room. The contemporary furniture was even to her liking. "You knew I would. My tastes haven't changed much since then."

"You're right, I did think you'd like it. Since it's furnished, there's not much decorating to be done, but we have free rein in my office. How about we decorate it before you leave?"

"I'm ahead of you there, Mr. Martin—I packed the items from your old office. I figured you'd want to use them."

Josh walked over to her and pulled her into his arms again. "You think you're smart, huh?"

"Very smart," she said, "and don't you ever forget it."

Josh watched the seven men file out of the conference room. Their reactions had been predictable. A couple welcomed him as their new boss, three others were ambivalent, and two of them resented him. "Why didn't you prepare me?"

"I wanted to see how you'd handle it," Carla answered from her seat across from him. "They let me see their…ah…displeasure…when I told them we were going outside to fill the position. You handled it well."

"I know how they feel and in their positions I'd feel the same way. They're good men. As long as they do their work, we'll get along fine."

"Good. Now that you've met your team, it's time to meet the corporate people. I'm hosting a dinner party for them Thursday night. You and Gloria are the guests of honor."

"Thank you, we'll be there," Josh said, though he wondered if Gloria would be able to make it on such short notice.

"Don't thank me so quickly. I get something out of this too. Though the brass let me run this facility as I see fit, I likc to give them the opportunity to commend my decisions."

"Well, I won't argue with you there. The more I learn about this job, the more I like it. I don't think I could have asked for a better match with my skills and interests. And," he added, "I know you couldn't have found a better candidate."

Carla stood and Josh did the same. "I'm glad to hear it. Now, I'd better get back to my office so you can get on with your day. My secretary will get the details of the party to Debbie."

Josh remained standing after Carla had left the room. He wasn't just blowing smoke when he'd told her how much he liked this job. It was a better fit for him than the job at General Electronics had been. He shook his head at the thought that it took getting fired and being out of work eight grueling months to get to this point. Maybe one day he'd be able to say that it was worth it. Not today, but maybe one day.

He picked up the phone and dialed Gloria's office. Her secretary answered. When she told him Gloria was in a meeting, he asked, "What's her calendar look like for Thursday and Friday?"

"A departrnent meeting Thursday afternoon and a division meeting Friday morning."

Not exactly good news, he thought. Josh thanked her and hung up. Gloria's meetings complicated things. Should he tell her about the party and let her make the decision or should he not mention it?

"Mr. Martin, your wife is on the line," Debbie said after she poked her head into the conference room. "I can transfer the call in here if you like."

"That won't be necessary. I'm on my way back to the office."

Josh followed her to his office. He picked up the phone and pressed the blinking button. "That was a quick meeting."

"Not quick enough. You were hanging up when I walked through the door. Was there something special you wanted to talk about or were you just missing me?"

Josh smiled. Her flirting caused him to remember the last night they had spent together. It had been less than a week, but he missed her. "Both. Carla's hosting a dinner party for us. A really big event. All the corporate guys are coming."

"That's great. This means a new dress."

Josh paused before speaking. "Thursday night."

Josh felt her thinking. "Not this Thursday?"

"Yes, this Thursday. Do you think you'll be able to come?"

Again she was thinking. "There are a couple of things on my schedule. It's going to be hard to move them around, but let me see what I can do."

She would try. That was good enough for now. "Thanks, Gloria. I know this isn't much notice."

"I should know something in a couple of hours. I'll talk to you then."

Gloria stared at the handset she had just placed on the phone. Why hadn't she told Josh she couldn't make it? She had two important meetings this week—Thursday afternoon and Friday morning. How was she going to get into Raleigh for a Thursday night dinner party? It was obvious she couldn't make the meetings and the party. The most sensible thing to do was to call Josh and tell him about the meetings. He'd understand. She picked up the handset and dialed three numbers before hanging up.

This is a very important dinner party for Josh, she thought. At his level these parties were as important as board meetings. She knew it and she knew he knew she knew it. Unfortunately, her meetings were just as important to her career. How could she explain her absence to attend a dinner with her husband? She hadn't been in her new job long enough to give a reason like that.

Maybe the party could be rescheduled. This was pretty late notice anyway, she reasoned. His company would understand problems with the date better than hers would, since her meetings had been scheduled for over a month and Josh's had only been scheduled today. Yes, Gloria thought, that's the reasonable thing to do. She'd call Josh and see if he could get the party rescheduled. Next week would be perfect.

She picked up the phone to tell Josh her suggestion. This time he was in a meeting. She hung up and breathed a telling sigh. She was actually nervous about his response. She didn't want him to think she didn't want to come, especially after the way she had acted after her interview the last time they were together.

Now was too soon in their commuter marriage to make these types of decisions, she thought. She wondered if she and Josh would ever get a break. They seemed to move from one crisis to another. Just when it seemed they were getting it together, something else happened. It wasn't fair.

Gloria laughed at herself. Fair? What's fair got to do with it?

A knock at her door interrupted her thoughts. "How's the VP today?" Foster Dixon asked. "You have a few minutes for a friend?"

"Sure. Come on in." She welcomed the interruption.

Foster swaggered into the room. There was no other way she could think to describe the way he walked. The man obviously had no problem with self-confidence. Although sometimes his self-assuredness rankled. Today was one of those days. "What are doing down here today? More gossip or is this actually official business?"

Laughing, he took a seat across from her desk. She had known he wouldn't be offended. The man didn't get insulted easily. "I wouldn't call it gossip exactly," he said.

"Okay, then, let's call it news. Have you heard any more news on my career? Am I up for another promotion so soon?"

"Ambitious, aren't we? That's consistent with the other news that I've heard."

Gloria strummed her fingers on her desk, impatient for Foster to get his news out. "Come on, spill it. I can see you're dying to tell me."

"Well, the word on the street is you and Josh are separated."

Gloria's fingers stopped strumming the desk. She knew the

gossip mill was notorious, but she'd never expected this. "Where did you hear this?"

"Doesn't matter. Is it true?"

"Of course it's not true. You saw Josh and me at Portia's party. I'm surprised you didn't nip that rumor in the bud yourself. You're slipping, Foster."

Foster shrugged. "That was then, this is now. So you're telling me Josh hasn't moved to North Carolina?"

Gloria knew she shouldn't be surprised that the details were out, but she was. She and Josh had decided to keep their commuter marriage quiet for a while. Well, it seemed the while was over. "Josh is in North Carolina, but we're not separated."

Foster's frown showed his disbelief. "Unless I'm mistaken you're still here in Georgia."

"Don't be smart, Foster, it doesn't become you. Josh was hired by Carolina Microelectronics. He's working there, but we're still very much married, very much together. It's called a commuter marriage."

Foster lifted a finger to his chin and began to move his head up and down as if he were pondering some deep philosophical problem. "A commuter marriage? That Josh is a strange guy. If you were mine, you can bet I wouldn't be in North Carolina without you."

"Well, now, that's a moot point since I'm not yours."

"Not for lack of trying on my part."

Every conversation they had ended this way. "Foster..."

Foster must have sensed his time was running out so he stood up to leave. "Let me know if you get lonely in that big house all by yourself."

She raised a questioning brow at him. "The door, Foster." He gave her a puppy dog smile, and God help her, she returned it. "Leave. Now."

When he opened the door, Portia walked in. "Fancy seeing you here, Foster."

"Don't make anything out of it, Mommy. I'm leaving."

Portia watched him leave and closed the door behind him. "Josh hasn't been gone a month and Foster is already making a move on you."

"He's not making a move on me. He's flirting like he always does. You know Foster."

Portia took the seat Foster had vacated. "That's the problem. I do know Foster."

Gloria knew of only one way to keep Portia's determined mind off Foster Dixon and his intentions. "How's my godchild doing today?"

Gloria knew her ploy had worked when Portia placed her hand over her stomach and adopted a look that could only be described as "glassy-eyed." "Of course, it's too early for me to feel any movement yet, but I do think I'm getting bigger. What do you think?"

Gloria held back the grin that threatened to spread across her face. Portia's stomach was as flat as it had always been. "I think I can see a little thickening around your waist."

Portia nodded her head in agreement. "I thought it was too early to start with the maternity wear, but I may need to. I don't want to look like I'm bursting out of my clothes."

Gloria picked up a pencil and began striking through some words on the pad in front of her. She didn't know what she was striking through, but she knew if she looked Portia in the face, she would laugh and Portia would be hurt. In that moment, Gloria realized that she had finally adjusted to Portia's pregnancy. She no longer envied her friend's good fortune. She was happy for Portia and that happiness was in no way colored by the problems she and Josh were having. "Well, I wouldn't say you're bursting at the seams yet. You have a few more weeks at least."

Portia looked skeptical. "If you're sure?"

Gloria did look at her then and she had to laugh. "I'm sure, Portia. I'll be the first one to tell you when your clothes start getting too tight."

Chapter 11

Josh packed his briefcase and prepared to go home. He thought about calling Gloria, but decided to wait. She'd said she would call him. If he didn't hear from her by ten, he'd call her.

He picked up the briefcase and headed for the door. The ringing phone stopped him.

"I'm glad I caught you," Gloria began. "I wasn't able to reschedule my meetings. Is there any chance the date for the party can be changed? They didn't give us much notice."

Josh placed his briefcase on the desk and sat down. He pinched his nose in frustration as he thought of a response. "There was nothing you could do?"

Josh could tell from the silence that she didn't appreciate the question.

"You didn't give me much notice," she said. "There wasn't a lot I could do. What do you want from me?"

I want you to be my wife. "Forget I said anything. At least you got back to me today. I'll talk to Carla about rescheduling."

"Ask her if she can give a couple of dates. Or at least, if she can give more notice than before."

Yes, I wouldn't want to inconvenience you. Josh caught the words before he said them. Instead he said, "I'll see what I can do. Well, I'd better get out of here. Maybe I can catch Carla before she leaves for the day."

"Does everybody there work late hours? It's after six, I called you at home, and when you didn't answer, I decided to try you at work."

Josh knew his working late hours was nothing new. He had

always done so. Why was she making a point of it now? "Well, I don't know about everybody else, but since I'm the new kid on the block, I'm out to do a good job. Now, I do need to hang up. I'll talk to you later tonight."

He stared at the phone after he hung up. He hadn't really expected her to make the party so he didn't know why her call had upset him so. He had a good job now and he was determined to do well at it. Things were looking up. Why then did this tension still exist between him and Gloria?

Josh picked up the briefcase and left for Carla's office. He wasn't surprised to see her seated at her desk with the door open.

"Do you have a few minutes?" he asked from the doorway.

Carla looked up from the papers she was reading to smile at him. "Sure, come on in. What can I do for you?"

Josh took the seat in front of her desk. "It's about the party Thursday. We have a problem with the date."

"That's not a problem. It was a bit much to expect you to be available on such short notice. We'll plan something else. This time with your schedule in mind."

Josh relaxed. Until she had spoken, he hadn't realized how tense he was. Thinking about it, he knew he had overreacted. He'd have to apologize to Gloria. "What will you do about Thursday?"

"Don't worry about it. You can meet everyone during the day. The party can wait."

That settled, Josh didn't have anything more to say. "I'd better go so you can finish up. I know you don't want to be here much later."

Carla smiled again, as if she knew something that Josh didn't. "I like the hard work and the long hours," she said. "Don't look so surprised. I bet you do, too."

Josh thought about it. She was right. When the work was good, the hours flew by for him. He was a goal-oriented guy and new projects with new problems always invigorated him. "I figure if you're going to work at a job forty hours a week, for forty or fifty years, you should enjoy it."

"That's my motto, too. You'll find that hard work is rewarded here at Carolina Microelectronics. We take the eager beavers and we work them hard. And we reward them well. Very well."

That was the sales pitch that had sold Josh on the company. He was the eager beaver. He was hungry. That period of unemployment had been a blow to his ego. This was his chance to get back what he had lost.

"You have what we look for, Josh. You're smart. That's a given. But you also have an edge. You want it. You want it all. I could tell during the interview. You strike me as a man who knows what he wants and who's willing to do what it takes to get it."

There was something ominous about the way she spoke. Was she really complimenting him or was she issuing a challenge? She had read him well and that was all right, but he sensed there was something more in her words and that something made him uncomfortable.

"You're a pretty good judge of people," he said, trying to be neutral. "But I'd better get out of here or you won't finish your work."

Josh stood up to leave the room. The look in Carla's eyes told him she knew he was uncomfortable with what she had said, but that it didn't matter to her. Josh walked out of the office without another word.

Once he was in the hallway, he wondered again at her words. Was there a hidden message in there for him? He had known Carla was a single-minded woman, but that hadn't bothered him. In fact, it had drawn him to her. He liked her determination. He was impressed by what she had accomplished at Carolina Electronics. Hell, he even envied her a little, though he'd never admit it to anyone.

Get a hold of yourself, he thought. You're getting paranoid. Stop looking for problems where there are none.

Gloria couldn't sleep. Though it was late and she wanted to get out of bed, she didn't want to risk waking Josh. He had been tired when he had gotten in last night and she knew he needed his sleep. Besides, she was still somewhat miffed about his reaction when she couldn't make the party and she assumed he was still upset with her. She hadn't mentioned it last night and neither had he. Part of the reason was the lateness of his arrival and the other was simple avoidance. At least, that's what it was for her. She didn't know about Josh. Although he had held her close all night, he hadn't made a move to get any more intimate. She wondered if that was a sign he was still upset.

Gloria thought about the plans they had today with Marilyn and Elliot. She was glad to be seeing the couple again. Though she had first formed a relationship with Marilyn, she was finding that Elliot was a good guy himself. Since she had referred him to one of her co-workers about a loan, she had talked with him regularly about the financing of his business.

Elliot was such a simple guy, unlike Josh in so many ways. Elliot just wanted his dream. The money didn't seem to matter that much to him. And Gloria knew there would be money and lots of it. Elliot's idea for fuel efficiency was a winner. He had gotten the financing at her bank with little trouble.

She smiled when she thought about Elliot's response when she'd told him he had gotten the loan. He had picked her up, swirled her around, and given her a big kiss. He had been embarrassed about the kiss and had apologized profusely. She had only laughed at him. Too happy for him to think much about it then. It was then that he had suggested that the two couples celebrate when Josh came home for the weekend. So she and Josh were spending the day with Marilyn and Elliot.

She heard Josh stir next to her. Unsure of what his mood would be, she held herself still so that he wouldn't know she was awake. When she felt him leave the bed, she let out a deep sigh. When she heard the shower go on, she got out of bed, grabbed some clothes from her closet, and went to the bathroom down the hall to shower.

She wasn't in the shower long. She was surprised to see Josh leaning against the vanity with his arms crossed when she stepped out. She quickly pulled the towel around herself. "Good morning," she said, feeling stupid for trying to hide her nakedness from Josh.

"Is it?"

Did Josh want to argue this morning? she wondered. She hoped not, because she didn't. "Yes, it is a good morning. Seems like a great day to take the boat out."

"I wasn't referring to the weather."

She gave a sheepish smile. He did want to argue. "Okay, Josh, what were you referring to, if not the weather?"

Josh turned around so that she could see his face in the mirror. Her first thought was that they were an attractive couple. His dark brown complexion complemented the light-brownness of hers. Her soft features, his strong ones. Yes, they were an attractive couple. "I'm sorry I was so tired when I got in last night, but I've been busting my tail at work. Are you still angry with me about the party?"

Her anger left when she saw the sincerity and concern in his eyes. "Not anymore."

"I'll say it again. I'm sorry I overreacted. Now, how's your work going?"

She relaxed at his apology. "Pretty exciting right now. I'm working on the financing for two developments—the Turner Hill Mall and the strip shopping center on Cascade."

"How did you pull that deal together? I thought the Turner Hill Mall was dead."

Gloria shook her head as she applied her foundation. "Almost. The South DeKalb Chamber never gave up on it and the financing finally came through. The mall will be a boon for that whole area."

Gloria saw pride and interest in Josh's eyes. "A boon for you, too. That's great, Gloria. What's this about Cascade?"

She was happy to talk with Josh about her work again. It had been a long while since she felt comfortable doing so. "That's my special project. A few of the businessmen in the Cascade area came to me with an idea. They want to open a strip shopping center that houses only small business—no chains. They see the population exploding in the area and they want to make sure that some of the money stays in the community. What better way than to have local businesses serve the local community?"

"Sounds like a good idea, but can they pull it off?"

"It's going to take some time and we've still got a lot of planning to do, but I think I can line up the financing."

"Your bank is being very generous these days."

Gloria took that as a compliment. In her new position, she had found a new sense of purpose and satisfaction. She'd never considered herself a community activist, but she found herself assuming that role in her projects. And she liked it. And she wanted to do more of it. She wanted to direct the bank along the lines of more community development, more support of local businesses. There was money to be made financing chains relocating to the Atlanta area, but she knew there was an untapped market in financing local businesses. "Hey, we're just in it to make money."

"The bank might be, but it's more than that with you. I'm proud of you. You're doing a great job."

Gloria could tell from his expression, if not his words, that his thoughts were elsewhere. She wondered if he was beginning to see why she didn't want to pull up stakes and leave Atlanta so quickly. She was doing things here. Things that mattered to her and the community. She hoped Josh could see that, too.

"I'm glad you were able to help Elliot," he said.

Gloria placed the cap back on the eyeliner, done with her eyes. "I can't take credit for that. All I did was point him in the right direction. That business plan you helped him pull together was the real winner. The loan office had nothing to question."

"Are you getting modest on me? I know you put in a good word for him and that word removed any doubts the loan officer may have had. I think Elliot knows that too. That's why they've invited us out to the lake today. I didn't even know they had a boat."

Gloria was pleased with Josh's praise, but she was also embarrassed. "They don't. They've borrowed a friend's boat. Elliot knows how much time we used to spend on the water and he wanted to do something special for us."

"So, you and Elliot have been spending a lot of time together?"

The question was innocent enough, but Gloria paused in the application of her lipstick to check Josh's expression. There didn't seem to be anything in the look he was giving her. "He's called me a few times. He looks at me as sort of an advisor."

"Has he asked you to be his partner yet?"

Gloria laughed at that. "In fact, he has. He was joking, of course. It was right after he got the loan. How did you know?"

Josh shrugged his shoulders. "It was just a guess. He asked me about it before I left for Raleigh."

"Elliot asked you to be his partner? You never told me that."

Josh turned around and leaned back against the vanity. She could no longer see his face in the mirror. "There was nothing to tell. The position in Raleigh is a lot more stable than a partnership with Elliot."

She turned to look at Josh's profile, her makeup all done. "I guess you're right, but I think Elliot is going to make a lot of money. He and Marilyn deserve it too."

Josh fingered the towel that Gloria had wrapped about her. "You're right about that. And so do we."

Gloria's attention focused on Josh's fingers. She wondered if he was going to unknot the towel. "So do we what?"

"Deserve good things," he said.

Before Gloria could comment, the phone rang. Josh's finger stopped moving on the towel and his eyes met hers. She stepped back and the towel fell to the floor.

"They'll call back," she said.

Josh and Marilyn sat around the table on the upper deck. Marilyn talked while Josh listened, or rather, tried to listen. His attention was constantly being drawn away to the sound of Gloria's laughter. She and Elliot were "manning the ship," as they called it.

"You haven't heard a word I've said, have you?" Marilyn asked. Her question brought his gaze to her face.

"I'm sorry, Marilyn. What were you saying?"

"Don't be sorry. It's endearing to watch you watch her with so much love in your eyes. You two probably wanted to spend

some time alone today. Elliot and I should be sorry for interrupting your time together."

Josh hadn't realized his thoughts were so obvious. He did
want to be alone with Gloria and he was jealous that she was
spending her time laughing with Elliot instead of laughing with
him. It wasn't that he didn't trust them or even that he suspected
them, but he wanted all of Gloria's attention. Their time together was precious to him since they had so little of it. "You're
our friends. We appreciated the offer."

"But it would have been more romantic if we'd just offered
you the boat?"

Josh laughed. "I think we'd better end this whole line of conversation."

She laughed too. "How's the new job?" she asked.

Josh told her about the job and his new boss.

"I'm glad you like it there," she said when he'd finished.
"How are you handling the commute?"

Josh glanced over at Elliot and Gloria again. "It's hard. I want
her with me."

"That's only natural. Just keep telling yourself it's only for a
few months."

He wished. From what Gloria had said about her job this
morning, Josh knew she really didn't want to move. And he admitted to himself, he didn't blame her. "Yeah. Just a few
months."

"You don't sound too sure about that. Do you want to talk
about it?"

Josh realized Marilyn was concerned and that she wanted to
be helpful but he didn't feel comfortable discussing his marriage
with her. "Thanks for the offer. I may take you up on it one day."

Marilyn reached out and placed her hand across his. "We're
here for you and Gloria if you need us. Anytime."

Josh nodded, then stood up abruptly. "I'll see if I can give Gloria and Elliot a hand." When he reached Elliot and Gloria, he
asked, "What's so funny?"

Elliot looked at Josh and then back at Gloria. He and Gloria
fell into laughter once more. "You had to be there," Elliot of-

fered. When Elliot finally stopped laughing, he asked Josh, "Enjoying the trip so far?"

"Sure, but I don't think I was much company for Marilyn, though. You'd better go see about her."

Elliot again looked from Josh to Gloria and back again. "I can take a hint. I'm outta here."

Gloria was still smiling as she watched Elliott walk over to his wife.

"You and Elliot seemed to be having a lot of fun," Josh said.

Gloria nodded and began tying back the sails. "He can be a funny guy at times."

"I bet."

Gloria stopped what she was doing to look at Josh. She smiled before she said, "I don't believe it, you're jealous."

"I'm not jealous."

"Yes, you are. Don't deny it. You're jealous of Elliot. Why?"

Josh looked away. "I want you all to myself. You should be laughing with me, not with him."

She loped an arm around his waist and kissed him. "And, I'd rather spend my time with you, but they invited us out and we have to be sociable."

"You're right, but all I can think about is this morning and the way we made love. I want to make love to you again."

Gloria felt the lower part of her body grow warm. "I want that too. Just think how much better it's going to be tonight when we finally get home. Anticipation is a great aphrodisiac."

Josh grunted and pulled her closer to him. "If I live that long."

Gloria felt his erection and she laughed. "You'll live."

He grunted again. "You're going to have to stand here awhile. If we walk back over to Elliot and Marilyn now, they're to know what's on my mind."

Chapter 12

Damn, Gloria thought, we've got to do something about this gearshift. She wanted to get closer to Josh, but the gearshift prevented her from moving as close as she liked. Determined to get some action started in the car, she leaned across the gearshift and placed her arms around his shoulders.

"You'd better watch yourself, Gloria," Josh warned.

She ignored him and put her tongue in his ear. When he moaned, she asked, "Something wrong, Josh?"

"Stop it, Gloria, I'm trying to drive. I don't want us to have an accident, do you?"

Gloria moved her attention from his ear and began to place hot kisses down his strong jaw. "Stop what?" she asked with a tinge of innocence.

"You know what you're doing," he said. His hands gripped the steering wheel and his eyes focused on the road.

She moved her hand to rest on his chest and continued her kisses. "You don't like it?"

He cut his eye in her direction. "You know I like it. That's the problem. I like it too much."

Her hand slipped from his chest to rest on his thighs.

"Gloria," Josh warned. He dropped one hand from the steering wheel and placed it atop hers.

She inched her fingers up his thigh, ignoring his feeble attempt to stop her movements. "This isn't affecting you, is it, Josh? It's not like you're about to run off the road or anything."

He cut his eyes in her direction again and the passion she saw in them almost made her forget the game she was playing. Josh wasn't playing, and as soon as they got home, she would pay for her actions. She shivered at the thought.

When Josh returned his attention to the road, Gloria's fingers resumed their motions. Evidently, Josh had decided to stop fighting her because he moved his hand back to the steering wheel.

"You're going to get it when we get home," he said. "Yes, you're going to get it."

When she looked down at the bulge in his pants, she knew he was right. She was going to get it when she got home. The thought made her warm all over.

She kissed him again on his jaw while her fingers made their way to the bulge in his pants. When she grabbed him there, the car swerved.

"Dammit, Gloria, you're going to get it."

She laughed.

When Josh pulled the Saab into the driveway, he was literally bursting at the seams. Gloria had settled back in her seat, looking as innocent as a Sunday School teacher. She was going to pay for what she had done to him and pay big.

He watched as she unbuckled her seatbelt. When she moved to raise the latch to open the door, he asked, her, "Where are you going?"

When she looked at him, he groaned and pulled her to him, gearshift be damned. No way was she getting away from him with a look like that in her eyes. She was just as affected by her sexual antics as he was.

He held her with one hand and lifted the steering wheel to its highest position with the other, all the while sliding his seat as far back as it would go. That done, he managed to position her so that she sat on his lap. Awkward positioning, but comfort was not his prime consideration now.

"You know you're going to have to pay up now, don't you Gloria?" he asked.

She adjusted herself on his lap, trying to get closer to him. With her hands positioned on either of his shoulders, she asked, "How much do I have to pay?"

When he reached under her blouse, she sighed. Her arms automatically lifted as he pulled her blouse over her head to expose her lace bra. "A lot," he answered as he unsnapped her bra and slipped the straps down her arms. He inhaled her scent as he threw the bra into the back seat with her blouse.

"God, you have beautiful breasts," he said, his mouth greedily attacking first one breast, then the other.

He heard the rumbling sounds from the back of her throat and he knew she was getting her payback. With much self-control he pulled his mouth away from her breasts. "What? Nothing to say? Cat got your tongue?" Before she could answer, he captured her mouth for a ravaging kiss. He couldn't get close enough to her.

He ended the kiss and pushed her away from him.

"Let's go inside," he whispered, done with his game and ready to get down to business.

"Why do we have to go inside?" she asked. "I don't want to move until you give me what you promised."

"But we'll be more comfortable inside," Josh offered. When she rose up from him and, with the skill of a contortionist, removed her shorts and panties, he knew the tables had turned.

"Gloria," he warned.

She looked down at him, her eyes glazed with a sensuous mist. "Don't you want this?" She didn't wait for his answer. She unzipped his shorts, lifted him out of his shorts, and directed him into her entrance.

It had been past midnight when they had finally come into the house. Their time in the car had been exciting. And the night in bed had been even better. It was as if their sex life had taken on a new life. It had urgency that Gloria once thought they had lost.

She felt Josh stir behind her and she snuggled closer to him. "Good morning," she said without turning around to look at him.

He pushed his arousal against her buttocks. "Very good morning."

She pushed her hips more tightly against him. "Don't you ever get tired?"

"Not of you," he said, placing a kiss on the base of her neck.

She turned around to face him. "You always say the right thing. Do you know that?"

He kissed her lips. "And you always do the right thing. I enjoyed our drive home."

She placed a hand on his chest, moving her fingers through the light film of fur that covered it. "I told you."

"Told me what?"

She placed a kiss on his chest. "So you've forgotten."

"Forgotten what?"

She continued with light, feather kisses across his chest. "Shame on you, Josh. You did forget."

He placed a hand on either side of her head and lifted her face to his. "What are you talking about?"

She smiled. "The challenge that you made when we were in Bermuda. So, how does this weekend stack up against the one we just had in Raleigh?"

He laughed. "You mean you planned that garage escapade?"

"Did you enjoy it?"

He pulled her to him. His Gloria was turning wanton on him. Maybe this commuter marriage would work after all. "Maybe I should show you how much," was his answer.

Gloria walked through the house reliving the day she and Josh had shared after they'd finally gotten out of bed.

They'd had brunch with Dexter and Portia and had spent the early part of the afternoon with them. Josh had been in a rush to leave afterward and now he was gone. She missed him already. It was an ache that she guessed she would have to get used to.

The ringing telephone cut short her musing. It was Elliot looking for Josh. "You just missed him. He left no more than ten minutes ago."

"It's just as well. I promised Marilyn that I wouldn't bother you guys today, but I wanted to get Josh's opinion on something before he left."

"You can always call him in Raleigh. You have his number, right?"

"Yes, I've got it. Maybe I will give him a call. I don't suppose you'd want to look over my idea, would you?"

Gloria smiled at his manner. "Why not? Why don't you two come over and plan to stay for dinner."

"Sounds good, but it's just me. Marilyn went to visit a friend's mother in Columbus. She won't be back until later tonight."

"Well, why don't you come over?" she asked.

"I have a better idea. Why don't we go out? This is something we can discuss over dinner." When Gloria hesitated, he added, "I owe you, Gloria. You've done so much for us already. Let me do something for you."

She responded to the pleading in his voice. "Okay. As long as it's nothing fancy."

"You choose the place. How about I pick you up in about an hour and a half—say, six o'clock?"

"You don't have to pick me up. I can meet you there."

"I don't want you driving home by yourself after dark," he explained. "Even if we meet there, I'll have to follow you home so you may as well let me pick you up."

"Okay, I'll see you around six."

After Gloria hung up, she realized she was glad to be getting out of the house and away from her thoughts. She wondered what Josh would make of her dinner with Elliot. Elliot without Marilyn. She had been flattered by his jealousy on the boat yesterday. Though there was nothing, would never be anything, between her and Elliot, it was good to know Josh thought she was attractive enough to worry about. She shook her head, tossing those thoughts aside, and wandered into the bedroom to find something to wear.

Elliot picked her up promptly at six and they went to the Olive Garden for dinner. She listened to his idea and gave her opinion. They went back and forth on some issues before reaching a compromise. They were both feeling good about the evening when they left the restaurant.

On the drive home he asked about her work and she told him about the Cascade project.

"Seems like it's keeping you busy," Elliot observed.

Gloria nodded. "It is, but it's worth it. It means a lot to the small businesses in the area. It's important for the people in that area to keep their money in the community as long as possible."

Elliot pulled into her driveway then. She was about to invite him in for coffee, but he spoke first.

"It was good of you to help me out," he said. "I really appreciate it. You and Josh have both helped me tremendously. I don't know how I'll ever repay you. One of you should reconsider and become my partner. You deserve to get something out of this business."

Gloria wanted to reach over and touch his cheek, in a friendly gesture, of course. "This is your dream. We're just glad to be a part of it. We've enjoyed watching you embrace your success."

Was Elliot blushing? she wondered. He was a fair-skinned man, so the faint, reddish tint of his cheeks could be a blush.

"It's not success yet," he said, "but it's close. So close I can taste it."

"This is something you deserve. You took your unemployment which could have an ending, and made it a beginning. I'm impressed."

Yes, he was blushing, Gloria said to herself.

"I couldn't have done it without Marilyn," he continued. "She supported me, and I mean more than financially, when I really needed it. I'll never be able to repay her for that."

He sounded so forlorn as he spoke that she wanted to reassure him. "She doesn't want to be repaid. She did it because she loves you. It's her dream, too. I envy you both."

They were silent for a while. "You and Josh seem to be adjusting well to your commuter marriage."

She nodded. "It's hard but we love each other and we're determined to see this through."

"I know this is none of my business, but I don't think this commuter marriage is such a good idea. Married people should be together."

It was so simple for Elliot. Too bad it wasn't that simple for her and Josh. "Ours is a special case. We don't want to be apart, but there was no other way."

"We all make choices. You and Josh had a choice. You chose to be apart rather than to be together. That I don't understand. I would never choose to be apart from Marilyn."

Gloria felt her defenses rise. "It's complicated, Elliot. Josh has to follow his dream just like you had to follow yours. I'm supporting him in that, but I have dreams too. Should I have given up my dreams to follow him? Should he have given up his dreams to stay with me?"

"I'm not saying you should have followed him, but I figured one of you needed to give in. You both made choices," Elliot continued, shaking his head, "but I can't see myself having made those same choices."

Her anger was immediate. "So, Mr. High and Mighty, you've judged Josh and me and found us lacking, is that it?"

Elliot reached for her hand. "No, that's not it at all. I care about you and Josh and I want you to be happy."

Gloria snatched her hand away and flung open the car door. She wasn't going to sit here and listen to Elliot's judgments. The things he had said had hit too close to home. At one time, she would have followed Josh anywhere. Why had she put her career before their marriage this time? She knew the answer, but she didn't like it and she knew Elliot wouldn't approve of it. Well, who the hell was Elliot to judge her anyway? She hopped out of the car. "Good night, Elliot," she said with obvious sarcasm. "I had a great time."

She heard Elliot say something but the words didn't register in her brain. She stormed to the front door, unlocked it, and let herself in. Once inside, she began to pace. Elliot and his opinions. Who asked him anyway? That's the problem with friends. They always gave too much advice. This kind of stuff she expected from Portia, not from Elliot. What did Elliot know about her marriage anyway? He couldn't even plan his own business without her help.

The more Gloria thought about his comments, the angrier she became. She wondered how many other people were judging her, looking for her marriage to fall apart. Well, other people didn't know about her and Josh. Their marriage was as strong as ever. This commuter arrangement was only temporary.

One good thing had come out of this, though. Josh would no longer have reason to be jealous of Elliot because Gloria was never going to see him again. That meant she wouldn't see Marilyn either, but she figured that was best. Marilyn probably shared Elliot's feelings anyway.

Chapter 13

Josh needed to leave early to meet Gloria's flight. Early was probably the wrong word. He wasn't leaving early; he just wasn't staying as late as usual. He had planned a romantic weekend that he knew Gloria would like. He could see it now. He'd whisk her into the townhouse for a candlelit dinner. Then, after dinner, he'd take her to the bedroom, where he had strewn red roses across the bed. The perfect beginning to the perfect weekend.

And they needed this weekend. In the last few months, their times together had been hit and miss, at best. If not her schedule, then his, had prevented them from getting together as planned. They hadn't been together, without the interference of work, since the weekend of their boat trip with Marilyn and Elliot. And that seemed so long ago, which was why Josh had planned such a special time this weekend.

And that's why Josh was so impatient with today's meeting. As soon as this meeting ended, his perfect weekend could begin. Would Carla never finish? he wondered. These Friday afternoon meetings were the only things he didn't like about his job. Who scheduled Friday afternoon meetings anyway? And these meetings always lasted until six. That wouldn't be a problem if he and Gloria weren't commuting. But it was hell when he had to make an eight-hour drive to Atlanta or a run to the airport to pick up Gloria.

Finally, Carla was wrapping it up. He'd be out of the building in fifteen minutes. Twenty at the most. A quick stop in his office and then he'd be gone.

He saw the message propped on his desk as soon as he walked

into his office. Don't let this be some major problem, he thought. He walked to the desk and picked up the note. From Gloria. Don't go to the airport, it read. Call her.

Damn, he thought. What was going on? He knew, but he didn't want to know. He flopped down in his chair and punched in her number on the telephone keypad. She picked up on the first ring. "Why are you still in Atlanta?" he asked.

"I'm sorry. I can't make it this weekend. The Cascade businessmen want a meeting tomorrow morning. We've run into a snag with the financing. It's an emergency, Josh. Please understand."

Josh didn't say anything. He thought about the townhouse. The dinner. The bed. His plans. Their weekend. All gone. And she wanted him to understand.

"Say something, Josh."

"I'm disappointed you can't make it," he said. *That was calm. That was good.*

"I'll make it up to you. I promise."

Sure. She had no idea of the plans he'd made and she was talking about making it up to him. What could he say?

"I know you're upset and you have every right to be," she went on, "but this couldn't be helped. The Cascade people could blow this whole deal if I don't handle it just right. Help me out here, Josh. Tell me you understand."

"It's not that I don't understand. It's that I don't believe it."

"I knew this would happen. I knew you wouldn't understand. I'm trying to make the best of our situation. What more do you want from me?"

I want to come first. Before work. Before clients. Before projects. "Let's just forget it, Gloria. You can't come. Don't worry about it. I'll drive down instead."

When she didn't respond, he asked, "You do want me to come home, don't you?"

"Of course, I want you to come home," she began. "It's just that I'll be so busy. I'd hate for you to make the trip and then I can't spend any time with you. You know how upset you were the last time you came home and I worked all weekend."

Josh couldn't believe what he was hearing. Gloria's work had never been that important in the past. "I wanted to see you, but if you're going to be busy, I'll stay here."

"I'll make it up to you, Josh," she said again. "I promise."

He had heard that before. "I know you will, Gloria," he said, but he didn't mean it. He didn't think she had any understanding of how important this weekend was to him. So, how could she make it up to him?

"Call me tonight?"

What else did he have to do? "Sure. Right now I'm going to head out of here. I'll talk to you later."

After they hung up, Josh sat at his desk and stared at the phone. Carla unexpectedly walked in. "Problems, Josh?" she asked.

He looked up and saw her walking into the office. She took a seat in front of his desk. "No problems."

"Couldn't tell it by looking at you. You look like you've lost your best friend."

For some reason that made him laugh. That was exactly the way he felt. Gloria was his best friend and he felt as if he was losing her and there was nothing he could do about it. "Gloria and I had plans for the evening and she has to work. So, I'm left to myself."

"I'm sorry it's taking her so long to find work here. I thought it would've been much easier."

"She's had some offers. It's just that her job in Atlanta is perfect. She hasn't found anything comparable. We're hoping she will and soon."

"So do I. By the way, I'm having dinner with Tom Kennedy and his wife tonight. You're welcome to join us if you like. No business. Just dinner. Tom's a good person to know. We're meeting at Dominic's around seven-thirty. You can just show up if you don't find anything else to do."

Josh's first inclination had been to turn down Carla's invitation, but at seven o'clock he was at Dominic's, looking for her and Tom. He saw Carla first. She was seated at the bar and she had changed clothes. He was surprised he even recognized her.

That slinky red dress was a lot different from what she usually wore to work and her hair was down, not pulled back in its normal bun.

He walked over to her. "I see I'm not as early as I thought."

She turned on her stool and he saw that the dress didn't even come mid-thigh. When Carla went casual, she went casual. "No, handsome, you're right on time," she said.

He couldn't form a response. Was Carla coming on to him? He looked around. Where were Tom and his wife? He didn't know what to do. Damn, this was awkward. "Are you all right, Carla?" He knew that was a dumb question, but he couldn't think of anything else to say.

When she laughed, he knew he had said the wrong thing. "What's so funny?"

"You," she said. "Hi, I'm Darlene, Carla's sister. Carla's twin sister. I'm meeting her here tonight before her dinner."

Josh knew he visibly relaxed and then he was more embarrassed. She had stopped laughing, but she was still smiling like the cat who had swallowed the canary.

"You knew I thought you were Carla, didn't you?"

She nodded. "People mix us up all the time, even though we have totally different personalities, not to mention—" she looked down at her dress "—different tastes in clothes. Didn't it throw you a little to see Carla dressed like this? Unless my sister has changed drastically in the last day, she'd never wear an outfit like this."

Josh had to agree with her. But since she looked exactly like Carla, he had assumed that Carla had varying tastes in clothes. "You enjoy doing this, don't you?"

She smiled that smile again. This time it was contagious. "Carla's friends and co-workers are usually such stuffed shirts. It's fun to see their reaction. You must be new since most Carolina Micro people know me and they're used to me. How long have you been here?"

"Almost four months," Josh answered.

She extended her hand. "Welcome to Raleigh. I hope you're here to stay."

He took her hand. "Thanks. I hope I'm here for a while my-self."

"Married?" she asked.

He was taken aback at the question, but he answered it by showing her the ring on his finger. "Almost two years."

"Talk about bad timing."

Josh knew she was flirting with him, but it was a harmless flir-tation. "I'll take that as a compliment."

"It was. You know, it figures."

"What figures?"

"All the good ones are taken."

He laughed outright at that. "How do you know I'm a good one?"

"Don't tell me I'm wrong. A man who looks like you can't be bad. Well, you could be, but it would be a good bad."

He laughed again. She was charming. And sexual. Very sex-ual. "You're outrageous."

"I'll take that as a compliment. Have a drink with me while we wait for Carla."

Josh took the bar stool next to hers and ordered white wine. He didn't have to say much because Darlene kept up a steady stream of conversation. She told him all the twin tricks she and Carla had played over the years. The stories gave him another picture of Carla. One that was much different from the Carla he knew from work. He filed that information away to think about at a later time. Now, he just wanted to listen to Darlene.

"Where's your wife?" Darlene asked. No topic was taboo for her. "I can't believe she let you out alone at night. I wouldn't if I were her."

Josh really didn't want to talk about Gloria with Darlene. It made him feel guilty. He and Darlene were engaged in harmless flirting, but he knew Gloria wouldn't approve. "She's working."

"She needs better hours. There are some women out here who consider a man without a date on a Friday night as avail-able whether he's married or not."

"Are you one of those women?" He knew as soon as he asked that he shouldn't have.

She turned to look at him. "I haven't been in the past, but

there's something about you that makes me think I need to reconsider my position."

After she said that, she turned around and sipped her drink. All his words about harmless flirtation went out the window. Her last statement had been said in all seriousness. He knew he should get up and leave right now. He was about to do that when she started in with another Carla-Darlene story. He couldn't leave in the middle of her story, could he? That's what he told himself while he sat there and listened to her soothing voice as she told her funny stories.

Gloria told herself over and over that this meeting was important. That this was part of her job. A part she liked, even.

"Mr. Thompson, we're going to work it out. They can't take the land. You have the deed."

The gray-headed Mr. Thompson shook his head. "I've seen it happen before, Mrs. Martin. You know how those big companies are. They can do anything."

Gloria smiled. She knew Mr. Thompson knew she was right, but he needed someone to hold his hand. He was getting pretty close to having his dream of owning his own store in the neighborhood where he grew up and he was getting antsy. Understandable.

"They can't do anything and you know it. You're just worried about the meeting tomorrow. Everything is going to be fine."

"She's right, Grady," Mrs. Thompson chimed in. "You're just getting jittery. Now calm down or Mrs. Martin is going to regret she agreed to give us the money."

Grady Thompson took his wife's hand in his. "We're putting up all the money we have in the world. My wife's security, the money we could leave for the kids and grandkids. Maybe we're too old to open a restaurant. Maybe it won't work and we'll lose all our money."

Mrs. Thompson shook her head. She was a petite woman, at least a hundred pounds lighter and six inches shorter than her bear of a husband, but Gloria knew Mrs. Thompson was her husband's anchor.

"Enough of that, Grady. You're exaggerating and you know it. Now we need to get out of here so Mrs. Martin can go home. Her husband will be upset with us as it is. It's almost ten o'-clock."

Mr. Thompson grudgingly stood up. Gloria knew he could have talked the rest of the night, but Mrs. Thompson was right. She did need to get home. She'd hated to cancel her trip to Raleigh this weekend, but it couldn't be helped. She had to meet with the Cascade investors tomorrow. In addition to being the one to pull the financials together, she had become a source of support and strength for the merchants. The support role was a new one for her, but she enjoyed it.

After she had led the Thompsons out of her office, her first thought was to call Josh. She picked up the phone to dial his number, but she changed her mind and put it back down. She knew Josh would still be angry that she hadn't made the week-end and she couldn't blame him. But she couldn't help it either. She was in the middle of this project and she had to see it through. And tomorrow was another full day of meetings. She knew her schedule was playing havoc with their weekend plans, but there was nothing she could do about it until the projects were wrapped up.

She sighed a long sigh and promised herself that she would make this weekend up to Josh. She didn't know when, but she would. With that thought in mind she packed her briefcase and left the office.

By the time Gloria arrived home, she had thought of a way to salvage some of this weekend with Josh. If she couldn't be with him in the flesh, the telephone would have to do and she was sure she could make it as interesting as any of those 900 num-bers. It'd be something different too.

First, she took a long, hot bath and massaged her skin with the perfumed lotion that Josh liked so well. She pulled a light, blue negligee from her closet and put it on. She felt sexy just thinking about what she had planned. She knew Josh was going to love it. She turned back the covers on the bed and climbed in.

She was about to pick up the phone when she realized she had forgotten the wine. She got out of bed and went to the kitchen for the wine. She couldn't have a seduction scene, even a telephone seduction scene, without wine, she reasoned.

Once she was settled back in bed, she picked up the phone and dialed Josh's number. "Hiya, handsome," she said when the phone was answered.

"This is Josh," was the response she got. "Leave a message at the tone."

She called every fifteen minutes until she fell asleep. The last time she looked at the clock it was one twenty-five.

When Josh woke up Saturday morning, he didn't remember much of the dinner with Carla and Tom and his wife, but he did remember Darlene. He was thinking about her when the phone rang. It was Gloria.

"I tried to call you last night," she said. "But you weren't home. What did you do?"

"I had dinner with some people from the office."

"I'm disappointed that I didn't get to talk with you, but I'm glad you weren't alone. I'm sorry again about the trip."

"Let's not keep bringing that up. What time is your meeting this morning?"

"I'm on my way out of the door now. I just wanted to hear your voice. I love you, Josh."

"I love you, too, Gloria." Josh hung up. He did love Gloria, but he had flirted big time with Darlene. And it had been fun. He wasn't doing anything or thinking about doing anything, but he had enjoyed her company a lot.

That was part of his problem, Josh thought. He hadn't made any friends in the time he had been in Raleigh. He was working a lot of hours so he didn't usually miss it, but this weekend he didn't want to be alone. He didn't want to miss Gloria because missing her made him angry with her. So, he reasoned, the best thing he could do for his marriage was to keep from missing her. Armed with that rationale, he now had to find something to do today. Darlene had mentioned a Greek festival on the Chapel Hill campus. He could pull out his fraternity T-shirt and trek over there. What better way to meet people?

Josh went upstairs and dressed in his fraternity T-shirt and jeans. He got his map, and after finding and circling the campus, he headed for his car. As he drove to the campus, he told himself over and over that he was going only to meet people, make a few friends. His trip had nothing to do with Darlene's comment that she'd be there all day. Besides, with the number of people that usually went to a Greek festival, the odds of him running into Darlene were slim to none. No, he wasn't looking for Darlene. He wanted to meet some of his fraternity brothers.

He continued to tell himself this until he pulled into the University parking lot. As luck would have it, Darlene pulled up in the space next to him. He looked over at her and smiled.

Chapter 14

"What are you doing here on Saturday?"

Gloria looked up from the contracts on her desk and saw Foster Dixon leaning against her office doorway. "This is my office, my building. What are you doing here? Slumming?"

Foster pushed away from the doorjamb and moved to the chair in front of her desk. "I had to go by the library. What's your excuse?"

"Cascade. I met with the principals today."

Foster leaned forward in his chair. "How's that going?"

Gloria wondered at his tone. She knew there had been talk about the project. Some of the other vice presidents didn't think it was worth the effort she was expending. "What have you heard?"

He leaned back. "Don't go paranoid on me. I haven't heard anything." He paused. "Much."

"What does that mean?"

"There's been some talk. They say you're going out on a limb for no reason. That you could have picked a safer project."

"And you? What do you think?"

He waved a hand in her direction. "Come on, Gloria. This project is peanuts. If you close the deal, who'll care? If you don't close it, it'll be a mark against you. I thought you were smarter than that."

"I'm disappointed in you, Foster. When the black community comes together to do something for itself, there is always a bunch of nay-sayers. It surprises me that you're one of them. I can't believe you don't see the merit in this project."

Foster stood and leaned over her desk. "I'll tell you what I see. I see a Florence Nightingale trying to save the world."

Gloria leaned toward Foster until they were almost nose to nose. "I'll tell you what I see. I see a black man who's forgotten what it means to be black."

Foster moved back, stung. Gloria had hit her mark. "Is that what you really think? You think that I don't care."

She didn't really think that. She hadn't really thought about it. "What am I supposed to think when you say you don't see the importance of this project?"

Foster pinched his nose. "My problem is not with the project. It's with your timing. Do you have any idea how hard it will be to get another project like Cascade if you fail with this one?"

She had thought about it, but not much. One of her investors had pulled out, but she knew she would find the money. She had to. "I won't fail."

"Whether you fail or not has nothing to do with you, Gloria. That's what I'm trying to tell you. This matter is engulfed in politics. You know, there are other investors interested in that area. Investors with a lot more money. Some people around here are hoping that you don't pull it off. Those other investors will mean more revenue for the bank. A lot more."

She knew he was right. Some people were waiting for her to fail. "Are you one of those people?"

Foster lifted both arms in the air. "How can you even ask that?"

"Just checking. Things are getting hairy around here. I wish Portia were around. I could always count on her support." This wasn't the first time she had thought about her friend. The workplace wasn't the same without her.

"I don't want you to blow this out of proportion. Not everybody is against you. There are those who are pulling for you, those who are wondering why the bank hasn't taken on more of these projects."

She raised a brow in his direction. "Huh?"

"No 'huh.' There are those who are very impressed with what you're doing. I admit, they're the minority, but you do have some people pulling for you. Louise, for one."

She was glad her boss was on her side, but her boss wasn't a friend. Portia was a friend. She could express her insecurities to a friend. She couldn't do that with her boss. "That's good to know."

They were silent for a moment, then Foster asked, "How is Portia?"

Gloria didn't know how she was. They hadn't spoken since Portia left on maternity leave. "She's fine."

"She sure surprised me, leaving like that. I thought she would have stayed around until the baby came."

Gloria had been surprised herself when Portia had told her she was leaving early. She talked about wanting to decorate the nursery, get ready for the baby. Portia had even chosen an extended leave instead of the three months she had originally talked about. Gloria shook her head. It was as if she and Portia had changed lives. Portia had been the one concerned about leaving her job. Gloria had wanted to stay home with the baby. Things surely had changed over the last year.

Foster snapped his fingers in her face. "Earth to Gloria?"

She looked up at him. "Sorry, Foster, what were you saying?"

He repeated what he had said, but Gloria tuned him out again as soon as he began talking. Her thoughts were still on Portia. She missed her friend and she regretted the distance she had put between them. A part of her blamed Elliot and his commentary. Seeing Portia made her feel guilty. Guilty because Portia's priorities seemed to be in the right place, while hers were questionable.

Foster literally ran into Portia the following Monday morning. "Hey, you'd better watch where you're going, little mother."

"Oh, hi, Foster. I'm sorry. My mind was somewhere else. What brings you downtown today?"

"I should be asking you that. I'm meeting with Eleanor. What are you doing here?"

"I just thought I'd drop by and say hi since I was downtown."

"Shopping?"

Portia grinned. "I have to have everything ready for my kid when she gets here, don't I?"

Foster laughed. "You know, I never would have thought you'd take mothering so seriously, but you're having a ball, aren't you?"

Portia placed her hand on her protruding belly. "I never thought it either, Foster. But it seems I've just fallen into it. I thought being home would drive me crazy, but I'm really enjoying it."

"Well, it shows. Maybe you ought to give some of that spirit to your girl Gloria."

"What do you mean by that?"

He shrugged his shoulders. "She seems to be strung a mite too tight. Things not going well with her and Josh and this commuter marriage?"

Portia thought Foster was probably right, but she wasn't going to gossip about her best friend. Even though she hadn't seen much of that best friend lately. She knew her pregnancy made Gloria uncomfortable, but she wasn't sure if jealousy or something else was the cause of that discomfort. "That's just wishful thinking on your part. You'd love it if things weren't going well with Josh and Gloria. You'd try to move right on in, wouldn't you?"

Foster had the decency to be honest. "I've never hidden my feelings for Gloria. If Josh messes this up, I'll be more than ready to step in. But right now I'm worried about her. She's too wrapped up in these projects."

"Gloria's always taken her job seriously. What's wrong with that?"

Foster shook his head. "Maybe I'm wrong, but I think you should talk with her. Unless I'm reading her wrong, she could use a friend right now."

That was all Portia needed. She would see Gloria today and they would discuss whatever it was that was causing the strain in their friendship. She missed her friend and she hoped Gloria missed her too. "I'll stop by her office on my way out. Thanks, Foster. Maybe you aren't the lecher that I've made you out to be."

Foster laughed. Before he walked away, he said, "Don't be too sure about that. There's more than one way to go about a task."

Portia watched him walk away with an almost smile on her face. Gloria had better be careful, she thought.

"Have you been avoiding me?"

Gloria looked up and saw Portia's head poked in her office doorway. She didn't answer immediately because Portia was partially correct. "Don't be silly. Come on in."

As Portia walked into the office, Gloria felt a familiar pang of jealousy. Portia looked as if she were about to deliver any minute now. Gloria hadn't realized the strength of her feelings about Portia's pregnancy. It still pained her to see her friend. She and Josh didn't need a baby now. She knew that. They needed to get their work situations settled before even considering a family. Then, why did looking at Portia's stomach make her feel so empty inside?

Portia eased down in the chair and put her hands on her stomach. "You didn't answer my question. Have I done something to offend you?"

Gloria felt guilty about the way she had treated Portia. "It's nothing you've done. It's me."

"It's okay if you don't want to talk about it," Portia said.

Gloria smiled. Portia was not being herself this Monday morning. It was very much unlike her not to want to talk about anything. She wondered if pregnancy had mellowed her some. A part of her hoped not. "No, I do want to talk about it. Do you have some time?" At Portia's nod, Gloria told her about the conversation with Elliot that had been gnawing at her.

"Does what he said bother you because you think he's right?"

"I'm not willing to say yet that I think he's right, but he has a point. Why would I choose this job over following Josh? Does that mean I don't value my marriage as much as I value my job? What kind of wife am I?"

"Hold on a minute here," Portia said. "First of all, you didn't choose your job over Josh. You compromised with him. He needed to take the job in Raleigh and you gave him a way to do so. That sounds like a good wife to me."

Gloria wondered how she could have forgotten how supportive Portia was. She had done herself and Portia a great disservice by distancing herself. She needed her friend now more than ever. "But did we do the right thing? Could we have done something else? If we were more in love, would we have done something else?"

"There's no right or wrong. You made the best decision you could at the time. Has it been working?"

Gloria shook her head slowly. "Not really. Our work schedules are so busy that our plans for swapping weekends aren't working out with any regularity. It's like we have two separate lives." The Cascade project was consuming more of her time than she had planned. Time that she and Josh had planned to spend together.

"Damn. That's not good. What's it like when you are together?"

Gloria remembered her last visit to Raleigh. *Cordial* was the first word to come to mind. They hadn't argued. It was as though they were determined to have a good weekend. If not arguing meant a good weekend, then they had achieved their goal, but using any other measure the weekend had been a failure. They had made love, but that, too, was cordial.

"So, what are you going to do about it?"

"Do? What can I do?"

"Come on now. If this were a problem with venture capital, you'd already have your game plan in hand. This is no different. You've got to get to work, girlfriend. That is, if you want to save your marriage. But if you don't, then—"

"Of course I want to save my marriage. Why would you even say something like that?"

Portia slid out of her chair and raised herself up. "I'm calling 'em like I see 'em. You're sitting around pouting about something somebody said about your marriage instead of trying to fix what's wrong with it. Doesn't sound like the right use of your energies to me, but then, what do I know?" When she reached the door, she turned and said, "Join Dexter and me for dinner sometime. We miss you."

Gloria stared at the door after Portia had waddled out. What had started out as an encouraging conversation had quickly turned defensive. Well, Portia could have given her some advice. Portia always gave advice. Hell, Elliot giving advice and Portia not giving advice. Was she in the Twilight Zone or what?

She wasn't in the Twilight Zone, but she knew she was at a critical point in her life and in her marriage. When she had married Josh, everything was so clear. They would get married, get established, have a family. Josh's job loss caused the plan to get off track. Now that Josh was employed again they were back on track. Or they should have been. With the raise Josh had gotten in his new job, they had already restored the savings they had depleted so money was not an issue. They were on track for Gloria to get pregnant and quit work. Therein was the problem. Did she still want to get pregnant? If she did, did she want to quit work?

She knew how her mother would have handled a situation like this. Her mother would have had the kids and continued the career. That was her mom. She had done it all. Or she had tried. She kept everything orderly, all right, but she was not the wife and mother that Gloria wanted to pattern her life after. No way. Not that women couldn't do both. It was just that her mother hadn't done it well. Gloria always felt that her mother valued her career above her family. She had vowed not to repeat that mistake.

That's why Elliot's comments had hurt so much. They made her realize how much she had changed. It discouraged her to think that she had lived so long with such unrealistic thoughts. How many families today lived on one salary? What made her think she and Josh could? No, when Josh had lost his job, she had realized how fortunate they were that she was working. It made her shiver to think how they would have fared if they'd had a couple of kids and she hadn't been working. She was glad to have gotten the reality check.

And, she admitted, it wasn't only the money. It was the work. She loved it. In her new position, she could do things that made a difference in people's lives, in the community. Didn't she have a responsibility to do that? If she left the bank, would her replacement be as sensitive to the concerns of the African-American community as she was? She didn't think so. No, if she gave up her job, it would be a loss for her and for those members of the African-American community that she could help.

This didn't mean that she no longer wanted kids; she did. But she knew she wouldn't stop working when she had them. No, she would do both. Besides, she had come to realize how much she enjoyed her work. And like her mother, she felt that her work was important. She thought that Josh knew now how important her work was to her, but she didn't know if Josh had concluded that she didn't want to quit her job even to have children.

Children? How could she think about children now? It took two people to make a baby, and with the small amount of time she and Josh spent together, it would be a miracle if she got pregnant. Especially since she was still taking the pill.

Chapter 15

Josh did a double take on the date on his desk calendar. It couldn't be, he thought. It couldn't be. But it was. His anniversary was coming up in two weeks. He couldn't believe he had let it slip up on him like this.

He got out of his chair and walked over to the windows, his hands in his pockets. What was happening to him and Gloria? They were growing apart. That's what was happening. They were too busy. Too busy for each other. But not too busy for Darlene, a small voice said.

Josh pushed the thought away. Things with Darlene hadn't changed. They were friends. Nothing more. He was still in love with Gloria. They just weren't making time for each other as they should. Too many things were more important than their time together.

He walked back to his desk and looked again at his calendar. He had a meeting the Friday of his anniversary weekend, but he was going to cancel it. He and Gloria would have this time together regardless.

He picked up the phone and dialed her number. "I'm asking you for a date. The weekend of the tenth. You have to go. No excuses allowed. What do you say?"

"I say, yes," she whispered. She had realized the date herself only yesterday. It had pained her to think that Josh had forgotten. Thank God he had remembered. "I almost forgot."

"Sweetheart, we have to do something about this."

She knew he was right. Four months into this commuter marriage and they both had to acknowledge that it wasn't working as they had planned. Gloria knew that much of the blame lay at her feet. Her work was consuming more of her time than she had planned, but what could she do? Now that she was in this Cascade project, she had to see it through. "What are we going to do, Josh?"

She heard him sigh and she knew she had given the wrong answer. "Let's just enjoy our anniversary. We'll talk about everything else after our trip."

Gloria didn't argue. She wasn't all that anxious to discuss their commuter marriage anyway since she still didn't have any answers. "Where are we going?" she asked, changing the subject.

She heard the smile in his voice. "I'm not telling you."

"Tell me. You know I'm going to find out anyway."

Josh laughed then. It wasn't a real laugh, but it was close. "That's one thing I don't have to worry about. There's no way for you to search through the closet here in Raleigh before the trip."

Gloria was leaving for the airport when the phone rang. She was tempted to ignore it, but she thought it might be Josh. "Yes," she said.

"Gloria, it's Dexter. We're at the hospital. Portia's in labor."

Gloria dropped her bag. "How is she, Dexter?"

"The baby's early, but the doctors say they're both fine." The words rushed out of Dexter's mouth. "I've been with her, but they made me leave the room while they do some tests." He put his hand to his head. "You don't think anything is wrong, do you?"

Gloria withheld a smile. Dexter was nervous and it was so endearing. He probably needed her support more than Portia did. "How about I come down and sit with you?"

"Would you, Gloria? I'd really appreciate it. I'm a wreck right now."

She smiled. "Sure, Dexter, I'll be there in twenty minutes. Sit tight. Everything's going to be okay."

Gloria hung up the phone and took a deep breath before making her next call. "Portia's in labor," she said when Josh answered the phone.

"Are you at the hospital?"

"No, I'm still home. I was on my way to the airport when Dexter called. I told him I'd be there in about twenty minutes. I'm sorry, Josh."

"Don't be sorry. I'll take a flight down tonight and meet you at the airport. We don't want to miss the birth of our first godchild. We have the rest of the weekend to celebrate our anniversary."

Gloria let out the breath that she had been holding. She didn't know what she would have done with Josh's anger. "You're not mad?" It was more an observation than a question.

"I'm disappointed, but I'm not mad. I want to be there for Dexter and Portia. I should be able to get to the hospital in the next few hours. Why don't you go over there? Tell Dexter I'll be there as soon as I can."

"I love you, Josh."

"I love you too."

Portia delivered the baby an hour before Josh's cab dropped him off at the hospital. He found Gloria standing in front of the nursery glass staring at the baby. He watched her, wondering, all the while knowing, what her thoughts were. He walked over and stood behind her, placing his hands on her shoulders. "Which one is it?" he asked.

Gloria pointed to the third bassinet from the left. It was pink.

"A girl," Josh said, his voice full of awe. "She's gorgeous. Have they named her yet?"

Gloria nodded. "Paige," she said, her voice muffled by what he expected had been tears. "They named her Paige."

Josh pulled Gloria back against him. "How is Portia?"

"She's fine."

"And how are you?" he asked, turning her around so that he could see her. He was right. She had been crying. He wiped her tears. "Happy tears, I hope."

She nodded again. "You should have seen them," she said, her voice stronger now. "I don't know who was more excited, Portia or Dexter."

"Where's the happy father?" Josh looked around the empty corridor.

"He's with Portia. He's spending the night with her. Do you want to visit with them?"

"No, we can come back in the morning. I'm sure they want to be alone tonight."

"I think you're right."

"Are you ready to go home?" he asked. When she nodded yes, he took her hand and led her out of the hospital.

They were quiet for most of the ride home. Josh watched Gloria even as he drove. Her hands rested protectively across her stomach. He didn't have to guess where her thoughts were.

"Do you think we'll be able to reschedule our trip?" he asked.

"I don't know, Josh," she answered absently. "My schedule is pretty busy and will be until this Cascade thing is settled."

"I don't remember you working this much before. Is it my overactive imagination or are you really working more?"

"It's not you. This project is taking a lot out of me."

"Does it have to?"

She didn't like the question because she didn't know how to answer it in a way that would make him understand. "Right now, it does, but it should be over soon." She went on to tell him about the snafu that had come up in the Cascade project.

"Do you think you're going to be able to pull it off?" he asked.

"Yes." Her answer was immediate. "This project is too important for me to let it fail."

Josh heard the surety and passion in her yes answer and it saddened him. Where would they be if she had that same passion for their relationship.

Josh was already in bed when Gloria finished in the bathroom. His gaze caught hers as soon as she walked through the door and he never let it go. She slipped the straps of her gown down her arms as she walked toward him. By the time she reached the bed, the gown and her underwear were on the floor. She stood before him naked.

Josh responded to his wife's nakedness by reaching out his hand to her. When she took it, he squeezed it tight and pulled her to him. Her eyes widened when she saw that he was also naked. His heartbeat increased.

When her silky skin touched his, he felt her heat. Or was it his? Maybe it was theirs. It really didn't matter. What mattered was that this was their anniversary and they were together. They had made it through two years of marriage. But would they make it through a third? an unbidden voice pushed through his mind. He shook his head slightly to force the thought away. But it was too late. The damage had already been done.

Gloria saw the flash of uncertainty pass across Josh's face and she wondered what had caused it. She touched her hand to his face and pulled him closer to her. "I love you," she said. "I've always loved you."

But will you keep loving me? he asked silently. Will we always be together? He couldn't bring himself to ask the question aloud. He did the easier thing. He kissed her. No, he ravaged her mouth. It was as if this kiss had to bind him to her. He pushed deeper into her mouth, crushing her body to his. When she moaned, he wondered if he was hurting her. A part of him knew he should ease up, but he couldn't. If he eased up, he would lose her.

Josh lay awake listening to the rapid beat of his heart, stroking his hand down Gloria's back as she lay contented on his chest. It would take him a while to get over this last bout of sex. He'd had orgasms before, but not like this. He had come and come and come. Maybe she'd get pregnant, he thought, then our problems would solve themselves.

Gloria lifted her head from his chest. A grin covered her face. "Have you been taking Superman shots or something?" she teased.

Josh couldn't help but grin. His masculine ego received the well-deserved stroke. "Do you think we made a baby?" he asked.

He would have sworn the light in her eyes dimmed. "Maybe" was all she said.

He squeezed her to him. "I hope so."

Gloria lay her head back down on his chest and chided herself for not telling him the truth. But, she reasoned, she hadn't really lied. There was a chance she could be pregnant. Come on, Gloria, her conscience poked, how can you be pregnant if you're still taking birth control pills?

Gloria wanted to push her conscience away, but she couldn't. She should have told him. She should have told him a while ago. She'd gotten back on the pill the weekend Josh had gone to San Francisco. It seemed such a reasonable move then. Now, it seemed like betrayal. A lie. How would Josh respond when he found out? She didn't know and she wouldn't find out today because she wasn't going to tell him.

Chapter 16

"You do this well," Darlene said when Josh handed her the next stack of T-shirts.

"You think I missed my calling—I should've been a T-shirt vendor rather than a corporate engineer?"

She shrugged her shoulders. "That's not what I meant. It's just that you seem so comfortable here. Sometimes you corporate honcho types have problems doing the small tasks. You're more comfortable giving orders."

"There's a time for everything and today's a day for fun. Being the boss can be a burden. I'm sure you know that from your sister."

Darlene shook her head. "Carla's not like that. She lives and breathes her work. Wherever she is, whatever she's doing, she's the plant manager. Look at her now."

Josh looked to where Carla was directing the sack race. Darlene was right. To look at Carla, you'd think she was planning a new clean room, not organizing a group of ten-year-olds for a sack race. "Your sister is intensive."

"About everything. To a fault."

Josh broke down the box that had held the T-shirts and folded it. "Do I detect a bit of hostility? I thought you and Carla got along well."

"We do. It's just that I find her intensity tiring. She was like this even as a child. I don't see how she keeps it up."

"So you went in the opposite direction?"

She punched him in the shoulders playfully. "I didn't know you were an armchair psychologist."

She hadn't answered his question, but he was willing to let it ride. "Are you planning to get into any of the games today?"

She looked at him as if he'd asked her to fly to the moon. "Two guesses."

Josh laughed. He had known from her outfit that she wasn't going to participate. The shorts might allow it, but the braless T-shirt wouldn't. "Do you usually come to these company gatherings?"

"Every now and then. This is my first one in about four years."

"Why this year?"

"I think you know the answer to that."

Was she saying she had come because of him? he wondered. "I don't think I do."

"I came to see that invisible wife of yours. Why isn't she here today?"

Gloria. Josh hadn't thought about her today. They had decided last weekend that she wouldn't come to this event since it was being held during the week. Unlike the other times when their schedules hadn't allowed them to share events, neither of them seemed upset or disappointed by this. After the failed honeymoon trip and Portia's new baby, they needed the time apart. That was good and bad. Good, because they were supporting each other and trying to work through this separation as best they could. Bad, because maybe they didn't expect much of each other these days.

"So, where is she?" Darlene asked again.

"Working."

"And she couldn't get away?"

Darlene had to know about their commuter marriage. Surely Carla had told her. "She had to work today and tomorrow. It would have been too much for her to come up today and get back to Atlanta tomorrow."

"What's she doing in Atlanta?"

"Come on, Darlene. You know that Gloria still lives in Atlanta."

She shook her head. "I knew no such thing."

He sighed as he realized Carla hadn't told her.

"Gloria and I have a commuter marriage. She's looking for work here and I'm looking for work in Atlanta."

"Is it working? I mean, are you enjoying this?"

"I'd be lying if I said it wasn't hard, but we're getting used to it."

She looked skeptical. "I don't know if I believe that."

"Why shouldn't you?"

"Because of us."

Josh froze in the middle of stacking the T-shirts. "What us?" he asked, but he knew what she was talking about. Since that Greek festival at Chapel Hill, he and Darlene had found themselves in the same company six or seven times. They always suggested that it was coincidence, but they both knew it wasn't. They enjoyed being together.

"If you don't want to talk about it now, we won't," she said, "but soon you're going to have to decide."

Josh didn't want to think about that. He knew what she was talking about. So far they could honestly say that they had a platonic relationship. The most they were guilty of was flirting, but they both knew that with only a small step from him, the relationship would move to something more. Did he want that?

Josh knew that what he did or didn't do with Darlene was directly related to the state of his marriage. He knew things weren't good between him and Gloria now and he knew a relationship with Darlene would only make matters worse. He still loved his wife and he wanted his marriage to work, but sometimes he wondered if there was any hope of that happening. He had racked his brain and had concluded there was nothing he could do to make things better. If he quit this job and moved back to Atlanta, their situation wouldn't be any better. They'd be under the stress of his unemployment. Now, they were under the stress of their separation. They couldn't win for losing, he thought.

"Have I scared you away?" Darlene asked.

He brought his attention back to her. He could walk away from Darlene now if he wanted to. But he didn't want to. "Me, scared away? Never."

She smiled at his words and they were back on the merry-go-round.

* * *

Two weeks later, Josh went to a fraternity gathering where Darlene just happened to be present. He got home a little after midnight. The evening had been an eye-opening one. The sexual attraction between him and Darlene had always been there. Now, it was getting out of hand. He wanted her. And he knew she wanted him. It would only take a word from him and she'd be in his bed. They both knew it. He suspected Darlene was counting down the days until he broke. If things continued to progress as they were, he knew his days were limited. Now was time for drastic action.

Josh picked up the phone and punched the number to his home in Atlanta. "Hello," Gloria answered in a voice full of sleep.

"I'm coming home in the morning. I need a few days off."

"What?"

He knew she was half asleep but he had to do this now. "I'm driving home in the morning. I'll be there in time to meet you for lunch. Can you do that?"

"Lunch? Yes, I think so."

She was still groggy and he hoped she'd remember their conversation tomorrow. "I'll come straight to your office."

"Okay. I need to go back to sleep now."

Before he hung up, he added, "I love you." He heard the click of her hanging up so soon after his words were spoken that he doubted she had heard them.

He had taken the first step. He was going home to fight for his marriage, his wife. The way he saw things, he and Gloria needed to end this separation. Their six months were up. Since they had always planned for Gloria to quit work when they started a family, he would suggest to her that they start a family now. Why shouldn't they? They were back on track with their original plan now that he was employed, so they could pick up where they had left off. It's a reasonable plan, he thought. He knew she was tied to her job and he was willing to give her enough time to settle her two biggest projects. After that, he wanted her with him. He wanted them together.

As Josh got ready for bed, his thoughts turned to the possible objections Gloria could have to his proposal.

What if she didn't want to have a baby now? He disregarded that one as a low probability. He knew she would love to have a little girl like Paige. No, that shouldn't be an objection.

What if she didn't want to leave her job? That was an easy one. He'd suggest that she take a leave of absence instead of quitting.

What if she didn't want to move to Raleigh? That wasn't an option. The whole point was for them to be together. The whole point was for them to be together. If he was going to be the working spouse, she would have to go where he was.

What if she didn't want to sell the house? He knew that could present a problem. That house represented many of their dreams. They could buy a house in Raleigh. Somehow he'd have to convince her to sell the house in Atlanta. Holding on to it was not a rational option.

Josh got into bed and finally faced the question that was forever in the back of his mind. What if she said their marriage wasn't worth the changes he was asking of her? That would be a killer. He had no answer for that. She had to still love him. She had to. But what if she didn't? Josh fell asleep without an answer.

Neither Gloria nor her secretary was present when Josh arrived at her office, so he waited. He was pretty anxious, though he tried to hide it. He had gone over every possible scenario in his mind during the trip down. They were going to work this out. They had to.

He sat in Gloria's chair with the back of the chair facing the door. He heard her voice and was about to turn around and greet her when he heard a male voice. For some reason, he didn't turn around.

He heard them move to the conference table. "About the Cascade financing," Gloria said. "What do you think of the numbers?"

Josh heard the shuffling of paper.

"Seems like a good deal for the borrowers. Couldn't the bank have gotten a higher interest rate?" The male voice belonged to Foster Dixon.

"I take that to mean it's a good deal."

"Let's not get into that again. When are you going to learn that this bank is not a charitable organization? We're here to make bucks. Big bucks."

Josh heard Gloria's laughter and could imagine Dixon's leering smile. The man was forever in Gloria's face.

"This is a good deal for the bank and you know it," she said. "A higher interest rate would be criminal since this is a community project."

"What else do you have for me?"

"That was it. I just needed some feedback on this package before I submitted it. It's going to fly. I know it."

Now get up and go, Dixon, Josh thought. You've done your duty.

"How about lunch?" Foster asked Gloria.

"Not today. I'm having lunch with Josh. As a matter of fact, I'm expecting him any minute now."

Dixon laughed and Josh wondered what was funny. He didn't have to wait long to find out.

"Come off it, Gloria. Josh might be Superman but not even he can go out to Atlanta for lunch, or are you telling me that he's moved back to town?"

The bastard, Josh thought. Trying to make a move on my wife. Josh felt like turning his chair around and telling that Dixon bastard exactly what he thought.

"No, he hasn't moved back to town, but he's going to be in town for a few days. Of course, you're invited to have lunch with us."

"Right," Foster said, his words dripping with sarcasm. "Like I want to have lunch with you and Josh. No, the invitation was for you only."

"I don't know why you keep pursuing this. You know I'm committed to Josh."

Good girl, Josh thought. Tell him.

"I was beginning to believe that until this ridiculous commuter marriage. No man in his right mind would leave you like that."

Josh heard more paper shuffling, then Gloria said, "I'm not getting into this with you again. Thanks for reviewing the file."

Her words sounded pretty final so Josh assumed she was signaling Dixon to leave. He was right.

"Okay, Gloria. I'll back off or now, but when you get tired of waiting for that guy to come to his senses, I'll be waiting."

"Then you'd better be prepared for a long wait," was Gloria's response.

"I've always felt that anything worth having was worth waiting for. And you're definitely worth the wait."

This guy was reaching back to lines from the seventies, Josh thought.

Josh heard Gloria's office door close and assumed that Foster was gone. He was about to turn around in his chair when Gloria caught the back of it and turned the chair around. She gasped when she saw him. "You scared me. Why didn't you say something to let me know you were here?"

"I started to, but when I heard Dixon's voice I decided not to intrude on the meeting. How is Dixon these days?"

"Foster?" Gloria was relieved their banter hadn't gone further. "Foster is still Foster."

"So, he's been giving you the rush while I've been away?"

"Like I said, Foster is still Foster. He's harmless. You heard the conversation."

"He didn't sound harmless to me. The guy pledged to wait until you got tired of me."

Gloria leaned over and kissed Josh on the nose. "You're jealous and it's cute, but not necessary. You heard me tell Foster that he was in for a long wait."

Josh got up from Gloria's chair so she could sit at her desk. "Has he always been that bad?"

"How about the Crab House for lunch?" she asked, effectively changing the subject. "I have a craving for seafood."

"Craving?" Josh wondered if Gloria had been thinking about babies as much as he had.

"How about it?"

"Fine. Wherever you want to go. Can we leave now?"

"Sure. Let me check my messages first."

They decided to walk to the Crab House since it was only a few blocks from Gloria's office. They both had the special Chef's Seafood Salad. In a quiet booth in the back, they discussed their work.

"Congratulations on the financing for the Cascade project." At the question in her gaze, he added, "I overheard you and Foster talking about it."

"Thanks. It was touch and go for a while, but now it's all done but the final paperwork. I'd guess two months tops."

"That's good. How's the Turner Hill project going?" If it were wrapping up, now would be the perfect time to bring up his ideas.

"Most of the work on that is done too. At least the part that I'll be involved in."

So far. So good. "So any other heavy hitters on your plate?"

She shook her head because she was chewing. "I'll be talking to Louise about that in the next few weeks. I've got my eye on a shopping center in South Fulton. How are things at Carolina Micro?"

If they were going to make a move, they'd have to make it before she got the South Fulton project, Josh thought. There was no doubt in his mind that she would get it. "We're as busy as ever. I'm overseeing an expansion that includes a new clean room. When it's up and running, the required direct and indirect support will increase my staff by seventy-five people."

"That's great," she said, but she was uneasy. Josh was building an empire, a life, in Raleigh. "How's Carla?"

"She's still the same. A little rough around the edges but she knows her job and she does it well."

"Good. And I'm glad that you've started to make friends outside of work. Your fraternity affiliation really panned out, didn't it?"

Josh's thoughts went immediately to Darlene. "Yeah, it did. The guys have kept me from being too lonely."

She winked at him. "I don't know if I like the sound of that. I hope it doesn't mean that you don't miss me."

Josh laughed because Gloria was being coy. "No, it just means that I'm not miserable with loneliness. I miss you a lot."

"And I miss you. This separation has been a lot harder than I expected."

She'd given him the perfect opening. "Yeah. I've been thinking a lot about that. I think I have a solution for us."

"Have you found a job here?" she asked in a high-pitched tone.

"No, that's not it. I thought that since neither one of us was having success in that area, we needed to explore something different."

"Don't keep me in suspense. What's your idea?"

"I've been thinking that we should start our family. We were at that point when General Electronics caved in. Now that we're back on our feet, it's the perfect time."

The silence was loud. He could hear her thinking. She didn't like the idea. It was taking her too long to answer. "What do you think?" he asked.

"I'm surprised, Josh. I didn't expect this as your solution. How can we think about having a baby when we don't even live together?"

Josh thanked God that he had gone through the scenarios. "That's what's so good about it. We had planned for you to stop work when we started a family. So, you can move to Raleigh and we'll be together."

"You've thought this out, haven't you?"

He nodded. "What do you think of the idea?"

Gloria looked at her watch. "I think we don't have enough time to get into this now. I have to get back for a meeting. Let's table this discussion until I get home tonight."

Josh nodded his agreement and signaled for the check. He knew it was going to take some energy to get Gloria to agree with this idea. But he knew he could do it. He had to. Too much was at stake.

Gloria could barely concentrate on the meeting. Her thoughts were on Josh and their lunch conversation. So, he thought the solution to their problems was for her to get pregnant and move to Raleigh. Exactly what she had feared.

There was actually nothing wrong with Josh's proposal. It

would have been perfect if she were the same person that she had been when they married, if she'd had the same goals. But she wasn't and she didn't. How was she going to make him understand that?

She thought he had seen how important her work was to her, but she must have been wrong. If he had understood that, he would never have proposed this solution. Well, she thought, Josh had one thing going for his idea if nothing else—timing. If she were to leave, now, with her major projects drawing to a close, was the perfect time.

"I'd like to see you in my office." It was Louise. Gloria knew the meeting was over because everyone was leaving. She hoped Louise hadn't noticed how distracted she was.

When she was seated in Louise's office, Louise said, "It's time to choose. Which one do you want—South Fulton or Alpharetta?"

Her answer was automatic. "South Fulton."

Louise pushed the folder that had been lying in front of her over to Gloria. "Somehow I thought that would be your choice."

South Fulton was written on the cover in big, bold red letters. Gloria opened the folder and scanned the first page. "I thought this was going to be a shopping center. This says medical complex."

Louise nodded with a knowing smile. "And look at the numbers."

"God! This is five times the amount that was needed for the shopping center."

"You're right and it's yours. It goes without saying that you're lucky to get this. Not that you aren't deserving, but pull this off and you're minutes away from your next promotion."

Gloria thought it ironic that this would happen on the same day as Josh's plan to change their lives. How could she even consider leaving now? A medical center in South Fulton. A project that would mean so much to that community. A project that would take at least a year to pull together. At least.

"I knew you'd be excited," Louise was saying. "The folks upstairs were impressed with the way you handled Cascade. The publicity it generated for the bank was invaluable. They were anxious for you to get this one. Aren't you going to say something?"

All Gloria could think about was the discussion that she and Josh were having tonight. She needed more time. She needed Josh to understand that.

"Gloria," Louise said, "I've never known you to be speechless. Say something."

"You know I love community projects. The hospital is just the type of project I wanted next. I need to look over the file, but I'm excited about it."

"Good. Take the time you need. We need to get a game plan together within the next month. I'll leave it to you to do that. Let's get together the middle of next month to see how you've sized it up. How's that?"

"Great, Louise."

Gloria left the office with conflicting feelings. A part of her couldn't wait to tear into the file. Another part of her was afraid to even open it. If she opened it, she knew there was no chance of hell she'd go along with Josh's proposal.

Chapter 17

Josh was listening to Gloria, but she couldn't believe what he was hearing. "We agreed on six months and it's been six months. You have to move to Raleigh," he said.

Gloria stood and began clearing the dishes from the table. He followed her into the kitchen.

"Aren't you going to respond?" he asked.

Gloria put the dishes in the sink and began rinsing them. "You aren't listening to me, Josh."

He grabbed her hand and turned her around. "Will you please stop with the damn dishes? This is an important conversation we're having."

Gloria removed her hand from his, pulled out one of the dinette chairs, and took a seat. "Okay, you have my full attention. Now tell me again that I should quit my job."

Josh put his hands on the back of the chair facing hers, but he remained standing. "Don't make me out to be the heavy here, Gloria. Our plan has always been for you to quit work when we start a family. Well it's time to start a family."

"Says who? Don't you think we should make that decision together?"

Josh flopped down in the chair. "I thought we had already decided," he said softly. "It seems you've changed your mind."

"It's timing, Josh. I'm not ready to have a baby." She knew she was hurting him, but she had to tell him how she felt.

"I could see how you responded to Portia's pregnancy. You can't tell me that you don't want a baby."

He was right. She did want a baby. Just not right now. They

both needed to find work in the same city first. "What if you're out of work again, Josh? What then?"

That was it. She had gone for the jugular. What could he say? "That won't happen."

"You promise?"

Josh stood up and presented his back to her while he went through the motions of getting a glass of water. She had him there. He couldn't promise. "We didn't go broke this last time, did we? Anyway, I'm more prepared now than I was last time. I don't have all my eggs in the Carolina basket."

"I'm scared, Josh. Scared. It was difficult when it was just the two of us. Think what it would have been like with a couple of kids. You have to admit that my working helped."

"You're right it did. But that was then and this is now. We can't live our lives based on what bad things might happen."

"Neither can we afford to be naïve about this. From a financial perspective, I need to keep working."

Josh pulled out his chair and sat again. "Look, Gloria, I don't have a problem with your working. If you want to go back to work after you have the baby, I'll support that decision. It won't be my preference, but I promise I'll support your decision. But that still doesn't address our present problems. This commuter marriage is not working. We're growing apart."

She knew he was right. She just wasn't ready to accept his alternative. "We'll just have to do better with our schedules…"

Josh jumped up of his chair. "Come on, Gloria. Wake up and smell the coffee. It's not going to work. You don't want another job, so you're never going to find something you want in Raleigh."

He was right. "What about you? I don't see you interviewing here in Atlanta."

Josh shook his head back and forth. If she couldn't see what was happening to them, there was nothing he could do. "I looked for nearly eight months before I went to Raleigh. I've told you once and I'll tell you again. There's nothing here for me."

"There's nothing in Raleigh for me."

"What about me, Gloria, don't I count for something?"

"I could ask you the same question. Why do I have to give up my job?"

Josh was beat and he knew it, but he had to give it one more chance. "How about we compromise? You take a leave of absence. We see how it works in Raleigh. We think some more about a baby. This way you won't have to give up anything." Even as Josh said this, he knew it was risky. They were continuing to postpone a decision that they had to make. He would force it now, but he wasn't sure he'd get the answer he wanted. "So, what do you say?"

"I don't know, Josh. I'll have to think about it. Taking a leave of absence is better than quitting outright."

Josh hadn't got what he wanted. He had wanted her to put their marriage before her career. He had wanted her to believe in his ability to take care of her and their children. But she hadn't. He couldn't fault her reasoning, but where did reasoning leave them? She was in Atlanta. He was in Raleigh. Darlene was in Raleigh. And he needed a wife.

"Let me know when you decide what you're going to do, Gloria," Josh said as he got in his car for the drive back to Raleigh on Sunday morning. She said something, but he didn't bother listening. He started the car and pulled out of the driveway.

The tension between him and Gloria had intensified since their discussion Friday night. The more he thought about the situation, the angrier he became. Gloria was selfish. He wasn't asking her to quit her job, just to take a leave of absence. She'd think about it, she said. Well, he hoped she made the right decision. For both of them.

The message light on his answering machine was flashing when he walked into the house. His first thought was that Gloria had come to her senses. He rushed to the machine and pressed the PLAY button.

"Call me," the voice. "I'm in the book."

It was Darlene. Josh pressed Rewind and then Play again. He did this three times.

He knew what he was doing when he went for the phone book. This was the first time Darlene had sought him out, called his house. He could have told himself that he had to return the call because it had something to do with work. Maybe Carla had an emergency. But he knew that wasn't it. No, Darlene called because she had gotten tired of waiting for him to make a move. She was forcing his hand and he knew it. Hell, he'd half expected it. That was why so much had been riding on his trip to Atlanta.

He found Darlene's number and jotted it down on the pad next to the phone. Was this the moment of truth? What would he say if he called? What would she say?

He picked up the phone and dialed six of the seven digits written on the pad before hanging up. He couldn't do it. He couldn't coldheartedly betray his marriage vows. And he knew that's what he'd be doing with that phone call.

Josh finally saw Darlene Friday night in the bar at Dominic's. She was wearing the red dress she had worn the first night he had seen her. It was an understatement to say that she looked good.

He watched her take a seat near the end of the bar. Before she was fully seated, some guy was making a move on her. She smiled at him, but obviously she turned him down because he soon walked away.

She saw Josh when she turned to watch the man walk away. Without a second thought, she walked over to his table.

She looked around before taking a seat. "You've been avoiding me, Josh Martin. And now you're out drinking alone. Could there be a connection between the two?"

"How do you know I'm alone?" he asked. "Gloria could be here with me."

Darlene smiled and took a sip of her drink. "I don't think so, Josh. Something tells me you're very much alone."

Josh belted down his gin and tonic and signaled the waiter for another. This was his fourth, maybe fifth, drink of the evening. "Darlene, the psychic."

"Don't be mean," she said, though she didn't appear insulted by his comment. "I may be the only friend you have right now. Why didn't you call?"

Josh drank from the fresh glass the waiter had brought him. "I think you know the answer to that. I'm a married man, Darlene."

"You could have fooled me. I never see any wife around."

Josh grimaced. "I'm not interested, Darlene. I'm perfectly happy in my marriage."

"Right. That's why you're out drinking yourself silly. What happened? Did the little woman let you down again?"

Josh knew Darlene had no idea how close to the truth she had gotten. Gloria had called this afternoon saying she couldn't make her scheduled visit to Raleigh this weekend. He wasn't surprised as much as he was hurt. He had hoped Gloria would have come to a decision about moving to Raleigh, but it seemed that all of her energy was directed toward her work. She probably hadn't even thought about them, their marriage. He reconsidered that thought. Maybe there was nothing to think about. Maybe her decision was already made and she just couldn't bring herself to tell him. That conclusion had led to his first drink and then his second and then his third...

"Afraid to answer the question, Josh?"

Josh put his glad down and looked at Darlene. At this moment, he hated her. At this moment, he wanted her more than he ever had. He took the last drop from his glass. "I'm leaving."

He swayed when he stood up and Darlene got up to help him. "How many drinks have you had tonight?"

Josh thought it was only five. Maybe it had been more. "A few."

"More than a few, I'd think. You're not driving home."

Josh pulled a few bills from his wallet and threw them on the table. "Like hell I'm not."

Darlene followed him to the parking lot, where he fumbled with his car keys. He tried to open the door, but he couldn't find the slot. "I need a little help here."

Darlene took the keys from him and dropped them in her purse. "You do need help. And I'm going to give it to you by driving you home. My car is over here."

Josh was in no mood to argue so he followed her to her car. He felt light-headed and his vision was fuzzy. The movement of the car out the parking lot didn't help matters any. By the time they reached his townhouse, he knew he was going to have a terrible hangover in the morning.

Darlene helped him to the door, fished through his keys and let them both in. He made it as far as the couch before he fell, more than sat, down.

"Thanks for driving me home," he said.

When she didn't respond, Josh looked around but he didn't see her. "Darlene," he called out. He thought about getting up to look for her, but his light-headedness made him remain seated.

When she finally came into view, he asked, "Where were you? Didn't you hear me calling you?"

"I heard you. I was just checking out the place. Nice bachelor pad you have here. Ready for bed?"

Josh knew it was another invitation. "Yes, but you're going home."

Darlene smiled and leaned over to take his arm, pulling him up from the sofa. "I don't think you're going to be able to navigate those steps without my help, so be nice."

Josh didn't say anything, but he allowed her to help him up the steps to his bedroom. Once there, he sat on the edge of the bed and kicked off his shoes. He unbuttoned his shirt after a few false starts and flung it on the floor in front of him. He removed his belt, but he had trouble with his pants. He was able to pull them down past his hips, but Darlene had to grab both legs and pull them off. He opened his mouth to say something, but suddenly he was so very sleepy.

Darlene pushed him on the bed. "Just go to sleep. I can let myself out."

She lifted his legs and placed them on the bed. He was asleep before he could thank her.

Darlene looked at his sleeping body, clad in only his undershorts. She had known from their first meeting that Josh would bring nothing but heartbreak her way. And she had been right. She looked at him now and she knew she was in love with him.

As crazy as it sounded, she was in love with Josh Martin. Married Josh Martin.

She sat on the bed next to him and wondered how she could have allowed this to happen. A married man. A married man in love with his wife. She knew Josh loved Gloria. That she had never doubted. What she had doubted and what had given her hope for a relationship with Josh, was that she wasn't so sure that Gloria was in love with him. She knew that if Josh were her husband, she wouldn't be content to be separated from him the way Gloria was. No, Gloria didn't love Josh and she didn't deserve him. Josh deserved a woman would love and support him the way he needed to be loved and supported. Darlene thought she was that woman.

She looked at her watch. It was after midnight and she was tired. The prospect of driving home didn't appeal to her. She looked again at the sleeping Josh and made her decision. She stripped down to her camisole and panties and climbed in next to him.

Gloria still didn't have an answer. She loved Josh and she wanted to be with him, but she was afraid to be without a job. She hadn't realized until lately how much of her self-esteem was wrapped up in her work. Could she make him understand that? Did she understand it?

The drive from Atlanta to Raleigh had given her some thinking time and she knew in her heart that she wanted to have that baby and be with Josh. She would tell him that when she surprised him with her visit.

Her thinking had started in earnest Friday night. After she had hung up from telling Josh that she wasn't going to make her trip, she had faced some truths about herself, him and their relationship. Josh was right that the commuter arrangement wasn't working. There were too many times, too many reasons, that she had let other things come first. So, even though she should be working this weekend, she wasn't going to. She was about to put Josh and their marriage first. Something she should have been doing since he moved away.

She pulled her car into the driveway and went to the door. She used her key because she wanted to surprise him. Once inside, she tiptoed up the stairs to his bedroom. Easing the door open, she walked slowly into the room. The blinds were closed, but the early morning light shone through the slits. Josh, dressed only in his undershorts, was asleep on the bed. Her heart filled with love for him. She moved to the bed, dropping her clothes among the one he had discarded earlier.

When she sat on the bed next to him, she was naked. Instead of kissing him, she looked at him for a long while, thinking of the life they had shared so far and the bright future that lay before them.

As she leaned down to kiss him awake, a strip of white cloth caught her eye. She reached behind him and picked it up. She thought her eyes were playing tricks on her, but she was wrong. It was a half-slip. A woman's half-slip.

She held the slip in her hand, not wanting to face the reality of what it meant. She let her eyes wander to the clothes that were strewn across the floor. She wondered how she had missed them when she walked in. A dress. A bra. Shoes. None hers.

Her heart was breaking and there was nothing she could do to stop it. Should she wake Josh? What would he say if she did? What did she want him to say?

Oh, my God. Why hadn't it occurred to her before? The woman was still in the house. Gloria quickly put her clothes back on, gathered up the woman's clothes from the floor, and started through the house looking for her. She checked the bathroom first. No one there. Then she went downstairs. The light was on in the kitchen. She wondered why she hadn't noticed that when she first came in? She knew why. All her thoughts had been centered on seeing Josh. Nothing else had registered.

She walked toward the kitchen. As she got closer, she heard someone humming. Then she saw her. It was Carla, Josh's boss. Gloria couldn't believe it. Josh and his boss. She didn't know what she was going to say or do, but she had to face this woman who was sleeping with her husband.

Carla stood at the stove, half-naked and humming while she scrambled eggs. Bitch, Gloria thought. The nerve of this woman, standing in my kitchen, cooking my food.

"You and Josh have some extra work to catch up on last night, Carla?" Gloria asked.

Darlene turned around. She was shocked but she recovered quickly. "Who are you?"

Bold bitch, Gloria thought. "Surely you haven't forgotten me. I'm Josh's wife, Gloria. But then maybe it's to your advantage to forget about me. Makes it easier to carry on an affair with Josh, doesn't it?"

Darlene removed the fryer from the flames and cut off the gas. She turned to Gloria. Without bothering to correct Gloria on her identity, she said, "Josh and I are friends."

"Friends?" Gloria could have scratched the woman's eyes out then. "Right. Look, I'm not here to have a conversation with you. I want you the hell out of my house."

Darlene looked around the kitchen. "Your house? How much time have you spent here, Gloria?"

"Look, I want you out of this house now." Gloria walked over to Darlene and pushed her clothes into her hands. "Get your clothes on and get out."

Darlene laid the clothes on the counter and began to dress. "You don't want him, Gloria, and I do. Why don't you let him go?"

"Who are you to tell me what I want and don't want? Josh is my husband and I'm not letting him go. Not for you, not for anybody."

"Maybe you won't have to. Maybe Josh will make that decision for you."

Gloria reached out and slapped Darlene, then yelled, "Get out of this house now."

Darlene seemed unable to move. The slap had surprised her. Little Gloria had more spunk that she had given her credit for. "Why don't we ask Josh what he wants? He's upstairs, you know. Still asleep. He had a *long* night."

Gloria didn't miss the innuendo in Carla's words. She walked to the front door and held it open. "Get out."

"What's going on down there?"

Both women looked to the stairs. Josh stood there in his undershorts.

Chapter 18

Josh looked from Gloria to Darlene, then back to Gloria. "It's not what it looks like."

"Get this woman out of my house, Josh."

Josh walked toward Gloria. "Don't come near me," she said. "Just get her out of here."

Josh looked to Darlene. "Thanks for bringing me home last night."

Darlene nodded at Josh, then looked over at Gloria. "My car is in the garage. She has to move her car from the driveway so I can get out."

Gloria slammed the front door and said to Josh, "You get her out of here." She then stomped up the stairs.

She first went to their bedroom, Josh's bedroom, but she couldn't stand it there, so she went into the other bedroom and sat on the bed. Agitated, she got up and began to pace the room. It all began to crash down on her. Josh had cheated on her! He had actually slept with somebody else. Not somebody else.

He'd slept with his boss. She couldn't believe it. What a fool she'd been.

She wondered how long it had been going on. She'd had an uneasy feeling about Carla since their first meeting. That understated beauty of hers. Well, it hadn't been understated today.

Gloria sat down on the bed. Was Carla the reason Josh had agreed so readily to this commuter marriage arrangement? Had he planned to sleep with her from the beginning?

Before she could reason out an answer to that question, Josh walked into the bedroom. "It's not what it looked like, Gloria."

She looked up at him. How could she have been such a fool? "I find her clothes strewn across your bedroom floor—"

Josh held up his hand. "Hold on here. What are you saying?"

"Her clothes were strewn across your bedroom floor and she was standing half-naked in your kitchen. How does that look from your position, Josh? From mine, it's pretty obvious what went on."

Josh shook his head like an innocent. She was amazed that he could muster a look of surprise, no shock, at her words.

"I don't know what you walked in on, but nothing happened between Darlene and me," he said. "I got a little drunk last night and she brought me home. I fell asleep and I thought she went home."

"Obviously, she didn't. And obviously, she slept here. With you. In your bed."

"I didn't sleep with her. I don't know what you found when you got here, but you have to believe me. I did not sleep with Darlene."

It registered that Josh called her Darlene. "Is Darlene some other woman you're seeing? That was Carla."

Josh walked toward her. "Carla? No, that wasn't Carla. That was Darlene."

Gloria held up a hand and Josh stopped in his tracks. "Stop the lies, Josh. I've met the woman before."

"I'm telling you that wasn't Carla. It was her sister, her twin sister, Darlene."

"Twin sister? You're sleeping with your boss's twin sister." She laughed a hysterical laugh. "You like living dangerously, don't you."

"No, I'm not sleeping with her. And yes, she is Carla's sister."

It didn't matter who she was. Josh had broken their vows. He had brought another woman into their home and made love to her. "I can't believe you would do this to us, Josh. How could you after all we've shared?"

Josh looked at his wife standing away from him, tears, hurt, and anger in her eyes, and he knew this was the lowest point in his life. He never thought they'd come to this. He blamed himself. He had already told her that nothing happened with Darlene, but she didn't believe him. Maybe it was because he didn't say it with much conviction. The sad truth was he didn't remember. The last thing he remembered was Darlene helping him up the stairs.

He was ready to swear that nothing had happened between him and Darlene. How could it? He was drunk.

"I'm telling you that nothing happened. Darlene is my boss's sister, for God's sake."

Gloria laughed. If he hadn't been looking at her, he would have sworn it was a happy laugh. "Did you know that I was jealous of Carla when I first met her? Seems I was right to be so. It must have been easier for you to fall into the sack with the boss's sister rather than the boss."

Josh went to her and grabbed her with both hands. "I did not sleep with her. Why can't you believe me?"

She looked at his hands on her arms. "Take your hands off me." When he didn't move, she added, "Now. Take your hands off me now."

Josh dropped his hands. He moved to put them in his pockets and realized that he wore only his undershorts. God, what a situation this was.

"She was practically naked when I found her in the kitchen this morning. Her clothes were strewn all around your bedroom. How do you explain that?"

Josh couldn't explain it. He couldn't remember. He cursed himself for drinking like that. There was really no excuse for it. God, he was just like his father. He hadn't hit Gloria like his dad hit his mother, but he had hurt her to the same degree, if not more. Right now he hated himself. "I can't explain it. Just know that I'd never intentionally hurt you. Trust me."

"You don't ask much, do you, Josh?"

"We can get past this, Gloria. It doesn't have to hurt us."

She laughed that laugh again. "Doesn't have to hurt? You must be joking. Do you know what your Darlene asked me?"

Josh had no idea what Darlene had said to her. He had rushed her out of the house so quickly that he hadn't had time to question her. "What?"

Gloria met his gaze. The hurt he saw reflected there made him hurt. "She asked me to let you go. Seems she knows a lot about our personal life. How did she get it? Pillow talk?"

"Dammit, Gloria. It's no secret that we don't have a traditional marriage. Most people here know that you still live in Atlanta."

"Don't even think about blaming me for what you did with Darlene."

"I'm not blaming you. I'm just saying that some people think our being apart means there are problems in our marriage."

"Right now, Darlene is the problem in our marriage. How long have you two been dating?"

"Dating? What the hell are you talking about?"

Gloria sat on the side of the bed again. "You said she brought you home. I assumed you had gone out together."

"Well, you assumed wrong. She saw me in a bar, and when she noticed I was a bit drunk, she offered to drive me home. End of story."

"Not according to Darlene. She didn't try to hide the fact that she wants you. Are you telling me that you didn't know she felt this way?"

Josh hated that question even though he had known it was coming. Yes, he knew Darlene's feelings, but he'd never encouraged them. But he hadn't done anything to discourage them either, and that was his mistake. "I knew."

"Did you discourage her interest?"

"Yes."

Gloria got up then and walked over to him. For the second time this morning, she slapped somebody. "I know you well enough to know when you're lying, Josh." She brushed past him and ran down the stairs.

Josh followed.

"What did you do with my keys?" she asked.

"Where are you going?"

She found the keys on the kitchen counter. "I'm going back to Atlanta. There's nothing here for me." She walked past him to the front door. She opened it and asked, "Where's my car?"

When he didn't answer, she asked again, "Where the hell is my car?"

"It's in the garage. I moved it earlier."

She closed the door. "I see. You moved it when your girlfriend moved hers out of the garage. To hell with you, Josh Martin." Gloria stomped through the kitchen and out the door to the garage.

Josh watched her leave and he could think of nothing else to say. The garage door went up and she backed out. Without another look at him, she sped off down the street.

Josh pressed the button on the garage door control panel, causing the door to come down, and walked back into the house, closing the door behind him. He looked around the kitchen and saw that someone, Darlene, had been preparing breakfast. He wondered again what had happened between them. Had Darlene really spent the night in his bed? If she had, had they had sex together?

He was angry with Darlene for what she had said to Gloria. If she had told Gloria they were just friends and explained what had happened the night before, he and Gloria might have been able to work this out. But, no, Darlene had her own agenda.

He could only be a little angry with Darlene though, because he knew he had led her on. He had allowed her to think that there might be a chance for them. There was only one person that he could be angry with and that was himself. And maybe, Gloria.

If Gloria had listened to his plea last weekend, none of this would have happened. He would have been in Atlanta helping her pack instead of in some bar getting drunk. Still, he knew that was no excuse.

The drinking had gotten him into trouble. If he hadn't been drunk, Darlene wouldn't have come home with him and set this horrible chain of events in motion. Yes, it was the drinking.

After she had turned off their street, Gloria realized she wouldn't be able to drive much farther. She was beginning to shake with nerves, and the tears falling from her eyes made it difficult for her to focus on the road. She headed for the main highway, where she hoped she could find a hotel.

Somehow she managed to register and get to her room. Once there, she stopped trying to keep herself together and let the emotions have free rein. It started with a wail, the sound of a wounded animal. She heard the sound and it startled her at first. Then she realized the sound had come from her.

Josh called Gloria in Atlanta every fifteen minutes after the time he thought it would have taken her to drive home. Either she wasn't home or she wasn't answering the phone. He prayed nothing had happened to her on the way. If something had happened, surely he would have been contacted. So, he assumed she wasn't answering his calls. He couldn't much blame her. He didn't know how he was going to fix this. He had checked the airlines and decided to take a Sunday afternoon flight to Atlanta. She needed some time. He'd give her some, but not much. They had to get this settled. Gloria needed time to adjust to her feelings, but too much time would allow her imagination to go overboard.

He had just dialed her for the fifth time Sunday morning when his doorbell rang. He wondered who was visiting at this hour. It wasn't like he had lots of guests.

He opened the door and was surprised to see Darlene standing there. "What do you want?" he asked.

Darlene pushed past him and came into the house. "Where's the missus?"

Josh stood at the door, not bothering to close it. Darlene would be leaving soon. "What did you tell her, anyway?"

Darlene sat on the couch. "You may as well close the door, Josh. I'm not going anywhere until we talk. And I know Gloria's not here."

Josh closed the door and walked over to her. He deliberately chose to sit in the chair opposite her and not on the couch next to her. "Okay, what do you want to talk about?"

"Us."

Josh shook his head. "I tried to tell you this yesterday, Darlene. There is no us. There can never be any us. I love my wife."

"But your marriage isn't working," she explained. "Can't you see that?"

Josh didn't like her attitude. It was one thing for him to think that his marriage wasn't working, but it was a whole other thing for someone else to sit in judgment. "You're way out of your league, Darlene. I'm not giving up on my marriage. Can't you get that through your head?"

"No, I can't. I thought you would know that about me by now. I don't give up easily when there's something I want."

Josh stood and walked over to sit next to her. "I know I've led you on, Darlene, and I'm sorry, but I'm not leaving my wife and that's final."

Darlene looked up into his eyes and smiled. Her look reminded him of a look he had seen once in Carla's eyes. A look that made him wary. "I know you mean what you're saying, Josh. At least you mean it for now. But my guess is things are going to change. Your little Gloria is not very happy right now."

Josh knew there was no reasoning with Darlene. All he could do was get her out of here so he could get to the airport. He stood and she stood, too.

"Okay, I'm leaving," she said. You have my number." With that, she sauntered to the door and let herself out.

Josh stared at the door after her. At this moment he wished he'd never met her at Dominic's. After all that had happened, he was still attracted to her.

Gloria checked her answering machine, and as she had expected, all the messages were from Josh. He had no idea she was still in Raleigh. She debated stopping by the townhouse on the way home to give them one more chance at a reasonable discussion. She didn't make a conscious decision, but she found herself in front of the townhouse. She didn't stop, but she slowed her speed long enough to read the license plate of the car parked in the driveway. She didn't know why she was surprised—she had looked like a vanity plate kind of girl. Gloria sped away, the Darlene moniker firmly planted in her mind.

Josh was seated at the counter when Gloria walked through the kitchen door. She had known he was there because his car was parked in the garage. That had given her a few minutes to get herself together, to prepare what she was going to say to him. When she saw him, all that preparation went away. She was raw emotion.

"What are you doing here?" she asked.

He faced her, meeting her eyes. "I live here, remember?"

"Hmmph," was her response. She walked past him to the stairs, headed for their bedroom. When she walked through the bedroom door, the smell of betrayal met her. Even though she had found Josh and Darlene in the other house, somehow they had also invaded this bedroom, this bed. She backed out of the room, bumping into Josh in her rush.

He pulled her into his arms. "What's wrong?"

She jerked away from him. "I can't stay in that room. Not with you. Not without you." She moved on down the hall to one of the guest bedrooms, consciously not choosing the one Josh had slept in when he'd moved out of their bedroom.

He followed her down the hall and would have followed her into the bedroom, but she slammed the door in his face and locked it. He stood outside the door and twisted the knob. "Open the door, Gloria. We need to talk." When she didn't answer, he added, "Please open the door."

"There's nothing to talk about," came her voice from the other side of the door. She remembered Darlene's car in his driveway earlier this morning and wondered if he had made love to her before leaving Raleigh. Would the pain ever stop? She didn't even find peace in sleep. In her dreams she saw Josh making love to that woman.

"There's a lot to talk about. Our marriage. I love you, Gloria. I don't want to lose you."

Gloria sat on the bed, her head in her hands. She wanted to cry but she couldn't find the tears. They were all gone. She was one mass of shivering pain. "You should have thought about that before you went to bed with your girlfriend. Did you love me then? Were you thinking about our marriage then?"

"How many times do I have to tell you that I did not sleep with her?"

When would he stop lying to her? Even if he hadn't slept with Darlene last night, he would have in time. His look told her that. The boldness that Darlene exhibited with her was not just bravado. She had reason to believe she had a chance to take Josh away from Gloria. Gloria knew Josh had given her that hope. "What was she doing at the townhouse then? Is she the maid?"

Josh leaned against the door. "I told you. I was drunk. She drove me home. Can't you believe that? Gloria?"

"I drove by the townhouse this morning. Her car was parked in your driveway."

Josh fought for a response. There was no right answer. If he lied, she'd know. If he told the truth, he'd be in more trouble.

She lay back on the bed, eyes wide open, and stared at the ceiling. "Your lack of response answers the question. Now, will you please leave me alone?"

She wished she could erase the entire weekend from her memory. The scenes kept playing over and over in her mind. There was no way to escape them. She'd never forget the pain she'd felt when she'd seen the woman's clothes in their bedroom. Or when she'd found her half-naked in their kitchen. It was all such a nightmare. And then the humiliation of standing there arguing with that whore about her own husband. God, she couldn't believe she'd actually done that.

What was she going to do now? Everything was different. She and Josh weren't special anymore. They were just people. People who had lost sight of each other. People who had a sham of a marriage. The tears began to flow then. She wasn't cried out after all.

Josh dragged himself back to their bedroom and sat on the bed they had shared. He lay back and remembered all the good times they had shared. In bed. And out. He squeezed his eyes shut and blocked out the other thoughts that fought with these happy ones. Images of Gloria's face when he'd walked in on her and Darlene Saturday morning. That was a look of hurt and anger that he'd never seen on her face before. And he was the cause of it.

If only he could undo this whole relationship with Darlene. He should never have encouraged her. It was all his fault. What was he going to do?

Chapter 19

Gloria was glad to go to work Monday morning even though she'd have to deal with Foster Dixon, who was shepherding the South Fulton deal. Finally, she could concentrate on something other than the problems in her marriage. Josh had gone back to Raleigh, thank God. She couldn't deal with him right now.

As if he heard her thinking about him, Foster walked into her office. "Ready?"

"Of course," she said. She got up from her desk and walked over to the conference table. "Let's get started."

Gloria was surprised at how well she and Foster worked together. For all of Foster's machismo, he was a team player, soliciting her ideas and considering her opinions. Not once did he make a personal overture.

"How about lunch?" he asked when they were finished.

Feeling good about their accomplishments, she said, "Sure, I could use a break."

They ended up at Mick's on Peachtree. Mick's brought thoughts of Josh, which she quickly shoved aside.

She ordered the pasta instead of her usual grilled chicken salad. Again, she wanted to keep thoughts of Josh at bay. Unfortunately, Foster ordered the salad.

"What's the matter?" he asked.

Surprised and embarrassed that her emotions were so close to the surface, Gloria shook her head. "Everything's fine."

"Good," Foster said. "I don't want you having second thoughts about lunch with me. I couldn't believe my good fortune when you decided to come without your chaperon."

Gloria laughed softly at his reference to Portia. "I usually need a chaperon with you. You can be bad sometimes."

Foster took a drink from the Coke the waiter had delivered to the table. "What was different about today? I really didn't expect you to come."

Gloria didn't want to talk about her reasons. She had told herself that she had come because Foster had behaved so well at the meeting, but she knew there was more to it than that. And that reason concerned Josh. "Maybe I just felt adventurous today," she said with a coy smile.

Foster nearly choked on his drink, though his recovery was admirable. "If I didn't know you better, I'd swear you were flirting with me."

She smiled, but said nothing.

"Well, well, well. Has Josh been a bad boy?"

That was the wrong thing to say. It hit too close to the truth. She never would have agreed to this lunch if things weren't strained between her and Josh. "Discussions about Josh are off-limits."

"Okay, pretty lady. I don't want to talk about him, anyway."

Gloria smiled again. This was what she needed. To feel desirable and attractive. Josh's betrayal had made her question her desirability and attractiveness. It was clear now why she had decided to lunch with Foster. She wanted him to confirm those things that Josh had caused her to question.

When they got back to Gloria's office, Foster asked, "How about dinner one night this week?"

She hesitated before answering. Did she really want to do this? "I don't know."

"I don't bite," he said with a grin.

"I'm not too sure about that."

"I'll make it easy for you. We can make it a working dinner. A brainstorming session of financing alternatives for South Fulton."

What's the harm in a little dinner? she asked herself, ignoring her conscience. "Okay, how about Thursday? That'll give us both time to think more about South Fulton."

* * *

Josh endured Monday morning. His thoughts were with Gloria, so concentration on work was impossible. Amazing, he thought, how the actions of one night could so drastically affect his life. Everything that he held dear was in jeopardy. Gloria and his marriage. They were what was important. How had he lost sight of that?

He had done nothing but think since Saturday. He wondered how things had gotten so far out of hand. How did he end up leaving Gloria in Atlanta in the first place? Married people are supposed to be together. Job or no job, they should've been able to work it out in Atlanta. Why hadn't they been able to do that?

That was the million-dollar question. Their marriage had been rocky every since he'd lost the General Electronics' job. He had thought this new job would help put those problems behind them. Looking back on it now, he realized how naïve they both had been. If they couldn't work out their problems together, they sure as hell couldn't work them out apart. Maybe that was what Elliot had tried to tell him. But he hadn't listened. And look where it got him. He should have taken Elliot's counsel more seriously. After all, he and Marilyn had made it through the rough patch in their marriage. Hindsight, he thought, was always twenty-twenty. Maybe he should have taken Elliot up on his partnership offer.

Josh knew he had to do something. Before Saturday's incident, he had hoped Gloria would move to Raleigh. Now, that was out of the question. She wasn't going to move and he didn't blame her. What woman in her right mind would give up her job and move away from a home she loved to follow a man she couldn't trust to be faithful to their marriage vows? Not Gloria.

He knew, too, that he and Gloria couldn't work out their problems apart. So, he had to move back to Atlanta. He picked up the phone and called Elliot. "Are you still looking for a partner?" he asked.

"You can't do it," Carla said.

"Watch me," Josh responded. He was surprised at Carla's attitude.

Angela Benson

"You have a contract with Carolina Electronics and I'm holding you to it. If you leave, I'll have you in court so fast, your head will spin."

He had seen that look on Carla's face before, the hard-driving, do-anything-to-get-the-job-done look that made him uneasy. "That doesn't make sense. Why would you go to all that trouble? Let me out of the contract and we can forget the bonus compensation that I've earned. I have to move back to Atlanta. Now."

Carla got up from her seat, walked around, and sat on the edge of the desk to face him. "And I need you here. Maybe we can work out some kind of compromise. I can give you a month's leave, six weeks tops."

He caught her gaze and held it. "That's not good enough. I need to move." Too much is at stake, he added to himself.

Carla went back to her chair and sat down. "Well, I won't let you out of the contract and you won't accept my compromise. Unless you can come up with another alternative, I'd say you're stuck."

At that moment, he wanted to swipe that silly smirk off her face. "I understand your position, Carla, and I know I'm asking a lot, but there's no way I can fulfill the terms of that contract."

She picked up a pencil and began writing on the ledger in front of her. Without looking up, she said, "I suggest you get back to work."

Josh stared at her for a few long seconds before leaving her office. He strode back to his office, slamming the door behind him. There was no way he was going to allow this job to cause him to lose his marriage. There was more than one way to skin a cat and to get out of a contract.

The phone range and Josh picked it up. His "hello" sounding more like "What do you want?"

"It's Elliot. I got your message. Are you serious about coming into business with me?"

"I'm willing to talk about it. That is, if you're still interested."

"Hell, yes, I'm still interested. When will you be in town again?"

"This weekend." He'd have plenty of time to talk with Elliot since he had a feeling Gloria wouldn't be doing too much talking. At least, not to him.

"That's great. We'll talk then. I'm excited about this, Josh. I could sure use your help."

"From the little I've heard from Gloria, it seems you're on your way. I'd understand if I'd waited too late to take you up on your offer."

"No way. I'm not letting you out that easily. I need you, all right."

They said their goodbyes and Josh hung up. He wondered again why he hadn't considered Elliot's offer seriously when he had first made it. If he had, he wouldn't be having these problems in his marriage now. Well, it was too late to go down that road again. He had made what seemed like the right choice a few months ago. Only in the glaring light of hindsight was it so obvious that the choice was wrong.

Foster postponed his dinner meeting with Gloria until Friday night. She was surprised that she had such a good time with him. They talked business, but he also provided that confirmation of her womanliness that she so needed. And he provided it in such a way that she could still feel that she had been faithful to her marriage vows.

When he got back to her house, he invited himself in for coffee. Against her better judgment, she allowed him in.

Foster followed her into the kitchen to help with the coffee. When she reached up to pull the coffee canister from one of the higher shelves in the cabinet, Foster came up behind her.

"I'll get that." He came so close that his chest touched her back, then he reached up and got the canister. When he placed it on the counter in front of her, he rested both of his hands facedown on the counter on either side of her. She stood trapped in the middle of his arms.

She didn't know what to say or what to do. It had been such a nice evening that she didn't want to put a pall on it. So, picking up the coffee canister, she turned within his arms and smiled up at him, the canister the only thing separating them. "Thanks. Now, can you let me out of this car?"

Foster smiled back at her, but he didn't move. "You are the most beautiful woman I've ever known," he said. "I've thought that from the first day we met."

God, she needed to hear those words. Needed to know that someone other than Josh found her attractive. But she knew this situation could easily get out of hand. Flirting was okay, but she wasn't ready for anything more. A picture of Darlene flashed through her mind. Maybe she was. "Foster…"

"Don't, Gloria. For this one night, let me tell you how I feel. For a few minutes, let's pretend you aren't married. Hell, Josh doesn't even exist." When she would have interrupted, he added, "Just a few minutes. If you want me to go away after I've had my say, I will. But if you want me to stay, I'll do that too."

She looked up at him and saw the sincerity and love in his eyes. She wondered how she could have missed the depth of his feelings for her. All this time she had thought he was just flirting, but the look in his eyes told another story. Foster Dixon was in love with her.

He saw the recognition in her eyes. "You never knew?"

She shook her head. It was as if she was in some sort of trance. Maybe she never saw it because she only looked for love in Josh's eyes. "I'm so sorry, Foster."

He removed the canister from her hands and put a finger to her lips. "Don't say anything more. Let me have this time with you. Okay?"

She didn't say anything more. She just stood there thinking about this man who loved her. She knew then that there was more to Foster Dixon than she had ever imagined. It caused something inside her to open up and she knew that this was a moment that she wanted too. Not a lifetime, because she still loved Josh. But a moment. A moment to get herself back after that awful run-in with Josh and Darlene. A moment to show this wonderful man that she appreciated what he was doing for her.

Josh found them like that. Foster's body hid Gloria from his sight, but he heard Foster's words and he didn't see Gloria try to get away. Anger rose up in Josh like a fountain and before he knew it, he had stormed over and pulled Foster away from Gloria. He turned Foster around and punched him in the jaw.

Foster, too surprised to block the blow, was knocked off balance. Gloria stood with her mouth open, looking from Foster to Josh and back again. Finally she said, "Josh, I didn't know you were coming in tonight." She could have kicked herself as soon as the words were out of her mouth.

Josh glanced at Foster. "That I believe. Was I interrupting something?"

Gloria decided this was a conversation they needed to have alone. She looked at Foster, who was rubbing his jaw. "Are you all right?" she asked. When he nodded, she said, "Let me walk you to the door. Josh and I need to talk. Alone."

Foster nodded at Gloria, but his look sent daggers at Josh and he didn't move to follow Gloria out of the room.

"Foster, please don't make this situation more difficult than it already is."

Foster brushed past Josh and followed Gloria out of the kitchen. At the front door, he asked, "Are you sure you're going to be okay?"

Gloria nodded. "He's not going to hit me, if that's what you mean. More than that, I can't answer."

"I'm sorry if I've caused you any problems, but I had to tell you how I felt. It's been eating me up for years. Maybe now I can get over you. That is, unless you decide you do feel something for me."

"Oh, Foster, I'm in no position to feel anything for you. Regardless of what happens with Josh and me, you should go on with your life. There's some lucky woman out there just waiting to make you happy. Don't waste your love on me." She reached up and kissed him on the cheek. "Thanks for dinner and everything else. You'll never know how much the evening meant to me, how much I needed what you gave me. I'm just sorry I couldn't give you more."

Foster stared at her for a few seconds as if willing her to love him back. Then he nodded and headed for his car.

Gloria eased the door shut and leaned her head against it. Josh's voice caused her to turn around. "What did you say?" she asked.

"You heard me. I asked how long you've been seeing him."

Gloria saw the hurt in Josh's face and a part of her was glad that she was able to hurt him. Another part of her wanted to hold him in her arms and let him know that no other man had taken his place. Instead, she brushed past him and went back to the kitchen.

Josh followed her. "Are you going to answer my question?"

Gloria put the coffee canister back in the cabinet. She no longer wanted coffee. All she wanted was to go to bed. Alone. "I'm going to bed, Josh. I'm not going to stand here and be interrogated by you."

Josh watched her leave the kitchen as if nothing had happened, as if he hadn't seen her standing in Foster Dixon's arms. That bastard. Josh wished he'd given him more than one punch. He couldn't believe it. The guy was in his home, making time with his wife.

Josh pulled out a dinette chair and sat down. It was too much. First, him and Darlene. Now, Gloria and Foster. What was happening to his marriage? His life? Would he ever get back what he had? At this point, he really didn't know. All he knew was that, right now, he hurt as he had never hurt before. And the worse part of it was that he had brought it all on himself.

He put his head in his hands and cried.

Chapter 20

Josh looked for Gloria after he got up the next morning, but she wasn't in the house. She may have eluded him this morning, but she couldn't avoid him forever. He'd see to it. It was probably good that she wasn't in now since he was scheduled to meet with Elliot this morning.

An hour later, he was in Elliot's garage. "So, you've decided to join me in this venture. I'm glad, but something tells me it's not just the great opportunity that I've put before you that led you to this decision."

Josh knew Elliot deserved an explanation. If they were going to be partners, they needed to be honest with each other. "You're right. It's not just the opportunity. I think I should have seen that earlier." When Elliot didn't respond, he continued, "I also should have listened to your advice on this commuter marriage. It's not working."

Elliot took two chairs from a table, offered one to Josh, and took a seat himself. "I'm really sorry about that, Josh. Marilyn and I both hoped you and Gloria would pull it off."

"Well, we couldn't. And now I need to get back to Atlanta to save my marriage."

"Is it that bad?"

Josh nodded. "It's worse than you think. Gloria thinks there's another woman."

"And why would she think that?"

Josh looked at his hands because he didn't want to see the look on Elliot's face. "Because there was."

"Josh! I don't believe it. Not you. You didn't cheat on Gloria."

He looked up at Elliot. The shock and disbelief that he saw didn't surprise him. "No, I didn't, but I came close. And she found out. I have to move back to save my marriage."

In a way, Elliot felt relief at Josh's words. Maybe now he could let go of the guilt over what he had said to Gloria that night. "I'm sorry it took these circumstances to bring you back, but I'm glad to know that I'll have you on my team. I need you, Josh."

"That's good, because I need you too. There's something else you should know."

"What's that?"

"Carolina Electronics is making noise about not letting me out of my contract. I think it's a scare tactic, but I thought you should know."

"Can they really do that?"

Josh nodded. "I signed the contract so I'm legally bound, but I don't see why they'd want a disgruntled executive. I've offered to forgo all bonus compensation. That should be enough to satisfy them."

"Could they make you stay?"

"Technically, but it'd take a court battle and I don't think they're up for that."

"If they are, would they win?"

"Unfortunately. I'm trying not to think about that. I just want you to know that all our discussions are based on that assumption that I can get out of the contract. Is that okay with you?"

Elliot nodded. "Of course, I'd like it better if everything were settled, but I can dangle for a while."

"I should know within the next month. How's that?"

"Hey, I want you with me and I'll take you any way I can get you."

"Good then. Now that we've gotten all that out of the way, let's talk shop. Where do things stand?"

Josh spent the rest of the morning going over Elliot's plans for his first production run. By lunchtime, he was excited about their prospects. He knew they would make a lot of money if they did everything right.

"Do you want to stay for lunch?" Elliot asked. "Marilyn would love your company."

"Not today, maybe some other time. Has Gloria talked to Marilyn about our problems?"

Elliot shook his head. "If she has, Marilyn hasn't told me. Actually, we haven't seen much of Gloria lately."

"Maybe it's been too difficult for her, knowing that you two made it through your rough time and we didn't."

Elliot nodded, but he knew the real reason Gloria hadn't been around. It was him. He had overstepped his boundaries. He knew he had to come clean with Josh about it. "That's not all of it."

Josh looked up at Elliot. "What more is there?"

"I told Gloria how I felt about your commuter marriage arrangement."

"And she didn't take it too well," Josh finished for him. "What exactly did you say?"

"I don't remember exactly, but I know she took my comments to mean that I thought you and she had misplaced priorities."

Josh nodded. "Well, you were right."

"But that doesn't help me with Gloria. We haven't spoken since then."

Josh clapped Elliot on the back. "Don't worry about it. You told Gloria the truth and she wasn't ready to handle it. I wasn't ready then either, but I am now."

"Do you think you and Gloria will work things out?"

Josh only knew what he wanted. "I know we will," he said and added a silent prayer that he was right.

"Maybe he's telling the truth," Portia said, her gaze on the napping Paige in the stroller in front of their bench. "Maybe nothing happened."

Gloria lifted a brow in Portia's direction. "You've got to be kidding. Josh was lying to save his ass."

Portia took her eyes off her baby and looked at Gloria. "Maybe not. Josh is an attractive man and women today will do anything to get an attractive man. Maybe it happened the way

Angela Benson

he said. She brought him home and he fell asleep. Everything else could have been her doing."

Portia had no idea how much Gloria wished she could believe that. Unfortunately, she didn't have the luxury of wishful thinking. "It was more than that. You didn't see her and you didn't hear what she said. Something was going on between them. Even if he didn't sleep with her that night, they were involved."

"I still can't believe it. Not Josh."

"I guess you don't want Dexter to be like him, now, do you?"

Portia looked away from Gloria and toward the mime who was performing in the park. "Maybe the rub-off worked the wrong way and Josh is being like Dexter."

"What do you mean by that?"

"Dexter has…ah…strayed in the past."

Gloria touched Portia's arm and Portia looked at her with tears in her eyes. "Portia? When? Why didn't you tell me?"

"It was the second year we were married. I think it only happened once. And I didn't tell you because it was too painful and our friendship was too new."

"Oh, I'm so sorry, Portia. I can't imagine going through something like this alone. I knew I had to talk to you. If I had known it would be painful for you, I—"

Portia patted Gloria's arm. "That's all right. I'm just glad I can be here for you."

"How did you deal with it, Portia? You and Dexter seem to have recovered very well. I would never have guessed."

"It was very difficult. The most difficult thing I've ever done. My whole world crashed when I found out."

Gloria understood those feelings because they were hers exactly. How did you get past them? she wondered. "How did you find out?"

"She called me. Can you believe the nerve of that bitch? She said that she was sleeping with my man, and if I didn't believe it, I could find his car at her house at a certain time."

"Oh, no Portia. What did you do?"

"I hung up on her, but I couldn't forget the call. Though I told myself over and over that I would trust Dexter, I checked it out.

Dexter said he was going to a basketball game with a few friends. An hour or so after he left, I drove by her house. His car was parked out front."

"God, Portia. You didn't go in, did you?"

"No. I couldn't go in. I didn't want to see them. Sometimes I think that's why we could get past it. If I had seen them together, I don't think I would have been able to erase the picture from my mind."

The picture of Darlene in the kitchen of the Raleigh townhouse flashed in Gloria's mind. "That's the way I feel. Even though I didn't see them in bed together, I saw her standing in his kitchen in her panties and camisole. She was cooking breakfast like she lived there. I can't get it out of my mind."

"You're going to have to find a way to deal with it or you and Josh don't stand a chance."

"I know that. I just don't know how to do it. What did you do after you saw Dexter's car?"

"Somehow I drove myself back home. I don't know how, because I cried all the way. I still couldn't believe it. I told myself over and over that there was some other reason that he was there, but deep down, I knew there was no other reason."

"Did you confront Dexter about it?"

She nodded. "When I got home, I sat on the living room couch and waited for him. I sat there for almost three hours waiting for him. You can imagine the thoughts that went through my mind. Those were the longest three hours of my life. Anyway, Dexter knew something was up as soon as he walked through the door."

Seeing her friend's distress, Gloria became concerned that this conversation was too much for her. "Portia, you don't have to do this. I'm sorry I brought it up. Let's talk about something else."

"That's all right, Gloria," she said. "I want to talk about it." Then she continued as if she was reciting facts about a project at work. "First, I told him about the call. I remember very clearly what he did next. He sat next to me and he took my hand. He looked into my eyes and told me that he loved me. At that moment, I hated him. How could he say that he loved me, when he had just been with another woman? I didn't say anything, I just got up and went to bed. In the guest room."

"And that was it?"

Portia shook her head. "Not by a long shot. That was just the beginning. The next day Dexter told me he had ended it with her and begged my forgiveness. But I had to put him through hell first. Betrayal like that does something to your insides. Your self-esteem goes straight to hell. I felt like I had to get back what he had taken. I thought I had to find that in another man's arms."

Gloria had thought the same thing and tried it with Foster. "Did you?"

"I tried, but I couldn't do it."

"Because you still loved Dexter?" Gloria asked.

Portia shook her head. "I couldn't do it because I still loved myself. If I had done it, I may never have gotten my self-esteem back. No, what I did, or didn't do, I did for myself. Not for Dexter."

"Is that when you decided to forgive him?"

"I think so, but we still weren't out of the woods. Even though I had forgiven him, I still don't trust him. The trust he had to earn. And only time brought that about."

Time. One thing Josh and Gloria didn't have with their current living arrangements. "To look at you two now, you'd never know it."

Portia smiled a smile that lit up her whole face. "I'm not saying that we aren't happy, but there are scars. The wounds heal, but the scars remain. We're not the same people that we were then. Our marriage isn't the same. Something like that changes you. You have to change to get past it."

"Did you ever think about walking away from the marriage?"

"I did walk away in my mind. That's how I endured the initial pain. In my mind, our marriage was over."

"But it wasn't."

"No, it wasn't. Dexter kept it together. He wouldn't allow me to throw it away. And now I'm glad he didn't. Are you thinking about walking away?"

"Not really. I don't know. I just know that every time I see

Josh's face, I remember all I saw that morning. Therefore, I don't want to see him. The memories are too painful. I just want to forget."

Portia touched her friend's hand. "That's normal, Gloria. You have to take care of yourself. You aren't responsible for Josh's feelings right now. You have to do whatever it takes to make it through the day."

"So much for our perfect marriage and relationship, huh?" It seemed so long ago that she had thought she and Josh had a perfect marriage and relationship.

"Not necessarily. You and Josh can still have a marriage if that's what you want. There's no reason you can't."

"I don't see how, Portia. I can't even think about making love with Josh again. It turns my stomach to even think about that."

"That's normal, too. You're human, Gloria, and you're having a human reaction to an awful situation. Take your time. You and Josh have plenty of time to make a decision about your marriage. I still believe that Josh loves you."

She wanted to believe that too. "How could he do it if he loves me?"

"Who knows what was going on in his mind? But I do know that you two have to acknowledge what happened before you can move on. If Josh did it, he needs to fess up. If he didn't, he needs to make you believe him."

Gloria didn't think she'd ever believe Josh wasn't guilty of something, but there was no need to go through that again with Portia. "I guess we'll start on this tonight. I left home this morning before he got up. I just couldn't bear to see him, but I know I can't avoid him forever. We'll talk tonight and he'll leave tomorrow. Then, I'll have some peace. But not until he's out of my house and out of my sight."

Josh was there when she walked through the door. She made for the stairs to avoid talking to him, but he called to her. Knowing she couldn't continue to avoid him, she walked into the living room where he was seated on the couch.

"I missed you this morning," he said.

She was in no mood for chitchat. "What do you want, Josh? I don't have all day."

He patted the couch next to him. "Sit down, Gloria. We need to talk."

She looked at the couch, then took a seat in the chair opposite him. "What do you want to talk about?"

He began quickly, "For the record, I didn't sleep with Darlene." When she would have interrupted, he said, "Listen, I know what it looked like, but I didn't sleep with her. I was drinking and she brought me home from the bar. Evidently, after I had fallen asleep she pulled off her clothes and got into bed with me. I swear I didn't touch her."

"And I suppose you have some land in Florida that you want to sell me?"

He ignored her question because he understood her pain. "The most I'm guilty of is flirting with her."

"Come off it, Josh."

"And leading her on. But I didn't do it because I loved her. I did it because I missed you."

Gloria stood then. "Right. You flirted with her because you missed me. I'm not going to let you make this my fault, Josh. It was your fault, not mine."

"What about what I saw between you and Foster Dixon. I could accuse you of sleeping with him."

"You could."

"That's all you're going to say? You're not going to deny it?"

"You'd like that, wouldn't you? If I slept with Foster that would somehow absolve you of what you've done. Well, I didn't sleep with him. I went to dinner with him."

"And that's all?"

"No, that's not all. I learned something last night. I learned that even if you don't love me, Foster does. I don't know how, since God knows I've never encouraged him, but he does. I never thought I'd need to hear those words from another man, but I needed to hear them that night."

Each word she spoke pierced his heart. He felt her pain and

he felt his own. It was almost unbearable. "Did they make a difference?"

"I don't know, Josh, I just don't know." With that, she ran up the stairs and to the bedroom she was now using.

Josh knew things looked pretty bleak for them now. Gloria still didn't believe he hadn't slept with Darlene. And he couldn't much blame her. It was a flimsy story. Now this complication with Foster Dixon and his declaration of love. Well, Foster was in for a fight if he thought Josh would give Gloria up. No, Josh had just begun to fight.

Josh prepared breakfast for both of them Sunday morning. He wanted one more chance to talk with her. When she didn't come down, he took a tray upstairs. He was relieved when she granted him entry into her room after his knock.

"What are you doing?" she asked.

"Serving you breakfast in bed."

"Well, it seems guilt brings out the best in some people." She looked at the food on the tray. French toast with maple syrup, scrambled eggs, bacon, hash browns, and orange juice. "And all my favorites, too. Why, Josh. You've outdone yourself."

Josh would have smiled, but her voice was laced with sarcasm. He ignored it. He had to if they were going to save their marriage. "I hope you enjoy it."

She grunted, but she picked up a fork and stabbed it into the French toast. She cut off a square and popped it into her mouth.

He pulled a chair up to the bed. "I'm moving back to Atlanta."

"Whatever for?" was her flip response.

He kept telling himself that she was hurt, so he tried to ignore her attitude. "I'm quitting Carolina and going into business with Elliot. What do you think about that?"

Elliot, boy, had he called it right, Gloria thought. If only she had listened to him instead of getting angry. "Why would you want to go into business with Elliot? I thought you were the big corporate mogul."

At least he had gotten her interest. "Some things are more important than work."

"Like what?"

"Like us. Our marriage."

"It's a little late for that, wouldn't you say?"

"I don't think it's too late. I love you, Gloria. I always have and I always will. I know you don't believe me about Darlene, but it's the truth. I swear it. And someday you'll believe me."

His words touched her but she couldn't let him continue. She wasn't ready yet to soften toward him. "Nice speech. Do you want me to clap?"

"No, I want a chance to prove myself to you. That's all I ask. Will you do that?"

Chapter 21

How could he even ask me that? she thought. "I can't make any promises right now, Josh, and I'd advise you not to make any hasty decisions."

"What are you telling me?" Josh choked out the question.

She pushed the breakfast tray away from her. "I need time and I don't know how much time. All I know is that what I saw that morning hurt worse than anything I've ever felt. That pain is still with me. I have to learn how to handle it before I can begin to think about what's next for us."

Josh didn't like what he was hearing. He needed her to give him some hope. "We've shared too much to let this end what we have." When she didn't respond, he asked the question that he most feared the answer. "You do still love me, don't you, Gloria?"

She looked at him, knowing the tears in his eyes were matched by tears in her own. "Right now, all I feel is pain. I can't feel anything else."

Josh got up and took the tray from the bed. He had to get out of the room while he still had his emotions under control. When he reached the door, he turned back to her. "I'm not giving up on us. I'll give you the time you need, but I'm not giving up on us." With that, he opened the door and left the room.

Gloria lay back down on the bed and closed her eyes, not bothering to wipe at the tears that seeped through her eyelids. She knew Josh was hurting, but there was nothing she could do to ease his pain. He'd have to deal with it alone because she needed all the energy she had to keep herself from falling apart.

* * *

Josh's mind was made up. He was leaving Carolina Electronics and Carla would have to deal with. He walked into her office Monday morning to tell her that.

She glanced up when he walked into the office, then went back to what she was writing without saying a word.

"Carla, I need to talk with you."

When she finally looked up at him, her smile and her relaxed manner took him off guard. He wondered what she was up to. "And what did you want to talk about?" she asked.

"Our discussion last week. I'm sure we can work out something."

She put down her pencil. "I don't know what more I can say. You have a contract. I've offered you time off. That's all I can do."

"You could let me out of the contract."

She smiled as if she knew something that he didn't. "That wouldn't be fair to you, Josh. You wouldn't want a reputation for reneging on your word, would you?"

He knew it was a threat. "Let's just say I'm willing to take the risk."

She shrugged her shoulders. "It's your career, but I think you'll find it fairly difficult to get another position if you break this contract."

Josh shook his head, not believing this conversation. "Why are you making this so difficult when you can hire somebody else?"

Carla picked up her pencil and twirled it between her fingers. "I have plans, Josh, and those plans include you. When I interviewed you for this job, I was also looking for someone who could one day take my place as Plant Manger. It just so happens that the time is coming sooner than I thought."

"Why would you be looking to replace yourself? That doesn't make sense."

She put the pencil down again and leaned forward. "Because when I leave this office, I'm going to an office at Corporate Headquarters, an office with Corporate Vice-President on the door. The corporate boys like you. They like the idea of your taking over here once I'm gone. You're not going to screw this up for me. And you shouldn't screw it up for yourself. You want this as much as I do. I know it. I saw it in you the first day we met. That's why I hired you."

Josh leaned forward. God help him, he was interested. He was still convinced that this was the best job he'd ever had, and even more so now with this new opportunity. He couldn't afford to be too hasty. "What kind of time are we talking about for these…ah…changes to take place?"

"A couple, three years, if things work out like I think they'll work out."

Josh sat back. Before he had walked through her office door, he had thought he couldn't get good luck if they were selling it on the street. And now this.

Well, maybe it wasn't good luck after all. It was an opportunity that he had to turn down regardless of how good it was, because it wasn't worth giving up his marriage.

"If you give the option of taking a six-week leave," he said, "I'll have to take it, but I must tell you again that it's very unlikely I'll be back. Given that, I'll understand if you withdraw the offer."

Carla stood, a satisfied smile on her face. "Let's have this talk again in about six weeks." He stood when she walked around her desk to escort him to the door. "Now, get things lined up in your office and be sure to let me know when you're leaving."

When Josh got back to his office, Darlene was seated at his desk. Oh, hell, he thought, here we go again.

"What are you doing here?" he asked.

She didn't bother getting up. She just looked up at him. "I'm having lunch with my sister so I stopped in to say hi."

Given the low cut of the dress she wore, he seriously doubted lunch with Carla was all Darlene had in mind. "Well, you've said it. Shouldn't you be getting to your sister's office?"

When she stood, he knew she had more on her mind than lunch with Carla. The dress fell across the tops of her thighs. He acknowledged again that she was one fine woman. "There's no need to be mean, Josh," she purred. "I thought we were friends."

Josh walked past her to his chair. He picked up a pencil and pretended to write. "Our friendship ended the night you got into my bed."

She sat on the desk and leaned toward him. When he looked up, he saw what she wanted him to see. "You know that's where you wanted me. I dare you to deny it."

He pushed back his chair so she wouldn't be so close. He may have thought it, but it was only a fantasy. He knew that now. And he had known it that night. "I admit we may have gotten our signals crossed earlier and I may have led you on, but I'm telling you now that I love my wife and I'm not giving up on my marriage. You need to find yourself somebody who's interested. It's not me."

She slid off the desk and walked to the door, undaunted by his comment. "I'll see you around, Josh. You take care now."

Josh shook his head. Women. The three in his life were driving him crazy. Carla, Darlene, and Gloria. Well, he needed to get two of them out of his life and he was starting with Darlene.

"Your mind's not on the work, Josh. Do you want to talk about it?"

Josh looked at Elliot, who was seated at the desk across from him. Elliot had brought a new desk into the garage for Josh. It was a bit crowded, but they knew it was only days before they found suitable office space. "I'm losing her, Elliot," he said. "I'm losing her and there's nothing I can do."

"I don't know what to say. What's going on with you two?"

"She hasn't spoken to me since I got in Sunday. It's Tuesday and she's still either too busy or too tired. We don't eat dinner together. Nothing. I could have stayed in North Carolina."

"You knew she was going to need some time. Just be patient."

"That's what I keep telling myself, but it's hard. I didn't do anything, and I'm getting tired of being treated like an adulterer."

Elliot only smiled. "It's been two days. Give it some time."

"But it seems like forever." They were both silent for a while. Josh hated his inability to exert any pressure in this situation, but all he could do was be there when she decided to forgive him.

"Enough of that. Let's get back to work. We should visit the site on Stone Mountain Industrial. I think it suits our purposes."

"You can't keep running from me," Josh said. It was Friday and things between him and Gloria weren't getting any better. "We have to talk. We've been living like strangers."

Gloria was seated on the bed in the guest bedroom that had become her haven. "I'm not ready. I need more time."

"And I've been trying to give you time, but think about me. Do you think it's easy for me to live in this house with you and not see you, not talk to you, not be with you?"

She didn't want to hear this. It still made her nauseous even to think of sex with Josh. She was nauseous a lot lately. "I told you not to make any rash decisions. You should have stayed in Raleigh."

"Is that what you really want?"

"I want you to leave me alone."

Josh walked over to her and pulled her up from the bed. The tears in her eyes ripped at his heart. "Don't you know that I love you? I'd never do anything to hurt you. You do know it, I can see it in your eyes."

God help her, he was right. She was still in love with him. And that was why she couldn't be around him, talk with him, be with him. She pulled away, not trusting herself not to respond to the need she saw in his eyes. "This is hard for you? Well, it's also hard for me. And I can't take it anymore."

"What do you mean by that?"

She stormed out of the room and went to the master bedroom they had shared, with him trailing behind her. "It means I can't take it anymore," she said, standing in her walk-in closet.

"What are you doing?" he asked.

She threw a suitcase on the bed, opened it, and began throwing in clothes from the closet and the chest. "Packing."

Josh watched her, not believing what he was seeing. "Packing? Where are you going?"

"I'm getting out of here. It's hard for you. It's hard for me. I'll make it easier for both of us."

Josh grabbed her arm as she pulled another garment from the middle drawer of the chest. "What are you talking about? You're not going anywhere. This is our home."

She jerked her arm away. "Watch me."

Josh watched as she flung garment after garment into the suitcase. When she tried to close it, it was too full. She grunted and pulled out another suitcase. She moved clothes from one bag to the other until she was able to close them both. Without a word, she pulled both bags from the bed and stumbled to the door under their weight.

Josh followed her out of the room. For some stupid reason, he wanted to help her with those bags. When she got to the top of the stairs, she dropped them beside her to take a rest.

"You can't just leave like this. Where would you go?"

She shook her head, breathless. "I don't know where I'm going. I just know I have to get out of here."

"You're not even going to give us a chance to work this out?"

"Work what out, Josh? Face facts. It wasn't just your…ah… encounter with Darlene. We've been having problems for a long time. Maybe they wouldn't have surfaced if you hadn't lost your job, but since that happened, we haven't really been a couple. Not really."

Josh rejected the truth he heard in those words. "All couples have problems. If they really love each other, they work them out."

She picked up her bags again. "Don't you see, Josh? That's it. Maybe we don't really love each other. Maybe we never have." She made her way down the stairs, stopping a few times to catch her breath. When she reached the bottom, she put the bags down again, walked to the living room table, and picked up her purse. Picking up the bags again, she stumbled out the front door.

Josh was left staring at the door as she closed it behind her. It was as if he were held in place by some invisible force. When he heard her car start, he was riveted out of his pose and out the door. He reached the sidewalk just as she pulled out into the street.

"Gloria," he called, but it was too late. She was gone and it felt as if she had taken a part of him with her.

* * *

As Gloria drove down the street, she remembered the last time she had left the house in anger. The night of their first fight. This time was different though. This time she didn't know if she'd ever be back.

She felt the tears build up in her eyes, but she was determined not to cry. She had cried enough. Now it was time for action. She had to find a way to pick up the pieces of her life. Then, maybe she could pick up the pieces of her marriage. Maybe.

When she stopped driving, she was in front of Portia's house. She wasn't sure of the welcome she'd get or what she'd do afterward, but she needed to talk to her friend.

"Gloria," Portia said when she opened the front door and saw her friend standing there. "God, I'm glad to see you. Josh called an hour or so ago and we've been worried since. Come on in."

Portia stepped back and Gloria followed her into the den. When they were seated, Portia asked, "What happened?"

Gloria wiped her hands down the side of her face. "What hasn't happened? I left home. I left Josh."

"Oh, Gloria. I'm sorry it came to this. Are you sure you couldn't work it out?"

Gloria shook her head. "Not now. I need to be on my own for a while. To think about what I want."

"I take it Josh didn't understand that need."

Gloria turned up her nose. "We argued. I left. Not exactly an amicable parting."

Dexter rushed into the room and kissed Gloria on the cheek. "I saw your car outside. God, am I glad to see you. What's up with you and Josh?"

Gloria looked askance at Portia. "I haven't told him," Portia said. "That's your decision."

Dexter looked from one woman to the other. "What are you talking about?"

Gloria nodded, then Portia got up and kissed Dexter on his forehead. "I'll get us some coffee. Have a seat and keep Gloria company until I get back."

Dexter watched his wife leave the room, wondering what was

going on. He looked back at Gloria. "What's up with you and Josh?" she asked again. "When he called here, he sounded out of control."

Gloria told him how she had left the house.

"But why, Gloria? You and Josh have a good marriage. Why can't you work this out?"

Portia walked back into the room before Gloria could answer. She handed them both a cup of coffee, settled herself on the arm of Dexter's chair, and reached for his hand. "Gloria found Josh in a compromising situation with another woman."

Dexter squeezed his wife's hand and then asked Gloria, "Are you sure?"

Gloria jumped up from the couch. "How can you ask me that? I saw her."

Portia stood up and pulled her friend into her arms. "Don't get upset, Gloria. Dexter didn't mean anything by that. He wanted to understand. We love you and Josh."

Dexter joined in their embrace. "That's right, Gloria. I can't believe Josh would do something like that. He loves you too much."

Gloria pulled out of their embrace. "What does love have to do with it?"

Dexter had a bewildered look on his face and he turned to his wife for direction.

"She knows about us," Portia said softly.

"Oh," was Dexter's only response. He walked back to his chair and sat down. Portia joined him. "You probably don't want to hear anything I have to say now, Gloria, but know that I never stopped loving Portia through the whole thing. I just thank God she was able to believe in me again. I hope that you'll give Josh the same consideration."

Gloria stared at her friends seated there in the same chair, offering comfort to each other. She knew it was difficult for them to discuss this, and she was touched that they cared enough about her and Josh to sacrifice their own feelings. "I love you both for what you're trying to do, but I'm not ready to do anything yet. I think I'd better leave."

"Leave? Where are you going?" Portia asked.

Anywhere but home. "I don't know yet. I'll find a hotel room until I can rent a place."

"You'll do no such thing," Dexter said. "You'll stay here with us. You and Josh may not be able to live together right now, but that doesn't mean we're no longer your friends."

"I couldn't do that. I wouldn't want to impose. Not with the baby…"

"That's why we need you here," Portia said. "You need to spend more time with your goddaughter. It'll be good for you both. And, God knows, I can use the company around here."

Gloria smiled and felt relief at their offer. She would feel better around friends. "But I won't be good company. I don't want to put a damper on your lives."

"We're going to worry more if you go someplace else, so you have to stay here."

"I'm still not sure…"

Dexter stood up. "Well, I am. Are your things in the car?" At her nod, he ordered, "Give me the keys."

Gloria reached for her purse on the couch and gave him the keys. "Are you sure?"

"Yes," they both said and then they laughed.

"Thanks a lot, you two," Gloria said. "I hope you don't live to regret this."

Chapter 22

"I'm sorry I'm late, Portia," Josh said. He pulled out a chair and sat down. "Why don't we go ahead and order? You must be hungry."

"Actually, I'm not."

Josh sobered. "Neither am I. How is she?"

"About as well as can be expected. She's working out her troubles. Between work and Paige, she keeps herself pretty busy. So busy she doesn't think about her problems."

"Damn," Josh said, his frustration mounting. "She needs to think about the problem and the solution. What am I going to do, Portia? I love her and I know I'm losing her."

Portia's heart contracted at the anguish she knew Josh felt. "I wish there was something I could say, but there isn't. You have to wait her out."

"I can't accept that."

"You don't have a choice."

"And that's what's killing me. My life is in her hands and I have no influence on her decision. Or when she's going to make it. This is impossible."

"It's impossible for her, too, Josh. Her world has been turned upside down. She needs time."

"She told you?"

Portia nodded.

"It's not true, you know. I didn't sleep with Darlene. Sure, I thought about it a couple of times. But each time I thought about it, I was angry with Gloria. It was never because of anything I felt for Darlene. It was always about what I felt for Gloria. Do you believe me?"

Portia nodded. "But unfortunately, I don't count."

"You do count. It's such a sick story that I'm glad somebody believes it. It gives me hope that one day Gloria will believe it too."

Portia didn't want to dash Josh's hopes, but she wanted him to be clear. "It's more than that, Josh."

He waited a few seconds before responding. "I know, but I've been telling myself that this was the major thing. Am I right?"

"In a way. But the only reason she can believe you were unfaithful is because of the way you two handled the unemployment thing. That made her think she didn't know you as well as she thought. That's why she can believe the worst about you."

Portia wasn't telling him anything he didn't already know. "Problems really compound, don't they?"

Portia nodded. "You can't run away from them. You have to solve them or you're right, they compound."

"And now I've got problems at work," he said aloud, though he was really talking to himself. "When it rains, it pours."

"Oh, Josh, I'd forgotten about that. How long are you going to be away from work?"

He gave a wry smile. "I'm working here."

"What? You're back in Atlanta for good."

So Gloria hadn't thought his move back important enough to tell Portia. "Unless I end up in court."

"That you have to explain."

Josh explained his partnership with Elliot and the lawsuit Carla had threatened.

"A lawsuit? Does Gloria know this?"

He shook his head. "We haven't talked long enough for me to tell her."

Portia covered his hand with her own. "I know you're hurting and right now you think you and Gloria may never get back together, but there is hope. Yours wouldn't be the first marriage to survive infidelity. Or supposed infidelity."

Josh was disappointed at the platitude. "Been reading Dear Abby?"

"Not quite. I lived it."

"You and Dexter?" Though he said the words, he didn't believe them.

She nodded. "Maybe you should talk to him."

"How are you this morning?" Portia asked when Gloria joined her for breakfast. Portia had been up for a while feeding Paige, then putting her back to bed. She was now on her second cup of coffee.

"Not so good," Gloria answered. "I feel awful."

"You've been having bad mornings ever since you've been here."

"I know. I must be worrying too much."

Portia drank from her milk glass. "Could be something else?"

"Like what?"

"You could be pregnant."

Gloria touched her stomach. "Pregnant? That can't be."

"You should know better than me, but you're showing the symptoms of the early months of pregnancy. When was your last period?"

Gloria searched her memory for the date. "I don't remember. I've had so much on my mind the last few months."

"Well, you should see a doctor."

"I don't think I'm pregnant." She couldn't be pregnant now. Not now.

"Even if you aren't pregnant, you need to see a doctor. You shouldn't be sick like this every day. You need to find out what's wrong."

"I know I'm not pregnant, but I do need to find out what's wrong, so I'll make an appointment with the doctor."

Pregnant. She was pregnant. She and Josh were going to have a baby. He'd be so happy about this. She went to the phone to call him. She hung up before she dialed the first number.

She couldn't tell him. Not now. So many things had changed. She didn't even know if they still had a marriage. She couldn't complicate the situation with a baby, could she?

"What did the doctor say?" Portia asked as soon as Gloria walked through the door.

"You were right. I'm pregnant."

Portia ran to her and hugged her as best she could with a crying Paige in her arms. "I'm so happy for you. I know how much you've wanted a baby."

Portia's happiness almost made Gloria forget her situation. Almost. She nuzzled the baby fat of Paige's neck, loving its softness. "Josh and I wanted a baby. Oh, Portia, what am I going to do?"

"Come over here and sit down. You're getting all worked up for nothing."

Gloria followed Portia to the couch. "This should be one of the happiest days of my life and I feel so lost. What am I going to do with a baby?"

Portia gave Paige a sucky kiss on the cheek that made the baby gurgle. "You're going to love him or her. That's what you're going to do."

"That's easy for you to say. You and Paige have Dexter. How can I have a baby when my marriage is in the toilet?"

"This baby may be the best thing to happen to you and Josh," Portia said, settling Paige on Gloria's lap.

Gloria rubbed the soft hair on the baby's head. "How's that? Do you think I should go back to him because I'm pregnant? I hope that's not your solution."

"That's not what I'm saying."

"Well, that's what it sounds like. How can you say it's the best thing to happen to Josh and me?"

"Perspective and speed, Gloria. This baby is what's important. If you can't forgive Josh and continue your marriage with him, you need to make that decision and begin to plan a life for this baby. But if you can forgive and make a good life for you and the baby with him, you need to make that decision so you and Josh can enjoy this time."

"So you think the right thing for the baby is for me to go back to Josh?"

Portia shook her head. "How can you think that's what I want. I'm the one with the parents who fought all the time. No, if you love Josh and can forgive him, then go back to him. But if you don't and can't, then make a clean break so you can focus on your baby. And you do have other options."

"Like what?"

"Adoption and abortion."

Gloria pulled Paige closer to her breast. "What? You can't be serious. Why would I want to carry the baby to term and then give it away? That makes no sense."

"You didn't say anything about abortion."

"God forgive me, it did cross my mind. But I could only have done that if I'd never told anyone about the pregnancy. As soon as I told you, abortion was no longer an option."

"I'm relieved to hear it because I know how much you want this baby and I know you'll be a great mother. Besides, we could end up in-laws."

"Wouldn't that be something? I'm glad our children will be around the same age. They'll have so much fun together and so will we."

"You're right," Portia said. "It'll be a lot of fun."

"If I get past the next few months. You're right about one thing though. I don't have a lot of time. I can't keep sitting around here not making a decision. I have my baby to think of now. I have to deal with Josh and my feelings for him."

"Dexter is having dinner with Josh tomorrow night."

"Whose ides was that?" Gloria asked.

Portia removed the fussy Paige from Gloria's lap. The baby had responded to Gloria's mood change. "Mine. I had lunch with Josh the other day. He wants you back, Gloria, and he's lost without you. Plus, he has no idea what you're thinking right now. The man is scared. I thought talking to Dexter would help him. You're not angry, are you?"

"How can I be angry after all you and Dexter have done for me? I'm sorry that you have to bring up the ugly time in your marriage. Especially now with the baby and all. You two should be focusing only on happy times."

Portia kissed the baby on her eyes to dry her tears. "We can handle it. It's still painful for us. Dexter more than me, I think.

But we look at what we have now and we're glad we worked through it. I would hate to have missed the time I've had with Dexter since then."

Gloria felt the loving feelings she had always had for Josh bubbling up in her, but she wasn't ready yet to deal with them. "What else did Josh say when you had lunch with him?"

"Did you know he had quit his job at Carolina Electronics and gone into business with Elliot?" Portia asked.

"He said something about that, but I can't imagine Josh giving up that job."

"He hasn't actually quit yet."

"I knew it." Josh did a lot of big talking, but Gloria knew he wouldn't give up that job easily.

"It's not like that. He offered his resignation, but it was turned down. They won't let him out of his contract. If he's not back in Raleigh in six weeks, they're taking him to court."

"Can they do that?" Gloria asked.

"According to Josh. He didn't think they would go that far, but his boss seems pretty determined to keep him."

Gloria shook her head. "I don't understand that at all. Why would they want to keep someone that doesn't want to be there?"

Portia repeated what Josh had told her about Carla's expected promotion and what it could mean to him.

"Josh should have stayed there. There was no need for him to move back so suddenly."

"To him there was a reason. You and your marriage."

Their marriage, Gloria repeated in her mind. What had happened to their marriage? "Sometimes I can't believe we're even in this situation. Not Josh and me."

"And sometimes I feel it's partly my fault," Portia said.

"How could you think that?"

"Well, the commuter marriage was my idea. If you hadn't gone that route, you wouldn't be in this situation."

"There's no reason for you to feel guilty. Our problems lay at our feet. The commuter marriage interval just brought to light problems that had been simmering on the back burner."

"You don't blame me, even a little?"

Gloria shook her head. "Not even a teeny bit. You've been a lifesaver for me from the time we found out about Josh's job loss. I know I acted ugly when I found out about your pregnancy and I'm so sorry about that. You're my best friend and I love you."

"I love you too. It hurt but I understood it. And now you're pregnant."

"And now I'm pregnant. Can you believe it? I'm going to have a baby." For the first time since she got home, Gloria grinned.

"I never knew," Josh said. He and Dexter were seated in Josh's living room, drinking beer.

"It's not the kind of thing we discuss over dinner," Dexter said. "That was an important time for us. I guess you know that now."

Josh nodded and took another swig of beer. "You can say that again. I've never felt so helpless, so lost in my entire life."

"That's the feeling, all right. And if you're like I was, it's worse because you know it's your fault. What can you do in a situation like that?"

"What did you do?"

"I ended it, confessed, and begged Portia's forgiveness."

"That was it? Portia went for it?"

"Yes, but only after she put me through hell. For a while, I had myself convinced she was deliberately torturing me. I knew she was in pain and I tried to allow for that, but I was in pain too. And I had no one to turn to. Who understands a man who's cheating on his wife?"

Josh laughed a hollow laugh. "Another man who's cheating on his wife. Thanks for coming over, man. I needed to talk to somebody."

"Hey, that's what friends are for. Portia and I want you and Gloria to work this out."

"Do you think we have a chance?" Josh held his breath while he waited for an answer.

"Where there's love, there's always a chance. Do you still love her?"

He nodded. "One thing this situation has made me understand is just how much I love her. I lost sight of that in all the things we've gone through in the last year or so. Just how precious she is to me and how my life is nothing without her. I can't lose her, Dexter. It would kill me."

"You're not going to lose her," Dexter said.

"What makes you so sure?"

"Because she still loves you."

Josh perked up. "How do you know? Did she tell you?"

"It's nothing she's said. But I know. She's hurt because she loves you so much."

"Maybe it's wishful thinking. She wouldn't have moved out if she still loved me. Am I being a fool here? Is it already over?"

"It's not over, but you're going to have to give her time."

Time. "It's been almost two months. How much time does she need?"

"Until she feels she can trust you again. It's not that she doesn't love you. She just doesn't trust you. She's wondering if you really love her."

"I do love her, but how can I show her if she won't even talk to me."

"It's hard, I know. I've been through it. But in a way, she's testing you. You'll have to prove your love over and over before she's confident enough to believe you. What happened affected her self-esteem, Josh. She has to get that back."

Josh was still amazed at how much that single event had changed his life. "I can't believe that one incident can wipe out almost ten years of love."

"It wasn't just an incident, Josh. She thinks you broke your vows. That's major."

"I know, I know," Josh said, resigned to wait. "Well, tell me how she's doing, what's she's saying, everything. I'm starving for her."

Chapter 23

Gloria had just put Paige down in her crib for the night when the doorbell rang. She took a final look at the baby, hoping she would stay asleep, before heading down the stairs to get the door.

"I'm coming," she yelled as she raced to the door. Whoever was at the door was leaning on the bell. She wondered who it could be. She looked through the peephole and saw Josh standing there. Her heartbeat raced. She was glad to see him, but she didn't want to see him. He leaned on the bell again.

She opened the door and stepped back. "What do you want?"

He smiled as if she'd asked a pleasant *How are you?* "It's good to see you too. May I come in?"

She wondered why he bothered asking, since he didn't wait for an answer. He strode into the house as if she had invited him over. She closed the door and followed him into the living room, where he took a seat on the couch. She didn't bother to sit. "What do you want?" she asked again.

He looked up at her, his smile still in place. "To see my wife."

His gaze made her uncomfortable. God, he was undressing her with his eyes. She shifted her weight from one foot to the other and ignored the urge to grab a pillow from the couch and cover herself. "Tonight's not a good time, Josh. I'm babysitting for Dexter and Portia."

"It seems there's never a good time. When—"

The sound of the crying baby interrupted him. "I've got to go check on her," Gloria said.

A few minutes later, she came back downstairs, holding Paige in her arms. Something stirred inside Josh when he saw her holding the baby. It brought images of her holding their baby.

He watched her walk around the room, cooing to the baby. "What's wrong with her?" he asked.

Gloria stopped walking and gave him an accusing glare. "You woke her when you rang the bell."

Josh stood up and walked over to them. "Come here, Paige. Let Uncle Josh get you back to sleep." To Gloria's surprise, the baby went willingly to Josh. She even stopped crying.

Josh smiled down at the baby. "You're a good baby, aren't you?"

"When did you get so good with babies?" Gloria asked. She knew she sound antagonistic, but she didn't like the thoughts that were running through her mind now. Thoughts of her and Josh and a baby—the baby she was now carrying.

"I've always loved kids. You know that. We both have. That's why we wanted to start our family so soon." He lifted a brow in her direction. "Maybe you've forgotten that?"

He wasn't going to get to her that way, she thought. "I remember, Josh. Unfortunately, I also remember a lot of other things." There. She'd done it. She'd brought Darlene into the conversation.

It didn't seem to bother Josh. He went back to his seat on the couch and cuddled the baby in his arms. Paige's eyes were droopy and Gloria knew she would soon be asleep. "I wish we had one just like her," he said. He looked up at Gloria with love shining in his eyes. "You'd be a great mother. And I'd be a great father."

If only he knew how much she needed to hear that now. If only they didn't have these problems. "Right." The word was full of sarcasm.

"I have dreams of you pregnant, your middle swollen with my baby. I still want that, Gloria."

She didn't say anything, couldn't say anything. He had disarmed her with his words.

"Let's take her upstairs." The sound of Josh's voice broke the silence.

Josh got up and headed for the stairs and Gloria followed him as if in a daze. Once in the baby's room, he gently lay her in her crib. Gloria watched him observe the baby for a few minutes and she knew he had spoken the truth about wanting a baby. Now was the perfect time to tell him.

"Josh…" she began.

He put a finger to his lips to shush her and pointed to the door. She followed him out of the room. When she would have spoken, he shushed her again. "No more harsh words, Gloria. Not tonight. I know you're hurting and God knows I'll never forgive myself for what I've done to you. To us. But it has to stop somewhere. You have to decide if you want to continue in this marriage. I'm going to wait, but I won't wait forever. I love you too much for that."

She knew when he finished speaking that he was going to kiss her. She knew it and she could have stopped him. But she didn't. No, she wanted the kiss as much as he did. Even though she didn't know what she would do later, she knew that right now more than anything she wanted this man to pull her into his arms and kiss her.

Josh reached for her and pulled her to him. She went willingly, almost eagerly, into his arms. She peered up into his eyes and the love shone brightly for her to see. It was a familiar look on his face. A look she had missed for what seemed like forever. He slowly bent his head until his lip touched hers.

She told herself to let him do the work, let him kiss her. But her body betrayed her. This man was her husband, the father of the baby she carried. And tonight she needed him to hold her, to kiss her.

When his tongue slipped past her lips, her legs went weak. She tightened her hold on him to keep from falling. She heard Josh groan as he deepened the kiss even more and then she felt his hands at her breast. Somehow that touch broke the spell he had cast over her. She pulled away and moved to wipe her hand across her mouth, effectively removing his kiss. He stopped her. The pleading in his eyes caused her protest to die on her lips.

"Don't," he said. "We both needed that. There's no reason to pretend you didn't."

His stare kept her rooted in place. He lifted his hand and ran a finger down her cheek. "I do love you," he said. With that, he turned and ran down the stairs and out of the house.

"Josh was here last night," Gloria told Dexter the next morning over breakfast. Portia hadn't come down yet. "Did you tell him I would be here alone?"

Dexter pushed back from the table and yawned, obviously still tired from his late night with Portia. "No, I didn't tell him. I may have mentioned that Portia and I were going out, but there was nothing contrived about it. I didn't set you up."

Gloria took another bite of her dry toast. That was all she could eat this early in the morning. "What did you two talk about then?"

"He's hurting, Gloria. He knows he screwed up and he wants the chance to prove his love to you. It's frustrating that you won't talk to him. That's probably why he came over."

"What should I do, Dexter?" she asked, not really expecting an answer.

"You mean about the baby?"

She nodded, not surprised Portia had told him about her pregnancy. "You didn't mention that to Josh, did you?"

"I wouldn't do that. That's your job. When are you going to do it?"

She remembered the picture Josh had made when he held Paige the night before. She had almost told him then. "When we settle things between us. I don't want the issues to get confused. I have to go back to him because I love him, not because of the baby."

"Do you love him?"

"Yes." She was sure of that. "But he hurt me and I have to find a way to get past that."

"He says he didn't sleep with her." At Gloria's glare, Dexter added, "He doesn't deny flirting with her, but he's adamant that he didn't sleep with her."

"And you believe him?"

He nodded. "What reason does he have to lie? In a way, it'd be easier if he had slept with her. Then, he could confess and beg you to forgive him."

Dexter was partially right. It did irritate her that Josh wouldn't confess what he had done. If he would admit it, she could work on forgiving him. Now, she had to deal with his lying on top of everything else. "How does he explain her clothes strewn around his bedroom and in his bed?"

"He doesn't. He still maintains that Darlene brought him home from the bar and put him to bed. Alone. The sound of arguing woke him up the next morning. He was surprised to find it was you and Darlene."

At least Josh was sticking to the same story, she thought. She had to give him credit for that.

"If you don't think you can forgive him," Dexter said, "you need to tell him. Soon. He's turning his life upside down now in hopes that you two will work it out."

"You're talking about his job with Elliot?"

"That and the fact that he broke his contract when he left Carolina. They've held off on filing the lawsuit, but he's convinced they're serious. If you aren't going to take him back, he's enduring a lot for nothing."

"You're blaming me for Josh's problems? How fresh. If he could make a decision to come back here now, why couldn't he have done it before all this trouble?"

"I don't know. You'll have to ask him that. You can't expect to work out your problems if you won't talk to him."

Dexter got up from the table just in time to greet his wife and baby. Portia pulled the high chair near the table and deposited Paige in it. She took Dexter's seat while he prepared Paige's breakfast. After placing the food on the baby's tray, he gave his wife a goodbye kiss and left the kitchen.

"Feeling nauseous again this morning?" Portia asked.

"It's getting better. Dexter was telling me about his visit with Josh."

"What did he say?"

She shrugged her shoulders. "Nothing new really. The lawsuit from Carolina Electronics. Josh may have been too hasty in leaving, especially since they were offering him a promotion."

Portia buttered a piece of toast and took a bite. "He's here because you're here. Would you consider going back to Raleigh with him?"

Two months ago that had been her plan. Amazing how quickly things changed. "Maybe once, but not now. Too much has happened."

"I guess he has no choice but to stay here then. And if he stays here, they're going to file suit against him. This has been a hell of a couple of years for Josh."

Gloria hadn't thought about it like that but Portia was right. Josh had suffered a great deal of disappointment in the last two years. And now he was having to give up a perfect job situation. She wished it didn't have to be so. "We both have. It hasn't been exactly easy for me either."

"At least Josh has this partnership with Elliot. Do you think they'll make a go of it?"

Gloria nodded, though she was uneasy about the partnership with Elliot. More precisely, she'd been uneasy about her relationship with Elliot since their argument. "There's no doubt. It'll be a couple of years before they see any real money, but the concept will work."

"You sound pretty sure of that."

"I am. The bank financed the venture. It wasn't considered that risky at all."

"Thank God for Elliot."

Gloria wondered about that. Elliot needed someone like Josh to help him. She knew Josh's input had gone into the winning business plan. Yes, he and Elliot would make a good team. If only...

"What are you thinking about?" Portia asked.

"Nothing."

"I don't believe you. Something's on your mind."

"It's Elliot."

"What about him?"

"We had a run-in a few months back."

"A run-in? You had a fight with Elliot? About what?"

Gloria shook her head. "It wasn't a fight. He said some things about my marriage that I didn't appreciate."

"Oh."

"Yes. Oh. And guess what? He was right."

"Is that going to present a problem for you and him in the future?"

That was exactly her concern. If she and Josh worked out their problems, she didn't want her relationship with Elliot to cause problems for him and Josh. "I don't think so, but I'm not sure. I haven't seen him since then."

Portia wiped the baby's mouth. She turned her head from side to side in a manner which said she didn't understand Gloria. "As thorough as you are at work, it amazes me how you allow personal matters to linger. It's almost as if you think that if you run away from them or don't deal with them, they'll go away. But they don't. You do see that, don't you?"

It had been a week since Josh had seen Gloria, but it seemed like only yesterday. The kiss was still fresh in his mind and in his heart. It had given him the hope he needed to endure their separation. She was still attracted to him. He hoped that meant she still loved him.

If only his work situation showed some hope. Things were moving forward with Elliot and the business, but the threat of the Carolina lawsuit still hung over his head. His last conversation with Carla hadn't yielded a satisfactory resolution. She was still dangling the carrot of a promotion. It wasn't as attractive now as it had been when she had first mentioned it. No, that carrot had been dangled at General Electronics and the result had been his termination. Now was not the time to base any career or life decisions on what may or may not happen at a corporation. Josh had gone through a lot to learn that lesson, but learned it he had.

He was actually excited about the work with Elliot. He didn't understand why he hadn't taken him up on it when Elliot had first proposed the partnership. If he had, maybe his marriage wouldn't be in trouble.

This partnership was giving him a sense of control in his life that he hadn't felt in a long time. He and Elliot could make a go of it. The future was theirs to make. Right now, the money was practically nonexistent, but that was okay. He and Gloria had savings and those savings and her salary would tide them over until he began drawing a salary from the company.

His readiness to accept Gloria's help to make it through this period made him smile. She'd tried to tell him earlier that this was what marriage was all about. Two people working together toward a common goal. He wanted this partnership for both of them. He longed for the day he could share that with her.

The ringing doorbell interrupted his thoughts and he realized he didn't know what was happening in the game on the television. He flicked it off with the remote control and went to the door.

He opened the door to find Darlene standing there. "What are you doing here?" he asked.

She pushed past him and into the house without answering his question.

"Don't sit down, Darlene," he said. "You're not staying."

She made for the couch and took a seat as if she hadn't heard him. "I think I am. At least until I can give you a message from Carla."

Josh reluctantly closed the door and went over to sit in the chair across from her. "You don't expect me to believe that Carla sent you, do you? Surely, you can do better than that."

She threw her head back and laughed. "You do know me well, don't you? I wanted you to know that Carla isn't going to prosecute. She just hates to lose. That trait runs in our family."

"And what's that supposed to mean?" he asked.

"Loosen up, Josh," she said. "I'm apologizing for being a sore loser. I couldn't accept it when you chose your marriage. Even though I knew you were in love with your wife, I didn't think she was in love with you. That made you fair game."

"You make it sound like a hunting expedition. This is my life we're talking about here."

She sobered and he knew she was serious. "And mine too. It was a game between us, Josh. At first. We parried back and forth, we flirted. It hurt to know that I was just a diversion for you. I thought there could be something between us."

Josh felt like a heel. "I was wrong to do that. You're right, I never had any intention of breaking my marriage vows or starting something with you. I'm sorry I hurt you."

"I'm a big girl," she said, her playfulness back. "The way I figure it, we're even now."

"And how do you figure that?"

"I may have lost you, but you've lost your wife. I'd say you're hurt a lot worse than I am."

That hurt. It was true, but it hurt. "Is that why you came today, Darlene? To gloat? To be happy that my marriage is torn apart?"

She sobered again. "No, that's not the reason I'm here. I wanted to tell you that I did spend the night in your bed that night. After you fell asleep, I undressed and got into bed with you. I had plans of seducing you, but you were too out of it. When I woke the next morning and you were still asleep, I decided to prepare breakfast for us. That's when Gloria found me."

He rubbed his hand across his head in frustration. "God Darlene, why couldn't you have told her that?"

"Tell your wife, or even you, for that matter, that I placed myself in your bed, uninvited, with plans to seduce you?" She said it as if that were the most ridiculous thing she'd ever heard. "I don't think so."

"Instead you made Gloria think something had happened between us."

"She thought I was Carla and I didn't bother correcting her. She assumed we had slept together and I didn't bother correcting her on that either."

"What did you hope to gain?"

"I don't know. A part of me hoped she would leave you and then you'd realize that you loved me. She did leave, but you still didn't want me."

Josh never knew that Darlene cared so much. "What made you come here today to tell me all of this?"

She shrugged in a noncommittal way. "Simple guilt. It's all gotten out of hand. When Carla told me about your leaving and the lawsuit, I knew it had something to do with the day Gloria and I had the run-in. It wasn't that hard to figure out. Anyway,

I came clean with Carla. After I explained that our relationship might come out in court, she decided against the lawsuit."

"Are you sure about that?"

"Very. Carla doesn't want the family name dragged through the courts. Might get in the way of her plans."

He knew she was right about Carla. Her plans were more important than anything. He had been like that at one time, but he'd learned that plans could become prisons. People were important. Love was important. Plans were, well, they were just plans. "You didn't have to come here to tell me that. Carla could have called."

"I know that, Josh, but I felt I owed you. If you want me to talk with your wife or something, I'll do that. I don't know if she'll believe me, but I'm willing to give it a try. What do you say?"

Chapter 24

Gloria was tired when she woke up Saturday morning. Thoughts of herself, Josh, and the baby had her tossing and turning for most of the night. Outside forces were taking away the leisure she had with which to deal with her situation. She had to make a decision. The sooner the better.

She knew what she wanted. She just wasn't sure it was the right thing to do. Shouldn't Josh have to suffer longer for his indiscretion? Would she be a fool to forgive him so quickly? Would he do it again if she did?

The rational part of her knew that her forgiveness would have no bearing on Josh's future fidelity. But her emotions continually told her that if she made him suffer enough, he'd never betray her again. She needed to do something to give herself the security.

But on this Saturday morning, she knew there were no guarantees. If she took Josh back, there was no surety that he wouldn't stray again. The only surety would be her trust and faith in him.

Could she allow herself to trust him again? She wanted to. God knows, she wanted to. But before she could give in to her desire, she and Josh had to come to an understanding about what had happened. Either he had to tell the truth or she had to believe his version of the events of that fateful Saturday.

With that in mind, Gloria got out of bed and dressed. Breakfast was out of the question since her stomach was still playing tricks on her. She grabbed a piece of dry toast and hit the streets.

Elliot and Marilyn were having breakfast when she arrived.

She greeted Marilyn with a kiss on the cheek before asking to speak to Elliot alone.

"I need a man's view on this situation with me and Josh," she said to Marilyn. "Do you mind if I borrow Elliot?"

In answer, Marilyn gave her a compassionate hug, smiled at her husband, and left them seated in the kitchen.

"How are things going with you and Josh working together?" she asked.

"Great. Josh and I always got along well."

"No problems?" she asked. Now that she was here, she was getting cold feet.

He shook his head. "I'm sorry for what happened between us, Gloria. I didn't mean to sound self righteous."

"That's not why I'm here, Elliot. I owe you an apology. You were right about everything. Can you forgive me?"

A grin spread across Elliot's face and Gloria knew she was already forgiven. "Consider it done," he said.

"Good," she said. "You and Marilyn have been good friends to me and Josh, and I need to know that the friendships can continue."

"I don't think we'll have any problems." His eyes smiled for the first time since the conversation had started. "I'm glad we had this talk."

She smiled. "I'm glad we talked, too. I'm learning the value of keeping the air clear at all times."

"Now that we have that settled, when are you and Josh getting back together?"

She rose from her seat and smiled again. "Soon, Elliot, real soon."

Gloria recognized the car as soon as she saw it parked in the driveway. Her driveway. Her first emotions were anger and hurt. Anger that Darlene would dare come to her home. And hurt that Josh would allow it. Her first inclination was to speed past the house without stopping. She didn't do that though. Running away wouldn't solve anything. If she went into the house now, she might get the answers she needed. Though not necessarily the ones she wanted.

She pulled her car into the driveway and got out, taking care not to slam the door. She walked slowly to the front door; afraid of what she might see when she walked in. She considered ringing the bell, but decided against it. She needed to walk in unannounced.

She turned the knob and the door opened. She heard voices coming from the living room as she closed the door and walked quietly into the foyer. She knew she should make her presence known. That was the honest thing to do. But she didn't do it. She stood in the foyer, hidden from their view, and listened to their conversation.

As the words flowed between them, she felt the tension in her fade away. She felt as if a weight had been lifted from her. Josh had been telling the truth after all. He hadn't slept with Darlene. Her relief was so powerful that her knees almost buckled and she had to lean against the wall to maintain her posture.

"If you want me to talk with your wife or something, I would do that," she overheard Darlene say. "I'd be willing to give it a try. What do you say?"

"I appreciate your offer," she heard him answer. "But that's not what Gloria and I need right now. You aren't the problem. The problem is us. It's taken me a while to see it, but I see it now. This is something that Gloria and I have to work out."

"If you're sure," she heard Darlene say.

Gloria turned and left the house as quietly as she had entered. She had heard enough. Enough to make her happy. But also enough to make her sad. Josh was right. His supposed infidelity was only a part of the problem. They couldn't get back together just because that was resolved. No, they needed to address the bigger issues that lay between them. She hoped they had the courage to do that. Deep down inside she knew they did.

Gloria wasn't surprised when Josh showed up at Dexter and Portia's later that night. She was half expecting him. After greetings and some cursory conversation, Dexter and Portia left them alone in the living room.

"When I lost the job at General Electronics," Josh began, "I felt like a failure. No, it was more than that, I felt like history was repeating itself. I thought I was going to be like my father. And do you know what, I became him."

Gloria knew something special was happening between them. Josh was going back to the beginning, telling her things that had bothered him. Things that she had sensed, but that he wouldn't share with her. Her heart overflowed with love for him.

"I never told you about him. At least, not in any detail, He lost his job the year I was eleven. I'll never forget it. At first, there was no change. We were such a happy family. So close. There was always laughter around the house. Dad was a big kidder and he kept Mom and me laughing.

"But then he began to drink and he and my mother began to argue. His jokes stopped being funny and the laughter and playfulness around our house ended. One night I saw him hit her. They didn't know I was watching them. I wanted to help my mom but I was afraid my dad would hurt me. So, I waited until he left the house before going to her."

Tears formed in Gloria's eyes as he told her about the little boy who had been forced to grow up much too soon. She heard guilt in his voice, and sought to ease it. "You were a child, Josh, there was nothing you could do. I'm sorry you had to go through it."

"My mom and I never discussed what happened," he continued, as if she hadn't spoken. "I think she knew I saw it, but she never talked about it. Anyway, my dad died for me that night and I promised myself I would protect my mother from that point on."

"Oh, Josh," she said. She wanted to comfort him, but she sensed he needed to do this alone.

"Life was never the same for us. Even though Dad had another job by the time I was thirteen, we were never able to recapture what we had. It was as if we had become a different family. I can't really explain it. When I look back on it now, I see that I blamed my father and his job loss for everything. If only my dad had been able to keep his job, none of those things would have happened. We could have stayed the happy family. Of course, I never said any of this, but I'm sure my dad knew. I'm sure he did."

"You don't have to do this, Josh," she said again. His pain was almost unbearable for her. "You don't have to relive it."

"Let me finish, Gloria," he said. "I need to finish. For us, if we're going to have a life together. Anyway, I made it through high school and I actually felt relief when I left for college. My parents were killed in a car accident at the beginning of my sophomore year. Dad had been drinking. That was one habit he hadn't gotten rid of when he got his new job." His voice broke then and he wiped his eyes. He was silent for a few long seconds. "I've always felt that I could have somehow prevented the accident had I been there. I hadn't kept my promise to take care of my mom. It was my fault she was dead."

"Josh, that's not so. There was nothing you could do. It was an accident. You can't blame yourself for that."

"But for a long time I did. I stayed in school and dedicated myself to my studies. I never dated much before that but afterwards I stopped altogether. That's how I got the nickname *Iceman*. I didn't trust myself with women. Didn't trust myself to take care of them."

It was all making sense now. Somehow in his mind he had gotten his supposed responsibility with his mother mixed up with her. Somehow his not having a job meant he wasn't taking care of her.

"Then I met you." He looked over at her and smiled. "It was as if something inside me opened. You crawled inside me and all my defenses were gone. And the amazing thing was that I didn't fight it. I knew I loved you from that first day and I've never stopped."

The tears streamed down her face at his words. He did love her. How could she have doubted it?

"You remember how we used to talk about our future together. I loved making plans with you. And I loved seeing them come true. When I lost that job at General Electronics, something inside me broke. On the outside I tried to remain calm and optimistic. But inside I knew I was my father all over again. Fear crippled me and distorted my view of everything. My sole goal was not to become my father and here I was doing the same things he had done."

"No, Josh."

"My self-esteem, my manhood, my pride, all took a beating. Every job lead that didn't turn out, every interview that led nowhere. It was a constant battle to keep up a front of control. I was dying inside. And I began to feel that I was letting you down. Not living up to the life that I had promised you."

She remembered him saying something like that before. She had tried to reassure him, but obviously it hadn't been enough.

"I was really hurt the night I overheard your conversation with Marilyn and found out about your promotion. I knew then that things were getting away from me. That you were getting away from me. Then, when Portia announced her pregnancy, well, that was the last straw. I knew drastic measures were called for." He looked over at her again. "I knew you didn't want to move, but I had to go to San Francisco. I thought I was losing you and I couldn't lose you without a fight. I thought I needed a job, any job, to fight for you."

"Oh, Josh," Gloria cried.

"When the job in Raleigh came through, I had to take it. For me, for our marriage. At least, I told myself it was for our marriage. Now I know it was for me. With that job, I got back my self-esteem, my pride, my manhood. I know it sounds crazy, but that's how I felt."

"It doesn't sound crazy at all. You were hurting. I'm sorry we couldn't have helped each other out better then." She had harbored some not so positive thoughts herself. Thoughts she would have to confess, but now was not the time.

"I looked at Raleigh as the answer to our problems. I wanted to pick up with our dreams and plans as if nothing had happened. When you wouldn't make the move, my insecurities kicked in again. I wondered if I had taken too long, if irreparable damage had already been done."

She could see how he would have thought that.

"Now I know that my leaving and your staying here were the worst things we could have done. That's why I've left Carolina Electronics and started the partnership with Elliot. It's not just for me this time. It's for us. I want you to be a part of this company with me. I won't have a real salary coming in for a while. I need to know that you'll support me in making a decision like this. We have savings to last us a while. We saw a big boost in our accounts in the last year—with your promotion and my new job. It shouldn't be a hardship for us. I don't expect your answer right now, but I need to know soon if you're with me on this, if this is the right thing for us."

She was ready to answer him now, but he wouldn't let her speak.

"Now, for the matter of Darlene. I didn't sleep with her. She deliberately let you assume the wrong thing that morning. I swear that's the truth. All I have as proof is my word and my love for you. You've got to decide whether that's enough. If it is, I promise you I'll never hurt you like that again. And if it isn't, well…I can't think about that because I don't think I can live without you."

When he had finished speaking, he stood up and she knew he was going to leave without allowing her to respond to all that he had said. She followed him to the door, almost bumping into him when he turned around to look at her. He lifted a finger to her cheek. "I love you so much it hurts. I hope you'll give me the chance to prove it to you." Then, he gave her a gentle kiss on the lips, turned, and left the house.

Gloria stood there for a few long minutes with a finger against the spot on her lips that he had kissed. The man that just left was the man she had married. The man she wanted to spend the rest of her life with. He wasn't perfect. No, he was a little too macho in his outlook to be perfect. But he was hers and she loved him.

Gloria sat in the familiar bedroom she had shared with Josh since they had bought the house. It hadn't taken her long to unpack since she hadn't taken that much with her. God, it was good to be home.

She had decided last night that she was coming home today. She would have told Josh then, but he hadn't given her the opportunity. It was probably better this way. She'd surprise him with dinner and then she'd tell him her side of the story.

Everything was all set for six o'clock. She looked at the clock

on the nightstand. Josh should be home any minute. She had told
Marilyn of her plans and had gotten her promise to have Josh
out of her house by five-thirty. Yes, any minute now her life
would start again. She had so much to tell him.

Josh felt the difference the minute he entered the house. When
Gloria greeted him at the door, he wasn't sure what to expect.
She smiled and he took that as a positive sign.

"How was your day?" she asked as if she asked it every day.

"Fine. It was fine." What was she up to?

She kissed him softly on the lips. "Well, come on. Dinner's
ready."

She led him to the dining room, where the table was set for
an intimate dinner for two—champagne, candlelight, and all. He
looked over at her, a question in his eyes. "What are we celebrating?"

She took a seat at the table and smiled. "My coming home,
of course. Now are you going to sit or not?"

He wanted to sweep her in his arms and tell her how happy
he was, but he sensed that she had other plans. He took his seat
across from her. "I can't think of any better reasons for a celebration, Mrs. Martin."

She poured them both a glass of champagne and then lifted
her glass for a toast. "To beginnings."

He tapped his glass to hers. "Beginnings." He took a swallow
and found it wasn't champagne, but sparking cider. Different,
but good. Hell, water would have been good tonight. He had his
wife back. And for good, he hoped.

They didn't talk much after that, but the silence wasn't a bad
silence. No, it was a comfortable silence. A peaceful silence.
Their love filled the space between them. It was heaven to bask
in that love.

When they had finished their meal, Gloria suggested they
have more cider in front of the fire. Josh ached to hold her in his
arms. It had been so long. He didn't want to wait. He knew this
was her night, but he offered a suggestion. "What if we have our
drinks upstairs?"

Gloria felt her loins tighten at his words. It had been so long since they had been together. She wanted it. She needed it. She had planned to talk first, to clear the air between them. But now what she had to say didn't seem that important. She would show him instead. "That sounds like a good idea."

Josh reached for her hand, its softness a balm to every hurt he had felt over the last two years. He wanted to be gentle with her tonight, to show her how much he cherished her, how much he loved her. But he didn't know if he had that kind of control.

Gloria allowed him to lead her up the stairs to their bedroom. His quick intake of breath, followed by the passionate gaze that he sent her way, told her that he appreciated what she had done. There were flowers everywhere. Flowers and candles. And the bed, with its satin sheets, was already turned down.

She dropped his hand and went into the bathroom to put on the negligee she had bought especially for this night. As she undressed she realized that she was nervous. It had been a long time. And she had gained weight. She wondered if he would notice. If he would be pleased.

When she walked out of the bathroom, Josh was already in bed. He hadn't bothered covering himself, so she could see how ready he was for her. It made her weak. And wet.

The look in his eyes told her that he liked the gown. He leaned up on an elbow and reached out his hand to her. She placed hers in it and he pulled her down to him. "God, you're so beautiful," he said. "You drive me crazy. You always have."

She smiled a soft, feminine smile. The smile of a woman secure in her man's feelings for her. "I guess that means you like the gown?"

He pulled the straps from her shoulders. "The gown has nothing to do with it. As a matter of fact, the gown is in the way." He pulled it down farther until her breasts were uncovered. Then he grazed his fingertips across them. She shivered in response, and he met her gaze. "You're more beautiful than I remember. It seems even your breasts are fuller."

It was one of the changes the baby was making to her body. They were slight changes and it only made her wetter to realize he had noticed them. She would have responded to his comment, but at that moment he chose to flick his tongue against one of her nipples and all thought of anything but that left her mind. Not wanting the other breast to feel left out, he used his finger to tweak its nipple. She moaned aloud at the sensations his touch invoked.

It was taking all of Josh's control to go slowly. He wanted her so badly. The fact that she wanted him as badly didn't do anything to help his control. As he massaged her breasts, he felt her squirm against him. If she didn't stop, he was going to lose it. But he didn't want her to stop. What he wanted was that gown out of the way.

With his free hand and her help, they were able to pull the gown down her body until nothing separated them. He rubbed his hands down her back, her buttocks, and her legs. He was still convinced that she was the softest woman alive. He forced himself to leave her breasts and then took her mouth in his. God, he could lose himself in her kiss. Her response was more than he had hoped.

The kiss only made Gloria want more. She was impatient for Josh to be inside her. She felt she would die if he didn't come inside very soon. She pushed her hips against him to give him that hint and was frustrated the he didn't respond to it. She decided to take matters into her own hands.

She tried to pull away from his kiss so she could sit up, but he followed her, not ready yet to end the soul-searching, life-giving connection. In spite of that, she was able to position herself so that she could guide him into her entrance. When she felt him fill her completely, she knew she had finally come home.

Chapter 25

Fear snaked up Josh's body when he awoke alone in bed the next morning. Had it all been a dream? he wondered shaking his head slowly. No, it hadn't been a dream. He could still smell her perfume, and her side of the bed was mussed. Where was she?

As if she heard him, she strode naked from the bathroom. "Looking for somebody?"

His relief was palpable. "Welcome home, Mrs. Martin," he said once she was back in bed and cuddled in his arms. "I've missed you."

"I've missed you too." She squeezed him to her. "We almost lost each other, Josh."

"I wouldn't have let you go. I love you too much. I would have found some ways to keep us together. Even if it killed me." The words were strong and he meant them. She was everything to him.

"The things you said to me the other night at Portia's meant a lot. I had almost given up hope of your opening up to me. We've been so distant."

"That's in the past now," he said. They had made mistakes. Both of them. But dwelling on those mistakes wouldn't help. "Thank you for believing in me."

Gloria knew he was talking about Darlene and she wondered if she should tell him what she had overheard. No, she wouldn't tell him. "I never stopped believing in you. I just got a little scared, a little confused."

She could tell from his silence that he was waiting for her to say more. "It wasn't just you who lost a job; we lost a job. I was hurt you didn't allow me to share your pain."

"I couldn't, Gloria. I didn't know how. And I was too scared. Too ashamed."

"I know that now, but I didn't then. All I knew was that you were keeping everything inside and not letting me in. I think it hurt more since before that we'd shared everything. Then, all of a sudden we were walking on eggshells around each other. When you stopped sharing, I thought I should do the same."

"Would it help to talk about it now?"

Gloria breathed deeply and snuggled deeper into Josh's arms. Now was her time of reckoning. She had to give an accounting of herself so they could put the past to rest. For good. "I got scared. Here we were the perfect Buppie couple, not a care in the world. Reality hit when you lost your job. We weren't any different from anybody else. Our dreams weren't guaranteed. Maybe they were even unrealistic."

"It was a wake-up call for both of us. You can bet we'll never be that naïve again."

"Right, Josh. But neither can we go to the other extreme, which is what I started to do."

"What do you mean?"

"I started to focus on money and security too much. I needed guarantees. Guarantees that couldn't be provided."

"You mean, I couldn't provide them."

The pain in his voice would have stopped her, but the soothing touch of his hand up and down her arm let her know it was okay to continue. "In a way, yes. In spite of all the college and my success at work, my only real goal in life was to be a wife and mother. I wanted to be the mother that I never had. My family would come first."

"There's nothing wrong with that."

"You're right, it's not. But when you lost your job, I became my mother. The importance of my work went up. And that was as it should be. The problem was the way I blew it out of proportion. I began to do the what-if's—what if you lost your job again and I wasn't working, what if we had kids. My work became my security."

"There's nothing wrong with that either."

"Not by itself. But then I began to question our dreams, our plans. Who was I to think I could be a full-time mom? Everybody else works, why shouldn't I? I even began to sympathize with Mom. Maybe her need for security drove her to work so much. Surprisingly, that was a comforting thought. Better than thinking she loved work more than she loved me."

"I never knew you felt that way."

She shrugged. "Neither of us ever talked much about our families. They weren't happy stories, Josh."

He knew she was right. They had tried to build a life and a future together without dealing with the past. It hadn't worked. Thank God they had the chance to try again.

"Anyway, the thing about my mom confused me," Gloria continued. "Things weren't clear-cut anymore. I didn't know what was right or what was wrong."

"It's not a matter of right and wrong."

"That's what I finally realized. It really wasn't about right and wrong. It was about choices. About risks. About love."

"I reached that conclusion too after that awful Saturday in Raleigh. There was no compelling reason for us to do that commuter marriage. It was a choice, and I know now, a bad choice."

"You're right, of course. It took me a little longer to realize it though." It hadn't really become clear for her until she learned she was pregnant.

"This may sound corny," Josh said, "but I think our marriage is stronger because of what we've gone through."

"It's not corny. I remember Portia telling me that a year or so ago. I see now that she was right. We've gone through a rough passage and we're still a team. That makes me think we can handle anything."

Josh felt the same way. Except for one question that continued to play on his mind. "Do we need to talk some more about the incident with Darlene?"

"That hurt. More than you can imagine. More than I thought I could bear. I knew we were having problems, but it never occurred to me that you might be having an affair."

"I wasn't."

"I know that now."

"How can you be sure?"

"Because I'm sure of you. You love me and there's no reason for you to lie."

"That simple?"

She couldn't continue with the lie. "I overheard you and Darlene the other day."

Josh's hand stopped its soothing rub down her arm. "When?"

"I came by the house to see you, to tell you that I still loved you and I wanted us to work it out. Darlene was there. I know I was wrong, but I sneaked into the house and listened to your conversation."

When he didn't say anything, she asked, "Are you upset with me?"

He shook his head and his hand began its rub again. "Not upset. Even though a part of me wanted you to believe me based on my word alone, I was worried that the question would always be in the back of your mind. But since you know for sure, I won't have to worry about that. I'm glad you know."

"It took a lot for her to come here."

He didn't want to talk about Darlene. "Hmm…"

"She did keep you from going to court."

"But she caused a lot of problems for us. Don't get me wrong. I know a lot of it was my fault. I should have discouraged her. I'm just glad that part of our life is over."

"Me, too. And since we're clearing the air, you've never made me answer for the incident with Foster Dixon that night."

"I had a pretty good idea what was happening. You were vulnerable and Foster was taking advantage. He's never hidden his attraction for you."

"You never wondered if something more was happening?"

"No. I hit him because I knew what his intentions were and I knew that the only reason you were susceptible to him was because of what I had done. I hit him because I couldn't hit myself."

"You're right. I only turned to him because I was hurt. I never intended for anything to happen. Do you forgive me?"

"There's nothing to forgive. I love you and I'll never put you in a situation like that again."

They were quiet for a long time, enjoying the feel of being in each other's arms again. Josh broke the silence. "What do you think of my going into business with Elliot."

"If it makes you happy. I want you to be happy."

"And I want you to be happy, but that doesn't answer the question."

"I just hate that you're giving up the job at Carolina. Dexter told me about the promotion possibilities. Are you sure you won't regret it someday? You know, feel like you missed out on something big?"

He shook his head. "Like I told you before, I'm never going to be that naïve about business again. There are no more guarantees at Carolina than there were at General. That opportunity didn't mean much to me."

"So you're really excited about this partnership with Elliot?"

"Very much so. We're going to do great things."

Gloria nodded. "You and Elliot do make a good team."

"Correction. You and I make a good team. We're in this together, or we're not in it at all. Okay?"

"Okay."

"How do you feel about supporting us until the business starts to make money?"

"I'm glad you're willing to let me help, but you may have waited too late."

Josh felt a bubble of fear. "What do you mean by that?"

"Maybe I'm not interested in working much longer. Maybe I want that family that you've promised me."

Josh was overcome with joy. "You want to start our family now? I thought you wanted to wait awhile."

"That was fear talking. I want to have your babies and I want to stay home and raise them."

"Are you sure this is what you want?"

"Positive."

"Maybe I shouldn't go into business now. I could always go back to Carolina."

"No, you can't. We've decided. You're going into business with Elliot. We have money, Josh. At least enough to keep us going through the business startup. And I can still work and I want to keep working after the baby is born. Not full-time, but I want to work." She took a deep breath before continuing with her most important thoughts. "I'm good at my job, Josh, and I make a difference. This South Fulton project is going to mean accessible health care for that community, a predominantly black community. I'm the cause of the bank taking on projects like that and I want to see them take on more. I want to be a part of them doing more."

"You seem to have this all worked out. You must think you got pregnant last night. Was it that good?"

She decided not to tell him yet. She'd save that surprise for another time. "No, it was better than good."

Josh and Gloria sat on their private beach on the shores of Aruba. She sat between his legs while he rubbed the round mound that represented their baby. "I'm glad you wanted to come back here," he said. "I think we should do it every year."

"You think the kids would like it?"

"Kids?" he asked, his hands continuing their massaging motion across her belly. He hoped to feel a kick. Gloria had felt them, but he hadn't felt one yet. "Let's have this first one before we start talking about the next one."

Josh had been overjoyed to hear about her pregnancy. He saw the baby as evidence of their love and the cement that helped bring them back together after a rough time. "You do want more, don't you?"

"Only a dozen or so."

She placed her hand atop his on her stomach. "How would you feel about two this time?"

Josh's hands stopped their soothing movements. "What?"

"Twins. We're going to have twins."

"How? When?"

"The doctor told me a few weeks ago. I wanted to surprise you."

He hugged her to him, feeling that life couldn't get much better than it was right now. "Every dream we had is coming true," Josh said. "I love you, Mrs. Martin."

BETWEEN THE LINES

Prologue

"Reconsidering our plan?" Mathias Sanders asked his lifelong friend Randolph Mason. The fifty-five-year-old men had lost track of each other after high school, but they'd found each other twenty years later at a publishing convention. By then, Mathias had moved to Lamar, Alabama, a small town about two hours from Atlanta and owned the *Lamar Weekly News,* while Randolph had been on his way to becoming the chairman and CEO of New York-based Mason Publishing, now the largest black-owned publishing company in the country. The cement of their renewed friendship was common tragedy. Randolph and his then fifteen-year-old son, Jake, had been alone since his wife, Tammy, had succumbed to cancer some seven years earlier. Mathias and his then eleven-year-old daughter, Eleanor, had lost their Barbara suddenly to an aneurysm less than a year before.

"Not really," Randolph said, studying a recent photo of twenty-eight-year-old Eleanor. With her hair pulled back in a stern bun and her blouse buttoned to her neck, the girl defined "prim miss." But the expressive, brown eyes set in her beautiful mocha-complexioned face hinted at passion. "We aren't forcing them to do anything, Mat. We're only providing them an opportunity."

Mathias lifted a finger for the bartender to bring him another drink. "An opportunity," he repeated, then looked at Jake's photo on the bar next to Eleanor's. Thirty-two-year-old Jake had his father's strong chin, his big, alert, brown eyes, and his coarse, jet black hair. And from the stories Randolph had told over the years, Mathias knew Jake also had his father's integrity and strength. "Somehow I don't think that's how they're going to view it when they find out."

Randolph popped a couple of peanuts into his mouth. "*If,* my friend, *if* they find out. Let's think positively here."

Mathias raised his glass and took a swallow of his tonic water. He didn't drink alcohol. He never had. "Okay, I'm thinking positively. Eleanor *is* going to kill me *if* she finds out what I've done."

"You haven't *done* anything, Mat. And all we're planning is a business deal."

Mathias gave a "humph." "Yeah, business *and* personal."

Randolph ran a strong, lean finger around the top of the bowl of peanuts. He and Mathias had often discussed bringing their children together, but they hadn't thought they would be interested in each other. Until now. "We have to do this, Mat. For their sake as much as ours."

Chapter 1

Jake Mason rocked his right leg from side to side impatiently as he sat in the expansive living room of the Sanders home wondering how he had allowed his father to convince him to come to Lamar, Alabama, of all places. He'd seen enough of Lamar already to know there was a good chance he'd die of boredom before the three months he'd given himself to do this job were up.

He checked his Cartier watch for the fifth time. Four-thirty. Mr. Sanders was supposed to meet him at four. Where was he? Was punctuality something small-towners lacked? Jake hoped not, because he knew his eyes would be on the clock for the entire time he was here.

Jake stood, pushed his hands into the pockets of his suit pants, and began to pace. The cluster of picture frames atop the baby grand piano in the corner of the room near a set of French doors caught his attention. He strode over to the piano and scanned the photos. Most of them were of Sanders's daughter, Eleanor. Jake knew this because Mr. Sanders had given Randolph many of these same photos.

He took his hands out of his pockets and picked up the frame holding what he thought was Eleanor's most recent photograph. The bun that was apparently her favorite hairstyle made her face look stern and older than her years. But it was the buttoned-up blouse with the collar around her neck that made her look mousy. All she needed were the stereotypical wire-rimmed glasses. Jake placed the picture back on the piano, grateful that Eleanor held no appeal for him. A romantic entanglement with Sanders's daughter was the last thing he needed.

The sound of splashing water caused Jake to look toward the French doors. A pool, he thought. So small-towners *did* believe in swimming. Thank God for that. He could use a swim now himself. It was hot in Alabama in the summertime.

He walked to the French doors and peeked through the white lace curtains. There was a pool, all right. An Olympic-size in-ground pool that made his mouth water.

The splashing continued but Jake didn't see anyone. He opened the door and started in the direction of the sound. Maybe Mr. Sanders had gotten so engrossed in swimming that he'd forgotten their meeting. Jake could understand that.

By the time Jake reached the pool, the splashing had stopped and a figure that he immediately knew wasn't Mr. Sanders stood drying her legs with a fluffy white towel. Damn, what a pair of buns on that honey, he thought. She stood bent over from the waist with her back, rather her buns, to him, all chocolate and glistening from the water.

Jake's eyes traveled her body, starting with the full hips covered with a thin strip of white cloth that gave new meaning to the word *thong.* He'd heard of thong bikinis, hell, he'd seen them, but this honey wore a one-piece suit in white that had less material than a lot of jockstraps he'd seen. His eyes continued their trip down her long legs and he couldn't help but wonder how it would feel to have those legs wrapped around him. His lips curved in a smile. Maybe Lamar, Alabama, wouldn't be so bad after all.

If Jake could have formed a rational thought, he would have made his presence known with an introduction, but he couldn't so he continued watching the beauty. When she stood to her full height, he was surprised that she wasn't very tall, five-four at most. With those Tina Turner legs, he wouldn't have been surprised if she'd been six feet tall.

Turn around, honey, he pleaded silently. He had to see her face. Everything else was exactly as he liked it. Though he didn't consider himself a hair man, there was something about the wet mane plastered against her shoulders that made him want to shout.

Turn around, he pleaded again. He felt his breathing quicken when she started walking away from him. He opened his mouth to call after her but he heard someone call his name. He closed his mouth and squeezed his eyes shut. *Damn Mr. Sanders's timing.*

Jake made his way back through the French doors, dismayed he'd missed meeting what was probably the most exciting woman in this one-horse town.

"Jake, my boy," Mr. Sanders began. He walked over and grabbed Jake's hand, pumping it for a few seconds before saying, "Damn," and pulling Jake into his arms for a bearhug.

"I can't believe this is our first meeting," Mr. Sanders continued. "I feel like I've known you forever."

Jake couldn't help but smile at the greeting. The older man's enthusiasm was contagious. "I feel the same way, Mr. Sanders. Dad has talked so much about you and your daughter that I feel I know you, too."

Mr. Sanders smiled and Jake knew then that the fifty-five-year-old man had probably been hell with the women in his younger days. Jake knew all too well how women responded to the sincere smile of a good-looking man, and he had no doubt Mr. Sanders had been an attractive young man. He still was. He was tall, Jake's height, about six feet. He had the same salt-and-pepper hair Randolph sported and the same muscular build, but there the similarities ended. There was an openness in Mathias Sanders's face that Jake had never seen in his father's.

"Have a seat, my boy," Mr. Sanders said as he walked to the eight-foot upholstered couch that stretched in front of the idle brick fireplace. "How do you like our town so far?"

Jake's thoughts went immediately to the woman who had been in the pool. He liked *her,* but he couldn't tell Mr. Sanders that. "It's certainly *not* New York."

Mathias Sanders laughed, a rich full laugh that caused the wrinkles around his eyes and mouth to become more pronounced. "You're right about that, but give us a chance. Lamar is not such a bad place."

It didn't really matter to Jake if Lamar was a bad place or not. This assignment was exactly what he needed to prove his capabilities to his father and to himself. And he was going to do it. Big Time. And his father would be so impressed, he'd beg Jake to take a lead role in Mason Publishing.

Jake only wanted to do the job he'd been assigned and get out of this town and on with his life. He also wanted to find out who the woman was at the pool, but he didn't have the nerve to ask. "About the paper, Mr. Sanders—" Jake began, but Mathias interrupted him.

"Not tonight, Jake. Tonight is family time. We'll have plenty of time to do business later. Now tell me some more about yourself and what you've been doing. Maybe you can add to what your father has already told me."

Jake settled back against the pillows on the sofa, giving up on his plans for a business discussion tonight. He told Mr. Sanders about his recent trip to Asia, leaving out most of the exciting things he'd done and the exotic women he'd met.

"You're a lucky young man, Jake. You should be glad your father encouraged your travels. A man needs broad horizons. So does a woman. I wish I could get my Eleanor to see that." Mathias laughed, but this time the wrinkles around his eyes didn't get involved.

Eleanor. How quickly Jake had forgotten about her, while thoughts of the beauty by the pool refused to leave his mind. "Eleanor doesn't like to travel?"

Mr. Sanders shook his head. "I sent her off to college in Georgia, but she came right back home. Never wanted to go anywhere."

Jake detected a bit of sorrow in Mr. Sanders's voice and he wondered what caused it. "Like they say, different strokes for different folks."

Mr. Sanders laughed as Jake had hoped he would. "Maybe you're right, Jake. Eleanor is different, all right."

Jake agreed with him, but he had a feeling it would be rude to say so.

"Have you seen her around here?"

Jake shook his head and his thoughts returned to the beauty by the pool. That certainly hadn't been Eleanor. There was no comparison between the beauty and the mousy-looking woman in the photographs. Maybe the beauty was her best friend. Some beautiful women surrounded themselves with less attractive friends to make themselves look better. He hoped the beauty he'd seen wasn't that shallow. Not that it would matter to him if she was. He was only here for three months and she could make the three months seem a lot shorter if—

"Don't you think so, Jake?" Mr. Sanders was saying.

Jake shifted his attention to Mr. Sanders and nodded. He didn't have any idea what the old man was talking about.

Eleanor wanted to scream. She should have said something, but she'd been too mortified to do much more than slink back to her cottage beyond the pool.

The nerve of that man. Just who the hell did Jake Mason think he was? Oh yes, she knew who he was. Even though she'd only gotten a quick glimpse of him as she'd toweled her legs, his face burned itself on the pages of her mind. How could she forget it? The man looked better in person than he had in the photos her father had shown her, and she hadn't even thought that was possible.

Jake Mason was one fine brother. Too fine, if you asked her. His tailored suit only enhanced his broad shoulders and slim hips. She could tell that much even though he'd been over a pool's length away from her. And that leer that masked itself as a smile across his mahogany-colored face was enough to make lesser women weak in the knees. It wasn't fair that a man could be so attractive.

And he had to know it. It took a man very secure in his looks to stare at a woman the way Jake had stared at her. Either that or he was crazy. And she didn't think Jake Mason was crazy. No,

Jake Mason was used to staring at women, and unless she was way off base, she was sure women usually returned his stare with one suitably welcoming.

Well, she wasn't one of those bimbos and she wasn't going to act like one of them. She was a woman. A liberated woman. And she hadn't appreciated Jake's appraisal. She wasn't a piece of meat to be ogled at by some man like a dog would ogle a juicy bone. The man had been practically smacking his lips as he'd stared at her upturned bottom. She could have died when she'd looked through her legs and glimpsed him staring at her. If wishes came true, the ground would have opened up and swallowed her right there. Better yet, it would have opened up and swallowed Jake.

She tightened the towel she had wrapped around herself and quickened her steps. She needed the security and safety of her home now. Knowing she was fully out of his sight, she broke into a run for the last fifty feet to her door.

She dropped the towel on the hardwood floor of her living room as soon as she entered the front door. By the time she reached the marble tile of her bathroom, she'd discarded the suit as well. She turned on the water in the shower, adjusted the shower head, and stepped in. Leaning back against the tiled walls, she let the water massage her body. The soothing warmth was a welcome balm to her muscles, but it did nothing for her attitude. No, it'd take more than warm water to restore her good spirits. Nothing short of getting Jake Mason out of Lamar would do that.

Fifteen minutes later, Eleanor stepped out of the shower refreshed, but still peeved. She toweled off with another of the fluffy white towels she'd bought in nearby Welles, loving the sensuous feel of the soft cloth against her naked skin.

Dry, Eleanor tossed the towel aside and reached for the perfumed lotion she always used. After seating herself at the bathroom vanity, she massaged the lotion into her skin. The soothing sensation felt sinfully good.

Finished, she got up and reached for the robe she kept hanging on the bathroom door. She removed it from its hook, but she didn't put it on. Rather she walked from the bathroom to her bedroom and threw the robe across the treadmill that held most of the clothes she had *not* worn that week.

Eleanor loved being naked. She often thought that if it wouldn't kill her father, she'd join a nudist colony. Since she knew that act would indeed kill him, her only alternative was to turn her home into a mini-nudist camp. It was why she kept her blinds closed and her drapes drawn at all times.

Thoughts of Jake Mason entered her mind again. She was tempted to call Carl Winters, her childhood friend and the paper's top investigative reporter, and ask if he'd gotten the results from the background search she'd ordered on Jake Mason, Randolph Mason, and Mason Publishing, but she didn't do it. She knew Carl would probably hang up on her anyway. She'd been bugging him about results since she'd given him the assignment a couple of days ago. The last time she'd spoken with him, he'd told her not to call him again.

Who was Carl to tell her when to call? she asked herself. She was paying for his services. She could do whatever she wanted. She reached for the phone on her black lacquer nightstand. It rang before she could pick it up.

"Hello," she said, hoping the call was from Carl.

"Hey, girl," her friend Megan began. "Do you want to go over to Welles tonight? Victoria's Secret is having a sale."

Eleanor sighed, glad to hear from her friend, but disappointed the call wasn't from Carl. She really needed the information on Jake. She'd hoped to act on it at dinner that night. "I can't tonight. I'm having dinner with Dad and a business associate."

"That fine brother you've been talking about?" Megan asked. Eleanor found the enthusiasm in her friend's voice disgusting. "How about I come over and have dinner with ya'll?"

Eleanor rolled her eyes. Sometimes it amazed her that Megan was her best friend. "Not tonight. Tonight's all business."

"But I want to meet him."

Eleanor flinched at the whine in her friend's voice. She and

Megan were both only children, but she hoped her own behavior wasn't as spoiled as Megan's. "You'll get to meet him. I promise. But not tonight."

"Are you interested in him? Is that why you don't want me to meet him? I thought you said you weren't interested in him."

Goodness, Eleanor thought, how had she allowed herself to get into a discussion about men with Megan on a night when she didn't have four hours to waste? "I'm not interested in him, Megan. We're discussing business tonight. I don't think this is the right time for you to make your move."

The silence made Eleanor think Megan was considering the truth in those words.

"When will you introduce us? You know there aren't many good men here in Lamar. If you're not interested, then I definitely am."

Eleanor glanced at the nightstand, at the miniature grandfather clock that had been her mother's. "It's getting late, Megan. If I don't hang up, I'm going to be late for dinner."

"Well, you tell that brother about me now. I want his appetite whetted before he meets me."

Eleanor rolled her eyes again. When Megan was between men, which she always was, she got a bit desperate. She'd been that way since she and her mother had moved to Lamar and the two girls had become fast friends. The other eighth-grade kids had called them "the odd couple" and the name had stuck. The beautiful Megan and the smart Eleanor. Nobody could figure out what they had in common, but everybody knew they were best friends. An odd couple, but an inseparable one. "I've gotta go, Megan. Let's go shopping tomorrow. I'll tell you all about Jake then."

That seemed to appease Megan because she hung up without much protest. Eleanor jumped up and went into her closet to find something suitable to wear. Since she'd already given Mr. Mason an eyeful, she wanted to be sure her dress for dinner bespoke of the woman she truly was.

She settled on a navy Carole Little suit and a bone blouse with a baby doll collar. The ensemble would cover her from neck to mid-calf, revealing nothing of her shape and in no way hinting at the navy French-cut silk panties and matching lace bra she'd have on underneath. Satisfied she'd picked the perfect outfit, she strode to the kitchen for a bite to eat before dinner. When she arrived at her father's house tonight, she didn't want hunger to distract her. Her task tonight was to grill Mr. Mason and find out the *real* reason for his and his father's sudden interest in the *Lamar Daily News.*

Jake placed the last of his underwear in the chest in the Sanders guest room, still amazed at how quickly Mathias, as he had instructed Jake to call him, had convinced him to move into his home though Jake had been determined to stay in a hotel or find a rental unit. Mathias was almost as bad as Jake's father. Neither man understood the meaning of "no" and both pushed until they got their way.

"A young man should enjoy himself, see the world, experience life," his father had told the young adult Jake when he'd expressed an interest in working for Mason Publishing. "You don't have to work, Jake."

Jake had tried to explain that he knew he didn't *have* to work; he *wanted* to. But Randolph hadn't listened. And over the years Jake had found it easier to go along with his father's wishes. He'd learned early that a man with money could always find things to do with his time—and his money.

Over the years Jake had engaged in one venture after another, and though he'd made a great deal of money, he'd never found his niche, a spot where he could stay and flourish. Sometimes he blamed his father for his rolling-stone-like relationship with work. But he knew much of the responsibility lay squarely at his feet. He could have dug in his heels at any time, but he hadn't.

He shook his head, forcing the negative thoughts away. He'd been surprised and honored when his father had asked him to work this deal with the *Lamar Daily.* Not because it was a big deal, but because this was the first time his father had *asked* for his help. He'd work this deal, all right. He'd come up with a proposal so fantastic his father would regret waiting so long to give Jake a place in the family business. Yes, with this deal Jake would prove to himself and his father how capable he really was.

Jake turned back the homemade quilt on the generations-old four-poster bed and stretched out to pass the time until dinner. He hadn't planned to live in the Sanders home, but it appeared that was exactly what he was going to do. The room, furnished with a desk, nightstand, and armoire, or chifferobe, as Mathias had called it, that matched the bed and chest, was comfortable, which was all Jake needed.

Well, he also needed privacy, but maybe that could be arranged. He wouldn't even consider bringing a woman to Sanders's home. Hopefully, the beauty at the pool had her own place with enough privacy for their pursuits. He still didn't have any idea who she was, but he guessed she was one of Eleanor's friends. Hopefully, he could get Eleanor to introduce him.

Eleanor entered the patio doors of her father's house promptly at six. Though she would deny it, she was anxious about meeting Jake. She wondered what he would think of her appearance tonight. Well, it really didn't matter as long as he realized that the Eleanor he was going to do business with was this Eleanor and not the Eleanor he'd seen by the pool.

"Eleanor, you're finally here," her father said when he walked into the living room with Jake trailing behind him.

"You make it sound like I'm late, Dad. It's only six," she answered her father and smiled in Jake's direction. Her eyes drank in the sight he made in the tan Armani suit that molded to his form like a woman to her lover. Casting those thoughts aside, she extended her hand. "Welcome to Lamar, Mr. Mason."

She noticed the twinkle in Jake's eyes. Was he thinking about their earlier meeting? Or did he know where her thoughts had been? She sincerely hoped not.

"Mr. Mason's my father, I'm Jake," he said in a deep baritone voice flavored with a hint of New York accent. He took her hand in both of his and squeezed it softly before letting it go.

Eleanor felt the tingle from her hand up her arm and down her body all the way to the toes of both her feet. Heavens, she had to get control of herself. It was just as she'd figured. Jake Mason was a womanizer. He probably expected her to swoon at his feet. She flashed what she hoped was a haughty smile that only partially turned up the corners of her mouth. "Jake it is then."

Mathias clapped Jake on the back and said to him and Eleanor, "Why don't we have a before-dinner drink?"

While Mathias prepared their drinks, Eleanor and Jake seated themselves. Unfortunately for Eleanor, she and Jake both chose the couch. She wondered if he did it on purpose. Did he know how flustered he made her? Was he thinking about their earlier meeting?

"So you're interested in our paper, Jake. For the life of me, I don't see what Mason Publishing wants with a small-town paper like ours."

Jake allowed his gaze to travel from the bun atop her head, to the string of pearls that lay around the prim collar of her blouse, to the navy pumps on her feet before focusing on the lipstick-less lips that had mouthed the accusation. And it had been an accusation. He was sure of it. "I asked my father the same thing, Eleanor. His interest surprised me as well."

Eleanor bristled. It was one thing for her to wonder about Jake's intentions for her paper, it was a whole other thing for him to suggest that the *Lamar Daily* wasn't worth his time. She leaned toward him and spoke softly, but clearly. "Well, I know you don't see it and that's why I want you to know right up front that I'm going to fight you all the way on this. Your dad may have used his friendship with my father to persuade him that this was a good deal for us, but I don't believe it for a minute."

Mathias brought their drinks before Jake could comment, which was probably good since Jake hadn't formed a comment. Well, he mused, it seemed there was more to Little Eleanor than he'd first thought. She might dress like a mouse, but she definitely had a mouth on her.

"Are you two getting to know each other?" Mathias asked with obvious hope that they were.

The saccharine-filled smile that Eleanor gave her father almost made Jake laugh.

"Of course, Dad. I think Jake and I are coming to an understanding. Aren't we, Jake?"

Jake took a swallow of his drink, which turned out to be sparkling water, before answering. When he did, he spoke to Mathias. "Eleanor was telling me what to expect during my stay here in Lamar."

Mathias took a seat in the wing chair next to the couch. "I'm sure Eleanor will help you get settled. Even though you won't be here very long, we'll make you as comfortable and as welcome as we know how. Won't we, Eleanor?"

Eleanor lifted her glass to her lips and gave her smile again. "He can count on it, Dad."

Jake coughed to cover up the laughter that bubbled up in his throat.

"I was thinking that maybe we could have a party to introduce Jake around."

Eleanor coughed then and Jake knew she was choking on the idea of giving a party for him. "Now, Dad, maybe Jake's not interested in that. He'll probably be going home every weekend anyway."

Jake smiled what he hoped was a good imitation of Eleanor's fake smile. "On the contrary, I'm here for the duration." Her eyes widened and he added, "At least until our business transaction is complete. Your dad has even offered me his guest room. It seems I'm going to be a member of the family."

Chapter 2

Jake watched the corners of Eleanor's lips droop and that fake smile slip from her face. She was good, though. She recovered so quickly that if she hadn't already made her feelings clear, he'd question whether he'd really seen the change in her expression.

She smiled in the direction of her father, then said to Jake, "He forced you, didn't he?" Before Jake could answer, she turned to her father. "Dad, I'm sure Jake was only being nice. I'll help him look for a place tomorrow."

"No, you won't, Eleanor," Mathias said. "Jake is staying here and that's that. I won't hear of my best friend's son staying in some run-down apartment."

Eleanor placed her glass on the cocktail table in front of her. "The Ferguson house is empty. I'll see about renting that for Jake."

Mathias shook his head. "That doesn't make sense. Jake can stay here. Besides, I get lonely in this big house all by myself."

Jake saw Eleanor roll her eyes toward the ceiling. He wanted to laugh. He had the feeling Mathias often used his "loneliness" as a ploy to get his way.

"Right, Dad, but let's think about Jake."

Jake watched the conversation ping-pong between Eleanor and her father. It irritated him that they were discussing him as if he weren't present. Even though he agreed with Eleanor that he'd much prefer to stay somewhere else, for some perverse reason, he couldn't let her have her way. "I kind of like the idea of living near someone I know," he offered. "And since I know only you and Mathias, I think here is great." He took a long swallow of his drink. "Unless you know of a place near where you live?"

Eleanor shot him a look that said she knew he was toying with her. He acknowledged her with a smile.

"Well," Mathias began, "you get to live near both of us. Eleanor lives in the cottage out beyond the pool."

Jake couldn't let the opening pass. He glanced over at Eleanor. "Still living at home," he said, then shrugged his shoulders in disdain. "I guess it's cheaper." He delighted at the ire that flashed in her big, brown eyes, knowing his tone left no doubt to what his real thoughts were about a twenty-eight-year-old woman still living at home.

"It's not the money," Mathias said. "It's the pool."

Jake pulled his eyes from Eleanor's pinched face and looked at Mathias. Thoughts of the pool brought thoughts of the beauty he'd seen. He wasn't too sure now that Eleanor would introduce him to her friend. He might have to fend for himself. "So, she's a swimmer?"

Mathias gave a "humph." "More like a fish. She and Megan make sure that pool gets more than enough use."

Megan. That must have been who she was. "That must have been Megan I saw in the pool when I arrived earlier."

The sound of Eleanor's choking brought Jake's eyes back to her.

"What's wrong with you, Eleanor?" Mathias asked, leaning toward her.

She patted her hand against her chest and shook her head. "I'm fine, Dad, something went down the wrong way."

Mathias looked at her for a few long seconds as if he wasn't sure he could believe her. Jake saw his concern and felt a bit envious of the relationship between this father and daughter.

"All right, then," Mathias said, "but be careful. Why are you drinking so fast anyway?"

Eleanor's eyes widened at her father's question and she glared in Jake's direction. He knew she would give her dad an earful because of that comment. He also knew she'd wait until he was gone.

"So," Jake asked Eleanor, "was that your friend Megan I saw earlier in the pool?"

"Right, Jake." Eleanor thought he was being sarcastic.

"Maybe you could introduce us sometime."

She studied his face. Was this man kidding or did he really not know that she was the woman at the pool? "You're serious, aren't you?"

The question in his eyes was immediate.

Eleanor felt as though she'd been punched in the stomach. He really didn't recognize her. And after the way he'd stared at her. Lusted after her. He didn't even know who she was. The cad didn't even recognize her. Though she hated to admit it, she was hurt.

"Megan was here today?" Mathias asked. "Why didn't you invite her to dinner?"

Eleanor slowly moved her head from side to side. By the way her father was carrying on, you'd think Jake was a visiting relative instead of a business associate planning to gobble up their newspaper. Where was the man's head these days? "I didn't think it was appropriate to invite Megan to a business dinner, Dad." There was no mistaking the censure in her voice.

Mathias stood and pointed at the two younger people as if they were disobedient children. "You two are too much alike. All you think about is business. Well, this is more than business and you had better face it. Randolph and I have been friends for years and no business deal is going to stop that. Now come on, let's eat dinner."

It was the longest dinner Eleanor had ever endured. And the most infuriating. Her father obviously thought Jake's presence ranked right up there with the Second Coming. He hung on to every word the man said. And Jake Mason said a lot. About nothing. The amount she'd learned about Mason Publishing's intents for their paper could be held in a thimble. The man was closemouthed. Yes, closemouthed and smart. He was weaseling himself into her father's confidence just as his father, Randolph, had done. Her father was being set up like the fatted calf. She had to help him because he was too blinded by the Mason men to even know he needed help. She shook her head in dismay.

"Something wrong, Eleanor?" Jake asked.

Eleanor directed her gaze to him. Had he been watching her? Had he finally realized she was the woman in the pool? She flashed him a smile. "No, everything's great, Jake. Just great."

Jake sat back in his chair. He'd actually enjoyed the dinner and he'd had to refine his opinion of Miss Eleanor. Although she was a bit homely, she did have spirit. And he liked that. He liked her. And he liked baiting her.

"So when do you think we should have the party, Eleanor?" Mathias asked. "We want Jake to feel welcome."

Eleanor cut a glare in Jake's direction, before turning to her father. "I don't know, Dad. We're going to be awfully busy."

Mathias waved his hands in dismissal. "You're always busy. What about Megan? She could plan it for you, couldn't she?"

Eleanor knew Megan would love that. "What about Ms. Delaney? She could do it."

Mathias shook his head at her reference to his one-day-a-week housekeeper. "No, Megan is the right person. I still can't believe you didn't invite her to dinner."

Eleanor didn't want to get back on that again. "Okay, Dad," she said, "I'll ask her." She looked at Jake. "She wants to meet you anyway."

"She wants to meet me? Why?"

Eleanor looked away from him and played with the dessert pudding Ms. Delaney had prepared. Never would she tell him she'd showed Megan his picture. The man was conceited enough as it was. "Well, Dad talks about you all the time." When she saw the smug, masculine, too-good-looking-for-words expression cross his face, she couldn't help but add, "Megan doesn't think anybody could be all that Dad has made you out to be."

"Eleanor," Mathias warned. "What's wrong with you tonight. Jake's our guest."

Jake laughed. "That's all right, Mathias," Jake said. "I'm beginning to think of Eleanor as the bratty little sister I never had."

Eleanor opened her mouth for a retort, but nothing came out.

Mathias stared at Eleanor and chuckled. "You've done the impossible, Jake. You've made Eleanor speechless."

Eleanor slammed the door to her cottage and kicked off her shoes. Jake Mason, hah. The man was a joke. A *big* joke. She just hoped the last laugh wasn't on her and her father. She slipped off her jacket, blouse, and skirt and threw them on the floor with the clothes she had pulled off earlier in the day, then trekked to her kitchen for a drink. Something strong. She pulled out a two-liter bottle of RC Cola and lifted it to her lips, welcoming the burning sensation in her throat. She took only a few swallows before dropping the bottle from her lips. "Oooh, that was so good," she said aloud, then placed the bottle back in the refrigerator and trooped to her bedroom.

She pulled off her bra and panties, hung them on the treadmill, then plopped down on the side of her bed and picked up the phone. Her eyes caught the time on the clock. Eleven-thirty. My how time flies when you're having fun, she thought dryly. She pushed aside any consideration for the time and punched in the seven numbers.

"Hello," Carl answered. She was glad he didn't sound as though he'd been asleep.

"Hi, Carl," she said, "this is Eleanor."

"I know who it is, Eleanor. The question is do you know what time it is?"

Eleanor turned away from the clock, propped her feet up on the bed and leaned back against the headboard. "It's time you gave me some information on Jake Mason and Mason Publishing, that's what time it is."

Eleanor held her breath. She didn't think she could stand it if Carl told her to call back in the morning. When he released a resigned sigh, she knew she'd hit paydirt.

"The report'll be on your desk in the morning. Can't you wait until then?"

Eleanor didn't answer and Carl didn't repeat his question. Eleanor knew the loser would speak first.

"Okay, Eleanor, what do you want to know?"

She smiled. "Everything. Start at the beginning and tell me all."

Carl told her about the beginnings of Mason Publishing, the company started by Randolph Mason and his wife, Tammy. He told her about their happy marriage, the birth of their son, and the struggle they had had to start their business. When he told her how Tammy Mason had died of cancer the year Jake Mason was eight years old, tears formed in her eyes.

Tears for the little boy Jake who'd lost his mother and tears for herself and the mother she'd lost. The tears streamed down her cheeks and fell on her naked breasts as Carl told the story of a driven Randolph Mason, a man determined to make something of his life for himself and his son. The tears began to dry as Carl told her about the ruthless takeovers Randolph Mason had executed during his tenure as CEO of Mason Publishing. The man didn't seem to have a heart, at least not when it came to business.

"What about the son? What about Jake? What's he been doing?" She wished for the hundredth time this week she'd paid more attention to her father's news of Jake over the years. But no, she'd been too focused on his good looks and her silly dreams and fantasies of a knight in shining armor to remember a word her father had said.

"Your typical rich man's son. Travels. Dibbles and dabbles in various business concerns. He must have the golden touch, because he's made a good amount of money without very much effort."

Eleanor pondered that information. Not that it surprised her. Jake had the typical Playboy profile—good looks, lots of money, and plenty of time. "Why did his father send him here?" she asked aloud, though the question was really to herself.

"That, I don't know," Carl answered. "This is the first project Jake has done for Mason Publishing. Maybe his father thought it was time he assumed some responsibility in the family business."

Eleanor wiggled her toes and stood up to stretch, the phone

cradled between her ear and her naked shoulder. "Has he had any experience at all in the publishing industry?"

Eleanor imagined Carl tapping his pencil to his forehead in impatience. "Nothing formal. Though I doubt he could be Randolph Mason's son and not know something about the business."

"I'm not too sure about that. What did he study in college?"

Carl was quiet.

"He did go to college, didn't he?"

"He went," Carl answered.

Eleanor knew he was holding back some information and she wondered why. "What is it, Carl? I know there's more."

"He graduated from Yale."

Yale. She was impressed. "What was his major?"

"Drama."

Eleanor howled. Drama. So, Jake Mason had entertained thoughts of becoming an actor. Must have been his good looks. And he must have found out looks weren't enough.

"Did he ever do any acting?"

"Not professionally. It seems his real interest was his track career."

"He ran track?"

"Almost made the Olympic team. He was good."

"I bet," Eleanor said. He probably had lots of practice running from one woman to another.

Eleanor asked Carl a few more questions before ending the conversation. She could hardly wait to read his report in the morning. After she hung up, she pirouetted around the room. So, Jake Mason was a would-be actor and athlete. She laughed out loud at the thought. She knew now he'd never take her newspaper. He wasn't even in her league.

Mathias opened the door to his den, looking over his shoulder as he did so. He didn't see anyone, so he rushed into the room, quickly closed the door, and practically ran to his desk. After he sat down, he pulled off his glasses and wiped his eyes with his forefinger and thumb, grateful he'd made it through tonight's dinner. Once again he wondered if he and Randolph were doing the right thing. He picked up the phone and punched in Randolph's New York number.

"I've been waiting for your call," Randolph said when he answered after the first ring. "How'd it go?"

"I'm not too sure, Randy," Mathias began. "Eleanor didn't seem to like Jake much. She was downright mean to him during dinner. Not like herself at all."

Randolph leaned back in his chair. He was pleased. Of course Eleanor resented Jake's presence and what he was trying to do. He wondered why Mathias didn't understand that. But then he knew why. Mathias still saw Eleanor as his little girl, not as a woman. He suspected that was the reason for Eleanor's conservative nature. But Randolph had a gut feeling that below that conservative exterior was a woman who could warm his son's heart and his bed. She couldn't be Barbara and Mathias's daughter without inheriting some of their passion. Randolph and Mathias had shared enough over the years for Randolph to know that Mathias and Barbara had shared a loving and passionate union that rivaled his marriage with Tammy. In his opinion, a man couldn't ask for more. "How did Jake respond to her?"

Mathias liked Jake. Had liked him before he met him, and meeting him had only confirmed his feelings. Jake was a good man. Good enough for his Eleanor. But not if Eleanor didn't want him. "You've got a great boy there, Randy. I guess I would say he tolerated Eleanor."

"Tolerated her? What exactly did the boy do?"

Mathias gave a half-smile at Randy's reference to his son as a boy. He knew that was exactly how Randolph saw Jake. As a little boy. A little boy who needed his father's direction and guidance. But the Jake that Mathias had met wasn't a little boy. He was a man.

Mathias wondered again how different the boy would have been had someone other than Randolph been his father. Not that Randolph hadn't done the best he could. Mathias knew he had. But Randolph was such a strong man. Maybe too strong for a son who loved him as much as Mathias was sure Jake loved him.

"I mean Jake handled himself well. He didn't let Eleanor put him on the defensive." Mathias sighed. "And she was trying to put him on the defensive. No doubt about it."

She's exactly what Jake needs, Randolph thought. Someone to push him and make him stand up for what he believes in. That and someone to love him as his mother had loved Randolph. Randolph firmly believed that the love of a good woman made a difference in a man. Made a man a man. He knew that's what loving Tammy had done for him. And he wanted that for his son. "Well, keep me posted. Are your plans all set for tomorrow?"

Mathias and Randolph went over their plans one by one, making sure they hadn't missed anything. When they were finished, Mathias hung up and sat in his den for a long while wondering over the rightness of what they were doing. When he started getting sleepy, he picked up his glasses and left the den to get ready for bed.

Chapter 3

Eleanor arrived at the newspaper office early the next morning. She wanted to make sure she was there before Mr. Jake Mason arrived. It made her angry even to think about it.

She picked up the *Welles Daily*, the *New York Times*, and the *Wall Street Journal* from the mat in front of the building, unlocked the door, and headed for her office. Her mind screamed when she saw the additional desk in her already cramped space. A desk for Jake.

She dropped down in her desk chair, threw the papers and her briefcase on her desk, and propped her feet up. She could almost strangle her father. How could he even consider merging their paper with Mason Publishing?

She remembered her mother bringing her to the paper for lunch with her father when she'd been a child of about seven. She'd loved coming here where her daddy worked. He always made her feel like a princess. He was the king, her mom was the queen, and she was the princess.

Sadness settled around her heart. "I miss you so much, Mom," she said softly.

Eleanor still remembered the first day she'd come to the newspaper office without her mother. Mrs. Lewis, the woman her father hired to care for her, had brought her. But it wasn't the same. Her father must have understood because he'd allowed her to stay with him until he was ready to go home. And that became the pattern for their lives.

Every day after school Mrs. Lewis would pick Eleanor up and

drive her to the newspaper office. She'd do her homework while her father and his staff worked on the next week's edition of the paper. When she was finished, her father would give her some small task to do around the paper. "This is our business," he'd say. "You need to learn it."

And that was the beginning of her love affair with the *Lamar Daily.* Throughout high school, she continued coming to the newspaper after school. And her assignments progressed from the trivial to substantive reporting.

When her father changed from a weekly paper to a daily paper during her junior year in high school, she'd even had her own column, "Lamar High Live." Because her high school didn't have a newspaper, her father gave classes to interested students about running a paper. Not just the journalism end, but the business end. Her father always said you needed to know your business. His encouragement led her to study journalism in college and then to go for her MBA.

She'd been back in Lamar at the paper about six years now and she enjoyed every minute of it. She'd missed her father and the paper while she was away. And she'd come back full of ideas. When her father had settled on just being the publisher and made her managing editor two years ago, she felt she'd gotten her head. There was so much she could do, so much she wanted to do. At the top of her list was starting a monthly magazine targeted at African-American families. She'd already added a weekly insert to the *Lamar Daily* to test the concept, but that was only the beginning.

Eleanor wanted a magazine with national distribution, but they didn't have the capital to start it now. Neither she nor her father had considered outside funding. He'd taught her early on that, when people put in their money, they wanted some control. And she and her father both prided themselves on being able to make decisions for the paper without having to deal with bureaucratic red tape. There were only the two of them to consider.

Until now. That's what she didn't understand. Why would her father bring in Randolph Mason and all the red tape of Mason

Publishing? The planned merger seemed to go against everything he'd taught her. She shook her head. She could only conclude that Randolph Mason had somehow tricked her father into believing a deal with him would be different. But she didn't buy it for a moment.

She smiled as she got up and put fresh water in the coffeemaker. Too bad Randolph hadn't sent in the big guns. He probably thought it wasn't necessary when dealing with a couple of hicks like her and her father. Well, she'd show Mr. Mason precisely what he was up against. She'd make the older Mason regret he'd ever sent his drama-trained, track-running son to manage this deal.

She went back to her desk and picked up the *Welles Daily*, flipping quickly through its pages. Finding no news of interest to her or the residents of Lamar, she closed that paper and picked up the *Times*. She did the same with the *Wall Street Journal* before turning around in her chair and clicking on her computer to check the wire for any late-breaking stories.

"Morning, Maxie," she heard her father say to the newsroom secretary, who must have arrived in the last fifteen minutes.

"Morning, Mathias," Maxine Walters said. Maxine was an attractive, almond-skinned, slightly graying woman about her father's age and she'd had a crush on him for as long as Eleanor could remember. She didn't understand why her father didn't know it. Everybody else did. No one called Maxine Walters anything other than Maxine or Ms. Walters. No one except Mathias Sanders.

"This here is Jake Mason. He's going to be with us for the summer. He and Eleanor will be sharing an office."

"Nice to meet you, Ms. Walters," came Jake's smooth voice. The man was a born charmer.

"Eleanor in her office?" her father asked, cutting off any conversation that may have started between Jake and Maxine.

By the time she heard Maxine say "Yes," her father and Jake were walking through Eleanor's office door. She stood and greeted them.

"How come you left so early this morning?" her father asked. "I'd planned on the three of us having breakfast then driving in together."

Eleanor had guessed that was his plan and she'd deliberately set out to circumvent it. The smirk on Jake's face told her he knew that.

"There were some things I needed to do this morning," she lied. She knew and her father knew she was rarely in the office this early. Maxine was usually the first one in, and Maxine usually made the coffee.

"Anything I can help you with?" Jake asked solicitously.

She turned and glared at him. "Thanks, Jake," she said sweetly. "But I don't think you can help." The unspoken words, *with anything,* hung in the air.

"Well," her father interrupted, "I'll leave Jake to you, Eleanor. Show him around the newsroom, the press room, you know the drill." He looked at his watch. "I'll meet you two for lunch at, say, one o'clock."

"But Dad—"

"That's fine, Mathias," Jake interrupted. "Eleanor will probably need a break from me by that time. I have a million and one questions."

"I'll bet," Eleanor muttered under her breath.

"Good," her father said, backing out of the office. "I'll see you two later."

Eleanor stared after him. She and her father had to talk. She was not going to baby-sit Jake Mason, drama graduate and track star. She had *real* work to do and none of it included teaching Jake about the newspaper business.

"This my desk over here?" Jake asked, forcing Eleanor's attention to him.

"No, it belongs to Bill Clinton," she answered, rolling her eyes.

Jake dropped his briefcase on the desk. "You'd better stop rolling your eyes like that before they get hung in that position."

Eleanor rested her hands on her hips. "Why are you really here, Jake?"

He sat down in his chair and leaned back with his hands behind his head. "You already know. The *Lamar Daily* is merging with Mason Publishing. I'll decide how to position it with the rest of our holdings."

Eleanor rested against the corner of her desk and crossed her arms. "We don't need you to position us, Mr. Mason. We already have a position and plans for our growth. We don't need you or your father's money."

Jake dropped his hands from behind his head and leaned forward. "That's not what your father said."

"That's not what your father conned my father into agreeing to, you mean."

"That's not what I meant at all. Your father doesn't seem to be the kind of man who can be easily conned." He shrugged his shoulders. "But then I've only known him a day."

He'd backed her into a corner. To maintain her position, she'd have to agree that her father was a pushover where Randolph Mason was concerned. She wasn't ready to do that yet. She stared at Jake for a couple of long seconds before getting up and heading for the door. "Come on, if you want the tour." She left the office without looking back.

"Megan's on the line for you, Eleanor," came Maxine's voice over the intercom just as Jake and Eleanor returned to the newsroom after Eleanor's halfhearted tour. Jake wondered why Eleanor cringed at the words.

"What's the matter?" he asked. "I thought Megan was a friend of yours." Plus, Jake wanted an introduction to her in the worst way.

Eleanor's gaze met his. "Tour's over." She turned and marched back to her office, closing the door behind her.

Jake watched through the window in the wall separating Eleanor's office from the rest of the newsroom as she picked up the phone. She saw him and turned her back to him. He smiled, then proceeded to enter the office and plop down in his chair. She turned and gave him a look he was sure cast aspersions on his parentage. He grinned. Obviously, she'd forgotten he was sharing her office.

"Maxine has to stop announcing my calls over the intercom like that," Jake overheard her whisper.

He shook his head. So that's why she'd cringed. She didn't like her business broadcast over the intercom system. He didn't see what harm it did, but obviously it irritated her.

Jake didn't bother to pretend he wasn't listening to her call. It seemed her friend Megan was leaving town for a while. Damn! He hoped she wasn't going to be gone for long. He wanted to meet her.

"See you in a couple of weeks," Eleanor said, then hung up the phone and turned to Jake. "Common courtesy says you don't listen in on other people's conversations."

Jake shrugged. "There are no secrets in a newsroom. Even *I* know that."

Eleanor pointed to the green metal desks scattered about the room outside her office. "There's no privacy out there. This is *my* office. There is privacy in here. And if we're going to get along, you'd better understand that."

Jake reached across her desk and picked up her copy of the *Times*. "I'll try."

"You'd be wise to do better than try. I'm not afraid of you, Jake Mason. Or of your high-powered father and his Mason Publishing."

Jake lowered the paper so he could see her. He would have grinned but she was so wound up, he didn't think she'd appreciate it. "What are you so bent out of shape about? Ease up some, Eleanor. We're going to be cramped in this office for a long time. Let's try to be friends."

"Friends?" Eleanor said the word as if it were a curse. "You must be joking. We can't be friends. You're the worst kind of enemy."

Before Jake could respond, a wiry, copper-complexioned brother in gray dress slacks, a white button-down shirt, and a black tie stuck his head in the office door. "Eleanor, they want you down in advertising. Seems there's some problem with the ads for today's edition."

Eleanor jumped out of her chair and rushed past the man and in the direction of the advertising manager's office. Jake watched her strut off, and as he did, he wondered why she was so upright.

"Don't let her get to you," the man said. "She's all right. You'll get used to her."

"And how long will that take?"

The man smiled. "A while." He extended his hand. "I'm Carl Winters. You must be Jake Mason."

Jake shook the hand. "Nice to meet you, Carl."

"Has Eleanor introduced you to everybody yet?"

Jake shook his head. "We went on a tour, but not many people were around when we started."

"Come on, then, I'll do it. And maybe even get you a cup of coffee."

Jake got up and clapped Carl on the back. "I'm glad I met you, Carl. Eleanor had me wondering if that Southern hospitality I'd heard so much about was a myth."

Eleanor was grateful when the waitress removed their lunch dishes. She was ready to leave this restaurant and Jake's company. And her father's. The man was completely taken in by the smooth-talking Jake. It was so unlike her father.

"It sure is hot here," Jake said. By his tone, you'd think he'd made some brilliant discovery.

Her father pushed back from the table. "Why don't you and Eleanor go for a swim? She goes at lunch most days." Mathias winked at Jake when Eleanor gasped. "She didn't know I knew."

"It's not like I was trying to hide something from you," Eleanor countered. "There has been no reason to discuss it."

"That's not important now, Eleanor," her father said in dismissal with a wave of his hand. "Why don't you take Jake here and the two of you hit the pool for a while?"

"Maybe another day. I usually swim instead of lunch, not

after." She glanced at Jake. "I'm sure Jake doesn't want to go swimming on a full stomach."

Jake didn't give her father time to respond. "She's right, Mathias. We should've gone before lunch or instead of it. But it's a good idea. Maybe we'll do it tomorrow."

Yeah, right, Eleanor thought. And tomorrow Hell will freeze over. "Maybe."

"Good, good," Mathias said. "Now how did things go this morning?"

Eleanor listened while Jake told of her tour and the introductions made by Carl. She waited for him to comment on her lack of courtesy, but he didn't and she wondered why. As if he'd read her thoughts, Jake turned to her and smiled.

Heaven help her, that smile made her insides quiver. The man was a practiced flirt. He wasn't her type at all. And heaven knows, she wasn't his. She'd have to keep her traitorous emotions in check. She was *not* going to be one of Jake Mason's small-town conquests. Megan could have him.

"Mathias Sanders, there you are."

It was Mrs. Thompson. The elderly woman cornered her father at every opportunity trying to get free publicity for one of her projects or another.

"Good afternoon, Mrs. Thompson," her father said, standing up and reaching for the older woman's age-spotted hand. "It's good to see you. Won't you join us?"

Eleanor hoped Mrs. Thompson had other plans. Lunch with her and Jake would be more than she could stomach.

"No, no," the gray-haired woman said. "I'm meeting my bridge club. I stopped to tell you how much we appreciated the story you ran on our Bridge Club Tournament. Those were some good pictures, too. Too bad you didn't get any of me."

Eleanor picked up her napkin to hide her smile. Mrs. Thompson never changed. She glanced at Jake and saw he didn't bother to hide his smile.

"Well, you know we couldn't run photos of everyone. We do our best." Her father gave her his biggest smile. Goodness, he was as bad as Jake. "Have you met my new partner, Jake Mason?"

"Your new partner," Mrs. Thompson said. "I thought this might be Eleanor's beau." She extended her hand to Jake. "Nice to meet you, Mr. Mason. Welcome to Lamar."

Jake stood up. "Thank you, Mrs. Thompson. It's a pleasure meeting you." His hundred-watt smile flashed and Mrs. Thompson blushed. A sixty-plus-year old woman blushed. Eleanor wanted to kick Jake.

"Are you married, Mr. Mason?" Mrs. Thompson asked.

Eleanor could have kicked Mrs. Thompson then.

Jake smiled. "Not yet. But then they don't have Southern belles like yourself where I'm from."

Eleanor watched as Mrs. Thompson batted her eyelids. Goodness, the older woman was flirting with Jake.

"Eleanor, dear," she said, addressing her for the first time, "this is a good one. You'd better keep an eye on him."

Jake smiled again and Eleanor wished she had the nerve to slap that smile off his face. Thank goodness Mrs. Thompson floated over to her friends at a distant table before Eleanor could make a comment. Jake's laughter brought her attention to him.

"What's so funny?" she asked.

"Small towns," Jake answered with a huge, mocking grin on his face. "I think I'm going to like it here."

Eleanor knew he was having fun at her expense, but her father spoke before she could put him in his place.

"We like to think our town has a certain charm." He cut a glance at Eleanor. "How's the party planning going? We want Jake to meet the people of Lamar. Have you spoken to Megan about helping you plan it?"

No, she hadn't, and she was hoping her father would forget it. No such luck. "Megan's out of town. She won't be back for a couple of weeks."

"Well, damn. Where did she go and why did she have to go now?"

Eleanor glanced at Jake. "She had some personal business to take care of."

Mathias turned to Jake. "I guess this means we'll have to put off your party until she gets back. You don't mind, do you, son?"

"Not at all, Mathias. Eleanor is doing a great job of making me feel welcome."

"I'll bet," Mathias muttered.

Jake laughed. "Like I said before. She's the bratty little sister I never had."

Eleanor stood up, slapping her napkin on the table. "Since the two of you seem to like talking about me as if I'm not present, I'll leave and you can continue." She grabbed her purse from the back of the chair. "Besides, some of us have work to do."

Before Eleanor reached the door, she knew she had behaved badly. What was wrong with her? Why was she acting this way? It didn't take her long to figure out why.

Jake Mason.

Chapter 4

Eleanor wasn't surprised when her father entered her office, shut the door, and closed the blinds. She wondered where Jake was.

"What's wrong with you, Eleanor? Why are you so rude to Jake? And to me, for that matter?"

Eleanor placed the layout she was studying on her desk. "You don't have to say it. I know I've been out of line."

"That's an understatement," he said. The "young lady" at the end of the sentence sounded as loud as if he'd spoken the words.

"Why are you doing this, Dad? Why are you giving them control of our paper?"

Mathias released a heavy sigh before he sat in the chair at Jake's desk. "We've been over this before, Eleanor." He searched her face before continuing. "Randolph and I have talked about going into business together off and on over the years."

Eleanor leaned forward in her chair. She didn't like what she was hearing. "But why this, Dad?" she asked, her lips tight.

"Don't use that tone with me, young lady," he said in the inflection he'd used long ago, when she'd complained about wanting to stay up beyond her bedtime. "This is still my newspaper and don't you forget it."

Eleanor wanted to roll her eyes at her father's oft-used phrase, but she knew if she did, she'd get a lecture and her schedule for the afternoon would be shot. "I'm sorry, Dad, but I don't see why you want to merge the *Lamar Daily* with Mason Publishing."

Mathias stood up, put his hands in his pockets, and faced the window to the newsroom. Eleanor stood to her full height of five-four and pulled on her father's arm to turn him around. She hated having to look up to him. It was one of the things that helped keep her a child in his eyes. "Dad?"

"It'll be good for us, Eleanor. Think what it would mean if we were a part of Mason Publishing. Some of the changes you want to see around here could actually happen with the Mason Publishing money behind us. It's a great opportunity."

Eleanor knew he was right. It was a great opportunity. In fact, too great. "What do they get out of it?"

"What?"

"Mason Publishing? What do they get out of the deal? I see what we get, but what do they get?"

Alarm flashed in Mathias's eyes and he looked away again. "You know Randolph and I have been friends for years. He understands he won't get as much out of the deal as I will, but he think there's money to be made with the *Lamar Daily*."

Eleanor wasn't so sure. The *Lamar Daily* hadn't made much money over the years. Maybe with some changes they could do better, but she didn't think they'd ever become rich. No, that kind of potential was not in their newspaper. The *Lamar Daily* was a good small-town paper, but that's all it was. "Randolph Mason didn't get rich buying small-town papers, Dad. And something tells me an astute businessman like him knows how to keep business and personal matters separate. There must be something in this deal for him."

"Don't look a gift horse in the mouth, Eleanor," Mathias warned, looking at her again. "You're getting what you wanted. You should be happy."

Eleanor knew there was no discussing this with her father. In Mathias's eyes, Randolph Mason could do no wrong. "I don't want this merger to happen, Dad. What if Mason Publishing starts telling us how to do our business? We've always counted ourselves lucky that we didn't have to cut through a lot of corporate red tape. Why do you want to subject us to it now?"

"This is *another* corporation. This is Mason Publishing. And Randolph Mason is my best friend. You worry too much."

She didn't think so, but there was no use telling him that now. "If he's not planning to make any changes in our business, what's Jake doing here?"

Mathias shook his head. "It's still a business deal, Eleanor. Randolph thinks this paper is the place for Jake to get involved in the business."

"But why now? Why us?"

"That was Randolph's call. Jake's overseeing this deal. He's here and you have to work with him in addition to sharing office space with him." She would have interrupted, but Mathias continued. "I know you don't like his sharing your office, but we don't have much space. And since he'll be working mostly with the two of us, it was either have him share your office or have him share mine." He smiled. "And since I'm the boss around here, you got the office mate."

"I still don't like it, Dad," she said, meaning more than sharing her office.

Mathias touched his daughter's cheek. "I know you don't, sweetheart. But you have to deal with it. You can work with Jake and me or you can work against us. Either way, this deal with Randolph is going through."

Jake chose that moment to make his appearance and Mathias dropped his hand from Eleanor's face. He gave her a final pleading look, then said, "I have an afternoon meeting with the mayor. I'll see you two tonight."

Jake watched Mathias leave and he knew instinctively words had passed between father and daughter. From the uneasy look in Eleanor's eyes, he guessed the conversation had not been a pleasant one. For some reason Jake couldn't name, he wanted to comfort her.

"So, what are we doing this afternoon?" he asked.

"About lunch—" she began slowly.

"Yes," he interrupted, "I enjoyed that tasty Southern cuisine." He hoped she understood why he couldn't let her finish. He didn't want her to apologize. He felt an apology would somehow take away from the tenuous and strange relationship they were forming. In fact, Jake enjoyed sparring with Eleanor. It thrilled him to see her all riled up. It was more than obvious she didn't want him in Lamar. And she had no intention of allowing him to make any changes in the way they ran the newspaper. But that didn't matter. Somehow he knew the two of them would work through their differences.

Eleanor stared at him a few seconds. "This afternoon we lay out tomorrow's paper and edit the editorials and columns."

Jake knew she didn't understand why he didn't want her apology but he was glad she accepted his gesture. He grinned. "Where do we start?"

At ten o'clock the next morning, Eleanor dropped down in her office chair, kicked off her low-heeled black pumps, and propped her stocking-clad feet on her desk, wishing it was time for her lunchtime swim. It had been a heck of a morning. Columnists. She couldn't live with 'em and she couldn't live without 'em. She'd spent the better part of the morning arguing with Tempest Tanner, their most temperamental *and* most popular columnist, about her treatment, or rather, mistreatment, of the recent demise of one of Lamar's oldest residents. Eleanor shook her head. For some reason columnists couldn't comprehend slander and libel. Maybe it's because the newspaper would be liable and not the individual columnist.

Eleanor crossed her legs at the ankles, leaned back in her chair, and attempted to run her hand through her hair. The barrette that kept her black hair in a bun on top of her head stopped her fingers and she had to settle for rubbing her hands across her head. Some days she wished she could wear her hair down, but she knew wearing it up made her look more mature, more professional.

Eleanor lifted her wrist and checked the time on the Spelman watch she'd bought at the last class reunion. Two hours. Two hours and she could escape for a refreshing dip in her father's pool. Nothing relaxed her like a swim. She'd been on the swim team in high school and college. She'd been told she could have been a competitive swimmer, but she enjoyed swimming too much for that. If she allowed it to become a job, what would she do for relaxation?

And if she was lucky, she could go to the pool without Jake as she'd managed to do yesterday after work. He'd spent this morning with her father and she hoped their meetings would keep them occupied through lunch and her swim.

"Call for Eleanor from Horace," came Maxine's voice on the intercom.

Eleanor made a mental note to speak with Maxine again about the intercom, then picked up the phone.

"Oh, no," she said when she learned Horace Page was in the hospital with a broken hip. "Don't hesitate to call us if you need anything, Mrs. Page. My father and I will visit Horace today."

After a few more exchanges Eleanor hung up the phone. "What am I going to do?" she asked herself.

"About what?" was Jake's response.

So he was back. "Horace Page is in the hospital."

Jake sat on the corner of his desk. "Horace? That's the sports reporter, right?"

Eleanor nodded. "And the sports editor is in Alaska on a four-week vacation. Who's going to cover sports while they're out?"

"There has to be somebody. You've got about twelve people on the news staff."

"Everybody's busy. We don't have anybody."

"Get a freelancer," Jake suggested.

"This isn't New York, Jake. The closest thing we can get to a freelancer is a sports reporter from the high school."

"Do that. How hard can the job be anyway? Even I've heard the old newspaper saying, *Sports is entertainment; not brain surgery.*"

She leaned a finger against her cheek and considered his words. "You've heard that, have you?"

Jake flashed his trademark grin. "Publishing's in my blood."

"It is, is it?" Eleanor said, an idea forming in her mind.

"Of course. Just like it's in yours."

Eleanor snapped her fingers. "You're right. And I've thought of the perfect solution."

"See, I knew you could do it. Are you going to go with one of the high school kids?"

Eleanor shook her head. "Actually I was thinking of someone a bit more mature."

"Who?"

"You."

"Me."

"Yes, you. Didn't you say a high school kid could do it? Well, if publishing is in your blood, you can do it, too."

Jake stood. "Me? A sport reporter?"

Eleanor scooted around to her desk. "Don't sound so surprised, Jake. I know you can do it. After all, everybody knows sports is entertainment, not brain surgery."

Jake's mouth dropped open, but no words came out.

"You can do it, can't you, Jake?" Eleanor baited, knowing Jake wouldn't be able to resist her challenge.

"What's my first assignment?" he asked, suitably insulted.

She scribbled the name of the school on a slip of paper and handed it to him. "Girls basketball at the high school. Take a photographer with you. Ben's available."

The Lamar High School gymnasium was very different from the gymnasiums Jake remembered from his high school days. The building was old, the bleachers were older, and the kids somehow seemed younger. Basketball in the summer was new to him, too, but Ben had explained that Lamar did things a little differently since the school system ran on a year-round schedule.

Ben led him to the press box, which was really the seat next to the scorekeeper, a little blue-haired woman, who smiled at Jake, but who couldn't seem to concentrate on much more than keeping track of the score.

Ben handed Jake a sheet that put names to the numbers on the jerseys and for the next hour Jake engrossed himself in girls' basketball. During timeouts and quarter breaks, Jake's eyes roamed the spectators that filled the gymnasium. They came in all shapes, sizes, and ages—children, parents, grandparents. It seemed the game was more than a high school game; it was a community event.

When the game was over, Ben introduced Jake to the school principal, the girls' coach, and other members of the Lamar High coaching staff. Jake was feeling like a member of the community when he left.

As he climbed into the sports van with Ben and headed back to the paper, he felt a sense of accomplishment. He didn't consider himself a reporter and he hadn't come to Lamar to be a reporter, but he'd been assigned a job and he'd done it. Well, he'd done part of it. He had enough notes for a story. Now, he had to write the story.

"You're all right, Jake," Ben said when they reached the office, then he ambled off in the direction of the darkroom.

"So are you, Ben," Jake said, but he knew Ben didn't hear him.

Jake walked into the newsroom, ready to work on his story. Eleanor met him at the door. "How'd it go?"

"It went," was all he said. "Now I have to get the story written. I want to make deadline." He stepped past Eleanor and strode to his desk.

Eleanor stared at him. "You're going to write the story *now?*"

Jake looked up from the computer screen. "If I can get this computer to work." He flicked a button, and when the screen didn't light up, he raised the terminal off the desk a little. "How old is this equipment anyway?"

"About fifteen years."

Jake lowered the computer. "Fifteen years? It's ancient."

Eleanor perched on the corner of her desk. "You're right, our equipment is ancient. But according to my father, Mason Publishing will infuse us with enough money to modernize."

"Is that what your father said?" he asked absently, still fiddling with the terminal.

Eleanor confirmed.

"And how much will this modernization cost Mason Publishing?"

Eleanor gave a figure and Jake whistled. "That's a lot."

Eleanor shrugged her shoulders. "To us, maybe. But certainly not to you. That sum is a drop in the bucket for Mason Publishing."

He stared up at her. "So you think we're going to be the gravy train for the *Lamar Daily?*"

"There's no way my father would consider this deal if Mason Publishing couldn't provide enough money to do the things we want to do around here."

Jake forgot about the terminal and his article and gave her his full attention. "What other things do you want to do?"

Eleanor moved to sit on her desk chair. "A new computer system is first. One of those pagination systems. That would make us more efficient as well as enhance the look of the paper. Next, we'd want funds to add a Sunday edition. I know we'd get the advertising support, but we need up-front capital to get started. Then, we want to start a magazine targeted at African-American families."

Jake smiled at her. "You don't want much, do you?"

"A paper is like a life. You have to dream big. That's what we're doing."

"So you don't think you'll get all the things you've named?"

Eleanor nodded. "I think we'll get the things I mentioned, but there are a dozen other things I'd like to see us do." She grinned. "I'm willing to go slowly. I don't want to break Mason Publishing."

Jake returned his attention to the computer. "I bet." He slapped the side of the computer terminal. "What's wrong with this thing?"

"Stop hitting it like that," Eleanor admonished. "Let me see." She walked to his desk and leaned over his shoulder. Ignoring the rich smell of his cologne, she hit the Control and Reset keys. The machine seemed to take forever to reboot. She leaned away from him as it did so.

"What did you do?" he asked, oblivious to the effect he was having on her.

"I rebooted the machine. You should be ready to go in a minute or so."

"I hope so."

She leaned over his shoulder again. "Okay." She pressed the Enter key twice. "There you go. It's ready."

Jake hit the insert key and clicked a couple other keys, then turned around and smiled at her. She couldn't help but smile back. The man was gorgeous.

"Thanks, Eleanor. It's working. I'll have to remember to reboot when I'm having problems." He turned back around and started on his story.

Eleanor remained behind him for a few seconds. She didn't understand Jake Mason. She'd been sure he'd come here to destroy the paper she'd known her whole life, yet here he was as excited as one of the high school kids about the story he was writing. What was it with this man?

"Make sure to save," she said before she went back to her desk and flicked on her computer. She might as well use this time to edit tomorrow's stories. After about twenty minutes, she heard Jake.

"Dammit," he said.

"What's wrong now, Jake?"

She heard the click of a couple of keys and the machine started to reboot. "I've got it covered."

Eleanor went back to her work.

"Dammit, now I can't find my story."

She heard him hit the side of the terminal again. "What'd you do?" she asked, getting up and walking over to him.

He looked up at her. "The keyboard froze, but I rebooted like you did before. Now I can't find my story."

Eleanor hit the Retrieve function key to view the file listing. "What's the name of the file?"

"Name? I didn't get that far. The keyboard hung when I was about three-quarters done."

"Uh-oh."

"Oh, no, I don't like the sound of that."

Eleanor gave him her first real smile, then touched his shoulder. "It wasn't saved. You lost your story. I'm sorry."

"Damn. Now's a fine time for you to tell me." He slapped the computer terminal on its side again. "Stupid machine doesn't even have an auto-save feature."

Eleanor chuckled as she went back to her desk. "Don't blame the machine, Jake. It's old and it doesn't have a mind or any modern features. It only does what you tell it."

"What's that supposed to mean?" Jake said, his voice raised.

Eleanor knew when to retreat. "Nothing. Just don't forget to save this time."

"You can bet on it," he muttered, then hit the side of the terminal again.

Randolph picked up his phone on the first ring. He knew who was calling.

"So what's happening on the Jake and Eleanor front?" he asked as soon as Mathias came on the line.

Mathias chuckled. "Jake became a reporter today."

"A reporter? Jake?"

Mathias laughed again, then repeated the story of the hospitalized sports reporter.

Randolph joined him in laughter. "So how'd he do?"

"According to Eleanor, he lost his story twice in the computer. But he got it done."

Randolph filled with pride. It wasn't that he was surprised Jake could do it. He knew Jake could do anything he set his mind to do. No, Randolph was more surprised Jake had done it. And apparently had enjoyed doing it. "What did Eleanor think of that?"

"I think it may work in our favor, Randy. She's thinking about him in a whole new light. She only made three negative comments about him tonight at dinner and those were inconsequential. I think the way he handled that story has made her reexamine her first opinion of him."

"Good. Good. Maybe we're getting somewhere."

"Don't get too excited. We still have a long way to go."

"I know. I know. But this is a start in the right direction. What's next?"

"I've told Eleanor to throw a 'Welcome to Lamar' party for Jake. She's hesitant to do it, but I've cornered her into asking her friend Megan to help."

"Megan? The teenage hormone you used to talk about?"

Mathias laughed. "She's not a teenager anymore."

"Do you think that's wise, Mat? Having this Megan around Jake? What if Jake gets interested in her instead of Eleanor?"

"I don't think that'll happen. Jake isn't Megan's type."

Randolph harrumphed. "I've never met a woman who didn't think Jake was her type. What makes this Megan different?"

"Megan's a flirt, Randy. Personally, I think she's in love with one of my reporters. No, you leave this to me. Megan is the ingredient we need here. She'll flirt and Eleanor'll be jealous. You watch."

"You sound pretty confident for a man who only a few minutes ago told me not to get too excited."

"I know, I know. But you should see them together, Randy. They're going to be a great couple."

"I hope you're right, Mat. I hope you're right."

Chapter 5

Coffee with Carl had become a part of Jake's routine in the nearly two weeks he'd been in Lamar and this morning was no different. Initially, Carl had allied himself with Jake to protect him from Eleanor, but now Jake felt they'd formed a real friendship.

"How was the game yesterday?" Carl asked, sipping from his coffee mug, his legs propped on his credenza.

Jake rolled his chair across the padded floor and threw the day's edition on Carl's desk. "You'll have to read it in the paper."

Carl placed his cup on his desk and picked up the paper, opening it to the sports section. "Not bad for a rookie."

"A rookie? I'm a reporter of experience. I've gotten more bylines in the last two weeks than most new reporters get in a couple of months. Hell, I may even get a Pulitzer for that track story."

Carl laughed. "Don't wait on that Pulitzer, Jake. If anybody in Lamar gets a Pulitzer, it'll be me."

"Keep telling yourself that, friend," Jake joked, knowing Carl was right.

"Hey," Carl protested, "not you, too. I don't get enough kudos around here as it is. I thought a big-city boy like yourself appreciated my worth."

Jake sobered. "I do and so do Mathias and Eleanor." Carl was the paper's most capable journalist. It was an odd day for the *Lamar Daily* when the headline story carried a byline that didn't belong to him. Jake wondered what kept a journalist of his obvious talent in Lamar. Carl would be hell at a larger paper and get a lot more exposure, too.

Carl grunted. "Mathias appreciates me, but I'm not too sure about Eleanor. Sometimes I think she still sees me as her geeky friend from school."

"I didn't know you and Eleanor were in school together," Jake commented. He'd thought he and Carl were about the same age. Now he wondered if Carl knew Megan and, if so, how well.

Carl nodded. "For twelve long years. For a while we were pretty close friends, but that was B.M."

"Excuse me?"

"Before Megan." Carl picked up his coffee mug again. "Eleanor and I were geeks together until Megan."

The hurt in Carl's tone surprised Jake. It seemed out of character for Carl to harbor ill feelings about something that had happened years ago. Jake wondered about it, but he couldn't miss the opportunity to learn more about the mysterious Megan. "What happened when Megan came along?"

"She and Eleanor became fast friends." Carl shook his head. "What an odd couple they were. That's what the kids called them, the Odd Couple."

"Megan was the slob?" Jake asked, thinking of the Oscar character. He knew without asking that Eleanor had to be Felix.

"That's not why they called them the Odd Couple. It was because they were so different."

Jake could imagine. The beautiful, alluring Megan and the prim, unassuming Eleanor. Well, maybe unassuming wasn't correct. Eleanor had too much mouth to be considered unassuming. "The beautiful and the plain, I can see that."

"You got it right. Megan was gorgeous, even in eighth grade. Eleanor could be a looker, but she doesn't know it."

"So Megan is still gorgeous?"

Carl sneered. "So gorgeous she has her own fan club."

Jake nodded. From the little he'd heard about Megan, he could understand why the men of Lamar had formed a club for her. Obviously, Carl wasn't a member.

"Too bad she's the president," Carl added.

Jake laughed. "So Megan is a bit self-absorbed."

"More like a *lot* self-absorbed."

"You sound like you don't like her."

Carl stared at Jake a few seconds before speaking. "Nobody *doesn't* like Megan."

Jake wanted to follow up on that, but before he could, Carl pushed away from his desk and stood. "I've got to see Wanda in composition. I'll talk to you later."

Jake stared after Carl, wondering what he meant by his last statement about Megan. Eleanor found him that way.

"What's on your schedule for this morning?" she asked.

When Jake looked at her, Carl's words about Eleanor sounded in his ears—*Eleanor could be a looker, but she doesn't know it.* The words had escaped him when his friend first spoke them, but now they registered. For the first time since he'd been in Lamar, he assessed Eleanor—really assessed her, not as his father's best friend's daughter, not as a bratty younger sister, not as a business rival, but as a woman.

He studied the bun atop her head and wondered how she'd look with her hair down. He realized now that he didn't even know how long her hair was. It was a rich, dark brown and appeared to be very thick, though he couldn't really tell from the way she had it rolled up on her head.

"Is something wrong with my hair?" Eleanor asked, patting the bun to make sure it was in place.

Her question brought Jake's attention to her face. "No, nothing's wrong with your hair." But you have beautiful big, brown eyes, he added to himself.

"Then why were you staring?" she asked, clearly not believing his words. "I'll go check it out myself."

Jake couldn't help but watch the gentle sway of her hips as she walked away from him. He knew it wasn't a practiced walk, merely the walk of a woman comfortable in her body. For once he appreciated the distance from the newsroom to the bathrooms. Though Eleanor wore a skirt that fell to her knees, he could see she had strong, firm calves and trim ankles and that made him think her thighs would be strong and firm, too.

Disappointment settled around him when she entered the bathroom door and he could no longer see her. It was probably a good thing. Now was not the time for sexual thoughts about Eleanor. No, he had come to Lamar to do a job. Not to get involved with the daughter of his father's best friend.

He dropped down in his chair. He wished to hell Megan would hurry up and get back.

Eleanor leaned against the bathroom door, grateful for the protection it provided from Jake and the emotions he stirred in her. Why had he been staring at her? At first, she'd really thought something may have been wrong with her hair. But when he'd looked in her face, she'd known his thoughts had nothing to do with her coiffure. No, Jake Mason had been assessing her attributes as a female. And, heaven help her, she wasn't sure if she'd measured up to his standard of womanhood. At least not dressed the way she was.

She walked to the mirror and stared at herself. She'd never before questioned her dress. She dressed for authority, not for allure, deliberately choosing the conservative outfits that some considered unfashionable. And that hadn't been a problem until now. Until Jake. Now she had thoughts of silk miniskirted suits in bold colors.

She'd been hurt when Jake hadn't recognized her as the woman at the pool and she secretly hoped that one day he'd laugh and tell her it was all a joke, that he'd known all along it was her. But that hadn't happened in the two weeks he'd been there and she was pretty sure it wouldn't happen until he met Megan.

At least, she hoped he'd make the connection after he met Megan. Surely, he'd know Megan wasn't the woman by the pool. Heaven help her, she'd kill him if he didn't figure out then that she was the woman.

Hearing the bathroom door open, Eleanor quickly stepped into an empty stall. What was she doing? she asked herself. Why was she hiding out in the bathroom trying to unravel the feelings Jake Mason aroused in her? Once again, she wished the man had never come to Lamar. This time, she acknowledged the paper wasn't the only thing she was afraid Jake Mason would steal.

No, right now Eleanor was concerned about Jake Mason stealing her heart.

Jake couldn't keep his eyes off Eleanor. He'd covertly observed her all afternoon. A couple of times she'd caught him staring, but he'd averted his gaze each time, and since she hadn't said anything, he figured she hadn't thought much about it.

He'd learned a lot about Eleanor. First, she chewed the end of her pen while she worked. Though he'd seen pens with chewed ends here and there around the newsroom, he'd never really thought about them. Now he knew they were Eleanor's pens.

What surprised him more was how cute she looked while she chewed. She'd put the pen in her mouth, push it in and out a couple of times, then play with the tip with her tongue before grasping it with her full, unpainted lips. There was something erotic in her every motion. He was almost relieved when Mathias came by to talk with her.

"I need to steal Eleanor for a while, Jake," the older man said.

"Fine, sir," Jake said, with a grin. "I'll make the most of the privacy."

Eleanor grinned back and he noticed her whole face lit up with that grin. Why hadn't he noticed that before?

"Don't get too comfortable," she said. "I'll be back. Soon."

Eleanor followed her father to his office, glad to get away from Jake. She'd thought things would get better as the day went on, but they hadn't. He was still staring at her. Well, maybe not staring, more like observing. She'd been tempted to ask him if he liked what he saw, but she wasn't sure she wanted to know his answer.

"You seem to be dealing with Jake a lot better," her father said after she was seated in the burgundy leather visitor's chair in front of his massive oak desk.

She tried not to think how much easier it would've been to put Jake and his desk in this large office rather than her smaller one. "Well, you know what they say, 'Keep your friends close and your enemies closer.'"

Mathias sighed. "Jake is not the enemy, Eleanor. We're all on the same side."

"I hope you're right," she muttered.

"Of course, I'm right. Look how he pitched in with the sports reporting. He could have snubbed his nose at doing that menial reporting job that you gave him, but he didn't. He did what was best for the paper."

"Okay, Dad, I get your point," Eleanor said. She couldn't deny that Jake had done a good job. She'd been surprised by his enthusiasm for the project. And more than a little pleased. His actions made her wonder if she'd initially judged him too harshly. Jake Mason was proving hard to dislike.

"Now," her father said, interrupting her thoughts, "have you given any thought to the specifics you want from our merger with Mason Publishing?"

She wished she could say she didn't see any potential for good to come out of the venture, but that would be a lie. "Sure I've thought about it. If they're going to give us money, you bet I can spend it. But I want to make sure the money doesn't come with strings attached."

"Yes, yes, yes. You've made your position clear. Have you discussed any of your ideas with Jake?"

Eleanor shrugged her shoulders. "I've mentioned some projects I'd like to see funded."

"And what was his response?"

"He said something about a gravy train."

Mathias laughed. "So Jake thinks we want to milk Mason Publishing."

"As if we would actually do that. They probably have so much money they don't know what to do with it."

"I'm sure you're wrong there. Randolph is my friend, but as you've said before, he's also an astute businessman. The only guarantee we made was that the newspaper will remain in our control. They can't sell it or break it up without our agreement and everybody keeps their job. Including you and me. Other than that, everything's up for grabs."

"Everything?"

"Everything. That's why it's important you work with Jake on this. Randolph has given him a free hand with this deal."

"Why this deal, Dad?" Eleanor asked for the tenth time since she'd learned of the deal. Maybe this time she'd get a satisfactory answer. "Jake's not a newspaperman. That much is obvious."

Mathis sighed, leaned back in his chair, and twirled a pen in his hand. "Like any parent, Randolph wants Jake to take over for him someday. And he thinks this deal is the project to bring Jake in the fold."

"And you think Mr. Mason is going to support whatever Jake decides?"

Mathias nodded. "That's what I know."

Eleanor had figured as much. But there was one point on which she wasn't sure. "And are you going to support me?"

"You know how much I love you, Eleanor, and I want to see you happy."

Eleanor knew her father's hedging wasn't a good sign. "I know that, but it doesn't answer my question."

Mathias dropped his pen on the desk and leaned toward her, concern in his eyes. "Are you happy, Eleanor? Really happy?"

"Of course, I'm happy, Dad. Do you think I'm not?"

He searched her face for any sign that she wasn't telling the truth. "I worry about you sometimes. Trapped in a small town, with this small paper. You're a young woman. You should experience life beyond Lamar."

Eleanor felt a tightening in her chest. "I am experiencing life. As you always say, 'If it didn't happen in Lamar, it didn't happen.'"

The old newspaper saying her father used so much didn't make him smile this time.

"You know what I'm talking about, Eleanor. Sometimes I think I did you a disservice by encouraging you to spend so much time here."

Eleanor got up from her chair, walked around her father's

desk, and hugged him. "That's not true. You were and still are the best dad a girl could have. I love you, Dad."

"I know you do, sweetheart. I know you do."

Eleanor took comfort in her father's embrace, but she realized he hadn't answered her question. She'd let it go for now, but soon she would demand an answer.

Eleanor began dropping off her clothes as soon as she walked through the door of her cottage. By the time she reached her bedroom, she was nude and her phone was ringing. She picked it up on the second ring.

"So how is handsome doing?"

Eleanor welcomed the cheery sound of Megan's voice. She reclined on the bed and prepared for a long conversation. "When did you get back?"

"Who said I was back?"

Eleanor laughed. "You're too cheap to call long distance."

"Ahh, you know me too well. So, how is the fine brother from New York doing?"

"Thriving. He's enjoying the sights and sounds of Lamar."

"I bet he is. The man is probably bored out of his mind. But I'm sure I'll be able to fix that. *If* you ever get around to introducing me, that is."

Eleanor knew her friend was right. It was time Jake met Megan. She couldn't wait to see his expression when he learned she wasn't the woman at the pool. "Well, you won't have to wait long. Dad wants you to plan a 'Welcome to Lamar' party for Jake."

"All right," Megan whooped. "Be sure to give Mr. S. a big kiss for me. If he was a little younger, I'd have my eye on him."

Eleanor chuckled. "Don't even think about it, Megan. If Maxine hasn't gotten his attention in all these years, you don't stand a chance. Besides, I don't think you're stepmother material. Though it would be fun to call you Mom."

"Don't even joke about something like that, Eleanor. You calling me Mom. It gives me chills. You still haven't told me about handsome. You haven't decided that you want him, have you?"

"Of course not," Eleanor answered a bit too quickly.

"You're sure?"

"Yes, I'm sure. He's not my type."

"Your type is a whole other conversation, Eleanor. I don't think you know what your type is. Now before you get your panties all twisted because of that statement, tell me what Jake's been up to."

Eleanor's flaring temper quickly faded. "He's our interim sports reporter."

"What? You're kidding! New York Jake is covering local sports? You *are* going to bore the man to death."

Eleanor chuckled again. "Believe it or not, he's enjoying it and he's good at it."

"I bet it hurt you to say that."

Megan was right, but Eleanor was not about to tell her. "And he's become good friends with Carl."

"Now I *know* the man is leaving town soon. Carl would bore a dead person. I don't believe you, Eleanor. Why are you putting him around all the dull people? If it wasn't so late, I'd come over there and introduce myself to him tonight."

"How did you know he was staying here?"

"Earth to Eleanor. This is Lamar, remember? There's no such thing as a secret. Especially secrets about a man as attractive as Jake. Everybody's talking about him."

"You stopped by the beauty shop today, didn't you?"

Megan laughed. "You know I had to get my weekly do and catch up on the gossip."

"I don't see how Betty gets anybody's hair done as much as she talks."

"Don't knock it. Betty has all the news."

"You're telling me," Eleanor said. Everybody in Lamar knew what a gossip Betty was.

Megan proceeded to tell Eleanor the latest news from the Betty hotline.

"Hey, why don't you have lunch with me tomorrow?" Eleanor suggested after all the gossip was discussed. "Drop by the office a little before noon and I'll introduce you to Jake."

"It's about time you invited me, girl. I was planning to show up on my own if you hadn't."

"I sorta figured that."

"Be sure to invite Jake to lunch with us."

"Don't worry. I'll invite him. I may even invite Carl."

Megan snorted. "Don't even think about it. The brother needs to get away from Carl. I'm telling you Carl is the dullest man I ever met. He was dull in high school and he's even duller now, if that's possible."

"You've never liked Carl, have you, Megan?"

"He's too much of a Goody Two-shoes. Even when we were kids, he was always judging me. Who's he to judge me?"

Eleanor laughed. "You're just upset because Carl is the only man in Lamar you don't have wrapped around your little finger."

"Like I'd even be interested in Carl. Please. I want a real man, not a boy."

Eleanor felt again that Megan protested a little too much when Carl's name was mentioned. She was almost sure Megan had a crush on him, though she'd never been able to get her to admit it. "If you say so, Megan. But I still may invite him to lunch with us."

"Hey, that might be a good idea. You can talk to Carl while I get to know Jake a little better. Better yet, why don't you go to lunch with Carl and leave Jake with me. I'll take good care of him."

"I bet you would," Eleanor said, ignoring the flame of jealousy that flared up in the middle of her stomach.

Chapter 6

Jake couldn't get Carl's words out of his head. *Eleanor could be beautiful, Eleanor could be beautiful.* He was about to agree with him. From where Jake sat, Eleanor needed to loosen up on the dress. The woman gave new meaning to the word *conservative*. She could also do something with her hair. He wanted to see it in a style other than that old maid's bun she wore every day.

Not that he didn't know what she was doing. He did. Eleanor was the corporate woman to the T. Her professional image was one of no-nonsense work.

He shrugged. Maybe it was because she worked for her father. He noticed she had a difficult time with the older members of the staff. They still wanted to treat her like a teenager. He knew her getup was part of her barrier against that, though he didn't think it was working.

"Here comes trouble." Carl leaned his head in Jake's office. "Megan has hit the floor."

Jake stood and walked to the door. "How do you know?"

"Don't you feel the rumbling in the foundation?"

"What are you talking about?"

Carl folded his arms across his chest and leaned back on the desk nearest Jake and Eleanor's office. "Don't you hear all that chatter in the hallway? It's Megan time."

Jake kept his expression clear, but he felt the excitement bubble up in him. He was finally going to meet the woman by the pool. Anxious, he straightened his tie.

Carl shook in head in disgust. "Not you, too."

"What?"

"Megan's already got you under her spell and you haven't even met her." Still shaking his head, he continued, "I thought you were different. I knew I was the only sane male in Lamar. Now I wonder if I'm the only sane male in the country."

"Are you sure about that, friend?"

Carl dropped his arms and straightened. "Of course I'm sure," he answered with what Jake thought was a mite much enthusiasm.

"If you say so."

"Yes, I do say so."

Jake clapped Carl on the back. "Don't get all upset. So you don't like Megan. In a way I'm glad. It leaves the field clear for me. If you were interested, we'd have to duke it out for her."

Carl snorted. "You must be kidding. I'd never fight over Megan. Though that's the kind of stunt that would get her attention."

"Let's be glad it won't come to that. You're going to introduce me, though. Aren't you?"

Carl walked away from his perch and back to his desk in the middle of the newsroom. "You don't know Megan. She'll introduce herself. She probably knows all about you anyway. That woman is telepathic where men are concerned."

Jake was getting bored with Carl's attitude. He said he disliked Megan more than he showed it, he thought.

While Carl went back to his work, Jake paced in front of his office and waited for Megan to walk through the newsroom door. From everything Carl had said about her, he knew she'd be pleased to find him waiting. And he *did* want to make a good first impression.

Eleanor walked through the door first and she was more animated than Jake had ever seen her. Her eyes sparkled and her laughter was light, but full. There was even more pep in her step. When he saw the tall woman with short, tight brownish-red curls next to her, Jake's heart dropped. This was Megan?

As Eleanor and the redhead approached, Jake became more certain the woman was indeed Megan. There was something blatantly sexual about her. He felt it even from a distance. She was the kind of woman who called out to men without opening her mouth. And she was the kind of woman to whom men always responded. But she wasn't the woman from the pool. Her hair was too short and the wrong color and she was too tall. No, she wasn't the woman from the pool.

When she saw him, she flashed him a smile he was sure made weaker men pant. He merely returned it with one of his own. He saw the change in her expression and knew his response was not what she'd expected.

Jake watched the two women approach him. Eleanor and Megan were the Odd Couple, all right. Megan in her bright red miniskirt and jacket was fire, and Eleanor in her cold navy blue female version of the power suit was ice, or at least that's what they seemed.

"You must be Jake," Megan said, extending her hand to him.

He pulled her hand to his lips in mock Southern gallantry. Carl groaned at the action, then turned his chair away from them. Eleanor rolled her eyes. Megan merely took it as her due.

"Why, Jake, they told me you were a Northerner. Where did you learn Southern charm?"

Jake rubbed her hand with his thumb before releasing it. "I've always felt the woman brings out the charm in a man. Now, if they had women like you in the North, maybe Northern charm would be as well known."

"You're pouring it on a bit too thick," Carl muttered from his seat not five feet from them.

Megan leaned close to Jake, but spoke to him in a voice loud enough for Eleanor and Carl to hear. "Don't mind Carl. He was raised in the South, but he's no gentleman."

"I heard that, Megan," Carl said, still facing away from them. Jake noticed he was doing a pretty good job of showing disinterest.

Megan turned to Carl. "Jealous, Carl?"

"Of what?" He still didn't turn around.

Megan frowned then turned back to Jake without answering

Carl's question. "Are you free for lunch? It looks like Carl will be too busy to go. What a shame." Her smile said that was the best news she'd had in days.

Jake laughed, then noticed Eleanor wasn't smiling. She was watching him and Megan as though she expected something. What? "Where are you going for lunch?"

"Virginia's," Eleanor answered. "It's Megan's favorite place."

Megan folded her arm under Jake's as if she did it every day. "And you must go with us. We have to get to know each other better."

Jake laughed. "I thought that was supposed to be my line."

"We don't stand on formality around here, Jake," Carl said, finally turning around. He stared directly at Megan though he spoke to Jake. "You'd better watch out, she'll probably make a pass at lunch."

"Carl," Eleanor chastised.

Megan said nothing. She merely stared at Carl, then flecked nonexistent lint from her jacket in Carl's direction and turned back to Jake. "If you two are ready, we can go. I don't see any need for Carl to tag along. Do you, Eleanor?"

Eleanor sure did see a reason for Carl to tag along. He could be her companion. From the way things were going so far, Megan and Jake would spend the entire lunch flirting. And she'd be sitting there like a fifth wheel.

She knew she could bow out, claiming she had work to do, but she didn't want to. She wanted to be there when Jake realized she was the woman by the pool. She could tell by the change in his expression when he saw Megan that he'd correctly concluded Megan wasn't the woman.

Eleanor knew too that Jake had done what most people did when she and Megan were together. He'd compared them. Strangely enough, she felt his comparison didn't find her lacking. That was a first.

"I can think of a good reason for Carl to come along," Eleanor said, getting back to Megan's question.

"What?" Megan's tone said she seriously doubted it.

Eleanor looked from Jake to Megan. "I'm just a chaperone. You two may need somebody to hose you down."

Sometimes Eleanor wondered how she and Megan remained friends. Today was one of those days. Megan was in rare form.

"You're so funny, Jake," Megan said for the umpteenth time, each time needing to touch Jake's wrist lightly as if to prove she was telling the truth.

Eleanor could have gagged. She shot a glance at Carl. His response was pretty much the same. He was on his fourth drink; thankfully he wasn't drinking alcohol.

"You're going to rub the skin off his wrist if you keep rubbing on it," Carl commented, then dropped his napkin on the table and stood up. "Excuse me," he said, "I need to get some air. It's getting pretty thick in here."

A part of Eleanor wanted to get up and follow Carl, but another part of her wanted to stay right there with Megan and Jake. Somebody had to keep the two of them in line.

"What's his problem?" Jake asked, referring to Carl.

Megan dismissed his question with a wave of her hand. "Carl has so many problems. Who knows which one is bothering him today."

Jake sat back in his chair and lifted his glass to his lips. "What's up with you and Carl? You two act like quarreling lovers."

Megan's eyes flashed anger. "Don't even go there. Carl is definitely *not* my type, wouldn't be my type if he were the *only* man on the earth."

Jake shot a glance at Eleanor and she read the question in his eyes. His perception surprised her. He'd figured out what it had taken her years to conclude. She nodded her head slightly and Jake directed his attention back to Megan.

Jake and Megan flirted for the rest of lunch, pausing occasionally to include Eleanor.

"I know you swim, Jake," Megan said, batting her eyelashes. "Eleanor has invited me over for a swim after work. Why don't you join us?"

598   *Angela Benson*

Eleanor almost choked on her coffee. This was what she wanted, yet it wasn't. If Jake went swimming with them, he'd definitely figure out she was the woman in the pool. She'd hoped he would have figured it out during lunch but he hadn't.

Jake looked at her. "I don't have any games to cover tonight. You won't mind, will you, Eleanor?"

"Why would I mind?" she asked, with a shrug of her shoulders. "You're living in the house. You can use the pool when you wish."

Jake smiled at Megan. "I'll see you after work, then." He turned to Carl, who had returned to the table. "Are you game?"

Carl snorted. "I can only stomach so much of Ms. M in a single day. I think I'll pass."

Jake smiled first at Megan then at Eleanor, before lifting his glass to them. "It seems I've lucked out, ladies. I'll have the two of you to myself. I'm enjoying living in Lamar more by the minute."

For the first time since she'd taken on the managing editor's job, Eleanor watched the clock for quitting time. She couldn't wait for the swim party this afternoon. She glanced over at Jake. She couldn't wait to see his reaction when he found out she was the woman by the pool. She hoped he swallowed his tongue.

Then she wondered what he'd do. Would he start to flirt with her like he'd been flirting with Megan? A part of her hoped he would, so she could shoot him down. Yes, it would give her great pleasure to be the one that got away from Jake Mason, Mr. Irresistible.

"We're going to have to start discussing plans for the paper," Jake said.

Eleanor looked up at him. "So soon? On Monday, you will have been here two weeks and you're ready to start making plans. That's kind of quick, isn't it?"

"I don't think so. Anyway, I said we needed to start, not that we needed to finalize anything."

"Okay, then. When do you want to start? This weekend?"

Jake shook his head. "Monday is soon enough. I plan to have some fun this weekend."

Eleanor wondered if he'd asked Megan out. No, Megan probably asked him to go dancing at the Farmhouse, a local hangout for the adult crowd. She'd have to wait and ask Megan about it because she definitely wasn't going to ask Jake.

"Monday's fine with me," she said after checking her calendar. "How about first thing in the afternoon? One o'clock, okay?"

"It works for me." Jake didn't bother to check his calendar. "Well, I'm outta here. I guess I'll see you at the pool."

"You sure will," she said after he left the office. She waited a good fifteen minutes before packing up her briefcase and following after him.

Eleanor heard the voices and splashing water before she reached the pool. She stopped a few steps behind the hedges that separated her yard from the pool grounds, adjusted the white thong swimsuit she'd worn the first day Jake had seen her, and took a deep breath.

She stepped from behind the hedges. "Hi, you two," she said in as calm a voice as she could muster. Megan, dressed in a red one-piece mallot, and Jake, in black trunks, sat on the far end of the pool. "How's the water?" She dropped her fluffy white towel on the plaid lounger and dived into the pool to join them.

The water was the right temperature to make her forget her worry. She used broad strokes to swim to the side of the pool and join Megan and Jake. When she reached them, she hoisted herself up next to Megan.

Pushing back her mane of dark hair, she smiled. "The water's great. Why aren't you guys swimming?"

Megan put a proprietary hand on Jake's knee. "I wore him out. He needed his rest."

Eleanor looked at Jake for the first time, and when she saw his expression, she wanted to shout her joy. From the cold look in his eyes, she knew he'd figured out who she was.

"Enjoying yourself, Jake?" she asked.

"It was you," he said, his voice full of accusation.

Megan looked at him. "What are you talking about?"

Jake wouldn't take his cold eyes off Eleanor. "You made a fool out of me."

Eleanor grabbed the towel behind Megan. "I did no such thing. You made a fool out of yourself."

"What are you two talking about?" Megan asked, clearly not liking being kept in the dark.

"Jake thought I was you."

"What?"

Eleanor explained about the day Jake had seen her at the pool.

Megan turned to Jake. "Why did you think she was me?"

Jake glared at Eleanor. "Who else could the woman I saw have been? I surely didn't think it was Eleanor."

"What's that supposed to mean?" Eleanor said, recognizing an insult when she heard one.

"Yeah, what does that mean?" Megan repeated. "How come you didn't think it was Eleanor? She lives here, after all. I don't."

"I'd seen her pictures," Jake muttered.

"What did you say?" Megan asked.

Eleanor didn't have to ask. She'd heard him. He'd seen her pictures and had concluded there was no way it could be her. She was definitely insulted.

"I'd seen her pictures," Jake said more clearly.

Megan chuckled. "What pictures? When?"

Jake explained about the friendship between their two fathers and the pictures they exchanged each year at the publishing convention.

"What did her pictures look like?" Megan asked, clearly enjoying Eleanor's discomfort.

Jake's eyes roamed Eleanor from head to toe. What Carl had said was an understatement. Eleanor was more than beautiful. She was a toasted goddess. "I'm sure you've seen the ones on the piano in the living room. In them, she certainly doesn't look like she's looking now."

Megan turned to Eleanor. "See. I told you to stop dressing like some old woman."

"I don't dress like an *old* woman, as you put it, Megan. I dress like a *professional* woman. If I listened to you, I'd be dressed like a hooker."

"You know that's not so. There are a lot of professional outfits you could wear that wouldn't make you look so stern and old."

"I think I'm old enough to pick my own clothes, Megan."

"From what you've been picking lately, I'm not so sure. Anyway, it's not so much what you wear. It's how what you wear hides who you are."

"And who am I, Megan?" Eleanor asked calmly.

Jake cleared his throat and both women turned to him. They had forgotten he was there. Clearly, this was an argument they'd had before.

"Sorry," Megan said sheepishly. "We always get carried away when we discuss this particular topic. But don't you think I'm right, Jake? She's gorgeous, but you'd never know it by what she wears every day. Tell her."

Jake read Eleanor's discomfort—no, it was more than discomfort—with the topic. "I don't think I want to get in this."

"You're already in it," Megan corrected. "You said that after seeing her pictures, you never would have thought she could look this good."

Jake shot a pleading glance at Eleanor. "That's not exactly what I said."

"Not in so many words," Megan relented. "But it's what you meant."

"Look," Eleanor said, tired of the entire discussion. "We came here to swim. Let's swim."

"You owe me an apology."

Eleanor's eyes flashed her surprise at Jake's statement. "I recognized you. It's your problem if you didn't recognize me."

"I didn't see your face," Jake murmured.

She shook her head in disgust. "And I can guess why. From what I saw, your eyes were focused on another part of my anatomy."

Jake's gaze dropped to her thighs and she knew he was remembering her upturned bottom. "Oh," he said.

"Yes, oh," she said, wishing he'd stop staring at her.

"Well," he said, recovering quickly. "That doesn't matter. You still owe me an apology."

"Surely, you're joking."

"No, I'm not. You should have told me it was you. You've had me going on and on about meeting Megan since I've been here."

"Hold on a minute," Megan said. "This is beginning to sound like you're disappointed about meeting me. I don't think I like the sound of that."

Jake threw up both hands. There was no reasoning with them this afternoon. "Southern women. Who needs them?" He grabbed his towel and stomped off to the house.

Chapter 7

Megan stared after Jake. "What's wrong with him?"

"Right now, I don't know and I don't care." Eleanor stood up. "I thought you came here to swim. Let's get in the water."

Megan jerked her friend's hand, causing her to sit back down. "You like him, don't you?"

"He's all right."

"This is me you're talking to, Eleanor. There's nothing wrong with it. He's a fine brother. And he seems interested in you, too."

Eleanor squashed the hope that sprang up in her chest. "He's interested in anything in a skirt."

Megan shook her head. "I know men. And that man is interested in you. He was probably curious even before he saw the *real* you."

Eleanor paddled her feet in the water and it splashed up her leg. "Now I know you're crazy." But memories of Jake's gazing at her in the last day or two flooded her mind. Was he interested in her?

"I don't see what the big deal is. He's a grown man and a fine one to boot. Go for it!"

Eleanor paddled faster. "There's nothing to go for. Anyway, I thought you were interested in him."

"I was, but only if you didn't want him."

"I don't want him."

"You may not want to want him, Eleanor, but you *do* want him."

Megan was too right. Eleanor's feelings for Jake had sneaked up on her. Sure, she'd been attracted to him from the beginning, but that was physical. In the past couple of weeks, she'd grown to like him as well. And she'd developed a begrudging respect for him after seeing the way he handled his sports assignments. But her emotions were too new to share with Megan right now. She'd share them, but not now. "What about your feelings for Carl?"

Megan's eyes jerked away. "Now I don't know what you're talking about."

"Sure you don't."

"What's that supposed to mean?"

"It means this game you and Carl are playing. When are you both going to admit that you care about each other?"

Megan snorted. "I also care about stray cats."

Eleanor decided to stop prying. Maybe Megan wasn't any more ready to talk about her feelings for Carl than she was ready to talk about her feelings for Jake. She stood and dived into the pool. What a pair they were!

"I thought you said they were beginning to like each other," Randolph said, thumping his Cross pen on the desk pad.

"They were until this little mishap this afternoon," Mathias responded with impatience.

"So what happened?"

"How do you expect me to know?"

Randolph jumped up out of his chair. "Hell, Mat, you're right there with them. Jake's living in your house. Eleanor's living in your backyard. And they both work for you. Why don't you know what happened?"

A moment of intense silence preceded Mathias's muttered response. "It was something to do with a swimming pool."

Randolph eased back down in his chair and waited for Mathias to tell his story. Mathias always did this when he was tense. No amount of pushing would make him speed up the telling of his tale. "What happened with the pool?"

Mathias explained the mix-up Jake had made with Eleanor and Megan.

Randolph chuckled. "So Eleanor's female vanity took a beating when Jake didn't recognize her."

"And Jake's male ego took a beating when he found out it was Eleanor in the pool and not Megan," Mat finished for him.

"That's a good sign. It seems to me things are moving along according to plan."

"Well, you must be seeing things I'm not seeing."

Randolph's secretary came in and beckoned him. "Stop worrying, Mat. Things are coming along fine. I've got to go."

Carl stood on his toes and let the basketball fly out of his hands. Swoosh! "That's the game, man," he said, grinning. "I told you I was good."

Jake dropped down on the pavement, grabbed the blue towel next to him, and wiped the sweat from his face. "You're not that good. I'm out of it today."

Carl sat next to him, leaned back on his elbows, and stretched out his long legs. "Excuses, excuses."

"You'd better watch it. It's only a game."

"I bet you'd be singing a different tune if you'd won instead of me."

Jake shook his head. "Man, if I had on those red polka dot shorts, I don't think I'd be saying much of anything. Win or lose. Where'd you get those things anyway?"

"I don't really remember," Carl said, looking down at the his dotted shorts before looking over at the regulation New York Knicks shorts Jake wore. "Not everybody has designer sportswear."

"Don't even start. I've had enough arguing for one day."

Carl chuckled, then reached behind Jake for the water bottle. "Eleanor and Megan got you down."

Jake snorted, shaking his head. "Those two women are crazy. I didn't come to Lamar to get mixed up with crazy women."

Carl took another sip from the straw in the water bottle. "Why did you come to Lamar, Jake?"

Jake shot him a quick glance. "You know why."

"I know what you've said, but I have a feeling it's more than that."

Jake thought about playing off Carl's question, then decided against it. "Have you ever felt the need to prove yourself?"

Carl nodded. "I was the class nerd. I felt the need every day and I still do."

"Well, I was never the nerd. I was Mr. Cool. No worries. No responsibilities." He stopped for a minute to gather his thoughts and was glad that Carl didn't interrupt those thoughts. "But that's not who I really was."

"So why did you act that way then? To get girls?"

Jake shook his head. "I wish it had been something as simple as that. No, my reasons were a bit deeper."

Again, Carl waited without questioning.

"It's almost like my father wanted me to be that. He seemed more comfortable with me in that role than me working with him."

"You were a kid, Jake. Your father probably wanted you to act like a kid."

Jake wished that were true. But it wasn't. He'd stopped being a kid a long time ago, but his father's attitude toward him hadn't changed. At least, it hadn't until this assignment in Lamar. Finally, his father had given him a job in Mason Publishing. And he was determined to present his father with a proposal for this merger that would make the older man question why he hadn't asked for Jake's help before.

Unfortunately, Jake had been in Lamar almost two weeks and he hadn't come up with a fresh angle on the deal. Not yet. But he knew if he kept digging, he'd find the angle he needed.

Carl punched him in the arm then stood up. "Come on, man. I think we both could use a cold beer."

"Strike!" the umpire called.

Jake grimaced. It didn't appear that his team was going to win today. His team. He'd been Carl's assistant coach for less than an hour and he already felt it was his team. He already had plans for the next practice. The Johnson kid needed to loosen his grip on the bat. The Woods boy should have been playing third base instead of center field. Yes, he had some ideas he was sure could improve this team.

"Enjoying yourself, man?" Carl asked, coming back into the dugout.

"Great, man. Look at that kid's swing. He needs some work. He's gripping the bat too tight."

Carl clapped him on the back. "Does that mean you're going to work with us while you're here?"

Jake nodded. He was glad he'd called Carl yesterday after the women had sent him running from the pool. Their quick game of one-on-one followed by a night of beer drinking had helped to ease his anger at Eleanor's trickery. He admitted trickery might be too strong a word, but he still insisted Eleanor should have told him she was the woman at the pool.

He allowed his glance to slide over to the first row of bleachers, where Eleanor stood talking to a member of the cheerleading squad. She looked great in her white denim shorts and pink T-shirt. Jake smiled when he thought about a baseball team with cheerleaders. He'd never heard of that before, but Carl had explained that the parents of the boys on the team had daughters who wanted to participate but who didn't want to play. Thus, the baseball cheerleading squad.

"She looks good, doesn't she?"

Jake didn't bother pretending he didn't know who Carl was talking about. "Very good." Good enough to eat, he thought to himself. He remembered then that this was the second time Carl had commented on Eleanor's looks. He'd assumed the two didn't really get along, but now he wondered. "You don't have a thing for Eleanor, do you?"

"Who, me? You must be kidding."

For some reason, Jake took exception to Carl's comment. "What's wrong with Eleanor?"

"There's nothing wrong with her if you want a woman who thinks she knows everything."

Jake laughed. Carl was right. Eleanor did think she knew

everything. He wondered how much of that was real and how much of it was a part of her professional persona. "What about Megan? Does she think she knows everything?"

Carl snorted. "No, Megan thinks she *is* everything."

Jake shook his head. It was as he had figured. Carl had it bad for Megan. He had it so bad he didn't even realize he had it. The poor sod. Megan was making his life miserable and he didn't even understand why. Well, Carl didn't have to worry about Jake making a move on Megan. No, his interests lay a little closer to home. He glanced over at Eleanor again. She might think she knew everything, but he knew a thing or two himself. It'd be fun figuring out who knew the most.

"Strike three. You're out," the umpire yelled. Pulling off his cap and mask, he said, "Game's over."

As the boys marched out of the dugout, Jake clapped them on the shoulders. "Good game, guys. We'll get 'em next time." He heard Carl saying similar words and reminding the boys about their next practice.

"I don't know who feels worse, me or them," Carl said after the last boy had filed out.

"Take my word for it," Jake said, gathering the last of the equipment from the dugout. "They feel worse."

Carl picked up the ball basket. "Maybe you're right. Hey, you played sports in college, didn't you?"

Jake nodded. "I ran track. Almost made the Olympic team."

"That's right and you majored in drama."

Jake stopped and looked at Carl. He didn't talk much about his rebellious Yale days. He'd majored in drama to irk his father. Jake had thought his father would force him to choose a major that would be useful in Mason Publishing. But it hadn't happened. Randolph had only encouraged his interests. And Jake had been too stubborn to change his major after that. "How'd you know?"

Carl was silent.

"How did you know?"

Carl shrugged as if it wasn't important. "I must have read it somewhere."

"Come on, man. There's more to it than that. I'm sure you didn't read it *somewhere*. How'd you know?"

More silence.

"You did a background check on me, didn't you?" Jake didn't wait for a response. "Whose idea, Mathias's or Eleanor's?" Jake knew the answer but he asked anyway.

"Eleanor's," Carl answered reluctantly.

"Damn!" Jake slapped his cap against his thigh. "I know it. What's on that woman's mind? What right does she have to go digging around in my background?"

"Hey, man," Carl said, placing a calming hand on Jake's shoulder. "It wasn't like that. Eleanor was worried about your plans for the paper. You don't know what this paper means to her."

Jake sat down on the bench. "Why don't you tell me?"

Carl dropped the ball basket and sat next to Jake. "Eleanor's mother and father bought the paper when Eleanor was a baby. The paper was a weekly then. Anyway, a black couple owning a newspaper in a small, predominantly white Southern town was a big thing at the time. They experienced some problems early on, though you wouldn't know it now. The people of Lamar have grown used to it and to them. The paper is her family legacy. Naturally, she has strong ties to it and she'll do anything to protect it."

"So why did Mathias agree to go into business with Mason Publishing?"

"That's the question Eleanor has been asking since she found out about the deal. That's why she asked for the background check on you. She was looking for anything that would help her understand her father's actions."

"And did she find anything?" When Carl hesitated, Jake added, "I'm not asking you to be disloyal. I'm trying to understand the real situation here."

"No, she didn't find anything. She still doesn't know why her father wants this deal."

"So she's not buying that he wants the money Mason Publishing has to offer?"

Carl stood up. "You'll have to ask her that. I've probably said too much as it is. Now let's get out of here."

Jake eased up from his seat and followed Carl out of the dugout. Eleanor and a pretty, dark-skinned little girl with a head full of braids were the only people left in the park.

"We're waiting for Kia's mother," Eleanor said when they asked why she was still there.

"How long will she be?" Jake asked solicitously.

"Oh, it shouldn't be long now. Don't worry about us. You two go on."

Jake looked at Carl. "You go on, man. I'll wait here with Eleanor and Kia."

"You don't have to do that," Eleanor protested. "I told you her mother'll be along any minute now."

Jake dropped down on the bench next to her. "Then I guess I won't have long to wait, now will I?" He smiled at the little girl. "Hi, Kia. Did you enjoy the game?"

The little girl, who couldn't have been more than seven, smiled a gap-tooth smile up at him and bowed her head up and down.

"Do you want to play baseball when you're older?"

She smiled but this time she shook her head.

"How about being a cheerleader?"

This time she bowed her head up and down vigorously.

"Can you do any cheers now?"

She looked up at Eleanor.

"You can talk to him. His name is Mr. Mason."

She looked back at Jake. "Miss Eleanor has been teaching me one, but I haven't learned it yet."

Eleanor tousled the little girl's braids. "You're getting better each time we practice. Before you know it, you'll be able to do all the cheers you want."

The little girl gave Eleanor a look of pure adoration and Jake's heart turned over. He was about to say something more when the little girl jumped up.

"Mommy, Mommy," she called in the direction of a late model, well-worn blue Ford Escort.

Eleanor stood and held the little girl's hand as the child's mother got out of her car and headed toward them. "Yes, it's your mommy."

"Thanks, Eleanor," the mother said, giving the little girl a hug. She was dressed in a brown plaid uniform so Jake assumed she was a waitress. "I'm sorry I'm late. I had a problem with the car."

Concern clouded Eleanor's eyes. "Nothing serious, I hope."

The woman shook her head, then glanced at Jake. Eleanor introduced him. "Winifred Carlisle meet Jake Mason. Jake's working at the paper for the summer."

"A summer job?" Winifred asked.

Jake smiled at her. "Something like that." He tugged at one of Kia's braids. "You have a great little girl here."

Some of the fatigue left Winifred's eyes as she smiled at her little girl. "The best. And I'd better get her home. You're probably tired, aren't you, punkin'."

"Can we get ice cream, Mommy?"

Winifred looked up at the adults. "I guess she's not that tired. But I'd better get her home. Thanks again, Eleanor. Nice meeting you, Mr. Mason."

"See you next week, Kia," Eleanor said, waving goodbye to the little girl.

"I didn't know you were a cheerleading instructor," Jake said as much to himself as to her. There were a lot of layers to Eleanor and he wanted to peel each one of them away.

Eleanor turned back to him. "I'm not. Kia's a little girl who needed a friend."

"And you're a big sister."

She didn't smile. "You make it sound as if I'm doing something extraordinary. I'm not."

"Just doing your part, huh?"

She did smile then. "Something like that. How about you? When did you become a coach?"

He shrugged. "I've always been involved in sports. But I guess you already know that."

She had the decency to blush, and to him, it made her look even cuter. "How would I know that?"

He tugged on her arm and she plopped down next to him. "Give it up, Eleanor. Carl told me about his investigation."

"He had no right to do that. He's my employee. I'll speak to him tomorrow."

"You'll do no such thing. We're partners now and Carl will not be called on the carpet for telling me something I need to know."

"We're not partners," she muttered.

Jake leaned closer. "What was that? I couldn't hear you?"

"I said, 'We're not partners.' Yet."

"And you don't want us to become partners, do you?"

"How'd you guess?"

"I'm not stupid. You've expressed your dislike from the first day we met, but I thought you were warming up to the idea of our business relationship. Was I wrong?"

Eleanor stood up. "I thought you said we would talk about this on Monday. Let's keep to that schedule. I have plans tonight, and if we get into this discussion, my evening will be ruined. Deal?"

Jake stood up, resolved to wait until Monday to have their talk. "Deal."

Eleanor nodded and proceeded to walk to her car. He followed her. "So what are you doing tonight?" he asked casually. He really wanted to ask *whom* she was going out with. He didn't think she was seeing anybody.

She stopped walking and glared at him. "Going out." She resumed walking.

Okay, he could take a hint. Especially when it was as subtle as a sledgehammer. "Megan going with you?"

"If you're interested in Megan's schedule, you should call her. I'm sure she gave you her number."

"What if it's not Megan's schedule I'm interested in?"

She stopped again when she reached her two-seater sports car. After taking a deep breath, she said, "Don't even think about it. I'm not interested. Definitely not interested." She pulled the keys out of the pocket of her shorts, opened the door, and slid into the driver's seat.

When she reached to close the door, Jake held it open. "You can't run from me, Eleanor."

She jerked on the door and he released it. "Watch me." She turned on the ignition, quickly put the car in gear, and backed out of the graveled parking lot, kicking up dust as she left.

Damn, Jake thought. There was nothing he liked better than a challenge. He knew pursuing Eleanor was a tricky move since he was there on business. Business with her. He also knew he was about to do something he'd regret. But he couldn't stop himself. Eleanor drew him the way bees drew honey.

Chapter 8

Jake looked up from his desk when Eleanor walked in the office Monday morning. "Good morning," he said with cheer.

Eleanor nodded. "Good morning."

He studied her dark suit, sensible shoes, and high-cut blouse but still wondered why he hadn't known the woman in the pool. Now that he knew who she was, it was obvious. When she removed her jacket and rose up on her toes to hang it on the coat stand, he noticed the way her blouse curved around her full breasts and the way her skirt clung to her generously rounded buttocks. It didn't take much effort to remember how the rest of her looked. The swimsuit she'd worn that day had left little to the imagination.

She turned around and glared at him. "Let's not forget this is a place of business."

He deliberately let his gaze wander teasingly from her trim ankles to the head that sported the usual bun. "And I've got nothing but business on my mind."

She opened her mouth to respond, but apparently changed her mind. She closed her mouth instead and went to her chair, dropping her morning papers on her desk.

Jake got up. "Want some coffee?"

She eyed him suspiciously, but handed him her cup. "Thanks."

"No problem," Jake said and left the office.

Eleanor slumped down in her chair. This was going to be harder than she'd imagined. Jake Mason did things to her. She had to be strong.

Jake returned to the office with her coffee. "Here you go."

When Eleanor took the cup, her fingers brushed against his and his gaze met hers. "Sorry," she mumbled, not knowing which was hotter, the coffee or his hand.

"No problem," he said, looming over her.

She turned around to her computer and pulled up the latest AP stories, hoping he'd take the hint and she wouldn't have to tell him to get away from her.

"What's new this morning?" he asked, leaning over her shoulder, so close she could smell his cologne.

She mumbled off the titles of the first few articles.

He pointed his finger to an article on redistricting. "Open that one."

She wanted to tell him to go to his own terminal and look at it; instead, she hit the space bar twice and the file opened.

"Those are some good quotes from your esteemed senators. Are you going to use them?"

She shook her head. "I'll let Carl decide. He's doing a story on local response to redistricting. If he wants to incorporate the quotes, we'll do that. If not, we'll run them as a separate story."

She breathed her relief when Jake picked up his cup and moved away from her.

"Are we still meeting after lunch?" he asked.

She'd forgotten about the meeting. "Sure."

He nodded and went back to his desk and to work. She watched him covertly while she pretended to go through her morning ritual of reading the papers. If only he—

"Eleanor," Maxine's voice on the intercom interrupted her thoughts, "they need you in composition. They're having a problem with the layout."

Eleanor went to composition. After solving the problem there, she spoke with Carl about his story, then one thing led to another, until the paper was ready and sent to the press. When she was done, she wanted more than anything to go home and take a cool dip in the pool. But she had that meeting with Jake.

"Lunch?"

She jerked her head away from her terminal and her thoughts back to the present. "What are you doing here?"

He grinned a wide mouth grin. "My office."

She rolled her eyes. "What are you doing back so soon? I thought you had an interview."

He flopped down in his chair. "I did. It didn't take long. The coach is an easy guy to talk to. How do you guys keep him in Lamar?"

She shook her head. "Really, Jake, you make it sound like he's in a cage. He's here because he wants to be."

"If you say so."

"It's hard for you to believe people actually enjoy living here, isn't it?"

"Not people. The coach. I'm sure he could get a position in a bigger town, a bigger school, more prestige."

"Bigger doesn't necessarily mean better. The man is living here because he likes living here."

"Are you here because you like living here, Eleanor?"

Memories of the night Jake had arrived in Lamar filled her mind. He'd shown his distaste for her decision to continue living at home then. "Yes, I'm here because I like it here."

"Maybe you're here because you're afraid to go anywhere else?" he murmured under his breath.

"What did you say?"

"Nothing."

"I heard you," she accused. "What do you have against small-town living, Jake? Have you ever considered that you're the one who's afraid? It's much easier to hide in a big city than it is in a small town."

Jake was still thinking about Eleanor's words when they met for their afternoon meeting. For some reason her accusation that he was hiding stuck with him. He wondered what signals she'd picked up to make her say that. When she entered the closet-size room they called a conference room, he had to force himself to discuss the scheduled topic when he really wanted to discuss her comments.

"Have you thought much about this merger?" he asked, once they were settled across the conference table from each other.

"I've done nothing but think about it since Dad mentioned the plans to me."

He lifted a brow in her direction. "I've got a feeling I'm going to have to listen to your little jabs all afternoon. So why don't you get it all off your chest before we get started?"

She leaned toward him. "Okay, let's do that."

He tossed his pen on the table. "Shoot."

Eleanor picked up his pen and pointed it at him. "Number one. My father and I have prided ourselves on running this paper with no interference. We do what we want, when we want—"

Jake lifted a finger. "Correction. You do what you want when you can get the money. I think that's why I'm here."

She shot him a warning glance. "We don't want to, will not, lose that autonomy."

She waited for him to interrupt again, but he only nodded.

She took a deep breath. "Number two. We're concerned that though Mason Publishing initially agrees with number one, somewhere down the road things will change."

"That's why we have contracts," Jake said, interrupting again.

She ignored that comment. "Number three. You and I have to be the voices of reason here. Our fathers' friendship is the basis for the business relationship and that makes it a risky proposition. I don't think either of them has really thought this through."

Jake nodded. "You might have a point there."

Her eyes registered her surprise. "You're actually agreeing with me?"

He leaned toward her. "You've gotten our roles confused. You've been the one with the hostility, not me."

"Touché."

"Have you talked to your attorney about your, ah, three points?"

"Of course. Now what's on your mind?"

He reached for his pen. "Number one," he said and she knew he wanted to grin. "Mason Publishing cannot afford for this newspaper to become a money pit."

"A money pit? What are you talking about?"

"You've mentioned before that the one positive for this whole deal is the dollars Mason Publishing brings to the table. Well, each expenditure must be justified. We can only spend money where we think we can earn it back."

"So, you're a bottom line kind of guy?"

"Aren't we all? You have an MBA. You know how businesses work."

"How did you know I had an MBA?"

"You aren't the only one with access to an investigating staff."

She was impressed. "Two for you."

He grinned. "Number two, which is really related to number one. This is a business deal, not a personal one. All decisions will be made on the basis of what's best for the business, all the businesses, of Mason Publishing."

She pointed her finger at him. "And that point conflicts with my points one and three. I cannot and will not abdicate control of the *Lamar Daily* to Mason Publishing. We must keep control. On that point, I'm inflexible."

"It's also a point on which I'm inflexible. Our fathers agreed on some basic tenets which I'm forced to uphold. Beyond that, you're going to have to trust us, Eleanor."

"Trust *you?*"

"Yes, trust us to make good decisions."

Eleanor wanted to dismiss Jake and end this meeting, but she couldn't. Her father wanted this deal and it was up to her to fight for the best terms possible. She had to compromise with Jake. She hoped she didn't live to regret it.

"What do you say? Will you trust me?"

Eleanor looked into his eyes and she understood he was asking about more than their business negotiation. "Let's take it day by day. If you show yourself to be trustworthy and if you work in good faith toward the paper, maybe then we can talk about trust."

Jake nodded, seeming to understand that was all he was going to get. "All right. Let's go through your points again in a little more detail. I'll have our accountants in New York run the numbers and we'll see where we are."

Jake stared at the calendar on his desk. Five weeks. He'd been in Lamar five weeks and he hadn't made much headway on his plan to impress the hell out of his father. All he'd done was get frustrated by a stern miss who was a knockout in a white swimsuit.

Maybe it was because she was the first woman he'd seen in Lamar, Jake reasoned. Maybe that was why she stayed on his mind all the time.

Jake shook his head. There was no use lying to himself. The woman at the pool had stayed on his mind true enough, but Eleanor had become an obsession. And when he'd asked her out, she'd had the nerve to turn him down as if he were some horny schoolboy.

But it was her supposed disinterest over the last week that irked him most. He'd never been treated with disinterest by a woman before.

So he had a plan to turn Eleanor's disinterest into interest. Although it wasn't an entirely ethical plan, it was close enough to one that he could execute it without too much guilt.

When he saw Eleanor glide down the hallway toward their office, he garnered enough courage to execute the first step of his plan.

"How's it going?" she asked, entering the office.

"I need to talk to you about something, Eleanor." He shut their office door and closed the blinds on the glass window facing the newsroom.

"Is something wrong?" she asked, anxiety filling her words.

"In a way," he said in a whisper.

"Speak up, Jake."

He moved closer to the desk, but didn't raise his voice. "It's about Carl and Megan. I think they need our help."

"Carl and Megan? What are you talking about?"

His look said he thought she was dense. "You do know he's in love with her, don't you?"

"In love? Carl's in love with Megan?"

Jake nodded his head. "I know when a man's in love."

She smirked. "I bet you do."

"Look, this isn't about me. It's about Megan and Carl. I like them both and I hate seeing them so miserable."

Megan didn't seem to be miserable. She had gone out with two different men over the weekend. "What do you think we can do about this anyway?"

"Matchmake," he said, as if he'd originated the idea. "You and I could be matchmakers."

"No way." She shook her head. There was no way she was going to get mixed up in Megan's love life. Sure she thought there was more to Megan and Carl than Megan would admit. But Eleanor knew her friend well enough to know she wouldn't appreciate any interference.

"I thought you were Megan's friend."

"I am her friend. Her best friend. That's why I'm not getting involved in any matchmaking scheme you may have in your mind." She lifted a brow. "If you're smart, you'll stay out of it."

He collapsed in his chair. "I can't just do nothing. Carl is driving me crazy complaining about Megan. If you won't do it for him, do it for me."

She had to smile. "It can't be that bad."

"It's worse than that. That man has it so bad he doesn't know if he's coming or going." Jake knew he was pouring it on a little thick but he couldn't stop himself. "Can't you see it?"

She nodded slowly. "They argue too much for there not to be something there."

"Yes, it's either love or hate. And I don't think it's hate."

"Well," Eleanor hesitated. "Neither do I."

"So you'll work with me?" Jake pressed.

"I'll think about it."

Jake grinned as if he'd won the lottery. "We can't discuss this too much at work." He motioned toward the door and the glass window. "The staff is probably wondering what we're doing in here now. Why don't we get together over dinner and discuss it? How about tonight?"

Chapter 9

Mel's Diner. The name on the revolving sign in front of the faded white diner was vaguely familiar to Jake. He rushed around to the passenger door of his leased sports sedan in time to close the door behind Eleanor.

"I can do some things for myself," she said to his unasked question.

"So I see." He put his hand to her back and ushered her through the screened door. He thought he'd stepped back in time when he saw the three white men in beige painter's outfits seated on the faded blue plastic seats of the metal bar stools. His gaze roamed to the score of people seated in the matching booths. It occurred to him that he and Eleanor were the only black faces in the place.

"You come here often?" he asked with obvious sarcasm.

Ellen gave a light chuckle. "All the time."

"Do we take a seat or wait to be seated?"

"We wait. Somebody will take care of us soon."

Jake noticed the two women in short, pink, apron-covered waitress uniforms busily serving the already seated customers. One was a kooky-looking brunette with beady eyes. The other was a nondescript redhead with a welcoming smile.

"Hi there, handsome. Nice buns."

Jake looked to his left and saw a bleached blonde with a beehive hairdo and a mouth full of chewing gum giving him the once-over.

"Where'd you find this one?" the gum-chewing beehive asked Eleanor.

"This is Jake. He's working with us down at the paper. I thought you would have heard by now."

She looked Jake over again and he actually felt as if she was undressing him with her eyes. "Well, now, maybe I did hear something."

Eleanor looked up at Jake and chuckled at the expression on his face. "You'd better leave him alone, Flo. I don't think he can take it."

Flo continued to smack on that gum. "I kinda think Jake, here, could handle anything. And I get the feeling he's handled a lot."

Eleanor laughed again. "Show us to a booth before Jake passes out."

As Jake followed Eleanor and Flo to a booth in the middle of the restaurant, he couldn't help but notice the exaggerated movement of Flo's hips.

"Here you are, folks," she said, handing them each a laminated menu. "Just holler when you're ready to order."

Jake watched Flo's switch as she walked away from them and to another table.

"See something you like?" Eleanor asked.

Jake turned to her and saw the humor in her eyes. "She's a piece of work."

Eleanor laughed, then slipped out of her navy jacket and placed it on the seat next to her. "That's an understatement. Flo's a landmark around here."

"Mel's Diner. Flo. Somebody in this town got a TV complex or something?"

Eleanor nodded. "I wondered if you'd even notice. Didn't know if the TV show *Alice* went over well with you Northerners."

"It didn't. At least, not at my house."

She ignored the comment. "Mel McKissic was a big fan of the show. When it was canceled he begged, borrowed, and some say stole to get the money to open this place. When it opened, Flo was here. Nobody knows where he found her."

"You're kidding."

She shook her head. "It was a big thing last year when Mel and Flo got married. It took up the entire page of the Thursday Living section."

"That much space, huh?" He chuckled.

Eleanor nodded. "That kind of story would have run in the Sunday edition, if we did a Sunday edition."

Jake raised a hand. "This meal is to discuss Carl and Megan, not the newspaper. Let's save that for the office."

"Okay, what do you want to eat?"

Jake picked up his menu. "What do you suggest?"

"The meatloaf is the best."

Jake scanned the items on the menu. Liver and onions, chicken steak, chicken gizzards. "I think I'll take the meatloaf."

Eleanor picked up his menu and hers and waved them in the air. Flo was at the table in a matter of seconds. She took their orders and left.

"Waving the menus above your head is a unique way of getting the waitress's attention," he commented.

"You should tell Flo that. It was her idea. She said people waving their hands confused her since people in Lamar were waving all the time. She didn't know if they were waving for her to come over or if they were waving at one of their friends across the room."

"I'm getting scared," he said.

Her eyes widened. "Why?"

"That explanation actually made sense."

Eleanor laughed and her face brightened and softened. He'd love to see her like that when she sported that white swimsuit. Then he'd want to see that sparkle in her eyes dim with passion.

"Do you really come here often?" he asked to keep his thoughts away from dangerous subjects.

"Not often. Just when I need to get away and think."

"So why'd you bring me here?"

She lifted her shoulders slightly. "It's private, in a way, and we can discuss Megan and Carl without worrying about the wrong people overhearing," she said, wondering if there was more to it than that but not yet ready to think about it.

He seemed to accept that answer, but his eyes searched hers as if trying to find out more. He clasped his hands and leaned forward. "Now what are we going to do about Carl and Megan?"

Eleanor shifted back on her bench seat. Was it her or was Jake invading her space again? "This dinner was your idea. I thought you were the one with the plan."

Jake relaxed and sat back. "I can't believe you don't have one. How have you lived with those two this long?"

Eleanor lifted a hand to her hair, brushing it lightly. It was time to take the bun down; it was starting to itch.

"Why don't you take it down?" Jake said as if he'd heard her thoughts. And unbutton a few buttons on that blouse while you're at it, he added to himself.

Eleanor looked at him, not sure if she should take his suggestion, then she smiled and got her purse. "I'll be back in a minute."

Eleanor felt Jake's eyes on her as she made her way to the women's room, and she liked the feeling. She pushed open the door then walked to the mirror above the first sink.

She placed her purse on the metal ledge above the sink and took the pins out of her hair. After placing the pins in her purse and taking out her brush, she shook her head, causing her mass of dark brown hair to fall about her shoulders.

Eyeing herself in the mirror, she toyed with the top button on her blouse. "What the hell," she said and undid first the top button, then the second. "That should keep Mr. Mason on his toes."

She brushed a few unruly strands in place, then put her brush back in her purse and left the rest room. Flo was seated at their booth when she got back and Jake was laughing.

Flo looked up at Eleanor. "Back already? Jake and me were getting acquainted some." Flo stood up and Eleanor slid back in the booth. "Loosening up, are you, honey?" Before Eleanor could answer, Flo went on. "Well, I can see how this man could make you unbutton your blouse. He'll, he'd make me do a little more than loosen a few buttons. And he just might be the one man, other than Mel, that is, to see me without this beehive."

"Mel's a lucky man," Jake said, taking Flo's hand in his larger one. "If I thought I had a chance, I'd give him a run for his woman."

"Go on with you," Flo said, pleased with Jake's comment. Eleanor didn't miss the slight squeeze she gave his hand before she released it.

Unless Eleanor's eyes were deceiving her, Flo's strut had gotten worse. She rolled her eyes. "What did you do to her?"

Jake poured each of them a glass of iced tea from the pitcher Flo had brought. "I didn't do anything to her. She's a nice woman. We were having a little fun. You do know about that, don't you?"

"About what? You making a pass at everything in a skirt?"

"No, having fun. That is a concept that you understand, isn't it?"

"What do you think?" Eleanor watched his gaze travel from her hair to the top of her breasts. It took all her strength to keep from fastening one of the buttons on the bone collarless blouse she'd worn with her navy suit.

"I think you're gorgeous."

She cleared her throat. It got so stuffy in the diner she wanted to fan herself, but she wouldn't give Jake the satisfaction of knowing how much he affected her.

Flo returned with their meals and saved her from having to respond to his comment.

"About Megan and Carl," she said once she'd recovered her composure. "What do you think we should do?"

"We need to keep putting them together. They don't see each other enough."

"But when they do, they argue and take shots at each other the entire time. Remember the day Megan came to the paper?"

Jake laughed. "Of course I remember. They're a real fire and ice couple."

"More like oil and vinegar."

"You aren't fooled by their show, are you? Those two love each other."

Eleanor took a pat of butter and smeared it across her dinner roll. "And you think if we put them together enough, they'll finally admit their feelings."

Jake nodded. "It's takes a lot of energy to fight against their emotions the way they do. If nothing else, they're going to tire themselves out. Then they'll have to face their feelings."

There was some merit to Jake's idea, but there was also a major hole. "But who's going to referee in the meantime?"

"Us."

"I kinda thought that's where you were going."

"Cheer up. This could be fun. They may even make us god-parents."

"You like kids a lot, don't you?" she asked, thinking about him helping Carl with the Little League team.

He nodded. "Part of being an only child, I guess."

It was the same for her. As a child she'd often wished for a brother or sister and she'd always loved babies. Children were still dear to her, which was one of the reasons she spent time with little girls like Kia.

"You know about that, don't you?" he asked when she didn't say anything. "We do have something in common."

Eleanor knew he was talking about their mothers and having lost them when they were young. "I think our mothers, even more than their shared childhoods, is the bond between our fathers."

Jake nodded. "My father thinks a lot of Mathias. I know they talk on the phone a lot and they see each other every year at the damn conference."

"Yeah, I remember the first year Dad brought home a photo of you."

Jake grinned. "You do?"

She arched a brow. "I bet you don't remember the first one your dad brought home of me."

"Oh, yes I do. I think that's who I still expected you to be. A little girl."

"I'm not that, am I?"

He grinned. "Not in the ways that count."

Heaven help her, she blushed. "You haven't changed much over the years."

"Now that has to be an insult."

"No. I was about eleven at the time. You must have been about fifteen. And I thought you were the handsomest boy I'd ever seen, my own personal knight in shining armor."

"Girlish infatuation," he said in earnest. "What do you think of me now that you're a woman of the world?"

Eleanor smirked. "Now, I think you're fishing for compliments."

He laughed and she felt tremors along her spine. "You can't blame a guy for trying."

She sobered. "No, I guess I can't."

They ate in companionable silence. After they had placed their dessert order, Jake asked, "Do you miss her much?"

She knew he was talking about her mother. "All the time. You?"

"Not all the time. But a lot."

They were silent again and in that silence a bond formed between them. They both hoped it would last.

Eleanor stepped out of the shower, grabbed a towel, and ran to answer the ringing phone.

"Where have you been? I've been calling you all night."

She put Megan on the speakerphone and dried herself with the towel. "Sorry about that."

"Take me off that speakerphone. You know I hate it."

Eleanor tied the towel around her chest, clicked the speaker button, and picked up the receiver. "Satisfied?"

"Now that's more like it," Megan continued. "Where were you?"

Eleanor had hoped to keep her meeting with Jake a secret, but now she realized that was merely wishful thinking. "I had a dinner meeting."

"No, you didn't. You went out with Jake, didn't you?"

Damn. "We had a dinner meeting."

"You can't fool me. If it had been a simple dinner meeting, you would've told me. There was more to it than that."

The accusation in Megan's voice made Eleanor wonder why she'd agreed to help with Jake's plan. "How are plans coming for Jake's welcome party?" Though she'd back-peddled on this party from day one, she knew it was the only topic Megan would warm to quickly.

"I know you're changing the subject, Eleanor, but fortunately, it's a subject I want to talk about. Everything is on for this Saturday."

"Has everyone been invited?" Eleanor asked, realizing that by the time of the party Jake's visit to Lamar would be half over.

"Yes, yes."

"Did you invite Carl?"

"Sure," Megan answered, a little too quickly.

"Megan—"

"Do we have to invite him?"

"You know we have to invite him. He's practically Jake's best friend in this town."

"Okay, okay. I'll call him myself."

"And be nice."

"I'm always nice."

"To most people, but not to Carl. Why is that, Megan?"

"All right, if you talk to me about Carl, I get to talk to you about Jake."

Eleanor was silent. She had the sneaking suspicion Jake had set her up. "I told you nothing's going on."

"Yeah, right."

Carl picked up the baseball bats and placed them in the rack stand. "So you went out with Eleanor last night. How was it?"

Jake leaned back on the bench. The little guys had all gone home from practice and he and Carl were cleaning up. Well, Carl was cleaning up while he watched. "It was a date."

Carl sat next to him. "I thought you were interested in Megan."

Jake shot him a sideways glance. "Would it bother you if I was?"

"Why should it bother me?"

"I don't know. Maybe you're interested in Megan."

Carl shook his head. "Never. Megan is nothing but a tease. Always has been. Always will be."

"I don't think so, Carl. She's a nice woman who likes to have fun. What's wrong with that?"

"She's not *my* kind of woman," Carl said with finality.

Jake decided to take another tack. "What do you think about Eleanor?"

Carl snorted. "In her way, she's as bad as Megan. You're the first man that's come along to shake her up a little." Carl punched Jake in the shoulder. "Thanks, man. It's good to see old Eleanor rattled."

Carl's words encouraged Jake, though he wasn't sure how accurate they were. "I don't know about all that."

"Take my word for it. I've never seen Eleanor so taken off balance by a guy. Where Megan's MO is to come on to everything in pants, Eleanor's is to push 'em away before they get too close." Carl laughed.

"What's so funny?"

"I used to think Eleanor was bossy by nature. Heaven knows, she bossed me around in those Before Megan days. But I figured out her bossiness is a tool she uses to keep people at a distance. The only people to get close are Megan and her father. Even knowing that, she still gets on my nerves."

Jake smiled. "Don't let 'em get to you so much, Carl. I think they like it. I bet Megan likes to set you off. Maybe if you pretended she didn't bother you or if you came on to her the way she comes on to men, she wouldn't bother you so much."

Carl looked at Jake and shook his head. "I guess I didn't tell you everything. Megan flirts with everybody. But me. Obviously, I'm not worth her energy."

"That's my point. Either you show her it doesn't matter or you give her the treatment she gives all the other men."

Carl seemed to think about Jake's suggestion. "And what would that get me?"

"You say you get satisfaction from seeing the way I keep Eleanor off kilter. Think how much satisfaction you'd get from seeing Megan off kilter."

Carl got up and grabbed the ball basket. "I'll think about it. Let's go."

Chapter 10

Jake admired Eleanor's firm hips and legs as she turned over on her back. It was time to execute step two of his plan.

"You've got to be kidding."

Jake handed her a towel. "No, we have to do this."

Eleanor took the towel and wrapped it around her chest. "We have to pretend to be a couple to help Carl and Megan? I don't think so, Jake. This sounds like some cheap trick on your part."

Jake threw up his hands. "If that's the way you feel about it, we won't do it. But I'm telling you, when Carl sees my success with you, it'll encourage him with Megan."

Eleanor eyed Jake suspiciously. "Explain to me again how this is going to help Megan and Carl."

"Well, we can go out and invite them to go with us."

"We could do that without being an item."

Jake shook his head. "I don't think so. Why would we be together so much?" He cleared his throat. "My reputation leads Carl to believe I'd have a romantic relationship with a woman, not a platonic one."

"Your reputation?" Eleanor sighed. "Carl's probably right."

"And the way I figure it, if I'm not interested in somebody, your friend Megan is going to be putting the moves on me so hard she and Carl won't have time to focus on each other."

Eleanor knew he was right about that. Megan had already promised to take her sights off Jake if Eleanor was interested. "So, what's our first step?"

Jake grinned. "You're going to go along with it?"

She shrugged, knowing he had the upper hand. "What choice do I have?"

"That's my girl. I figure our first event will be this 'Welcome to Lamar' party that you and Megan are planning. You can be my date."

She held up her hand. "Wait a minute. Everybody doesn't have to know about this ruse. Why can't we keep it to Megan and Carl?"

Jake sat down on the chaise next to her. "You yourself said there are no secrets in Lamar. Plus, if everybody knows, we have more legitimacy."

"Yes, and more people nosing in our business. You don't know about small-town romances, Jake. They become the fodder for local gossip."

"Look at it this way. We may not be able to control what people say, but we can definitely control what's printed in the paper."

Eleanor totally missed his attempt at humor. "What about my father? What's he going to think? Maybe we should tell him."

Jake hadn't thought about the fathers. He certainly didn't want them getting any ideas. "Yes, that's a good idea. Why don't we tell Mathias tonight? How do you think he'll respond?"

"He'll think it's a stupid idea, but he'll go along with it because he likes Megan and Carl."

Jake rubbed his hands together. "Well, then, it seems we have it all planned. Let's go for another dip." Jake dropped his towel and dived into the pool.

Eleanor watched as he swam the length of the pool in record time. Slowly, she dropped her towel, walked to the edge of the pool, and dived in. Why did she feel as though she'd dived into the biggest mess of her life?

"Hell, Mat, they aren't supposed to be matchmaking. They're supposed to be falling in love."

Mathias leaned back in his chair. Their scheme seemed to be falling down around their heads every day. "Don't tell me, I know. Now what are we going to do?"

"I don't know, but leaving them to their own devices is not working. We have to do something."

"We've already done something, Randy. We're the ones who set this whole thing up. Maybe we've done enough."

"And maybe we haven't. I have an idea."

Mathias rubbed his head. "Oh, no, not another one."

"Come on, Mat. Work with me on this. I'm hosting a gala next Friday and I think Jake and Eleanor need to attend."

"And how, pray tell, are we going to convince them to do that?"

"Tell them I'm interested in a progress report on their work on the merger. That should do it."

"Won't it seem strange that you're inviting Eleanor?"

"No, I don't think so. Tell her it's a chance for her to meet me and some of the players in the New York office. If she's as skeptical about this venture as she was in the beginning, she'll jump at the chance."

Mathias knew that part was right. Eleanor would consider it her duty to attend and to check out Randolph and his business. "Maybe I'll come along, too."

"Not this time, Mat. Make some excuse for not coming. Your Eleanor needs to do this one alone. Maybe being away from you and her familiar surroundings will push her and Jake closer."

"I'm not too sure about that," Mat said slowly. "Eleanor has this friend in New York. Some man who's been in touch with her over the years. He even came to Lamar one time."

"Damn. It could be a problem if she's with anther man instead of Jake."

"Hey, what if you invited Carl and Megan along on this trip? Since Jake and Eleanor are pretending to be a couple for their sakes, they can't very well spend all their time with other people."

"You're a genius, Mat. That should do it."

"So what excuse will you use to get Megan and Carl to make the trip? Megan's not exactly involved in the newspaper business."

"Not me, Mat, you. You know both of them. Think of something. I'll talk to you later."

* * *

"Just pretend you're in Victoria's Secret," Megan said, tugging on Eleanor's arm to get her into Modern Woman, the trendy clothes shop for professional women.

Eleanor's pulse raced as she entered the upscale shop. The mannequins in the conservative yet modern miniskirted suits practically called out to her. It wasn't that she didn't like this kind of clothing. She did, but didn't think it was right for the office. She needed to project a strong, business image at work, and she didn't think a miniskirt provided that image.

Megan approached a mannequin dressed in a deep burgundy linen-silk blend suit near the front of the shop. "Now this is you."

Eleanor reluctantly touched the fabric and closed her eyes. It felt so good to touch, sensual almost.

"See, I knew you would like it," Megan said. "This *is* you."

Eleanor opened her eyes, her hand still touching the fabric. "The fabric feels good, but I'm not sure about the skirt."

Megan walked over to a rack and flipped through the suits. "Here's one in your size. Try it on."

"I don't know, Megan," Eleanor said, taking the suit in her hand. "I can't wear this to work."

"Sure you can," Megan said, leading the way to the dressing room. "Women are doing it every day. Come on, Eleanor, this is the nineties. Women don't have to dress like men or like schoolmarms to show their authority."

Eleanor slipped into the dressing room and quickly removed her tan slacks but kept on her matching silk shirt.

"While you're trying that on, I'll look around for some other things you might like. Keep that on until I get back though," Megan warned from outside the dressing room door. "I want to see you in it."

Eleanor stepped into the skirt first, pulling it up over her silk panties, then positioning it at her waist. After she'd zipped and fastened the button, she evaluated herself in the mirror. She admitted her legs looked good in the short skirt, but when she thought about Maxine and the others in the office, she began to tug on it to see if it would go farther down her thighs. No such luck.

Megan knocked on the door as she slipped on the jacket. "Let me see," she said.

Eleanor quickly fastened the double-breasted jacket and twisted the lock on the door. "Come on in."

"Wow," Megan said, her hands full of clothes. "You look great. We should have done this a long time ago."

Eleanor tugged on the skirt again. "It looks good, but the skirt is way too short to wear to work."

Megan hung the clothes on the hook next to the mirror, then swatted Eleanor's hands. "Leave the skirt alone. That's the way it's supposed to fit. And nobody's going to say anything except to ask why it took you so long to stop dressing like an old woman."

Eleanor rolled her eyes. With friends like Megan, a girl didn't need any enemies. She pointed to the clothes Megan had brought in. "I suppose you want me to try on all of those?"

Megan grinned. "This is only the beginning. We have all day."

"Aggg…" Eleanor groaned, then reached for the white sheath that dipped low in front and back. "And where will I wear this?" she asked. "Surely you don't think I can wear it to work?"

"No, silly," Megan said, easing out of the dressing room. "You can wear it to Jake's welcome party. I can't wait to see his face when he sees you in it. You'll knock him dead."

Eleanor put the sheath back on the hook while she removed the suit, ignoring the frisson of pleasure that teased her belly at the thought of Jake's response to her in the sexy white dress.

She studied the suit after she'd put it back on its hangers. Yes, she'd take it. Maybe she'd wear it on their trip to New York.

That settled, she turned her attention to the white sheath and she couldn't stop the grin that spread across her face. She couldn't wait for Jake to see her in it.

Jake's arm resting on her waist distracted her. She'd been so anxious to see his reaction to her new outfit that she hadn't considered the effect Jake in a casual black suit and black shirt would have on her. "Nobody's looking," she whispered, glad for an excuse to put some distance between them. "You can drop your hand now."

"But it feels so good." He grinned down at her, squeezed the small of her back, then dropped his hand.

She stepped away from him, resisting the urge to tug on the short, form-fitting white sheath Megan had convinced her to buy. The man had a way of making her feel naked, which was odd since she was a woman who normally reveled in her nudity. "How are you enjoying your party?"

His eyes caressed her body. "I couldn't have asked for anything more."

She felt her skin warm to his words. Though she was sure this was a practiced assault, it didn't lessen its effect. "I'm sure my father will be glad to know you're having such a great time." Eleanor's eyes roamed the room and found her father trapped in discussion with Mel and Flo. A short space from him, Ms. Delaney and Maxine huddled together.

"How about you? Are you glad I'm having a good time?"

"So, so," she said, distracted by the whispered argument that seemed to have developed between Maxine and Ms. Delaney. She wondered what that was about.

"You sure know how to crush a guy's ego."

She placed her hand on his arm. "That's not it. It's just that I don't think Carl and Megan are paying us any attention." She inclined her head in the direction of the dance floor where Megan, in a fire-engine-red cocktail dress, danced with Winifred's brother, Wesley. "Megan's having a great time. Without Carl."

Jake moved a step closer to her. "It sure seems that way. Where's Carl?"

Eleanor pointed to a corner near the punch bowl where Carl, in what could best be described as a basic black Sunday-go-to-meeting suit, stood conversing with Mrs. Thompson and Tempest Tanner. "I don't think he cares about us or Megan."

Jake massaged her bare shoulder, his hand burning the skin he touched. "Don't worry so. I'm sure they're very aware of each other. Why don't we hit the dance floor? Maybe that'll get their attention."

She gave him a skeptical look, but allowed him to lead her to the dance floor Megan had made out of the Sanders living room. Megan had outdone herself with this party. The small tables surrounding the dance floor and the serving tables aligning the walls made the room seem almost like a nightclub. The banner proclaiming WELCOME TO LAMAR, JAKE across the mantel made it clear who the star of this event was.

As her luck would have it, a slow tune played as soon as they hit the dance floor. She looked up at Jake. "Did you plan this?"

He pulled her into his arms. "I'm lucky."

Eleanor didn't bother to comment. She rested her head on his chest and enjoyed the feel of his body against hers.

"You're the softest woman," he murmured against her hair as his arms caressed down her back.

She smiled against his shirt and tightened her hold on his waist. "You don't feel so bad yourself."

"Hey, are you flirting with me?"

She heard the grin in his voice. "If you have to ask, I must not be doing a good job of it."

"Well, well, well."

"Don't get carried away," she warned, responding to the smugness in his voice. "This is an act for Carl and Megan, remember?"

"Now that wasn't nice. You get my hopes up. Then you dash them. You could break my heart."

Eleanor didn't think it would be his heart that would break. More than likely it would be hers. "I bet you've broken a lot of hearts."

"Not me," he said in earnest. "I don't make promises I can't keep."

"Somehow I don't quite believe there aren't some hearts out there with your knife in them."

He squeezed her to him. "You'd be wrong. And I must be losing my touch. You're standing here in my arms in this romantic atmosphere and you're talking about other women in my life. I know I'm losing my touch."

She chuckled. "I don't think you have anything to worry about in that department."

"Does that mean I'm getting to you?"

She considered avoiding his question, but decided against it. "It means you could get to me if I let you."

"And why won't you let me?"

"Because I don't want my heart broken."

He tilted her chin up and brushed her hair back so he could see her face clearly. "I wouldn't break your heart, Eleanor."

The sincere words made her knees weak. His gaze rested on her lips and she knew he was thinking about kissing her. Heaven help her, she was thinking about kissing him. Instead, she cleared her throat and lowered her head back to his chest.

When the dance was over, he took her hand in his and led her over to where Carl still stood talking to Mrs. Thompson.

"You look so lovely tonight, dear," Mrs. Thompson said, reaching for Eleanor's hand. "You should wear your hair down more often."

Eleanor accepted the compliment easily. Almost all of the guests had complimented her new look.

"I'm glad to see at least one of my most favorite young people is finding romance," the older woman continued. "Carl, here, has spent the entire evening talking to me when he should be finding himself a young lady."

Carl groaned.

"Maybe he's looking for a woman with a bit more experience, Mrs. Thompson," Jake suggested with a masculine twinkle in his brown eyes.

"Oh, go on, Jake," Mrs. Thompson said, then slapped his hand coyly. "I was telling Carl there are quite a few available young women here in Lamar."

"I can find my own women, Mrs. Thompson," Carl said with a tinge of annoyance.

"Well, you don't seem to be doing a good job of it, young man. How many of these young women have you talked with tonight?"

"That doesn't—"

"Yes, it does, young man. It tells me you need my help. Now, I'm going to mingle around here and find a young woman for you. You wait and see."

"But Mrs. Thompson—"

She patted his cheek. "You can thank me later, son. Now let me get out here and find you a young woman."

Eleanor and Jake laughed at Carl's chagrined expression.

"You'd better follow my lead and find your own woman, man," Jake said, pulling Eleanor closer to him.

Carl placed his glass on the lace-covered refreshment table. "I've had it. I'm out of here."

"Carl," Eleanor called after him, but he didn't stop. He headed straight for the door, then practically ran out of it.

"I thought he'd never leave," Megan said from behind them.

Eleanor turned around. "Where'd you come from? I thought you were dancing."

"I was, but the guy I was dancing with had two left feet and fifty arms." She lifted her hands and examined her nails. "Not exactly my type."

Eleanor leaned into Jake. "Sometimes what we're looking for is right under our noses."

"Well," Megan said, "the only thing under my nose right now is my top lip. Believe me, if there was another one like Jake around, I'd know it."

Eleanor looked up at Jake. "I think that's a compliment."

"Thanks, madam." Jake gave an exaggerated bow.

Megan reached for Jake's hand. "Mind if I borrow your man here for a whirl around the dance floor?" she asked Eleanor.

Eleanor slipped from under Jake's other arm. "Of course not."

Jake planted a quick peck on her lips and whispered, "Don't be jealous now. You're the only one for me."

Eleanor touched her hand to the place he had kissed and wished she was the only one for him.

Jake slapped his hand on the steering wheel. "Shut up! Both of you, shut the hell up!"

"Jake…" Eleanor said, placing her hand on his arm to calm him.

Jake shook her hand off. "I've had enough of them, Eleanor. They're worse than kids." He wondered why he'd been crazy enough to think Megan and Carl loved each other. In the week since the welcome party, they'd almost driven him insane with their constant bickering. Now, this drive to Atlanta was turning into a nightmare.

"I don't know why you invited her on this trip in the first place," Carl sneered. "What does she know about newspapers anyway? What does she know about anything?"

"Do what Jake said and shut up, Carl," Megan shouted. "Mr. Mason invited me because I'm Eleanor's best friend. And if you don't like it, you can go back to Lamar. We'll have a much better time if you don't come."

Eleanor turned around in her seat and pointed at them. "Jake is about ready to pull this car over and throw you both out. Now get yourselves together."

Megan crossed her arms and moved closer to the door—any closer and she would have to get out. "It's his fault."

Carl shot Megan an accusing stare. "You need to grow up, Megan. Look at yourself, pouting like a child."

"You don't—" Megan was about to get wound up again.

"If you two say one more cross word to each other," Jake said through tight lips, "I'm going to stop at the next exit and put you out. You got that?"

"Yeah."

"Yes."

Eleanor turned back around in her seat. "Do you think that was necessary?"

Jake glanced at her. "It made them shut up, didn't it?"

"But you don't mean it, do you?" Eleanor whispered.

"Like hell I don't," Jake answered, loud enough for Megan and Carl to hear. "One more set of cross words from them and they won't be going to New York. At least, not with us."

This time Eleanor believed him. She turned once more to look at Megan and Carl. They hugged their respective doors, staring out the windows with smirks on their faces. They were about an hour from the Atlanta airport and Eleanor wasn't sure they were going to make it.

"What are they doing?" Jake whispered.

Eleanor turned back around in her seat. "I think it's called a Mexican standoff."

Jake chortled. "Enough about the dueling brats. Are you excited about this trip?"

If Eleanor could talk freely, she'd tell Jake she was disappointed Carl and Megan had come along. Their presence meant she and Jake had to continue their roles as budding lovers and that meant Eleanor couldn't spend time with her old college friend, Franklin. "I'd be more excited if we didn't have to baby-sit."

Jake grimaced. "I know the feeling." He'd been excited about having Eleanor to himself in New York. But when he'd found out she intended to spend all her time with Franklin, he'd been disappointed. Learning Carl and Megan were coming had restored his excitement. But in spite of what their presence would mean in New York, he was dead serious about leaving them if they acted up again.

Eleanor touched his arm. She'd started to do that a lot lately. She was really getting into her role. "You must be happy to get back to your old stomping ground."

"I am. I'm also looking forward to showing you the sights. I'll love seeing the city through your eyes."

That warm feeling that was becoming her constant companion filled Eleanor's stomach. "I've been to New York before."

"Not with me. I want you to see *my* New York."

They were both silent for a while, enjoying each other's company. Eleanor reveled in the masculine approval Jake had given her new burgundy miniskirt suit. Though she had to fight the urge to tug on the skirt, she was glad she'd given in to Megan's urgings and updated her wardrobe.

"You've traveled a lot, haven't you?" Eleanor asked a while later.

Jake smiled at the memories. "For as long as I can remember. After my mom died, I started going with my father on business trips. We didn't go far because we didn't have much money, but where he went, I went."

"That must have been great. I know I loved spending time with my dad when I was younger. As a matter of fact, I still do."

"Yeah, those were good times. As I got older, Dad decided I needed more structure in my life so we stopped traveling as much and I settled down to the life of an ordinary child. Not as exciting."

"Did your dad still travel?"

Jake gripped the steering wheel with both hands. "That was the downside. By then, we had more money and his trips were for longer periods of time. But he made up for it during the summers. That's when we traveled together."

"Sounds like you and your dad are close."

"We were."

"What happened?"

Jake had asked himself that question. He wasn't sure if there was an answer. "Things changed. I got older. Dad got busier."

"That's too bad," she said, and he felt she meant it.

"It's all right. Overall, Dad's a good guy," Jake said absently. "He wanted me to be happy, but he didn't understand that being with him made me happy."

Sounded like her dad, Eleanor thought. "My dad always said he wanted me to travel, get away from home, but I never got the feeling he meant it. He wanted me with him."

"You liked that?"

"A lot."

"I hear a 'but' in there somewhere."

She looked out the window. "Sometimes I wonder what my life would be like if I hadn't come back to Lamar when I graduated from school."

"Where would you have gone?"

"New York."

"Your friend Franklin?"

She nodded. Franklin seemed so long ago. He'd been the first man she'd ever loved.

"Was he more than a friend?"

"He asked me to marry him."

The words hit Jake like a sucker punch. He was taking Eleanor back to the arms of a guy who'd asked her to marry him. "Why'd you turn him down?"

She smiled. "I didn't want to leave Lamar. My dad needed me."

"Do you ever regret it?"

"Not marrying Franklin?"

She'd asked herself that question many times over the last few years. "I don't regret not marrying Franklin, but I do wonder how different my life would have been had I been a bit more adventurous."

Jake wondered if she still had feelings for the guy. "How did you and Franklin meet?"

Eleanor smiled. "Jealous?"

"I think it's natural. The new beau is always a little jealous of the old beaus. Especially the ones who made marriage proposals."

"The new beau?"

Jake inclined his head in the direction of the back seat to remind her of the roles they were playing for the benefit of Carl and Megan. "Don't you think I'm entitled to be a little jealous, Carl?"

"I say always keep a man a little jealous," Megan chimed in.

"He wasn't talking to you, Megan," Carl explained calmly. "He was talking to me. Do you think everything has to revolve around you?"

Jake looked at Eleanor and they both grinned. Thank God, they were almost at the airport.

Chapter 11

Jake saw his plans for the weekend begin to disintegrate right before his eyes. "You can't go back to Lamar. We're here. We've checked our luggage. We have our boarding passes. They're boarding the plane now."

Megan glared at Jake. "You don't tell me what to do. *You* threatened to dump me out of the car. I'm not going."

"Megan," Eleanor said, "be reasonable. How will you get back to Lamar?"

"Who said I was going back to Lamar? I have friends in Atlanta. Maybe I'll get a room and stay here until you guys get back on Sunday."

"Well, I'm ready to get on the plane," Carl said cheerfully. "She's right. She's a grown woman. If she doesn't want to go, she doesn't have to."

Jake didn't know who he wanted to strangle first: Carl or Megan. "This is childish, Megan. Get on the plane."

"I am not." Megan kissed Eleanor on the cheek. "You have a good time in New York." She shot a glance at Jake, then said loud enough for him to hear, "And I hope you see Franklin while you're there."

Eleanor grabbed one of Megan's hands. "Are you sure?"

"I'm sure. Now get on that plane before it leaves you."

"Okay," Carl said, taking Eleanor's other hand. "We're boarding now. Have fun in Atlanta, Megan. We'll see you when we get back."

Carl escorted Eleanor to the jetway and Jake followed. Megan stood behind waving.

"We can't leave her, Carl," Eleanor said.

"Of course we can," Carl whispered. "Anyway, you know as well as I do she's going to make a late entrance on the plane. Let's not beg her. She's coming. Megan wouldn't miss a free trip to New York and a Mason Publishing party for anything."

"I'm not sure about this, Carl. I don't think she's coming."

Carl shot Jake a glance. 'It's your call, man. Do we play it her way or mine?"

Jake looked back at Megan. She was still smiling. "Let's board."

When the stewardesses began closing the overheard compartments, Eleanor said, "I don't think she's coming."

"She is," Carl said, but some of his confidence was gone.

"She'd better hurry," Jake added.

Carl stood up. "I'll go get her. But this is the last time."

"Carl…" Jake said, but Carl was out of his first-class seat and through the door. "Damn, now they're both going to miss the flight."

The flight attendant closed the front cabin door as soon as the words were out of Jake's mouth.

"I'd say you're right," Eleanor said as the pilot began his push back from the gate.

"Damn!"

Eleanor touched his arm again. "Don't worry so. It's not that bad. Maybe they'll come to an understanding while we're gone."

Jake stared at her. "Do you really think so?"

She shook her head. "I'm beginning to wonder if this plan of yours is worth it. Megan and Carl may be a lost cause."

"Let's not give up yet." Jake didn't want to agree with her since he had ulterior motives for the plan, but he thought she was right. In his opinion, Carl and Megan were too inflexible to ever get it together. He didn't think they'd find *anyone* who'd put up with them.

"At least it works out for us."

"Works out?"

Eleanor took a magazine out of the seat pocket in front of her. "Yes, now we don't have to pretend to be a couple. You can visit with your friends and I can spend some time with Franklin."

Franklin. Exactly what Jake hadn't wanted. "Yeah, lucky us."

She looked over at him. "I'm sure your little black book must be burning a hole in your pocket. Do you think you'll be able to see all of your women this weekend?"

Jake could do nothing but go along with her. He wasn't about to admit he wanted to spend time with her if all she could think about was Franklin. "I'll hold a lottery. The winner gets to see me this weekend."

Eleanor laughed. "You're too much, Jake."

Jake laughed, too, but it was an empty laugh. His trip to New York was doomed. He wanted to strangle Megan. And he probably would as soon as he got back to Lamar.

He leaned back in his seat and closed his eyes. It had been a hell of a day.

Jake and Eleanor took a limo from LaGuardia Airport to the Mason estate in White Plains. During the thirty-minute ride, Eleanor questioned Jake about his father.

Jake's accessing gaze traveled from her crossed legs to the choker around her neck before meeting her eyes. "Why all the questions? I'm sure you've had Carl put together a file."

"Of course," Eleanor answered, uncrossing her legs and shifting slightly to pull her skirt farther down her thigh. "But I want to hear it from you."

A smile touched Jake's lips then he sank back in the seat and closed his eyes. "Next question."

Eleanor liked the relaxed look of his features. It made him appear more approachable. Vulnerable, even. "Why haven't you been more involved in your father's business?"

The twitch in his jaw told her the question was painful for him.

"My father didn't want me involved," he answered simply, but she sensed there was nothing simple about it.

"Why was that?"

Jake opened his eyes. "You're full of questions, aren't you?"

"You didn't answer me."

He closed his eyes again. He didn't want to discuss this with Eleanor because he had some of the same questions himself. "Why don't you save it until you meet my father. You *do* want to have something to ask him, don't you?"

Eleanor touched his knee. "But I want you to answer this one."

Jake grinned. "You're beginning to sound like Megan."

"Now that was a low blow," she said, allowing him to deflect her question.

"Ah, but it's true." Jake chuckled. "You and Megan are quite a pair."

"You can't seriously think I sound like Megan."

"You make it sound like an insult. It's not. It's merely an observation."

"Yes, but I was in the car with you while Megan behaved like a petulant child."

Jake opened his eyes and sat up. "You're being kind. She was at her best today."

"Don't try to change the subject. Do you seriously think Megan and I are alike?"

Jake nodded.

"You're the first person to say that. Most people think we're exact opposites. I suppose you know they called us the Odd Couple in school."

He nodded again. "I can see why they did that. That's the impression you two give. But it's a false impression. You're very much the flirt and spoiled little girl that Megan is and she's very much the reserved, stern woman that you are."

"Me, a flirt and a spoiled little girl? I don't think so. You must have me confused with someone else."

Jake rubbed her arm. "Now don't get mad with me. You did ask. Do you want me to continue?"

Eleanor nodded. "You certainly can't stop now."

"Take that evening at Mel's Diner. You wanted to play the flirt then, but you weren't sure about doing it."

Eleanor remembered taking her hair down, unbuttoning a couple of buttons of her blouse, and hoping Jake would notice.

"And don't forget that white bathing suit you wear. Definitely designed to get a man's attention."

"But that doesn't make me a flirt."

He ignored her comment. "And look at you now," he said, allowing his gaze to meander from her feet to the hair on her head. "Your legs were made for short skirts. And the way your hair falls in curls on your shoulders is maddening."

"Jake..." she pleaded, a warm breeze of passion raising her body temperature.

Jake stared into her eyes and she wondered if he knew the effect his words were having on her.

"I bet you were a virgin until you met Franklin. Right?"

Eleanor averted her eyes. He was right, but it wasn't his business, she decided. She wondered how he knew anyway, but she wasn't going to ask. She was sure she wouldn't like his answer.

He didn't wait for her response. "And my guess is, Megan is *still* a virgin."

Again he was right, though most people guessed Megan was sexually active. She liked men. A lot. But she didn't sleep around. She'd die if she knew Jake knew. "You'll have to ask her that," she said, wondering again how Jake knew so much. The man must have ESP where women are concerned, she concluded.

When he didn't continue, she met his gaze with her own. "Go on," she said. "I know you're not finished."

"When men look at Megan, their first thought is she's a firecracker. When they look at you, their first thought is she's uptight. What they don't know is you're probably hotter than Megan."

Eleanor felt herself grow warmer. "And how do you figure that?"

"That bathing suit. I doubt Megan would wear anything that revealing, even in the privacy of your pool. I'm hoping the only place you wear it is in the privacy of your own pool. Please tell me I'm right."

She wouldn't have answered him, but he sounded so grave she took pity on him. "You're right. Not that it matters."

"Oh, it matters, all right."

Eleanor refused to ask what that meant. "So you've got Megan and me all figured out?"

Jake nodded. "As much as a man can figure out any woman."

"And I'm sure you've been through your share of women."

He caught her gaze. "Why don't you ask me?"

Eleanor knew what he was talking about. "I know you've been through a lot of women. There's nothing to ask."

"If you ask, I'll answer."

"Why?"

"Because I'm basically an honest guy. I don't make promises and I don't lie. Keeps life simple."

She didn't know why she had to ask, but she did. His eyes told her he'd tell her the truth. "Have you loved any of them, Jake?"

He smiled as if he'd known that was the question she'd ask. "I've loved them all."

"Eleanor, dearest," Randolph Mason said, pulling her into his arms. "It's about time we met." He pushed her back and grinned at her. "I knew it. You're gorgeous."

Eleanor believed he meant it and his words made her feel gorgeous. She silently thanked Megan for coaxing her into the burgundy tailored suit with the miniskirt.

"You're not so bad yourself," she said and meant it. Randolph Mason was a very attractive man. His salt-and-pepper hair, his bright eyes and sparkling teeth. Not to mention the broad shoulders set off by his tapered suit. Jake got his good looks from his father.

"Hey, watch it now," Jake warned. "There are children in the room."

Eleanor saw the teasing glint in Jake's eyes. "I apologize, Jake. I see where you get it from."

Jake laughed.

"I know an insult when I hear one," Randolph teased. "My son is a perfect gentleman and so am I."

Eleanor rolled her eyes and spoke in an exaggerated Southern drawl. "Oh, is that what ya'll call it up North?"

Randolph's eyes danced. "What do you call it in Lamar?"

"Calculated charm."

Randolph laughed, then spoke to Jake. "She's a tough one, son. Are you surviving down there?"

Jake passed her a teasing glance. "We've had our moments. But I think we're on the right road now. What do you say, Eleanor?"

She nodded, getting into the spirit of the moment. Jake and his father's relaxed relationship warmed her. Maybe she'd misread the comments Jake had made during the ride from the airport. "It was touch-and-go for a while, but I think I have him trained now."

Randolph shot Jake a glance. "Trained, huh?"

Jake raised his arms in surrender. "What can I say? She's a slave driver."

"Well, this slave driver needs to freshen up," Eleanor said. "If you'll excuse me?"

"I don't know what I was thinking about, dear," Randolph said. He pressed the intercom and a uniformed manservant appeared in the door. "Jeffrey will show you to your room."

Jake watched as Eleanor left the library behind Jeffrey. When the door closed, his father said, "She's nothing like her pictures, is she?"

Jake turned to his father. "Mathias told you about the woman at the pool?"

Randolph nodded and walked around to his desk. "So what's been happening?"

Jake dropped down on the couch in front of the wall of built-in bookcases. "Not much. I've been trying to understand the paper."

"What do you think?"

"It's a nice, small-town paper, but I still don't see why you want it. Will you explain that to me again?"

"There's nothing to explain. Mat and I have been friends forever. We want this merger because of our friendship. It's your job to make it work as a business deal for Mason Publishing. Are you going to be able to do it?"

"Definitely," Jake said with confidence. He was still determined to do more than his father expected.

"Good, I'm counting on you."

Jake's shoulders set up a little straighter at that comment. His father was counting on him. There was no way he would let him down. In fact, he planned to impress the hell out of the older man. Once he knew from which angle to approach the new magazine that he and Eleanor had discussed, he'd be better able to draw up his deal-of-the-century. He couldn't wait to present his father with the final proposal.

Jake scanned the hotel ballroom later that night looking for Eleanor and wondering where she was. He wanted to see her, but he also wanted to see this guy who had spoiled his plans to be Eleanor's date for the gala.

"Are you looking for somebody, Jake?" Sherise's honeyed voice asked.

Jake looked at her and wondered when he'd lost interest. She was still the attractive, leggy, demure yet fun-loving diva he'd first met, but now his tastes hungered for someone with more mouth and less height. "I told you about Eleanor. She's supposed to be here tonight. Dad wants to introduce her around."

"Are you sure there isn't more to it than that?"

That got Jake's attention. "Jealousy doesn't become you, Sherise."

"And you're turning into a bore. I get the feeling I'm being used."

Feeling guilty, Jake immediately slid his gaze from her. She was right. He'd only invited her after he'd learned Eleanor was bringing Franklin. His plan had been to make Eleanor jealous. Now he realized how stupid that was. And how unfair to Sherise. "Look, Sherise, I'm sorry. Do you want to dance?"

Her eyes twinkled and he knew all was forgiven. He took her hand and led her to the floor. Luckily for him a slow Barry White tune played. He pulled her into his arms, glad they didn't have to talk anymore.

He sensed Eleanor's entrance into the ballroom and his head went up.

"Watch it, Jake," Sherise chastised. "Those are my feet you're stepping on."

"Sorry," Jake mumbled, his eyes still on Eleanor. He'd thought she was gorgeous before but tonight she'd gone beyond that. White was definitely her color, though he thought the strapless white gown could have used a little more material up top.

And he thought the guy on her arm looked a little bit too happy. He wondered what Eleanor had done to make the guy grin like that.

"Is that her?"

Sherise had stopped dancing and was now looking at Eleanor and her date.

"That's her," Jake said, taking Sherise's hand and leading her in Eleanor's direction. "I'll introduce you."

Randolph and his date for the evening reached Eleanor before Jake did.

"Here you are," his father said to him. "Good to see you, Sherise. Have you met our Eleanor?"

Randolph made the introductions then Eleanor introduced the tall, well-groomed man with her as Franklin.

Jake took his hand, sizing him up. "Glad you could make it. Eleanor speaks of you often."

Franklin placed an arm around Eleanor and pulled her to himself and smiled. "All good, I hope."

Eleanor touched the string of pearls around her neck and gave Franklin an intimate smile that made Jake's inside clench. "I only told the truth."

Franklin rewarded that answer with a kiss on her forehead. "Thank you."

Randolph took Eleanor's arm. "Come on. There are some people I want you to meet."

"Franklin?" Eleanor asked.

"No, you go on," he said, waving her away. "I'll be okay."

"Are you sure?"

Franklin winked. "As long as you look for me for the first dance."

"Deal," she said and let herself be escorted away by Randolph.

"Do you live in New York, Franklin?" Sherise asked, flashing the man a brilliant smile that Jake thought was exaggerated.

"All my life. You?"

"Brooklyn."

Jake observed Franklin as he talked with Sherise. What was it about this man that attracted Eleanor? Jake admitted he was handsome. And tall. And well groomed. Probably very successful, since Jake guessed his tuxedo wasn't a rental. And the guy was personable. Jake had to give him that.

But Jake didn't like him. And he knew why. Franklin had been engaged to Eleanor. And in Jake's opinion, that erased all the other positive attributes the man had.

Eleanor's jaw hurt from so much smiling. Randolph had introduced her to what seemed like over a hundred people. Thankfully, he did most of the talking so all she had to do was nod and smile. At other times that would have rankled her, but not tonight. Tonight she was glad because it gave her time to think.

So Sherise was the kind of woman that attracted Jake. She was surprised. For some reason, she'd thought Jake went in for blatant sexuality, not the demure sophistication she sensed in Sherise.

She guessed one really couldn't judge a book by its cover. She smiled at the thought and at the bald-headed man and his wife Randolph was now introducing. Jake always surprised her. First, his attitude at the paper. Then, his genuine concern for Megan and Carl. Now, his choice in women. Jake Mason was not a man to be pigeon-holed.

"I think I've waited long enough," a firm masculine voice whispered close to her ear.

She turned and smiled at Franklin. "I'm sorry I left you for so long. Thanks for being such a good sport about it."

Franklin took her drink from her hand and placed it on the passing tray of the floating waiter. "Now it's my time."

She turned to Randolph. "Please excuse me for a while," she said.

"Oh, sure, dear," Randolph said, looking from her to Franklin. "But be sure to come back in a little while. There are still people for you to meet."

Franklin placed his hand on her elbow and escorted her away from Randolph and company and onto the ballroom floor. "If I didn't know better," he said, "I'd think the elder Mason was trying to keep you away from me."

Eleanor stepped into his arms. "You've got to be kidding."

Franklin slipped his arms around her waist and pulled her close. "He wouldn't be the first older man interested in a pretty young thing like yourself."

"Pretty young thing?" she repeated. "You'd better be glad I'm in a festive mood or I'd have to call you on that phrase."

"Politically correct phrasing or not, the older Mason could be interested in you."

"No way. The man is my father's best friend."

"So?"

"So, they're practically brothers."

He turned her in a fancy turn. "There could be another reason for his interest."

He turned her again.

"And what's that?"

"Maybe he wants you for a daughter-in-law."

Eleanor stopped moving and looked up at him. "Now that's crazy."

He urged her into the dance step. "What's crazy about it? Maybe your fathers want to merge more than their businesses."

Eleanor shook her head. This conversation was ridiculous. "Are you jealous, Franklin? Is that what this is about?"

"Why would I be jealous? You're not my girl anymore."

He *was* jealous. She'd thought Franklin had gotten over their failed romance, but obviously he hadn't. "Maybe it was selfish of me to invite you tonight, but I wanted to see you."

He hugged her closer and she felt him relax. "I'm glad you invited me. You're very special to me, Roni." It was the first time he'd used his pet name for her in years.

"Oh, Franklin…"

He squeezed her. "There's no need for that. I'm fine. I'm not pining away for you, if that's what you're wondering."

The levity in his voice made her smile. "I'm glad to know that."

"I'm seeing somebody," he said a few seconds later.

"Is it serious?"

"More serious than any relationship I've had since you. I think she could be the one."

"Oh."

"Yes, oh. You'd like her. She's a great woman." He looked down at her. "A lot like you."

"Are you happy?" Eleanor questioned.

"Very. I didn't think I'd get over you, Eleanor. You broke my heart when you decided not to come to New York. I loved you, you know."

"I know," she said softly. She was happy for Franklin, but a part of her hated that soon he would no longer be hers. There was a sense of security in knowing somebody out there loved her. "Does she mind your being out tonight?"

He shook his head. "I told her the three of us would get together sometime this weekend. She wants to meet you."

"She does?"

He nodded. "She said she wants to meet the woman who helped make me a man."

Eleanor looked up at him. "You told her that." It was something he'd often told her though she never really believed he meant it.

When the song ended, Franklin led Eleanor out to the terrace.

She sat on the marble bench and he leaned on the marble railing in front of her. The night was clear and cool and the sky shone with stars.

"You've changed," he said.

"I'm older."

"And a little wiser," he added.

"I hope so."

"He'd be a good match for you."

"What are you talking about?"

"Jake."

"Jake?" she repeated.

"I think you already know that."

She didn't answer. She'd be lying if she said she wasn't attracted to Jake. He was an attractive man and that tuxedo showed off the contours of his body so well that her pulse raced. But finding him attractive and having a relationship with him were two different things.

But heaven help her, she had wondered about loving Jake Mason. He had a charm that practically disarmed her. And she sensed he was drawn to her as well. If they had met under other conditions, maybe—

"This is Franklin you're talking to, Eleanor," he said, interrupting her musing. "I think I know you better than anyone else in the world."

"But you're wrong this time."

Franklin sat next to her and took her hand in his. "I don't think so. Love doesn't always happen twice, Eleanor. I've been lucky. I loved you, but you didn't love me. Then I found Vicky. I love her and she loves me. I want you to find that. I want you to love somebody so much it hurts."

"Why do you want me to hurt?" she asked, deliberately misunderstanding what he meant.

"You know it's real when it hurts, when you've given all you think you have and you still have to give more. You know it's love when you're willing to dig deep to find the extra strength it takes to make the relationship work."

Chapter 12

Jake heard her laughter before he opened the door to his father's library. He was relieved she was back, glad she hadn't spent the night with Franklin.

"What's so funny?" he asked as he entered the library. Eleanor and his father sat on the leather couch studying what he recognized by its tattered cover as the family scrapbook. "Or do I have to ask?"

Randolph eased back on the couch and Eleanor closed the book. "Don't ask," Randolph said. "I was catching Eleanor up on the family history."

He had been telling Eleanor about his wife, Jake's mother. That meant he liked Eleanor. A lot. He discussed his late wife with very few people. "Don't believe anything he said about me."

"Oh, I didn't. He sounded too much the proud father. He had to be exaggerating."

Jake studied his father, wondering what he'd said and wishing he'd heard some of it. "What have you been saying?"

"I'm an old man," he said, standing up. "I'm entitled to say whatever I want."

Eleanor chuckled. "I see my father isn't the only one who's not above using age to get his way."

"Watch it, young lady," Randolph warned. "I'd hate to have to report you to your daddy."

Eleanor rolled her eyes. "Another similarity to Dad. You both seem to forget I'm an adult."

"Humor us. If you're lucky, you'll have children of your own someday and you'll understand." Randolph looked at Jake. "Entertain Eleanor for a while. I'm going to bed."

Jake saluted. "Yes, sir."

"Jake, you don't have to—" Eleanor interrupted.

Randolph waved his hand. "He wants to. If he didn't, he'd be at his apartment or still out with Sherise."

"Dad—"

"Okay, I'm going. See you two at breakfast."

As Randolph closed the door, Jake took a seat next to Eleanor and rested his arm on the couch behind her. "Did you have a good time tonight?"

"I sure did. Your father's a great host." She yawned. "I don't think I've ever met that many people in a single night before."

Jake chuckled. "How many names do you remember?"

She waved a finger in the air. "I remember a lot of names. Matching those names to faces, now that's another matter."

Jake casually propped his right leg over his left. "So, ah, did Franklin enjoy himself?"

Eleanor glanced at him. "I think so."

"That's good."

"I liked Sherise. She's a nice woman."

"Yes, she is." Jake checked Eleanor's eyes, hoping to see at least a trace of jealousy. Unfortunately, he found none.

"Is it serious?"

Jake caught her gaze. Maybe there was a trace of the green devil, after all.

"You don't have to answer that," Eleanor amended and he knew she wished she could take her question back.

"Oh, I don't mind. No, it's not serious. We're friends. She dates other people and so do I. We enjoy each other's company. Nothing more."

Eleanor nodded as though his answer didn't mean much to her. "I see."

He wasn't fooled by her gesture. "Do you?"

She gazed up at him, her eyes bright and her lips wet. He wanted to kiss her. He uncrossed his legs and decided to try it.

When he leaned his head down to her, Eleanor's mouth dropped open. "It's okay," he teased. "I don't bite."

She scooted back on the seat, away from him. "I don't think we should do this."

Jake followed her. "Do what?"

She looked up at him again and he took advantage of her open mouth and kissed her. When his lips met the softness of hers, sparks shot through his body. She was so soft, so sweet.

She didn't respond immediately, so he increased the pressure slightly, encouraging her to participate with him.

She pulled her mouth away from his. "Jake—"

"Don't talk. Kiss me," he ordered, taking her mouth in his again.

This time she gave. A little. Enough to make him want more. He leaned closer until he had her pressed into the back of the sofa.

"That's it," he encouraged. "Kiss me."

Eleanor moaned into his mouth and he felt her hands go up to his shoulders, pulling him closer.

"Oh, yes," he murmured, increasing the pressure even more. "I want you, Eleanor."

Her arms dropped from his shoulders and she eased her mouth away from his. When she lifted her gaze to his, he saw that her eyes were damp.

He touched his finger to her cheek. "I *do* want you," he repeated softly.

She looked up at him with clear eyes. "I want you, too."

He grinned. Hell, he felt good. "I kinda guessed that."

She grimaced. "How nongallant of you to say so."

"You're beautiful," he whispered, his finger tracing a path down her jaw. "And you smell so good."

She released her smile. "Now that's a lot better."

"What are we going to do about it?"

"Nothing."

"Nothing? We're both adults. What's stopping us?"

She eased away from him and stood before his father's desk. He liked the look of her—wet lips, hair ruffled from his hands.

"There's a lot stopping us," she said.

"Name one thing."

"Your plans for my paper."

He sank back into the couch, realizing they were going to do nothing about it. "That's business. This is personal."

She smiled sadly. "That's where we differ. The paper for me is personal."

He knew there was nothing he could say to change her mind. He wasn't sure he wanted to. He couldn't make any promises about the paper beyond the ones he'd already made. What he did there had ramifications far above the merger her father and his father had planned. No, what Jake did in Lamar was, to him, proof of what he could accomplish when he set his mind to it. It was evidence he could present to his father to show he was more than capable of doing a job well. No, there were no more promises he could make to Eleanor. "I understand," he said softly.

She gave another crooked smile and quietly left the room.

Eleanor eased up the stairs to her room, her senses still taut from her encounter with Jake. She wanted him in the worst way. She admitted to herself that what she felt had been building since she'd first seen his picture when she was a little girl.

Eleanor and Jake. She'd dreamed of kissing him long ago, but she'd never imagined how powerful such a kiss would be.

Eleanor and Jake. Colleagues and competitors. There was no way they could sustain a love affair given their working relationship. Jake had a job to do and she had to protect her paper. She couldn't let anything cloud her judgment about that. She couldn't let Jake use her for his purposes.

That thought took her by surprise. What if Jake was using her? Though she didn't think that was the case, she couldn't immediately dismiss it. Maybe if she held on to it, she'd be able to fight her attraction for Jake.

She undressed and climbed into bed. When she closed her eyes, visions of Jake loomed above her and her mind took her to the place that held the beauty of what it would be to share her body with him, to indulge herself with his body. Yes, she wanted him. And though she wasn't that experienced, she knew enough to know that making love with Jake would be exquisite.

She knew she had to stop thinking about him. If she didn't, she'd find herself going back downstairs to him. She wondered what he would do if she did. It didn't take much imagination to figure out that answer.

Her breathing increased when she heard him ascend the stairs. It stopped altogether when he paused outside her door. If he knocked, she didn't know if she'd have the strength to turn him away. She started breathing again when he left the door. She didn't know if she was glad or sad that he had gone.

She closed her eyes once again and tried to sleep. No such luck. Giving up, she climbed out of bed and went to take a shower. A cold shower.

"I'm telling you, I think we're getting someplace. Jake couldn't take his eyes off Eleanor all night."

"Are you sure, Randy?"

"Of course I'm sure. I think he kissed her tonight."

"At the party?"

"No, in my library here at the house."

"Did you see them?"

"Not exactly," Randolph hedged.

"What do you mean, 'not exactly'?"

"I left them alone in the library, then I listened outside the door."
Mathias chuckled. "No, you didn't."

"Well, for a few minutes I did," Randolph explained. "I wanted to know if we were getting anywhere. And we are."

"That's good. Be careful and don't get caught. Remember, they're not supposed to know we're matchmaking."

"I know, Mat. I'll talk to you tomorrow."

Eleanor bumped into Jake when he stopped suddenly at their arrival gate in the Atlanta airport.

"Why'd you stop?"

"I don't believe it."

She looked around him to see what had his attention. Her mouth dropped open when she saw Carl and Megan seated, practically in the same seat, swallowing each other's face.

"Do you think they were hit on the head and lost their minds since we left them on Friday?" she asked.

Jake recovered and started in the direction of Carl and Megan.

"I see you two didn't kill each other," he said.

Megan pulled away from Carl and stood up. Eleanor noticed she didn't let go of his hand. "Welcome back, you two. Did you have a good time?"

"We did," Eleanor answered. Jake and Carl, wearing a Cheshire-like grin that she'd never seem him sport, had some male eye discussion going so she knew he wasn't going to answer.

Megan smiled up at Carl. "I guess we're ready to go, sweetie." Carl rewarded her with a kiss.

Eleanor shot Jake a bewildered glance. "Sweetie?" she whispered.

Jake shrugged his shoulders, indicating he didn't know what was going on.

"So are you two going to tell us what happened?" he asked.

Carl draped an arm around Megan's shoulders and pulled her close. Leaning into him, she slid her arm around his waist. "It's a long story," Carl said. "We'd better walk while we talk."

Thankfully, the concourse wasn't crowded. If it had been, there would have been no way for them to walk four-abreast. And it seemed Carl and Megan were not about to release each other.

"Do you want to tell him or should I?" Megan asked Carl.

"You can start, cupcake." He kissed the tip of her nose. "I'll finish."

Eleanor saw the look that passed between them and knew there was a memory of sexual adventure associated with the words. Megan was no longer a virgin. She'd bet on it.

"Okay," Megan began. "I sat around for a few minutes after you guys had gotten on the plane, then I went to the phone to find a rental car and a hotel room. There were no cars available anywhere."

"She was muttering curses to herself when I found her," Carl said, his voice full of warmth.

Maybe aliens have invaded their bodies, Eleanor speculated silently. Surely this couldn't be the fighting couple she and Jake had left in the Atlanta airport two days ago.

Another affectionate smile passed between the couple. "Well, Carl came along and solved all my problems."

Carl chuckled. "Megan's memory is colored by the good time I showed her this weekend."

"Well," Megan agreed, "maybe I did scream at him a couple of times as he followed me down the concourse."

Carl laughed.

"And I may have slammed the cab door on him and ripped his jacket."

Carl laughed harder.

"And maybe, just maybe, I told the hotel desk clerk he was a pervert who'd followed me all the way from the airport."

Carl laughed yet harder.

"But the worst thing I did to my sweetie is that I locked him out in the hall when all he wore were his briefs."

Carl sobered. "Now that wasn't funny, cupcake."

Megan put a finger to his lips. "But I made up for it, didn't I, sweetie?"

"Yes, you did," Carl said, kissing her finger.

When they reached baggage claim, Megan and Carl volunteered to get the car while Jake and Eleanor waited for their luggage.

"Looks like I was right," Jake said as soon as the other couple was out of ear shot.

"About what?"

"All that tension between Megan and Carl. I think they're in love."

"Or lust."

"What's the difference?"

Eleanor's eyes widened. "If you don't know, there's no way I can explain it to you."

"Are you upset about something?" Jake asked, giving her a

quick glance before focusing on the conveyor that delivered the bags. "You've been acting weird all day."

Yes, something was wrong with her. Her cold shower the night before last had done nothing to quell her desire for Jake, while he seemed to have recovered with little effort. Obviously, he hadn't wanted her that much. "I'm fine. I just want to get home."

"So do I."

"You think of Lamar as home?" she asked, surprised at his words but also warmed by them.

He shrugged it off. "I like it there and I miss my team. Maybe there's something to be said for the slower pace. Hey, isn't that your bag?"

She watched as he retrieved first her bag, then his from the carousel. "Let's wait for them outside," he said, motioning to the door.

She followed him out, all the while thinking about his comments on Lamar. Was Jake becoming a country boy, after all?

Chapter 13

"You're blushing," Jake teased. They were about halfway to Lamar and already Carl and Megan had put on quite a show.

Eleanor lowered her head. "It's the moaning. Can't they kiss in silence?"

"When it's good, it's good. Why don't you talk to me? Maybe we can ground them out."

"What do you want to talk about?"

"Us."

There is no us, she said silently. "Okay, let's talk about the paper."

Jake chuckled. "If you insist."

"Did you tell your father about my plans? Every time I tried to speak with him about them, he deftly changed the subject."

Jake was grateful for his father's hands-off approach on this deal. The Old Man was really letting him handle the project. "As well he should. This is my deal. He doesn't make the decisions, I do. Didn't I tell you that?"

She grimaced. "You did, but I didn't believe you."

"Thanks for nothing."

"Don't be insulted. I never figured Randolph Mason to be the hands-off type."

Jake knew his father's hands-off approach was because this project was so small, but he didn't dare tell Eleanor that. "Mason Publishing is a big enterprise. He can't have his hands in everything."

"I guess you're right. How do you feel having total control?"

"Responsible. I want to do the right thing, the best job, for all the concerned parties." He wanted to exceed beyond any and all expectations his father had or had ever dreamed.

She patted his knee. "Do what I tell you and you'll be fine."

He sucked in his breath. "That's the first time you've touched me since Friday night."

That kiss. She'd wondered which one of them would mention it first.

"No comment?"

"No comment." She glanced back at Megan and Carl. Seeing they were oblivious to the world, all cuddled in each other's arms, she spoke freely. "We've already decided the kiss was the beginning and the end."

"You decided."

She smiled coyly. "Unless you can do what you want by yourself, I guess that means I made the decision for both of us."

"You're a tough woman. You know that?"

"I thought you said I was soft," she said, then gasped, wishing she could take the words back.

"Hey," Carl interrupted. "What are you guys whispering about?"

Eleanor was relieved at the interruption. Jake placed a hand on her knee, turned quickly to her, and mouthed, "Later."

"So you finally decided to come up for air?" Jake asked, glancing at them in his rearview mirror.

"If you want, Jake," Megan chimed in, "Carl and I can swap places and let you and Eleanor have the back seat for a while."

Eleanor turned around in her seat and glared at Megan. "I wouldn't trust you two. You'd probably try to sit in Carl's lap while he drove."

Carl captured Megan's lips for a quickie. "We'll have to try that, cupcake."

The look of pleasure and adoration on Megan's face was one Eleanor had never seen there before. After years of leading men around by the nose, her friend had finally been bitten by that old love bug. Eleanor was happy for her.

"Where did cupcake come from?" she asked.

Carl opened his mouth to answer, but Megan covered his mouth with her hand. "Don't you dare." Carl chuckled and Eleanor saw his tongue come out and caress Megan's hand.

Megan tore her gaze from him and looked to Eleanor. "I don't believe I almost let him get away."

Now Carl was the one who wore the satisfied look. Love looked as good on a man as it did on a woman.

Megan nudged Carl. "Tell her."

Carl frowned down at her. "I'll tell her later."

"Tell her now, sweetie. You know I can't keep a secret."

"Don't tell me you two got married?" Eleanor asked, shocked but at this point ready to believe about anything where these two were concerned.

They looked at each other and chuckled. "Well," Carl drawled. "There was this church."

Megan punched his arm. "Don't tease her." She turned to Eleanor. "No, we didn't get married."

Eleanor heard the unspoken "Yet." "What is it then?" she asked Carl.

"Megan and I have decided to take a vacation. Together. So I'm going to need some time off."

Eleanor relaxed. "You know that's no problem. You have enough vacation."

"Well, I was thinking about taking a month."

"A month? We can't do without you for a month. Not on this short notice. Who would fill in for you?"

Megan leaned forward. "We've already thought about this. Jake can cover for him."

"Jake?" Eleanor said, her voice high. She ignored Jake's quick glance at her.

"Yes, Jake," Carl said. "He took over sports. Now he can take over my assignments."

"But," she said, then stopped. She wanted to say "But sports was easy." Looking at Jake, she decided to change her words. "Jake didn't come to Lamar to be a reporter. He has other things to do."

"You don't think I can do it, Eleanor?" Jake asked and she knew she'd insulted him.

She looked at him. "Of course you can do it. That's not the issue."

"It sure does sound like the issue to me," he said, his eyes focused on the road, his lips tight.

"Whoa, you two," Carl said. "You're beginning to sound like another couple I used to know. Now, if you don't calm down, I'm going to put you out at the next exit."

Megan giggled.

"Now be cool," Carl continued. "We'll talk about this when we get back to Lamar."

Eleanor turned around in her seat and looked at Jake. His jaw was set in a firm line and she knew he was upset. She hadn't meant to hurt his feelings. Why did she always say the wrong thing where he was concerned?

Megan collapsed on Carl's chest. "I've never been this happy before," she said when her breathing returned to normal.

"I know," Carl said, lazily brushing her short curls with his hand. "Me either."

Megan tightened her hold on Carl. She was so glad she'd found him. And now that she had, she couldn't imagine her life without him. When she thought about the time she'd wasted arguing with him, fighting her feelings for him, she experienced a deep regret.

"I love you, Megan," Carl said softly, his hand still in her hair. She loved his touch, whether it was in her hair like now or all over her body as they made love. "I suppose I've loved you since we were children, since you first moved to Lamar. I even suppose you're the reason I never left Lamar."

Overwhelming joy filled her entire being. Carl loved her. She buried her face in his chest and squeezed him even tighter, tears filling her eyes.

He lifted her head so he could see her face. "Don't cry, cupcake. Tell me you love me, too."

The tears flowed freely now. "I do. I do. I do," she said, dotting his face with kisses with each pronouncement. "You're the best thing that's ever happened to me."

"I know," he said, and she heard the smile in his voice.

She looked up at him. "Don't get cocky with me." She pushed her pelvis against his. "I have my ways of getting satisfaction."

Carl groaned. "Don't I know it." He rolled over until she was under him, her beautiful face staring up at him. Everybody saw her beauty and he didn't mind, but he was glad he saw the woman inside where she was even more beautiful. And if possible, more desirable. He wanted to love her again so he lowered his head to kiss her.

"Not yet," she said, pushing at his chest with her arms. "I want to talk."

Carl groaned again and rolled to her side. Maybe this was part of being in love. She wanted to talk and he didn't mind. "Okay, cupcake, what do you want to talk about?"

Megan settled herself in Carl's arms, loving the cherished feeling he gave her. "Eleanor and Jake."

"Eleanor and Jake. Oh, no, I'm told the romance is over when your lady brings another couple to bed with you. That or she's into kinky." The smile was back in his voice.

"I'm serious," she said. "Don't you think they're perfect for each other?"

"Hmm…"

"The way I see it," Megan continued, "they're never going to find each other without our help."

"Oh, no," Carl began, feeling obliged to put up some kind of resistance though he knew he'd go along with her plan. "I don't think they need us meddling around in their affair."

"I'm not talking about an affair. I'm talking about Eleanor and Jake finding what we've found." She laced her hand with his and brought it to her lips for a kiss. "I want them to be as happy as we are."

He couldn't argue with that kind of logic. "What is it you propose we do?"

"I don't know yet, but I'll think of something."

Carl rolled her over onto her back and poised himself above her. "Think about them later. Try thinking about me now."

"At least this plan of ours is not a total failure," Mathias mused.

"What do you mean by that?"

Mathias snorted. "We got Carl and Megan together."

"Damn," Randolph said. "I don't believe this. I really don't believe it. This is your fault."

"My fault?" Mathias raised his voice. "How is this my fault?"

"You were supposed to get Carl and Megan on that plane," he accused. "Maybe if you had, Eleanor and Jake would be a couple by now."

"Don't go blaming me, Randolph Mason. Some things never change," Mathias muttered. "It's never your fault. You haven't changed since we were kids."

"Okay, okay," Randolph gave in. "It's nobody's fault."

"I know it's not my fault," Mathias stated adamantly.

"Well, now that that's settled. What are we going to do about Jake and Eleanor?"

"Okay, Eleanor." Jake opened round two of their negotiations Monday morning when they returned to work. He hoped it wouldn't go the full fifteen. "Let's try this again. When I look at the list of projects you want Mason Publishing to fund, they fall into three categories: community support, infrastructure, and growth. Do you agree?"

He waited for her nod.

"Now, of those three items, only growth interests me."

"I sorta figured that," she muttered.

"But do you agree with me?"

Eleanor leaned forward and he thought again how attractive she looked with her hair down. He didn't trust himself even to think about her gorgeous legs in that hot pink miniskirt suit.

"To a degree," she said, "but the other items deserve discussion."

"In due time. Let's talk about the idea you have for this

African-American family magazine." The more Jake dug into this project, the more apparent it became that his best angle was this magazine. The progressive concept filled a large void in the marketplace.

Eleanor stood up and framed an imaginary picture with her hands. "Picture this. The cover has a black-and-white silhouette of a man and woman in the foreground, and three children and two sets of grandparents in the background. The title, *Our Family,* is in bold black-and-gold letters across the top." She looked at Jake. "Are you with me so far?"

"So far. So good. I've got the cover. Now what's inside?"

"The purpose of the magazine is to foster and support the black family. So each issue would have that as its theme. With twelve issues each year, we could do three issues featuring kids; three on parenting; three on marital relationships; and three issues on dating relationships. Of course, there'd be something each month for all the groups."

"Where would issues related to elder care fall?" he asked, and her smile told him she was pleased with the question.

"I've thought about that and it can fall into one of the parenting issues or maybe kids or maybe even both. It's something we could work with. What's your first thought?"

He tapped his pencil on the table. "I like the idea of putting it in the kids issue. That way the focus won't be on age, but on the different roles we play in our lifetimes. From kid, to parent, to lover, to spouse. I like it."

"You do?" Eleanor asked, clearly pleased with his answer. "Oh, Jake, I've been thinking about this for so long and I couldn't see how we could make it work. We just didn't have the funds."

"Until Mason Publishing came along," he finished for her.
She nodded.

"Why didn't you take this idea to some venture capitalists? I'm sure you would have gotten financing."

Eleanor shook her head. "That's not the way we do business. We use our own money or money we can borrow on our own terms."

"We're back to the control issue."

She nodded. "Right. That's one of the first lessons my father taught me."

"And you learned it well."

That sounded like an insult to Eleanor. Before she could comment on it, he asked another question. "How do you expect this magazine to pay for itself?"

Eleanor sat on the edge of the table and it took all of his willpower to keep from staring at her legs. "As with most publications, we'll only expect circulation to pay for paper and staff. Ads will pay for everything else."

"And you expect national circulation and thus national advertising?"

"Exactly. I figure we'll start small and branch out. Thus, the need for outside capital. It's probably too risky to go national immediately. By starting locally, expanding regionally, then nationally, I think we'll have the best chance for success."

"You've got this all planned out, haven't you?"

She nodded again.

"And how much cash do you think you'll need to get started?"

Jake whistled at the number she threw out.

"It's not that much, Jake," she argued. "At least, not for what we want to do. Once the magazine hits the marketplace, we'll have more advertisers coming to us than we can handle."

Jake showed no emotion, but he agreed wholeheartedly with her assessment. As the first magazine in its market, *Our Family* would be guaranteed a strong showing. It would take any copycat publication a while to match their numbers. "Are any infrastructure improvements included in that number?"

She didn't cower. "A few."

"I bet. I'm sure you have all this documented." Again, he waited for her nod. "I'd like to get a copy. I think we may be able to hinge the deal on this magazine idea."

She beamed. "That's great, Jake. Now what about the community projects and infrastructure? You've experienced our computer system. You've seen the press and the photo shop. You know we need updating. It'll mean a classier product. And it'll mean more work from our existing pool of employees."

"That brings up another issue," he said, ignoring her concerns. "What about staffing the new magazine?"

"That's another place we have to spend money. We need journalists, but we also need recognized authorities to discuss key issues and provide alternatives. We also need staff to manage the day-to-day operations of the magazine."

Jake had already considered those factors. "What role will you play in *Our Family?*"

"I'd love to be managing editor," she said immediately.

"What about your role as managing editor of the *Lamar Daily?* You'd do both?"

That's where Eleanor was torn. In her wildest dreams, she kept her role as managing editor of the *Lamar Daily* in addition to being managing editor of *Our Family.* "I'd have to make a choice, I guess."

"Carl could probably take over as managing editor of the *Lamar Daily,*" he offered.

"No," she said quickly. "I want the paper to stay in the hands of the family. Not that Carl isn't a good man. If we have to use a nonfamily member, I'd rather that person be managing editor of *Our Family.* The *Lamar Daily* is family."

"You could really let someone else take over *Our Family,* your baby?"

She wasn't sure. She wanted them both. A part of her would willingly give up her role at the *Lamar Daily,* but another part, a stronger part, wanted to keep it. She didn't think too closely about why. She shrugged. "We do what we have to do. It would be a lot of fun, and not to mention challenging, to birth and nurture *Our Family* on a day-to-day basis, but I'll be happy to *see* it get done. I don't have to *do* it."

"I hear your words, Eleanor, but your heart's not in them."

"Maybe I'm getting like you, Jake. It's not about my heart. It's about business."

She knew he didn't buy it, but she was thankful he didn't pursue it.

"I don't think we can commit to the community projects you've talked about yet. We should focus on the magazine and the infrastructure needed to support it. We'll consider the community projects later."

Eleanor extended her hand. "Seems like we're working from the same page, Jake. We may be able to come up with a deal I can live with, after all."

Jake took her hand in his, and instead of shaking it, he caressed it. "We work well together."

She felt the sexual connotation of the statement all the way to her toes. She was as attracted to Jake as she'd always been. And if today's meeting was any indication, she had no reason to fear his plans for the paper. The roadblocks keeping them apart seemed to be disappearing. "The jury's still out on that, but it's looking pretty good."

"May I take that as a word of encouragement?"

She eased her hand out of his and strolled to the door. "You may," she said, opening the door of the conference room. "But just a little." She heard him chuckle as she closed the door.

Chapter 14

"He'll be back," Eleanor said, tugging on Megan's arm to get her attention.

Megan reluctantly turned to her. "I miss him already."

"You've got it bad, don't you?"

Megan put her hands to her chest and whirled around. "I'm in love," she sang. "I'm in love."

Megan extended her hands to Eleanor. Eleanor took them and joined in her dance, a dance they had made up when they were kids. "Me-gan's in lo-ove," Eleanor joined in. "Me-gan's in lo-ove." Pretty soon they collapsed on Eleanor's bed in a fit of giggles.

"Remind you of one of our slumber parties?"

Eleanor nodded. "We always ended up laughing ourselves silly and Dad telling us to get some sleep."

Megan chuckled. "We almost drove Mr. S. crazy."

"That's why we had to alternate our sleepovers between your house and my house."

Megan rolled over on her stomach and propped her head on her hands. "You know, for a while I wished your dad and my mom would get together. Then we'd have been real sisters."

"We *are* real sisters," Eleanor said.

"But you know what I mean."

Eleanor nodded. "I never thought about my dad getting married again until I was much older. Maybe senior year. I know I thought about it a lot when I was in college."

"When you were dating Frank-lin?" Megan always exaggerated the syllables of his name.

"Why didn't you like him?"

"I did like him."

"You certainly didn't act like it."

"It could have been that he reminded me of Carl. They're a lot alike," she said, then added, "on the surface."

Eleanor considered Megan's observation. The only similarity between the two men was that they both were of the glasses and pen protector set. First-class nerds. But Franklin had changed a lot—become cosmopolitan—since she'd first known him. "At this point, Megan, everybody reminds you of Carl."

Megan rolled over on her back and pulled a pillow to her chest. "He's wonderful."

Eleanor shook her head and rolled her eyes. "You're beginning to repeat yourself."

Megan threw the pillow aside and faced Eleanor. "I want you to have what I have with Carl."

Eleanor wanted it, too. "One day. Maybe."

"Was it like this with Franklin?"

"What do you think?"

Megan pondered the question. "I don't think it was. At this point, I'd follow Carl anywhere if he married me. You wouldn't follow Franklin."

Eleanor nodded. "I loved Franklin. But I think it was more a puppy love. He was the first guy who loved me and that by itself was intoxicating."

"I can't remember anyone before Carl," Megan said dreamily.

Eleanor threw a pillow at her. "Now I know you're exaggerating."

Megan retaliated with a pillow missile to Eleanor. "I'm not, and if you'd ever been in love, you wouldn't say that."

Eleanor took the pillow and held it in her lap. "If you say so."

"Come on, Eleanor. Loosen up. You and Jake seem to be getting a little closer. What do you think?"

Eleanor folded her hands and rested them on the pillow. "I have a confession to make," she said softly.

Megan raised up on her knees. "What is it? Are you pregnant?"

Eleanor's eyes shot up, but a burst of something akin to pleasure settled in her bosom at the thought of having Jake's baby. "Of course not. Are you crazy?"

"So what is it?" Megan asked as she sat back on her thighs.

"Jake and I were never a couple. We only pretended to be one to help get you and Carl together."

"What?" Megan asked, eyes wide.

"You heard me. We faked our relationship for you and Carl."

Megan's eyes filled with tears as Eleanor explained the plans she and Jake had made.

"You did that for us?"

Eleanor nodded and Megan pulled her into her arms. "You're my best friend and my sister, all right. I'm so grateful for what you and Jake tried to do for me and Carl."

When Megan pulled away, Eleanor wiped at her own now-damp eyes. "We knew two people who argued as much as you two belonged together."

"And I know you and Jake belong together. He's had you off your beat since he got here. Even Carl's noticed it."

"We're business associates," Eleanor stated emphatically.

"Understatement of the year. Did you sleep with him in your quest to get me and Carl together?"

Eleanor hit her with the pillow. "Of course not."

"But I bet you kissed him."

"Maybe."

Megan pushed her pillow away. "Maybe nothing. Come on, girl, tell me."

"Okay, I kissed him."

Megan jumped up and gave the high-five sign. "I knew it. I knew it. I told Carl…"

"You told Carl what?"

Megan settled back down. "Nothing. I didn't tell him anything."

"Yes, you did. Now tell me what it was."

"Don't bust your britches. Carl and I want you to be as happy as we are."

"And…"

"And we think Jake could be the guy for you."

She'd been having thoughts along that line herself. "Me and Jake?"

"Yes, you and Jake. You're perfect for each other."

"And why do you think that?"

Megan leaned back on the bed and smiled confidently. "Because he's the first man to make you get your panties in a snit."

"Want to go for a drink tonight?" Jake asked Carl after everybody had filed out of the conference room at the end of the weekly status meeting.

Carl grinned. 'Not tonight. My lady's waiting for me."

Jake walked over and propped on the edge of the table in front of his friend. "You've got it bad. You know that, don't you?"

Carl whirled around in his chair. "If this is bad, I don't think I could handle good."

Jake laughed. "I knew there was something between you and Megan."

"Well, you knew more than I did. I'm glad you and Eleanor decided to make us come to our senses before it was too late. Thanks, man."

Jake slapped him on the back. "It was nothing. Eleanor and I did it for ourselves as much as we did it for you and Megan."

"What do you mean by that?"

"If we didn't get you two together, you would've killed us with your constant bickering."

Carl gave a smile, then quickly sobered. "I love her, man."

At that moment, Jake felt envy deep in his bones. Though he'd dated many women in his lifetime and he'd loved them all, he'd never been *in love* with any of them. When he saw Carl like this though, it made him wonder what he'd missed. "I'm happy for both of you."

"Thanks, man." Carl leaned back in his chair, linked his fingers and rested them on his stomach. "Megan tells me things are heating up with you and Eleanor."

That was new to Jake. He leaned closer. "What did Eleanor tell her?"

Carl shrugged. "She mentioned something about a kiss."

So, Jake thought, Eleanor couldn't get that kiss out of her mind either. "Well, that's about the extent of what's happened."

"Don't discount it, man. A kiss is a good thing. Maybe somewhere along the line your playacting became real."

Jake shook his head. "I doubt it. Eleanor's not interested in pursuing a relationship with the enemy."

Carl chuckled. "You're still the enemy?"

He thought about their last discussion of *Our Family.* "I'm gaining ground, but I still have a long way to go yet."

Carl shook his head. "What are you going to do about it?"

"What can I do?"

Carl studied him, before shaking his head. "If you don't know, man. I can't tell you."

"Yeah, yeah. When a brother falls in love, he wants every other man to be in love."

Carl grinned, but he didn't deny it. "It's great, man. You should try it."

"You mean, Megan's great."

"She is."

Those simple words expressed to Jake the love Carl felt for Megan even more than his earlier declaration of love. "You're a lucky man."

"You're telling me. Can you believe a woman like Megan waited for me?" Carl shook his head, then spoke without waiting for Jake's response. "She was a virgin, man," he said, his voice full of awe. "I was the first guy she was with. Do you know how that makes me feel?"

So he'd been right about Megan. He did know women. "Would it have made a difference if she wasn't?"

"Maybe to her," Carl said.

"What does that mean?"

Carl looked up at Jake. "I was inexperienced, too."

"What?" Jake exclaimed. "You've got to be kidding. You mean, you'd never…"

Carl shook his head. "Never."

Jake stood up and slipped his hands in his pockets. "I don't believe this. How old are you?"

Carl began gathering his papers. "I'm twenty-eight, the same age as Megan and Eleanor. And don't go making a big deal about this. I can't believe I told you anyway."

Jake sobered, then clapped Carl on the back. "I think it's great for you and Megan."

Carl nodded. "It makes me glad I waited." Carl grinned as if he'd remembered a funny joke.

"What?"

Carl's grin broadened. "Now I can't seem to get enough. Fortunately, neither can Megan."

"You lucky dog," Jake said in good humor.

"I'm not a dog," Carl replied with mock pique. He stood up and put his papers under his arm. "My cupcake says I'm a sweetie."

Jake laughed as Carl strutted out of the conference room.

On Thursday night of his seventh week in Lamar, Jake stared out the French doors of the Sanders living room wondering if he should go to Eleanor. She'd fled his presence as soon as possible after dinner with him and her father. He reached for the door latch for the fourth time. Should he go to her?

He dropped his hand. If she didn't want anything to happen between them, then he should respect her wishes. He placed his hand on the door latch again. On the other hand, her position was going to drive them both crazy before the summer was over, so he'd be doing them both a favor by forcing the issue.

He snatched the door open and stepped outside before he talked himself out of making the trek to her cottage. He strode past the pool and followed the lane to her front door.

He lifted his hand to rap on the door, then dropped it. Was he ready to face the consequences of sleeping with Eleanor? He knew she wasn't a woman he could casually make love to, then walk away from. But then he'd never done that. Every woman he'd been with had known the score. When he was with a woman, he was faithful. Yes, serial monogamy was his MO. But when he was ready to move on, he moved on. And since he'd made no commitments, he felt no guilt.

But what about Eleanor? Not only was she a *special* woman, she was his business associate and the daughter of his father's best friend. What the hell was he doing knocking on her door?

Before he could answer that question, Eleanor opened the door and peeked out. The answer to his question no longer mattered.

"What are you doing here, Jake?" she asked, her breath coming in short spurts. He wondered what she'd been doing.

"I want to talk to you," he lied.

Her eyes squinted and he knew she didn't believe him. "I saw you at dinner. You could have talked to me then."

He grinned. "I don't think you'd want your father to hear the things I have to say."

"Jake…" There was a plea in her voice.

He put his hand on the door in an attempt to push it open farther. "Fifteen minutes. Give me fifteen minutes."

He saw the indecision in her eyes.

"You must have it bad for me," he challenged, studying the hand that rested on the door as if he were indifferent to her answer, "if you don't trust yourself to be alone with me for fifteen minutes."

She grunted. "It's not me I don't trust, it's you."

He grinned again. "Scared?"

"You wish," she said, stepping back from the door and allowing him to push it open farther so he could enter. "I hope I don't regret this," she said when he was inside.

He couldn't form a response. Actually, he couldn't close his mouth. As he admired her form in the thigh-length fluffy white robe, he wondered if everything she owned was white. And skimpy.

His eyes traveled her full length, causing her to pull the collar of her robe closer. Unfortunately for her, the action only caused her breasts to be better outlined. Unfortunately for him, the puckered nipples caused a similar response in his groin.

"You wanted to talk," she said, turning around and walking to the overstuffed white couch.

He followed her, again admiring the sway of the lush hips atop her long, firm legs. "Yes," he said, stalling for time to clear his mind. He deliberately sat next to her on the couch and pretended to ignore the raised brow she directed at him because of the action.

"I'm waiting," she said, apparently eager for him to get on with it.

Jake wondered again if he was doing the right thing. He shuffled through the magazines on the table in front of him, then picked up *Family Focus*. "Studying the competition?"

That was the right thing to say, because Eleanor immediately relaxed, leaned forward, and picked up a copy of *Southern Families*. "Yes, if you can call it that. These magazines aren't directed at African-Americans, but they demonstrate the concept. Look at this one. The article on the fading nuclear family is the kind of story I'd like to do in *Our Family*."

Jake looked at her, about the comment, but the sight of the tops of her breasts peeking out from her robe made him forget what he was about to say.

"What do you think?" she asked, her eyes sparkling with excitement.

I think I'm in trouble, he said to himself. "Let me see." He briefly scanned the article, glad for a reason to take his eyes off her yet disappointed he couldn't look his fill. "Not bad."

"Not bad?" She took the magazine from him and scanned the article as if to make sure it was the one she was thinking about. "How can you say 'Not bad'? That's exactly the kind of article I want us to do in *Our Family*."

Her eyes were shooting sparks now. He liked it. "I don't see anything unique about it."

She breathed deeply and he knew she was about to blow her stack.

"Maybe you don't know a good article when you see one," she said calmly.

He fought to keep from grinning. "Maybe." Pause. "Maybe not."

She threw the magazine down on the table and crossed her arms. "What did you want to talk about?"

He chuckled. "I liked the article, Eleanor."

She dropped her arms and rolled her eyes. "Then why didn't you say so?"

"Maybe I like to see you squirm."

Jake knew by the flash of passion in her eyes that the erotic picture his words painted in his mind was also painted in hers.

"I can't stop thinking about that kiss," he whispered.

"Jake…"

He reached for her hand and rubbed it between the two of his. "I bet you've been thinking about it, too."

She attempted to remove her hand from his, but he wouldn't release it. Instead, he pulled it to his lips and kissed it. "Your skin's so soft," he murmured.

"Don't."

He looked up at her and knew the passion in her eyes was mirrored in his. "Don't what? Don't want you? That's impossible."

"But—"

"But you're afraid?" He released her hand. "What are you afraid of, Eleanor?"

She lowered her eyes, but she didn't answer.

He leaned closer and placed a soft kiss on her exposed neck. "Are you afraid of what you're feeling?" he whispered.

She inclined her head more and he began a row of kisses up and down her thin neck.

"Tell me what you're feeling," Jake whispered. "Tell me, Eleanor. I see it in your eyes when you look at me. I felt it in your kiss when you kissed me. Everything about you tells me we'd be good together. From the gentle sway of your hips when you walk, to your puckered nipples that greeted me at the door, to the way you chew the ends of your pens when you're working."

"Jake," she murmured, inching away from him.

He pulled back and lifted her chin so that she stared into his eyes. "Can't you see that I feel the same way?"

She shook her head, but she didn't say anything.

He took her hand and placed it on his crotch. "Can't you feel how much I want you?"

She stared at the bulge, then flashed her eyes to his and quickly removed her hand.

"I want to touch you," he said, then raised his hand to the top opening of her robe and touched her chest. His eyes never left hers. "May I touch you?" he asked, but he didn't wait for an answer. He slid his hand down to a warm breast and covered it. His eyes closed at the pleasure that shot through him.

"Jake," Eleanor pleaded in a thick voice. Her hand covered his own and he opened his eyes.

"Do you like that?" he asked, tweaking her erect nipple.

A rap sounded at the door before Eleanor could answer.

Chapter 15

The interruption brought Eleanor to her senses and she finally had the strength and the desire to move away from Jake.

"Damn," Jake said when his hand fell away from her breast.

"Eleanor, it's me," Megan called from outside the door.

Jake dropped his head and muttered, "Talk about bad timing."

"I'd better get that," Eleanor said, straightening the collar of her robe.

She got up on wobbly legs, glared down at Jake, and headed for the door.

"What took you so long?" Megan asked as soon as Eleanor opened the door. "I've been knocking for five minutes."

Five minutes, Eleanor thought. Had she been so involved with Jake she'd missed five minutes of knocking?

Megan strode past her and stopped in her tracks as soon as she saw Jake.

He stood up. "Hi, Megan."

Megan, eyes dancing, turned around and faced Eleanor. "I'm sorry, girl, I didn't know you had company."

Eleanor strode past her and took a seat in the overstuffed chair next to the couch. "It's not company. It's Jake."

Megan made a beeline for the couch. "Hope I didn't interrupt anything?" She sat down next to Jake. "Actually, I hope I did interrupt something."

Jake laughed and Eleanor rolled her eyes.

"Where's your shadow?" Jake asked, then stood up and stuffed his hands in his pockets.

That dreamy look of love came over Megan's face. "Carl stopped by the house to see you. It didn't occur to us you'd be here. I guess he'll be along in a minute or so."

"I'm sure he will," Eleanor muttered. "He doesn't let you out of his sight for more than ten minutes at a time."

Megan ignored Eleanor. "Why don't you sit down, Jake? There's no need to rush off. Carl and I won't stay long."

"He was leaving anyway," Eleanor said, but Jake contradicted her words when he sat back down on the couch.

Megan grinned. "I guess he changed his mind."

Eleanor chose to ignore that. "What brings you and Carl out?"

"Oh, we wondered if you and Jake wanted to see that new Robert Townsend movie with us."

"Not tonight," Jake and Eleanor said at the same time.

Megan looked from one to the other and grinned. "No, I didn't think you'd be interested. Seems like you already have plans for the evening."

Carl's rap on the door saved Eleanor and Jake from having to respond.

"You'd better put on some clothes," Jake said to Eleanor, then stood up again. "I'll let Carl in."

Eleanor's mouth dropped open.

"Bossy, isn't he?" Megan said with a giggle. "But he has a point. Carl will probably be a little uncomfortable with you dressed like that."

Eleanor looked down at herself, remembering that she wore nothing underneath the skimpy robe. "I'll be back in a minute."

"I'll go with you." Megan got up and followed Eleanor to her bedroom. When the bedroom door closed, she dropped down on the bed and asked, "What was going on?"

"Nothing." Eleanor opened the sash on her robe and stepped into her closet. After slipping on a pair of satin bikini briefs, she pulled on a pair of jean shorts and one of her old high school T-shirts. First, she tucked the shirt into her shorts, then decided she best wear it out since her shorts were pretty short.

Megan grinned at her when she walked out of the closet. "I know it wasn't nothing. So tell me what happened."

"I don't want to talk about it now, Megan. Let's get back out there before Carl comes looking for you."

Megan got up from the bed. "Isn't he sweet?" she said in that dreamy voice.

"As syrup," Eleanor responded dryly.

"No need to be nasty, Eleanor. Just because you're having problems with Jake doesn't mean you have to be mean to my Carl."

Eleanor dropped down on the foot of the bed. "I'm sorry. I don't know what's wrong with me."

"I do, girl. You've got it bad." Megan moved to sit on the bed next to her. "You're falling for him, aren't you?"

All Eleanor could do was nod. In spite of all her efforts to stop him, Jake Mason had gotten under her skin. Deep. It was so stupid. Why did she have to fall for a man who was only going to be around for the summer, for about another five or six weeks to be exact. If she and Jake were different people, a long-distance relationship might have a chance. But they were who they were and she didn't see them in a long-distance relationship. Once he left Lamar, he'd forget her and her heart would break.

"Well," Megan said, in a sagelike voice, "the good news is he's fallen for you, too."

Eleanor stood up and slipped her hands in her rear pockets. "I'm not too sure about that."

"I am."

"What makes you so sure?"

Megan grabbed Eleanor by the shoulders and pushed her to the door. "A little bird named Jake has been talking to a little bird named Carl."

Eleanor stopped walking. "What did Jake say?"

"You know I can't tell you that. Carl thinks I can keep a secret. Now, let's get back out there. I miss my sweetie."

If Carl and Megan didn't leave in the next five minutes, Jake planned to throw them out. He took a quick glance at Eleanor.

Damn! She was getting increasingly uptight with each one of Carl and Megan's not-so-subtle jabs.

Any other time with any other woman, he could have enjoyed the other couple's antics. But not with Eleanor. Not where they were in their relationship. If they even had a relationship.

And if he didn't get Larry and Moe out of there, they didn't stand a chance of becoming a couple.

"Are you two sure you don't want to check out this new flick?" Carl asked, mischief in his smile. "We'd love to have you come with us, wouldn't we, cupcake?"

Megan's smile was all butter. "We sure would. Especially since you two don't have anything better to do."

Eleanor refused to be baited. "Why don't you *all* leave?"

Carl gave Jake an understanding smile. "I think she wants you out, too, man. I hope we didn't ruin your evening."

Jake wanted to wrap his hands around Carl's neck. "See you later."

"I guess we'd better go, sweetie. They're both being rude." Megan giggled. "They must be frustrated."

Carl guffawed. "That must be it."

Jake stood. "That's it. You two are outta here." He walked to the door and opened it. "It's been real."

"We can take a hint," Megan said, moving to the door. "I'll talk to you later, Eleanor." She giggled again. "Maybe I'll wait till tomorrow. You probably have a busy night planned."

Carl and Megan were still laughing when Jake slammed the door behind them.

Eleanor stood up. "You'd better go, too, Jake. It's getting late."

"That's not gonna cut it, Eleanor. We have to talk."

Eleanor didn't want to talk. She needed to think. "Not tonight, Jake. I can't handle it tonight."

Jake went to her and pulled her into his arms. "I'm sorry we were interrupted."

"I'm not."

He rubbed his hands up and down her arms. "Yes, you are."

She pulled back and looked up at him. "I don't like your bossy attitude. I know my own mind."

"Sure you do," he said, pressing her head back to his chest. This was his woman and he liked holding her. His woman. He'd never thought like that before, but he liked the sound of it.

He felt her relax in his arms. "What do you want from me, Jake? A summer fling?"

That question took him off guard. He didn't even like the sound of the word *fling* when thinking about Eleanor. But what did he want?

She pulled away from him. "You won't even admit that a fling is all you want?"

He wanted to tell her she was wrong, but he couldn't. This wasn't supposed to happen. He wasn't supposed to feel things for her. What had happened to his plans to work a deal that would make his father sit up and take notice? When had she become so important to him? "I want more than that."

The surprise in her eyes was clear for him to see.

"Don't look so surprised."

She shook her head as if to clear her thoughts. "What do you want, Jake?"

He couldn't answer her because he didn't know. He hadn't though much beyond his feelings for her *now*. He knew he cared about her. A lot. He knew a relationship with her would be different from any he'd had in the past. But he didn't know what that meant in practical terms. He didn't know where or how the relationship would progress. He was afraid even to think about it. He only knew he couldn't not be with her.

"I think you'd better go," she said finally.

"I don't want to go."

She smiled sadly. "I know, but you have to."

"But—"

She lifted a hand to stop his words. "Close the door on your way out. I'm going to lie down." She gave him a final look and left the room.

Jake stood rooted in place while she practically ran to her room and closed the door. *Damn! She was driving him crazy.*

Jake stared at her bedroom door for a couple of seconds, before taking the few steps that placed him only a door away from her. He lifted his hand to open the door, but he couldn't do it. He couldn't do it because he couldn't answer her questions. *Damn! Why did she have to make things so difficult?*

He turned slowly and walked out of her cottage, closing the door behind him. Maybe it was best, he told himself. He didn't need the complications that came along with Eleanor. No, he was much better off without her.

Maybe he could get Carl and Megan to introduce him to somebody else and he could keep his mind off Eleanor. Yes, that's exactly what he'd do.

Who was he kidding? he asked himself when he reached the French doors of the main house. There wasn't a woman alive who could keep his mind off Eleanor. He'd have to find a way to deal with her. And soon. God knows, he couldn't go through another night like tonight. Going unsatisfied was not a situation he found himself in often and he didn't like it. No, he didn't like it one bit. Thank God he hadn't had to resort to cold showers. Yet.

Eleanor released the breath she'd been holding as soon as she heard Jake's footsteps leave her bedroom door. She didn't know if she was glad or sad he hadn't opened the door and joined her in bed. Maybe she wished he had. Maybe that was why she'd stripped off her clothes and collapsed naked on the bed as soon as she'd closed her bedroom door.

It was all moot now that Jake was gone. At least, it was moot for the moment. Eleanor was mature enough to know that the feelings that raged between her and Jake wouldn't be denied forever. She and Jake would make love, and soon, as sure as the sun rose each day.

She rolled over on her stomach. Why was she delaying the inevitable? Maybe the wisest thing to do would be for them to go to bed, do the deed, and be done with it.

She eased up from the bed and headed for the shower. Yes, she and Jake needed to do the deed and get it over. There were only so many cold showers a woman could take.

Eleanor dragged into work the next morning after a nearly sleepless night. Thoughts of Jake and her own libido had kept her awake until early in the morning.

She grabbed a cup of coffee and hoped it would keep her alert enough to get out today's edition.

"Morning, Eleanor," Carl called. "Sleep well?"

Eleanor wanted to wipe that stupid grin off Carl's face. "Morning, Carl," she said and kept moving to her office.

She uttered a silent thanks that Jake wasn't at his desk. Hopefully, he'd be out all morning.

She dropped in her chair and began her morning ritual. Before long she was in her routine and her tiredness was forgotten.

"Morning, Eleanor."

The smooth silkiness of Jake's voice stopped the movement of her fingers. She glanced up at him. "Morning." She refocused on her screen and forced her fingers to move again.

She heard Jake settle himself at his desk and pick up his phone.

"So what do you think, Buddy?" she heard him ask.

Buddy? Who was Buddy? She didn't consider listening to his conversation as eavesdropping. No, they shared the same office and he talked loudly.

When his voice dropped to a whisper and she could no longer hear him, her fingers stopped their movement again and she leaned, ever so slightly, toward him.

"Do you want something, Eleanor?" Jake asked.

Busted, she sat up straight and resumed her keystrokes. "Oh, no."

"Look," she heard Jake say, "I'll talk to you a little later when I have some *privacy.*"

Eleanor heard the emphasis on the word *privacy* and knew it was for her. When she raised her eyes to him, he was staring at her, his eyes blazing with passion and something else she couldn't name. She gave a weak smile and returned her attention back to her keyboard.

She heard him hang up the phone then swagger over to stand behind her.

"You were eavesdropping," he whispered.

The spoken words couldn't have affected her more if he'd said *I want you.*

"I was not," she lied.

"You're lying," he said, so close his breath tickled the back of her neck.

She resisted the urge to swat him away. "I can't help it if you talk too loudly."

He moved away from her and sat on the edge of her desk. "You known what I like least about this office?"

"No," she said, turning around. "I don't."

"That damned window," he said, referring to the window in the wall separating her office from the rest of the newsroom.

He sounded so sincere that laughter bubbled up in her and spilled out.

"I love your laugh," he murmured.

His passion sobered her and she looked through the window out into the newsroom to gather her wits. Carl, a knowing grin on his face, had the audacity to wave at her. Maybe she should consider getting rid of the window.

"Did you sleep well last night?" he asked.

Praying the passion she felt didn't show in her eyes, she glanced up at him and shook her head.

"Neither did I."

They were both silent for a while.

"Is this easy for you?"

She shook her head. If he thought this was easy for her, she must be one good actress.

"So what are we going to do?"

She smiled crookedly. "We could close the blinds and go for it right here."

He inhaled deeply. "Don't tempt me."

She stared up at him, wanting to tell him he wasn't the only one tempted. Instead, she got up out of her chair and walked to the window.

"What are you doing?" Jake asked, his eyes wide with banked passion.

She twisted the rod and the blinds closed. "I'm yielding to temptation." She started to walk back to him, but she turned around and twisted the lock on the door. "We don't want any interruptions, do we?"

Jake's mouth dropped open, but no words came out.

"What's wrong, Jake?" she asked as she sauntered toward him. "This is what you want, isn't it?"

"Eleanor…" Jake warned.

She walked into the middle of his spread legs and his thighs tightened against her. When he groaned, she placed a hand on either of his shoulders and stared into his passion-filled dark brown eyes. She'd known this man less than two months, but she knew the place he'd found in her heart was forever. She didn't kid herself the relationship was forever, though. Jake's stay in Lamar was limited. She knew that and she accepted it.

"Two can play this game," Jake said, unbuttoning her jacket and pushing it apart.

She leaned her face closer to his and rubbed her jaw against his. "What game?"

Jake reached inside her jacket, encircled her waist with his hands, and pulled her tight against him. "You feel so good."

"Umm, you don't feel so bad yourself." She relaxed in his arms and tightened her arms around his shoulders. She thought she could stay in his arms forever. There was something sure and right about it.

"I want to kiss you."

She leaned away from him and his eyes repeated his words. "I thought you'd never ask."

She closed her eyes when his lips captured hers. When his tongue slipped inside her mouth, she knew this moment was only the beginning for them.

When he pulled away, they were both breathing heavily.

"Do you want to come over tonight?" she asked when she could get her breath.

He pulled her back for another long kiss. "What time?" he asked.

"I'll be there all night."

"All night?" he repeated.

"All night."

He pushed her away from him and looked into her eyes. "Are you sure?"

Her confidence slipped a little and she wondered if her feelings were one-sided. She stepped out of the circle of his arms, went back to the window, and was about to open the blinds. Jake's hand stopped her.

He turned her around. "Make no mistake about it, Eleanor. I want you. I want you so bad now I hurt."

She relaxed and dropped her head against his chest. "I want you, too."

He grunted. "And you're going to have me."

Chapter 16

Eleanor stripped out of her fifth outfit in the last twenty minutes. Why was Jake Mason making her so nervous? This wasn't her first date, nor was it her first time. Get a grip, she told herself. Jake is only a man.

"Right," she said, looking at the three piles of lingerie covering her bed. She never would have guessed she had this much lingerie. A piece here and a piece there over the years certainly added up. Her bedroom looked ready for a Victoria's Secret yard sale.

She opened the last drawer in her lingerie chest, praying the odds were with her. She pulled out garment after garment until there was nothing left in the drawer. And still she had found nothing to wear.

She pushed the piles of lingerie aside and dropped down on the bed. Maybe she should give up on clothes and greet him at the door in her birthday suit. She wondered what he would think of that.

She grabbed a pile of the lingerie in her hand and took it to the dresser. It didn't matter what Jake would think. She was going to be herself tonight. She stuffed the first pile in the dresser and went back to the bed for another. Finished, she propped her hands on her hips and stared at the third pile still on the bed.

Nodding her head, she pulled a white lace bodysuit from the pile and held it up in front of her. "This is it. This is what I'll wear tonight."

Satisfied, she picked up the remaining items and placed them back in the dresser. When she turned to head for the bathroom, the phone rang.

"Are you nervous?"

Eleanor dropped down on the bed. "What are you talking about, Megan?"

Megan chuckled. "Carl told me about the closed blinds and locked door at the office today. When you canceled our date for tonight, I figured you must have had other plans."

She should have known Carl would say something. He'd been grinning at her all day. "I don't know what you're talking about," she lied.

Megan chuckled again. "Sure you don't. Anyway, have fun tonight. I'll call you tomorrow and see how things went."

Megan hung up before Eleanor could respond.

"Damn," she said, then scrambled into the shower.

Twenty minutes later, she was dressed in her bodysuit, applying her makeup. Not too much, though, but she couldn't plan for a love scene without the proper look, could she?

She heard a knock at the front door as soon as she placed the cap on her lipstick. "Perfect timing," she said, grabbing her standard robe. "Let's make Mr. Mason wonder for a little while, at least."

Eleanor walked to the door, took a deep breath, then opened the door. At the sight of Jake standing there in a pair of beige pants, a white open-collar dress shirt, and aviator sunglasses, her knees went weak and she tightened her hold on the doorknob to keep her balance.

"Hi," she said, praying her voice sounded normal since her pulse wasn't. It seemed her heart rate had doubled in the few seconds she'd been standing at the door.

Jake pulled off the aviator glasses and handed her a single white rose. "Hi, yourself," he said, his eyes shining with passion.

When she saw the burning passion in Jake's eyes, she immediately felt exposed. And this was a rare feeling for her. She was comfortable with her body and usually relished her nudity. But not now. Now she wished for a longer robe. Maybe even jeans and a T-shirt. She ran her hand through her hair, which fell in soft curls on her shoulders.

"Aren't you going to take it?"

The laughter in his voice alerted her to action and she reached for the rose. "Thank you," she said, stepping back into the room. "Come on in."

"Thought you'd never ask."

Eleanor walked to the couch, twisting the stem of the rose in her hand, very conscious of Jake behind her. She wished again that she'd chosen to wear more clothes. She sat on the couch and Jake sat next to her.

"Ouch," she said, and dropped the rose on the table in front of her.

Jake placed the aviator glasses next to the rose and reached for her hand. "Did you hurt yourself?"

She shook her head. "It's nothing. I pricked my finger."

Jake pulled the injured finger to his lips and his eyes met hers. "Let me kiss it and make it better."

"That won't be—"

Jake's tongue on her finger sent a shiver of desire through her and her words were forgotten. After he kissed the injured finger, he moved on to each finger of her hand. Eleanor felt warmer with each touch of his tongue.

"That better?" Jake asked, his eyes now glazed with passion.

She reluctantly pulled her hand away, wondering what had happened to her courage. Had she really expected to go through this evening in a mechanical fashion—wham, bam, thank-you, ma'am—and have it done with? What had she been thinking?

Jake shifted in his seat. He wondered if taking her finger in his mouth had been a wise move. He'd known his desire for Eleanor was great, but he hadn't anticipated his desire would work against him. But that's exactly what was happening.

He glanced at Eleanor and took small satisfaction in knowing she was as affected as he was. No, her eagerness could only enhance their union while his could ruin the evening for both of them. And he definitely didn't want that to happen. He needed to slow things down.

"Nervous?"

She looked at him with wide doe eyes and all he wanted to do was take her to bed. "Who, me?"

He chuckled. "No, the couch."

She gave him the laugh he wanted. Except the laugh was as enticing as if she'd stripped naked before him. He cleared his throat. "What do you want to do?"

She stared at him and he would have sworn he heard her mind speak, *Go to bed.* "Do?"

"Aw, hell," he said and pulled her into his arms.

"What—"

"Don't talk." His mouth covered hers and he felt his breath leave his body. What was it about this woman that affected him so? The opening of her mouth below his stopped any action of his brain to answer that question.

Eleanor leaned closer to Jake, needing to touch him all over. Her arms wound around his neck as his tongue entered into a mating ritual with hers. This wasn't the first time she'd been kissed, not even the first time he'd kissed her, but for the life of her, she couldn't remember any kiss except this one.

She took a quick breath when Jake groaned, but was grateful when he took up his assault again. The pressure of his eager lips against hers made her squirm against him, but it was the feel of his smooth hands against the bare skin of her chest that made her moan and want to touch him in return.

Why did he have on so many clothes? she wondered. Shouldn't he take off some of his clothes?

She grew impatient and dropped her hands from his neck to his shirt, still holding up her end of the kiss. As his hand slipped to her lace-covered breast, she undid the first few buttons of his shirt.

He lifted his mouth from hers and stared into her eyes as his hand massaged her breast. She closed her eyes, not able to stand the intensity she saw in his coupled with the sensation his roving hands caused.

Jake stopped his massaging motion and she opened her eyes. Seeing the question in them, he gently pressed his lips to hers. When he pulled back, he brought the belt of her robe with him. "God," he said, pushing her robe off her shoulders onto the back of the couch.

The white lace that played peek-a-boo with the body he longed to possess mesmerized him. When he fingered the lace covering her right breast, she moaned again and her body lifted slightly from the couch.

Jake watched the play of emotions in her eyes and marveled that he could cause such abandon in her. When she closed her eyes again, he lowered his head to her right breast and lavished his tongue on its firm peak. The grainy sensation of her nipple against his tongue made his groin tighten. He was in trouble.

She didn't help his predicament any when she placed a hand to the back of his head and pulled him closer, all the while pressing her body more firmly against his. He groaned, then lifted a hand to tweak the nipple of her other breast. Now he wished he had another hand. Maybe even another mouth. There were so many things he wanted to do. With her. And to her.

He wanted to kiss her mouth again, but he didn't want to stop his attention to her breast. He opened his mouth and took in the nipple and felt he was actually being nurtured. He knew he'd die if he didn't get to sample the other breast.

When her hand fell limp from his head, he raised his head slowly from one breast and captured the other in both hands. He teased the extended nipple with his fingers before hungrily capturing its peak in his mouth. Yes, there was life in her breasts for him.

Eleanor's tongue slipped out of her mouth as spasms of desire shot through her body. With each movement of his tongue, each touch of his tongue, her body temperature rose and her need for him grew. She wanted to touch him, but she couldn't make her hand respond to her mind. It was as if her body was no longer under her control.

"Jake," she pleaded, wanting to touch him the way he was touching her.

He lifted his head and focused desire-glazed eyes on her while his hands continued to pull at her nipples. Somehow, she managed to mobilize her arms to pull him closer to her. "I want to touch you," she murmured.

She pushed his shirt off his shoulders. "Jake," she said again. "I can't get the shirt off."

He seemed to come out of his haze long enough to shrug out of the shirt and throw it on the hardwood floor.

Eleanor immediately leaned into him, splaying the fingers of both her hands across his broad, smooth chest. When he sucked in his breath, she gazed into his eyes and a feeling of pure desire swept over her at the knowledge that she could affect this man so.

"Oh, Jake," she cooed before lowering her head to his nipple and loving it with her tongue. The twitching in his limbs encouraged her motions and she moved her hand to play with the other nipple much as his hand had played with hers.

Her satisfaction with herself increased with each involuntary movement of his body. She was becoming accustomed to the role of seductress until she felt his hands slip to her pubis.

Jake noticed the hesitation in her movements when his hands touched the lace covering her mound, but she quickly resumed her assault on his chest. The feel of her soft lips against his chest coupled with the feel of the wet flesh of her mound against his hand made him ache. He knew it wouldn't be long now.

"Eleanor," he murmured, moving both his hands to her head to stop her motions. The passion in her eyes when she looked up at him was almost his undoing and he forgot what he wanted to say as his mouth swooped over hers.

She gave herself to him completely, pressing her body so tight against him he could feel the imprint of every piece of lace that covered her.

They were both breathless when he broke the kiss. She rested her head against his chest while he stroked her jaw with his forefinger.

Eleanor heard his labored breathing and was hard-pressed to

distinguish it from her own. She'd never felt as in tune with any human as she felt with Jake now. She knew he was as overcome with emotion as she was, and knowing they were equals in their feelings made her want him more.

Eleanor was ready when he moved his mouth to her ear and whispered, "Let's go to bed."

She kissed his forehead, placed her hand in his, then stood. She felt his eyes searing every inch of her as she led him to her bedroom and her bed.

She lay on her side on the bed and watched him remove his shoes and pants. When she saw his bikini briefs, she smiled. He definitely had the body for them—firm hips and thighs and everything in between.

An unbidden question as to the number of women who had thought that same thing entered her mind, and for the first time since he'd touched her, she became unsure of what she was doing.

"What's wrong?" he asked, his fingers in the waistband of his briefs.

"You've done this a lot, haven't you?"

He slipped the briefs past his hips and down his legs. Stepping out of them, he joined her on the bed and pulled her into his arms. "No you don't. There are only two of us in this room and I'm not letting you include some imaginary woman from my past." He kissed her lips lightly. "Understand?"

She forgot her question as he began his assault upon her senses again. He captured her gaze with his own while his hands eased under the straps of her bodysuit and pushed them down her arms.

When the lace covering her breasts fell away, his eyes darkened and she thought he was going to take the exposed flesh in his mouth again. Her disappointment when he didn't was acute.

He continued removing the lace from her body, his eyes getting darker and darker with each inch of revealed skin. By the time the lace covering her mound was removed, his eyes were practically black.

She licked her lips together as she lifted, first one leg, then the other, so he could remove the suit from her body entirely. When she was naked before him, his gaze left hers and roamed her body.

She burned with every touch of his glance. His gaze traveled her body leaving a trail of scorching flesh. A spot on her left shoulder burned especially hot and she wondered what he found so fascinating there.

Jake marveled at the beauty of her naked body. She was definitely the most beautiful woman he'd ever known. Her creamy brown skin drew him like magnets drew metal. There was no denying the hold she had on him.

He'd walked into this relationship with Eleanor knowing it was going to be different from other relationships he'd had, but he hadn't realized how different. He'd planned to leave Lamar when his job was finished and not look back. Now, he wasn't so sure he'd be able to. Hell, he wasn't sure he even wanted to.

Eleanor wondered what was happening between them. She knew as well as she knew her name she would never be the same after being with Jake. Her mind told her she should stop now, while she had a chance. Her body told her it was too late to stop and she didn't have a chance. Her body was right.

Eleanor couldn't stand it any longer. "Touch me," she said.

Jake honored her request by resting one hand on her stomach and using the other to pull her mouth to his. She sighed as they resumed the dance they had started in her living room.

Jake eased his body against hers. "I love the way your skin feels. So silky. So smooth. So soft. Oh, so soft."

His words made her feel as if her backbone had slid out of her body. His firm, warm skin felt as good to her, but she couldn't tell him. Her mouth's only purpose now was to kiss him. She moaned, her body a shivering mass of desire. She couldn't feel anything but her need for him.

And his raging need for her. Again, she was awed at the effect she had on him. She felt him, large and long, against her thigh and her body seemed to open up in anticipation of receiving him.

Jake wanted the evening to last longer, but he knew that was impossible. If he didn't have her now, he was sure he'd die.

"Eleanor," he whispered and slipped himself inside her warm, wet sheath.

"Jake…" she began.

He heard the awe in her voice and knew she experienced the same sense of rightness and oneness he felt. It was as though they were alone in the world, as if something bigger than the two of them was being set right by their union.

They moved together as if they'd made love thousands of times. She instinctively met his every thrust and anticipated his every desire. He found the most sensitive areas of her body with expert precision. They were one in every sense of the word.

Chapter 17

When Eleanor opened her eyes the next morning with Jake's strong arm resting across her stomach and his head resting against her still-sensitive breasts, she knew her life would never be the same. She lifted her hand and rubbed it lightly across his head while memories of their night of passion saturated her mind.

She had guessed Jake was an accomplished lover, but she'd never guessed the heights to which his tenderness would take her. From his first touch, she'd been his to do with as he wanted and she hadn't been disappointed. She smiled a satisfied smile. Each of the four times their bodies had joined was perfect.

Yes, their night had been perfect. And though Jake's touch brought long-dormant emotions to life, she knew their relationship had no future. She understood Jake had only given himself for the night and she accepted it. She wasn't sure if she wanted more anyway. At least, not from him.

She'd needed Jake the previous night and she didn't regret being with him, but that night would be their first and last encounter. She didn't want to start thinking of a future with him.

Jake shifted his head and moved his hand to her breast. She sucked in her breath when his fingers began their massage. "Jake," she whispered.

"Good morning."

She felt his smile against her skin and his fingers increased their pressure. Though her senses were awakened and she was more than ready to make love with him again, she didn't think it was wise. She grabbed his hands and stopped the movement of his fingers. "Jake, we can't."

He raised his head and gazed into her eyes. "Why can't we?"

The sensuous smile curving his lips made her ask herself the same question. She shook her head and pushed the stray strands of hair from her face while she tried to remember why they couldn't.

He took advantage of her bemused state and kissed her. The kiss was a teasing kiss, one designed to make her want. And make her want it did. She pulled his head closer to her and gave herself up to the moment. Why fight it? She'd tell him later they couldn't do this anymore.

Uncontrolled strands of Eleanor's thick, nearly black hair tickled Jake's nose and he awakened to the sight of her beautiful, supple form sprawled across his body. Her nipples burned against his ribcage and he wanted her again.

He wanted her again, but he wasn't going to wake her. He grinned a satisfied masculine grin. No, he'd play the role of the gallant Southern gentleman and let her sleep for a while longer since he'd kept her up most of the night.

He shook his head when he thought of his first impression of Eleanor. He would never again apply the words *stern* and *prim* to her. She'd been everything but that with him last night. And this morning. He smiled again. Maybe he'd continue to use the word *mouthy,* though, but it would refer to the way she spoke when she kissed him. He'd never enjoyed kissing a woman as much as he'd enjoyed kissing her. He'd heard kisses described as soulful before, but it was only now that he thought he understood what a soulful kiss was.

He pressed his arms around her and closed his eyes. The restful contentment he felt was new to him. Normally, when the after-sleep sex was finished, he was ready to go home. But not this time. No, this morning he was content to hold Eleanor in his arms.

The next time he opened his eyes, Eleanor was moving out

of the circle of his arms. He tightened his arms around her. "Don't go."

She struggled to lift her head and shift away from him a little. "I have to go to the bathroom."

"Oh," he said a little sheepishly and released her. "Hurry back."

He admired her naked body as she glided away from him. The swing in her hips caused his groin to tighten. He wanted her again and this time he wasn't going to play the Southern gentleman.

Eleanor quickly closed the bathroom door and leaned back against it, her legs weak. How could his looking at her do this to her? She knew why. Jake didn't *look* at her. He made love to her with his eyes. Though he hadn't touched her as she'd walked away, she'd felt his hands and his mouth all over her body. Her body was as taut as stretched wire and she knew only Jake could give her relief.

Eleanor moved away from the door and looked at herself in the mirror. She still looked the same, but she knew that was only because she looked on the outside. She knew if she could see the inside, she'd see the change in her. She knew her senses were heightened. The body she'd always been comfortable in was now foreign to her.

She touched her sensitive breasts. They were no longer breasts; they were fountains from which Jake had drunk. Her shoulders were paths on which he had planted kisses. Her stomach, a wasteland he'd developed. Her navel would never again be just an inny.

She reluctantly touched her hand to her sticky mound and she knew that somehow Jake had marked this place as his own. She had no doubt that no man would ever claim her as Jake had done. And even though she knew that, she wasn't sad. No, she was happy. Happy to have had this special moment with Jake.

But now the moment was over and she had to tell him to go home. She ignored the dreaded ache that settled across her now-heavy heart at the thought.

* * *

Eleanor bumped into Jake's naked body when she walked out of the bathroom.

"I missed you," he murmured, gathering her in his arms.

She allowed herself a glorious second in his arms, before pulling free. "We have to talk."

He nibbled along her shoulder and she leaned her head to the side to give him better access. "I'm talking already. Do you hear what I'm saying?"

She forced herself to move away from him. "Jake!"

"God, I want you," he said, his eyes dark and piercing.

He lifted her in his arms, took her back to bed, and settled her against his chest. He kissed her while his hands explored the already familiar contours of her body.

Her traitorous body responded to his touch and she gave in to her desire. What was one more time?

Eleanor fanned at the annoying hand slapping against her rump. "Ouch, stop it." She turned over and was rewarded with Jake's smile.

"I'm hungry," he said, grinning.

"You can't be serious."

He laughed and kissed her briefly before getting out of bed. "We'll have to wait for more of that. Now, I need food."

Eleanor pulled the pillow over her head so Jake wouldn't see the rush of blood to her face and also to keep her eyes from his very masculine body. "Go eat then."

He pulled the pillow away. "Come with me."

Had he said those words to her during the night? she wondered, then shook her head. She wasn't going to start looking for sexual innuendo in every statement he made. "I'm not hungry." Her traitorous stomach growled, making her a liar.

He laughed again. "Come with me. It's my treat."

"You don't have to do that." She wished he would hurry up and leave.

"Listen," he coaxed. "I'll even take you to Mel's."

A smile escaped when she thought of their first visit to the diner. "It's not open on Saturdays."

He pulled the covers away from her and made love to her with his eyes. "Well, if you won't go out with me, I guess I'll have to get my nourishment here."

Her nakedness worked against her. She hopped out of the bed. "Okay, let's go get something to eat."

He laughed at her. "Chicken."

"Is Jake still there?"

Eleanor brushed her hair back with her hand and looked over at Jake's sleeping form. After a late, late breakfast he'd coaxed her back to bed. She admitted that it hadn't taken much effort on his part.

"What do you want, Megan?"

Megan giggled. "I guess that means he's still there."

Eleanor heard Megan mumble something to someone in the background. It had to be Carl.

"Anyway," Megan said when she was back, "Carl and I were wondering if you two wanted to go dancing at the Farmhouse with us tonight."

Eleanor didn't want to go dancing. She wanted to be alone. She needed to think. One night with Jake had turned into almost two nights. She had to get him out of her cottage or they'd end up spending the entire weekend in bed. As if to confirm her prediction, Jake's hand reached for her in sleep and she knew then if they didn't go out with Carl and Megan they'd spend the rest of the night here in bed. "What time are you leaving?"

Megan mumbled something else to Carl, but Eleanor couldn't make out what it was. "Carl says we can wait for ya'll to get dressed."

"Megan..." Eleanor warned.

"Well, I'd understand if you two want to spend the rest of the evening in bed. I told Carl—"

"We'll go," Eleanor said, cutting her off.

"Good. Why don't you two drive over to my place when you get dressed?" She giggled again and hung up the phone.

"Megan has to stop giggling like some schoolgirl," Eleanor mumbled.

"What did you say?" Jake said, turning over to face her.

"Nothing."

He reached for her. "Well, come here."

Eleanor wondered how he could keep it up. Literally. "We can't, Jake. Megan and Carl have invited us to go dancing with them."

"I don't want to leave this bed."

She didn't either, but what she wanted didn't matter. This time she was going with her head instead of her body. "I want to go."

"We can dance here."

She rolled her eyes, knowing his kind of dancing would not be done standing up. "We've been in this house for almost two days."

He grinned. "Are you complaining?"

He knew full well she wasn't complaining. At least, not about what they'd shared. "We need to get out. This room is no longer big enough for the three of us."

Jake looked down at his aroused penis. "Well, my man, now she counts you as another person. I guess that means you made a good showing."

Eleanor slapped him across the chest and got out of the bed. "I'm talking about your ego, idiot! Your ego is the third person."

"Now, you've hurt his feelings, Eleanor. He thinks you don't like him."

She glared at him. "I'm going dancing. You can sit here and talk to yourself all night, if you want." She stormed into the bathroom.

Jake looked down at his penis. "Well, my man, I guess you'll have to wait for your dance. It seems the legs get the next workout."

Eleanor and Megan had gone dancing at the Farmhouse many times on many Saturday nights. They'd always made it a rule never to dance with one guy more than once and to always come home together. They'd never broken that rule.

Until tonight. Carl and Megan were so wrapped up in each other they pretended each song was a slow dance and stood in the floor holding each other. Well, sometimes they did those face-swallowing kisses that made Eleanor wonder how they could breathe.

She and Jake were a little more circumspect. But barely. For the fast dances, she did force Jake to put a few inches between them. But the slow dances were torture.

"I must be losing my touch," Jake whispered in her ear, his breath on her skin adding to the erotic haze she now found herself in.

She didn't understand what his comment meant. How could he think he was losing his touch? Their bodies were pressed so close that neither of them were able to move a muscle without the other feeling the full effects of it.

"What are you thinking about?" he asked when she didn't respond.

She shook her head, too weary at her lack of self-restraint this entire weekend to even speak.

"Want me to tell you what I'm thinking?"

She grunted and pressed her face closer to his chest. "I can guess."

He chuckled. "But I want to tell you."

She gathered the material of his shirt in her hands. "Jake…"

"I want to see your eyes widen when I enter you," he murmured. "Did you know you did that?"

Eleanor swallowed. Hard. That warm feeling that had been with her since Jake had entered her cottage yesterday got warmer.

"Then I want to hear your whimpers of pleasure as I—"

"Don't," she pleaded, pulling away from him and running from the dance floor.

Jake rushed after her but she thwarted his efforts when she entered the ladies' room.

A couple of minutes later, Megan stormed in.

"What's wrong with you? Jake's hovering outside that door like he's going to break it down."

Eleanor buried her face in her hands and tried to shake off the emotions she was feeling. It didn't work. When she dropped her hands, the feelings were still there.

"What's wrong?" Megan asked again.

"Nothing. Everything." Eleanor dropped down on the plaid plastic settee.

"Did he say something to hurt your feelings?" Megan asked, her voice full of concern.

Eleanor shook her head slowly and extended her hand to her friend. How could she explain what Jake did to her?

Megan took her hand and sat next to her. "Want to talk about it?"

"There aren't enough hours in the day."

Megan settled back on the settee. "I've got nothing but time."

"What about Carl? I don't think you two have been apart for this long since you've been together."

"He's all right. Anyway, I think he has his hands full with Jake." She brushed a wayward strand of hair from Eleanor's face. "If I hadn't come up when I did, I'm sure he'd be in here by now."

"What's with him, Megan?" Eleanor asked, truly bewildered by her actions and his.

"He's falling in love."

"In lust, maybe," Eleanor muttered.

Megan shrugged. "If that's what you want to call it."

"That's what it is," Eleanor declared. "Strong, strong lust."

"And great, great sex," Megan finished for her.

Eleanor laughed and some of the weight she'd been carrying feel away. "Extraordinary sex."

"So, what's the problem?"

The problem was that Eleanor feared she was feeling something much more than lust. Much, much more.

Carl reached across the table and stopped the glass that Jake put to his lips. "Drinking is not going to help."

Jake shook off his hand. He needed something, and though he knew it wasn't a drink, a drink was all he had. "It might."

"I don't know, man. You might regret this drinking later on tonight, if you know what I mean."

Jake placed the glass on the table. "It probably won't matter."

"Then why did you put the glass down?"

Jake ran a finger around the top of his glass. "Why do women play with a man's mind? Just tell me that."

Carl chuckled and leaned back in his chair. "Is that women in general or one, stubborn, know-it-all woman, in particular?"

Those words made Jake smile. "One stubborn, know-it-all woman who's also the sexiest, most desirable, and most giving woman I've ever met."

"Uh-oh."

"What?"

"Sounds like you've got a bad case of—"

Jake lifted a hand. "Don't even say it. Don't even think it."

Carl ran a finger down the side of Jake's drink glass. "They say the denial stage is first."

"I'm not denying anything."

"If you say so."

"I do."

"Okay."

"You don't believe me?" Jake asked.

Carl leaned forward and rested his forearms and elbows on the table. "I've been there, man. You can run, but believe me, you cannot hide."

"Well, I'm not running and I'm definitely not looking to hide."

"Uh-huh," Carl said. "So what happened with Eleanor?"

Jake shrugged. If he knew the answer to that, he wouldn't be sitting at this table dying to take a drink he didn't even want. "You tell me. You're the expert with women."

"My guess is, you and she are suffering from the same problem."

Jake didn't have to ask what the problem was. The word *love* had crossed his mind more than a few times in the last thirty-six hours. Usually it was preceded by *making,* as in *making love.* But there were a couple of times the lone word formed itself in his mind. "You think so, huh?"

"I think so."

Chapter 18

Jake took Eleanor's key and unlocked her door.

"You don't have to do this, Jake," she said, wishing he had allowed Carl and Megan to drive her home. She needed to get away from him. Their one night of do-it-and-get-it-over sex had turned into two days of glorious passion that would forever change her life. "I assure you I've been letting myself in for a while now."

He stared at her and pushed the door open. "Go in, Eleanor."

Eleanor sidestepped him and entered the house, stopping just across the threshold. "Well, thanks for a nice evening."

"A nice evening?" Jake practically yelled at her. "Is that all this was for you—a nice evening?"

No, it was much, much more than that to her, but she couldn't tell him that. He might want a summer affair, but she didn't. Her heart was already too involved. "There's no need to yell. I can hear."

"What's going on, Eleanor?" he asked, his voice a sensual whisper that caressed her skin as his hands had done earlier.

She grasped the doorknob tighter. "Nothing's going on. I'm tired and I want to get some sleep."

He shoved his hands in his pockets. "I don't want to leave."

Why was he making this so difficult? she wondered. Men with lesser egos would have taken a graceful exit at her sleep line, but not Jake. "Why do you want to stay?"

He leaned against the doorjamb. "I like being with you."

Heaven help her, her knees went weak. "You mean, you like sleeping with me."

"That, too."

She cleared her throat. She wasn't going to let him work his magic on her again. She knew it wouldn't take much for him to get back in her bed. She hated the weakness in her that made that true. "That's not enough."

He stood up straight and pulled his hands out of his pockets, all attempts at casualness gone. "What do you want from me?"

Everything. "Nothing."

He put his hands back in his pockets. "Nothing?"

"Look, Jake. We had a nice time. More than a nice time. But it's over. Let's not make more of it than it was. You wanted me. I wanted you. We both got what we wanted. Let's leave it at that."

"That's it?"

She nodded, then watched the play of emotions in his face. Anger and frustration reigned.

"Okay, then that's the way it'll be. See ya." He turned and made his way up the path to the main house.

Eleanor closed the door and leaned back against it. He was gone and she was glad. Nothing could become of them anyway. Jake was a big-city man with big-city plans. She was content in her small town working for her newspaper. She had been right to turn him away.

She dropped her purse on the couch and began shrugging out of her clothes. She was naked when she reached her bedroom and collapsed on the bed.

The feel of the fabric of the comforter against her naked skin sent shock waves through her. It was as if Jake had touched her skin. She jumped up from the bed and grabbed her robe, quickly sliding it on. She collapsed on the bed thinking about Jake. He'd invaded her body, her mind, and her life.

And he'd taken away her comfort in her own body.

Damn Jake Mason.

Jake made his way up the path and into the main house, all the while thinking about the thirty-six hours he'd spent in Eleanor's arms. He couldn't be angry with her, because he understood her. He'd known it would be different with her. And he'd been right. Though she hadn't said it, he knew she didn't want an affair; no, Eleanor wanted a relationship.

"Hi there, Jake," Mathias called when Jake reached the stairway leading up to his bedroom.

Jake turned and faced Mathias, who stood in the doorway of his office. "Hello, sir. How are you doing?"

"Fine. Fine. What have you been up to?"

For a split second, Jake thought Mathias knew exactly what he'd been up to. "Nothing much. Enjoying Lamar."

Mathias nodded. "So I see. You didn't come home last night."

Jake searched Mathias's eyes, but found no guile in them. "No, sir. I didn't. That's not a problem, is it?"

Mathias pulled off his glasses, took a white handkerchief from his jacket pocket, and wiped the lens. "No, that's not a problem. I was a little worried though."

Jake was immediately sorry for his suspicions. "I'm sorry about that, Mathias. I'm not used to having someone worry about me and my hours. You know, Eleanor may have been right. Maybe I need my own place."

"Nonsense," Mathias said quickly. He put his glasses back on. "That won't be necessary." He walked over and put an arm around Jake's shoulder. "I'm not going to put a cramp in your style."

Jake turned and allowed Mathias to lead him up the stairs. "That's not it, Mathias. I need some privacy."

Mathias dropped his arm. "Privacy, huh? I guess that means you've found yourself a lady friend."

Jake studied the older man's profile. He had the sneaking suspicion that Mathias *did* know about his evening with Eleanor. "Well, you could say that."

"Mind if I ask who the lucky young lady is?"

Jake was grateful they had reached the top of the stairs. Now, he needed to escape to his room. "I don't know if giving her name would be very chivalrous of me, Mathias," Jake answered, praying Mathias would let it rest.

Mathias nodded. "I see."

Jake sensed the older man wanted a response from him, but he didn't have one to give him. "I guess I'll say good night."

"Good night," Mathias said, but he kept standing there as though he was waiting for Jake to say something more.

"Good night," Jake said again and reached for his doorknob.

As Jake stepped into his room, Mathias asked, "This woman. Do you have feelings for her, Jake?"

Jake turned around and met Mathias's stern gaze. The older man *did* know he had spent the last evening with Eleanor. "Yes, sir," he answered in earnest. "I care a lot about her."

Mathias nodded, apparently accepting the truth in Jake's words. "That's good, Jake. That's very good. I'll see you in the morning, son."

Jake watched Mathias travel down the hall to his bedroom and close the door, then he entered his own room.

Mathias knew Jake was sleeping with Eleanor. Jake was sure of it. And Mathias was upset about it. Jake was also sure of that. And he couldn't blame Mathias.

Jake cursed himself. He'd known when he moved in here that starting something with Eleanor would cause problems. He'd thought it wouldn't become an issue. But it had.

He had to make a decision. He had to move out of Mathias Sanders's house or he had to stop thinking about Eleanor. Jake leaned back on the bed. He'd start looking for a place tomorrow.

Mathias sat in the rocking chair in the corner of his room. He called the chair his thinking chair. The chair had been Barbara's idea. This was where either of them sat when they needed to sort out a serious problem or if they were trying to find a solution to a tough situation.

Well, he was in a touch situation tonight. He knew Jake and Eleanor had spent last night and most of today together. And he wasn't naïve enough to think they'd been playing chess.

He got up from the chair, sat on the side of the bed, picked up his telephone, and dialed Eleanor's number.

"Hello," she mumbled.

"Hi, sweetheart. Were you asleep?"

"No, Daddy. I was just lying here."

He knew she was trying to mask the sadness in her voice, but he heard it and pain wrenched in his gut. "Are you feeling okay?"

"I'm fine," she said, her voice a little stronger. "How are you doing? I haven't seen you in a day or so."

"Fine. Fine."

He was silent.

"Did you want something special Daddy?"

He wanted to make all her hurt go away as he had done when she was a child. That was his job as her father. But he couldn't do it this time. And what hurt most was that he had caused her pain. "No, I didn't want anything."

"Okay, I think I'll hang up then. I'm getting sleepy."

"Eleanor?" he asked.

"Yes."

"I love you."

He heard her smile.

"I know you do. I love you, too."

"Good night, daughter," he said and hung up the phone. He dropped his head in his hands. What have I done to my baby? he asked himself.

The phone rang and Mathias considered ignoring it, but he picked it up. It was Randolph.

"He had sex with her," Mathias declared.

"Great!" Randolph exclaimed. "Now we're getting somewhere."

"Have you lost your hearing, Randolph?" Mathias said in clipped tones. "I said your son had sex with my daughter."

"I heard what you said, Mat. But I don't know what your problem is."

"My problem is that your son had sex with my daughter," Mathias repeated, his voice rising. "Our plan was for them to get married."

"Aw, come off of it, Mat. That's the way things work these days. First, sex, then marriage."

"I haven't heard your son say anything about marriage."

"Give them time. Don't forget your daughter is twenty-eight, not thirteen."

"What's that supposed to mean?" Mat shouted.

"Calm down, Mat. I didn't mean anything by it."

"Then why did you say it?"

"You talk about them like they're teenagers. They're adults, Mat. Don't forget that."

Mathias wrapped the phone cord tight around his wrist. If he was a drinking man, he'd be drunk by now. "She's my baby, Randolph. And she's no match for a playboy like Jake."

"Are you saying Jake took advantage of her?"

"You said it. I didn't."

"Maybe you got it wrong and your little girl seduced my boy."

"Get serious, Randolph."

"I am serious."

Mathias took a deep breath. This discussion wasn't getting them anywhere. "Look, I don't want to talk about this now. My little girl is hurting and your son is to blame. You'd better hope this scheme of ours doesn't blow up in our faces. Because if it does, you and your son will have to deal with me."

Chapter 19

"They can't do this," Eleanor exclaimed. "They can't do it."

Jake leaned back in his chair, determined not to be moved by the nervous motion of her tongue licking her lips. "They already did it."

"But how could they?"

Jake propped his legs on his desk and crossed his arms across his stomach. "Let's see. They probably made reservations. Drove to the airport. Got on the plane."

She rolled her eyes and sat on the edge of her desk facing him. "It's not funny. What am I going to do without Carl? You know he's our top reporter."

"If the loss of one man makes your paper fall apart, you've got more problems than Mason Publishing anticipated and we're going to have to reconsider our deal."

Eleanor smiled for the first time since she'd learned Carl and Megan had hopped a plan to the Caribbean for a couple of weeks. "Well, at least that would be one good thing to come out of this mess."

Jake dropped his legs from the desk. "There's no need to get nasty. Carl and Megan left. I'm still here."

I'm still here. The words repeated themselves over and over in Eleanor's mind. *I'm still here.* "Does that mean you're going to take over Carl's assignments?"

"Carl and I talked about it."

Eleanor's eyes widened and she gave him an accusing stare. "You've talked to Carl?"

"Yes."

"When?" she said, her voice rising. He knew she wasn't going to like his answer.

"Now, don't get all upset—"

"When?" she demanded.

"I spoke with him yesterday."

"Yesterday?"

"Yesterday." Jake had spent a rainy Sunday hanging around Carl's apartment with him and Megan. They'd tried to con Eleanor into coming over but she'd rejected the invitation. Jake knew she was thinking about that now.

"And nobody thought I needed to know?"

Jake dropped his gaze to his hands, which were folded on his chest. "It came up suddenly. One minute we were talking and the next minute Megan was on the phone making reservations."

"She could have called me. This is so unlike Carl."

"The man's in love, Eleanor. He's entitled to be a bit adventurous."

"Adventurous? More like irresponsible," she muttered. "He's taking on all of Megan's negative traits."

Jake got up and stood in front of her. "And you're blowing this way out of proportion. Maybe you're frustrated about something else?"

"And what, pray tell, would that something be?"

Jake shrugged his shoulders slightly. "What makes a woman frustrated on Monday mornings?"

Eleanor got up and strode to the window facing the newsroom. "Her top reporter unexpectedly leaving town for two weeks with her best friend."

"It could be that or it could be an unfulfilled desire of some kind."

His words floated out to her and kissed her cheeks, causing her to turn back to him. "Don't start with me this morning, Jake. I'm not up for it. Carl is gone and we have a paper to get out. I suggest you get started. It's going to be a hell of a long two weeks."

In a way, Eleanor was thankful for the chaos that Carl's absence caused in the newsroom. It gave her an excuse to ignore any tension between herself and Jake. And she welcomed that.

"Is Carl's headline story ready?" she asked Jake, who was totally engrossed in the article he was editing. She had to admit he'd pitched right in there taking up the slack for Carl's absence.

Jake hit the Enter key on the computer. "It is now."

"Do you want the byline?"

Jake laughed, but shook his head. "Carl would kill me. It's his story. All I did was check some facts for him."

"If you're sure?"

"I'm sure. It's Carl's story. If tomorrow's story ends up the headline story, then I'll take the byline."

"Fair enough," she said and went back to her terminal.

Two hours later, the paper was sent to press.

"We did it," Eleanor said, brushing her hair back from her face.

"Did you doubt we would?" Jake asked, wanting to run his hand through her wayward curls. He definitely preferred her new style with the curls falling to her shoulders to the old bun. All in all, he approved of the changes she'd made, from the tinge of lipstick on her soft lips to the short skirts and jackets she wore each day.

A smile curved her lips. "Not really. I didn't realize how much I depended on Carl."

"Maybe you should tell him that when he gets back," Jake suggested.

She stared at him for a long second as she considered his words. "Maybe I should."

"I've moved into Carl's apartment," Jake added casually.

"When did this happen?"

"Yesterday."

"You had a busy day yesterday."

He captured her gaze. "It's not how I wanted to spend the day, but I got a lot accomplished."

"That's good," she said and flicked on her computer, dismissing him.

"I think your father knows about us."

Eleanor turned around. "Knows what?"

"I think he knows I spent the night at the cottage."

"How could he know? Did you tell him? Tell me you didn't tell him."

"Calm down. Of course I didn't tell him."

"Then how does he know?"

"I wasn't home all weekend." Jake asked softly, "Does it bother you that he knows we slept together?"

His words slammed against her chest. "No more than it bothers any woman to know that her father is keeping track of her sex life."

Jake chuckled. "I wouldn't take it that far."

"That's because he's not your dad. How would you feel if your father knew?"

"That's why I moved out of your dad's house. What's between us is between us. I don't want to hide it from your dad or mine, but neither do I want to include them in our relationship."

She lifted a brow. "Relationship? I thought we slept together."

"I don't know about you, but one-night stands aren't my style. Is that all it was for you?"

After finishing her hundredth lap, Eleanor pulled up to the side of the pool and got out of the water. Unfortunately, her emotions were strung as tight now as they had been when she'd entered the water fifty minutes ago.

She grabbed her towel and marched back to her cottage knowing she'd have to hurry to get back to the paper for her dreaded 2 P.M. meeting with Jake.

"Need some help with that key?"

She jumped, then turned around at the sound of Jake's voice. "What are you doing here and why are you dressed for swimming?"

Jake gave a lazy grin. "Maxine told me you'd come home for a swim. I thought I'd join you, but I see I'm too late."

"Maxine talks too much," Eleanor said, turning away from him and opening the door.

He chuckled and the sound made her hands shake. "I don't think so."

She stepped across the threshold and turned to close the door, but she bumped into Jake's chest. "What—"

Jake took advantage of her surprise and gathered her to him for a kiss. "I've done nothing but think about you. I don't know how I made it this long without tasting you again."

She stopped her traitorous arms before they wrapped themselves around his waist. "Just what do you think you're doing?" she demanded, pulling away from him.

He stepped away from her and the glazed look of passion she expected to see in his eyes wasn't there. "That's my last invitation."

"Invitation to what?"

That lazy grin appeared again and the passion that had been missing in his eyes made its appearance. "Party. Carl's apartment."

"A welcome back party for Carl and Megan?" She didn't know why she'd asked. She wasn't going with him.

He shook his head. "This is a two-person party. I call it a 'More than a Summer Fling' party."

Understanding dawned and she leaned her head to the side slightly. "I don't think so."

Jake lifted her chin and kissed her again. She didn't try to pull away. "It's your decision." He stepped away from her. "I'll see you in the office at two," he said, then turned on his heels and left her standing in her doorway.

Eleanor touched her hand to her lips, which still throbbed from his kiss. What was Jake up to? she wondered.

Jake entered the conference room at exactly two o'clock, determined not to push Eleanor to make a decision about their relationship. He dropped down in the chair next to hers and placed a bulky manila envelope on the table. "Why do we meet in this room when we could talk in our office?"

"When the paper went from a weekly to a daily, Maxine decided we needed a conference room. Then she started bugging everybody to schedule meetings." She shrugged her shoulders. "It got to be a habit."

"This paper is really like a family, isn't it?" he said, more to himself.

She picked up her pencil and twirled it in her fingers. "Most small-town papers are. So what do you want to talk about?"

He wanted to say *Us*. Instead, he opened the bulky manila folder. "I've gotten some preliminary figures back from the guys in New York and I'd like to get your opinion on some things." He pushed a sheet of paper in her direction. "What do you think?"

Eleanor read the projections and cost estimates for *Our Family*. She looked up at Jake. "I guess my figures were slightly underestimated."

He raised a brow. "Slightly? I'd say *grossly* is a better word."

She focused on the spreadsheet again. "You're not cutting any corners. I had scaled back on some of my ideas to make the project more cost-effective."

"Are you complaining?"

She looked up at him again. "No way. As my father says, why look a gift horse in the mouth?"

Jake searched her face for guile and, seeing none, gave her a big grin. "Now Mason Publishing is a horse. Is that a step up from a gravy train?"

Eleanor laughed at his reference to an earlier conversation they'd had, and the tension in the room lessened. "I guess it is."

"Let's go over this line by line," Jake suggested.

Eleanor enjoyed every minute of their discussion. Jake shared her excitement about *Our Family,* and if he was able to get the support from Mason Publishing that he wanted, the magazine would be even better than she'd imagined.

"Oh, Jake," she began. "This is going to be great. I thought it would take us four years to get to where you want us to be in eighteen months. Do you really think we can pull it off?"

The joy in her eyes mesmerized him. "What do you think?"

She grinned from ear to ear. "With my brains and your money, we can't lose."

* * *

Eleanor drove around Carl's apartment building for the fifth time. She wanted to go in, but she didn't want to face the self-satisfied grin she was sure Jake would wear in greeting.

Yes, Jake had worn her down. Between his warm eyes, and his interest and support for her plans for the paper and *Our Family,* he'd gotten to her more quickly than if he'd sent flowers and sang ballads to her every day.

On her sixth spin past the building, she pulled into the parking lot. She was a modern woman—if she wanted to visit a man she could, she told herself. Other women did it all the time.

By the time Eleanor reached Carl's door, she realized she was not "other women." But she was also not a coward. She rapped on the door and held her breath.

It seemed hours before Jake opened the door.

"Hi," he said, with no trace of a self-satisfied grin.

"Hi," she repeated, feeling awkward he hadn't yet invited her in.

Jake stared at her, wondering if she was really there or if she was an apparition brought forth by his wildest fantasies. He reached out and caressed her cheek to assure himself she was real.

Eleanor held his hand to her face and smiled at him with comforting eyes. "Is something wrong?"

He grinned at her. "Not now." He dropped his hand and stepped back so she could enter the apartment. "Make yourself at home."

She walked in, allowing her gaze to take in the whole room. A nondescript brown plaid sofa, love seat, and chair took up most of the room. They were accompanied by a solid oak coffee table and two end tables, all dotted with magazines.

"You've never been here before?"

She moved her eyes from the first edition print hanging on the wall behind the sofa to Jake and shook her head. "I was never invited."

"Carl is not a wise man."

She smiled, accepting his compliment. "I don't know about that. He's always wanted Megan and now he has her. That sounds like wisdom to me."

"Or good luck."

She sat on the couch and crossed her legs. Jake didn't miss the expanse of thigh exposed when she did. "Do you really think it was luck?"

He couldn't think about much more than her warm brown thighs. "Maybe it was more than that."

Eleanor nodded. "He loves her. I like to think that it was destiny."

He sat on the coffee table in front of her. "I think a man makes his own destiny."

She uncrossed her legs and scooted back on the couch. "And what is your destiny, Jake?"

"You."

"Oh."

He leaned toward her and caressed her face with his eyes, before using his hands. "Yes, oh."

"Ah, but how long does your destiny last?"

He dropped his hand from her face. "As long as we want it to."

"Until you leave Lamar?"

He stood up, shoved his hands in the pockets of his khaki shorts, and turned away from her. "If that's all you want."

She sighed, then got up and stood behind him, wrapping her arms around his waist and resting her head on his back. "Why is it so hard to care about somebody, Jake? It's not supposed to be this hard."

He breathed deeply. "I don't know."

"I care," she said softly, "I didn't want to, but I do."

He felt her words attempt to penetrate the contours of his heart. "I care, too," he whispered.

She dropped her hands and moved to stand in front of him. "Say it again."

He cupped her face in his hands. "I care." He dipped his head to kiss her, and she opened her mouth to him. When he would have deepened this kiss, she pulled away.

"What's the matter?" he asked.

"Nothing." She kissed him lightly on the lips then took his

hand and led him back to the couch. "I want to talk for a while."

He nuzzled her neck. "We can talk later."

"Do you really mean that?"

He pulled back and looked into her skeptical eyes. "Well, maybe not." He sat back, pulling her into his arms. "What do you want to talk about?"

"Us."

"I thought we'd already done that."

She locked her fingers with his. "We *started* to talk."

He raised their interlocked hands and kissed her fingers. "Okay, let's talk."

"While I was driving over here, I told myself I was only coming to get my itch scratched…" She peeked up at him from beneath half-lowered lashes. "If you know what I mean."

"Thank God I'm a good scratcher." He nuzzled her neck again.

She moved away from him. "I'm trying to be serious, Jake."

"So am I."

She shot him an accusing glare. "You're doing this on purpose, aren't you?"

He directed his attention to her neck again. "Doing what?"

"Seducing me to stop me from talking."

"You can talk."

"But you aren't listening," she accused.

He pulled away from her and she saw the sincerity in his eyes. "I told you I care. And I do. God help me, I care more than I'd planned to. I came here to do a job for my father. I had no intention of falling for you. But I did."

She touched her hands to his face, her heart so full of love for him that she thought it might burst with it. "Thank you for telling me that. Now, don't you want to know why I'm here?"

He grinned, then pulled her into his arms. "I know why you're here."

"You do, do you?"

"Sure." He pulled her into his arms and sank back into the couch. "You're here because somewhere in the back of your mind, I'm still that knight in shining armor you fell in love with when you were a little girl."

She laughed. "I always thought you were too modest for your own good."

"I believe in honesty over modesty." He kissed her again, this time pressing his hand against her breast. "Can we stop talking?"

Chapter 20

Eleanor heard Megan's giggles and raised her head from Jake's nipple. "Oh, shoot." She moved to get off him and out of the bathtub, but he pulled her back.

"Stop it, Megan," came Carl's voice from beyond the master bedroom door.

"They're going to find us, Jake," Eleanor said, frantically pulling away from him. "Let me up."

"Eleanor," Megan called. "Where are you?"

Eleanor felt the rumble of laughter in Jake's chest before she heard it.

"I can't believe you think this is funny." She pulled at his arms again. "Let me go."

"What are you going to do, honey? Walk out there in your birthday suit?"

Eleanor covered her mouth with her hands. "My clothes are in your bedroom."

Jake grinned. "That's right."

"You can't hide, Eleanor," Megan sang. "I know you're here. I saw your car outside."

"Leave them alone, Megan," she heard Carl say. "I knew as soon as we saw Eleanor's car we should have gone back to your place, but no, you wanted to come in."

Eleanor shot Jake a pleading look. "Any chance they'll leave?"

Jake shook his head. "Kiss me and I'll tell you my plan."

"How can you think about kissing at a time like this? Tell me the plan now."

Jake tightened his sudsy arms around her and shook his head. "Kiss me first."

"I don't believe you," Eleanor fumed.

"Maybe they're in the Jacuzzi," came Megan's voice.

Eleanor turned widened eyes to the bathroom door. She closed her eyes when she heard Megan enter the master bedroom.

"Eleanor," Megan sang. "I'm going to find you."

Eleanor slapped Jake on the shoulder. "Do something. The bathroom door isn't lock. What if she comes in here?"

"Kiss me first."

"Oh, you," Eleanor said, then kissed him. She'd planned on a short kiss, enough to pacify him, but he had other plans. He began a slow melody with her mouth that almost made her forget her friend on the other side of the door.

"I know you're in there, Eleanor," Megan said.

"Leave them alone," Carl pleaded. "Sometimes you can be a pain in the butt, Megan."

Jake released Eleanor from the kiss. "That's right, Megan," he yelled. "Leave us alone. We're busy."

"I'm dragging her out of here, Jake, don't worry," Carl said in an irritated voice. "Sorry about this, Eleanor."

"Sometimes you can be a stick-in-the-mud, sweetie," Megan said. "I was only teasing them."

Eleanor hit Jake again. "That was your plan. What kind of plan was that?"

"Well, they aren't in here, are they?"

Eleanor rolled her eyes and pushed at his arms again. "Let me go."

Jake released her, but his body was so slippery she almost fell backward in the tub. She shot an angry glance at him. "Are you trying to kill me or what?"

Jake laughed. "You said to let you go, so I let you go. I'll hold you again, if that's what you want." He reached for her again.

She scrambled out of the tub. "No way. Keep your hands to yourself."

Jake wiggled his brows at her. "What about my other body parts?"

"This is funny to you, isn't it?" Eleanor said, grabbing a towel and wrapping it around herself. "It's all one big joke."

Jake stood up in the tub and Eleanor admired his soapy body. Goodness, he was a well-built man. From his broad shoulders to his tapered waist to his tight buns and thighs.

"See something you like?"

Eleanor looked up into his grinning eyes. "Nothing I haven't seen before."

He stepped out of the tub and grabbed himself a towel. "Does this mean the thrill is gone?"

She looked down at his erection. "Apparently not for you."

He rolled up his towel and swatted her bare thighs. "Now, don't go hurting my man's feelings. You ought to be proud of him, staying up through all this commotion."

"You know, Jake, sometimes I wonder what I see in you. You have the sensitivity of a door post."

Jake pulled her to him and let her feel him taut against her. "You talk too much, woman." He kissed her hard.

She gave herself to the kiss, admitting to herself it was somewhat erotic to think of her friends on the other side of the door while she and Jake made out.

Jake lifted his head. "Now that's more like it. Do you want to get back in the tub?"

Eleanor actually considered his proposal, but her more conservative self won out. She pointed to the door. "You first."

"Chicken," Jake said, tightening his towel around his waist. "Am I decent?"

"As decent as you're going to get," she said, pushing him toward the door.

Jake opened the door and peeked out, scanning the master bedroom. "The coast is clear. They must be in the living room."

Eleanor took a deep breath. "Lead the way then. Let's get this over."

She followed Jake through the bedroom, out into the hall,

hoping her prayers would be answered and she'd be able to get to the guest room for her clothes before Megan saw her. It was not to be.

"You're looking good in that towel, girl," Megan said as soon as Jake and Eleanor walked out of the bedroom door.

"We're a matching set," Jake responded, and Eleanor was glad he'd spoken. All she wanted to do was separate Megan from that silly grin she wore.

"So I see," Megan said, not taking her eyes off her friend.

Eleanor fingered her towel, then stepped away from Jake. "Well, I hate to disappoint you, but I'm going to change into something that covers a little bit more of my body."

Megan grinned. "I guess you'd better. I wouldn't want my Carl to get any ideas."

"Megan," Carl's voice came from down the hall. "Leave them alone."

Megan hunched up her shoulders and whispered, "I just love it when he goes Tarzan on me." With that, she turned and went down the hall to Carl.

Eleanor almost ran to the spare bedroom, a chuckling Jake in her wake. He grabbed her when her towel hit the floor.

"How about a quickie?"

She reluctantly pushed away from him. "You've really lost your mind. They could hear us."

He grabbed her again. "That's the point. A bit dangerous, a bit forbidden."

"No way." She pushed him away and quickly donned her black satin panties and a pair of white cutoffs. "Stop staring and get dressed," she ordered Jake, who stood studying her every move.

Jake looked as if he wasn't going to do as she suggested, then he tossed her bra to her. "Put this on so I can concentrate."

She quickly fastened the bra and slipped her T-shirt on over it. "Okay, slow poke, I'll see you when you're dressed." She dropped a kiss on his forehead as he riffled through his dresser looking for something to wear.

"You looked better in the towel," Megan said when Eleanor joined her and Carl in the living room.

"Thanks a lot." The sight of the two of them curled in each other's arms on the couch as if they'd been together forever caused a budding of envy to settle in Eleanor's stomach. "Why are you two back so soon? I thought you'd be away at least another day."

Megan pouted her red-glossed lips. "I wanted to stay, but Mr. Responsibility here started getting the guilts. He had to come back to the paper."

"Thanks, Carl," Eleanor said, then remembered a conversation she'd had with Jake about showing more appreciation for Carl. "We certainly missed you around the paper. It made me realize how much we count on you. I don't tell you often, but we really do appreciate what you do and we're glad to have you on our team."

The shock in Carl's eyes took Eleanor by surprise. "What?" she asked. "You don't believe me?"

Carl shook his head as if to clear his thoughts. "I never thought I'd hear you admit it."

"Well, even old dogs can learn new tricks."

Jake entered the room dressed in khaki shorts and a regulation New York Giants football jersey. "Who's an old dog?"

"Eleanor," Megan quickly chimed in.

Jake draped an arm around her shoulder. "I wouldn't call you a dog, honey. A tigress maybe, but definitely not a dog."

Eleanor colored, Megan laughed, and Carl grinned.

"What happened while we were away?" Carl asked.

Jake looked from him to Megan. "If you can't guess, it won't do me any good to tell you."

Megan giggled.

"Stop with the innuendo, Jake," Eleanor warned, slapping his wrists.

Jake dropped down on the couch and pulled Eleanor onto his lap, ignoring her discomfort in the company of Megan and Carl. In the almost two weeks Megan and Carl had been away, he'd gotten used to having her close. He wasn't going to give that up now. "Tell us about your trip," he said to Megan and Carl.

Carl and Megan told the story together, with Carl giving the highlights and Megan filling in the details.

After a few minutes of this, Jake whispered to a fidgety Eleanor, "You'd better stop wiggling before I embarrass us both."

Eleanor immediately stopped moving. Megan giggled, Jake groaned, and Carl resumed his story.

"Mat, you need to get away. You're worrying about them too much."

Mathias rested his chin on his hand propped on the desk. "I should never have let him move out."

"Come on, Mat. Jake is a grown man. There was no way you could make him stay at your house if he didn't want to."

Mathias leaned back in his chair and breathed deeply. "He's sleeping with her on a regular basis."

Randolph could barely contain his excitement. If Jake and Eleanor were sleeping together, maybe he'd have that grandchild a lot sooner than he expected. He didn't think it was wise to mention that to Mathias, though. No, Mathias wouldn't appreciate it. "Why don't you come up next weekend? I'm giving another party." When Mathias hesitated, Randolph urged, "Come on. It'll do you good."

"I don't know…"

"You're sounding like an old woman, Mat. You have to trust Eleanor. She's a grown woman. You need to treat her like one."

Mathias knew Randolph was right. His Eleanor was a good girl. And that was what had him worried. If Eleanor was sleeping with Jake, it meant she thought she was in love with him. He knew his daughter that well.

But Jake was the unknown. He knew Jake was a good man. But he was a man. And Mathias wasn't so old he didn't realize a man didn't have to be in love, or even in like, to have sex. Particularly good sex. "Do you think Jake cares about her, Randy?"

"I know he does," Randolph said without hesitation. "You

should have seen them when they were here, Mat. Jake couldn't keep his eyes off her." Randolph chuckled at the thought. "The only person that kept his attention more was her date. Jake may not know it yet, but Eleanor is the one."

"I certainly hope so. I don't want my little girl's heart broken."

Randolph sighed. "I can't promise her heart won't be broken, Mat. I loved Tammy, but there were times I thought my heart was going to split in half. I bet Barbara sent you through some rough times as well."

Mathias remembered with glad sadness the times he'd made Barbara cry and the times she'd driven him to beat his head against the wall. He shook his head. Why did love have to involve pain?

"You know I'm right, Mat," Randolph said, interrupting his thoughts. "Either one or both of them is going to feel like their heart is breaking before this is over."

"How can you be so calm about it? Aren't you worried about Jake?"

Randolph sighed. "He's my boy, Mat. Of course I worry about him. I worry about him growing old and alone. I worry about him looking back and regretting his carefree youth. I don't worry about him loving Eleanor. She's right for him. And when you first met Jake, you thought he was right for Eleanor."

"That was before he slept with her," Mat mumbled, not yet ready to give up his position.

"How about it, Mat?"

"How about what?"

"You coming to New York. It'll do you good."

"I'll think about it," Mathias hedged, not sure he wanted to leave town at this point. What if Eleanor needed him?

"You know, Mat, you and I have been the best fathers we knew how to be. But I think getting Jake and Eleanor together is the last thing we should do. They're grown. They need their own lives. And we need ours."

"What do you mean by that?"

Randolph cleared his throat. "Jake might not be the first Mason man to the altar."

Mathias straightened in his chair. "What are you saying, Mat?"

"Maybe I want to get married, too. Maybe I don't want to live out the rest of my days alone."

Mathias snorted. "You haven't exactly been alone."

"You know what I mean. I can't believe you haven't thought about it. Are you still seeing Maxie on the quiet?"

Jake grabbed the ringing phone on his way out of the office for lunch. Eleanor had already gone home for a swim and he thought he'd surprise her.

"Hello," he said, hoping this call would be short. He loved seeing Eleanor in her bathing suit.

"Jake, it's me, Buddy. Do you have a few minutes?"

Jake sighed. This was the second time he'd talked to his old college acquaintance, Broderick "Buddy" Hamilton, since he'd been in Lamar. "A couple. What do you want?"

"How about coming over to Welles for dinner? My old man wants to meet you."

Jake looked at Eleanor's chair. He'd done enough research on Hamilton News since his first conversation with Buddy to know Eleanor would consider his visit to the Hamiltons of Hamilton News Company a mistake. "What's this about?"

Buddy laughed. "Don't be paranoid. Consider it one college pal being hospitable to another. That's the benefit of a Yale degree. Networking. Contacts."

Jake leaned back in his chair. "So this is business."

"I won't lie to you, Jake. My dad and I have some ideas for the *Lamar Daily* we'd like to toss at you."

Tell me something I don't know. "Why aren't you discussing these ideas with the Sanders? It's their paper, after all."

"The word on the street is that Mason Publishing is taking over."

"Not taking over. There'll be a merger, but control of the paper will remain with the Sanders family."

Buddy chuckled. "Maybe that's the way it'll start, but you know as well as I do that the health of Mason Publishing comes first. Maybe we can make a deal that'll leave all parties happy."

"The question still remains: Why haven't you come to Sanders with this deal if it's so reasonable?"

Buddy sighed. "Sanders and his daughter are unreasonable. They aren't moved by money. They won't even listen to our plan."

"Maybe they have good reason."

"Look," Buddy defended. "What happened with the *Gaines Weekly* was a one-time thing. That's not the way Hamilton News normally does business."

Jake wasn't too sure. He'd become skeptical of Hamilton News when he'd learned how they'd bought the *Gaines Weekly* one day and dismantled it a week later, deciding it was more cost-effective to have the paper in a larger town nearby, which they also owned, do weekly inserts for Gaines instead of producing a weekly Gaines paper. "I'm not sure I believe that, Buddy."

"Come on, Jake. This discussion we want to have is bigger than any one newspaper, including the *Lamar Daily*. Much bigger. At least hear us out. If you don't like the deal, there is no deal. If you like it, then we can talk. No strings."

Jake looked at his watch. "I'll think about this, Buddy, and let you know. I have to go now."

Jake said his goodbyes, hung up, and rushed out of the office to meet Eleanor. His instincts told him to have the meeting with Buddy. Maybe he'd get some information that he could use to sweeten the Mason-Sanders merger.

Eleanor, dressed in his favorite white thong swimsuit, was already in the pool when he arrived.

"What took you so long?" she asked when he dived in after her.

"I'm a busy newspaperman. Emergencies come up all the time."

"Bah." She kicked water in his face and swam away from him.

"You're going to pay for that," he challenged, charging out after her.

After an hour or so of enjoying Jake's company, Eleanor swam to the side of the pool and hoisted herself out. "I'm tired."

Jake swam to her and grabbed both her legs in his arms. "I'm not," he said, eyes dancing.

"Oh, no, you don't," she said, knowing where his thoughts were. "We have to get back to work."

"You're the boss. You don't have to be anywhere."

She pulled away from him before she gave in to the temptation he posed. "Not today."

He lifted himself up and sat next to her. "What do you know about Hamilton News?" he asked casually, drying himself with a towel.

"They're scumbags as far as I'm concerned." She went on to repeat the story of the *Gaines Weekly.* "They come to us every year with some wacko idea or another. We don't even bother to listen." She paused. "Why the sudden interest?"

Jake stood up, extended his hand to her, and helped her to her feet. "I got a call from Broderick Hamilton."

She stared up at him, her fingers tightening on his hand. "What? Why is Broderick Hamilton calling you?"

"There's nothing to be excited about," he said, rubbing her hand with his thumb in an effort to calm her. "Buddy and I are old college acquaintances."

She released his hand and stepped back a few steps from him. "And?"

Jake picked up his towel and casually threw it across his shoulder. "And he wants to have dinner with me."

"Just dinner?" she questioned, her eyes sharp with skepticism.

He moved close to her and pulled her into his arms. "That's all. You're welcome to come along if you like."

Eleanor shook her head, then relaxed against him. "That's not necessary. You go if you want, but don't believe anything they tell you about the *Lamar Daily,* Jake. They've wanted our paper for a long time, but they're never going to get a piece of it."

Jake thought about her words, and wondered, not for the first time, if Eleanor was too emotional about the paper. He believed the sense of responsibility she felt for the paper kept her from doing some of the things she really wanted to do. He knew how much she wanted to work on *Our Family,* but she was going to deny herself that joy because she couldn't see turning over control of the *Lamar Daily* to anyone else.

That didn't seem right to Jake. He could hardly wait to dive into the new magazine and he wanted her to share that joy with him. Somehow he knew that his future and Eleanor's was with *Our Family,* not the *Lamar Daily.*

He made up his mind then. He was going to have dinner with Buddy Hamilton. What harm could it be to listen to what the man had to say?

Jake spread the final sheet on the desk in front of Carl and ran his index finger down the last column. "So what do you think?"

"I think Eleanor is not going to understand."

"I didn't ask you that," Jake said, knowing Carl was right. Since his meeting with Buddy last week, he'd tried to think of a way to tell Eleanor of his revised plans for the merger without her discarding them out of hand. But he hadn't come up with one. Yet. "I asked what you thought about the idea. Let me worry about Eleanor."

"It's a great idea, you know that. But is it worth Eleanor?"

"I told you. I'll worry about Eleanor." And he was worried about her. When he'd agreed to meet with Buddy, he'd had no idea the Hamiltons would suggest such a viable venture. When he'd heard their proposal, he'd known immediately that it was the angle he'd been looking for to impress his father. So, even though he knew Eleanor didn't trust the Hamiltons and wanted no association with them, he'd considered their deal. And when he'd presented a counterproposal with conditions that safeguarded the *Lamar Daily* and Mason Publishing, he'd been surprised and elated the Hamiltons had accepted it.

"Why will you worry about me?" Eleanor asked as she entered the office she shared with Jake.

Jake stopped his musing and got up, covertly turning over the pages he'd been showing Carl. "What are you doing here?" He bussed her cheek. "I thought you were taking the afternoon off."

Eleanor glanced at Carl. "Is he trying to get rid of me?"

Carl raised both hands. "I'm not in this." He nodded to Jake. "See you later, man."

Eleanor watched Carl leave the room, then turned to Jake. "What was that all about?"

Jake shook his head and pulled her to him. "Nothing."

"Jake, we shouldn't."

He touched his lips to hers. "And why shouldn't we?"

She gave in to the kiss, then stepped away from him. "We decided to keep our relationship out of the office. No kissing, no touching."

"But I like touching you," Jake said, walking toward her with a gleam of passion in his eyes. He reached behind her and closed the blinds. "I don't know why I didn't think of this before. We could reserve the conference room every day for about half an hour. I bet that would get Maxine going."

Jake backed Eleanor to the wall and placed his hands on either side of her head, effectively trapping her. She stared into his eyes and quickly dropped her glance. That look in Jake's eyes usually caused a similar one in her own.

"Look at me," he said, as if reading her thoughts.

She chose instead to duck under his arms and stand next to the door. "What were you and Carl talking about?"

Jake stopped in midstride. "I told you."

"No, you didn't," she said, shaking her head as the alarm that had been building in her stomach since Jake's dinner visit with Buddy Hamilton last week grew.

Jake walked to the desk and gathered up his papers. "I was telling him about my plans for the *Lamar Daily*."

Eleanor stiffened her back. "Your plans? I thought they were *our* plans."

Jake didn't look up. He hated lying to Eleanor, but what choice did he have? "You're right. Our plans. I meant our plans."

"Is there something you're not telling me, Jake?" She prayed there wasn't.

Jake looked at her and considered telling her the truth. "No," he said instead. He needed more time to plan what to say to her. "Come on, I'll take you to lunch."

Eleanor let Jake lead her out of their office. She tried to ignore the unsettling feeling in her stomach. Surely Jake wasn't keeping secrets from her about his plans for the paper. She had to believe that wasn't what he was doing.

Though she tried to ignore them, her suspicions grew during their lunch.

"Have you heard anything more from New York about your proposal for the magazine?" she asked when their plates were cleared.

Jake shook his head, but she noticed he didn't look her in the eye. "Don't worry. I'll let you know as soon as I know something."

Eleanor nodded, but she didn't believe him. She silently chastised herself for not grilling him after his dinner with Buddy. Against her better judgment, she'd allowed herself to trust him, to care for him. The uneasy feeling in her stomach told her that may have been a mistake. She prayed her feelings were wrong.

Chapter 21

When Jake pulled Eleanor into his arms later that evening, he knew he'd been wrong to keep secrets from her. He should have told her everything immediately after that meeting with Buddy so they could have mapped out a strategy together.

But he hadn't told her. And now she was suspicious. He knew he hadn't appeased her with that flimsy excuse he made for the conversation he was having with Carl. No, she hadn't bought it and he knew she hadn't bought it. And now he didn't know how to tell her what he'd done without making her upset with him. But he'd find a way. He just needed more time.

He pressed his mouth against her naked breast and gloried in the moan his touch drew from her. He didn't know what gave him more pleasure—the joy of touching her or the joy of knowing he pleased her.

She arched against him and he knew she wanted what he wanted. He lifted his mouth from her breast and moved it to her lips.

"I need you," Eleanor moaned into his mouth.

He needed her, too. He raised himself slightly, then lowered until he was buried within her.

He waited until she reached her pinnacle, loving the play of emotions that danced across her face, then he let go and took his own pleasure. When he'd emptied himself, he remained atop her, luxuriating in their connected bodies. Realizing he was much too heavy to stay atop her all night, he rolled to the side and tucked her into his arms.

"That was so good," she said softly then drifted off to sleep.

As he watched her sleep, he acknowledged this woman had stolen his heart. Somewhere along the line, he'd fallen in love with her.

"I love you, Eleanor," he whispered, then joined her in sleep.

Eleanor awoke with a start, surprised but relieved her quick movements hadn't awakened Jake. She slowly lifted his hand from her belly and eased herself away from him. She held her breath when he mumbled her name, then released it when he folded his hand under his head on the pillow they had been sharing.

She got up from the bed, rubbing her arms to ward off a chill caused by the thoughts that had troubled her sleep. Keeping her back to Jake, she scanned the room for the clothes she had so quickly discarded in her need to be with him.

After she'd found all the items, she quickly slipped into them. When she was dressed, she returned to the sleeping Jake. Her heart turned over at the satisfied and peaceful look on his face, so different from the anxiousness that had been there before they'd made love. She'd responded to that anxiousness, hoping he'd tell her what was on his mind. But he hadn't. He'd taken her in his arms and loved her as if he'd never let her go. If she didn't know better, she'd believe Jake was falling in love with her.

But she did know better. Jake hadn't made her any promises. She'd known when she'd first gone to bed with him that what they shared would be temporary. Yes, she'd known that with her head, but somehow the message hadn't made it to her heart.

Her traitorous heart had done her in. She was in love with Jake Mason. She'd probably fallen in love with him the day he'd lost his article in the computer. She smiled at the memory. But her smile quickly turned into a sorrowful frown. She was in love with Jake, but she no longer trusted him.

If only he hadn't been so tight-lipped about his conversation with Carl. It had been obvious they were discussing something he didn't want her to hear. He should have known she wouldn't be satisfied with his half-answers. Obviously, he hadn't.

If only he didn't need his father's approval so much. Though

Jake didn't talk much about it, she knew this assignment meant more to him than he let on. This assignment was his chance to show Randolph he could handle the responsibility of Mason Publishing. She knew that about him and she respected it because she understood it. In a lot of ways, Jake's relationship with his father was similar to hers with her father.

If only he'd told her the truth instead of lying to her. That was what really bothered her. If he'd respected her enough, cared about her enough to tell her the truth, she'd feel much better about the whole situation. She could handle a man making a business decision. She could fight that, but she couldn't handle lies, because they signaled other deceits.

If only.

Well, she couldn't deal in if-only's. Now she had to deal in what-ifs. What if Jake was planning the demise of the *Lamar Daily?* What if he'd only been sleeping with her to gain her confidence so he could destroy her? Keep your friends close and your enemies closer, the old saying repeated itself in her mind. Was what she and Jake had shared his attempt to keep his enemies closer?

She closed her eyes. There was no way she could look at this man who made her body sing and her heart race and believe he'd betray her. He couldn't after what they'd shared. She opened her eyes and drank in her fill of him. Could he?

She placed a soft kiss on his forehead. Thankfully, he didn't stir. She pulled away and wiped at the tear that fell against her cheek. She loved him, but she couldn't let him ruin the paper that was so much a part of her life.

She closed the bedroom door quietly as she left, thankful Carl now spent most of his time at Megan's. She couldn't handle running into him on her way out. Spotting her purse and car keys on the end table nearest the front door, she quickly picked them up and left the apartment.

She wanted to trust Jake, but she couldn't. Too much was at stake. She'd had him investigated before, but this time she'd have to do the investigating herself.

* * *

Jake patted the bed next to him. "Eleanor," he mumbled, then opened his sleepy eyes. "Eleanor," he called again, staring at the indentation in the bed that marked the place her body had been. Where was she? he wondered. "Eleanor," he called yet again, this time louder.

He threw back the sheet and climbed out of bed, stretching to relieve his tired muscles. He grinned. Maybe he could get Eleanor to join him in a nice, warm shower. He padded to the bathroom with that plan in mind.

"Eleanor," he said again, opening the bathroom door without knocking. He quickly scanned the room. She wasn't there.

Worried, he hurried down the hall to the kitchen and living areas, calling her name. Still no answer. Where was she? he asked himself.

He went back to the bedroom, dread building in his chest. Her clothes were gone He raced back to the living room, pulled back the curtains, and peeked out the window. Her car was gone. He dropped the curtain. Why had she left without waking him? She'd never done that before.

He went back to the bedroom and dressed in an old pair of shorts, hoping he'd find a note from her among the disarray in the room. No such luck. No note told him much more than any note could ever speak.

He'd taken a calculated risk tonight and he'd lost. He'd hoped he could keep his plans from Eleanor until he had them finalized, but then she'd overheard that conversation with Carl earlier today. He pounded his fist on his knee. "Damn."

He stood up and went into the bathroom. He needed an aspirin for this headache that had come on like gangbusters. He caught a glimpse of his face in the mirror on the medicine cabinet as he opened its door, and he stopped his motion.

Who was this man? he asked himself.

He shrugged. He'd thought coming to Lamar would help him answer that question for himself and his father. And with the revised plan he had for the merger, he knew he'd carve out a place for himself in Mason Publishing that would make his dad proud. Then why did the face staring back at him in the mirror look so grim?

He closed the cabinet door without getting the aspirin. Aspirin wouldn't help this headache. He needed to talk to Eleanor. He needed her to understand where he was coming from. Business was business, he would tell her. But even as he said the words to himself, he knew Eleanor wouldn't understand.

She may have understood yesterday. She may have even understood before he'd made love to her. But she wouldn't understand now. He knew how her mind worked, and he knew if she learned of his plans, she'd think he'd used her.

But he hadn't. Actually, the opposite had happened. He loved her. He knew that now. He had known it when he'd taken her in his arms. Hell, maybe he'd even known it the first day he'd seen her by the pool. God knows, his life hadn't been the same since.

He smiled to himself. Beautiful Eleanor. Mouthy Eleanor. Smart Eleanor. Sexy Eleanor. His Eleanor.

His Eleanor. That was how he thought of her now. That was who she had become to him. She was his and he wasn't going to lose her. He'd lost too much in his life. He'd had no control over losing his mother, but he could have fought harder to remain a part of his father's life. He would fight this time. He would fight for his father's respect and he would fight for Eleanor's love. He wouldn't let her push him away. And he knew that's what she was doing by leaving in the middle of the night. And he wasn't going to let his father down with this deal. Somehow he'd come up with a plan that was acceptable to him, his father, and his woman. He had to.

The phone rang. Again. Eleanor stood by her bathroom door and listened for Jake's voice after the beep. She'd successfully avoided all his phone calls and she wasn't going to break that record now.

"Pick up, Eleanor," Megan's voice called after the beep. "I know you're there. You can pick up. Jake's not here."

Eleanor sighed. Jake had camped out on her doorstep for the better of the morning, but she'd pretended she wasn't home. She should have known he'd go straight to Megan and Carl to find out where she was.

"I'm going to keep talking, Eleanor," Megan said. "So pick up the phone."

"All right, already," Eleanor said to the phone, then raced to pick it up.

"What do you want, Megan?" she asked in a tight voice. She wasn't going to discuss her relationship with Jake. She wasn't.

"What's up with you and Jake? The man is frantic. And he's got Carl frantic."

Eleanor tapped her feet impatiently as Megan droned on. When Megan stopped for her, she said, "I don't want to talk about him now, Megan."

"Oh, Eleanor," Megan said, and Eleanor heard the pity and concern in her voice. "Do you want me to come over?"

Eleanor dropped down on the side of the bed. This was why Megan was her best friend. She knew her and she cared about her. "That won't be necessary. I'm all right."

"No, you're not," Megan said quickly. "And neither is Jake. What's the problem? You'll feel better if you talk about it."

Eleanor wiped her free hand across her forehead and leaned back on her pillows. How she wished that were true. "Not this time, Megan."

"You're sure?"

"Not really," Eleanor confessed, disarmed by Megan's quick acquiescence. "But it's the best I can do right now."

"That bad, huh?"

Eleanor laughed lightly. "Not so bad I can't handle it."

"What are you going to do?"

Eleanor glanced over at the airline ticket on the dresser. "I'm taking a trip."

"Alone?"

"Very much alone."

"You need to think, huh? I can understand that."

Eleanor didn't bother to correct Megan since she *would* have time to think while on this trip. But the real reason for her trip was fact-finding. She needed to get the line on what Jake was up to. And she wanted to do it without Jake and her father looking over her shoulder. If things were as bad as she thought, she'd need the time alone to decide how to deal with them. If she was wrong, well, she didn't think she was.

"Where are you going?"

Eleanor's attention returned to Megan. "New York," she lied.

"Do you want me to go with you?"

"I appreciate the offer, but I need to be alone. Besides, I don't think I'd want you around me when you're going through withdrawal."

"Withdrawal? What are you talking about?"

Eleanor laughed again. "You'd miss too many Carl shots and you'd go into withdrawal. I can't handle that."

Megan laughed too and Eleanor heard her speak to someone in the room with her, someone she guessed was Carl. "Do you want us to come over tonight?" Megan asked when she came back on the line. "I could even come without Carl for a couple of hours. Withdrawal shouldn't set in that quickly."

"You're sweet to offer, Megan, but it's not necessary. I'm leaving for Atlanta tonight." That was true, and Eleanor immediately regretted telling Megan. She didn't want it to get back to Jake.

"I assume Jake doesn't know this," Megan said.

"You assume correctly."

"And you don't want him to know."

"Correct, again. Do you think Carl can keep a secret?"

"It won't be necessary," Megan said. "I guarantee you I'll keep Carl so busy tonight he won't have a chance to even think about Jake."

Memories of last night with Jake filled Eleanor's mind. She wished she could lose herself in him tonight. But that wouldn't work. She couldn't lose herself in the very person she was trying to get away from.

* * *

"She's not coming in today, man," Carl said Monday morning, flipping on his terminal. "We have to get the paper out without her. Think we can do it?"

"Where is she?" Jake asked, dismissing Carl's question.

Carl scanned the morning's AP stories. "Out of town."

"Out of town?" Jake flopped down in the chair next to Carl's desk. "When did she leave?"

"Yesterday morning," Carl said, his attention on the screen in front of him. "I think."

Jake grabbed the arm of Carl's chair and turned him around. "You think?"

Carl stared at Jake's hand on the arm of the chair, then glanced up at him. "I told you she wasn't going to like it."

Jake stood and rubbed his hand across his head. "She doesn't even know what I'm planning."

"Okay," Carl said, and turned around in his chair.

Jake turned the chair around again. "Okay, man, talk to me. What did she tell Megan?"

"What makes you think she told Megan anything?"

Jake stared at him. "I'm not in the mood for games, Carl. I've been up all night trying to figure out how to handle this situation with Eleanor and she's not here. Where is she?"

"You aren't going to like it…"

"Where is she?" Jake asked again.

"She went to New York."

"New York?" Jake repeated. Franklin was in New York. Had she gone to see Franklin? She couldn't have. Eleanor wasn't the type of woman to go from one man's bed to another's. He was sure of that.

"I knew you wouldn't like it."

"Why'd she go to New York?"

Carl shrugged his shoulders and turned back around to his screen.

Jake didn't even know why he'd asked the question. He knew why she'd left town. Oh, he might not know the specifics, but he knew part of the reason she'd left was to get away from him.

"Do you know how long she'll be gone?"

"Megan said a couple of days."

Jake considered joining her. They could use some time away from Lamar and the paper. Some time for the two of them. "Where is she staying?"

"I didn't ask."

"Maybe Megan knows," Jake said aloud, though he was really talking to himself. If he could find out where Eleanor was staying, he could join her and explain that this deal was good for everybody involved.

Carl turned around in his chair. "Leave Megan out of this, Jake. She's Eleanor's best friend. Don't put her in the middle."

Carl's strident tone surprised Jake. "But I need to see Eleanor. Who knows what she's cooking up in her mind?"

Carl stared directly in his eyes. "I don't think she could cook up anything worse than the reality of your plan, at least not in her eyes. Wouldn't you agree?"

Jake opened his mouth to say the situation wasn't that bad, but he knew it was. He knew what the paper meant to Eleanor. He'd rationalized his actions by saying *Our Family* was her future. Their future. But he knew that wasn't a decision he could make for her.

Eleanor wanted *Our Family,* but she was duty-bound to the *Lamar Daily.* She'd outgrown it, but she wouldn't or couldn't let it go. He'd thought he could help her break free, but maybe all he'd done was make her dig her heels in deeper.

Yes, he'd been wrong to make the decision without her. He'd known it when he'd held her in his arms last night. He wiped his hand across his face. Hell, he'd known it was wrong all along. That's why he hadn't told her about it, why he hadn't allowed her to decide.

Chapter 22

"So what are you going to do about it?" Megan asked after Eleanor told her what she'd learned of Jake's deception.

"I'm going to stop him," she said matter-of-factly. "No way is Jake Mason going to partner us with Hamilton News." She'd converted all her feelings of hurt and betrayal into determined vengeance. Jake Mason would pay for trying to use her and her paper.

"How?"

Eleanor shrugged. "I'm not sure, but believe me I'll come up with something."

"I bet you will," Megan muttered.

"What's that supposed to mean? You can't be siding with Jake on this."

"No," Megan began, twisting the top on her soda. "I'm not siding with him. He was wrong to keep secrets from you and he needs to answer for that. But I love you and I don't think you're facing your real feelings."

Eleanor snorted. She'd faced her real feelings and it hadn't been a pretty sight. Now was the time to put feelings aside and turn to action. "I see Jake for what he really is. I'm glad I found out before I—"

"Before you what? Fell in love with him?"

Eleanor didn't answer. She'd been about to say that but she couldn't because she knew it would have been a lie. She had been fool enough to fall in love with him. "It doesn't matter."

Megan reached over and touched her friend's knee. "It does matter. It matters more than anything."

"How can it matter when it's obvious he cares nothing for me?"

"I don't see how you can say that. It's not obvious to me."

Eleanor stared at Megan and wondered if she'd heard a word of Jake's deception. "He used me, Megan. He used me."

Megan sat back. "It doesn't look that way to me."

Eleanor rolled her eyes. Megan had turned into a Pollyanna ever since she'd fallen head over heels for Carl. "And how does it look to you, Dear Abby?"

"I think you need to face your real fears. Are you upset with Jake because of his plan or are you using that as an excuse to keep from following your heart?"

"I don't know what you're talking about."

"Sure you don't."

Eleanor lifted her lip in a smirk. "And what's that supposed to mean?"

"It means Jake's the first guy to come along and make you question your safe and perfect little world here. You seemed not to mind until he touched your precious paper. Why did that set you off?"

"You don't understand. The paper is my business, my career. I can't let him take it."

"Eleanor," Megan said softly. "The paper is not your mother."

Eleanor jerked her eyes away from Megan. "I never said it was. Why would you even say that?"

"Because you treat that paper like it's sacred. It's not. Sometimes I think that paper has more of a hold on you than your father does."

Eleanor jumped up. "That's just not true. I can't believe you're saying these things."

Megan didn't move. "I'm your best friend and I love you like a sister, but you're wrong this time. I don't want to see you throw away what you and Jake have because of some business decision."

"You don't understand. It's more than that. It's about Jake respecting my wishes. It's about him including me in his decisions. He didn't do either."

"Have you told him this?"

Eleanor shook her head. She hadn't spoken to Jake since the night she'd left him alone in bed. There was nothing to say.

"Now that's real mature of you." Megan sighed. "You have to let him explain."

Eleanor shook her head again. "I can't let him know how much I know. If he knows, he may take action to keep me from stopping him. I can't take that risk."

"But you can risk losing the only man you've ever loved because of your pride?"

"That's not it."

Megan watched her for a long second. "If you say so." She sighed again. "Do you want to go over to Welles tonight? Victoria's is having another sale."

Jake answered the door after her first knock. When she saw him, her heartbeat increased and the attraction that had always been between them flared. Thoughts of his plans for her paper doused the flames. She studied this man she'd loved and been loved by and wondered how she could have so misjudged his character.

It hadn't taken her long to learn of his plans. If she hadn't been so taken by him, she wouldn't have let things get as far as they had. Thank goodness she'd overheard him talking to Carl.

"Eleanor," he said finally. "Where have you been? I've been worried sick."

She brushed past him, determined not to let the concern in his voice deter her. She'd remembered many times while she was in Atlanta that he was a trained actor.

He closed the door, then followed her back into the living room. She didn't bother to sit down. "Why'd you do it, Jake?" she asked, hating the hurt that came through in her voice. She'd planned to handle this in a professional manner.

He reached for her and she moved away from him. "Just answer the question. Why'd you do it?"

He didn't flinch. "It's business, Eleanor."

Each word was a shot to her already aching heart. "Was what we shared in bed business, too?" she asked, her voice a whisper.

He reached for her again and this time she let him hold her. "How can you even ask that?"

She jerked away from him, hating the weakness she exhibited. She had to maintain some measure of dignity. "Because from where I'm sitting it looks like you were sleeping with me to keep me from questioning your actions. That was certainly one way of gaining my trust."

He flinched at her words and she was glad she'd hit her target. "How can you think so little of me after what we've shared?" he asked.

She gave an empty laugh and wondered where the sound was coming from. "Now, that's royal. How can I *not* think little of you, Jake? You've taken everything we've shared and thrown it back in my face. How could *you* think so little of what we've shared?"

"I did it for us—" he began.

She slapped him before he could finish his thought. "Stop lying to me. You didn't do this for me. You did it for yourself. For your own ego. It had nothing whatsoever to do with me."

He rubbed his jaw. "You're wrong."

"I wish I were," she said, marching toward the door. She had to get out of this apartment, out of his presence. She put her hand on the knob then turned around. "It's not over, Jake. I'm going to fight you to the end. Your plans aren't going to make it off the paper you've written them on. There is no way the *Lamar Daily* will get in bed with Hamilton News. You have my word on that."

"This isn't about the paper, Eleanor. It's about us."

She laughed that laugh again. "There is no us, Jake. There never was. At least, not in your mind. If you had thought of us, we wouldn't be having this argument now." She turned and swung open the door.

"You can't run from me, Eleanor," he called after her, repeating the words he'd told her early in their relationship.

She turned around and stared at him. "I never thought I'd need to, Jake, but I do. After all that we've shared, I don't know who you are."

Jake winced at the slamming of the door behind her. He was tempted to go after her, but he knew it was no use. What could he say? She'd said it all, and unfortunately, she'd been right on most counts.

Except for one. She'd been wrong about them. He'd never used her. He hadn't even planned to get involved with her. Lord knows, his life would be much simpler now if he hadn't gotten involved with her.

But he had. Against all reason, he'd fallen for his business associate and the daughter of his father's best friend. And now he couldn't let her go.

Eleanor bumped into Carl as she rushed out of his apartment.

"Hey, hey," he called, catching her by her arms to keep her from falling. "You'd better watch where you're going."

"Sorry, Carl," she mumbled and sidestepped him to continue to her car. She didn't want to talk now. Especially not to Carl. He'd probably been in on Jake's plans from the beginning. She'd talk to him tomorrow when she was calmer.

Carl grabbed her arm again. "Hey, what's the matter? You and lover boy have another fight?" He grinned. "You two fight as much as some other couple I used to know."

Eleanor couldn't smile with him. Her and Jake's relationship was nothing like the one he shared with Megan. "I can't talk about this now, Carl." She couldn't. She feared she'd cry if she did. And she wasn't going to give Jake Mason the satisfaction of making her cry.

"You love him, Eleanor, and he loves you."

His words were so confident that Eleanor met his gaze for the first time. "He told you that? Is that how he convinced you to betray me?"

Carl shook his head sadly. "I didn't betray you."

Eleanor was tired of lying men. "Are you saying you didn't know what Jake was planning for the paper?"

Carl had the decency to look away. "I knew, but only after he'd formed the plan. I told him you wouldn't go for it. I told him you wouldn't understand."

She believed him. "And what did he say?" she asked, but she knew. It was obvious. Jake didn't care what she wanted.

"He loves you, Eleanor," Carl said instead of answering her.

"Oh, Carl, come on. Don't use that line on me. Did he ever say those words to you?" She hated the hope that budded in her chest as she waited for his answer. She was still looking for some way to exonerate Jake.

"Well, not exactly."

Her hope died as quickly as it had bloomed. "Just like I thought. Good night, Carl."

He grabbed her arm again and made her face him. "Can you walk away from him, Eleanor? You know what moves him as well as I do. Maybe you don't love him after all."

"You don't have to use reverse psychology on me, Carl. I *do* love him. I've admitted that much to myself."

"Then you two can work this out."

She reached up and touched his face, her anger at him gone. He only wanted her and Jake to find what he and Megan had found together. "We don't have what you and Megan have. We never did. It wasn't meant to be for us."

He placed his hand atop hers. "If I'd given up on Megan, we wouldn't be together now."

Eleanor laughed and patted his jaw before dropping her hand. "You did give up on her, remember? You two could barely stand to be in the same room together."

"But I never gave up on her. Why do you think I stayed in Lamar all these years?"

She smiled. "I guess it wasn't the paper."

He shook his head, a look of wonder and amazement and love on his face. "I'm here because she's here. I don't think I could've left even if she'd married someone else."

"I envy what you have with Megan," she admitted. She'd thought she and Jake might have a chance at that but she now knew that had been a pipe dream.

Carl chuckled. "You envy us now, but I bet you didn't about two months ago."

"Good point."

"I'm not saying Jake didn't make a mistake, Eleanor. He did. But it's not one that the two of you can't get past." He touched his right hand to her cheek. "Take my advice. Don't make any decisions that can't be reversed and don't say anything you can't take back. Love is too precious to throw away."

Eleanor watched the clock, turning off the alarm before it went off at six o'clock. She hadn't needed to set it since she hadn't slept all night. She couldn't. Her mind was too full of thoughts. Thoughts of Jake. And her. In this bed. In his bed.

She threw back the sheet and slowly moved her pajama-clad legs to the floor. The room even felt different. But she knew it wasn't really the room. It was her. She wasn't the same woman she'd been before she met him. And she'd probably never be the same again.

She straightened her shoulders, got up from the bed, and made her way to the bathroom. In twenty minutes she was dressed and on her way to the main house for breakfast with her father.

He was seated at the kitchen table sipping coffee when she walked in. "Morning, Dad," she said and kissed his upturned forehead.

Mathias smiled at her, but she didn't miss the question in his eyes. "What a nice surprise! You haven't joined me for breakfast in quite a while. To what do I owe this pleasure?"

She turned her back to him and poured a cup of coffee from the coffeemaker. "Could it be that I wanted to have breakfast with you?" She turned back around and leaned against the counter.

Mathias pushed his plate away. "Out with it, Eleanor."

She reluctantly lifted herself from the counter and sat down at the table in front of her father. It was quiet in the kitchen this morning. Too quiet. "It's about Jake," she said slowly, running her fingers down the sides of her coffee cup.

Mathias placed his hands over her fingers and stopped their motion. "What did he do to you?"

The alarm in his voice surprised her. She squeezed his fingers briefly, then removed her hand and brought her cup to her mouth, taking a long swallow before speaking. "It's not what he did to me," she said, though it wasn't really true. It *was* about what he did to her, but that was not her father's concern. "It's what he's planning to do with the paper."

Mathias sat back in his chair, and Eleanor could have sworn she saw relief in his eyes. "I thought you two had come to a working agreement about the future of the paper."

"So did I." She gave a weak smile. "But Jake was a little smarter than I gave him credit for. It seems he had other ideas."

Mathias looked at his watch then stood up. "I'm meeting with the mayor this morning. I'm sure you and Jake will work this out."

She looked up at him and her heart broke. How could her father be so trusting of men so undeserving of trust? "Not this time, Dad. Jake has approached Hamilton News."

Mathias's eyes widened and he sat back down at the table. Eleanor had known the name of the newspaper consortium would get his attention. Hamilton News approached them at least once a year with a deal of some kind, but Mathias never considered any of their offers. "Why would he contact them?"

She should have been glad for the suspicion she heard in her father's voice because it meant he was taking off the rose-colored glasses where Jake and his father were concerned. But she wasn't. No, she hurt because she knew her father's so-called best friend's betrayal would cause him considerable pain.

"Why did he contact them?" Mathias asked again.

She looked down at her coffee cup, then brought her eyes up to meet her father's. "Money."

"Money?" Mathias repeated. "Why would Jake want money from them?" Mathias snapped his fingers. "Mason Publishing could swallow them up like that."

Eleanor shrugged her shoulders. This entire conversation was suddenly making her tired. "Maybe it's power. Who knows what's going through Jake's mind?"

"Power?" Mathias nodded. "Now that I can understand."

Eleanor couldn't believe her ears. Her dad obviously had a blind spot as big as the state of Alabama where the Randolph men were concerned. "Well, in his plan he gets both. Not only is Jake arranging a merger between Mason Publishing and the *Lamar Daily,* he's also bringing Hamilton News into the deal."

Mathias leaned forward anxiously. "What are you talking about?"

Eleanor cleared her throat. She was only going to say this once. "Jake wants to create Mason News, a wholly owned subsidiary of Mason Publishing. Mason News will be the beginning of a conglomerate of small-town newspapers. Of course, Jake will be president and CEO, and Buddy Hamilton, of Hamilton News fame, will be his second-in-command. He and Buddy plan to gobble up every small-town paper in the Southeast within five years. The *Lamar Daily* is their first conquest." Eleanor winced as she spoke the words. The pain of Jake's betrayal ran deep.

Mathias sat back in his chair. "Well, the boy has guts. I can say that."

"That's all you've got to say?" Eleanor yelled, infuriated at the calm in her father's voice. Had he completely lost his mind? "Jake and his father are going back on the spirit of this whole deal. If they partner with Hamilton News, where will our autonomy go?"

"Calm down, Eleanor," her father said, standing up again. "You're going to give yourself a heart attack. This is bad, but it's not that bad. I'll speak to Randolph."

Eleanor grabbed his arm. "It won't do any good, Dad," she warned. "Randolph has given Jake a free hand with this project. There's nothing he can do now without going back on his word to his son. We have to handle this ourselves."

"What do you think we should do, Mat?" Randolph asked after Mathias had repeated Eleanor's news.

Mathias was surprised at the calm he still felt. Ever since Eleanor had told him the news, he'd waited for his anger to surface. But it hadn't. "I don't know that we should do anything. Maybe we've done enough."

"You're willing to let Jake go through with his plan?" Randolph asked, obviously not believing that.

Mathias rubbed the bridge of his nose. "Maybe it's for the best, Randy."

"I don't believe what I'm hearing. You love that paper."

"Maybe that's the problem. It's a paper. Maybe it was wrong to have so much emotion invested in something that can't feel."

"What's on your mind, Mat?" Randy asked, knowing his friend too well.

"I've been thinking a lot about Barbara and about Eleanor since this morning. Maybe it's time for Eleanor and me to move on."

"What do you mean?"

"Well, the paper has played a large role in our lives since Barbara's death. I've always wondered if it kept Eleanor tied to Lamar. And to me." He sighed. "Maybe it's time for her to make the break."

"How does she feel about this?"

Mathias sighed. He knew his Eleanor was feeling a lot of things these days. She was angry with Jake because of his plans, but she was also hurt by what she read as his betrayal. "She's hurting, Randy, but she won't go down without a fight. Jake's in for it."

Randolph chuckled softly. "In a way, I'm proud of him, Mat. No, this isn't what I wanted, what we wanted, but it's something of his own doing. I can understand him wanting his own business without my interference."

"I feel the same way. Your boy is turning out to be quite a man. I hope my Eleanor will see it that way."

"I think she will, Mat. I know it sounds strange for me to say, but I think Eleanor is going to find herself in this, too."

"I hope you're right." Mathias knew his daughter was in pain, but there was nothing he could do about it. He and Randolph could step in and effect some changes on the business front, but it was her personal life that caused the greatest wounds. He hoped she and Jake would work it out.

"So we're going to wait it out, see what they do?"

Mathias took a deep breath. "That's all we can do." He was silent for a couple of seconds. "Did you ever think it would come to this?"

"No," Randolph said quickly. "Do you regret what we've done?"

Mathias thought hard. "No, I don't. Sometimes change is necessary. We knew all we could do was bring them together. Now it's up to them."

Chapter 23

Jake met his father at the Atlanta airport at noon the next day.

"How're things going, Jake?" Randolph asked, stirring his vodka and tonic.

Jake observed his father, still wondering about this impromptu visit. He knew his father well enough to know there was a specific purpose for the meeting. He wondered what it was. He hoped his father wasn't checking up on him. "Moving right along," Jake said, trying not to give away too much. He'd wait for his father to reveal his hand first.

"Have you and Eleanor worked out the agreement?"

Jake met his father's gaze, trying to decide if there was more to the question than the obvious. Not seeing anything, he shrugged. "We're making progress. I think you'll like the proposal."

Randolph nodded and took another sip of this drink. "I'm sure I will."

They were both silent for a couple of minute. Jake watched the red, white, and blue Delta jets through the windows while Randolph nursed his drink.

"I'm glad to have you working with me on this deal, Jake," his father said. "I know I was a bit heavy-handed when I gave you the assignment, but I'm proud of what you're doing. I wished we could have worked together sooner."

A lump formed in Jake's chest. He hadn't expected this. He cleared his throat. "Well, it's been good for me, too."

Randolph nodded again. "I want you to run this business

someday, you know." He grinned. "Not too soon, though. I still have a few good years left in me."

Jake grinned too and his shoulders straightened. "More than a few years, I hope."

"Yes, yes," Randolph said. "I'm sorry we didn't get started together sooner."

Jake ran his hand up and down his glass of water. "Why did it take so long, Dad?" Jake asked the question that had puzzled him for years. He held his breath while he waited for the answer.

"I don't really know." Randolph sighed. "After your mother died, I was lost. I didn't know what to do with a child. Your mother was the caretaker." A smile softened the older man's face and Jake wondered at the memory that triggered it. "Anyway, after she was gone, I did what I thought was best. I took you with me."

"There was nothing wrong with that. I loved being with you."

Randolph met his son's gaze. "I know you did, but that was no life for a growing boy."

"So you left me at home?" Jake couldn't keep the distaste out of his mouth.

Randolph winced. "I thought it was the right thing at the time. Your mother and I always wanted you to have a better life than we did. We didn't want you to struggle like we did."

"So you made sure I had the best of everything?"

Randolph nodded. "I tried. I tried my best." He cleared his throat and Jake wondered if he was about to cry. "I've always loved you, Jake. I missed you and I wanted you with me, but it wasn't fair to you. I had to work and you needed a regular life."

"I needed a father," Jake said softly.

Randolph released a long breath. "I know that now. Aw, hell, I guess I figured it out over the years. But it was too late, the damage had been done. We'd grown so far apart I didn't know how to reach you."

Jake nodded. They had grown apart. Sure, they talked often and saw each other regularly, but they didn't share their lives. He couldn't remember when they had. "I used to sit at your desk in your office at the house and pretend I was you." He slowly rolled his shoulders back at the memory. "I'm not sure if I wanted to be you or if I wanted to be like you. Maybe if I was more like you, you'd want to spend time with me."

Randolph's eyes did mist then. "I'm so sorry, son. Do you think you can forgive your old man?"

When Jake looked at his father, he knew the older man wasn't sure what his answer would be. "There's nothing to forgive."

"Yes, there is. I want you to forgive me for giving you things when I should have given you myself. I want you to forgive me for ignoring your interest in the business, our business, when you were younger. I should have encouraged that. I know that now."

Jake nodded. "Is that why you gave me the assignment in Lamar?"

Randolph raised his brow. "You didn't seem to be interested in the business anymore. I had to find a way to get you involved." He paused. "Why'd you take the assignment? You didn't have to, you know."

The memory of his father ordering him to take the assignment made him smile. "That's not exactly how I remember it."

Randolph laughed a rich, full laugh and his eyes cleared of their mist. "I was a bit forceful, but that's never stopped you from ignoring my wishes in the past. Why this time?"

Jake shifted in his seat. "I thought it was some kind of test and I wanted to prove to you I could do it."

"It was never a test, Jake. I had no doubts about your ability. Your will, maybe, but never your ability."

Jake examined his father's eyes and saw only his sincerity. His lips curved in a smile. "I wish I had been as sure."

"You're doing a good job. Hell, a great job."

Jake's chest puffed out at his father's words. "Thanks. It means a lot to hear you say that."

Randolph cleared his throat. "Well, you'd better remember it because it may be the last time."

"Somehow I already knew that," Jake said with a grin.

"So," Randolph began. "How's it really going here? I got a call from Mathias."

Jake's shoulders stiffened. So, his father had come to check up on him.

"Don't get all ruffled on me. This is still your deal. I'm here if you need me. I want you to know that."

Jake relaxed. "What did Mathias say?"

Jake nodded when Randolph finished telling him of the concerns Eleanor had expressed to Mathias.

"So she's right?" Randolph concluded.

"She figured out most of it," Jake said, then told his father the details of his plan.

"Whew, that's some deal you've worked. How did you get Hamilton News to agree to your terms?"

Jake leaned forward, warming to the topic. "This is all verbal. Nothing has been done contractually, as you know. Hamilton News has been trying to do this for a while. They saw the *Lamar Daily* as their first step. When we got involved with the *Lamar Daily,* they thought they could work a deal with us to get a piece of it." He shrugged his shoulders. "I countered. I hate to admit it, but I was surprised when they went for it."

Randolph was quick in his response. "Hell, that's the way it is with most big deals. You study, you plan, you make your pitch, and you hope like hell they go for it. How do you think I built this business?"

Jake grinned. "I thought you were a shrewd businessman, smarter than all your competition."

"That, too. But big business takes guts. And you've got them. Not everybody does."

"Well, some of the credit goes to Buddy Hamilton. He's stepped into his father's shoes and he's determined to make a new name for Hamilton News."

"Aha," Randolph said, after taking a sip from his glass. "I ought to call the older Hamilton for a drink to celebrate."

"You know, this isn't the response I expected from you."

"What did you expect?"

"For you to think I'd betrayed you by trying to carve out something of my own."

Randolph shook his head. "Never. You remind me of me when I was younger. I wanted to build something of my own. I understand those feelings in you. It's part of being a man."

Those were exactly Jake's feelings. He was relieved his father understood. Why couldn't Eleanor? "Too bad everybody doesn't understand that."

"Eleanor?"

Jake lifted his gaze in surprise. "How'd you guess?"

"I saw the way you two looked at each other when you were in New York. I'm not so old I've forgotten what desire looks like. Do you care about her, son?"

Jake nodded. "It's a difficult relationship. Hell, it may not even be a relationship anymore."

"She's that upset?"

"She doesn't trust Hamilton News and refuses to even consider our plans as a valid business decision. One that will benefit all of us. The paper is like family to her and she wants things to stay as they are."

"So you've talked to her about it?"

Jake shook his head slowly. "Not in any detail. She's not talking to me much these days."

"What are you going to do about that?"

Jake stared at him. "What can I do? She doesn't understand how important this is to me."

"And you don't understand how important the paper is to her?"

"That's not it. You don't understand—"

Randolph held up his hands. "I *do* understand. But now you're facing the decision I had to face with you. Do you make the best business decision or the best personal decision?"

Eleanor tucked her pen in her mouth and scrawled her options on the sheet in front of her. Option 1: Shoot Jake. Option 2: Run over Jake. Option 3: Strangle Jake.

She dropped her pen on the table, folded her hands across her stomach, and wished Randolph's flight would hurry up and arrive. She'd been waiting over two hours now and she was getting cabin fever.

She looked over at the bar and her gaze met that of a rather handsome, dark-skinned brother with a mustache. Any other time she might have smiled at him, but not today. Today she gave him a haughty glare that said she was unavailable and uninterested. Unfortunately, the man must have been dense for he hopped off the bar stool and made his way toward her table. Oh, no, she thought.

"Eleanor," she heard a voice call from behind her.

"Randolph," she said, relieved he was here. She stood and rose up on her toes and bussed his cheek. "Sorry," she whispered, "but that guy over there was about to make a move on me."

Randolph hugged her to him and chuckled. "At least the young man has great taste."

Eleanor moved away from the older man and returned to her chair. A cheerful feeling bubbled up in her as she remembered the last time she'd seen him. "You're too much, Randolph."

Randolph pulled out the chair next to her and took a seat. "So what's happening with you and Jake?"

"You don't waste any time, do you?"

Randolph signaled the waiter for a drink. "Time's too precious to waste. When you're my age you'll appreciate that."

"You and Dad certainly use your age to your advantage, but I don't see either one of you slowing down."

Randolph grinned at her. "Won't work, young lady. This conversation is about you and Jake, not about me and your father."

Eleanor met his gaze. "I think the issue is your relationship with my father. He entered into a good faith agreement with you, and your son has reneged on it. What are you going to do about it?"

The waiter delivered Randolph's drink and he took a sip before answering her. "I can see why Jake fell in love with you."

Eleanor swallowed hard. She hadn't expected that. "Let's keep this professional, Randolph," she said calmly. "Are you going to keep your word to my father?"

Randolph sighed. "Technically, Jake has adhered to the *law* of the agreement. And as for the *spirit* of that agreement, well, I've already spoken with your father about that. We've reached an understanding."

An understanding. That didn't sound good. "Exactly what kind of understanding are you talking about?" she asked slowly.

Randolph leaned forward and pulled one of her hands into his bigger ones. They were warm to the touch and she was somehow comforted by them. "Mathias understands this is Jake's project. My hands are tied."

Eleanor snatched her hand out of his. "Why are you doing this to us?" she asked. "My father thinks you're his best friend."

Randolph leaned back in his chair and brought his glass to his lips. "I am his best friend."

She snorted. "You sure have a funny way of showing it. Is that how you built Mason Publishing—by taking advantage of all your friends?" Randolph visibly recoiled at her words, but she didn't feel any triumph that her jab had hit. She stood and gathered her belongings from the table. "Yes, I know about the ruthless Randolph Mason, building his empire with no regard for anything or anyone but himself. My father was never in your league."

"You—"

Eleanor waved her hand in dismissal. "Forget it, Mr. Mason. I thought Jake was a bastard, but maybe I was wrong. Maybe he's just his father's son."

Eleanor turned on shaky legs, head held high, shoulders straight, and walked away from Randolph Mason.

"Eleanor," he called after her.

She stopped but she didn't turn around.

"Be angry with me. Be angry with your dad. Hell, be angry with Jake, but don't give up on him. He loves you and he needs you."

She stiffened at his words, wishing they were true. But they weren't. She swallowed deeply and continued out of the restaurant. She had work to do if she was going to keep her newspaper.

Chapter 24

Eleanor jumped when the smooth hand touched her shoulder and the keys to her cottage fell to her feet.

"I'm sorry," Jake said, bending over to pick up her keys. "I didn't mean to frighten you." He handed her the keys.

"What do you want, Jake?" she asked, trying to calm her shaking fingers so she could insert the key in the door.

"We need to talk."

He stood so close she felt his breath on her neck. "It's a little late for that now, isn't it?" She breathed a relieved sigh when she finally got the door open and slipped inside.

"You should have talked to me, Eleanor."

She turned around and faced him. "I should have talked to you?" she said, her voice rising. "You have some nerve, Jake Mason." She moved to close the door in his face, but he inserted a loafer-shod foot in the opening.

"We have to talk," he said. "Please."

The softness of his plea made her heart warm to him, but she couldn't give in to it. She couldn't let him use her again. "It won't do any good. I don't trust you, Jake. We should have talked before you made plans to sell out my newspaper."

He blinked rapidly and she wondered if his eyes were wet. They couldn't be, could they?

"I care about you, Eleanor. We can't end like this."

"You care about me? You care about me? Well, you have a funny damn way of showing it." She pushed the door against his foot, hoping the pain would make him move it. It didn't.

"I'm not leaving until we talk."

She could tell from the firm line of his lips he was telling the truth. She could let him in for a few minutes or she could stand there all night. She released her hold on the door and walked into her cottage.

Jake followed her. When he was seated on the couch, he began, "I know I should have told you about my plan..."

She wiped her hands across her face. She was so tired. "You didn't make any commitments to me, Jake. We both knew this was a business deal. I was a fool to trust you."

He winced at her words, then reached for her. She pulled back. "You weren't a fool."

She shook her head slowly. "Yes, I was. Every time I made love to you, I was a fool." She smiled a sad smile. "Did you get a kick out of it, Jake?"

"It wasn't like that."

She lifted a brow. "What was it like then?"

He didn't answer immediately, He wanted to tell her that he loved her and wanted a future with her, but he knew her anger would force her to throw the words back at him. He wanted to tell her that his actions were not premeditated, that his relationship with her hadn't been part of some diabolical scheme.

She stood up. "Just like I thought. I think you should go now."

Jake felt they had played this scene before. Eleanor asks how he feels and he holds back. Not this time. "I'm not through yet."

"I think you are," she countered, impatiently tapping her foot on the hardwood floor.

He looked down at his folded hands then raised his gaze to her. "I met with my father a couple of days ago," he began.

"This doesn't interest me, Jake," she said, but it did interest her.

"Anyway," he continued, as if she hadn't spoken, "we talked like we hadn't talked in a long time. He understands what I'm doing, Eleanor. Why can't you understand? Why does this have to come between us?"

She strode to the door and grabbed the knob. "Oh, I understand, all right. I understand that proving something to your father is more important than keeping your word to me. That's what I understand."

He shook his head. "I haven't lied to you, Eleanor. My only sin was keeping you out of my discussions with Buddy Hamilton."

"Don't forget selling out my newspaper," she added, her eyes full of anger and hurt. The anger he could handle, but it almost killed him to see the hurt. And to know that he had put it there.

"I haven't sold out your paper," he said calmly. "Buddy Hamilton—"

"I don't want to hear about Buddy Hamilton. You knew how I felt about Hamilton News and you still went behind my back and made plans to align my newspaper with them. Don't tell me you didn't think that would make me angry."

"I thought I could make you understand," he said, but he knew his words fell on deaf ears. Eleanor wasn't ready to listen to him. Yet. "I wasn't trying to hurt you. I was trying to help myself. And us. My plan can benefit both of us."

She dropped her hand from the doorknob and propped it on her hip. "The paper is everything is me, Jake. I've told you over and over that I want complete control. Why did you even consider a deal with Hamilton News? They're control freaks."

"It's not as bad as you think. They were willing to deal on a lot of issues."

Eleanor shook her head. "I don't want to hear it. This paper belongs to the Sanders family. I don't want anyone else involved in it."

"You were willing to let Mason Publishing become involved," he noted carefully.

"That's because I let you deceive me. Like a fool, I thought caring feelings were associated with your erotic touches. I was wrong." She eyed him. "What was I, Jake? A summer fling, after all?"

Jake stood up and went to her. "It wasn't like that. How many times do I have to tell you?"

She reached for the door and opened it. "You don't have to tell me anything again. Get out."

He touched her cheek with the back of his hand and she moved her head away. "I'm going to prove to you it was more than that for me."

He stepped out of the door and she slammed it behind him.

Eleanor settled back on her bed with the latest Evelyn Coleman mystery, hoping to take her mind off her troubles for at least a short time. Making that call to Hamilton News was the hardest thing she'd ever done. But she'd had to do it. If Jake had made a deal with the devil, she had to know the details of it before she could fight it. And at this point, she didn't trust Jake enough to believe his statement of the facts.

The sound of her doorbell startled her. She quickly jumped up from the bed, tightened the belt on her robe, and ran to the door. A part of her wondered if it was Jake. "Who is it?"

"It's me, Eleanor," her father's voice answered.

Eleanor sighed, not sure if she was happy or sad it wasn't Jake, then opened the door. Her father stood there still dressed from his day at the office. "Is something wrong, Dad?"

Mathias shook his head. "I wanted to talk to you. I haven't seen you much around the paper."

Eleanor stood back so he could enter the cottage. "Carl and Jake are taking care of everything, aren't they?"

Mathias entered the cottage and eased onto the couch. "Of course, but I still miss you. I've been worried about you."

Eleanor leaned against the mantel in front of him. "There's no need to worry. I'm taking care of business."

"That's what I'm worried about," Mathias muttered. He patted the space next to him. "Come over here and sit down."

She moved over to him. "What's wrong?"

He took her hand in his. "I don't want you to fight Jake on this."

"What?" She tried to pull her hand away but his hold tightened.

"You heard me. I don't want you to fight Jake on this."

"Why not?" she asked, wondering what Jake or his father had said to her father to make him give up so easily.

"Because we need a change around here."

"What did Randolph say to you, Dad? How did he convince you to go along with Jake?"

Mathias shook his head slowly. "Randolph didn't have to say anything. This is my decision."

She jerked on her hand again, but still he wouldn't release it. "I bet this is your idea. Just like it was your idea to bring Mason Publishing into our business. Why are you letting those people use us?"

"Is that what you think I'm doing?"

The tinge of sadness in his voice almost stopped her words. "That's what it looks like. First, you bring them here against everything you've ever taught me and now you're willing to let them throw our paper willy-nilly at Hamilton News. What's happening to you?"

Mathias patted his daughter's knee. "You're a good child, Eleanor. You always have been."

Eleanor wondered where all this was coming from, but she didn't have time to ask.

"I did my best to raise you after your mother died, but sometimes I wonder if I didn't do the wrong thing by bringing you into the paper so early."

She shook her head and tried to keep a lid on the anxiousness that was building in her. "You raised me right. And you did the right thing by bringing me into the paper. I loved you and I loved the paper. I still do. Don't you know that?"

"Maybe I do. But haven't you ever wondered what your life would've been like if you'd stretched your wings beyond Lamar? I've held you back, Eleanor. You were meant for greater things than a small-town paper."

Her heart rebelled at the words. "That's not so, Dad. I love working at the *Lamar Daily.* I love Lamar."

He rubbed his thumb across the back of her hand. "I know you're frustrated a lot, Eleanor."

"No more than any other newspaper managing editor," she said, dismissing his concern.

"I don't think other editors have to deal with reporters and columnists who've known them since they were kids and still treat them that way."

She smiled at his observation. "It's not that bad."

"And what about your idea for the magazine? Haven't you ever thought about dropping your duties with the *Lamar Daily* and pursuing that dream?"

Yes, she'd thought about it. More than once. But she'd never been able to do it. The magazine was a dream. The *Lamar Daily* was reality. It was her heritage. "The *Lamar Daily* is more than a paper."

He smiled sadly. "No, it's not. That's the problem. To us it's become more than a paper."

She looked toward the mantel, not liking the direction this conversation was taking. "And that's bad?"

"Not in and of itself. But when you look at the big picture, it takes on a different spin."

"And what's the big picture?" she asked, not sure she wanted to hear his answer.

He tightened his hold on her hand, and she turned to him. "The big picture is a grieving husband and his motherless daughter seeking refuge in the family business."

Tears quickly filled her eyes. "And what's wrong with that? At least we had some place to seek refuge."

"There's nothing wrong with it, but we sought refuge too long. Pretty soon we started hiding."

She wiggled her hands free of his and wiped at her eyes. What could she say? She'd never thought of it that way. She'd told Jake as much. "I don't think we're hiding."

"Then what are we doing? I'm a fifty-five-year-old man and I've been sneaking around with Maxie for almost fifteen years."

Eleanor's eyes widened. "You and Maxine? Fifteen years?"

Mathias nodded. "Me and Maxie. Fifteen years. I call that hiding."

Eleanor felt as if the wind had been kicked out of her. How could she have missed a fifteen-year relationship? "I knew Maxie had a crush on you, but I never knew you returned her feelings."

"That's because I didn't want you to know. I didn't want you to think I was cheating on your mother."

"But Mom was dead. How could you cheat on her? You could have told me. I would've understood and I would've been happy for you."

"Maybe."

"You don't think I would've been happy for you?"

"I don't know."

She leaned into him. "Oh, Dad. I'm so sorry you had to sneak around."

He patted her knee. "Don't worry about me and Maxie. We'll be okay. As a matter of fact, we're coming out of the closet."

"You're getting married?" she asked, not sure how she would feel if he said he was.

He chuckled. "I asked her, but she likes the status quo. Maybe when things change at the paper, she'll change her mind."

"So you have personal reasons for going along with Jake's plans?"

He nodded. "I used the paper for a lot of years to hinder my personal life. I think it's only fitting that now I use it to further my personal life."

Eleanor chuckled. "You and Maxie. I don't believe it."

"It's good to hear your laugher. I haven't heard much of it lately."

She sobered. "There hasn't been a lot to laugh about."

"Nobody ever said love was easy."

"Love?"

"That's what this is really about, isn't it, Eleanor? You love him, don't you?"

Carl opened the door as Jake was about to insert his key. "Hey," Carl said. "It's about time you got home."

"I'm glad I caught you before you left," Jake said, rushing into the apartment. "I need to talk to you. Can you give me a few minutes?"

Carl checked his watch. "I guess I can spare a couple of minutes. We have dinner reservations for eight."

Jake hung his jacket on the back of one of the kitchen chairs and sat down. "Come over here."

"What is it?" Carl asked, making his way to the table.

"I've been talking to Buddy Hamilton."

Carl whistled. "Don't I know it. Megan is practically spitting fire. I told you Eleanor wasn't gonna like it."

"Sit down. Sit down."

"Hold your horses, I'm sitting down. What do you want to show me?"

Jake pulled a legal pad out of his briefcase. "Here's the latest deal." He'd gone over the highlights with Buddy on the phone. He wanted one more meeting with him before presenting the plan to Eleanor.

Carl picked up the pad and began reading. Jake felt hope spring up in him when a smile slowly spread across Carl's face.

"So, what do you think?"

Carl clapped him on the back. "I think you should've come up with this deal first."

Jake wished he had. He'd almost lost the most important thing to him in his macho quest to impress his father. "What do you think Eleanor will say about this one?"

"She'll go for it."

"I hope so," Jake said, knowing she had to go for it. He couldn't go through his life without her.

"You finally realized what was important."

Jake gave a wry smile. "It took me long enough." His father's words about making the best business decision or the best personal decision had stuck with him and he'd been able to come up with a third alternative—a decision that satisfied both his business and his personal needs.

"I hate to say this…"

Jake grinned. "Go ahead and say it."

"I told you so."

Jake clapped Carl on the back. "Thanks for that, friend. The next time you give me advice about my woman, slap me if I don't listen."

Carl rubbed his hands together. "Can I get that in writing?"

Jake laughed.

Carl looked at his watch, then stood. "So when are you going to tell Eleanor?"

"As soon as I get a formal okay from Buddy."

"And when are you going to ask her to marry you?"

Jake's heart hammered in his chest. "As soon as I think she'll give the answer I want. I'm willing to wait."

"Take my advice. Don't wait. She's in love with you."

The hope that Eleanor still loved him kept Jake going. "From your mouth to God's ears. I can't live without her, Carl."

"Welcome to the club." He grinned. "Ain't love grand?"

As Eleanor closed the blinds in her living room in preparation for going to bed, she acknowledged the effect Jake Mason still had on her life. Her closing blinds? She couldn't remember the last time she'd had her blinds open. Since she'd walked around her house nude most of the time, it served her better to keep the blinds closed. That was before Jake Mason.

Tonight was an after-Jake Mason night and she was closing blinds that she'd had open all day. As a matter of fact, her blinds had been open every day since she'd gotten back from her fateful fact-finding trip. No use keeping them closed since she no longer walked around nude.

And Jake Mason was the reason she no longer walked around nude. She couldn't do it anymore. She couldn't bear her naked body without thinking of him and how he'd made love to her, so she kept herself covered. She sighed. She'd given too much of herself to him before she found out that he was undeserving.

After the blinds were all closed, she checked the lock on the front door and headed for the shower. She slipped out of her pink terry cloth sweatsuit and threw it in the hamper. She glimpsed her naked form when she walked by the bathroom mirror, but she quickly averted her eyes so as not to see herself. It was still too painful. She couldn't look at her breasts, her body, without feeling the caress of his hands, his mouth.

She stepped into the shower and let the warm water work its magic. In here, alone, she could relax. In here, for a short while at least, she could forget her problems.

When she was sufficiently relaxed, she turned off the shower, stepped out onto the cool tiled floor, and grabbed a towel to dry herself. Once she was dry, she slipped on her gown, then left the bathroom and climbed into her bed.

She closed her eyes, but sleep wouldn't come. That was not unusual in her post-Jake Mason world. She couldn't go to sleep without thinking about him, what she'd felt for him, and what she'd experienced with him.

Tonight her father's comments joined her regular thoughts. "You love him, don't you?" her father had asked.

She hadn't answered him, but she knew the answer. Yes, she loved Jake. She'd probably always love him. But she wasn't sure if love was enough. What was a relationship without trust?

She didn't trust Jake. He'd betrayed her as surely as if he'd slept with another woman. She shuddered at the thought, then shook her head. No, his betrayal hadn't reached that depth.

She turned restlessly toward the clock. Her mother's clock. How she wished her mother were here now! Relationships were almost too difficult for a woman to handle without an advocate. And her mom would have been her advocate. She was sure of it.

When she turned away from the clock and closed her eyes, she saw Jake the last night they'd made love. In his eyes, she saw love. Love for her.

She'd seen that same look in his eyes the day she'd confronted him in his apartment. And it had still been there when he'd confronted her at her apartment.

"I want you to love somebody so much it hurts," Franklin had told her. "You know it's real when it hurts, when you've given all you think you have and you still have to give more. You know it's love when you're willing to dig deep to find the extra strength it takes to make the relationship work."

Eleanor loved Jake. And though he hadn't spoken the words,

she believed he loved her. She'd walked away once from a man who loved her; could she do it again when she loved him back?

Eleanor arrived at the newspaper early the next morning. Again, she wanted to beat Jake in. She collected the papers from the stoop, tucked them under her arm, and let herself in. She smelled Jake's cologne as soon as she entered their office. A feeling of contentment washed over her and she could hardly wait to see him. After a night of soul-searching, she'd decided to put the past in the past and move forward with the future. A future that included Jake. It was a decision she believed her mother would commend.

She'd thought about going over to Carl's, but she decided it was more appropriate they meet on the grounds of the battle. Taking a seat at her desk, she flicked on her computer and pulled up the AP stories. It was good to be back in her routine again.

"Morning, Eleanor."

Jake's voice floated over her skin. She turned around and drank in the sight of him. "Morning, yourself," she said, noting that he looked tired. "What's wrong?"

He placed his briefcase on his desk and leaned back on its edge. "I should be asking you that."

She stood and sat on the edge of her desk facing him. Their knees touched, but she didn't pull away. "Why didn't you tell me?" she asked, no venom or anger in her voice.

He shrugged. "I didn't think you would understand." He moved his knee away. "And I was right."

She shook her head slowly. "I didn't understand your lying to me and your keeping secrets from me. You'll never know whether I would have understood the reasons for your plans."

He twisted around, pulled open the briefcase, pulled out a legal pad, and handed it to her. "Here's the deal. What there is of it."

She took the pad, never taking her eyes from his. "Why are you showing it to me now?"

"Read it." He ignored her question.

She handed the pad back to him. "I don't need to read it."

He stared at her hand for a long second then took the pad. "You're not going to give me chance to explain, are you?"

She heard the frustrated defeat in his voice. "There's nothing to explain. I've done a lot of soulsearching, Jake. And I know what I want." She walked over to the window. "You asked me once to trust you. Well, I'm going to trust you now." She twisted the cord and the blinds closed. His mouth dropped open.

"What are you up to, Eleanor?"

She sauntered back to him and draped her arms around his neck. "Do you love me, Jake?" She hoped her uncertainty didn't sound in her voice.

He clasped his arms around her waist and pulled her tight against him. "I've missed you so much."

"But you didn't answer my question." She pulled back from him and stared into his dark, inviting eyes. "Do you love me?"

He lifted his hand and traced a line down her jaw. "I didn't think I could love anybody the way I love you."

She bit her lip to keep back her tears of joy and fell back in his embrace. "I love you, too."

She reveled in the massaging motion of his hands along her back. When his hand moved around to caress her breast, she moaned.

He pushed her slightly away from him and captured her mouth in a life-giving kiss. They were both out of breath when he pulled away.

He touched his fingers to her lips softly, as if he were touching something precious. "Your lips are so soft. You can't know how it feels to touch them after having been apart from you."

She kissed his fingertip and captured his hand in hers. "Oh, yes I can. I've missed you more than you can know."

He stared into her eyes and she wondered what he was looking for.

"You don't mind about my plans for the paper?"

She kissed him softly on the lips. "This paper has been a part of my life for as long as I can remember. In some ways it filled the void left by my mother's death. So, I do care about your plans."

He rubbed his finger along her bottom lip. "Then why are you here with me now? Are you trying to torture me?"

She chuckled at the distress in his voice. "No, I'm not trying to torture you."

He pulled away from her and stood up. "What do you want from me, Eleanor?"

"All I want is your love." She rested her head against his back and wrapped her arms around his waist.

He turned in her embrace and looked at her with hard eyes. "And you want me to stop my plans. Is that what this is? Blackmail? I get you if I give up my plans."

Her heart filled with pain at the anguish in his voice. "I wasn't sure enough of your love to come up with a plan like that."

He buried his head in her shoulder. "You should have known."

"I'm not psychic, Jake. You should have told me."

"I did," he whispered against her skin.

She pulled back. "No, you didn't. Believe me, I would remember something like that."

"You were asleep."

"When was this?"

He kissed her lips. "The night you skipped out on me."

"I'm sorry about that."

"It doesn't matter," he said, but she knew it did.

"It does. I shouldn't have left like that, but I was afraid. You'd made such sweet love to me. I could almost feel your love. Yet I knew you were keeping something from me. I wondered if I was falling for an act." She smiled. "You do have acting training, you know."

"There was never any acting between us, Eleanor. Every time I've touched you, I've loved you." He slapped her bottom. "Don't you think we'd better open the blinds."

"Do we have to?"

He pushed her away. "We still have a paper to get out."

She walked to the window and opened the blinds. "Oh no," she said, covering her mouth with her hands.

Chapter 25

Jake turned and saw the smiling faces of Carl and Megan. "Damn!"

Eleanor dropped her hand from her face. "My sentiments exactly. Brace yourself, they're coming in."

"And what have you guys been doing in here?" Megan asked, wagging her finger at them. "We've been waiting for the blinds to open for the last hour."

Eleanor rolled her eyes. "Now that was an exaggeration of an exaggeration."

Jake looped an arm around Eleanor's waist. "To what do we owe the pleasure of your visit this morning?" He winked at Carl. "Maybe I should say, who?"

"We have an announcement," Carl said, pulling the blinds closed again.

"You're getting married!" Eleanor practically screamed.

Megan flashed the three-carat diamond on her left hand. "Yes, yes, yes."

Eleanor stepped away from Jake and enveloped her friend in a hug and soon both women were crying happy tears.

Jake extended a hand to Carl. "Congratulations, man."

"Thanks," Carl said, pulling Megan back to him. He kissed her forehead. "I couldn't let her get away."

"I had to drag him to the jewelry store," she said. "I thought he didn't want to marry me."

Carl shook his head. "That wasn't it. I wanted to pick out the ring myself. I wanted it to be a surprise."

She kissed him. "I love you, Carl Winters."

Jake caught the joyous look on Eleanor's face as she watched the engaged couple. She saw him looking at her and gave him a smile between her tears. He pulled her to him. "I love you, Eleanor Sanders," he whispered.

"Oh, Jake," she said.

Jake pressed a kiss on her forehead, cleared his throat, and said, "Come on, everybody. Let's stop with the crying. Eleanor and I want to take you two to dinner tonight to celebrate."

"Sounds like a good idea to me," Megan said. "I think we have a lot to celebrate. Do you two have an announcement to make?"

Jake grinned down at Eleanor. "Let's say we've called a truce. We'll keep you posted on any other developments."

Eleanor looked at her watch. "Sorry to break this up, guys, but we have a paper to get out."

"I told you she was a slave driver," Carl said to Megan as he led her out of the office.

Jake opened the blinds again. "The staff will be talking about us. Do you think we should say something to them?"

Eleanor shook her head. "I don't think we'll have to say anything." She pointed to the newsroom, where Megan and Carl had a group of people surrounding them. "They'll be too busy talking about Carl and Megan's engagement."

Jake grinned. "I wish this were the end of the day instead of the beginning."

Her eyes took on a glazed look and his groin tightened. "So do I," she said.

Jake cleared his throat again. It was going to be a long day. "I'd better get to work."

Eleanor didn't release his gaze. "Maybe you should."

Jake moved from one foot to another. "You'd better stop looking at me like that or they're going to have to get this paper out without us."

Eleanor grinned. "Is that a threat or a promise?"

"Eleanor," Jake warned, his gaze traveling from her feet to her head before settling on her lips.

Eleanor released her breath. "Okay, I get your message."

"You don't," Jake said with intensity. "But you will. I promise you that."

Jake went through the day in a state of sexual anticipation. He tried to keep his mind off Eleanor, but he couldn't do it. Her presence surrounded him and filled his every thought.

By lunchtime, he was exhausted.

"How about a swim for lunch?" Eleanor asked, a gleam in her eyes, and Jake understood the invitation was for more than a swim.

He licked his lips. "You certainly know how to hurt a man."

"What do you mean?" she asked, her eyes bright and inviting. "I only asked if you wanted to go for a swim."

"I can't," he said softly. "I'm really sorry, but I have a business meeting."

Her smile dimmed. "Oh."

"No, oh." He got up, walked to her desk, and sat on its edge facing her, his back to the newsroom. "I have a meeting with Buddy Hamilton."

"Oh," she said again, and he knew she was wondering at the wisdom of giving him her trust.

"I love you, Eleanor."

"I know," she said finally.

"And don't forget it. I'm going to make this right for us. Do you believe me?"

She wore a grave look as she considered his question. When the corners of her mouth turned up in a smile, though slight, he knew they were going to be all right.

Jake held Eleanor's hand for the entire drive from the restaurant where they'd had an enjoyable dinner with Carl and Megan to Eleanor's cottage. They didn't talk much, because there was nothing more to be said. He'd gotten a verbal okay from the Hamiltons today and he'd had to force himself to wait until they were alone to tell Eleanor the details.

He glanced over at her. She faced straight ahead and he wondered where her thoughts were. He knew she'd been taken aback by his lunch meeting with the Hamiltons, but she hadn't said anything. She'd given him her trust and she wasn't going to take it back. Her trust and confidence in him made him feel strong and capable. With a woman like her by his side, he knew he'd always take the high road.

She glanced over at him and smiled when he pulled up into her drive. He placed a soft kiss on her hand, then got out of the car and opened her door. He smiled at the memory of the first time he'd taken her out when she hadn't bothered to wait for him to do the task. He was glad she'd waited tonight.

When she grasped his hand to lift herself out of the car, he pulled and she fell into his arms. He crushed her to him, then pushed her back slightly so he could see her face. He lowered his head to kiss her and she closed her eyes in anticipation. He groaned, then rested his chin against the top of her head.

"What is it?" she asked softly.

"I can't kiss you now," he forced out.

"Why not?"

He gazed down into her questioning eyes. "Because if I kiss you now, we may not make it to the house."

Passion blazed in her eyes. "I see."

He turned up the corners of his mouth. "You don't, but you will."

He took her hand in his and led her into her house. It seemed to take forever to get the door unlocked, but finally they were in the house. As soon as the door closed behind them, he pulled her into his arms.

"It's been too long, Eleanor," he murmured. "I've missed you so much."

She wrapped her arms around his neck. "Oh, Jake."

The pressure of her breast against his chest made him moan. "I want to go slowly, and make this beautiful for you, but I don't know if I'll be able to. I need you so much."

She pressed a series of kisses along his neck. "Who wants to go slow? I need you too, Jake."

That was all he needed. He lifted her off her feet and carried her to the bedroom. His knees almost buckled when he reached the bed and she nipped at his ear. "Eleanor, you're going to make me come too soon if you don't stop."

"I can't stop," she said sluggishly. "I want you. Now."

He deposited her on the bed and would have pulled back to discard his clothes, but she wouldn't release the hold she had on his neck.

"No," she said. "Don't leave me. Please don't leave me."

He sank down against her. "I won't leave you. I couldn't leave you. You're my heart. Don't you know that?"

She lifted her head and pressed her mouth against his in answer. Jake lost all rational thought. Eleanor's passion consumed him.

Soon they were pulling at each other's clothes. She was as impatient to feel his naked body against hers as he was to feel hers.

When they were both finally naked, he was so taut he entered her with haste. "Did I hurt you?" he asked when she moaned loudly.

She rolled her head back and forth on the pillow and lifted her hips in rhythm with his. His thrusts were hard and fast, but he could do it no other way. He was glad when she reached her climax, because he knew he couldn't wait for her.

Eleanor awoke contented, but feeling a bit decadent. Blood rushed to her face when she thought about their earlier coupling. It had been wild and primitive. A necessity, not a desire.

She twisted in Jake's arms until she could see his face. Her heart turned over at the contented smile he wore even in his sleep. She knew exactly how he felt because she felt the same way.

Tonight had been different. Tonight there had been no pretense between them. With the confession of their love, they'd removed all barriers to the perfect expression of that love. They hadn't verbally spoken of a future together, but tonight she'd made that commitment as surely as if she'd accepted his marriage proposal.

Not that he'd made a marriage proposal. He hadn't, but she believed he would. Soon. And she'd be Eleanor Mason. Mrs. Jake Mason.

"What are you smiling about?" Jake's sleepy voice asked.

She kissed the tip of his nose, glad he was awake. "A girl has to have some secrets."

"Secrets? I thought we got rid of all those earlier tonight."

So she'd been right. He'd felt it, too.

"It was good with us before," he continued, his finger tracing a line along her lips, "but tonight was phenomenal. I now know what it means to be *one* with somebody. Do you understand what I'm saying?"

She nodded, not trusting her voice to speak. His words touched a chord in her heart and she knew theirs was a forever kind of love.

"I love you more than I thought I could love anybody. There's nothing I wouldn't do for you. Nothing."

"Oh, Jake," she moaned. The intensity of his words made her body warm with the need to be close to him.

He folded her into his arms. "I won't let you go. You know that, don't you?"

"I know," she whispered, feeling safe and cherished in his arms.

"Nothing will ever come between us again. I promise."

"I know that, Jake. You don't have to say it."

He brushed her hair back from her face. "Yes, I do. I want us to be like we were tonight forever. I don't ever want anything to come between us again. Not even our work."

"It won't, Jake. We'll make the right decisions for the right reasons."

He kissed her again, needing to touch her more. When the phone rang, his first impulse was to ignore it, but the singsong voices of Megan and Carl on the answering machine caught his attention.

"We'll understand if you two are busy and can't answer the phone," they began, then interrupted themselves with giggles. "We wanted to make sure you two knew you were the best man and maid of honor at our wedding." More giggles. "Or that could be matron of honor if you make it to the chapel before we do." More giggles. "Since you two haven't picked up, I guess we'll hang up and let you get back to what you're doing." More giggles and then dial tone.

Jake dropped his head in the space between Eleanor's neck and her shoulder. "They're outrageous."

Eleanor chuckled. "But they're perfect for each other."

He pulled back and looked at her. "And we're perfect for each other."

"Prove it," she challenged, a sensual gleam in her eyes.

"There's nothing I'd rather do," he responded and began to show her all the ways they were perfectly matched.

Chapter 26

Jake's face was the first thing she saw the next time she woke up. She wanted to wake up to that face every day of her life. "Good morning," she said, reading the love in his eyes.

He kissed the tip of her nose. "I love you, Eleanor Sanders."

A contented feeling settled in her stomach. She wanted to experience that feeling every day of her life. "And I love you, Jake Mason."

"Sit up. I want you to see something." He turned to the nightstand and brought out a legal pad like the one he'd handed her earlier when they were in the office.

She handed the pad back, then raised her eyes to him. "Why don't you tell me that it says."

"It's a new deal."

She smiled. "I kinda thought that."

"With Hamilton News."

"Oh."

He kissed her quickly on her lips. "No, oh. I didn't make the decision this time. We'll make it together."

She smiled, knowing that he wasn't talking about only this decision, but every decision they'd ever make. "Okay, what are our options?"

He kissed her again, lingeringly. "We can go with the original deal the two of us had mapped out. You stay at the helm at the *Lamar Daily,* and I take the helm of *Our Family.*"

She touched her lips to his again. "What's the next option?"

"Okay," Jake said, barely able to form a rational thought. He wanted her again. "We merge the *Lamar Daily* and Hamilton News and begin to build the largest consortium of small-town papers in the country."

"Hmm," she said, nibbling on his lips. "And who's in charge of this new consortium?"

"You and Buddy run the consortium, and I run *Our Family* as a separate entity."

She reflected on this possibility, the queasy feeling in her stomach about Buddy's involvement replaced by a cautious acceptance of the need for change. "Any more options?"

He couldn't resist one more kiss. "Same as the last. We merge with the Hamiltons. But Buddy and your dad run the consortium, while you and I build *Our Family* together."

She leaned into him, pressing her breasts tight against his chest. "I like the sound of that."

He pulled back, wanting to make sure he'd heard her correctly. "What?"

"You and I building our family together. I like the sound of that."

His heartbeat raced. "Does that mean what I think it means?"

She smiled at him. "Depends on what you think it means."

He pulled her into his arms and tilted her face up so he could see her. "Are you going to marry me, Eleanor?"

"I think that's what I said."

He crushed her to him, relief flooding his body. He and Eleanor had a future. After a few seconds of holding her close, he asked, "So which option do you want for the paper?"

"Which one do you want?"

"It doesn't matter. As long as I have you, it doesn't matter."

She pulled back and looked up at him. "What about your father? Which option will impress him most?"

He looked deep into her eyes and knew he was a changed man because of her. He'd come to Lamar to impress his father with a megabusiness deal. But somewhere along the line he'd fallen in love with a mouthy Southern miss who'd showed him what was really important. "I think Dad wants me to be happy. As long as my decision keeps you in my life and in my bed, he'll be impressed." He paused. "So, the choice is yours. I'm yours."

She squeezed him to her. "You and me and *Our Family*."

He looked down at her. "Are you sure this is what you want?"

She nodded. "I want a future with you, Jake. I want us to build something together. My father and my mother built the *Lamar Daily* and it'll always be my legacy, the legacy of our children. But I also want to give them something from us. A legacy started by you and me."

His eyes darkened and he kissed her again. When he lifted his head, he said, "I guess we have a deal."

She grinned. "Though I was never too high on the idea of a Mason-Sanders merger, I now think this alliance could be the best thing that's ever happened to me."

Epilogue

"Twins?" Mathias propped his feet up on the table in front of the couch in Randolph's library and stuck an unlit cigar in his mouth. "Can you believe they're going to have twins?"

Randolph lit Mathias's cigar, then got one for himself. He'd ordered four cases as soon as he'd heard Eleanor was pregnant. A second order for four more cases followed when he'd learned she was having twins. Not one to stand on tradition, he'd already started giving them away. "My great-grandmother's sister had twins. It's those strong Mason genes."

Mathias harrumphed, then tapped his cigar on the ashtray in front of him. "We did it, didn't we, Randy?"

Randolph pulled the cigar from his mouth and blew a circle of smoke. "I never doubted it, Mat. I never doubted it."

"Neither did I, Randy. Neither did I."